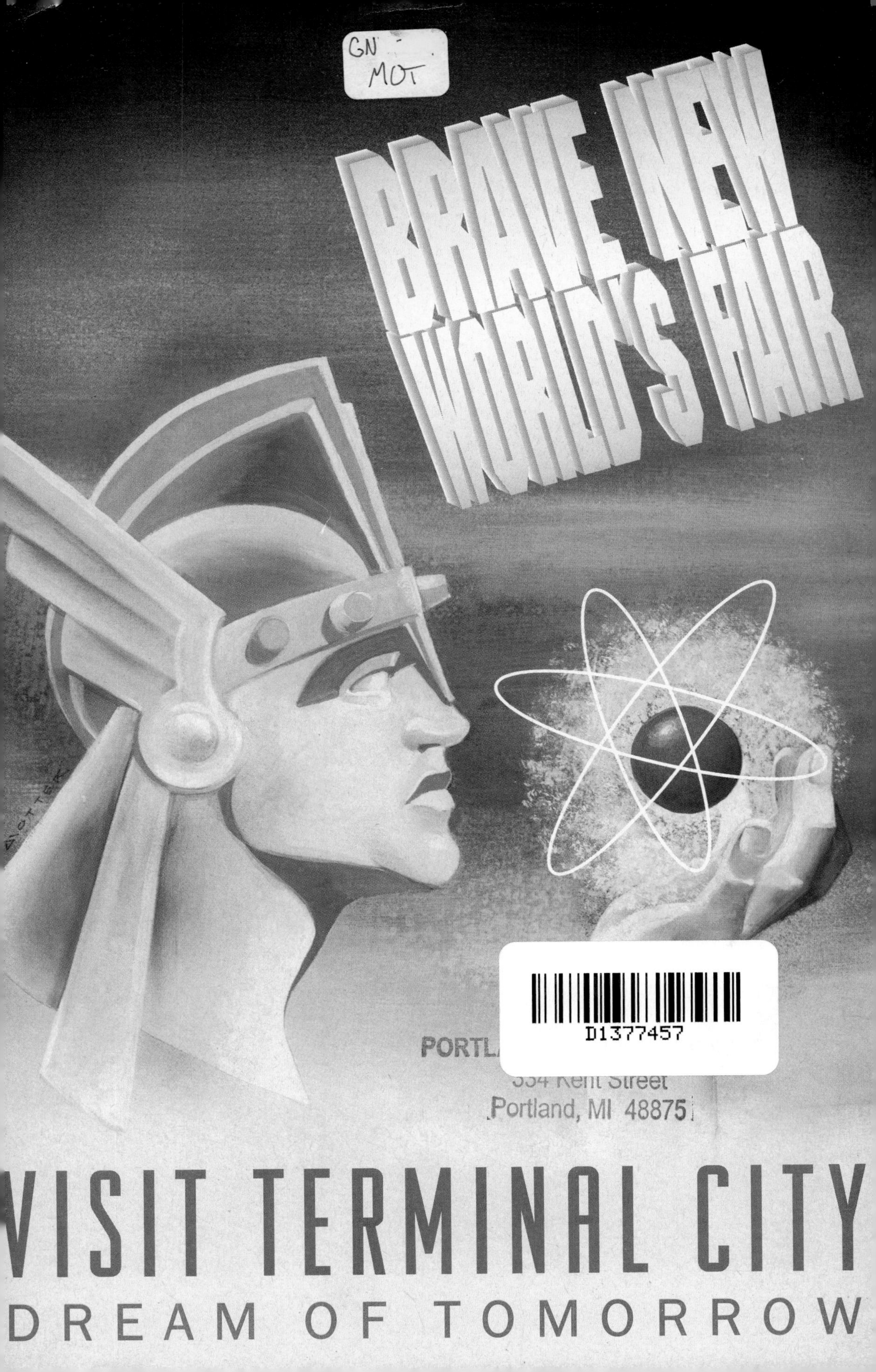
BRAVE NEW
WORLD'S FAIR
VISIT TERMINAL CITY
DREAM OF TOMORROW

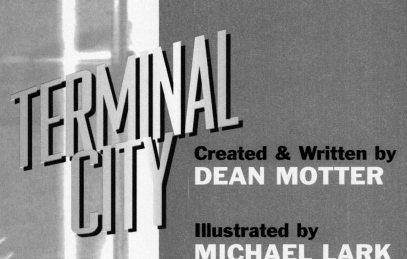

TERMINAL CITY

Created & Written by
DEAN MOTTER

Illustrated by
MICHAEL LARK

Colored by
RICK TAYLOR

Lettered by
WILLIE SCHUBERT

Original series covers by
MARK CHIARELLO
MATT WAGNER
DEAN MOTTER

Frontespiece by
DEAN MOTTER

INTRODUCTION

Was it Adolf Hitler who said, **"A city corrupts from the inside?"** *(Einen Stadt Gestink von der Inner)*

No, it wasn't, it was me and the German is completely bogus; but who cares, because everyone knows that putting a Nazi in the first sentence of an introduction is a surefire way of attracting the reader's attention. And you *are* paying attention—aren't you? So, let's get to the good stuff.

Terminal City lives up to its name. The main character, the City itself, embodies the terminus of all cities that abide in the parallel universe of Dean Motter's and Michael Lark's minds. In this comix novel, elements of George Orwell's *1984* and Aldous Huxley's *Brave New World* combine to give us a noir, retro vision of how the world might have ended up; or, for that matter, ended entirely. Noir, because Terminal City reeks of nightmares and of men dreaming through other men's bodies. Retro, because Terminal City is a metropolis that made it into the nineties, but actually stopped dead somewhere in the fifties. It's an odd mixture of Runyonesque eccentrics like Cosmo Quinn, Li'l Big Lil, Kid Gloves, and Eno Orez and everyday souls in search of themselves like Charity, Jezebel, Bonnie Bergman (B.B.) and Manual, the hapless bellhop.

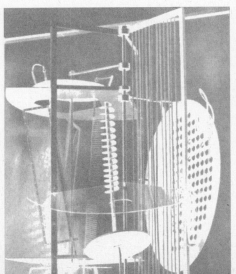

Terminal City is an urban zoo that barely contains the predators of the asphalt jungle. There are no trees, no flowers, no children, no Flower Children, no hope. Its heroes are ghosts—cast-off daredevils, disgraced champions and left-for-dead explorers—ghosts who must rise from the tombs of their forgotten pasts to struggle for the soul of the City, struggle against the swarms of thugs, riffraff, scum and psychopaths that crawl out of the rotting core of this corrupted metropolis.

It's a hard town. The people are hard. The shadows are hard. Even the drugs are hard. The crank of choice is Electrocaine—shock therapy meets nose candy. Not an easy world to get by in and few do, except for the ruthless and the pure. The ruthless rule and the pure hang like flies on the wall, witnesses to history, waiting for the time to act.

Sounds bleak, it is; but it's funny and strangely human for a comic-book series. Motter's sense of humor borders on the sneaky. Li'l Big Lil tells her gunsel chauffeur to "make a right at the old Lang sign," the evil Monkey Brothers are dubbed Hirno, Sino and Speekno and the octogenarian silent film star who drops in at the end carries the moniker Lance Boyle. My father was a punster, I'm a punster, how can I help but love this guy?

Well, introductions, like after-dinner drinks, should be short and sweet, so let's wrap this up. For me, *Terminal City* is a literate kid's dream come true, a character-rich novel with lots and lots of pictures. Welcome aboard; it's a great town to get lost in.

Peter Bergman
Los Angeles

Peter Bergman, a founding member of The Firesign Theatre,
is presently touring his one-man show
"1000 Ways To Survive The Millennium"
and producing "DRIVEN," the sequel to
his CD-ROM "PYST."

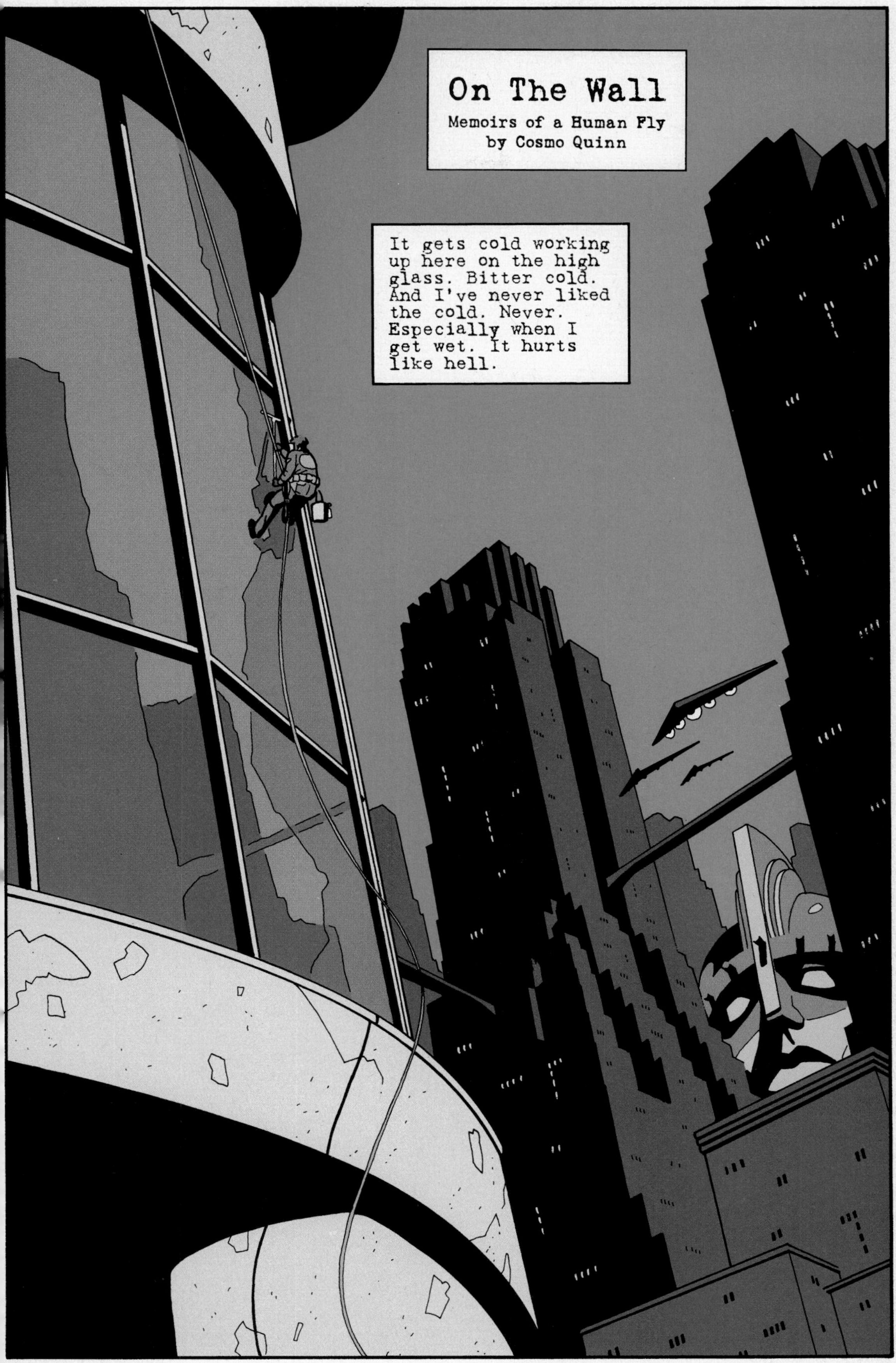

On The Wall
Memoirs of a Human Fly
by Cosmo Quinn
It gets cold working up here on the high glass. Bitter cold. And I've never liked the cold. Never. Especially when I get wet. It hurts like hell.

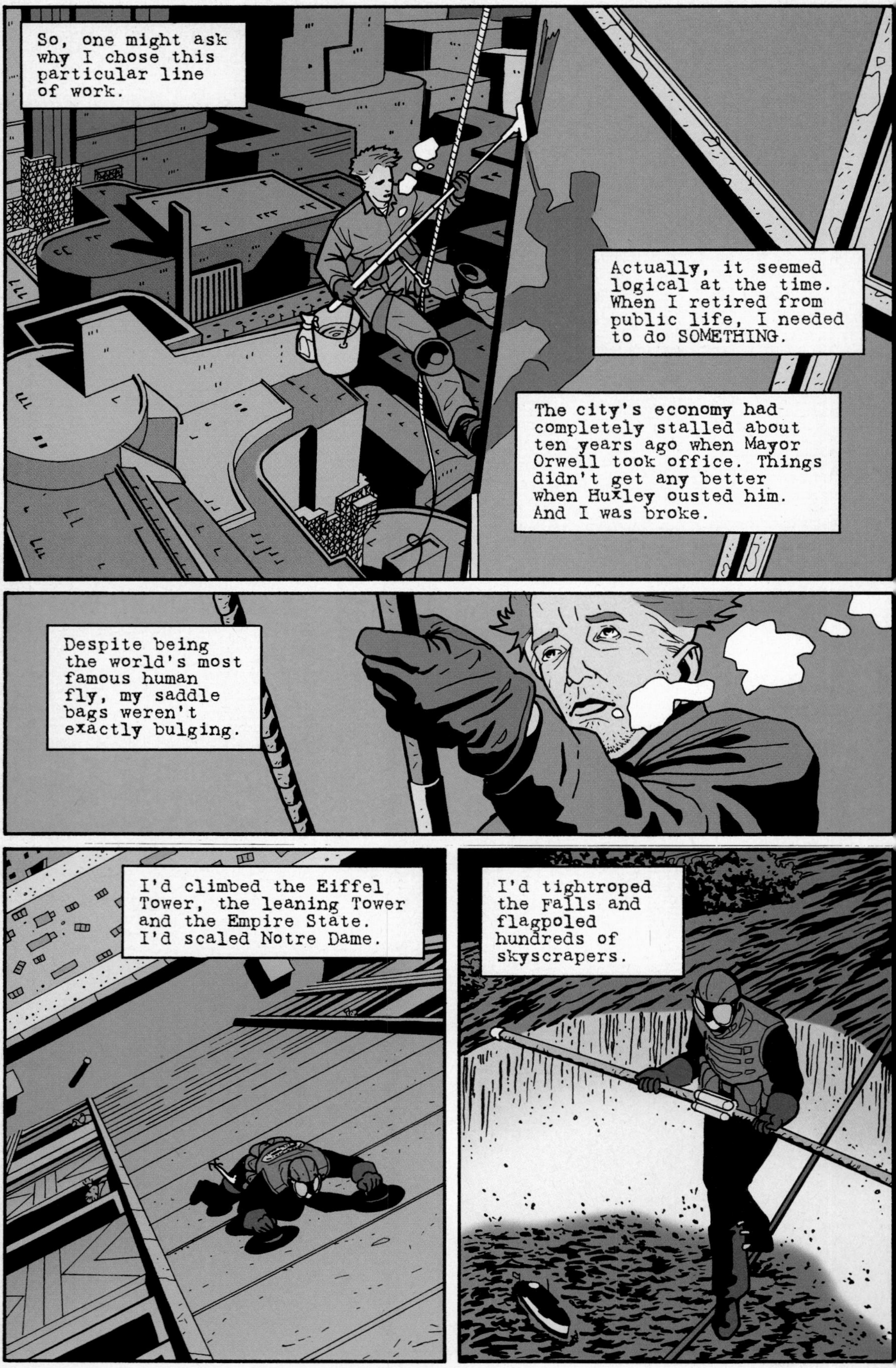
So, one might ask why I chose this particular line of work.
Actually, it seemed logical at the time. When I retired from public life, I needed to do SOMETHING.
The city's economy had completely stalled about ten years ago when Mayor Orwell took office. Things didn't get any better when Huxley ousted him. And I was broke.
Despite being the world's most famous human fly, my saddle bags weren't exactly bulging.
I'd climbed the Eiffel Tower, the leaning Tower and the Empire State. I'd scaled Notre Dame.
I'd tightroped the Falls and flagpoled hundreds of skyscrapers.

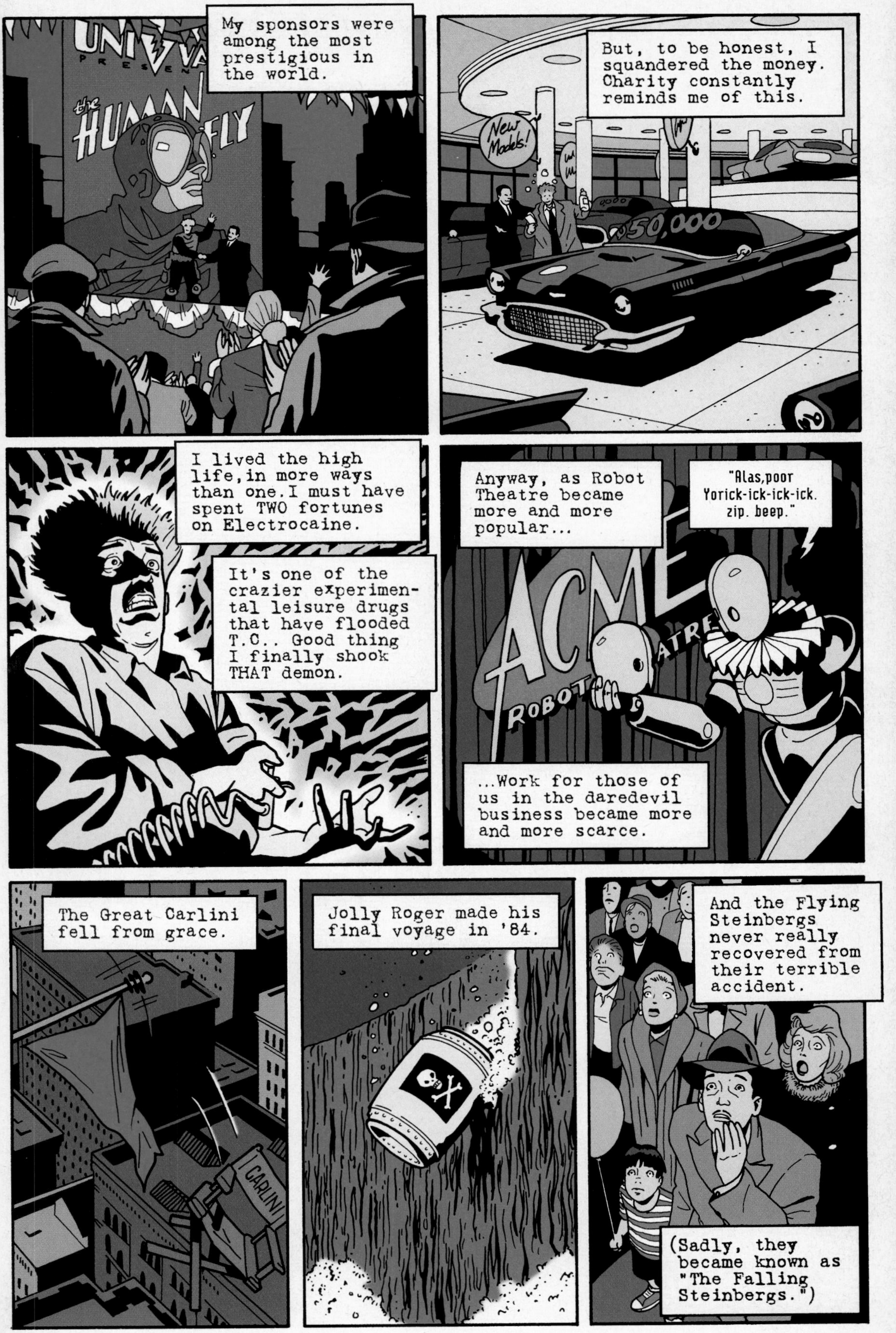
My sponsors were among the most prestigious in the world.
UNIVAX PRESENTS the HUMAN FLY
But, to be honest, I squandered the money. Charity constantly reminds me of this.
New Models!
$50,000
I lived the high life, in more ways than one. I must have spent TWO fortunes on Electrocaine.
It's one of the crazier experimental leisure drugs that have flooded T.C.. Good thing I finally shook THAT demon.
Anyway, as Robot Theatre became more and more popular...
"Alas, poor Yorick-ick-ick-ick. zip. beep."
ACME ROBOT THEATRE
...Work for those of us in the daredevil business became more and more scarce.
The Great Carlini fell from grace.
CARLINI
Jolly Roger made his final voyage in '84.
And the Flying Steinbergs never really recovered from their terrible accident.
(Sadly, they became known as "The Falling Steinbergs.")

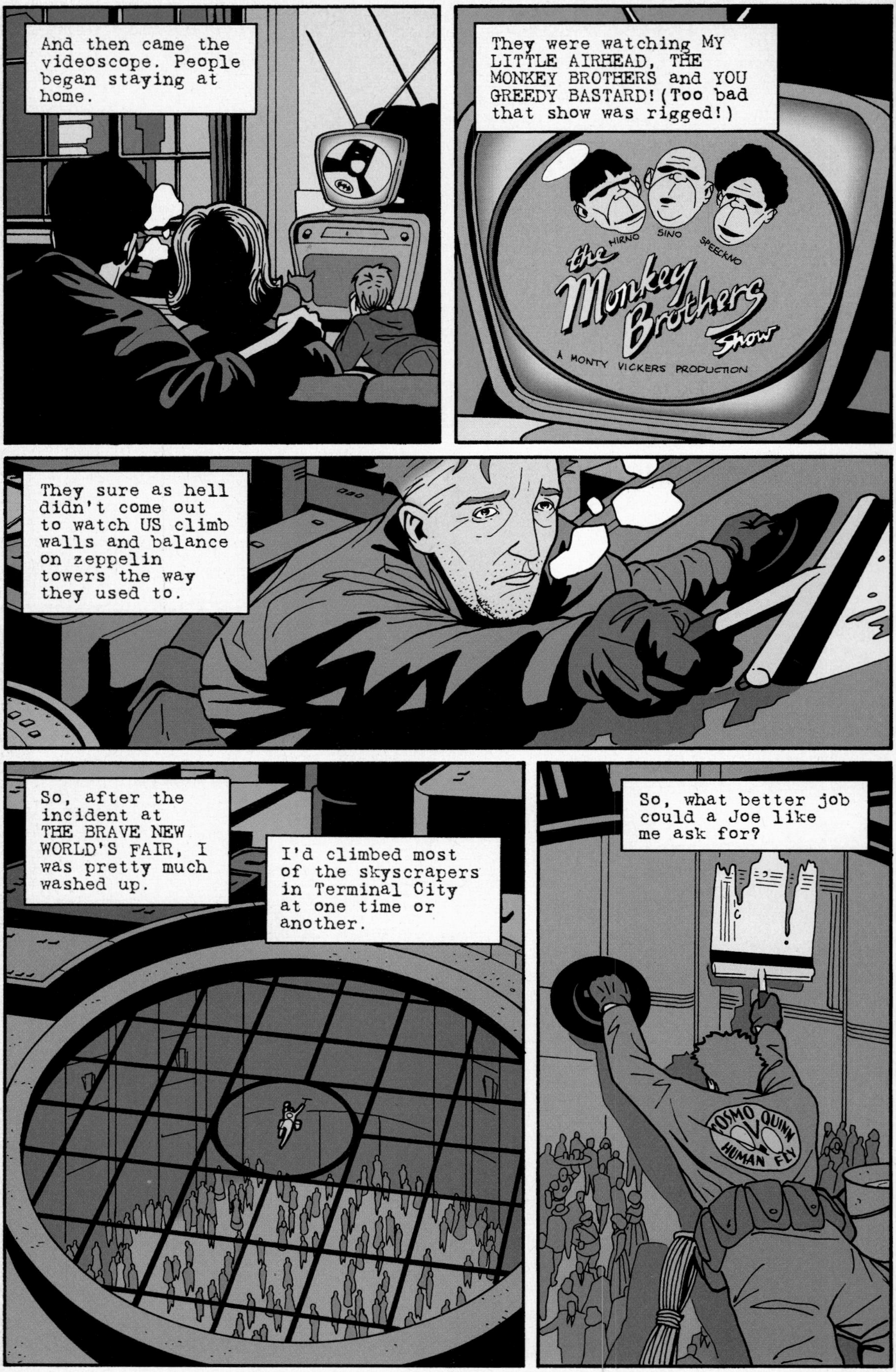
And then came the videoscope. People began staying at home.
They were watching MY LITTLE AIRHEAD, THE MONKEY BROTHERS and YOU GREEDY BASTARD! (Too bad that show was rigged!)
HIRNO
SINO
SPEECKNO
the Monkey Brothers Show
A MONTY VICKERS PRODUCTION
They sure as hell didn't come out to watch US climb walls and balance on zeppelin towers the way they used to.
So, after the incident at THE BRAVE NEW WORLD'S FAIR, I was pretty much washed up.
I'd climbed most of the skyscrapers in Terminal City at one time or another.
So, what better job could a Joe like me ask for?
COSMO QUINN
HUMAN FLY

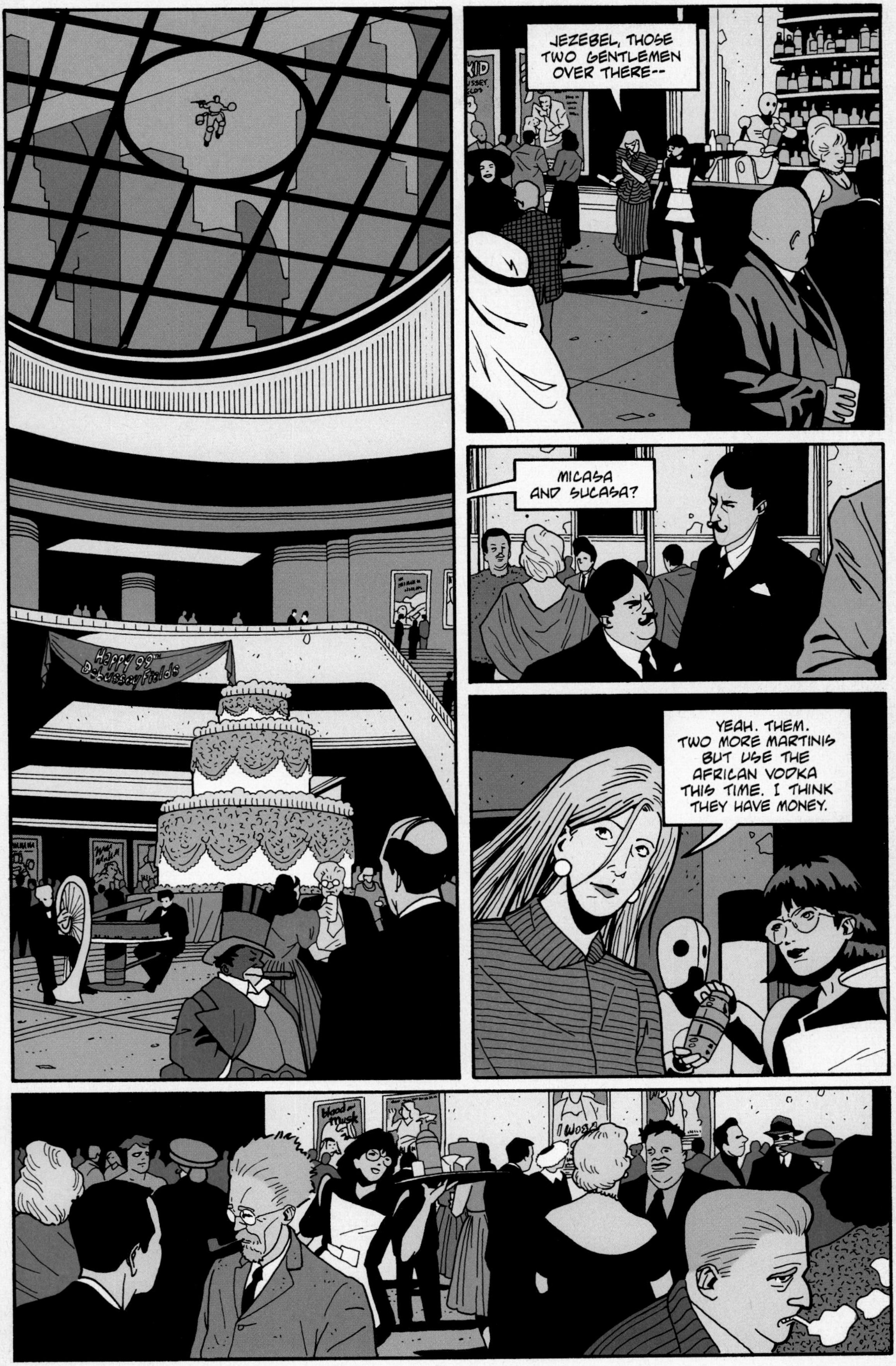

Happy 99TH Debussey Fields
JEZEBEL, THOSE TWO GENTLEMEN OVER THERE--
MICASA AND SUCASA?
YEAH. THEM. TWO MORE MARTINIS BUT USE THE AFRICAN VODKA THIS TIME. I THINK THEY HAVE MONEY.

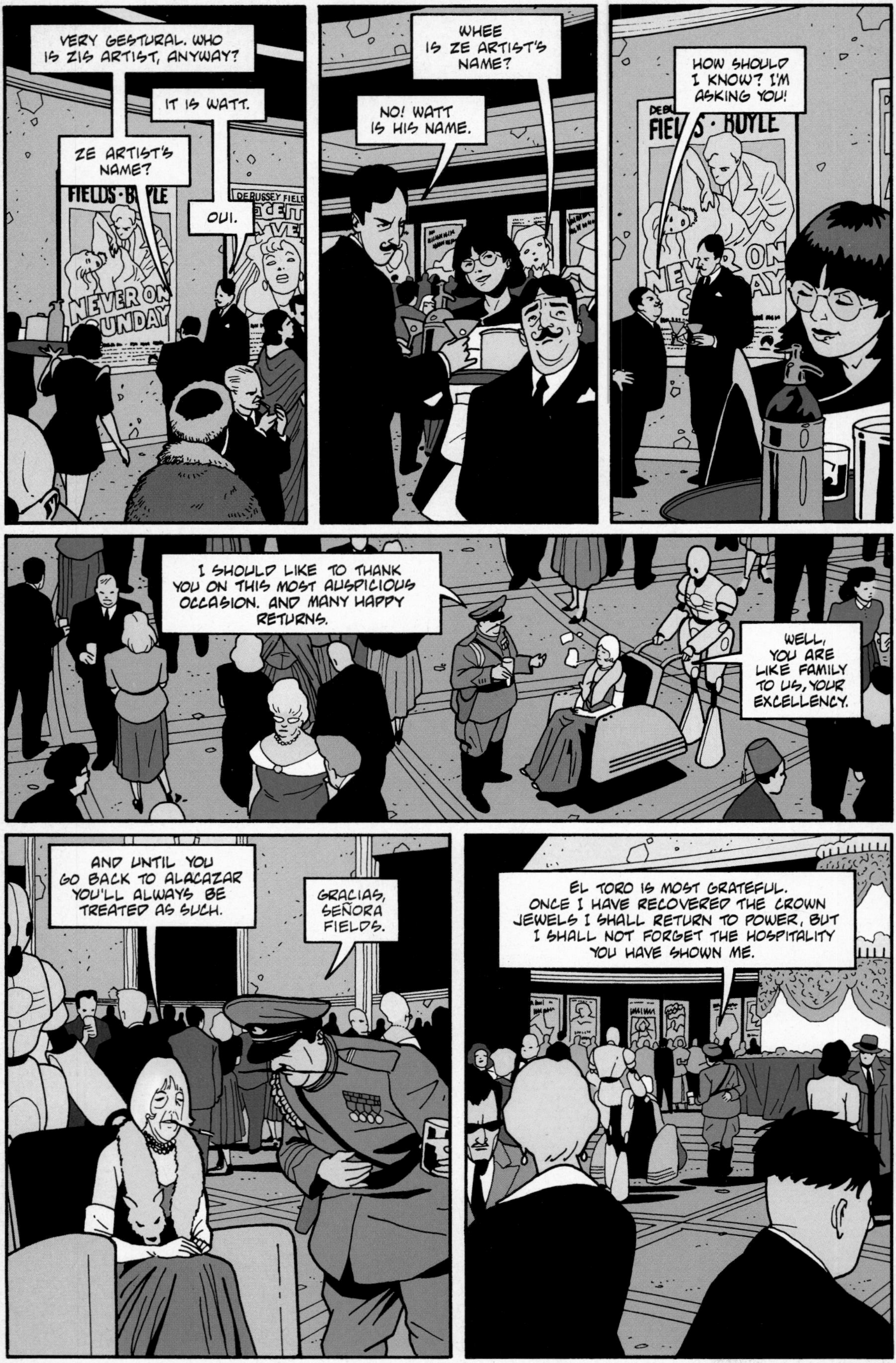
VERY GESTURAL. WHO IS ZIS ARTIST, ANYWAY?
IT IS WATT.
ZE ARTIST'S NAME?
OUI.
FIELDS · BOYLE
NEVER ON SUNDAY
DEBUSSEY FIELDS
WHEE IS ZE ARTIST'S NAME?
NO! WATT IS HIS NAME.
HOW SHOULD I KNOW? I'M ASKING YOU!
I SHOULD LIKE TO THANK YOU ON THIS MOST AUSPICIOUS OCCASION. AND MANY HAPPY RETURNS.
WELL, YOU ARE LIKE FAMILY TO US, YOUR EXCELLENCY.
AND UNTIL YOU GO BACK TO ALACAZAR YOU'LL ALWAYS BE TREATED AS SUCH.
GRACIAS, SEÑORA FIELDS.
EL TORO IS MOST GRATEFUL. ONCE I HAVE RECOVERED THE CROWN JEWELS I SHALL RETURN TO POWER, BUT I SHALL NOT FORGET THE HOSPITALITY YOU HAVE SHOWN ME.

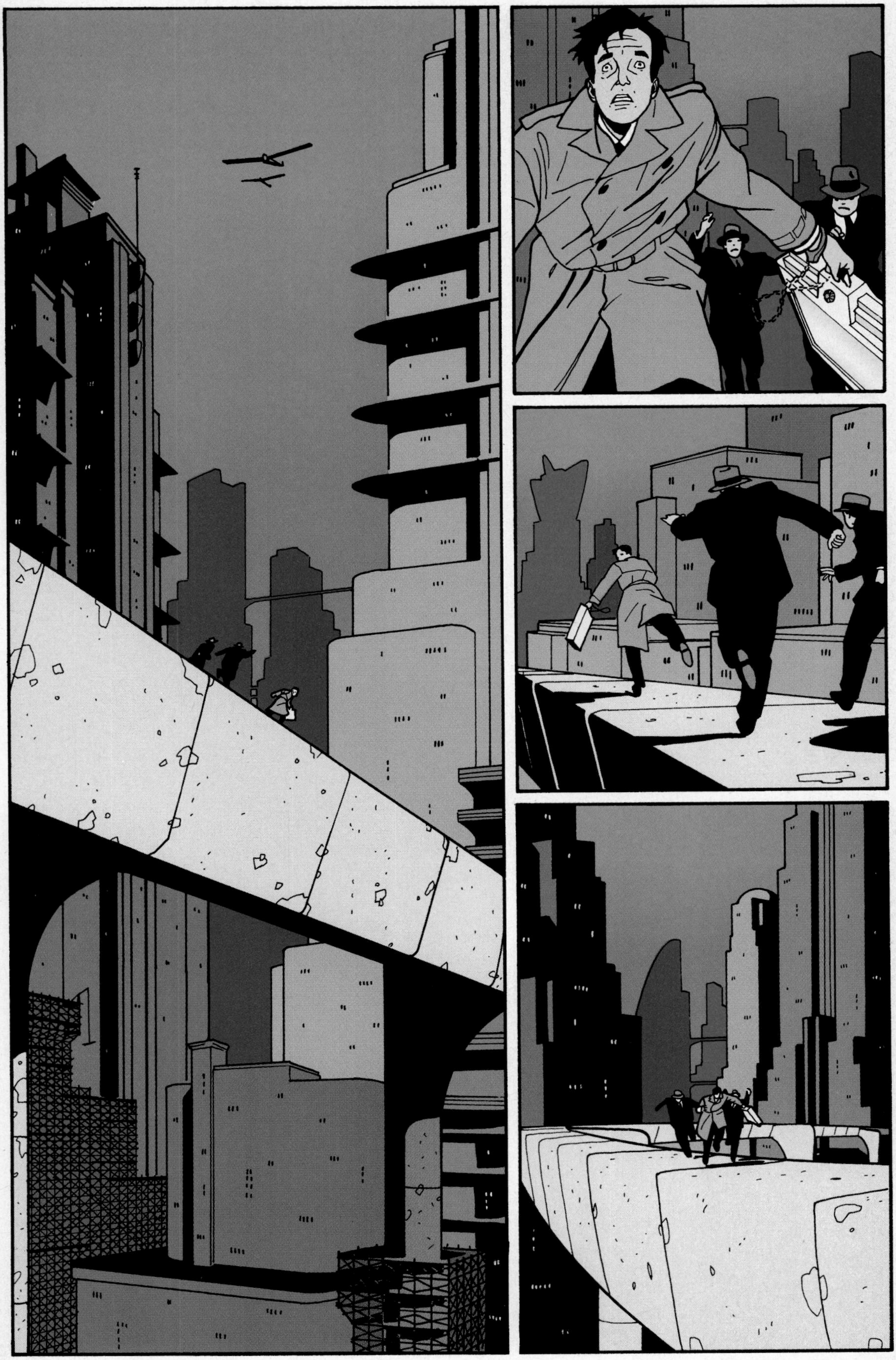

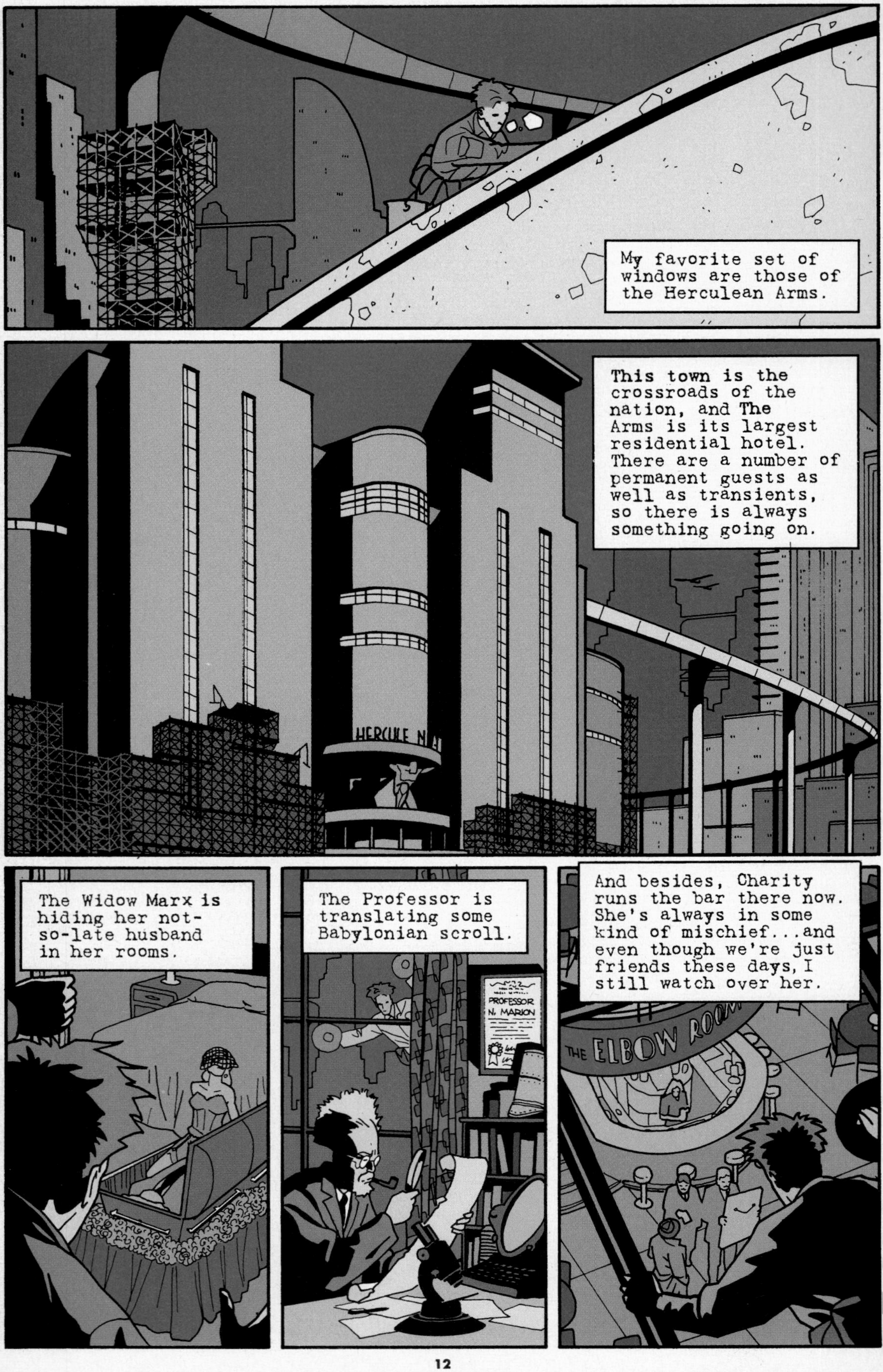

My favorite set of windows are those of the Herculean Arms.
This town is the crossroads of the nation, and The Arms is its largest residential hotel. There are a number of permanent guests as well as transients, so there is always something going on.
HERCULE N
The Widow Marx is hiding her not-so-late husband in her rooms.
The Professor is translating some Babylonian scroll.
PROFESSOR N. MARION
And besides, Charity runs the bar there now. She's always in some kind of mischief...and even though we're just friends these days, I still watch over her.
THE ELBOW ROOM

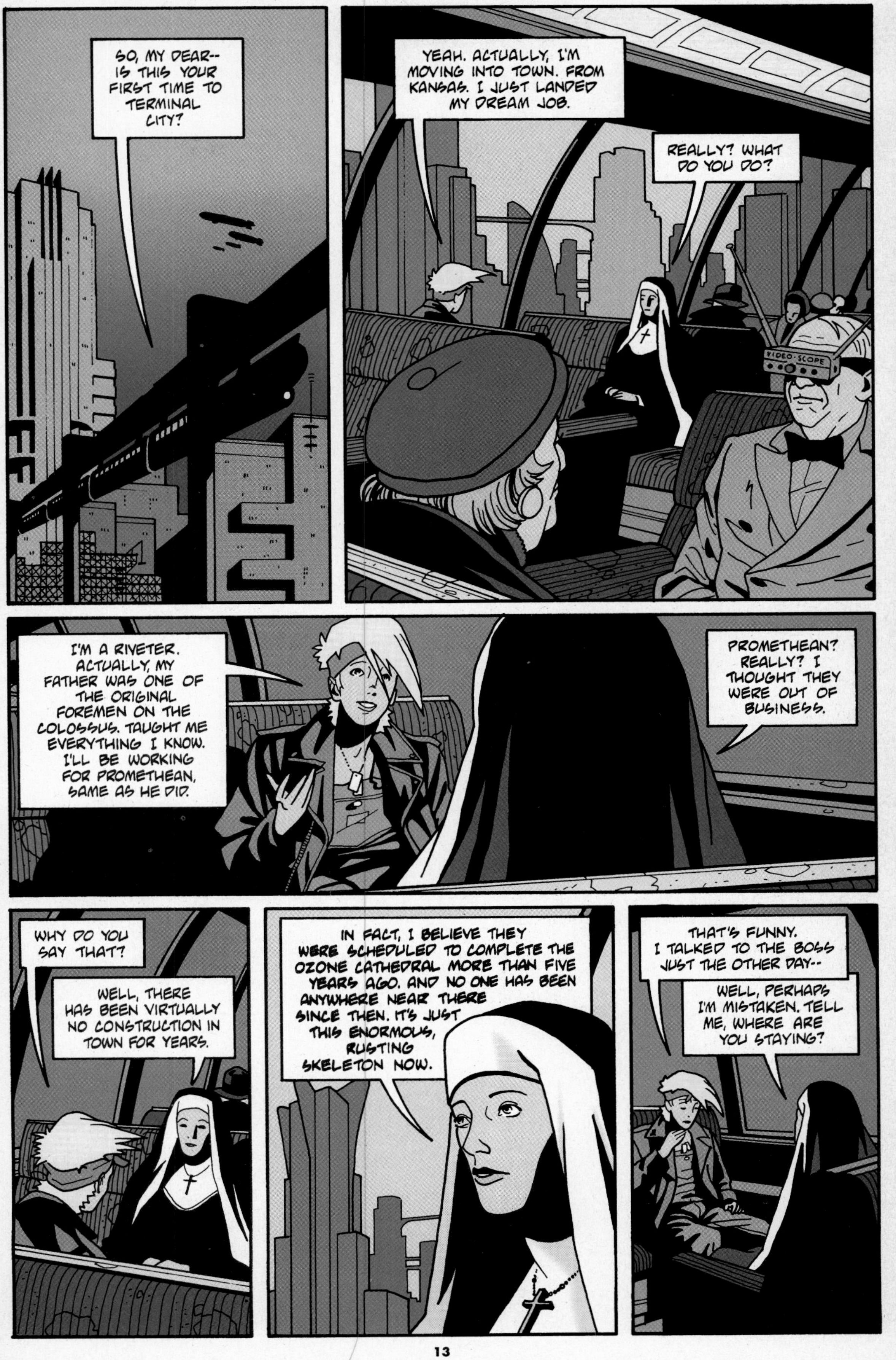
SO, MY DEAR-- IS THIS YOUR FIRST TIME TO TERMINAL CITY?
YEAH. ACTUALLY, I'M MOVING INTO TOWN. FROM KANSAS. I JUST LANDED MY DREAM JOB.
REALLY? WHAT DO YOU DO?
VIDEO-SCOPE
I'M A RIVETER. ACTUALLY, MY FATHER WAS ONE OF THE ORIGINAL FOREMEN ON THE COLOSSUS. TAUGHT ME EVERYTHING I KNOW. I'LL BE WORKING FOR PROMETHEAN, SAME AS HE DID.
PROMETHEAN? REALLY? I THOUGHT THEY WERE OUT OF BUSINESS.
WHY DO YOU SAY THAT?
WELL, THERE HAS BEEN VIRTUALLY NO CONSTRUCTION IN TOWN FOR YEARS.
IN FACT, I BELIEVE THEY WERE SCHEDULED TO COMPLETE THE OZONE CATHEDRAL MORE THAN FIVE YEARS AGO. AND NO ONE HAS BEEN ANYWHERE NEAR THERE SINCE THEN. IT'S JUST THIS ENORMOUS, RUSTING SKELETON NOW.
THAT'S FUNNY. I TALKED TO THE BOSS JUST THE OTHER DAY--
WELL, PERHAPS I'M MISTAKEN. TELL ME, WHERE ARE YOU STAYING?

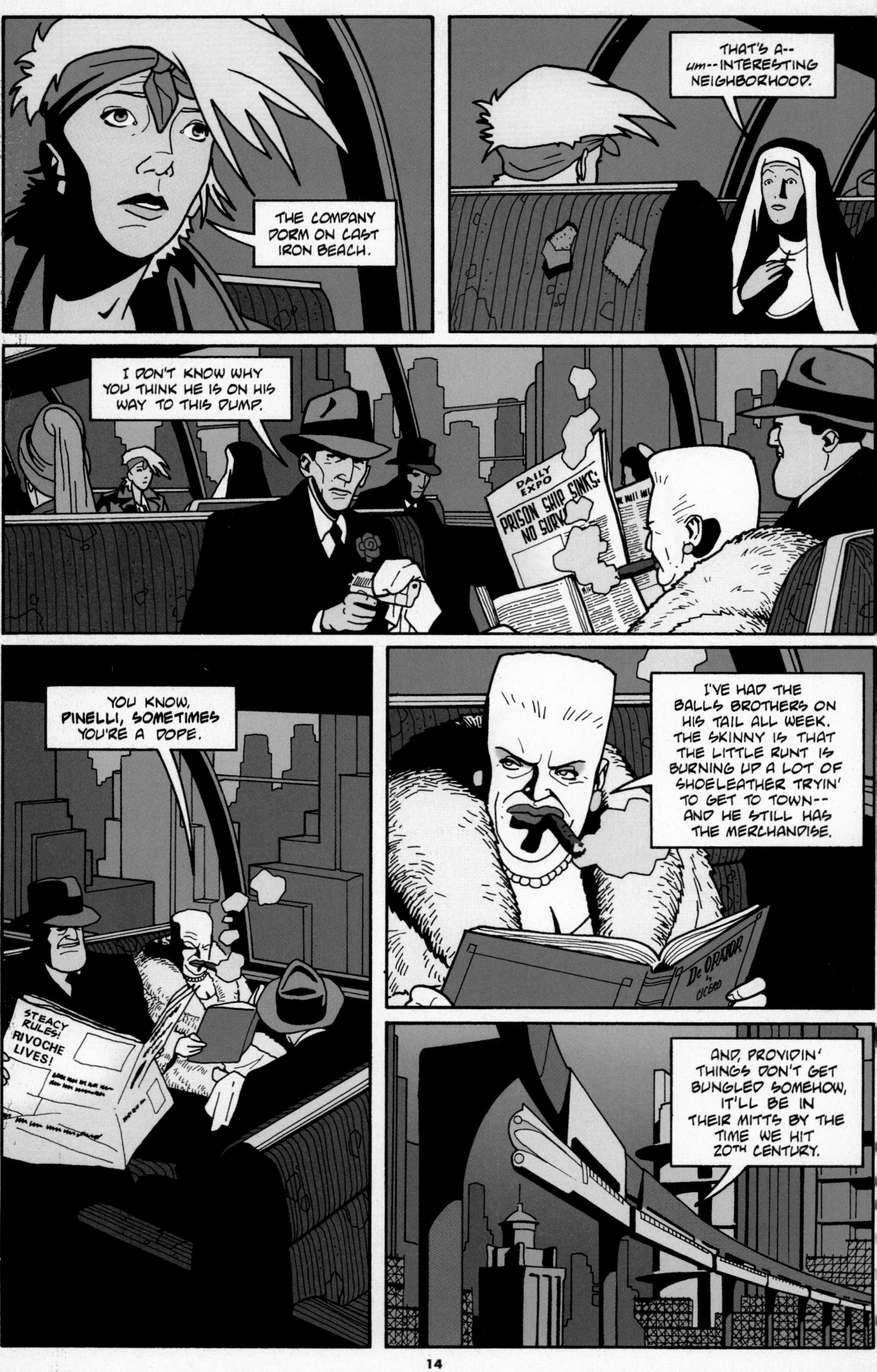
THE COMPANY DORM ON CAST IRON BEACH.
THAT'S A-- um--INTERESTING NEIGHBORHOOD.
I DON'T KNOW WHY YOU THINK HE IS ON HIS WAY TO THIS DUMP.
DAILY EXPO
PRISON SHIP SINKS:
YOU KNOW, PINELLI, SOMETIMES YOU'RE A DOPE.
STEACY RULES!
RIVOCHE LIVES!
I'VE HAD THE BALLS BROTHERS ON HIS TAIL ALL WEEK. THE SKINNY IS THAT THE LITTLE RUNT IS BURNING UP A LOT OF SHOELEATHER TRYIN' TO GET TO TOWN-- AND HE STILL HAS THE MERCHANDISE.
CICERO
AND, PROVIDIN' THINGS DON'T GET BUNGLED SOMEHOW, IT'LL BE IN THEIR MITTS BY THE TIME WE HIT 20TH CENTURY.

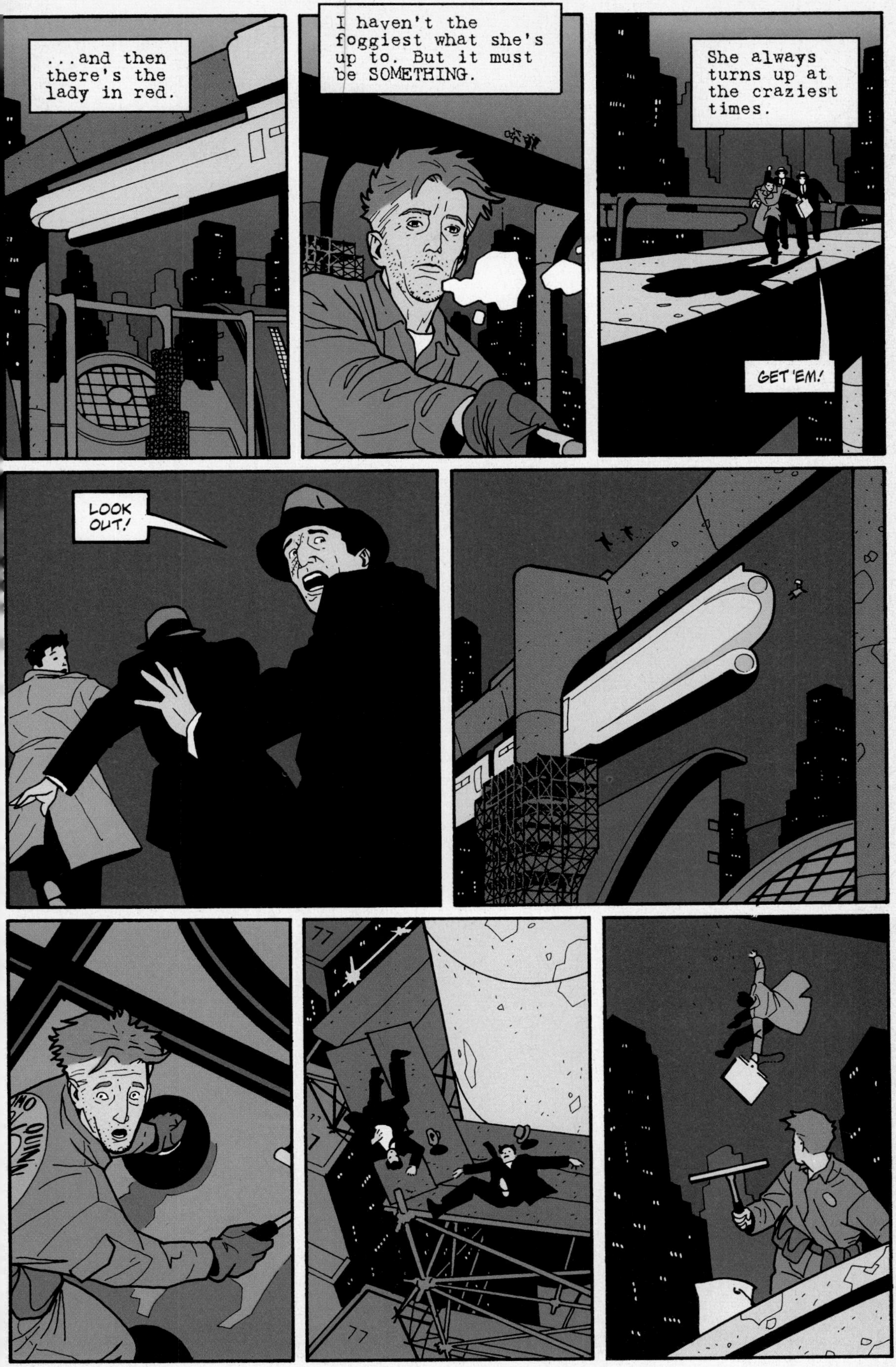
...and then there's the lady in red.
I haven't the foggiest what she's up to. But it must be SOMETHING.
She always turns up at the craziest times.
GET 'EM!
LOOK OUT!

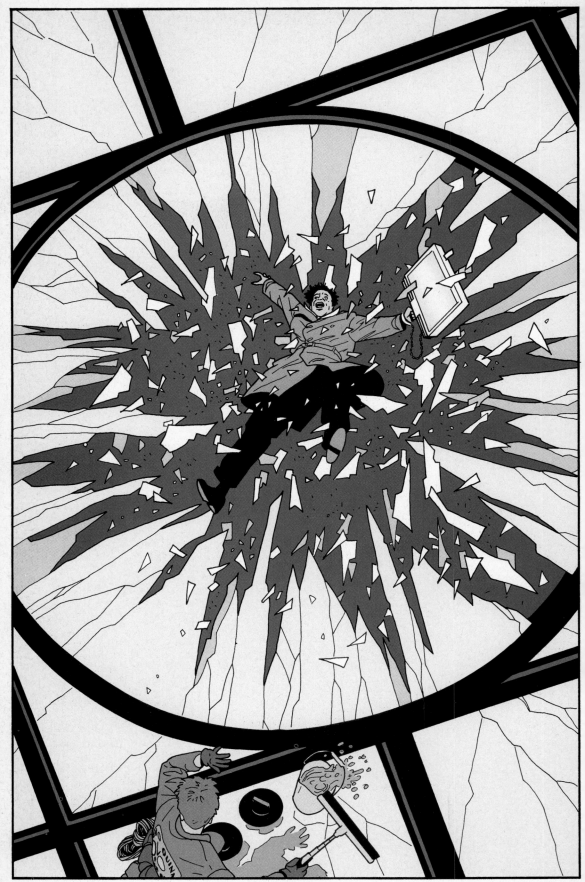

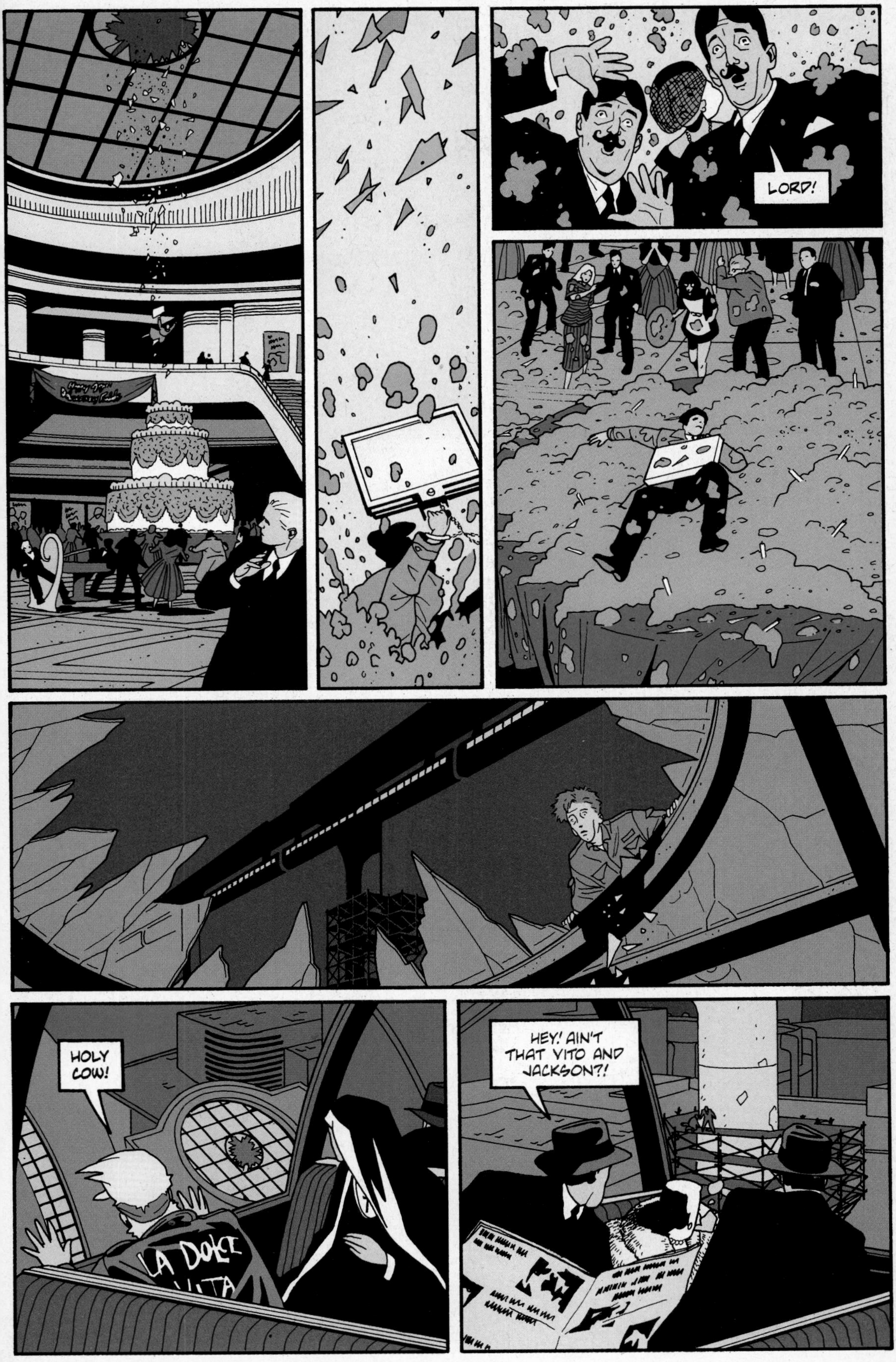
LORD!
HOLY COW!
HEY! AIN'T THAT VITO AND JACKSON?!
LA DOLCE VITA

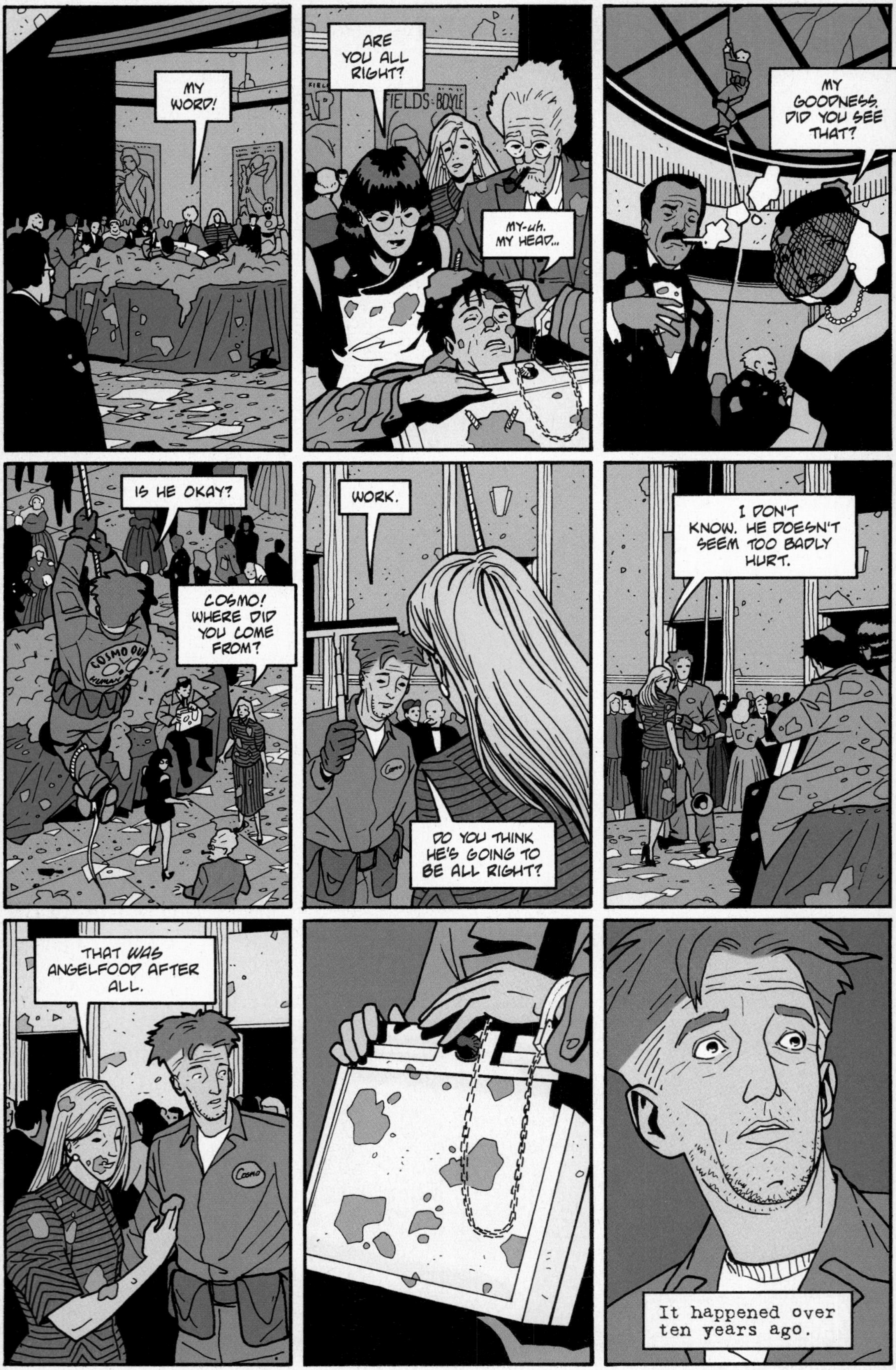
MY WORD!
ARE YOU ALL RIGHT?
FIELDS • BOYLE
MY-uh. MY HEAD...
MY GOODNESS. DID YOU SEE THAT?
IS HE OKAY?
COSMO! WHERE DID YOU COME FROM?
WORK.
DO YOU THINK HE'S GOING TO BE ALL RIGHT?
I DON'T KNOW. HE DOESN'T SEEM TOO BADLY HURT.
THAT WAS ANGELFOOD AFTER ALL.
It happened over ten years ago.

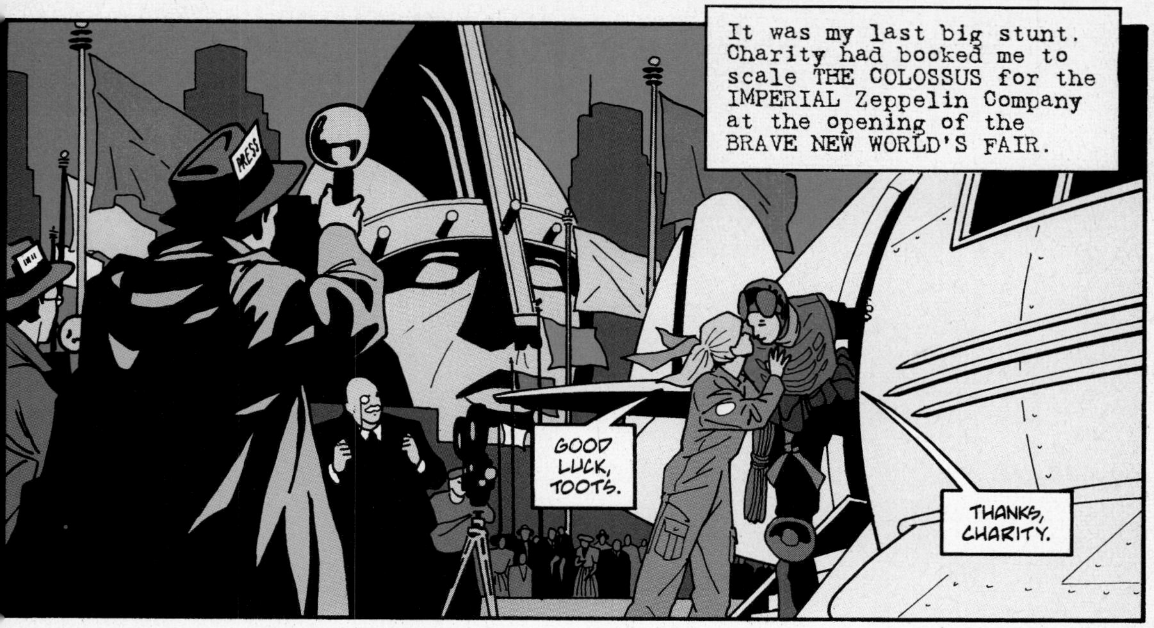
It was my last big stunt. Charity had booked me to scale THE COLOSSUS for the IMPERIAL Zeppelin Company at the opening of the BRAVE NEW WORLD'S FAIR.
PRESS
GOOD LUCK, TOOTS.
THANKS, CHARITY.

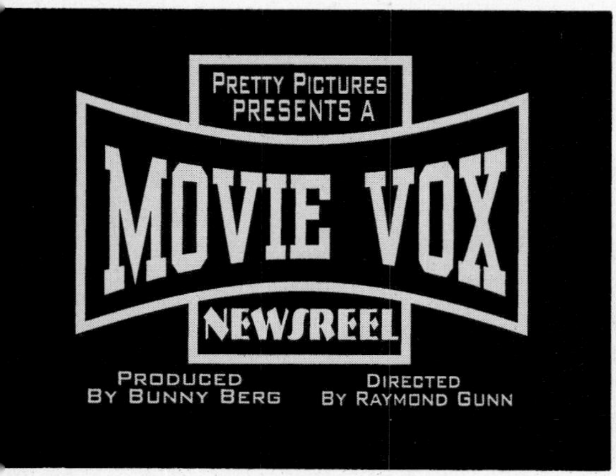
PRETTY PICTURES PRESENTS A
MOVIE VOX
NEWSREEL
PRODUCED BY BUNNY BERG
DIRECTED BY RAYMOND GUNN

THE PLACE IS
TERMINAL CITY.

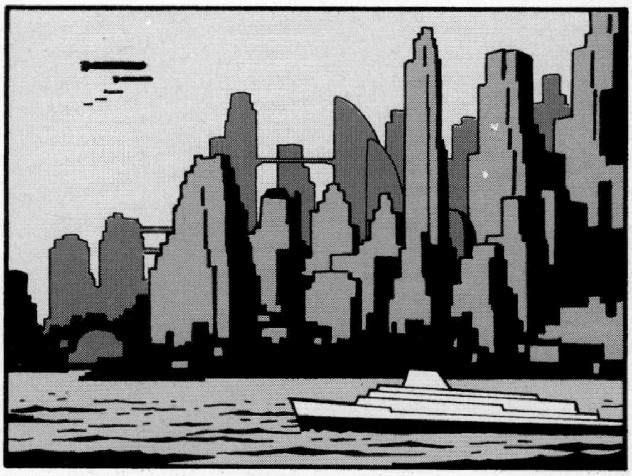

THE SITE OF THE
BRAVE NEW WORLD'S FAIR.

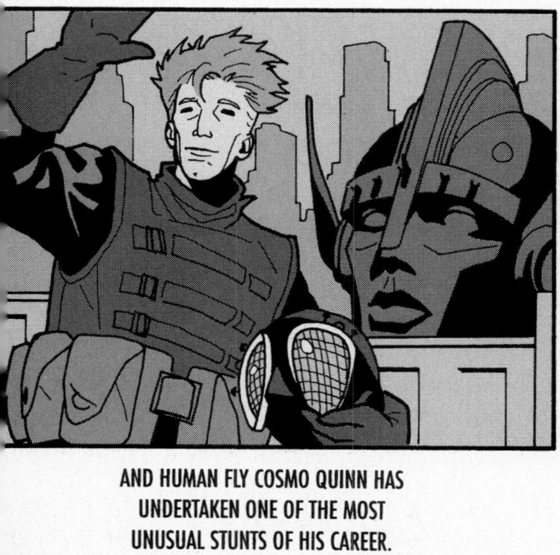

AND HUMAN FLY COSMO QUINN HAS
UNDERTAKEN ONE OF THE MOST
UNUSUAL STUNTS OF HIS CAREER.

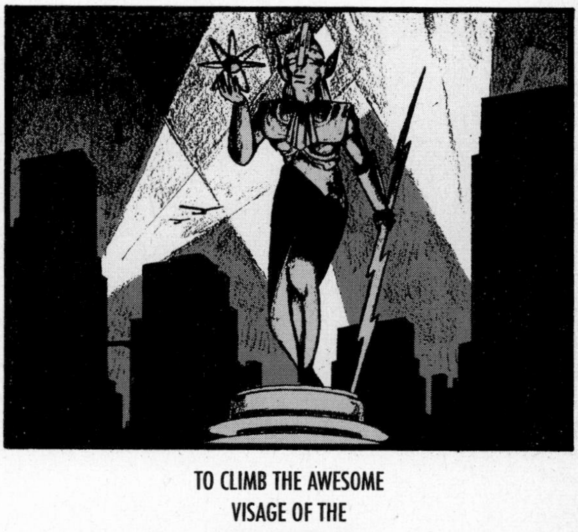

TO CLIMB THE AWESOME
VISAGE OF THE
COLOSSUS OF ROADS.

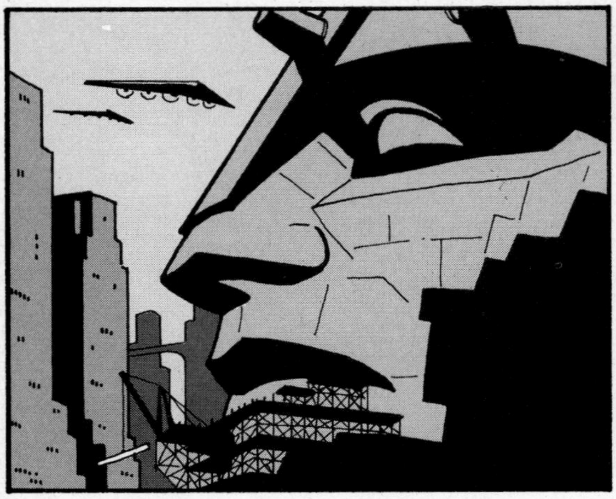

THIS, OF COURSE, IS MERELY THE HEAD OF WHAT WILL, WHEN COMPLETED, BE THE LARGEST STATUE OF ITS KIND EVER CONSTRUCTED. EVEN SO, IT IS AN IMPRESSIVE SIGHT.

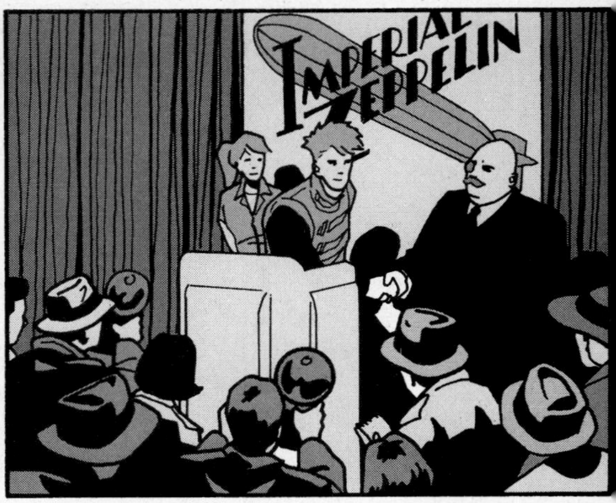
IMPERIAL ZEPPELIN

IT HAS TAKEN THE CREW OF PROMETHEAN CONSTRUCTION OVER FIVE YEARS TO COMPLETE THIS MUCH. WHEN FINISHED IT WILL BE A HEROIC SYMBOL, A MAJOR ZEPPELIN TERMINAL, AND AN IMPORTANT TOURIST ATTRACTION FOR THE MANY PEOPLE WHO PASS THROUGH TERMINAL CITY.

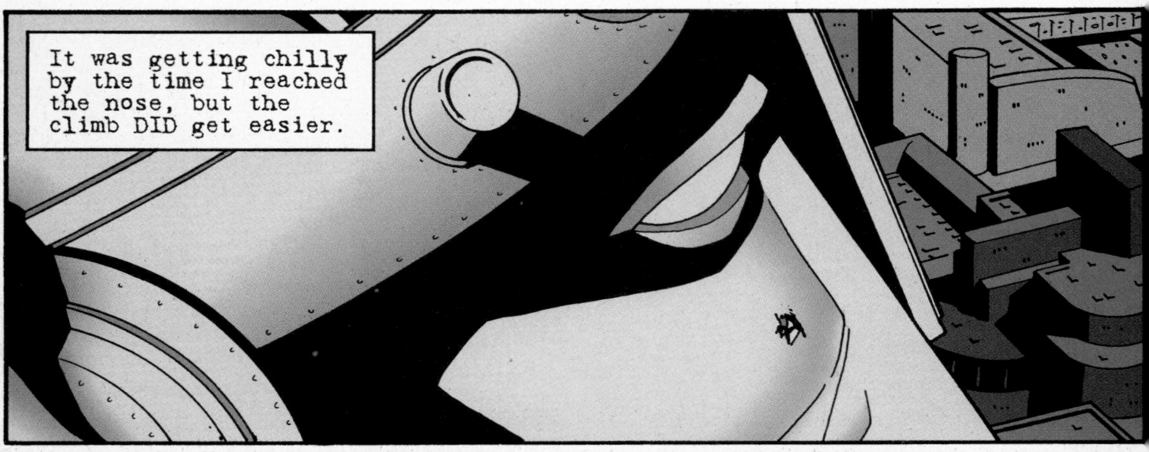
It was getting chilly by the time I reached the nose, but the climb DID get easier.

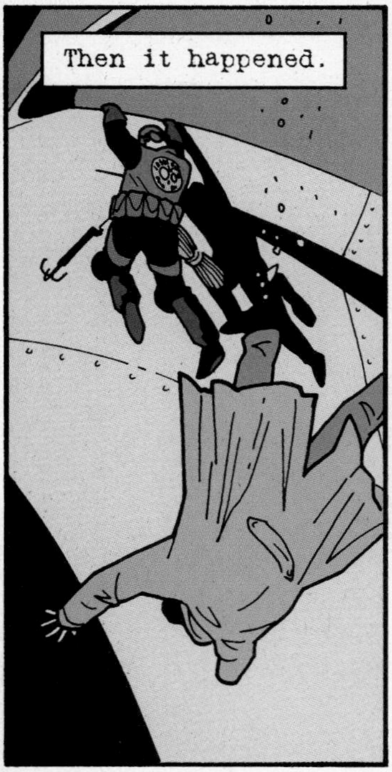
Then it happened.

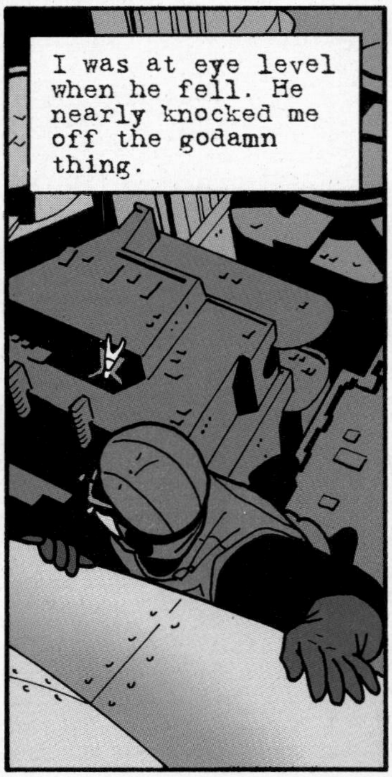
I was at eye level when he fell. He nearly knocked me off the godamn thing.

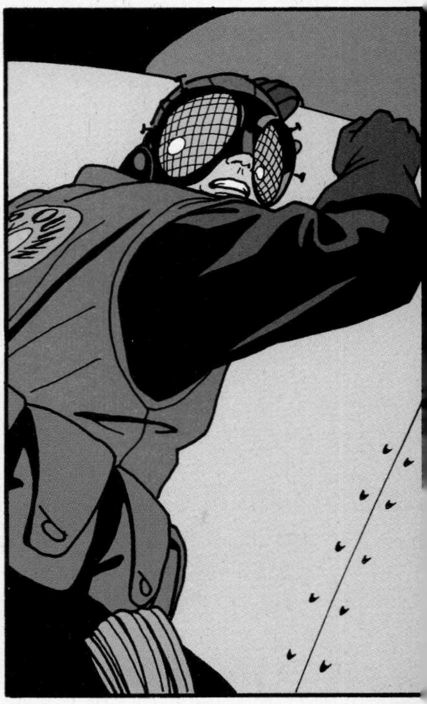

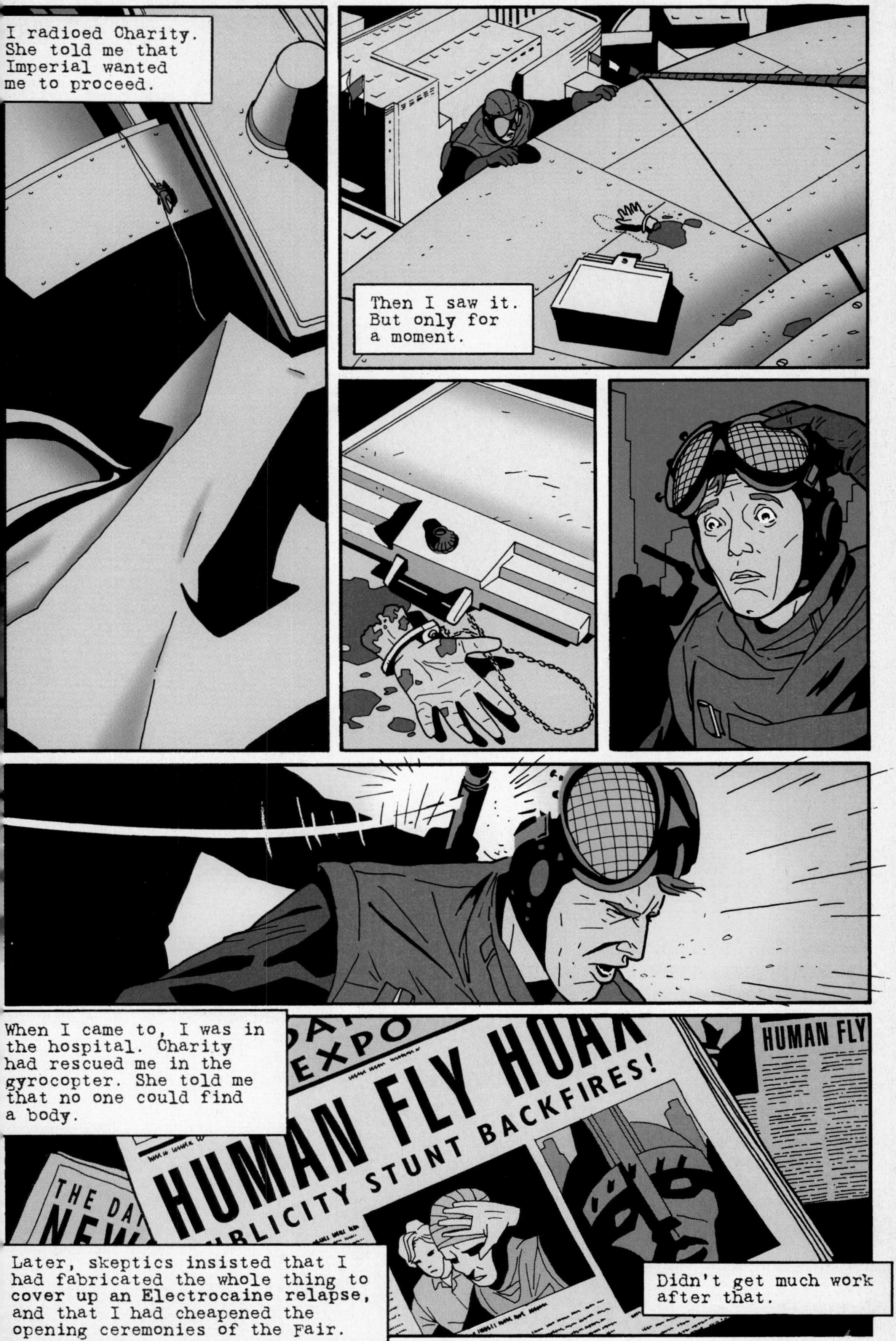

I radioed Charity. She told me that Imperial wanted me to proceed.
Then I saw it. But only for a moment.
When I came to, I was in the hospital. Charity had rescued me in the gyrocopter. She told me that no one could find a body.
EXPO
HUMAN FLY HOAX
PUBLICITY STUNT BACKFIRES!
HUMAN FLY
THE DA
NEW
Later, skeptics insisted that I had fabricated the whole thing to cover up an Electrocaine relapse, and that I had cheapened the opening ceremonies of the Fair.
Didn't get much work after that.

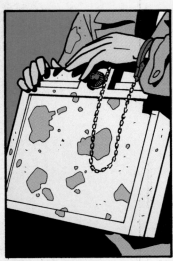

WHAT HAPPENED?

DON'T KNOW... WHERE AM I...?

YOU'RE IN THE ARMS, SUNSHINE.

THE ARMS...? WHOSE ARMS--?

THE HERCULEAN ARMS, YOUNG MAN. WHO ARE YOU?

WHO AM I...?

--I-I DON'T KNOW.

WELL, LET'S GET YOU CLEANED UP. AND THEN YOU CAN LIE DOWN.

JEZEBEL, WHY DON'T YOU PUT SOME ICE ON HIS HEAD AND THEN LET HIM REST IN ONE OF THE VACANT ROOMS.

ANYTHING YOU SAY, OH QUEEN OF THE NILE.

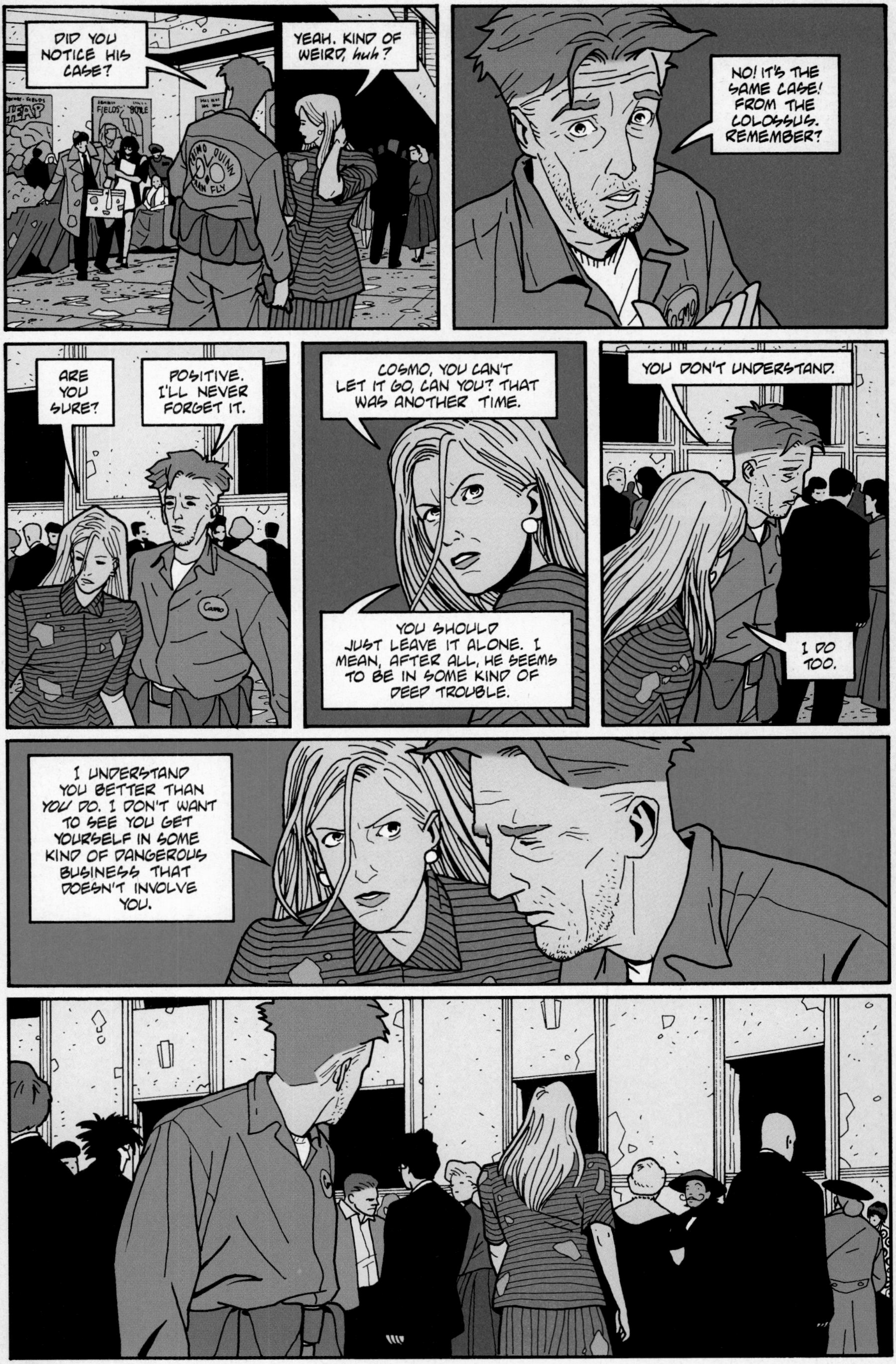
DID YOU NOTICE HIS CASE?
YEAH. KIND OF WEIRD, *huh?*
NO! IT'S THE SAME CASE! FROM THE COLOSSUS. REMEMBER?
ARE YOU SURE?
POSITIVE. I'LL NEVER FORGET IT.
COSMO, YOU CAN'T LET IT GO, CAN YOU? THAT WAS ANOTHER TIME.
YOU SHOULD JUST LEAVE IT ALONE. I MEAN, AFTER ALL, HE SEEMS TO BE IN SOME KIND OF DEEP TROUBLE.
YOU DON'T UNDERSTAND.
I DO TOO.
I UNDERSTAND YOU BETTER THAN YOU DO. I DON'T WANT TO SEE YOU GET YOURSELF IN SOME KIND OF DANGEROUS BUSINESS THAT DOESN'T INVOLVE YOU.

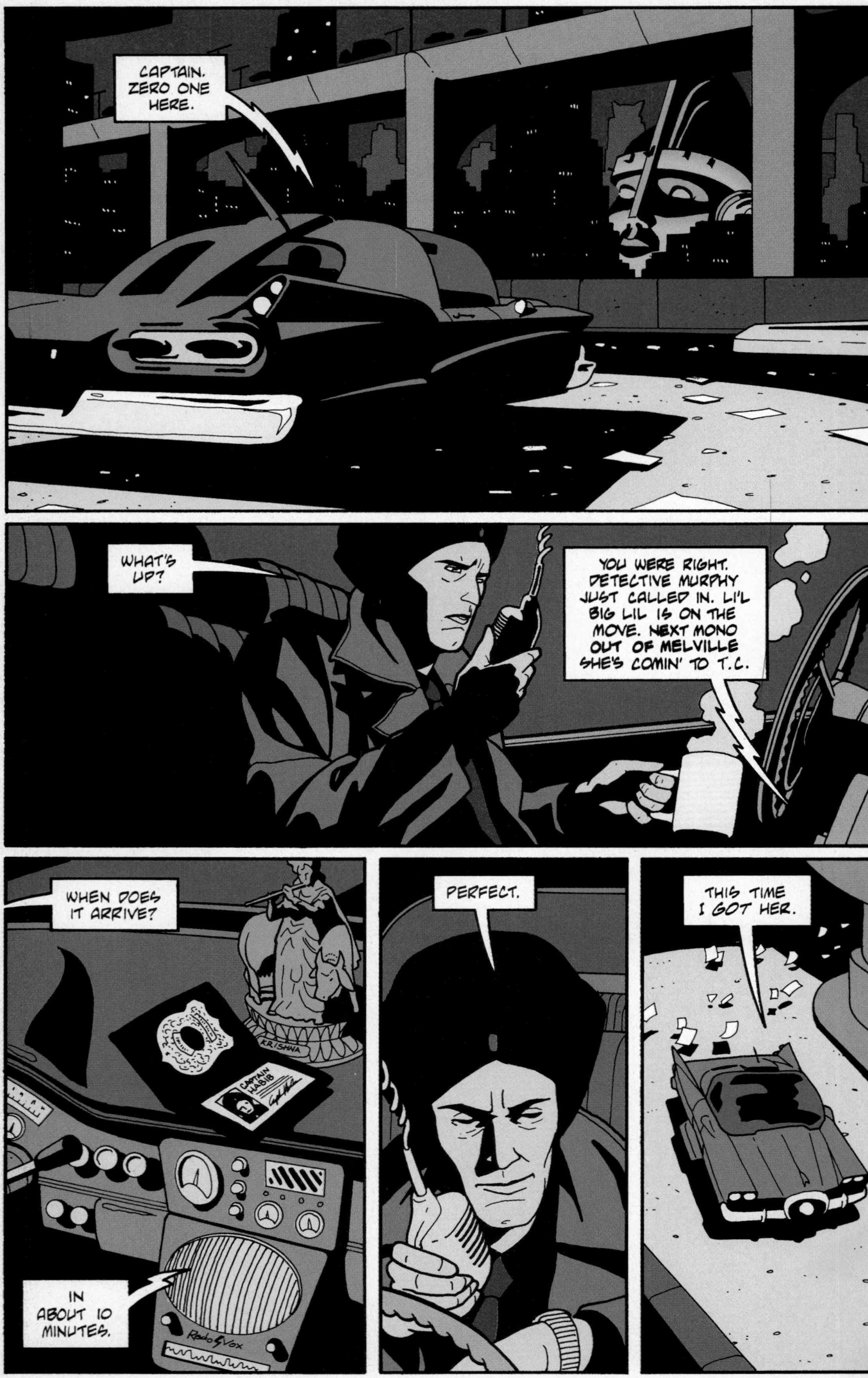
CAPTAIN. ZERO ONE HERE.
WHAT'S UP?
YOU WERE RIGHT. DETECTIVE MURPHY JUST CALLED IN. LI'L BIG LIL IS ON THE MOVE. NEXT MONO OUT OF MELVILLE SHE'S COMIN' TO T.C.
WHEN DOES IT ARRIVE?
KRISHNA
CAPTAIN HABIB
IN ABOUT 10 MINUTES.
PERFECT.
THIS TIME I GOT HER.

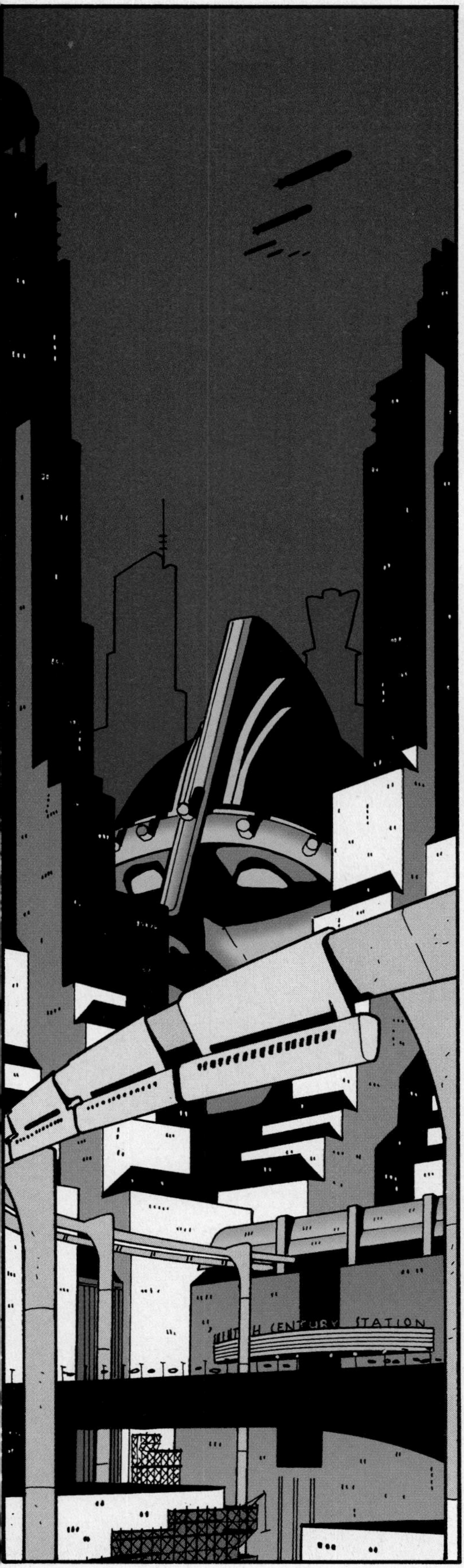
CENTURY STATION

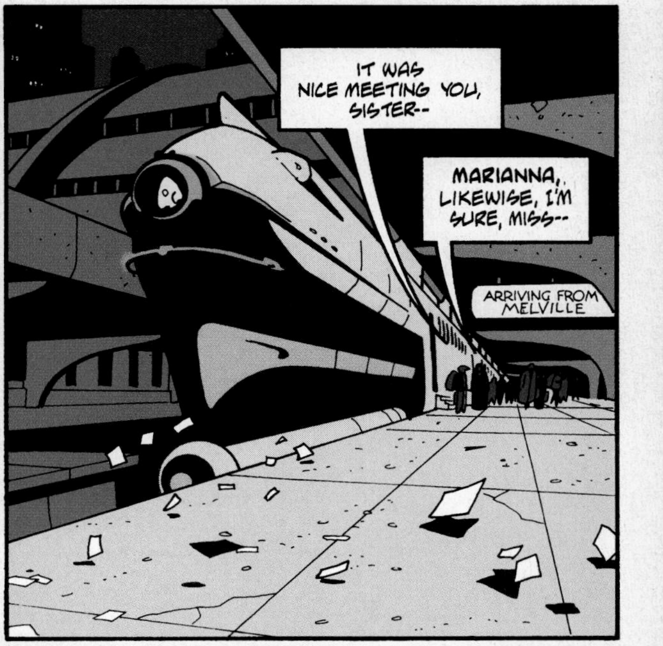
IT WAS NICE MEETING YOU, SISTER--
MARIANNA,. LIKEWISE, I'M SURE, MISS--
ARRIVING FROM MELVILLE

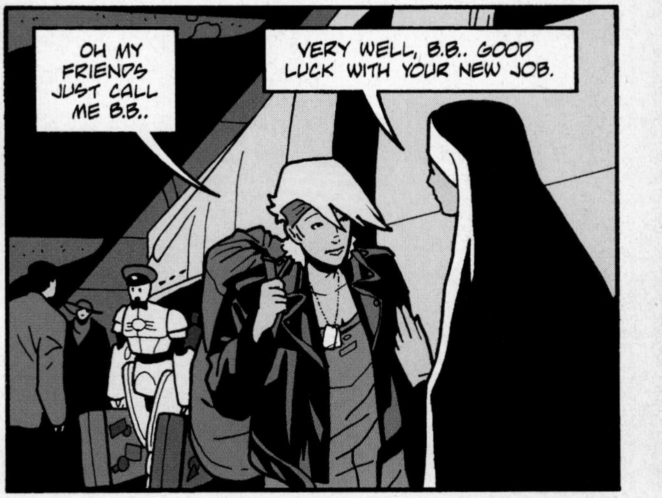
OH MY FRIENDS JUST CALL ME B.B..
VERY WELL, B.B.. GOOD LUCK WITH YOUR NEW JOB.

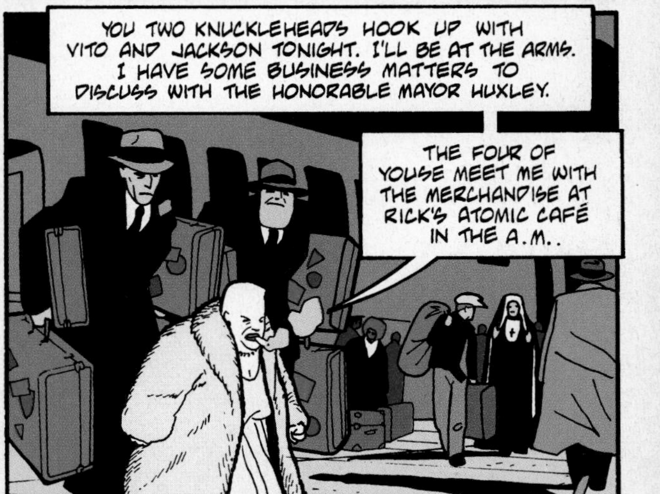
YOU TWO KNUCKLEHEADS HOOK UP WITH VITO AND JACKSON TONIGHT. I'LL BE AT THE ARMS. I HAVE SOME BUSINESS MATTERS TO DISCUSS WITH THE HONORABLE MAYOR HUXLEY.
THE FOUR OF YOUSE MEET ME WITH THE MERCHANDISE AT RICK'S ATOMIC CAFÉ IN THE A.M..

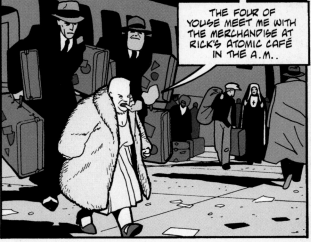

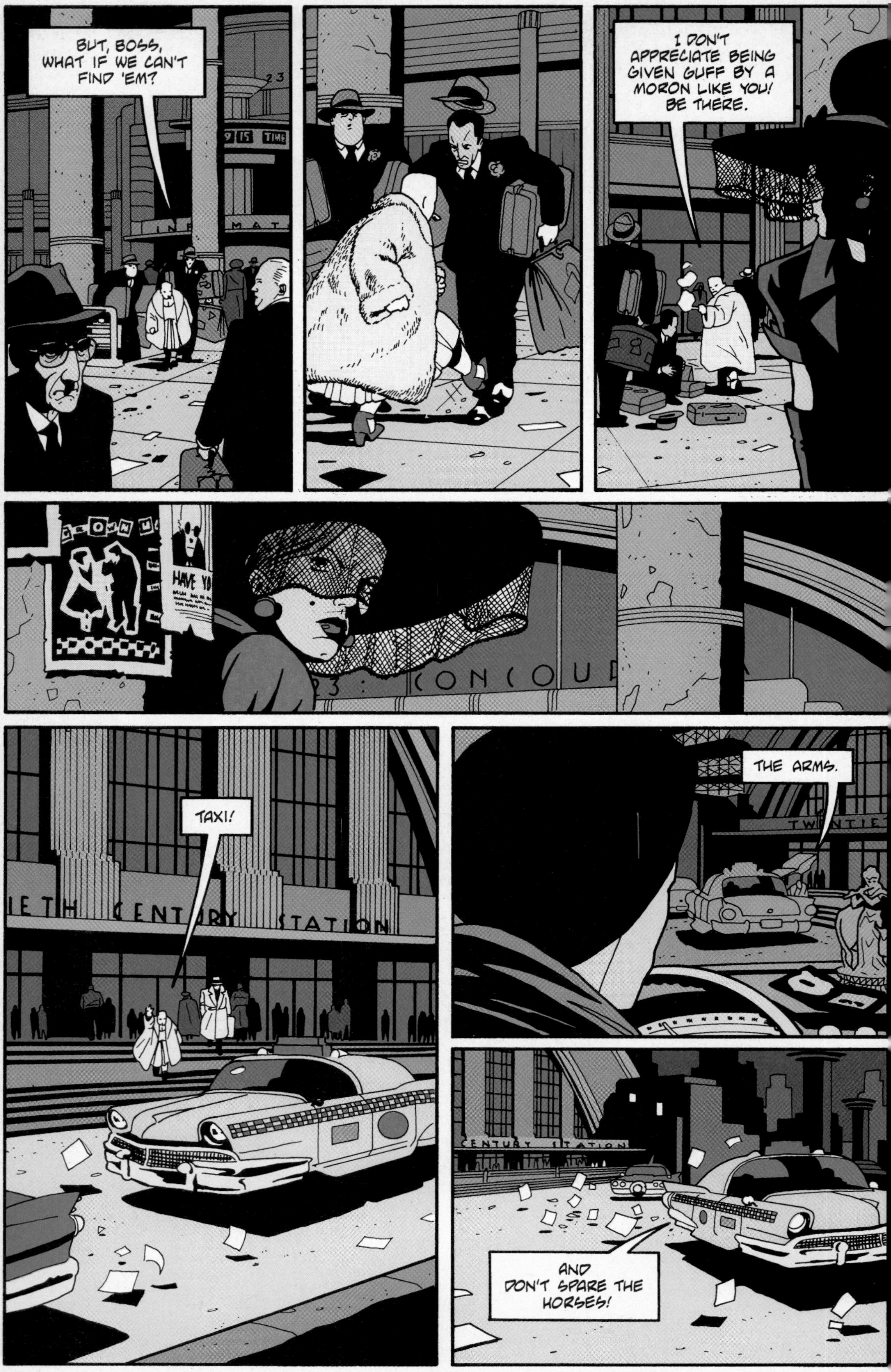
BUT, BOSS, WHAT IF WE CAN'T FIND 'EM?
I DON'T APPRECIATE BEING GIVEN GUFF BY A MORON LIKE YOU! BE THERE.
TAXI!
CENTURY STATION
THE ARMS.
AND DON'T SPARE THE HORSES!

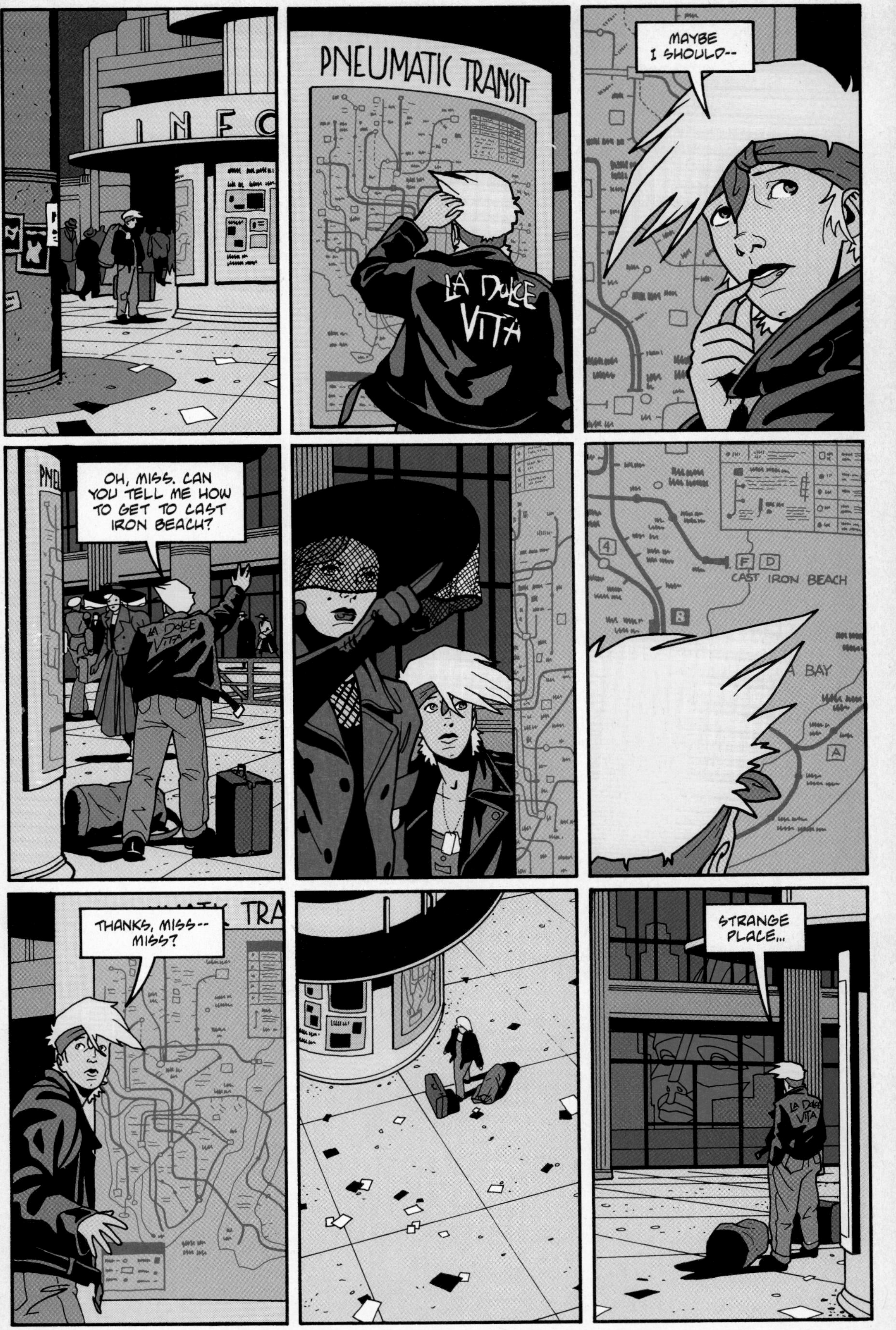
INFO
PNEUMATIC TRANSIT
LA DOLCE VITA
MAYBE I SHOULD--
OH, MISS. CAN YOU TELL ME HOW TO GET TO CAST IRON BEACH?
LA DOLCE VITA
CAST IRON BEACH
A BAY
THANKS, MISS-- MISS?
STRANGE PLACE...
LA DOLCE VITA

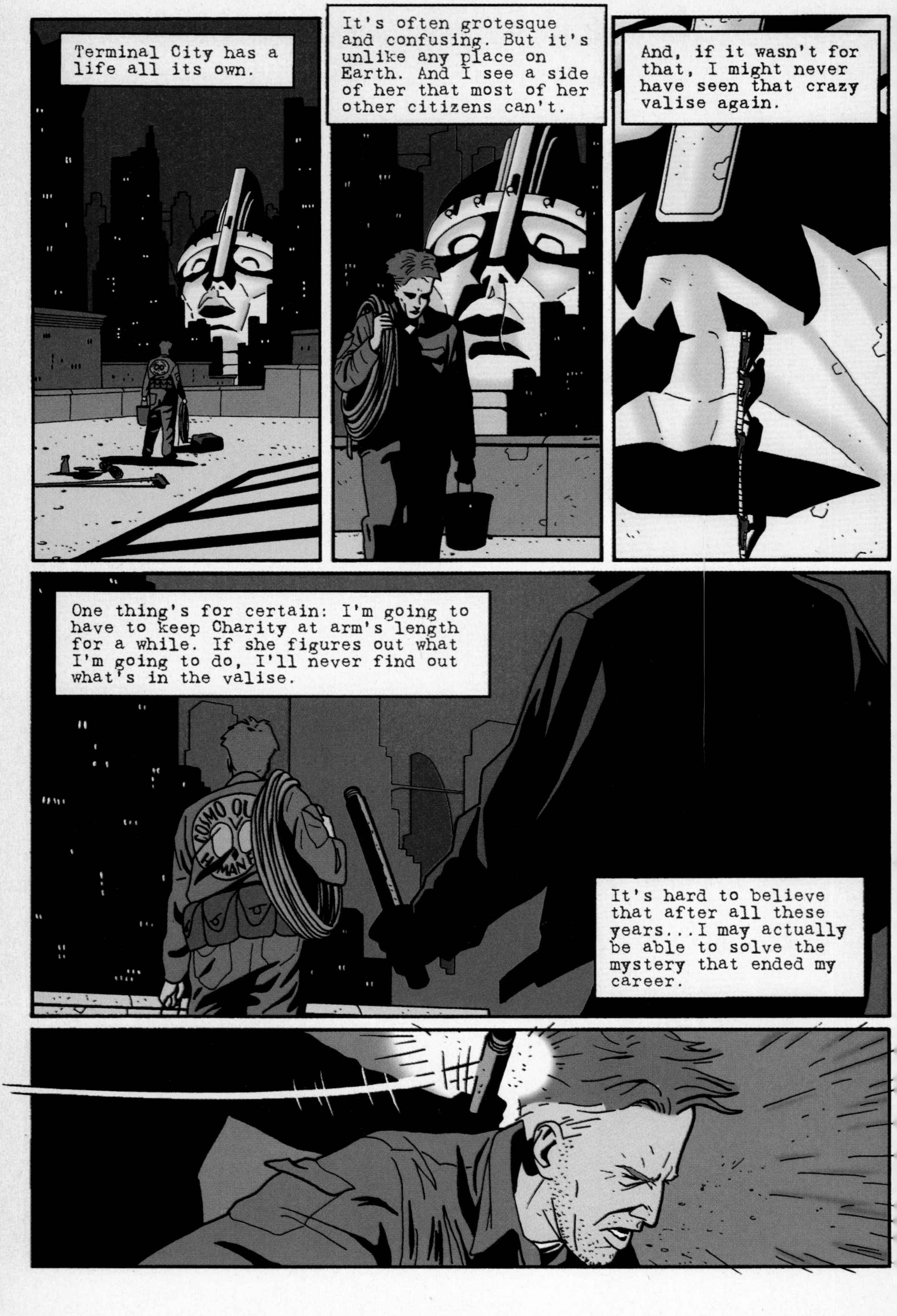
Terminal City has a life all its own.
It's often grotesque and confusing. But it's unlike any place on Earth. And I see a side of her that most of her other citizens can't.
And, if it wasn't for that, I might never have seen that crazy valise again.
One thing's for certain: I'm going to have to keep Charity at arm's length for a while. If she figures out what I'm going to do, I'll never find out what's in the valise.
It's hard to believe that after all these years...I may actually be able to solve the mystery that ended my career.

Episode Two

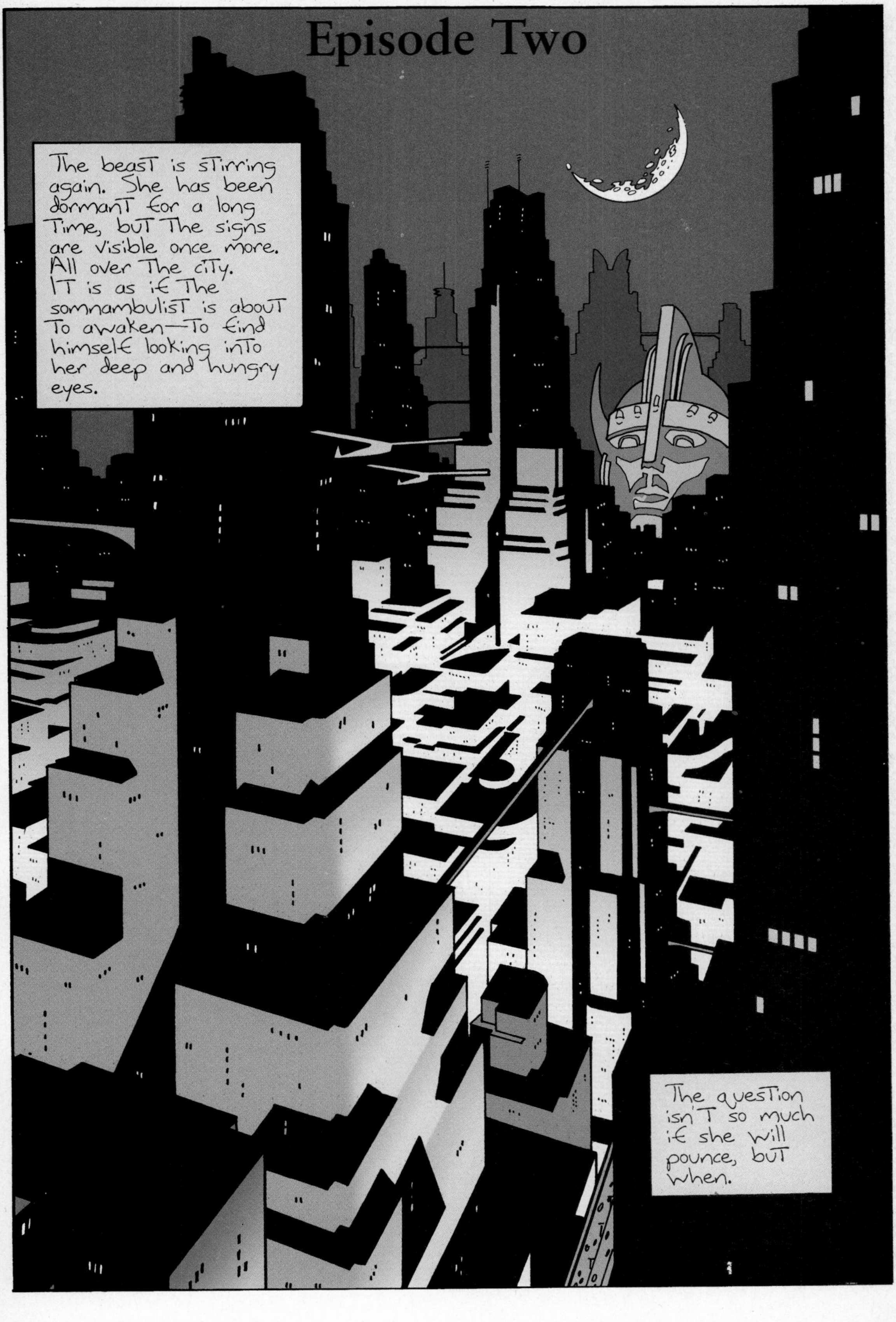
The beasT is sTirring again. She has been dormanT for a long Time, buT The signs are visible once more. All over The ciTy. IT is as if The somnambulisT is abouT To awaken—To find himself looking inTo her deep and hungry eyes.
The quesTion isn'T so much if she will pounce, buT when.

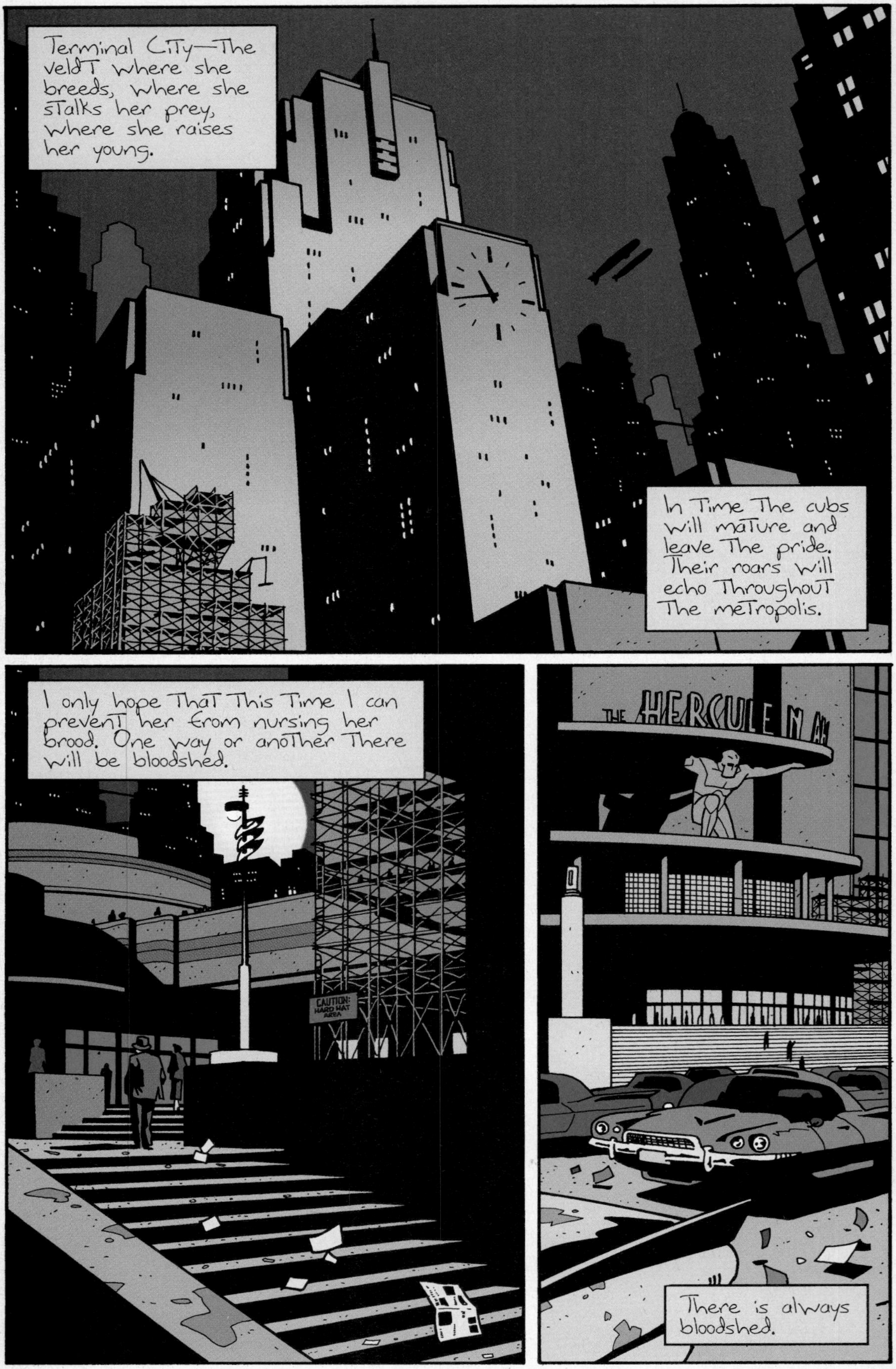
Terminal City—The veldT where she breeds, where she sTalks her prey, where she raises her young.
In Time The cubs will maTure and leave The pride. Their roars will echo ThroughouT The meTropolis.
I only hope ThaT This Time I can prevenT her from nursing her brood. One way or another There will be bloodshed.
CAUTION: HARD HAT AREA
There is always bloodshed.

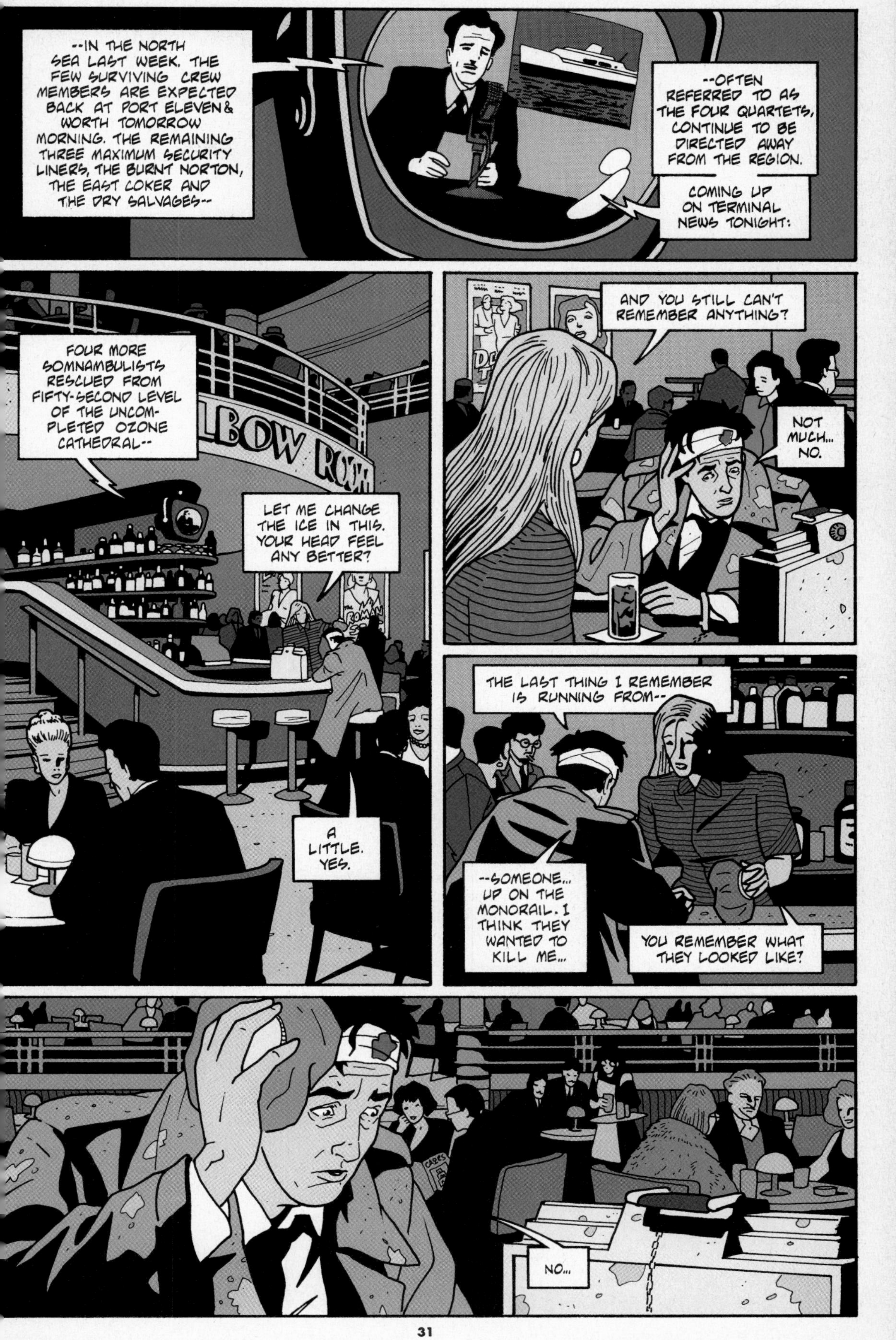
--IN THE NORTH SEA LAST WEEK. THE FEW SURVIVING CREW MEMBERS ARE EXPECTED BACK AT PORT ELEVEN & WORTH TOMORROW MORNING. THE REMAINING THREE MAXIMUM SECURITY LINERS, THE BURNT NORTON, THE EAST COKER AND THE DRY SALVAGES--
--OFTEN REFERRED TO AS THE FOUR QUARTETS, CONTINUE TO BE DIRECTED AWAY FROM THE REGION.
COMING UP ON TERMINAL NEWS TONIGHT:
FOUR MORE SOMNAMBULISTS RESCUED FROM FIFTY-SECOND LEVEL OF THE UNCOMPLETED OZONE CATHEDRAL--
LBOW RO
LET ME CHANGE THE ICE IN THIS. YOUR HEAD FEEL ANY BETTER?
A LITTLE. YES.
AND YOU STILL CAN'T REMEMBER ANYTHING?
NOT MUCH... NO.
THE LAST THING I REMEMBER IS RUNNING FROM--
--SOMEONE... UP ON THE MONORAIL. I THINK THEY WANTED TO KILL ME...
YOU REMEMBER WHAT THEY LOOKED LIKE?
NO...

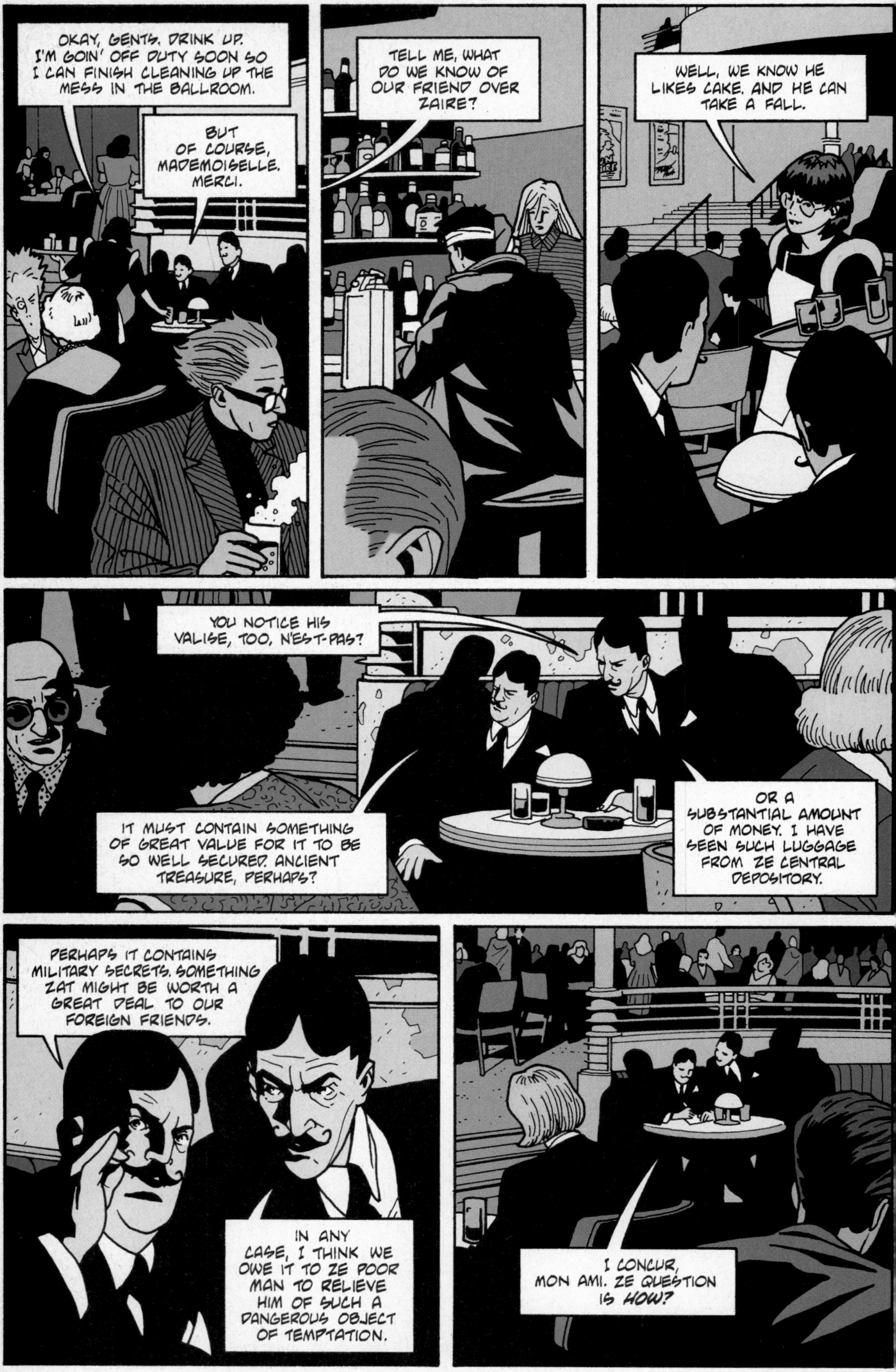
OKAY, GENTS. DRINK UP. I'M GOIN' OFF DUTY SOON SO I CAN FINISH CLEANING UP THE MESS IN THE BALLROOM.
BUT OF COURSE, MADEMOISELLE. MERCI.
TELL ME, WHAT DO WE KNOW OF OUR FRIEND OVER ZAIRE?
WELL, WE KNOW HE LIKES CAKE. AND HE CAN TAKE A FALL.
YOU NOTICE HIS VALISE, TOO, N'EST-PAS?
IT MUST CONTAIN SOMETHING OF GREAT VALUE FOR IT TO BE SO WELL SECURED. ANCIENT TREASURE, PERHAPS?
OR A SUBSTANTIAL AMOUNT OF MONEY. I HAVE SEEN SUCH LUGGAGE FROM ZE CENTRAL DEPOSITORY.
PERHAPS IT CONTAINS MILITARY SECRETS. SOMETHING ZAT MIGHT BE WORTH A GREAT DEAL TO OUR FOREIGN FRIENDS.
IN ANY CASE, I THINK WE OWE IT TO ZE POOR MAN TO RELIEVE HIM OF SUCH A DANGEROUS OBJECT OF TEMPTATION.
I CONCUR, MON AMI. ZE QUESTION IS *HOW?*

HOW COULD YOU MUGS LOSE HIM? HE'S HOOFING IT DOWN THE RAIL WITH THE GRIP CUFFED TO HIS WRIST. WHERE COULD HE GO?

BIG LIL IS GONNA BE PISSED.

WE'LL *FIND* HIM, ALL RIGHT?

YEAH, 'SHOEBOX.' ANYWAY, WE GOT WORD TO STREET-LIFE. IT'S ONLY A MATTER OF TIME. THE MAN'S GOT EYES EVERYWHERE.

YOU GONNA STAKE ME ON THAT?

I WOULDN'T WANT A PIECE OF *THAT* ACTION!

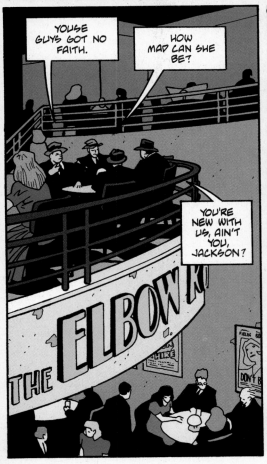

YOUSE GUYS GOT NO FAITH.

HOW MAD CAN SHE BE?

YOU'RE NEW WITH US, AIN'T YOU, JACKSON?

THE ELBOW ROOM

JUST HOPE LIL GETS HERE SOON, SO WE CAN GET THE SCREAMING OVER WITH.

SEARCH CONTINUES FOR PRISON SHIP SUNK IN NORTH SEA

LITTLE GIDDINGS STRIKES UNKNOWN OBJECT

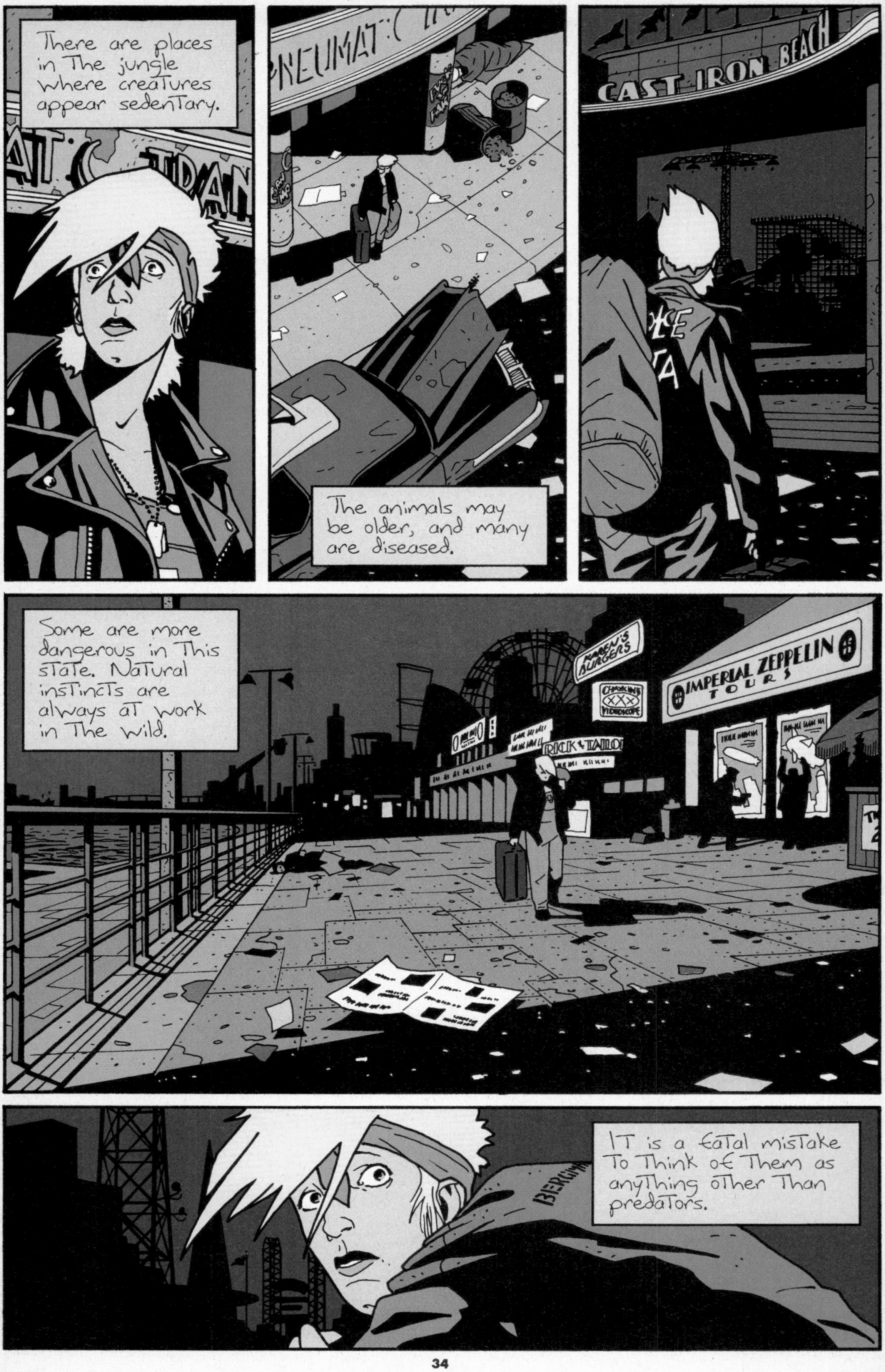
There are places in The jungle where creaTures appear sedenTary.
The animals may be older, and many are diseased.
CAST IRON BEACH
Some are more dangerous in This sTaTe. NaTural insTincTs are always aT work in The wild.
KAREN'S BURGERS
VIDEOSCOPE
IMPERIAL ZEPPELIN TOURS
IT is a faTal misTake To Think of Them as anyThing oTher Than predaTors.

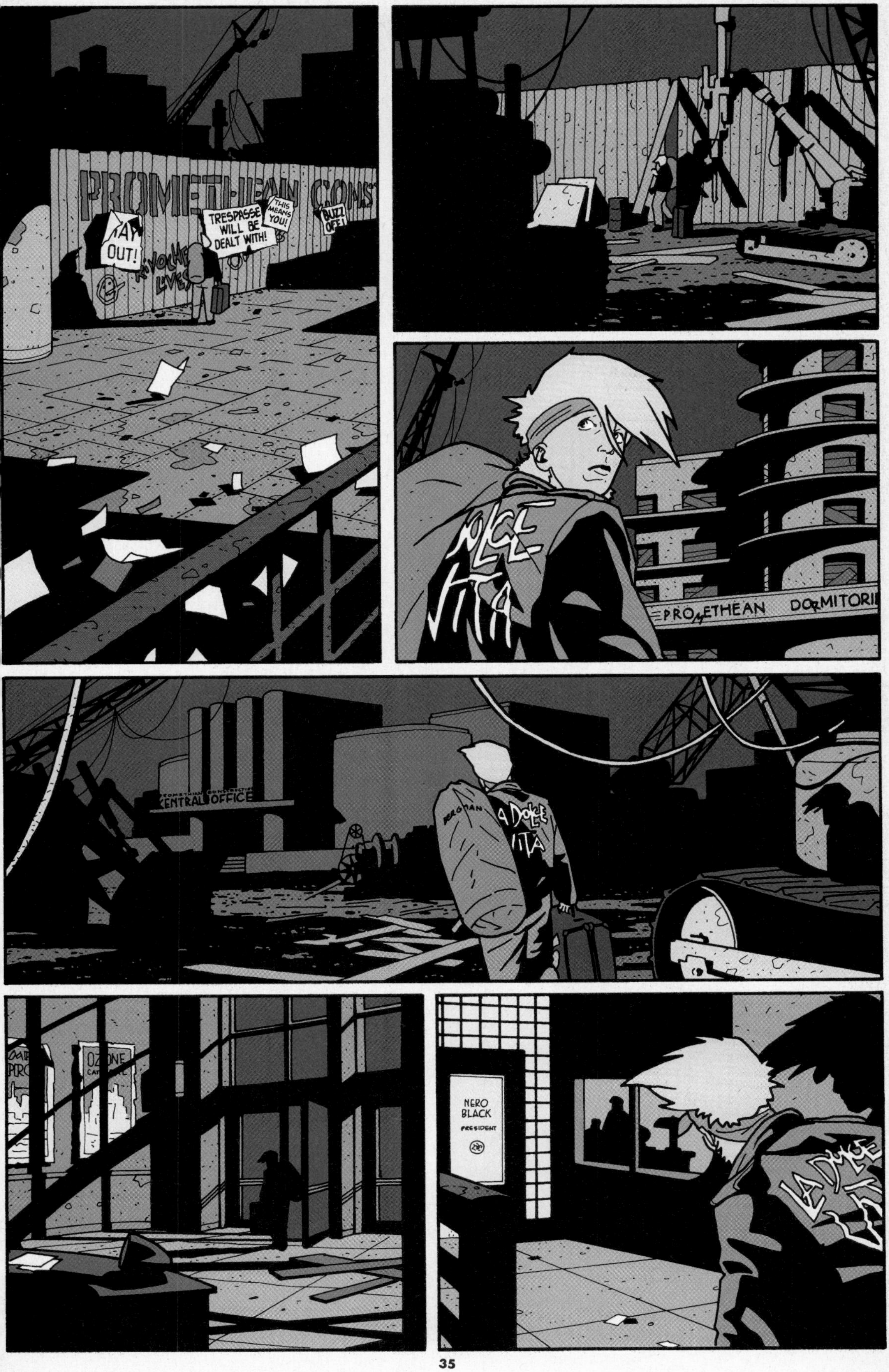
PROMETHEAN CONST
AY OUT!
TRESPASSE WILL BE DEALT WITH!
THIS MEANS YOU!
BUZZ OFF!
DOLCE VITA
PROMETHEAN DORMITORI
CENTRAL OFFICE
LA DOLCE VITA
OZONE
NERO BLACK PRESIDENT
LA DOLCE

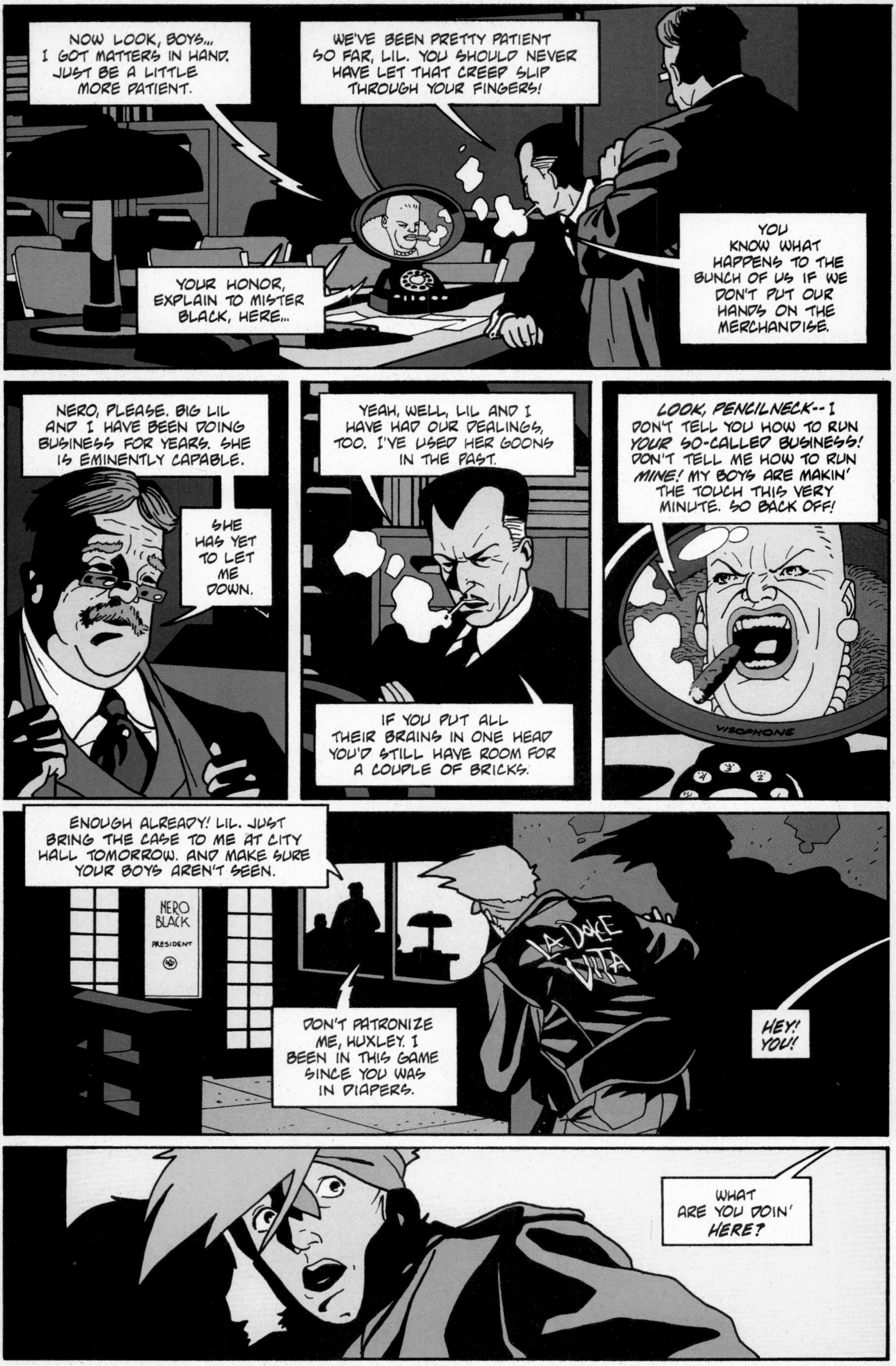
NOW LOOK, BOYS... I GOT MATTERS IN HAND. JUST BE A LITTLE MORE PATIENT.
WE'VE BEEN PRETTY PATIENT SO FAR, LIL. YOU SHOULD NEVER HAVE LET THAT CREEP SLIP THROUGH YOUR FINGERS!
YOU KNOW WHAT HAPPENS TO THE BUNCH OF US IF WE DON'T PUT OUR HANDS ON THE MERCHANDISE.
YOUR HONOR, EXPLAIN TO MISTER BLACK, HERE...
NERO, PLEASE. BIG LIL AND I HAVE BEEN DOING BUSINESS FOR YEARS. SHE IS EMINENTLY CAPABLE.
SHE HAS YET TO LET ME DOWN.
YEAH, WELL, LIL AND I HAVE HAD OUR DEALINGS, TOO. I'VE USED HER GOONS IN THE PAST.
IF YOU PUT ALL THEIR BRAINS IN ONE HEAD YOU'D STILL HAVE ROOM FOR A COUPLE OF BRICKS.
LOOK, PENCILNECK-- I DON'T TELL YOU HOW TO RUN YOUR SO-CALLED BUSINESS! DON'T TELL ME HOW TO RUN MINE! MY BOYS ARE MAKIN' THE TOUCH THIS VERY MINUTE. SO BACK OFF!
VISOPHONE
ENOUGH ALREADY! LIL. JUST BRING THE CASE TO ME AT CITY HALL TOMORROW. AND MAKE SURE YOUR BOYS AREN'T SEEN.
NERO BLACK PRESIDENT
LA DOLCE VITA
DON'T PATRONIZE ME, HUXLEY. I BEEN IN THIS GAME SINCE YOU WAS IN DIAPERS.
HEY! YOU!
WHAT ARE YOU DOIN' HERE?

THIS PLACE IS CLOSED!

OH-UH I'M NOT DOIN' NOTHIN'. I MEAN--IT'S JUST I WAS SUPPOSED TO REPORT FOR WORK, TODAY...AND A ROOM.

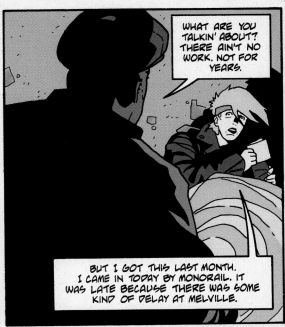

WHAT ARE YOU TALKIN' ABOUT? THERE AIN'T NO WORK. NOT FOR YEARS.

BUT I GOT THIS LAST MONTH. I CAME IN TODAY BY MONORAIL. IT WAS LATE BECAUSE THERE WAS SOME KIND OF DELAY AT MELVILLE.

PROMETHEAN ENTERPRISES

Recruitron Upper Response

To: Bonnie Bergman,
Please report to
Cast Iron Beach Compound
on May 14 for Employment Review...

Hmmm. SAY, YOU'RE BOSS BERGMAN'S KID, AREN'T YOU?

YEAH, HE WAS MY FATHER.

HE WAS A GOOD MAN. ONE OF THE BEST. SHAME ABOUT WHAT HAPPENED TO HIM.

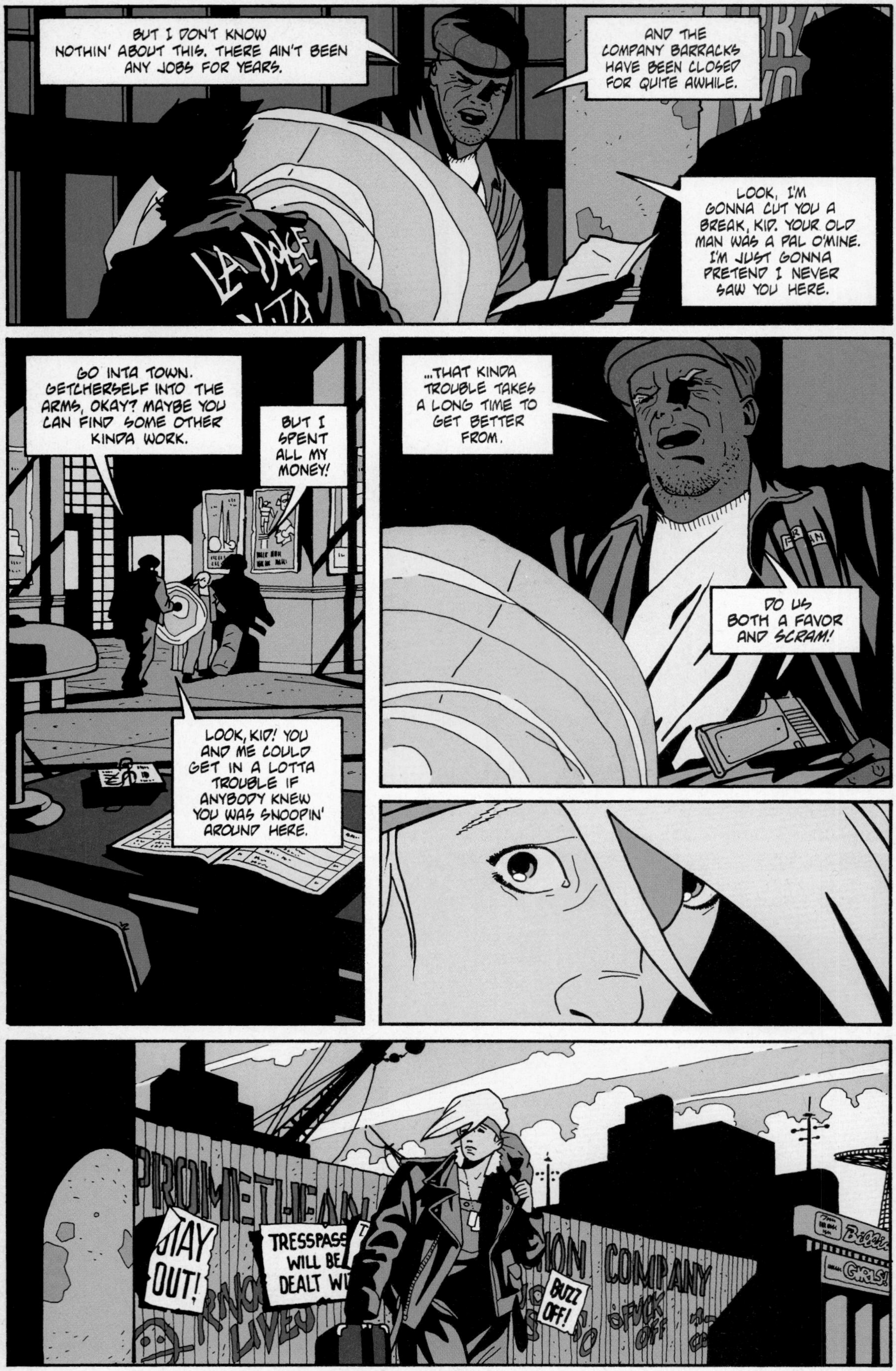

BUT I DON'T KNOW NOTHIN' ABOUT THIS. THERE AIN'T BEEN ANY JOBS FOR YEARS.
AND THE COMPANY BARRACKS HAVE BEEN CLOSED FOR QUITE AWHILE.
LOOK, I'M GONNA CUT YOU A BREAK, KID. YOUR OLD MAN WAS A PAL O'MINE. I'M JUST GONNA PRETEND I NEVER SAW YOU HERE.
GO INTA TOWN. GETCHERSELF INTO THE ARMS, OKAY? MAYBE YOU CAN FIND SOME OTHER KINDA WORK.
BUT I SPENT ALL MY MONEY!
LOOK, KID! YOU AND ME COULD GET IN A LOTTA TROUBLE IF ANYBODY KNEW YOU WAS SNOOPIN' AROUND HERE.
...THAT KINDA TROUBLE TAKES A LONG TIME TO GET BETTER FROM.
DO US BOTH A FAVOR AND SCRAM!
PROMETHEAN
STAY OUT!
TRESSPASS WILL BE DEALT WI
COMPANY
BUZZ OFF!
FUCK OFF
GIRLS!

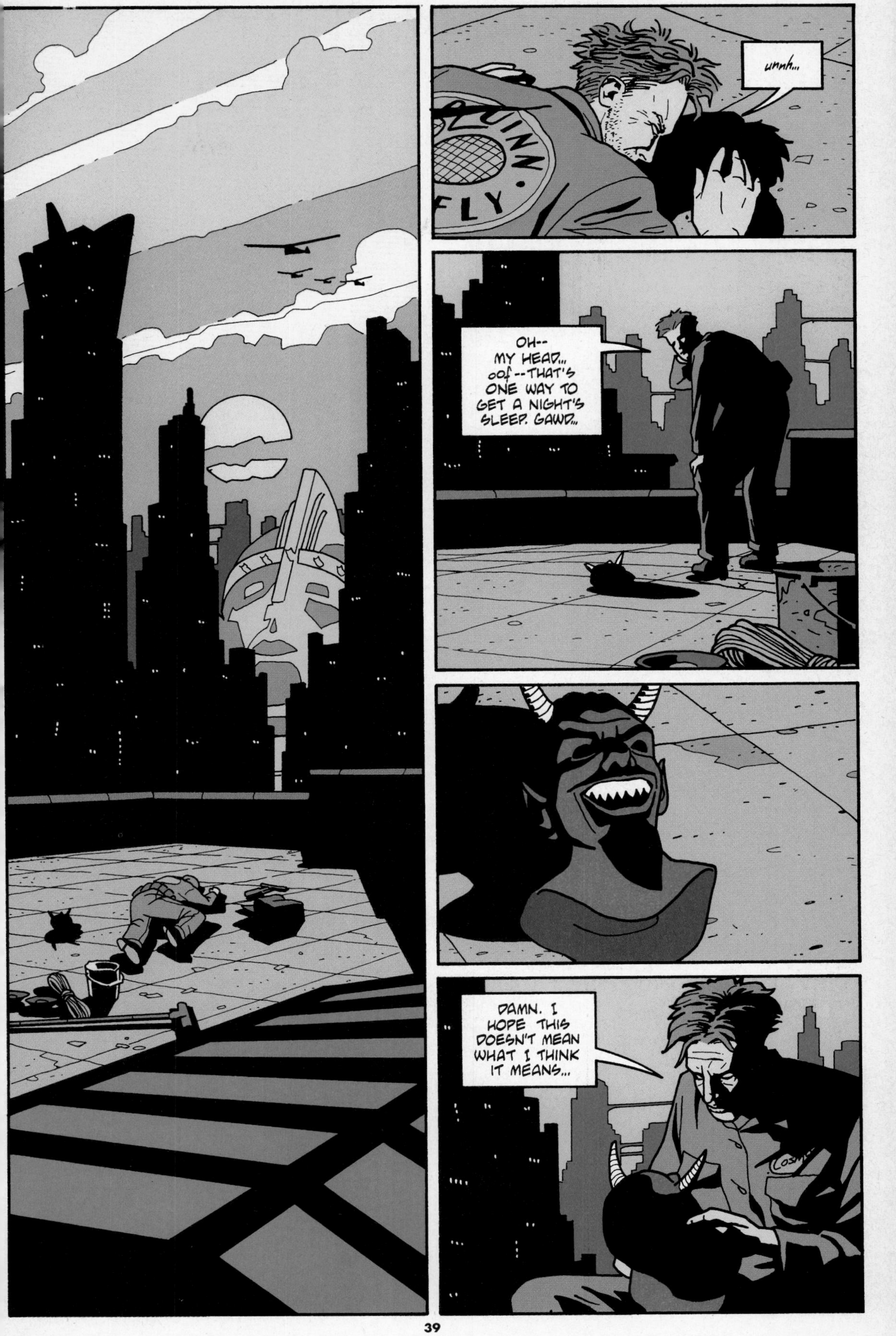

unnh...
OH-- MY HEAD... oof --THAT'S ONE WAY TO GET A NIGHT'S SLEEP. GAWD...
DAMN. I HOPE THIS DOESN'T MEAN WHAT I THINK IT MEANS...

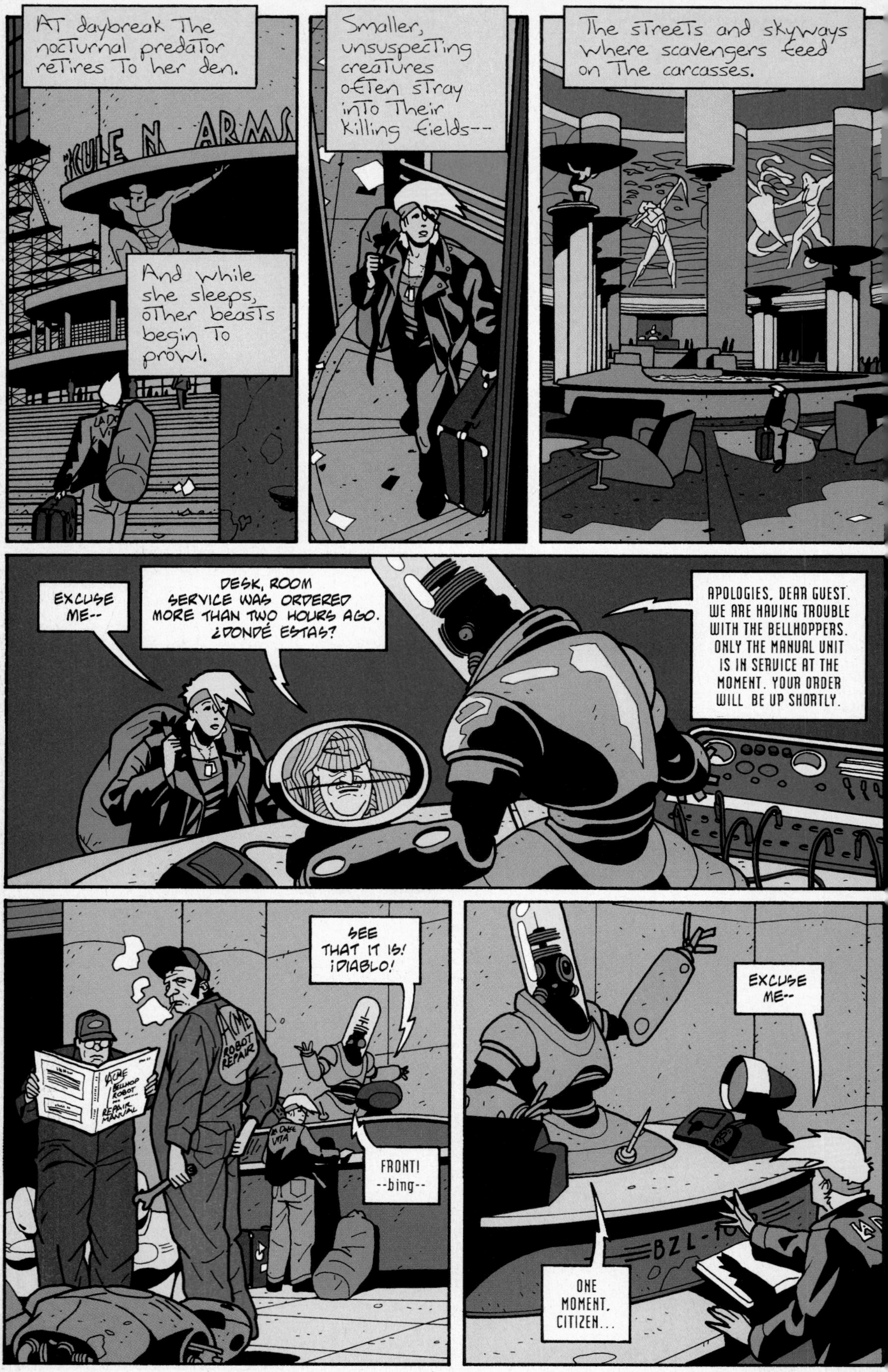
AT daybreak The nocTurnal predaTor reTires To her den.
And while she sleeps, oTher beasTs begin To prowl.
Smaller, unsuspecTing creaTures ofTen sTray inTo Their killing fields--
The sTreeTs and skyways where scavengers feed on The carcasses.
EXCUSE ME--
DESK, ROOM SERVICE WAS ORDERED MORE THAN TWO HOURS AGO. ¿DONDÉ ESTAS?
APOLOGIES, DEAR GUEST. WE ARE HAVING TROUBLE WITH THE BELLHOPPERS. ONLY THE MANUAL UNIT IS IN SERVICE AT THE MOMENT. YOUR ORDER WILL BE UP SHORTLY.
ACME ROBOT REPAIR
ACME BELLHOP ROBOT REPAIR MANUAL
SEE THAT IT IS! ¡DIABLO!
FRONT! --bing--
EXCUSE ME--
ONE MOMENT, CITIZEN...

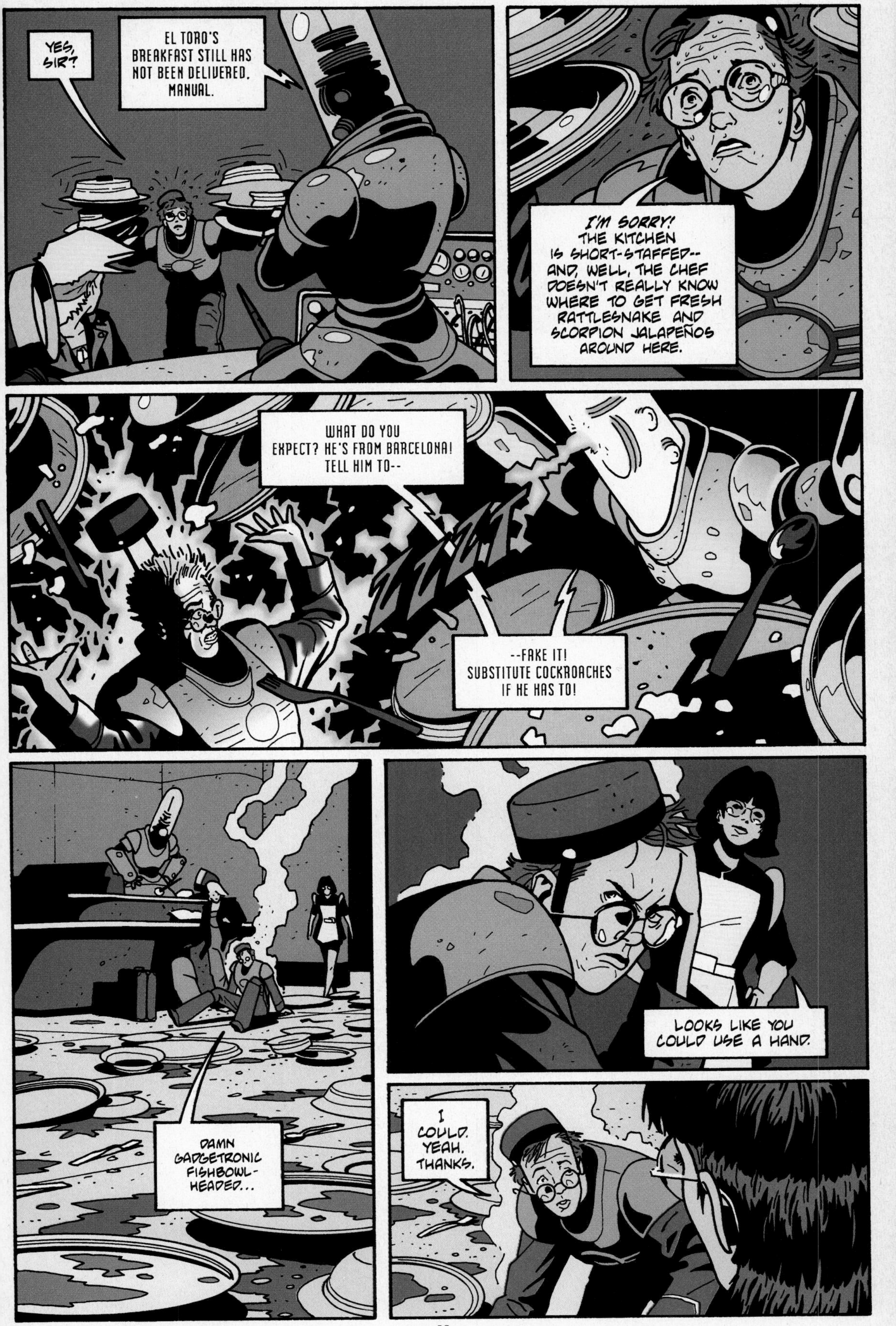
YES, SIR?
EL TORO'S BREAKFAST STILL HAS NOT BEEN DELIVERED, MANUAL.
I'M SORRY! THE KITCHEN IS SHORT-STAFFED-- AND, WELL, THE CHEF DOESN'T REALLY KNOW WHERE TO GET FRESH RATTLESNAKE AND SCORPION JALAPEÑOS AROUND HERE.
WHAT DO YOU EXPECT? HE'S FROM BARCELONA! TELL HIM TO--
--FAKE IT! SUBSTITUTE COCKROACHES IF HE HAS TO!
DAMN GADGETRONIC FISHBOWL-HEADED...
LOOKS LIKE YOU COULD USE A HAND.
I COULD. YEAH. THANKS.

NOW, HOW MAY I HELP YOU?

WELL, I'D LIKE A ROOM. BUT--HM-- I CAN'T AFFORD MUCH.

I SEE. THERE IS ROOM 1313. IT IS NOT A DELUXE SUITE. BUT THE CEILING HAS FINALLY BEEN REPAIRED. IT COULD BE MADE AVAILABLE AT A DISCOUNT. HOW LONG WILL YOU BE WITH US?

I'M NOT SURE. UNTIL I FIND A JOB, I GUESS...

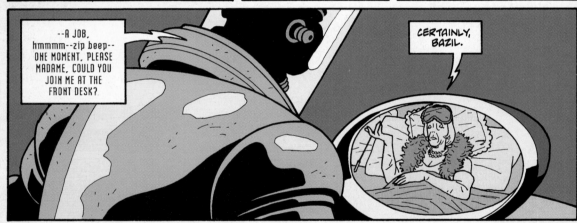

--A JOB, hmmmm--zip beep-- ONE MOMENT, PLEASE MADAME, COULD YOU JOIN ME AT THE FRONT DESK?

CERTAINLY, BAZIL.

-tick- SIGN HERE. MADAME FIELDS WILL BE DOWN MOMENTARILY.

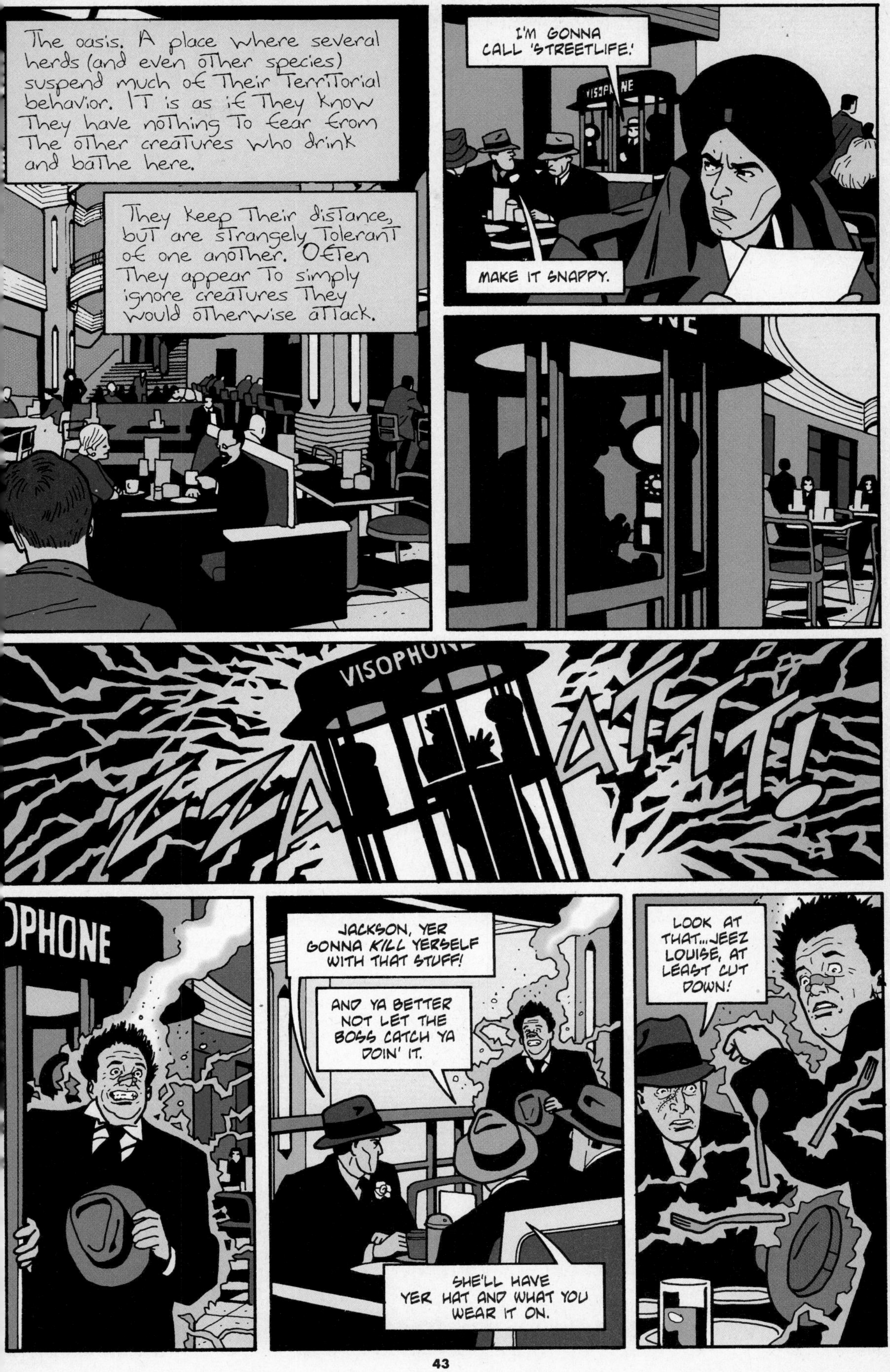
The oasis. A place where several herds (and even other species) suspend much of their territorial behavior. It is as if they know they have nothing to fear from the other creatures who drink and bathe here.
They keep their distance, but are strangely tolerant of one another. Often they appear to simply ignore creatures they would otherwise attack.
I'M GONNA CALL 'STREETLIFE.'
VISOPHONE
MAKE IT SNAPPY.
VISOPHONE
ZZZAAATTTT!
OPHONE
JACKSON, YER GONNA KILL YERSELF WITH THAT STUFF!
AND YA BETTER NOT LET THE BOSS CATCH YA DOIN' IT.
SHE'LL HAVE YER HAT AND WHAT YOU WEAR IT ON.
LOOK AT THAT... JEEZ LOUISE, AT LEAST CUT DOWN!

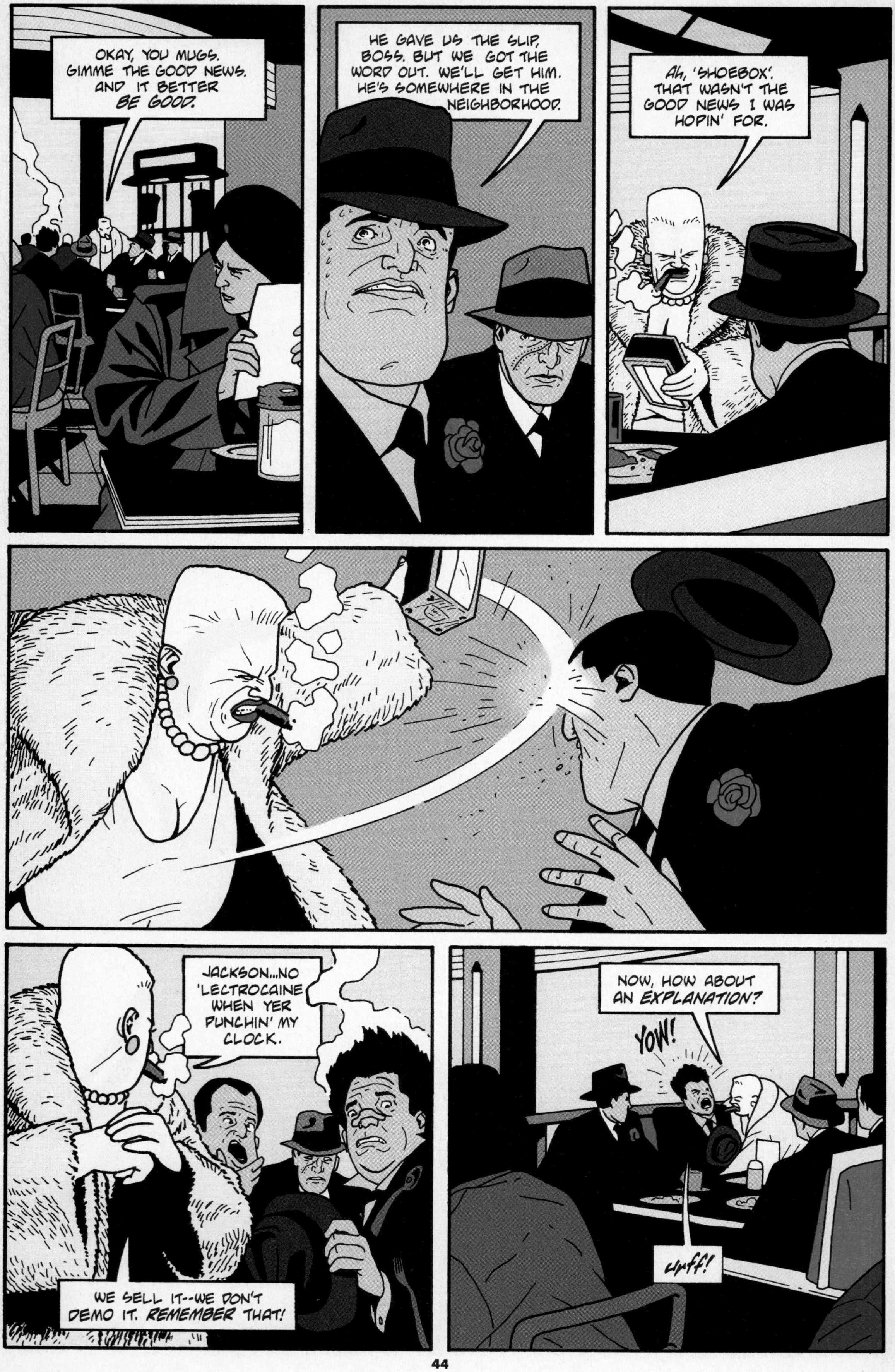
OKAY, YOU MUGS. GIMME THE GOOD NEWS. AND IT BETTER BE GOOD.
HE GAVE US THE SLIP, BOSS. BUT WE GOT THE WORD OUT. WE'LL GET HIM. HE'S SOMEWHERE IN THE NEIGHBORHOOD.
Ah, 'SHOEBOX'. THAT WASN'T THE GOOD NEWS I WAS HOPIN' FOR.
JACKSON...NO 'LECTROCAINE WHEN YER PUNCHIN' MY CLOCK.
WE SELL IT--WE DON'T DEMO IT. REMEMBER THAT!
NOW, HOW ABOUT AN EXPLANATION?
YOW!
unff!

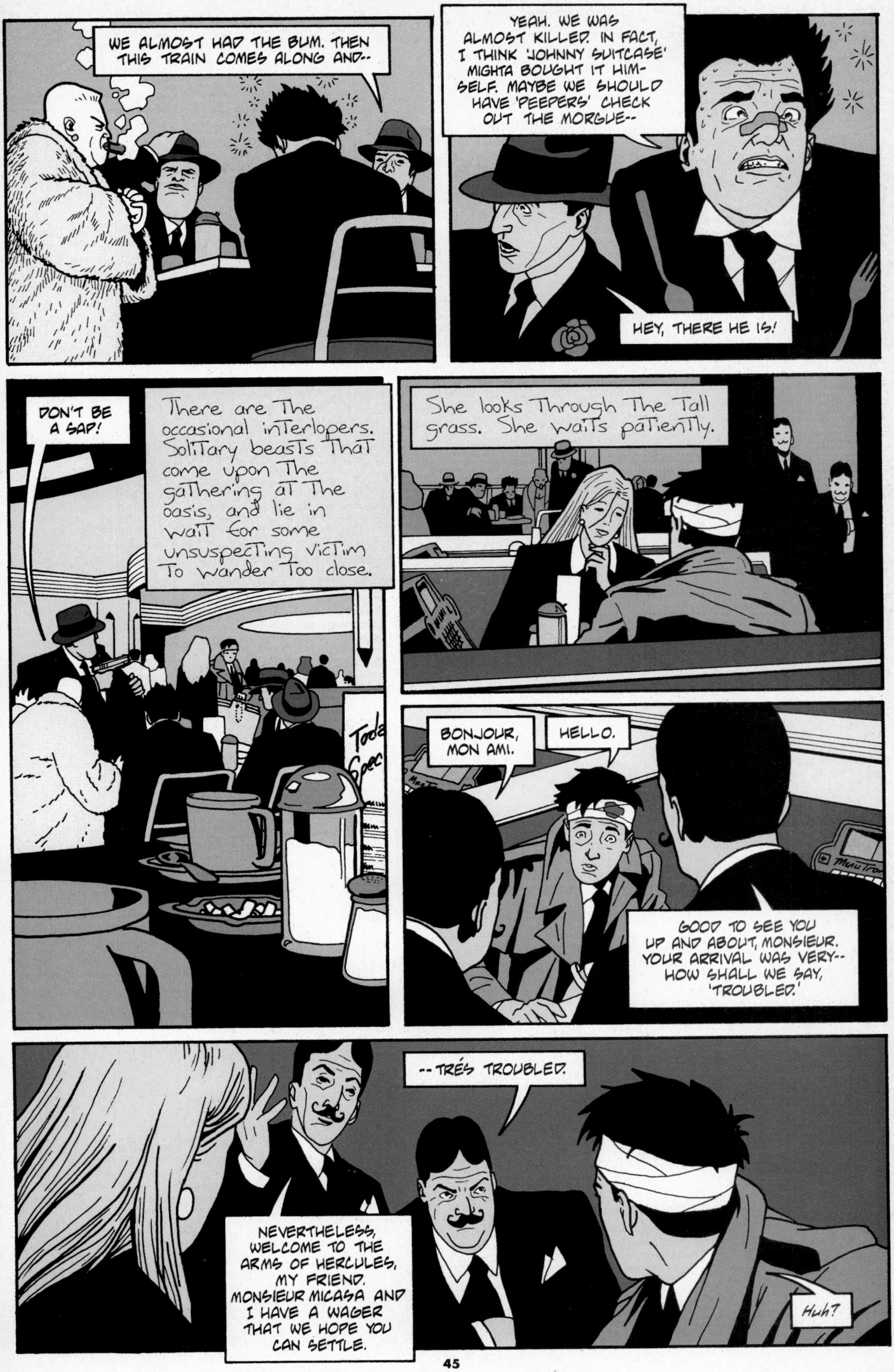
WE ALMOST HAD THE BUM. THEN THIS TRAIN COMES ALONG AND--
YEAH. WE WAS ALMOST KILLED. IN FACT, I THINK 'JOHNNY SUITCASE' MIGHTA BOUGHT IT HIM-SELF. MAYBE WE SHOULD HAVE 'PEEPERS' CHECK OUT THE MORGUE--
HEY, THERE HE IS!
DON'T BE A SAP!
There are The occasional interlopers. SoliTary beasTs ThaT come upon The gaThering aT The oasis, and lie in waiT for some unsuspecTing vicTim To wander Too close.
She looks Through The Tall grass. She waiTs paTienTly.
BONJOUR, MON AMI.
HELLO.
GOOD TO SEE YOU UP AND ABOUT, MONSIEUR. YOUR ARRIVAL WAS VERY-- HOW SHALL WE SAY, 'TROUBLED.'
--TRÉS TROUBLED.
NEVERTHELESS, WELCOME TO THE ARMS OF HERCULES, MY FRIEND. MONSIEUR MICASA AND I HAVE A WAGER THAT WE HOPE YOU CAN SETTLE.
Huh?

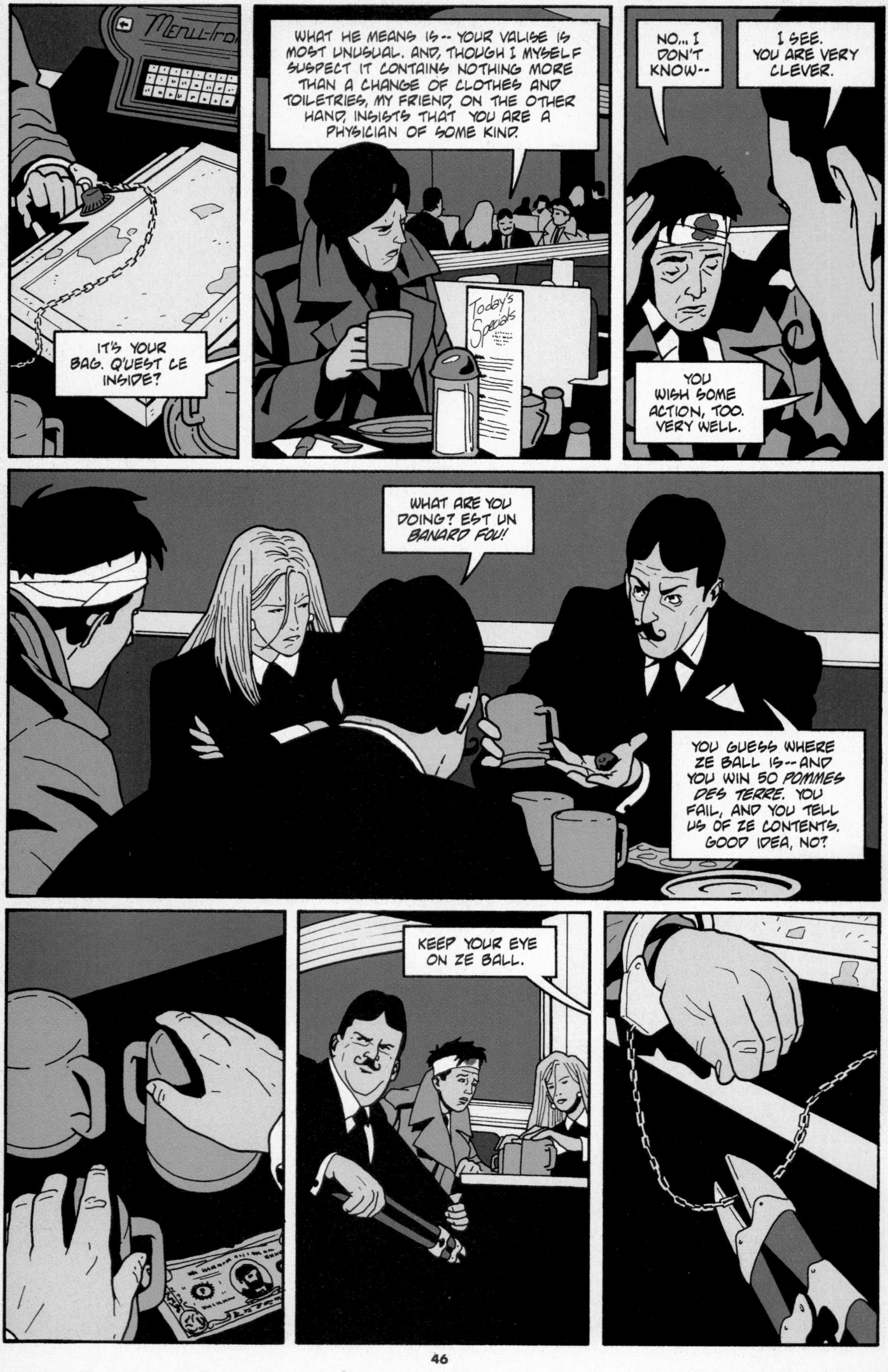
Menu-Tro
IT'S YOUR BAG. Q'UEST CE INSIDE?
WHAT HE MEANS IS-- YOUR VALISE IS MOST UNUSUAL. AND, THOUGH I MYSELF SUSPECT IT CONTAINS NOTHING MORE THAN A CHANGE OF CLOTHES AND TOILETRIES, MY FRIEND, ON THE OTHER HAND, INSISTS THAT YOU ARE A PHYSICIAN OF SOME KIND.
Today's Specials
NO... I DON'T KNOW--
I SEE. YOU ARE VERY CLEVER.
YOU WISH SOME ACTION, TOO. VERY WELL.
WHAT ARE YOU DOING? EST UN *BANARD FOU!*
YOU GUESS WHERE ZE BALL IS--AND YOU WIN 50 *POMMES DES TERRE.* YOU FAIL, AND YOU TELL US OF ZE CONTENTS. GOOD IDEA, NO?
KEEP YOUR EYE ON ZE BALL.

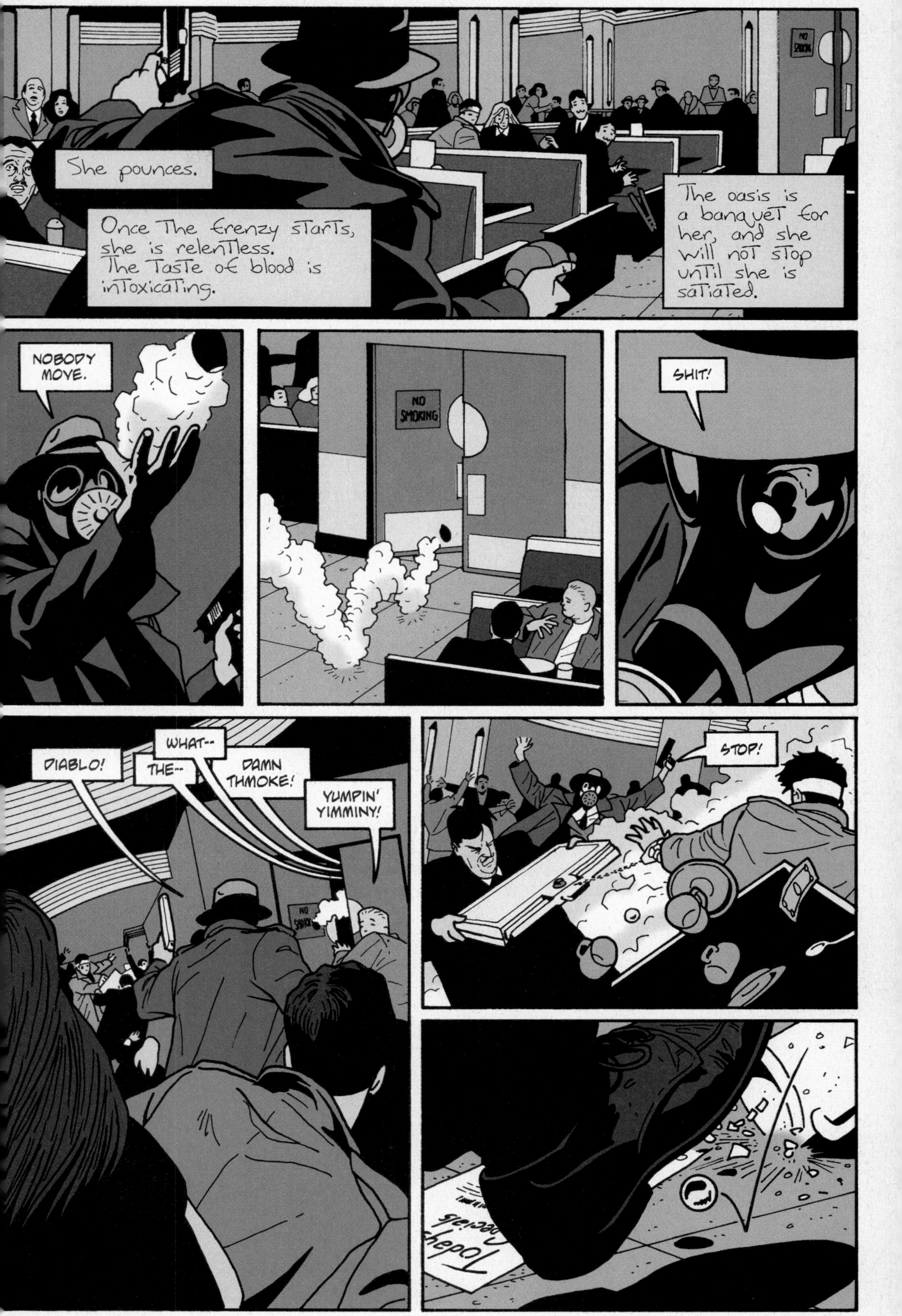

She pounces.
Once the frenzy starts, she is relentless. The taste of blood is intoxicating.
The oasis is a banquet for her, and she will not stop until she is satiated.
NO SMOKING
NOBODY MOVE.
NO SMOKING
SHIT!
DIABLO!
THE--
WHAT--
DAMN THMOKE!
YUMPIN' YIMMINY!
STOP!
Today's Specials

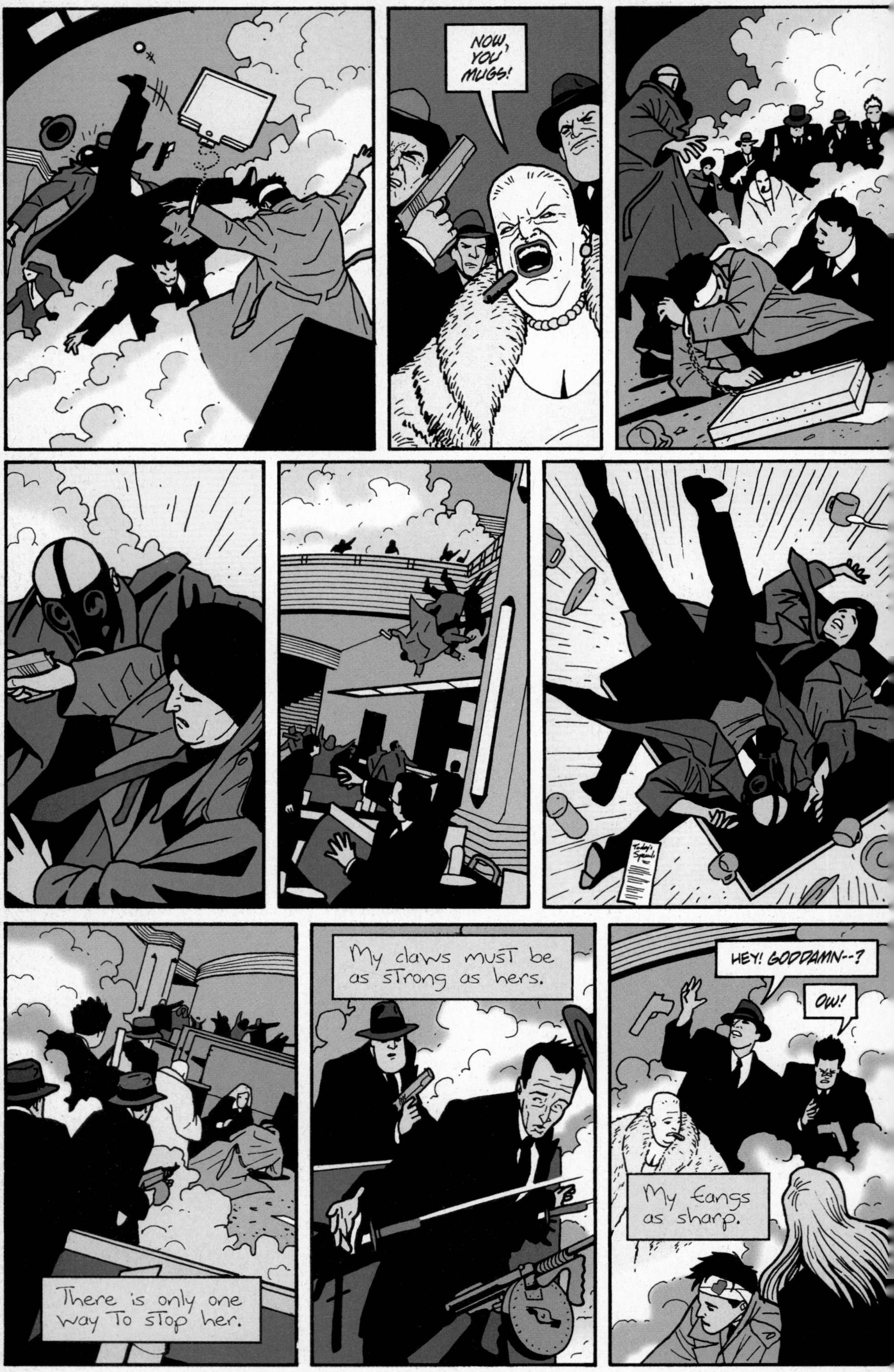
NOW, YOU MUGS!
My claws must be as strong as hers.
HEY! GODDAMN--?
OW!
My fangs as sharp.
There is only one way to stop her.

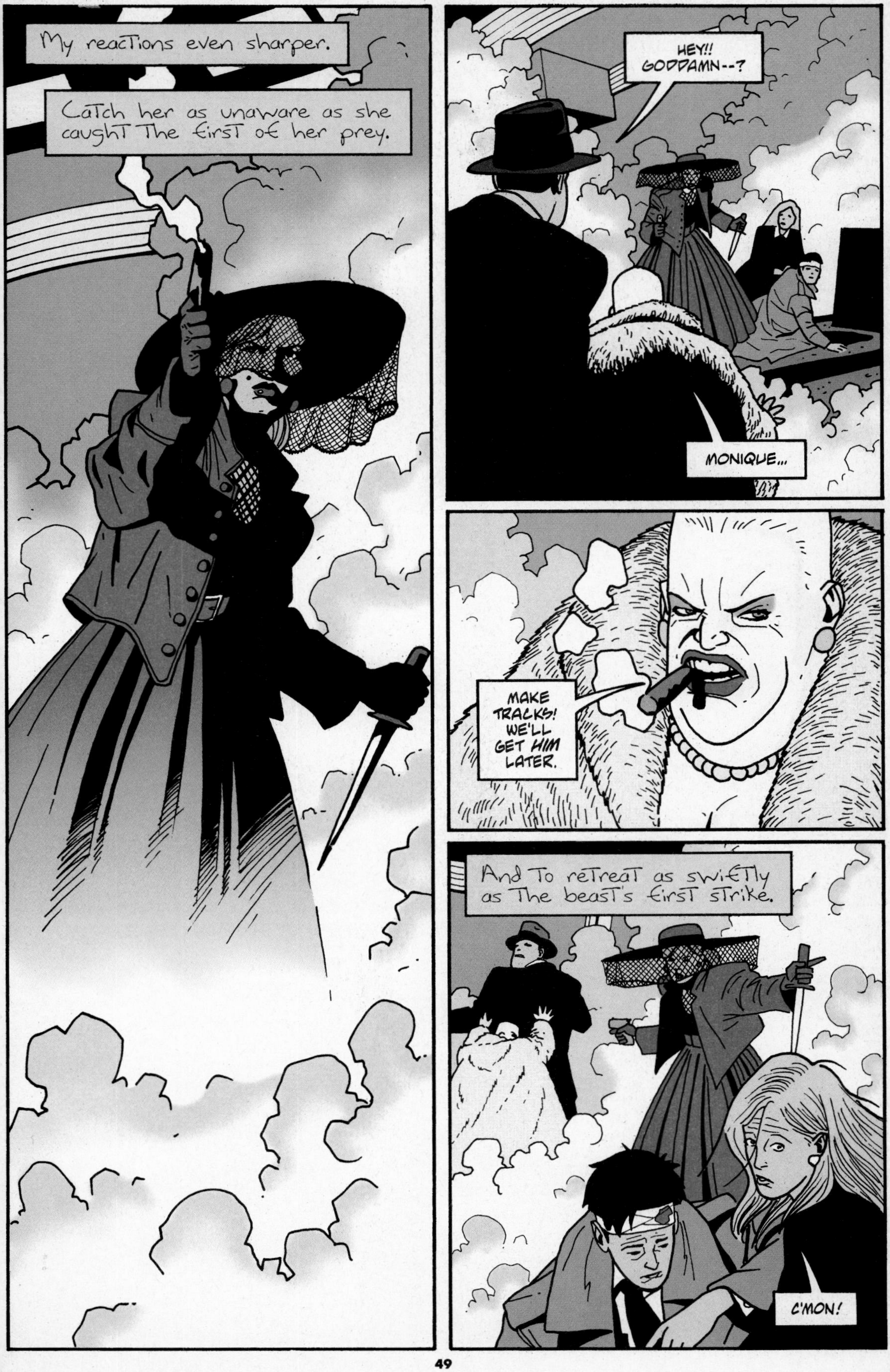
My reactions even sharper.
Catch her as unaware as she caught the first of her prey.
HEY!! GODDAMN--?
MONIQUE...
MAKE TRACKS! WE'LL GET HIM LATER.
And to retreat as swiftly as the beast's first strike.
C'MON!

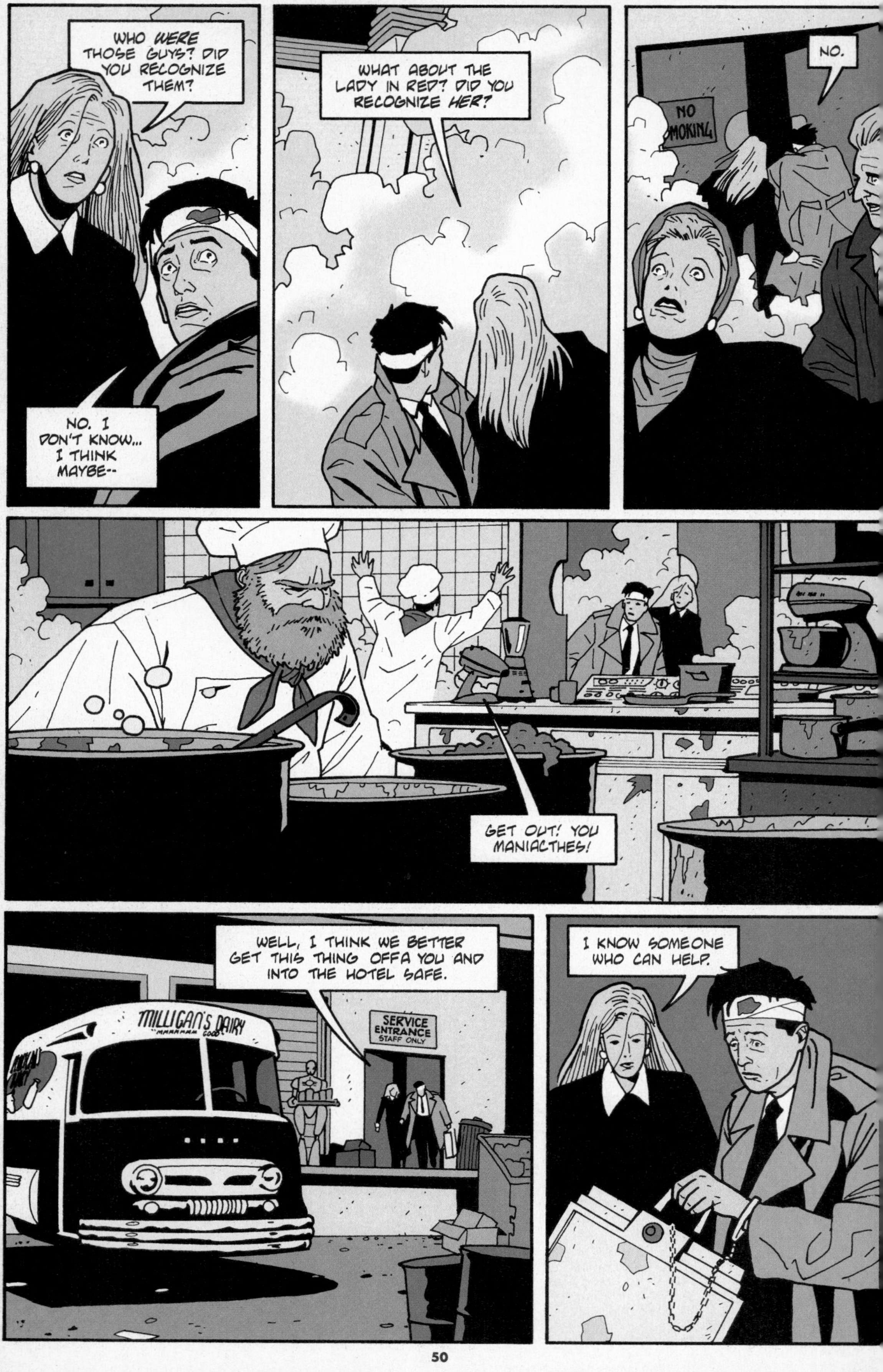
WHO WERE THOSE GUYS? DID YOU RECOGNIZE THEM?
NO. I DON'T KNOW... I THINK MAYBE--
WHAT ABOUT THE LADY IN RED? DID YOU RECOGNIZE HER?
NO.
NO SMOKING
GET OUT! YOU MANIACTHES!
WELL, I THINK WE BETTER GET THIS THING OFFA YOU AND INTO THE HOTEL SAFE.
MILLIGAN'S DAIRY
SERVICE ENTRANCE STAFF ONLY
I KNOW SOMEONE WHO CAN HELP.

THIS IS *CURIOUS!* THIS ACID IS KNOWN TO DISSOLVE *ANY METAL!*

IT'S NOT EVEN MAKING A STAIN.

I'VE NEVER SEEN ANYTHING LIKE IT. THE CASE SEEMS TO BE MADE FROM THE SAME MATERIAL.

CROWN JEWELS OF ALACAZAR
EYES OF NOSTRADAMUS

WHAT ABOUT THE LOCKS?

I DON'T RECOGNIZE ANY OF THESE CHARACTERS.

KNOK KNOK

OH, THAT MUST BE LUNCH.

HEY, BOSS. WHAT'RE YOU DOIN' HERE IN EGGHEAD'S?

OUR FRIEND HERE NEEDS SOME HELP. WHAT DO YOU THINK, PROFESSOR?

WELL... THE COMBINATION OF THIS IMPERVIOUS MATERIAL AND THESE UNKNOWN SYMBOLS WOULD LEAD ME TO HYPOTHESIZE...

THAT WHAT?

...THAT IT IS QUITE POSSIBLY NOT OF THIS EARTH.

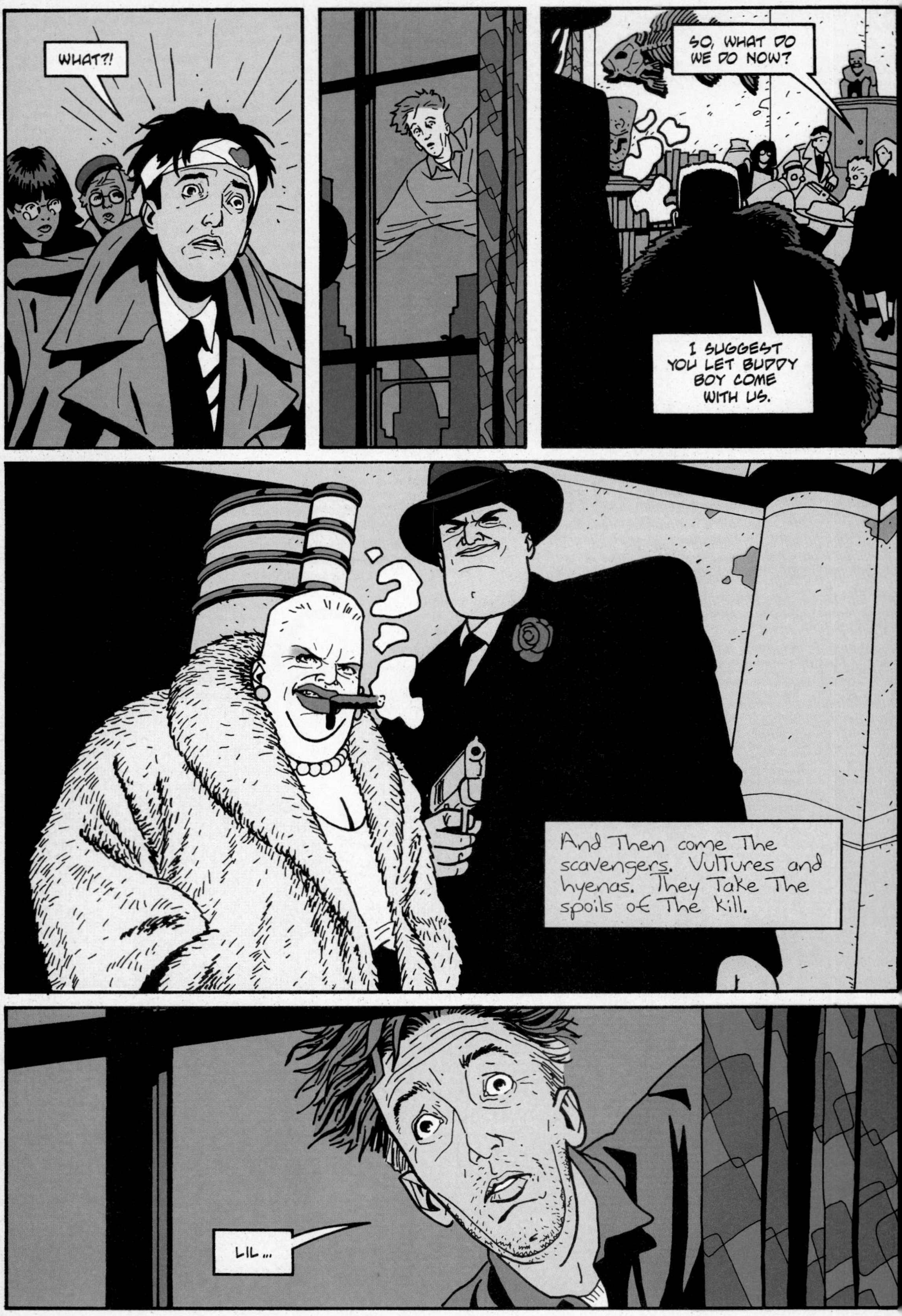
WHAT?!
SO, WHAT DO WE DO NOW?
I SUGGEST YOU LET BUDDY BOY COME WITH US.
And Then come The scavengers. VulTures and hyenas. They Take The spoils of The kill.
LIL...

Episode Three

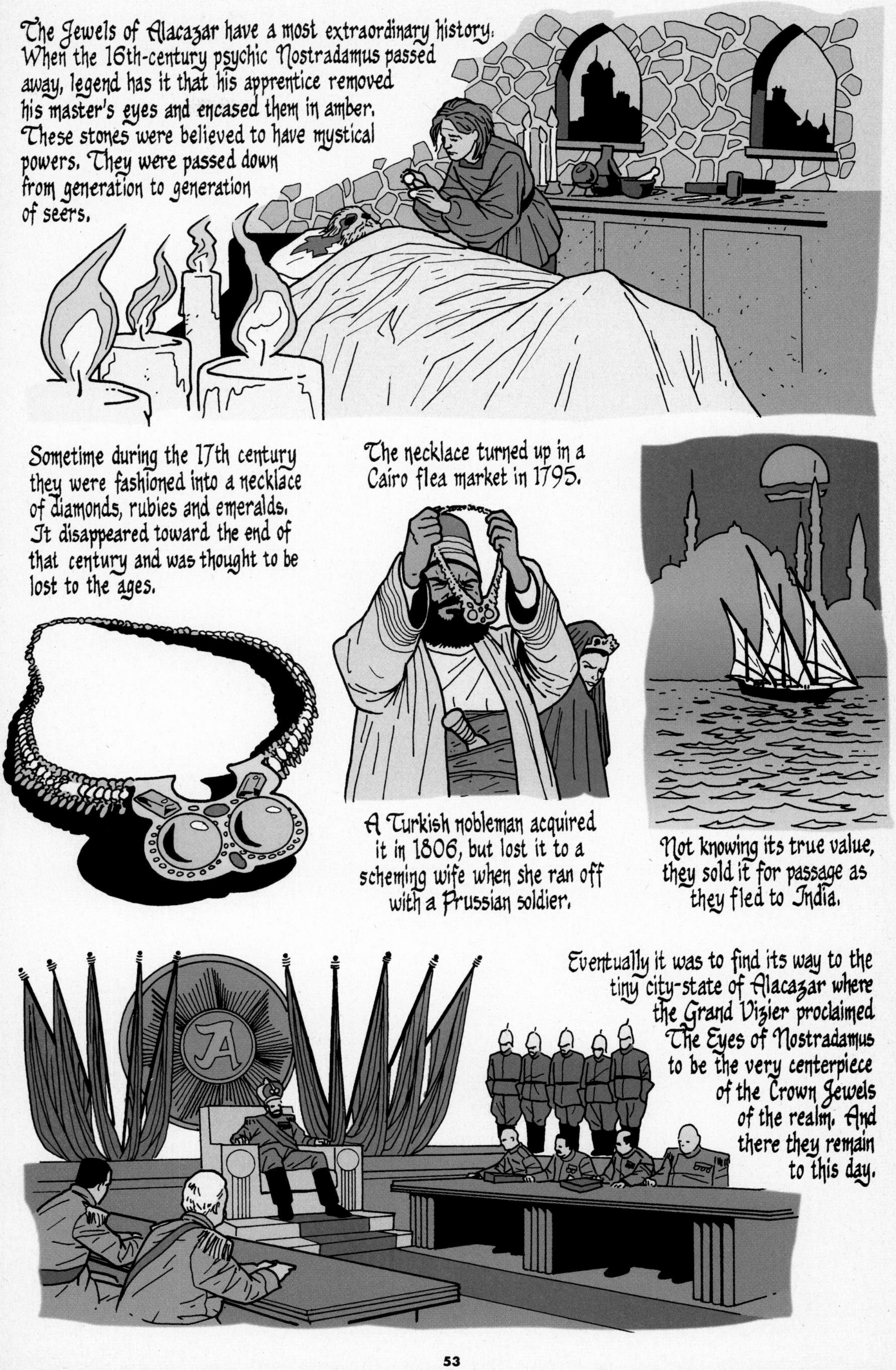
The Jewels of Alacazar have a most extraordinary history: When the 16th-century psychic Nostradamus passed away, legend has it that his apprentice removed his master's eyes and encased them in amber. These stones were believed to have mystical powers. They were passed down from generation to generation of seers.
Sometime during the 17th century they were fashioned into a necklace of diamonds, rubies and emeralds. It disappeared toward the end of that century and was thought to be lost to the ages.
The necklace turned up in a Cairo flea market in 1795.
A Turkish nobleman acquired it in 1806, but lost it to a scheming wife when she ran off with a Prussian soldier.
Not knowing its true value, they sold it for passage as they fled to India.
Eventually it was to find its way to the tiny city-state of Alacazar where the Grand Vizier proclaimed The Eyes of Nostradamus to be the very centerpiece of the Crown Jewels of the realm. And there they remain to this day.
A

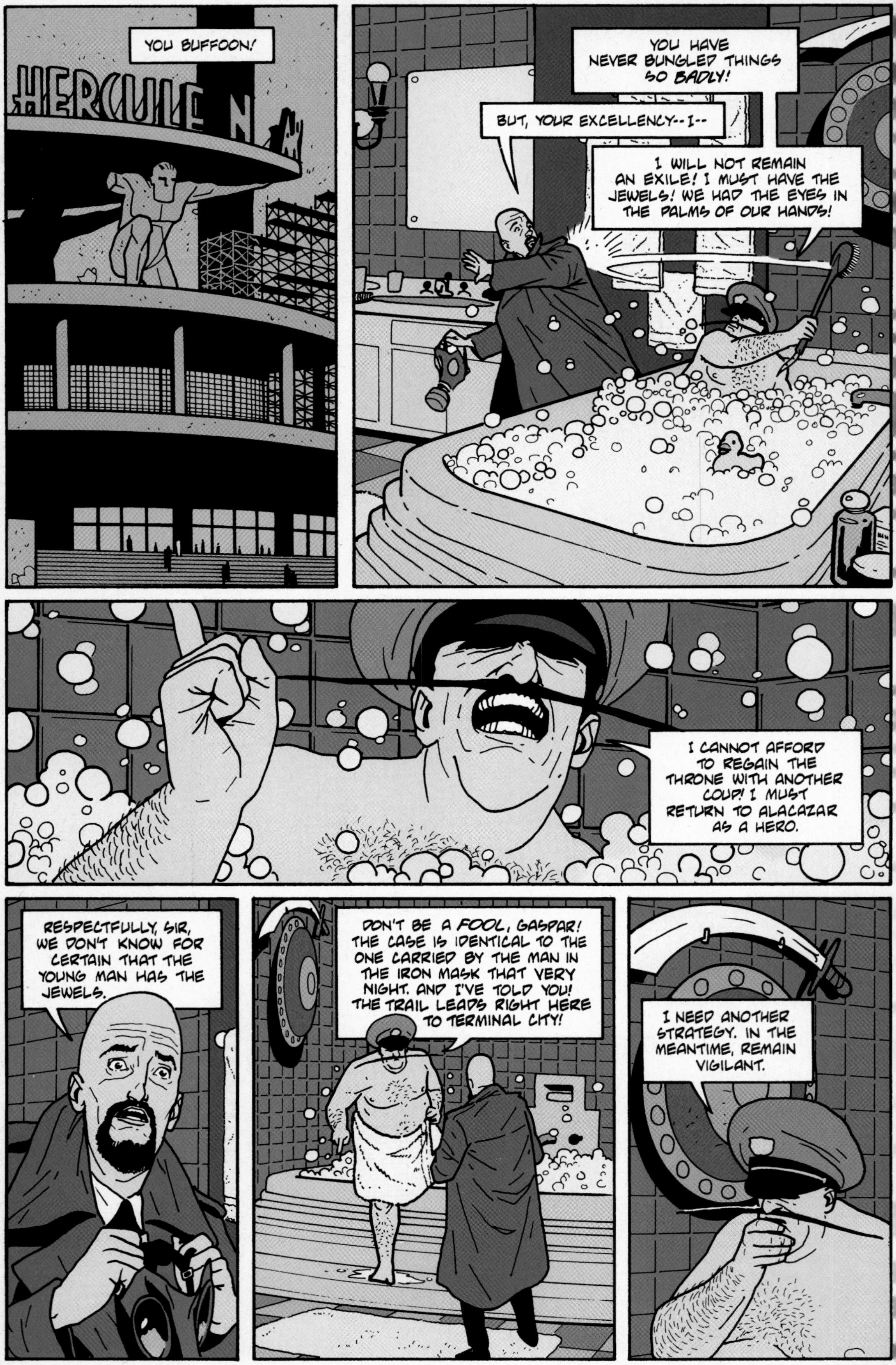
YOU BUFFOON!
HERCULE
YOU HAVE NEVER BUNGLED THINGS SO BADLY!
BUT, YOUR EXCELLENCY--I--
I WILL NOT REMAIN AN EXILE! I MUST HAVE THE JEWELS! WE HAD THE EYES IN THE PALMS OF OUR HANDS!
I CANNOT AFFORD TO REGAIN THE THRONE WITH ANOTHER COUP! I MUST RETURN TO ALACAZAR AS A HERO.
RESPECTFULLY, SIR, WE DON'T KNOW FOR CERTAIN THAT THE YOUNG MAN HAS THE JEWELS.
DON'T BE A FOOL, GASPAR! THE CASE IS IDENTICAL TO THE ONE CARRIED BY THE MAN IN THE IRON MASK THAT VERY NIGHT. AND I'VE TOLD YOU! THE TRAIL LEADS RIGHT HERE TO TERMINAL CITY!
I NEED ANOTHER STRATEGY. IN THE MEANTIME, REMAIN VIGILANT.

I REALLY SHOULDN'T BE RENTING THIS ROOM TO ANYONE. IT'S ONLY RECENTLY BEEN REPAIRED. BUT YOU SEEM LIKE A NICE YOUNG PERSON, AND CONSIDERING WHAT LITTLE YOU HAVE TO SPEND...

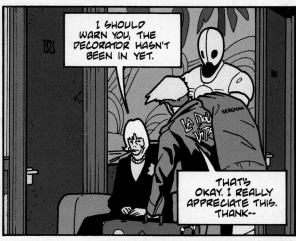

I SHOULD WARN YOU, THE DECORATOR HASN'T BEEN IN YET.

THAT'S OKAY. I REALLY APPRECIATE THIS. THANK--

--YOU.

WHAT--um-- HAPPENED HERE?

NOTHING REALLY. SOME SHOOTING. SOME EXPLOSIONS.

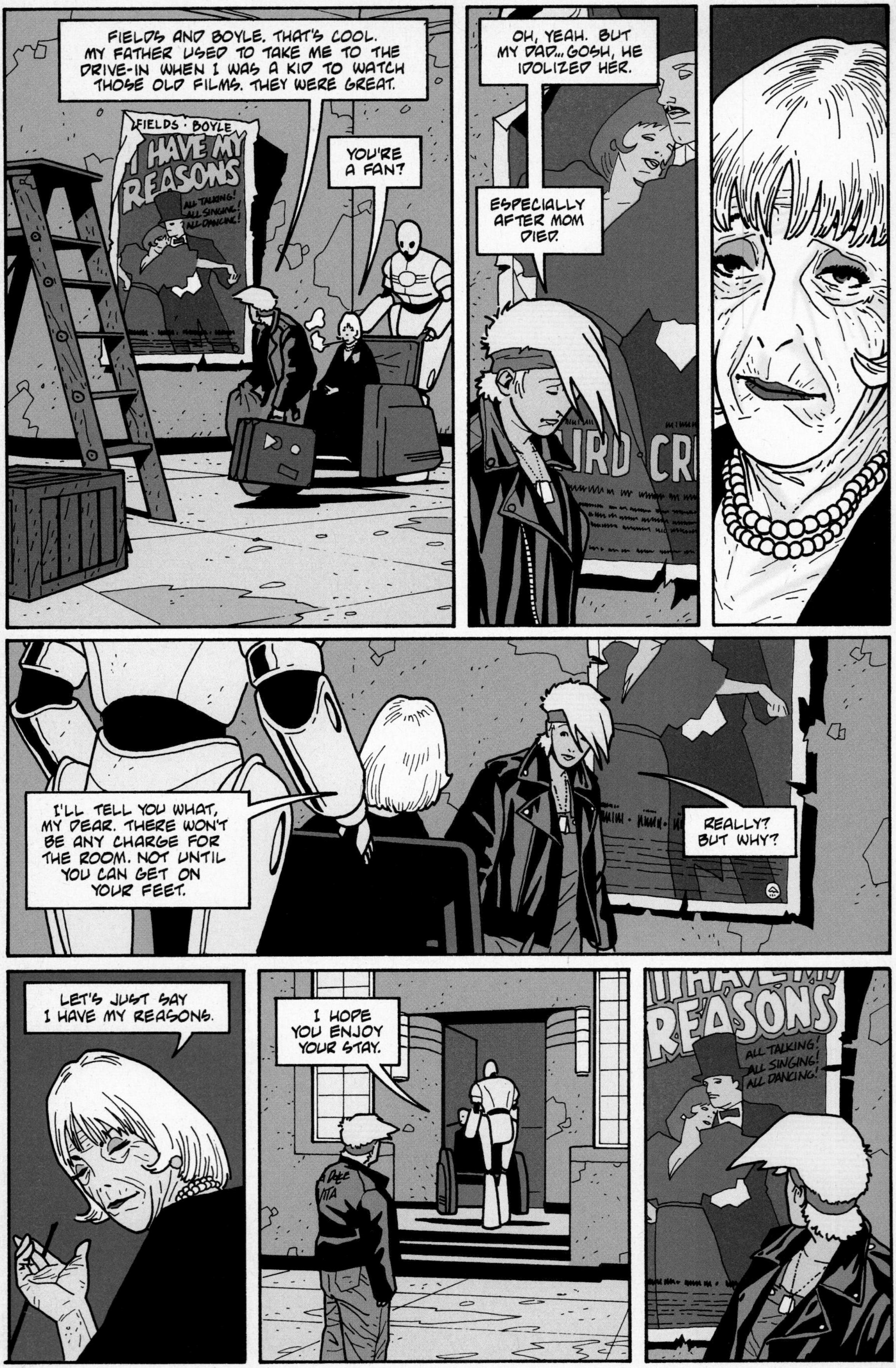
FIELDS AND BOYLE. THAT'S COOL. MY FATHER USED TO TAKE ME TO THE DRIVE-IN WHEN I WAS A KID TO WATCH THOSE OLD FILMS. THEY WERE GREAT.
FIELDS · BOYLE
I HAVE MY REASONS
ALL TALKING! ALL SINGING! ALL DANCING!
YOU'RE A FAN?
OH, YEAH. BUT MY DAD... GOSH, HE IDOLIZED HER.
ESPECIALLY AFTER MOM DIED.
I'LL TELL YOU WHAT, MY DEAR. THERE WON'T BE ANY CHARGE FOR THE ROOM. NOT UNTIL YOU CAN GET ON YOUR FEET.
REALLY? BUT WHY?
LET'S JUST SAY I HAVE MY REASONS.
I HOPE YOU ENJOY YOUR STAY.
REASONS
ALL TALKING! ALL SINGING! ALL DANCING!

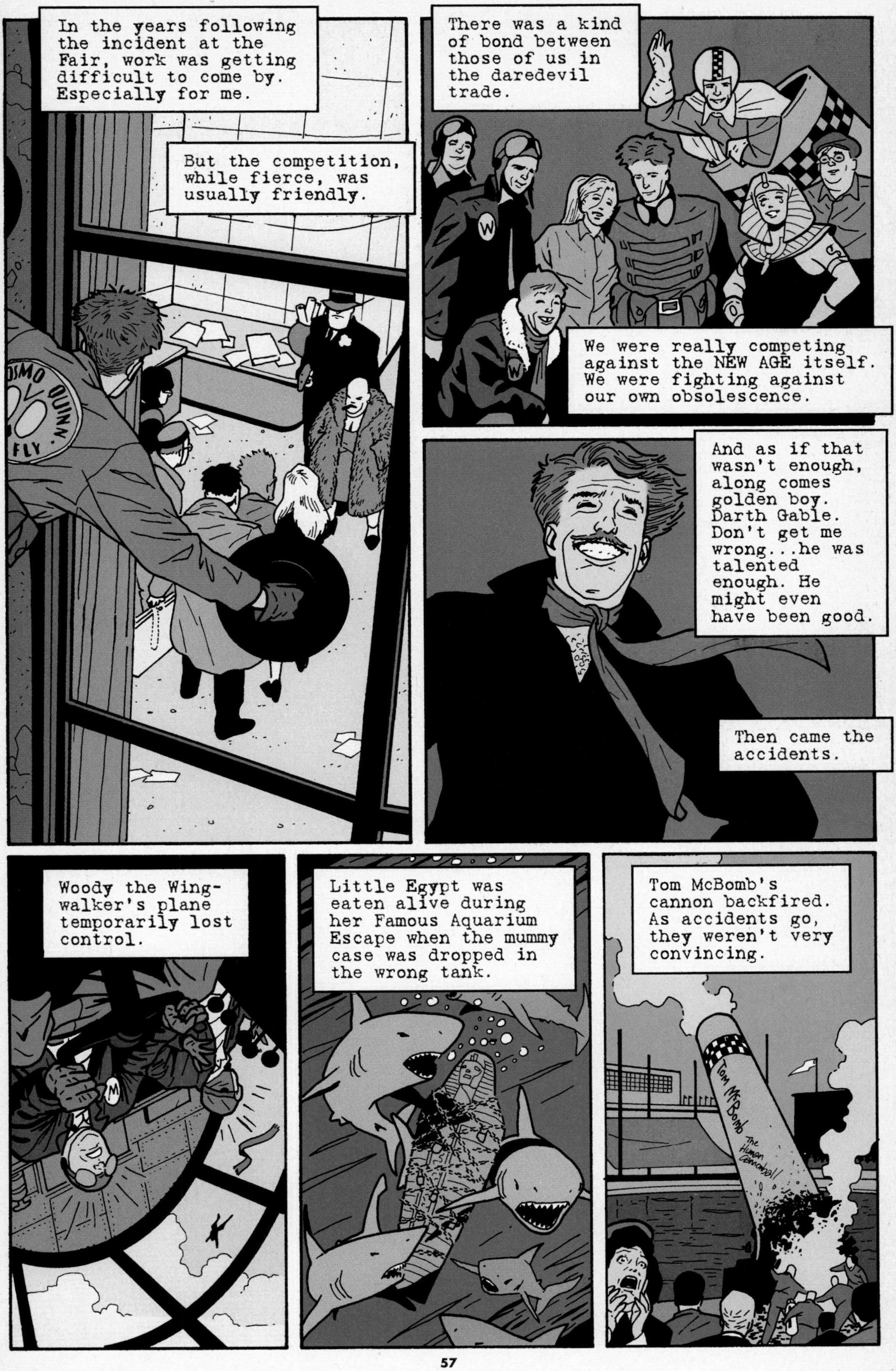

In the years following the incident at the Fair, work was getting difficult to come by. Especially for me.
But the competition, while fierce, was usually friendly.
OSMO QUINN
FLY
There was a kind of bond between those of us in the daredevil trade.
We were really competing against the NEW AGE itself. We were fighting against our own obsolescence.
And as if that wasn't enough, along comes golden boy. Darth Gable. Don't get me wrong...he was talented enough. He might even have been good.
Then came the accidents.
Woody the Wing-walker's plane temporarily lost control.
Little Egypt was eaten alive during her Famous Aquarium Escape when the mummy case was dropped in the wrong tank.
Tom McBomb's cannon backfired. As accidents go, they weren't very convincing.
Tom McBomb
The Human Cannonball!

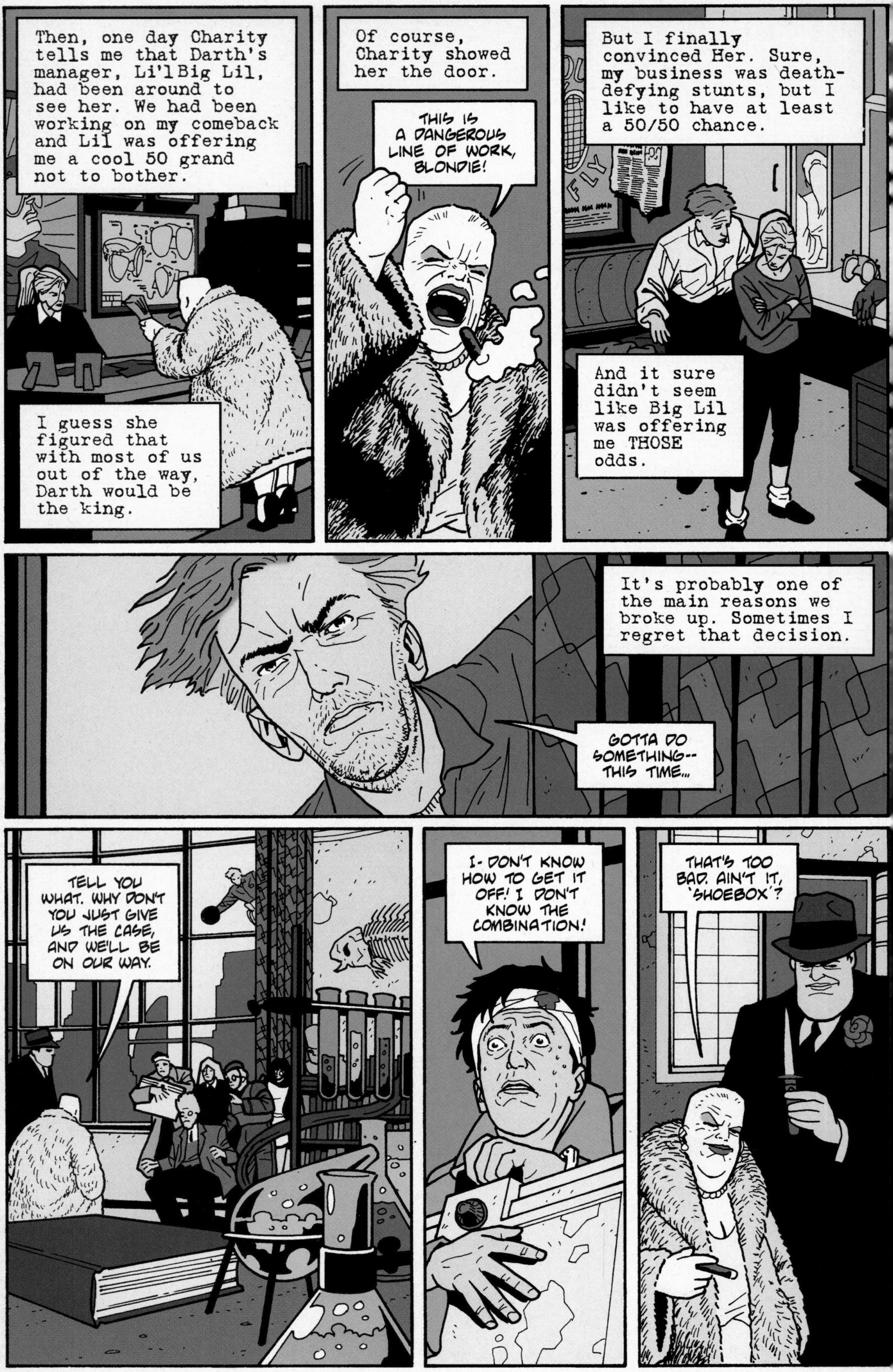

Then, one day Charity tells me that Darth's manager, Li'l Big Lil, had been around to see her. We had been working on my comeback and Lil was offering me a cool 50 grand not to bother.
I guess she figured that with most of us out of the way, Darth would be the king.
Of course, Charity showed her the door.
THIS IS A DANGEROUS LINE OF WORK, BLONDIE!
But I finally convinced Her. Sure, my business was death-defying stunts, but I like to have at least a 50/50 chance.
And it sure didn't seem like Big Lil was offering me THOSE odds.
It's probably one of the main reasons we broke up. Sometimes I regret that decision.
GOTTA DO SOMETHING-- THIS TIME...
TELL YOU WHAT. WHY DON'T YOU JUST GIVE US THE CASE, AND WE'LL BE ON OUR WAY.
I- DON'T KNOW HOW TO GET IT OFF! I DON'T KNOW THE COMBINATION!
THAT'S TOO BAD, AIN'T IT, 'SHOEBOX'?

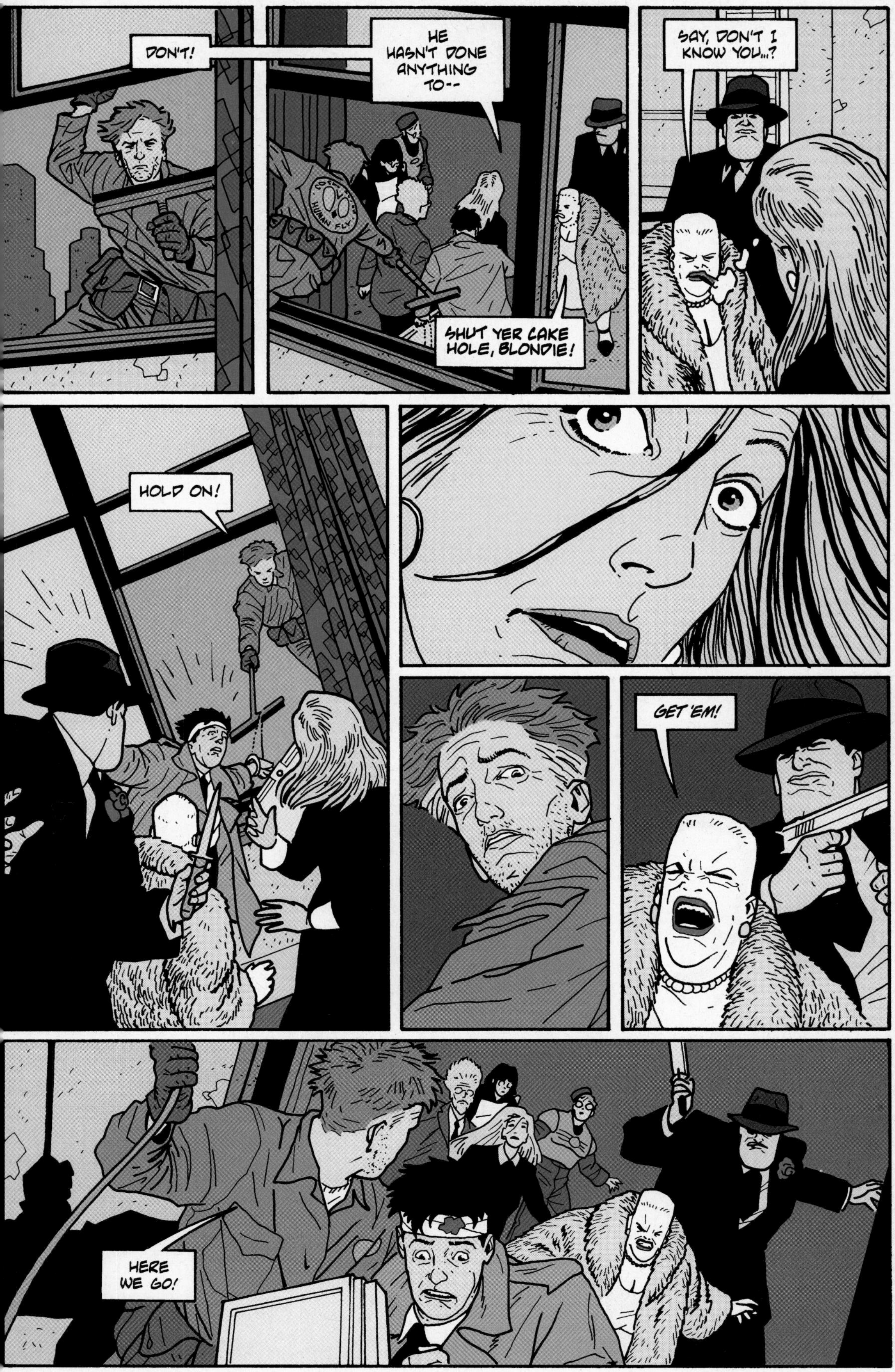
DON'T!
HE HASN'T DONE ANYTHING TO--
SHUT YER CAKE HOLE, BLONDIE!
SAY, DON'T I KNOW YOU...?
HOLD ON!
GET 'EM!
HERE WE GO!

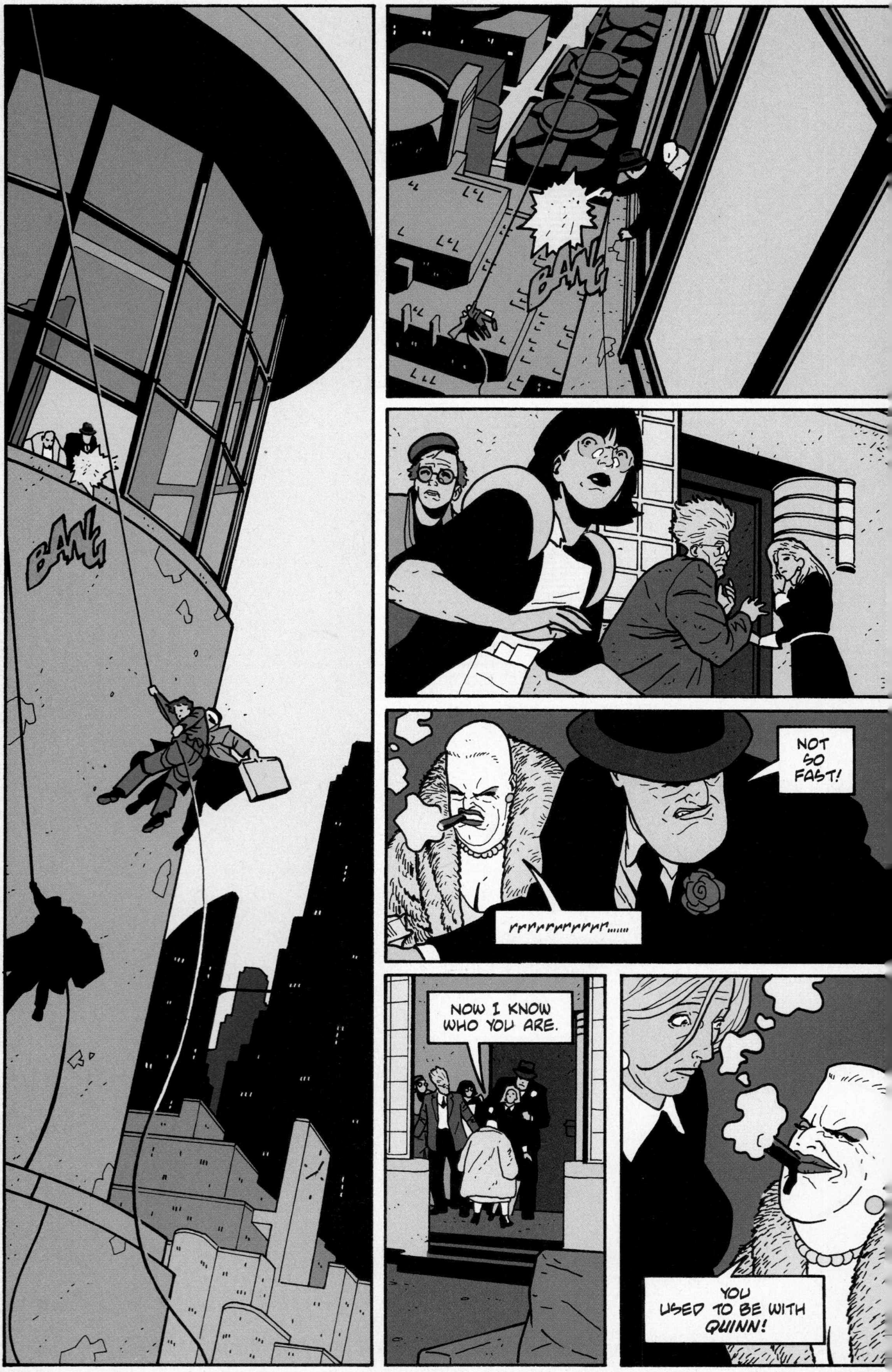
BANG
BANG
NOT SO FAST!
rrrrrrrrrrrr......
NOW I KNOW WHO YOU ARE.
YOU USED TO BE WITH QUINN!

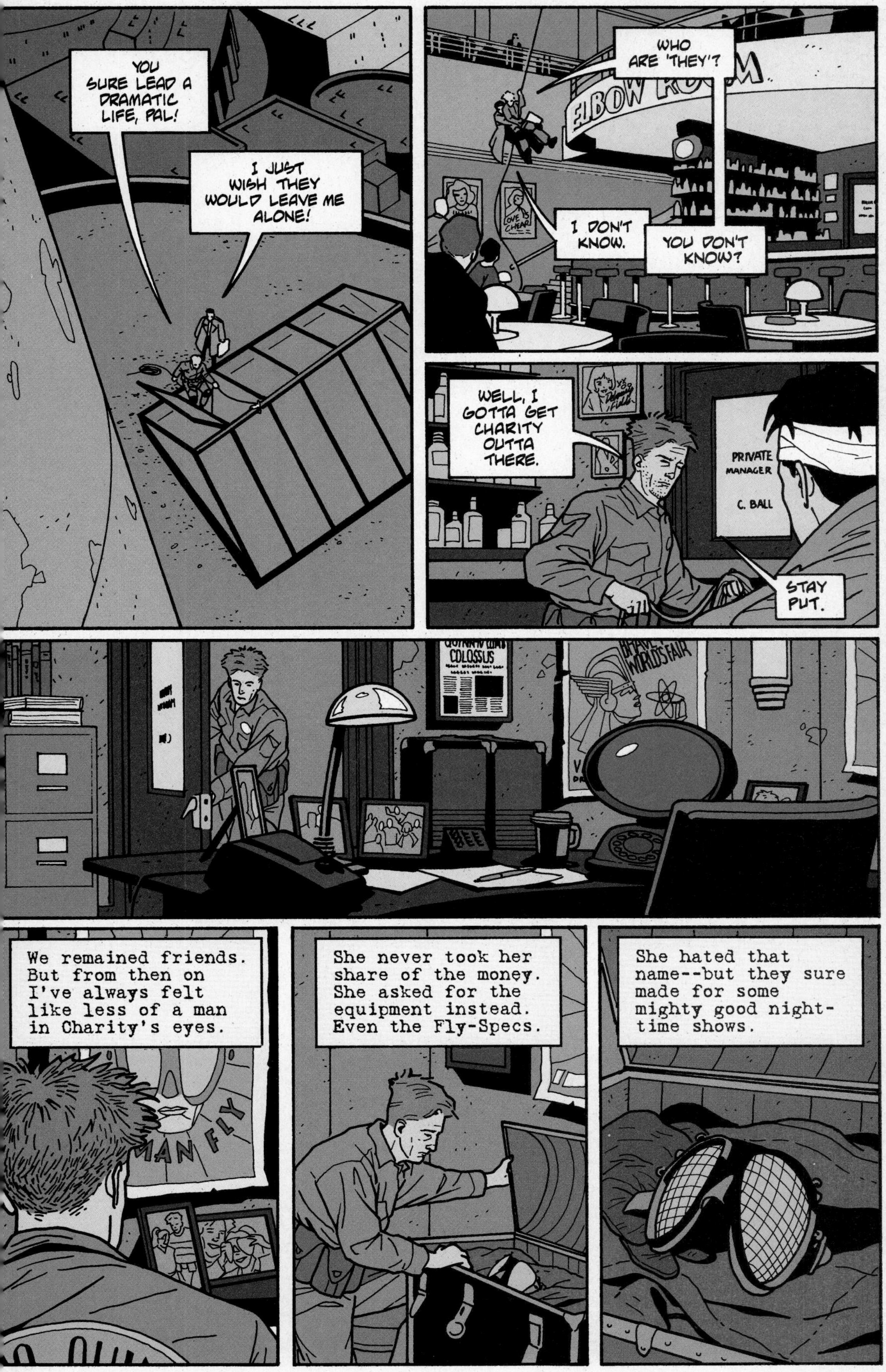
YOU SURE LEAD A DRAMATIC LIFE, PAL!
I JUST WISH THEY WOULD LEAVE ME ALONE!
WHO ARE 'THEY'?
I DON'T KNOW.
YOU DON'T KNOW?
WELL, I GOTTA GET CHARITY OUTTA THERE.
PRIVATE
MANAGER
C. BALL
STAY PUT.
COLOSSUS
We remained friends. But from then on I've always felt like less of a man in Charity's eyes.
She never took her share of the money. She asked for the equipment instead. Even the Fly-Specs.
She hated that name--but they sure made for some mighty good night-time shows.

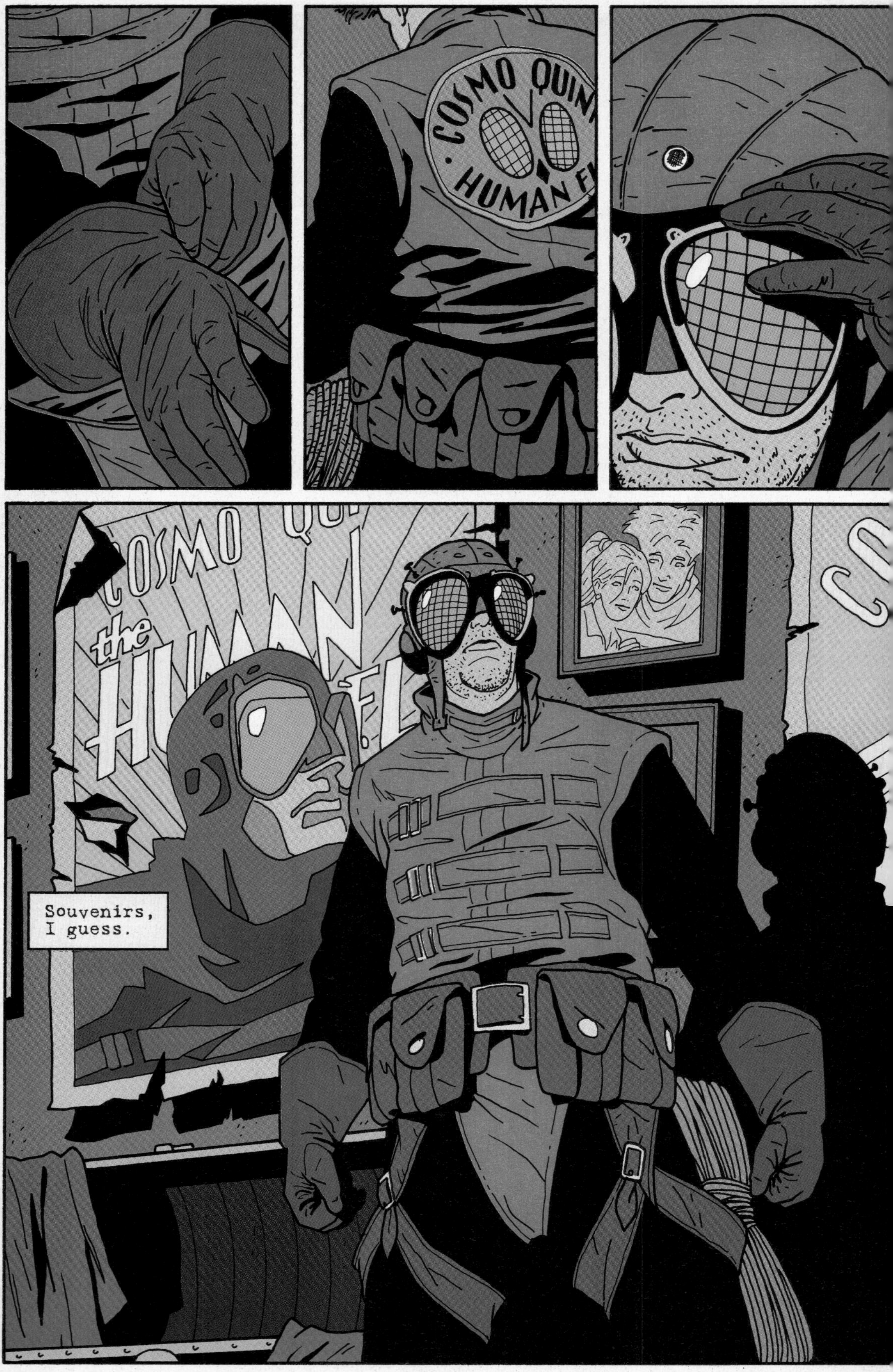
Souvenirs,
I guess.

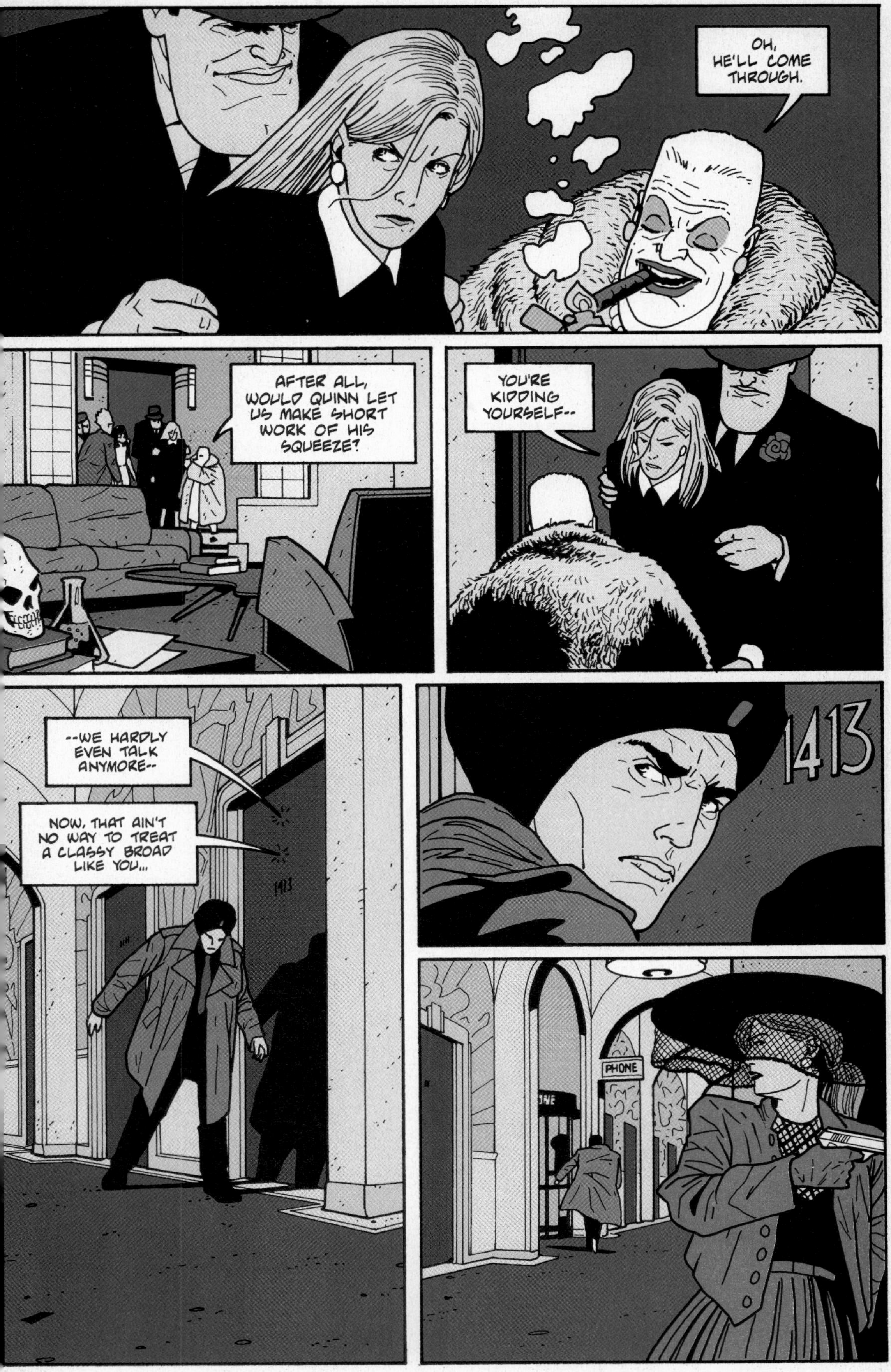
OH, HE'LL COME THROUGH.
AFTER ALL, WOULD QUINN LET US MAKE SHORT WORK OF HIS SQUEEZE?
YOU'RE KIDDING YOURSELF--
--WE HARDLY EVEN TALK ANYMORE--
NOW, THAT AIN'T NO WAY TO TREAT A CLASSY BROAD LIKE YOU...
1413
1413
PHONE

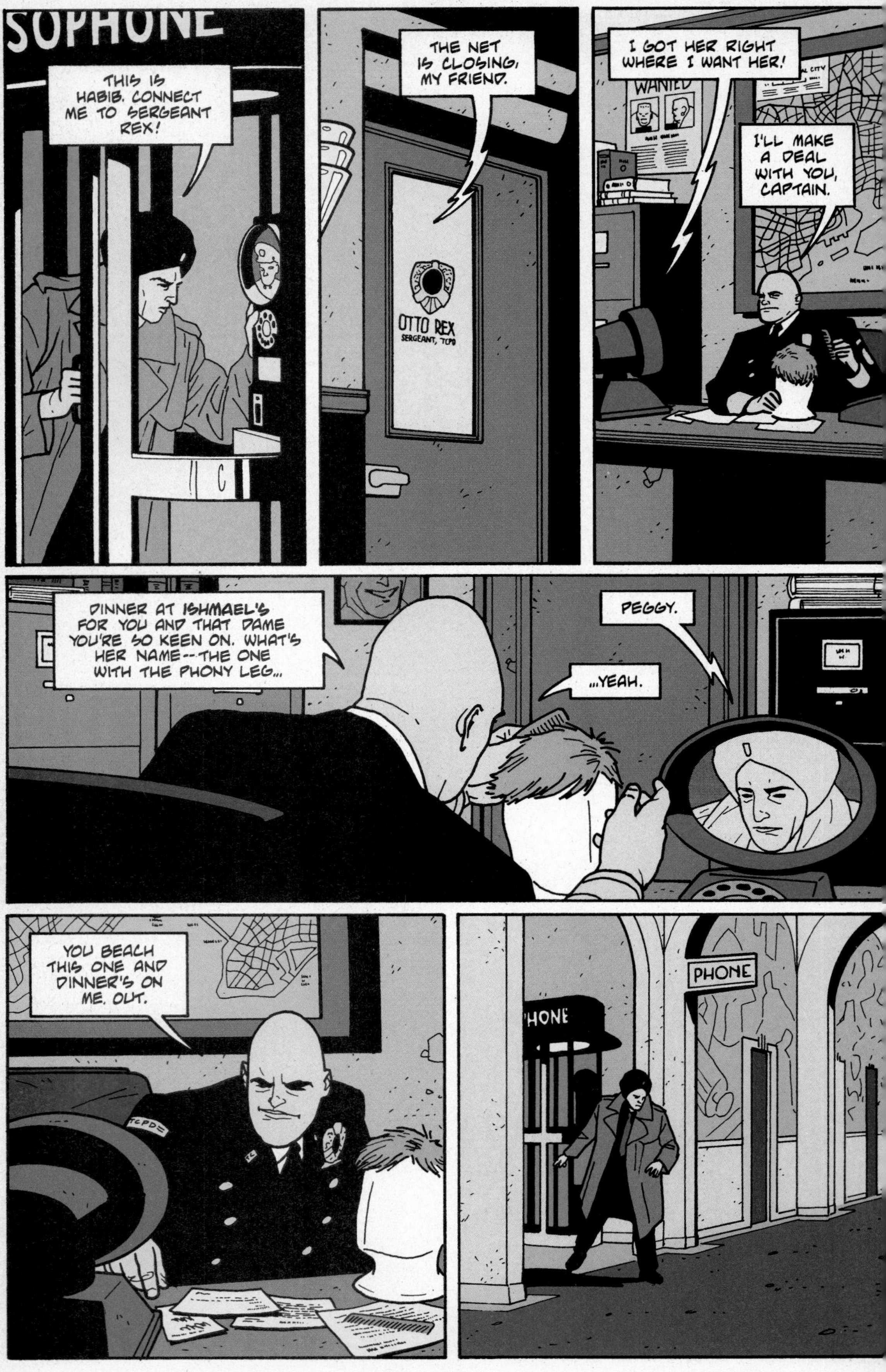
SOPHONE
THIS IS HABIB. CONNECT ME TO SERGEANT REX!
THE NET IS CLOSING, MY FRIEND.
OTTO REX
SERGEANT, TCPD
I GOT HER RIGHT WHERE I WANT HER!
WANTED
I'LL MAKE A DEAL WITH YOU, CAPTAIN.
DINNER AT ISHMAEL'S FOR YOU AND THAT DAME YOU'RE SO KEEN ON. WHAT'S HER NAME-- THE ONE WITH THE PHONY LEG...
PEGGY.
...YEAH.
YOU BEACH THIS ONE AND DINNER'S ON ME. OUT.
TCPD
PHONE
PHONE

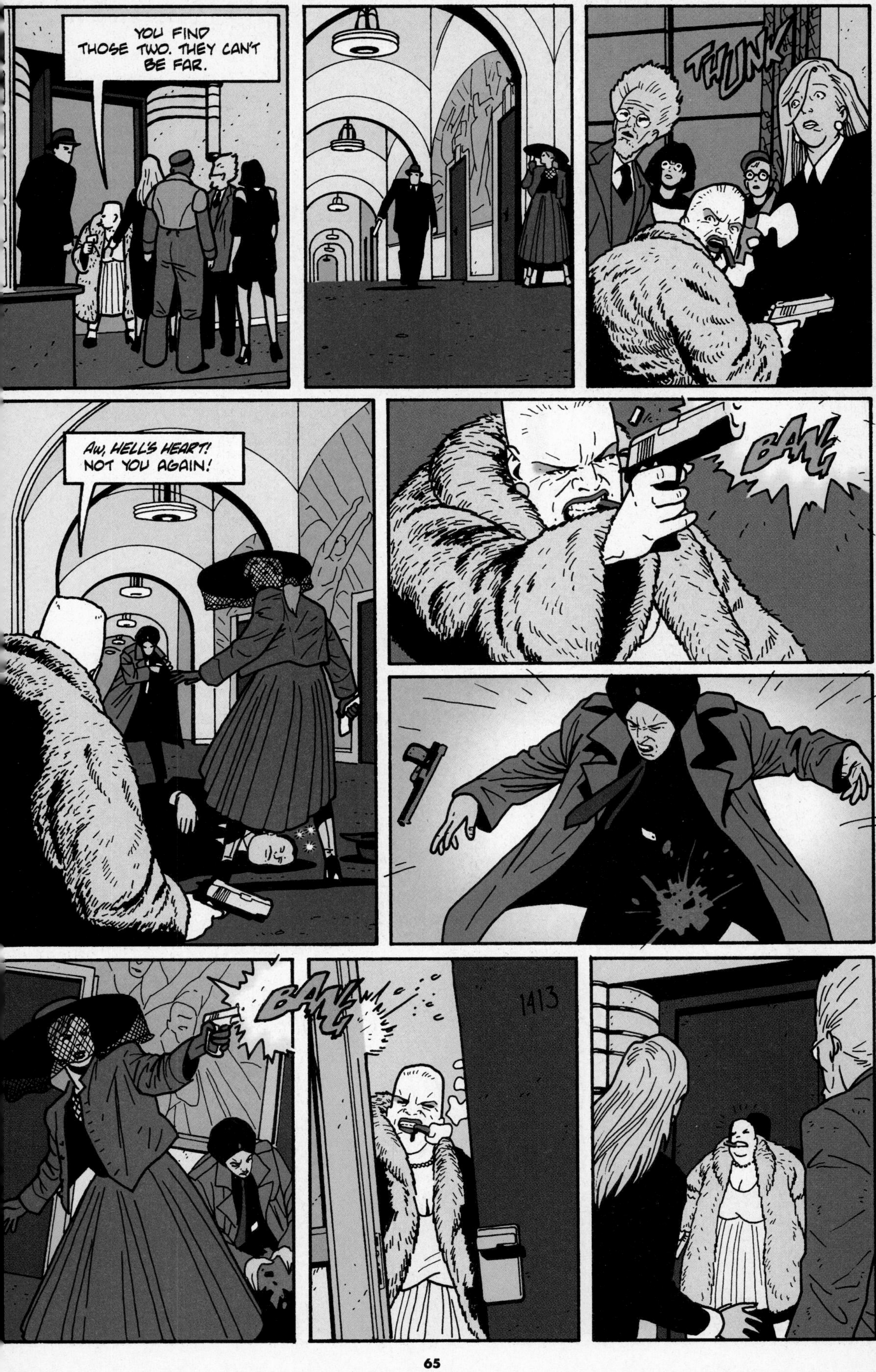
YOU FIND THOSE TWO. THEY CAN'T BE FAR.
THUNK
AW, HELL'S HEART! NOT YOU AGAIN!
BAM
BAM
1413

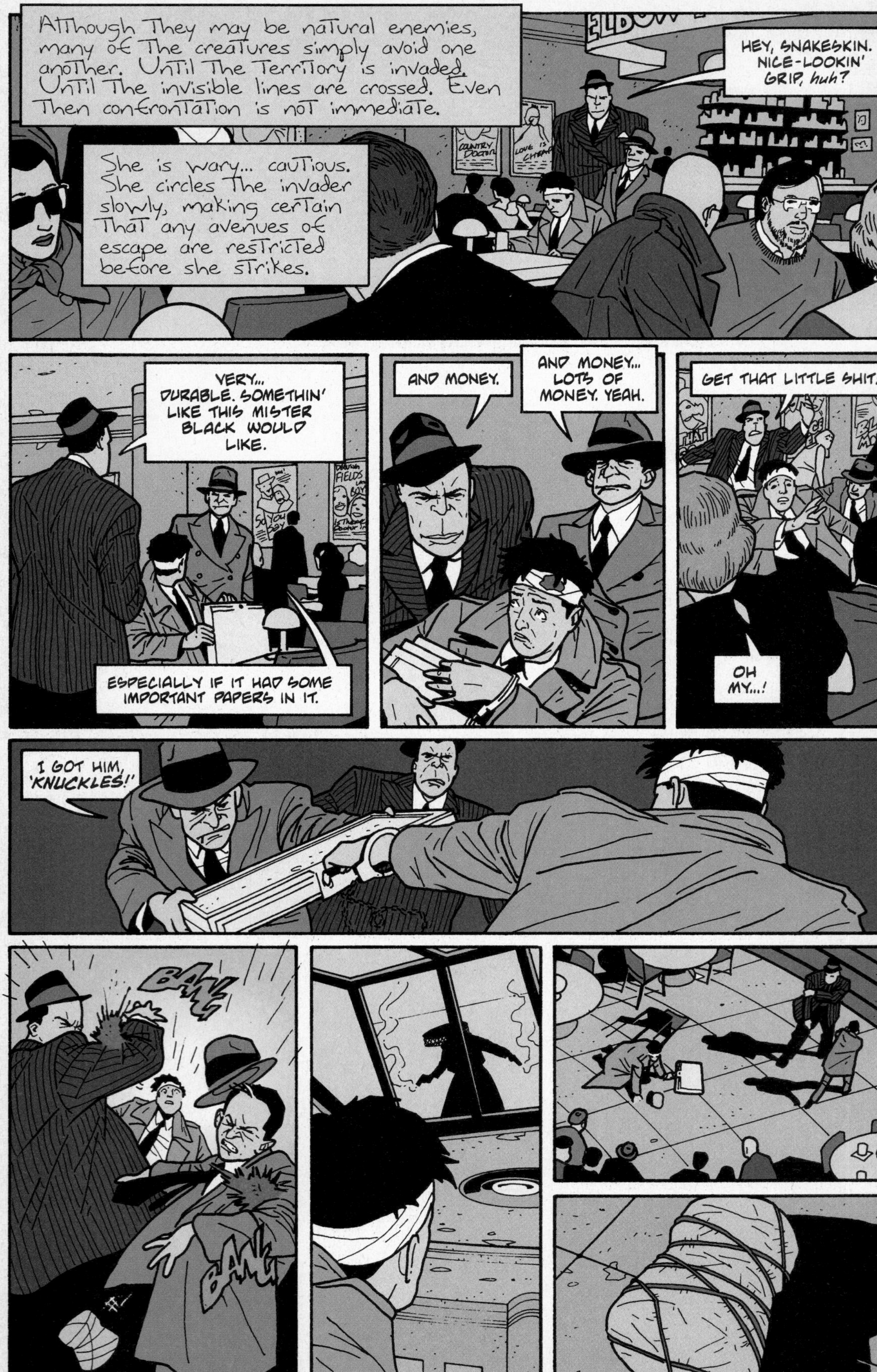
Although They may be natural enemies, many of The creatures simply avoid one another. Until The Territory is invaded. Until The invisible lines are crossed. Even Then confrontation is not immediate.
HEY, SNAKESKIN. NICE-LOOKIN' GRIP, huh?
She is wary... cautious. She circles The invader slowly, making certain That any avenues of escape are restricted before she strikes.
COUNTRY DOCTOR
LOVE IS CHEAP
VERY... DURABLE. SOMETHIN' LIKE THIS MISTER BLACK WOULD LIKE.
ESPECIALLY IF IT HAD SOME IMPORTANT PAPERS IN IT.
AND MONEY.
AND MONEY... LOTS OF MONEY. YEAH.
GET THAT LITTLE SHIT!
OH MY...!
I GOT HIM, 'KNUCKLES!'
BAM
BAM

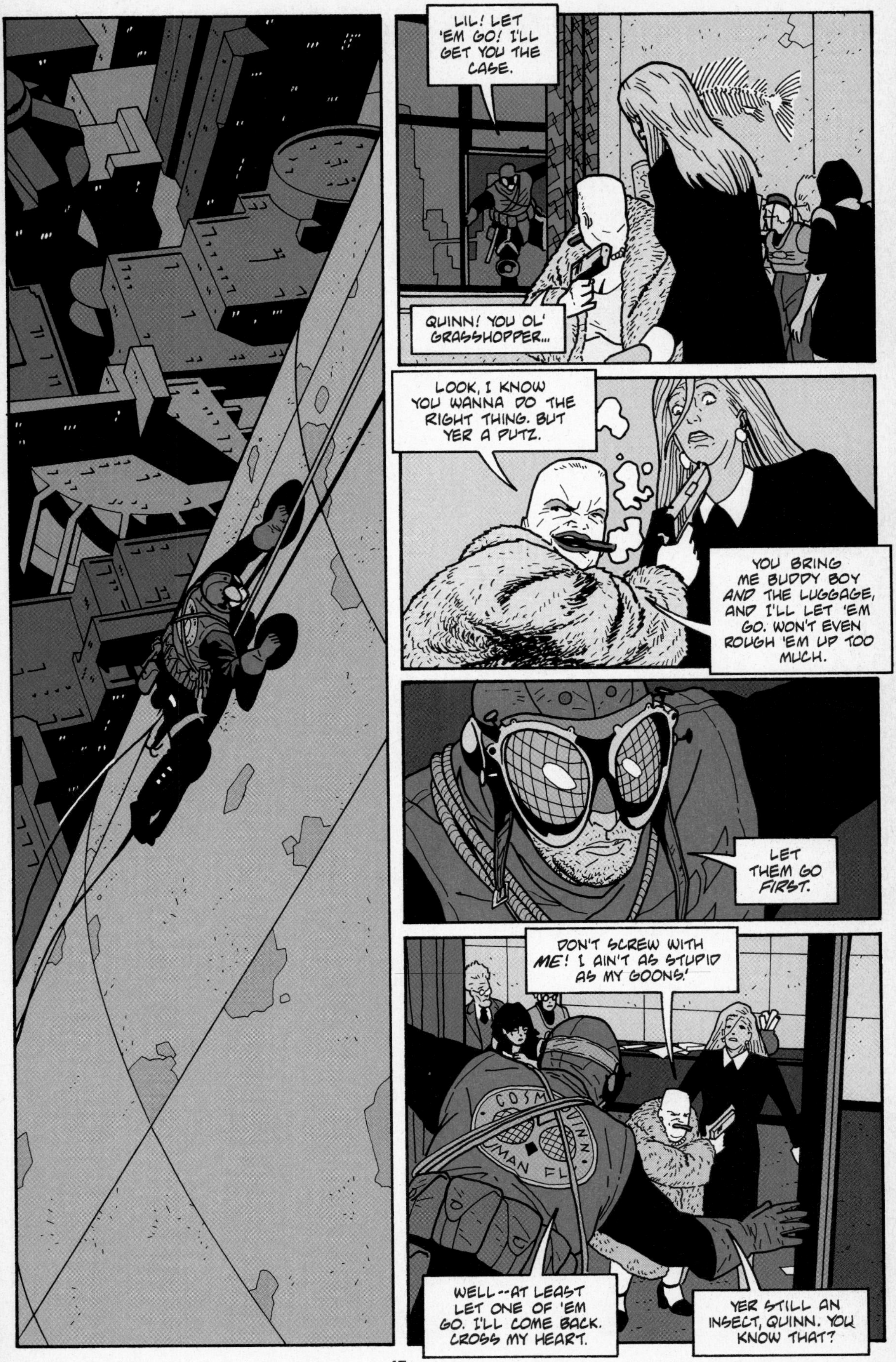

LIL! LET 'EM GO! I'LL GET YOU THE CASE.
QUINN! YOU OL' GRASSHOPPER...
LOOK, I KNOW YOU WANNA DO THE RIGHT THING. BUT YER A PUTZ.
YOU BRING ME BUDDY BOY AND THE LUGGAGE, AND I'LL LET 'EM GO. WON'T EVEN ROUGH 'EM UP TOO MUCH.
LET THEM GO FIRST.
DON'T SCREW WITH ME! I AIN'T AS STUPID AS MY GOONS!
WELL--AT LEAST LET ONE OF 'EM GO. I'LL COME BACK. CROSS MY HEART.
YER STILL AN INSECT, QUINN. YOU KNOW THAT?

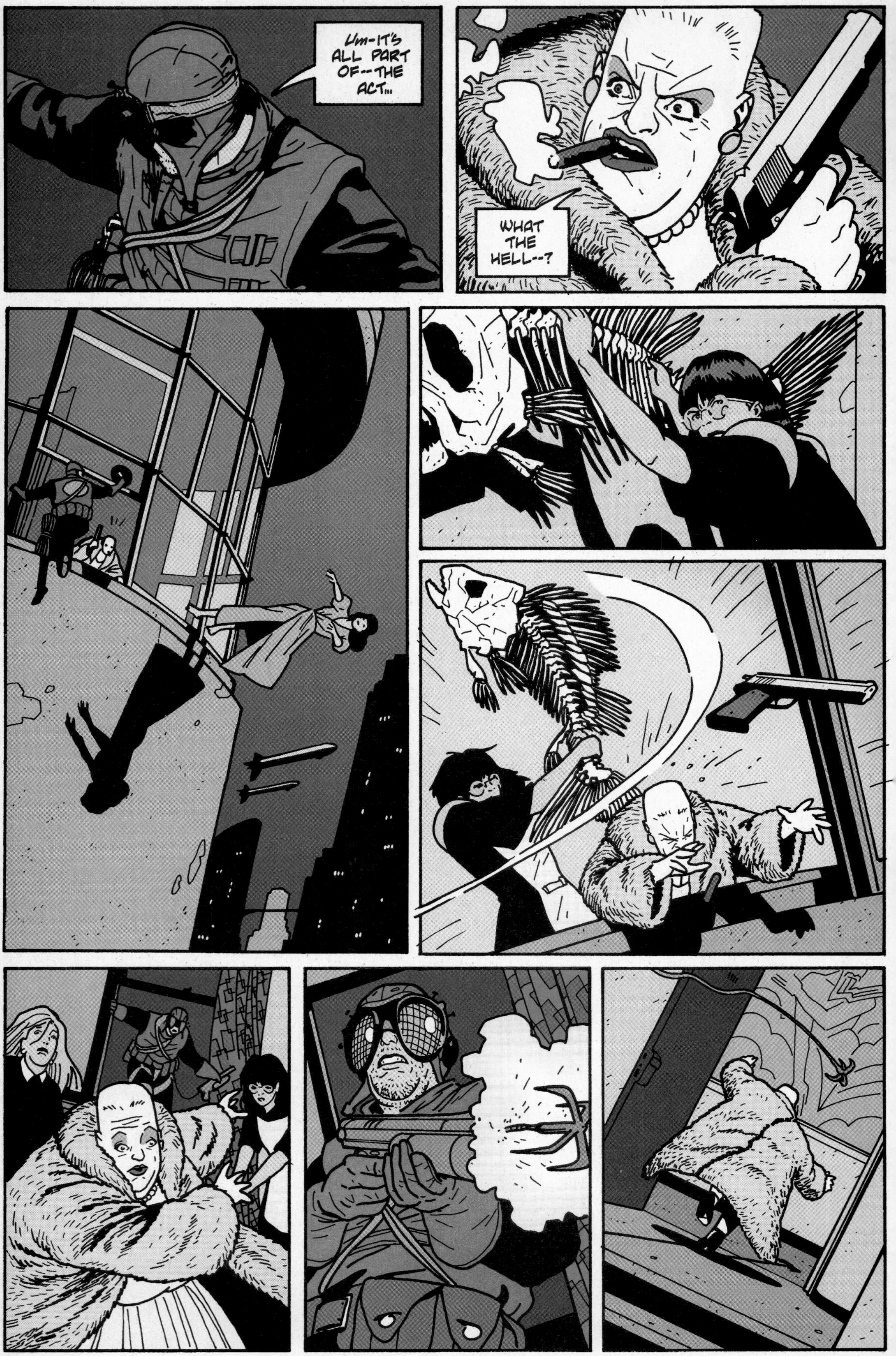
UM-IT'S ALL PART OF--THE ACT...
WHAT THE HELL--?

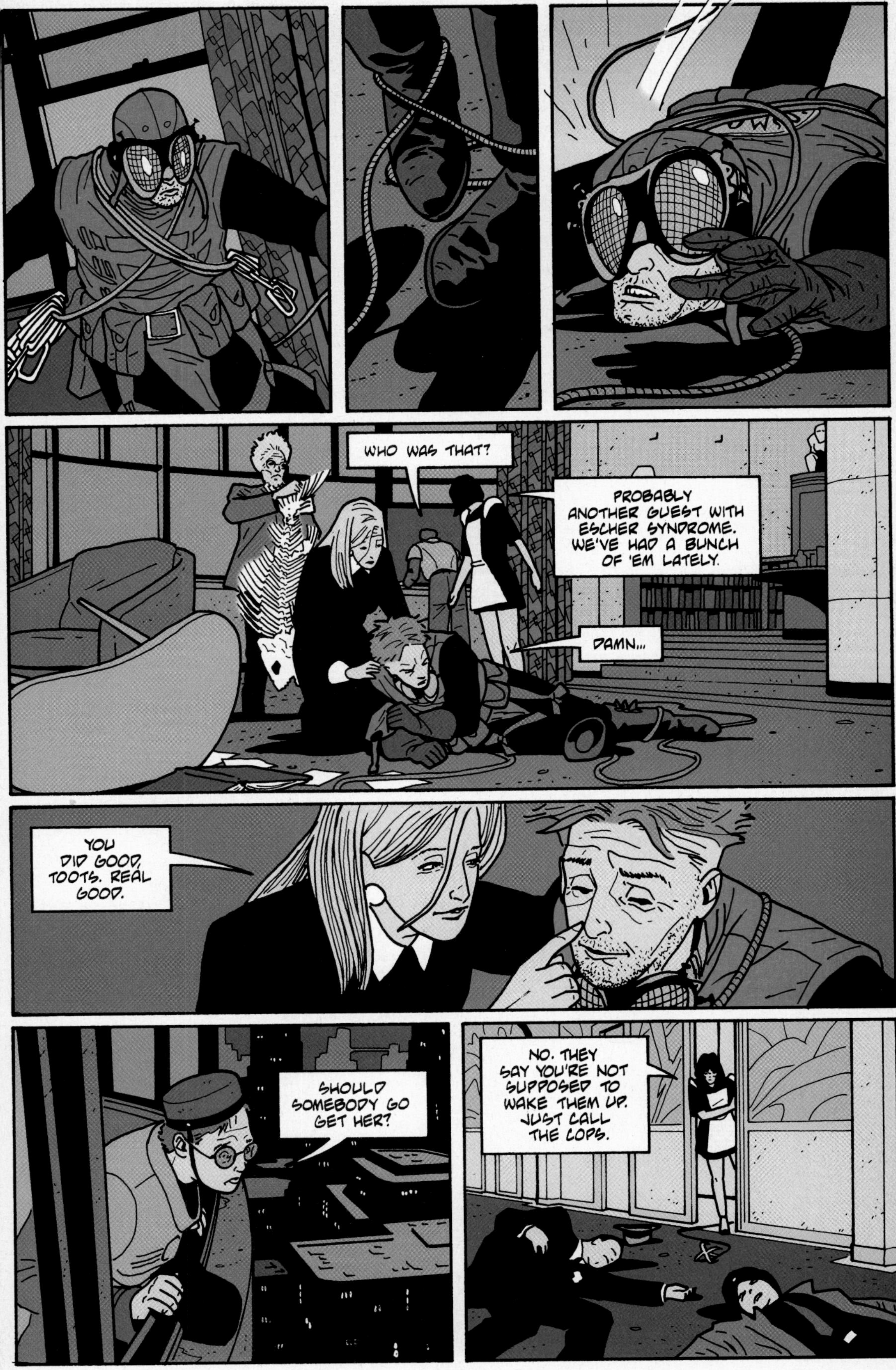
WHO WAS THAT?
PROBABLY ANOTHER GUEST WITH ESCHER SYNDROME. WE'VE HAD A BUNCH OF 'EM LATELY.
DAMN...
YOU DID GOOD, TOOTS. REAL GOOD.
SHOULD SOMEBODY GO GET HER?
NO. THEY SAY YOU'RE NOT SUPPOSED TO WAKE THEM UP. JUST CALL THE COPS.

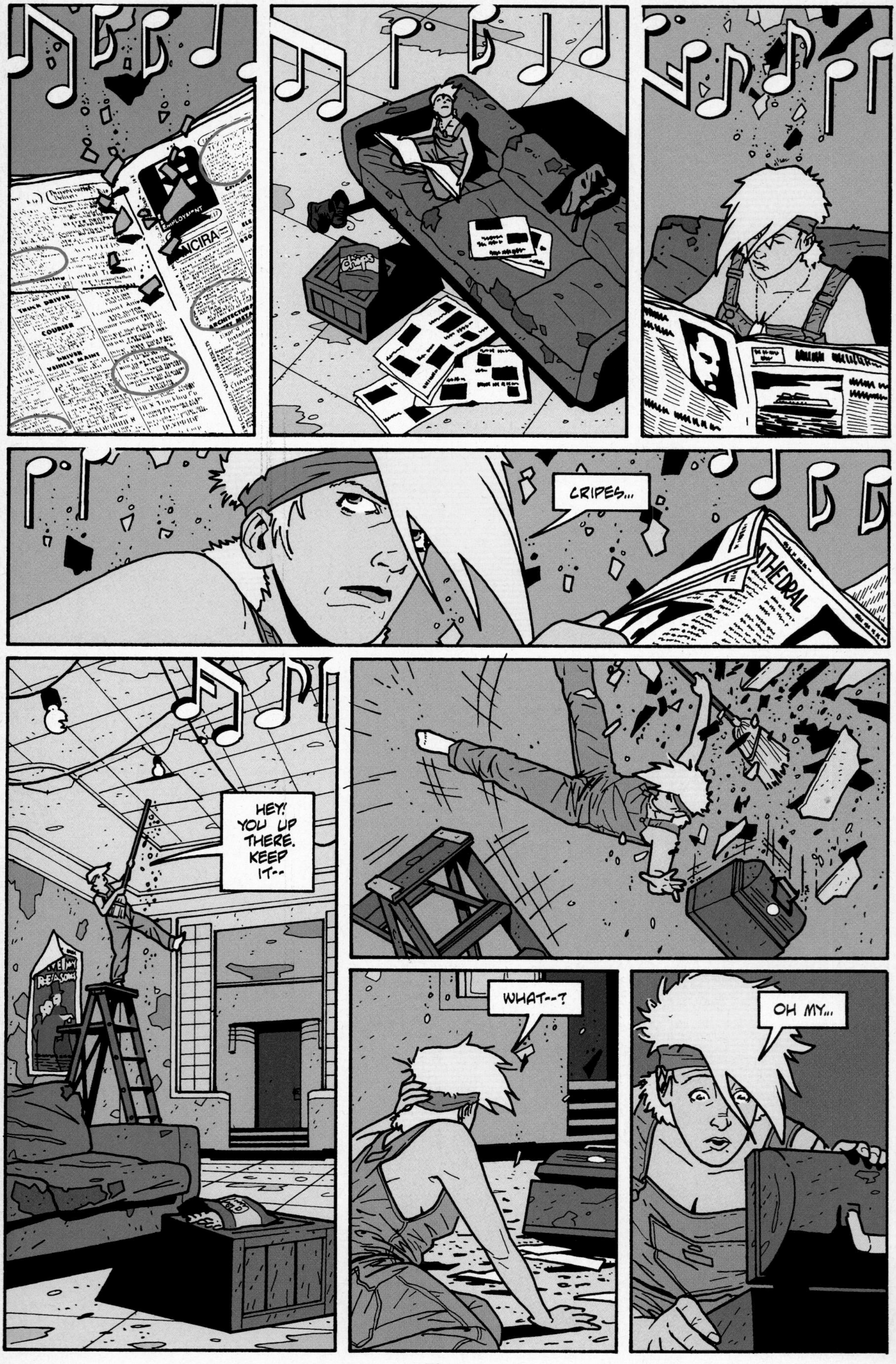
CRIPES...
HEY! YOU UP THERE. KEEP IT--
WHAT--?
OH MY...

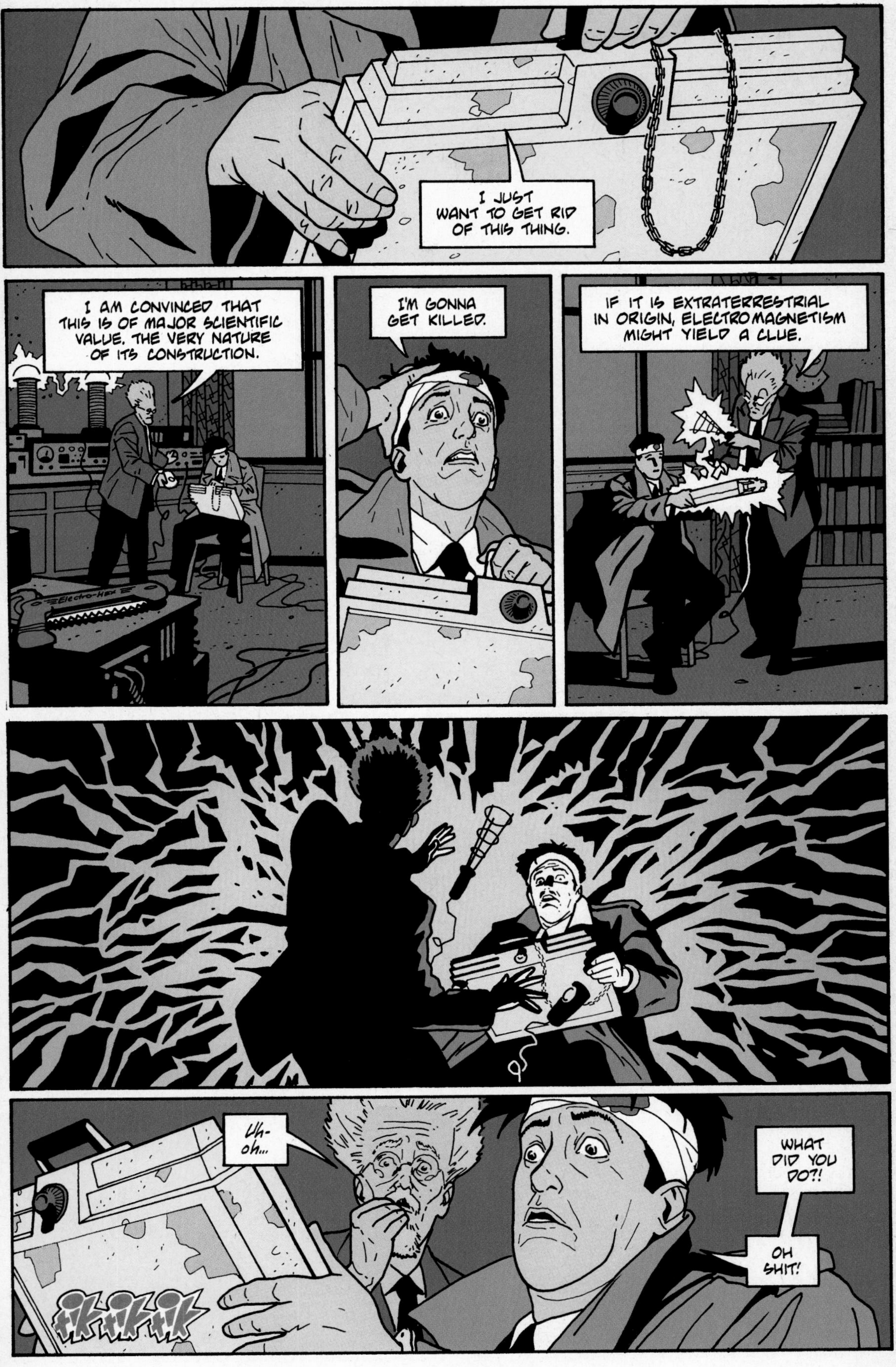
I JUST WANT TO GET RID OF THIS THING.
I AM CONVINCED THAT THIS IS OF MAJOR SCIENTIFIC VALUE. THE VERY NATURE OF ITS CONSTRUCTION.
Electro-Hex
I'M GONNA GET KILLED.
IF IT IS EXTRATERRESTRIAL IN ORIGIN, ELECTROMAGNETISM MIGHT YIELD A CLUE.
Uh-oh...
WHAT DID YOU DO?!
OH SHIT!
tik tik tik

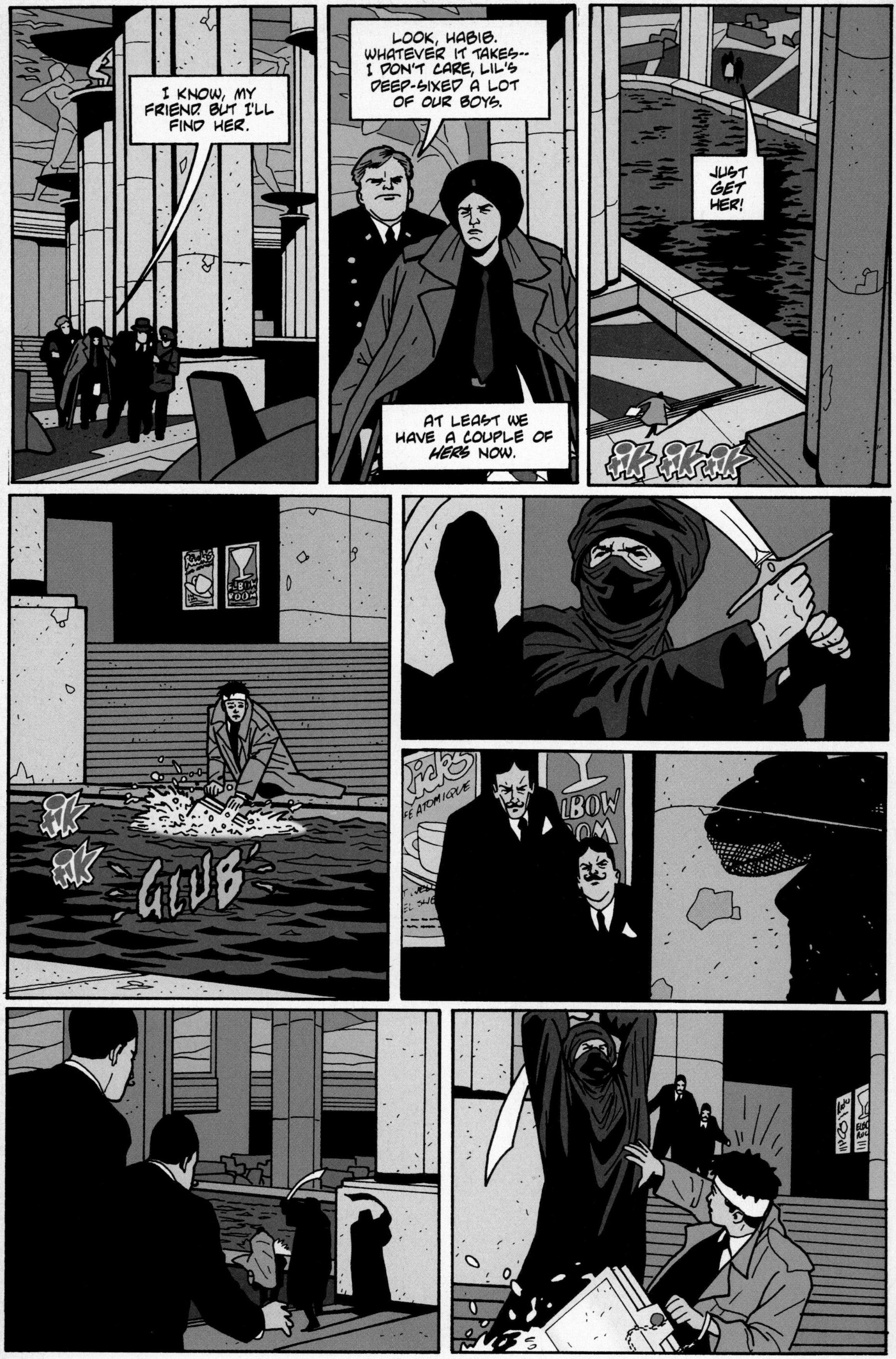
I KNOW, MY FRIEND. BUT I'LL FIND HER.
LOOK, HABIB. WHATEVER IT TAKES-- I DON'T CARE, LIL'S DEEP-SIXED A LOT OF OUR BOYS.
AT LEAST WE HAVE A COUPLE OF HERS NOW.
JUST GET HER!
TIK TIK TIK
ELBOW ROOM
TIK
TIK
GLUB
ELBOW ROOM

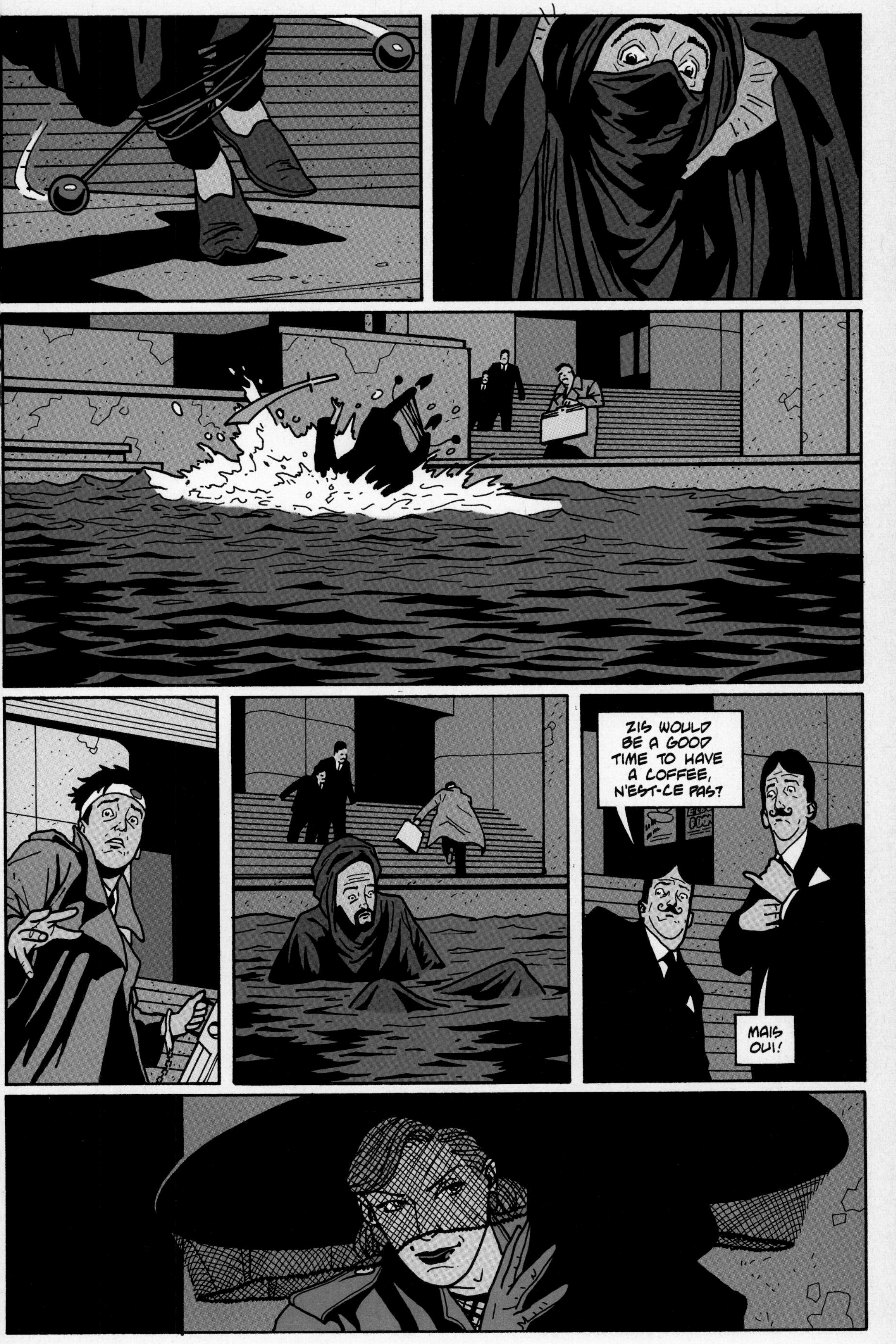
ZIS WOULD BE A GOOD TIME TO HAVE A COFFEE, N'EST-CE PAS?
MAIS OUI!

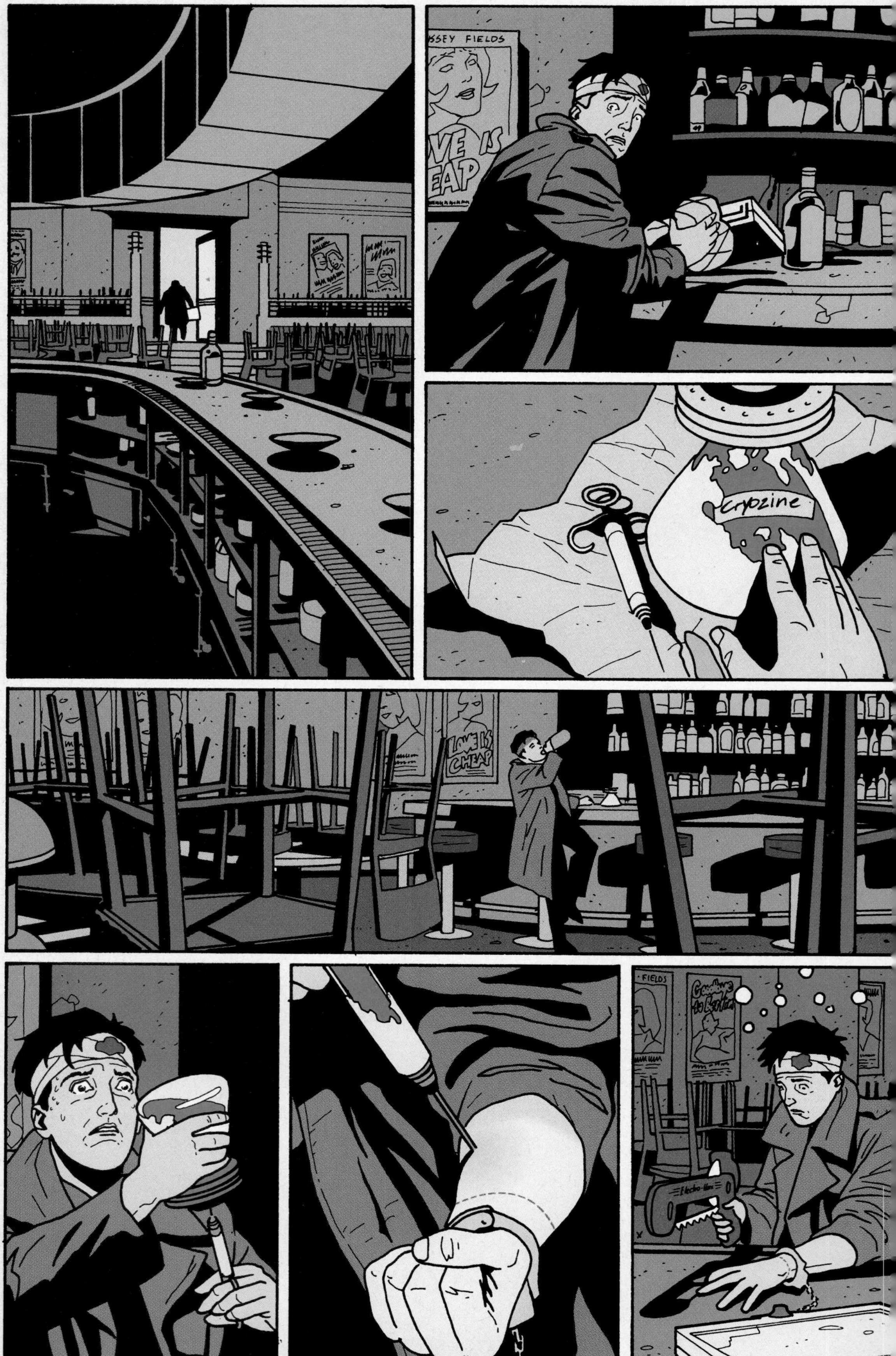
Cryozine
LOVE IS CHEAP
FIELDS

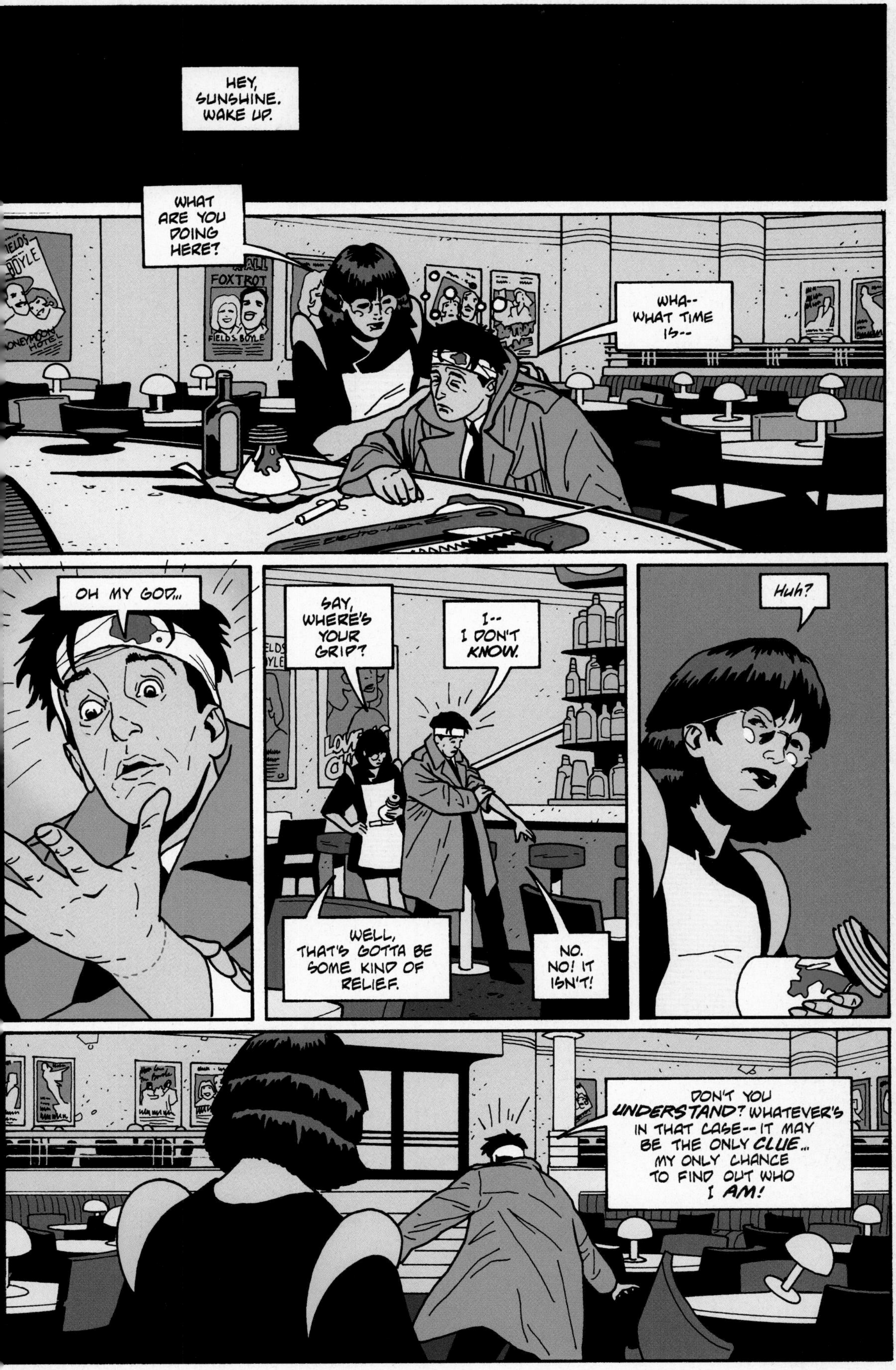
HEY, SUNSHINE. WAKE UP.
WHAT ARE YOU DOING HERE?
WHA-- WHAT TIME IS--
FOXTROT
FIELDS BOYLE
ELECTRO-HAX
OH MY GOD...
SAY, WHERE'S YOUR GRIP?
I-- I DON'T KNOW.
WELL, THAT'S GOTTA BE SOME KIND OF RELIEF.
NO. NO! IT ISN'T!
Huh?
DON'T YOU UNDERSTAND? WHATEVER'S IN THAT CASE-- IT MAY BE THE ONLY CLUE... MY ONLY CHANCE TO FIND OUT WHO I AM!

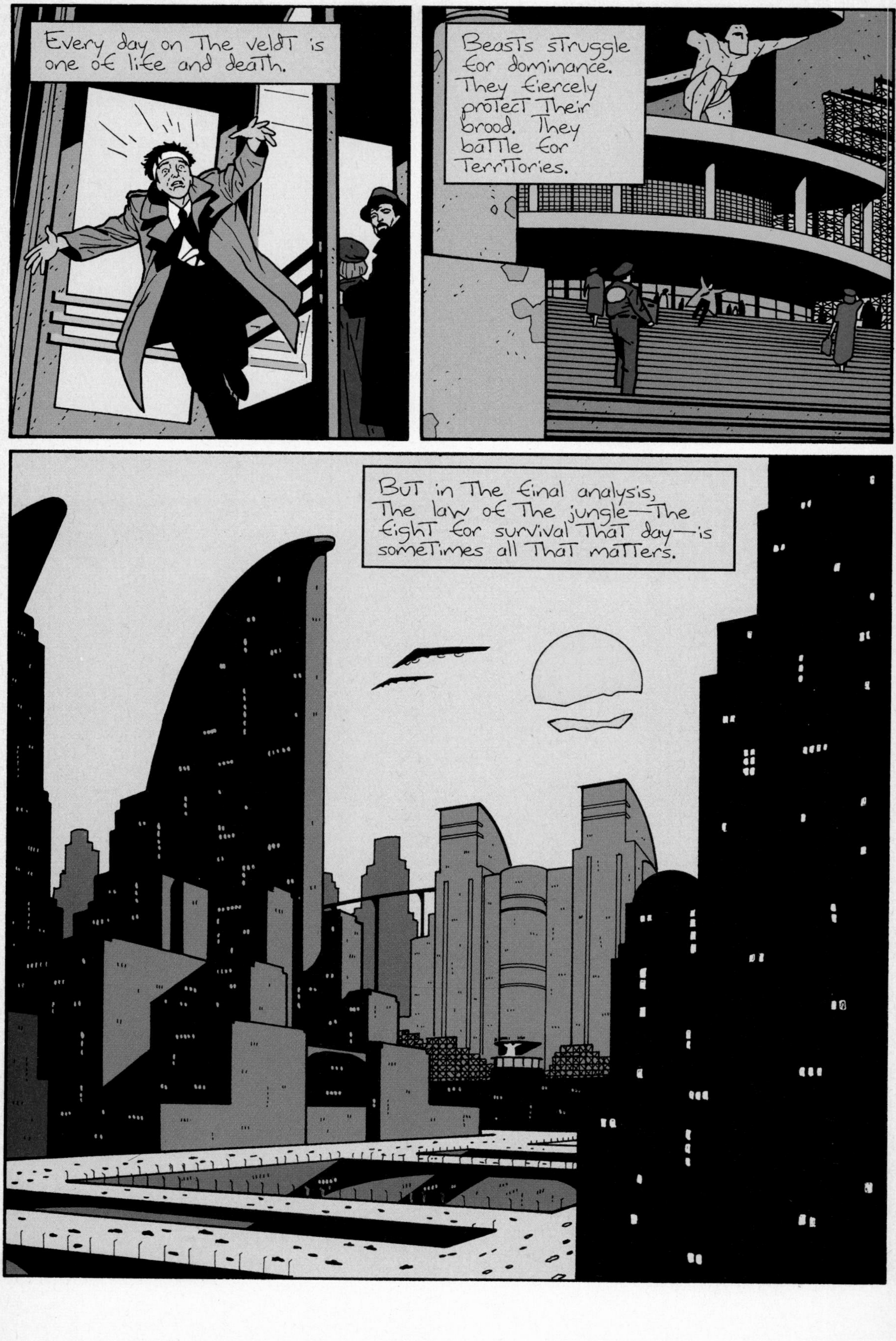
Every day on The veldT is one of life and death.
BeasTs sTruggle for dominance. They fiercely protect Their brood. They battle for TerriTories.
BuT in The final analysis, The law of The jungle—The fight for survival ThaT day—is someTimes all ThaT matTers.

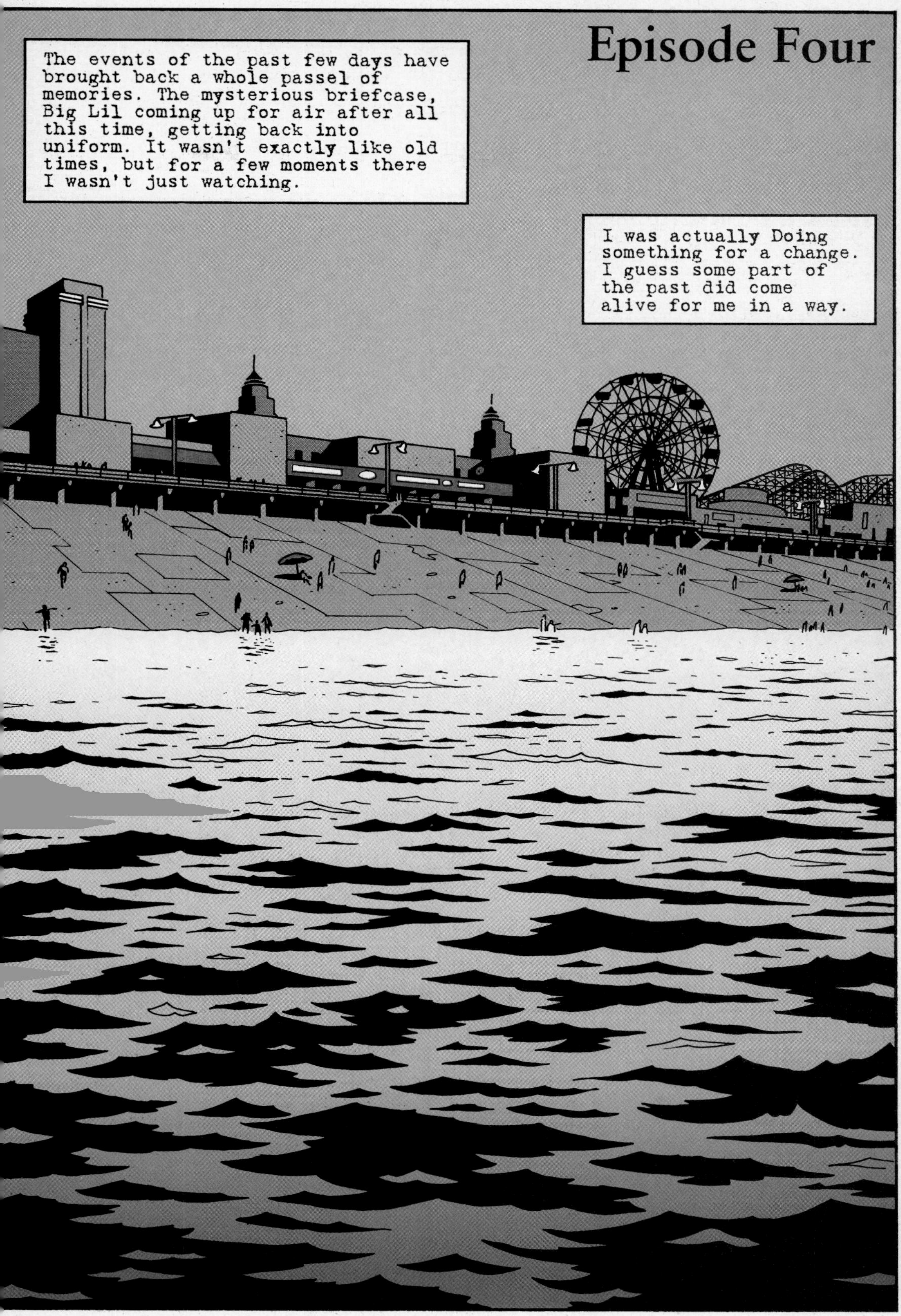
Episode Four
The events of the past few days have brought back a whole passel of memories. The mysterious briefcase, Big Lil coming up for air after all this time, getting back into uniform. It wasn't exactly like old times, but for a few moments there I wasn't just watching.
I was actually Doing something for a change. I guess some part of the past did come alive for me in a way.

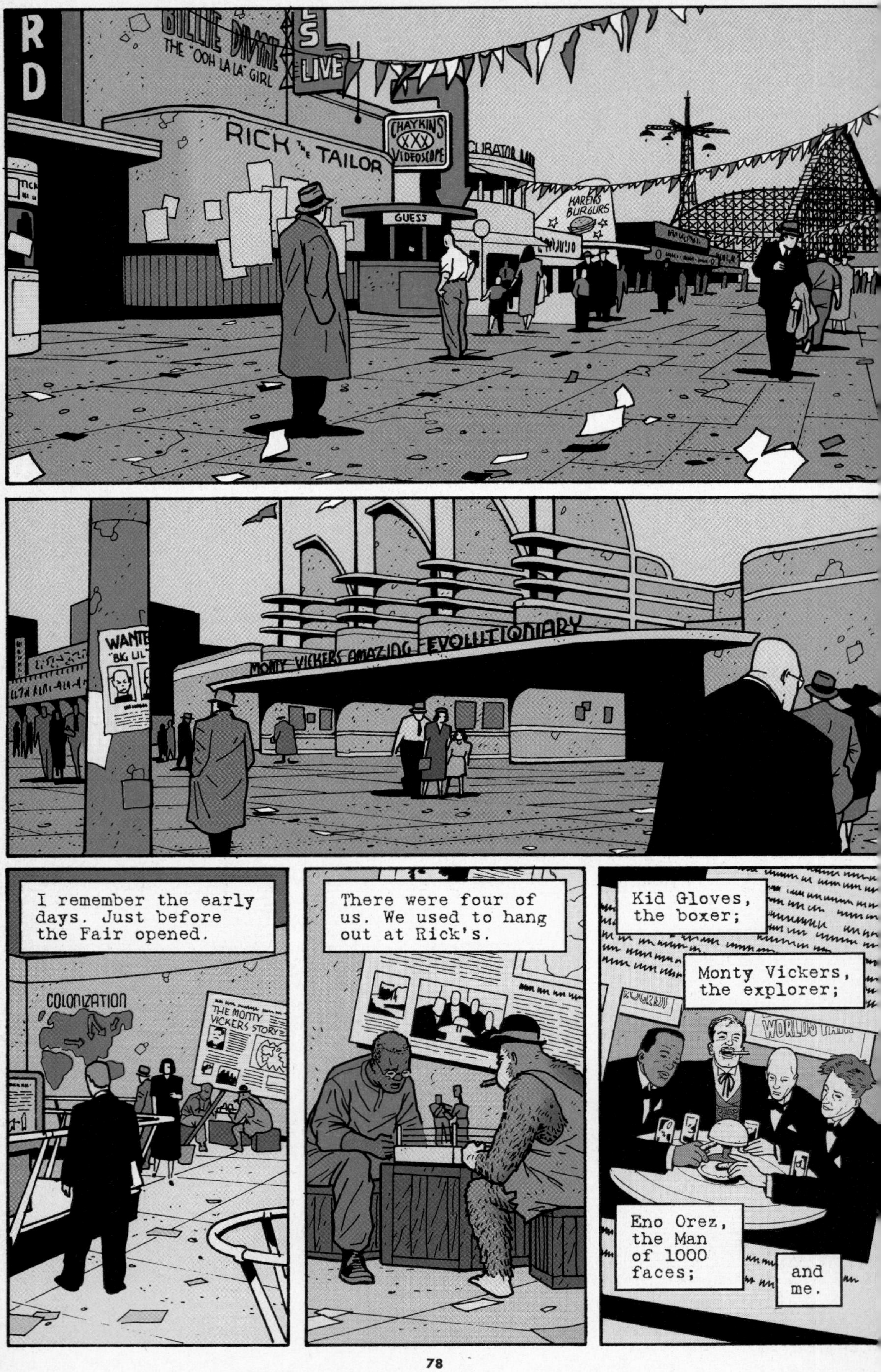
BILLIE DIVINE
THE "OOH LA LA" GIRL
LIVE
RICK THE TAILOR
CHAYKINS XXX VIDEOSCOPE
GUESS
KAREN'S BURGURS
WANTE
"BIG LIL"
MONTY VICKERS AMAZING EVOLUTIONARY
I remember the early days. Just before the Fair opened.
COLONIZATION
THE MONTY VICKERS STORY
There were four of us. We used to hang out at Rick's.
Kid Gloves, the boxer;
Monty Vickers, the explorer;
Eno Orez, the Man of 1000 faces;
and me.

We were on top of the world. Our tails were a-waggin'.

Monty had just returned from the Russian Steppes with the first specimens of the Abominable Snowman.

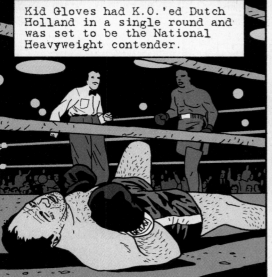

Kid Gloves had K.O.'ed Dutch Holland in a single round and was set to be the National Heavyweight contender.

And Eno had returned from his year-long tour performing before the Crowned Heads of Europe.

Each of us had been personally invited to participate in the opening of the BRAVE NEW WORLD'S FAIR.

Little did any of us know how things would turn out.

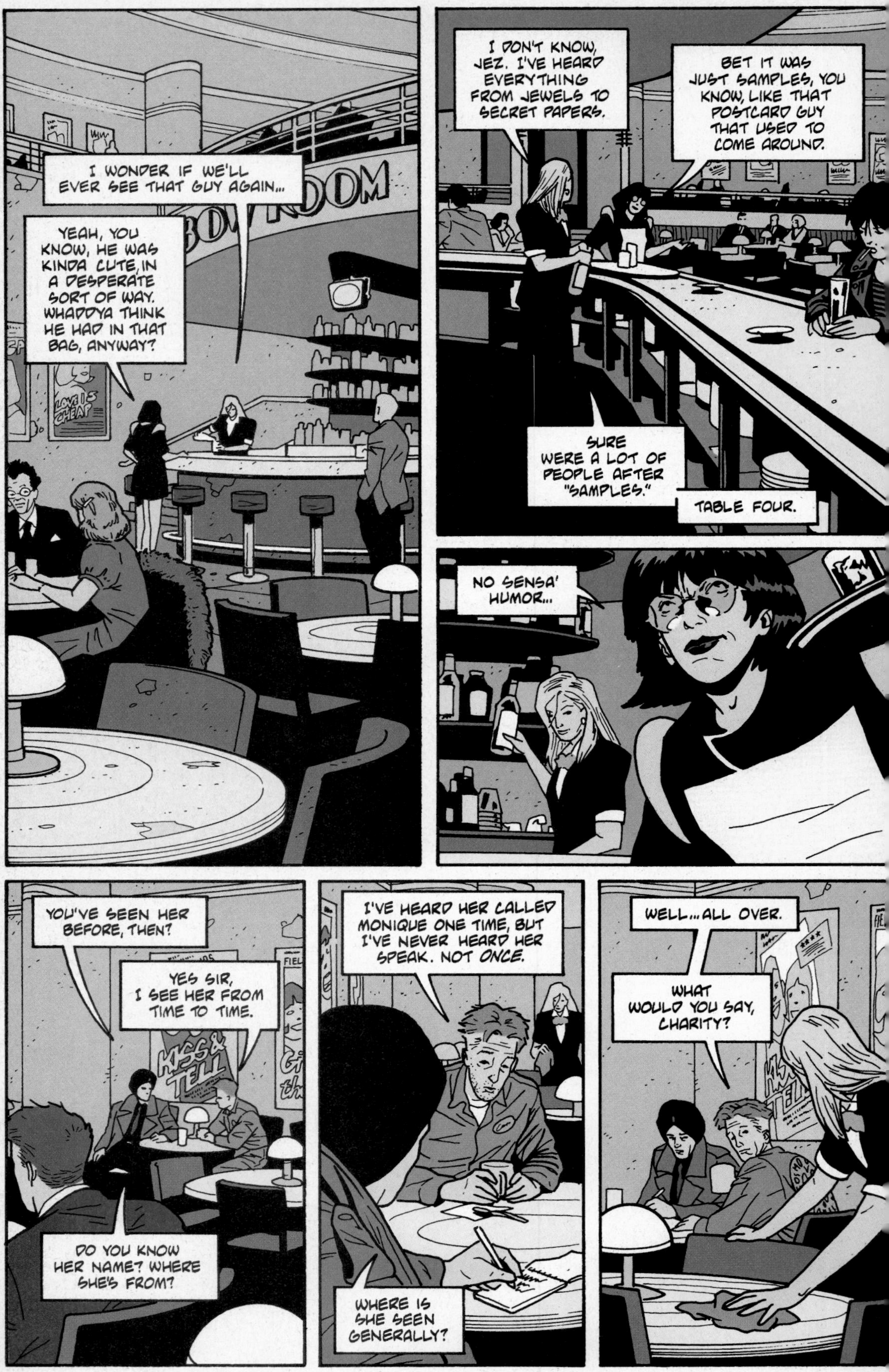
I WONDER IF WE'LL EVER SEE THAT GUY AGAIN...
YEAH, YOU KNOW, HE WAS KINDA CUTE, IN A DESPERATE SORT OF WAY. WHADDYA THINK HE HAD IN THAT BAG, ANYWAY?
BOW ROOM
LOVE IS CHEAP
I DON'T KNOW, JEZ. I'VE HEARD EVERYTHING FROM JEWELS TO SECRET PAPERS.
BET IT WAS JUST SAMPLES, YOU KNOW, LIKE THAT POSTCARD GUY THAT USED TO COME AROUND.
SURE WERE A LOT OF PEOPLE AFTER "SAMPLES."
TABLE FOUR.
NO SENSA' HUMOR...
YOU'VE SEEN HER BEFORE, THEN?
YES SIR, I SEE HER FROM TIME TO TIME.
KISS & TELL
DO YOU KNOW HER NAME? WHERE SHE'S FROM?
I'VE HEARD HER CALLED MONIQUE ONE TIME, BUT I'VE NEVER HEARD HER SPEAK. NOT *ONCE.*
WHERE IS SHE SEEN GENERALLY?
WELL...ALL OVER.
WHAT WOULD YOU SAY, CHARITY?

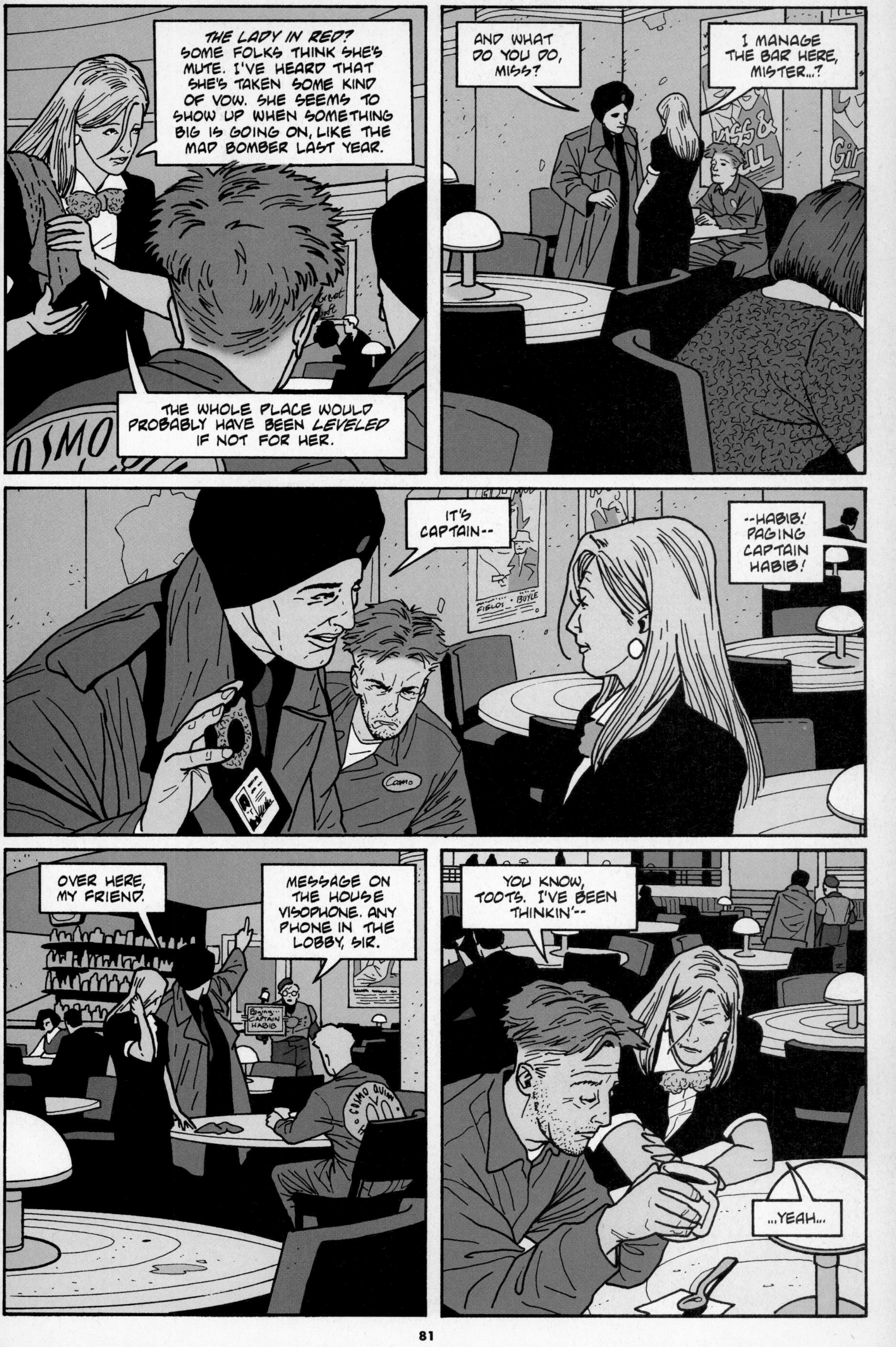
THE LADY IN RED? SOME FOLKS THINK SHE'S MUTE. I'VE HEARD THAT SHE'S TAKEN SOME KIND OF VOW. SHE SEEMS TO SHOW UP WHEN SOMETHING BIG IS GOING ON, LIKE THE MAD BOMBER LAST YEAR.
THE WHOLE PLACE WOULD PROBABLY HAVE BEEN LEVELED IF NOT FOR HER.
AND WHAT DO YOU DO, MISS?
I MANAGE THE BAR HERE, MISTER...?
IT'S CAPTAIN--
--HABIB! PAGING CAPTAIN HABIB!
OVER HERE, MY FRIEND.
MESSAGE ON THE HOUSE VISOPHONE. ANY PHONE IN THE LOBBY, SIR.
PAGING... CAPTAIN HABIB
YOU KNOW, TOOTS. I'VE BEEN THINKIN'--
...YEAH...

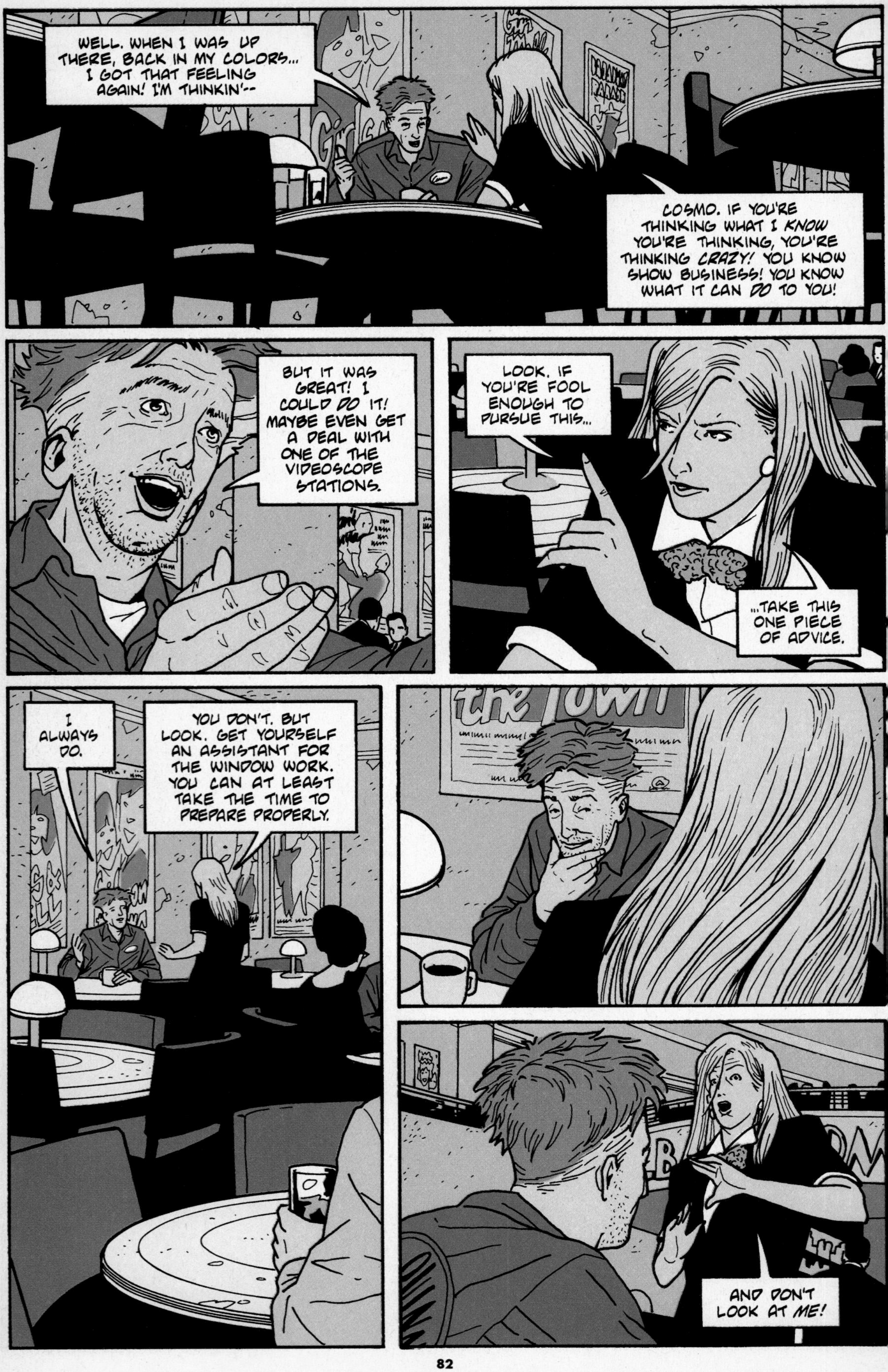

WELL. WHEN I WAS UP THERE, BACK IN MY COLORS... I GOT THAT FEELING AGAIN! I'M THINKIN'--
COSMO. IF YOU'RE THINKING WHAT I KNOW YOU'RE THINKING, YOU'RE THINKING CRAZY! YOU KNOW SHOW BUSINESS! YOU KNOW WHAT IT CAN DO TO YOU!
BUT IT WAS GREAT! I COULD DO IT! MAYBE EVEN GET A DEAL WITH ONE OF THE VIDEOSCOPE STATIONS.
LOOK. IF YOU'RE FOOL ENOUGH TO PURSUE THIS...
...TAKE THIS ONE PIECE OF ADVICE.
I ALWAYS DO.
YOU DON'T. BUT LOOK. GET YOURSELF AN ASSISTANT FOR THE WINDOW WORK. YOU CAN AT LEAST TAKE THE TIME TO PREPARE PROPERLY.
the TOWN
AND DON'T LOOK AT ME!

Monty was a curious hombre. A master showman, he traveled to strange, exotic lands and returned with all manner of trophies and unusual creatures (many believed extinct).

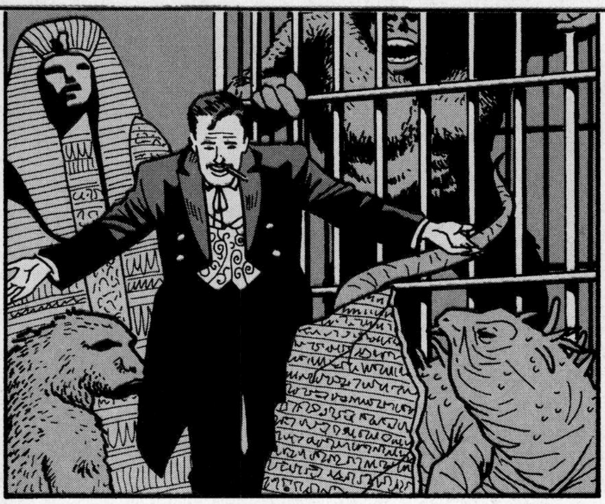

PROFILES IN ADVENTURE
TAKES A LOOK AT TERMINAL CITY'S MOST
COLORFUL CITIZENS.

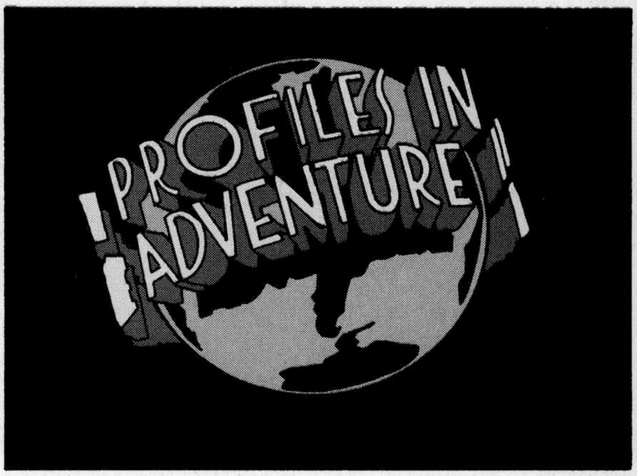
PROFILES IN ADVENTURE!

MONTY VICKERS. EXPLORER, ARCHAEOLOGIST, ANTHROPOLOGIST. TRAVELING WITH HIS INTREPID CREW TO THE FOUR CORNERS OF THE EARTH, THE INDOMITABLE MISTER VICKERS NOT ONLY SENDS BACK INCREDIBLE SPECIMENS AND ARTIFACTS, BUT REMARKABLE FOOTAGE OF HIS DARING EXPLOITS IN THOSE ROMANTIC LOCALES.

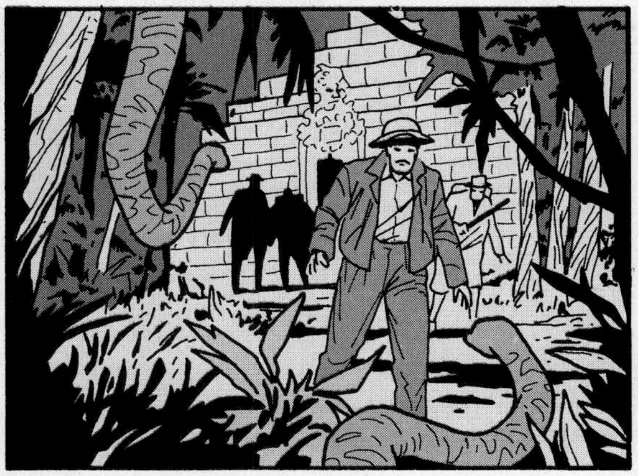

FOR THE OPENING OF THE BRAVE NEW WORLD'S FAIR HE HAS COMPILED A MENAGERIE OF THE MOST UNCOMMON EXHIBITS THE WORLD HAS EVER SEEN.

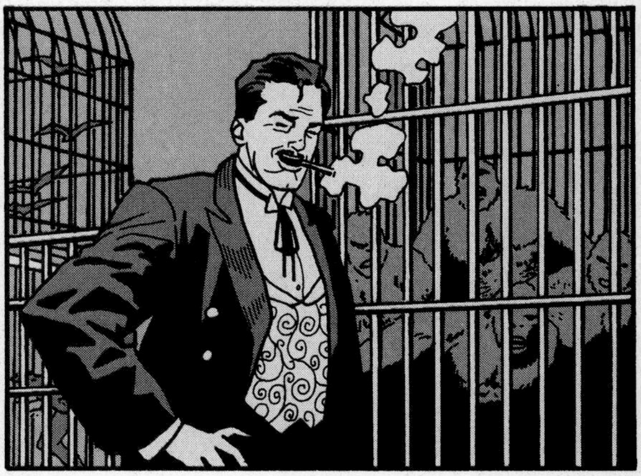

THE CROWN JEWEL OF HIS COLLECTION IS THE AMAZING EVOLUTIONIARY. THE ONLY COMPLETE LIVING COLLECTION OF HUMAN EVOLUTION IN EXISTENCE, IT CONSISTS OF FUR-COVERED LIZARDS, MONKEYS, CHIMPANZEES, GORILLAS, AND MISSING LINKS OF ALL KINDS— INCLUDING CRO-MAGNONS, HOMO ERECTUS, AND EVEN NEANDERTHALS.

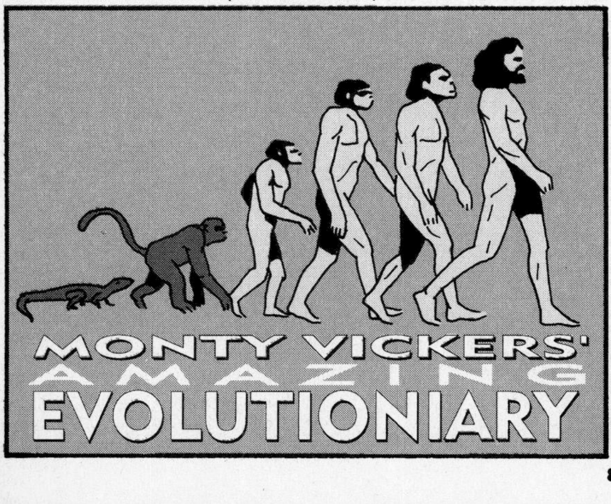
MONTY VICKERS'
AMAZING
EVOLUTIONIARY

MAYOR ORWELL HAS DEDICATED AN ENTIRE PAVILION TO THE COLLECTION. IT IS CERTAIN TO BECOME A STAR ATTRACTION OF THE FAIR.

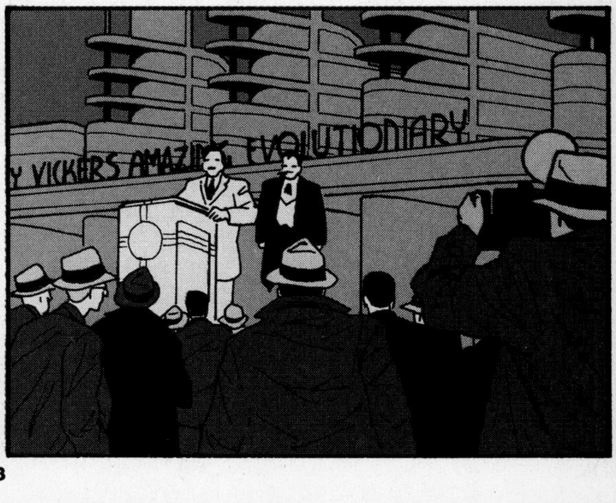
EVOLUTIONIARY

Monty's partner, Oliver DiMappe, envied the fame. Preferring to run the domestic end of things, he rarely went on the safaris, and consequently was almost never seen in the newsreels.

At the opening of the fair, Monty announced an expedition to Tibet.

He had made some earth-shaking discovery and promised to bring it back alive.

In true Vickers style he never revealed exactly what it was, but the public was wild with anticipation. Sponsors flocked to him.

The great Monty Vickers was always a sure bet.

Well, that is until the fateful trip. Vickers' plane vanished somewhere over China.

After a massive search effort, DiMappe sadly informed the world that he had uncovered evidence that Monty had absconded with the sponsors' money.

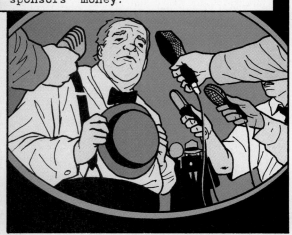

I didn't believe that story for a minute.

I've always been sure that RATTLESNAKE did Monty in.

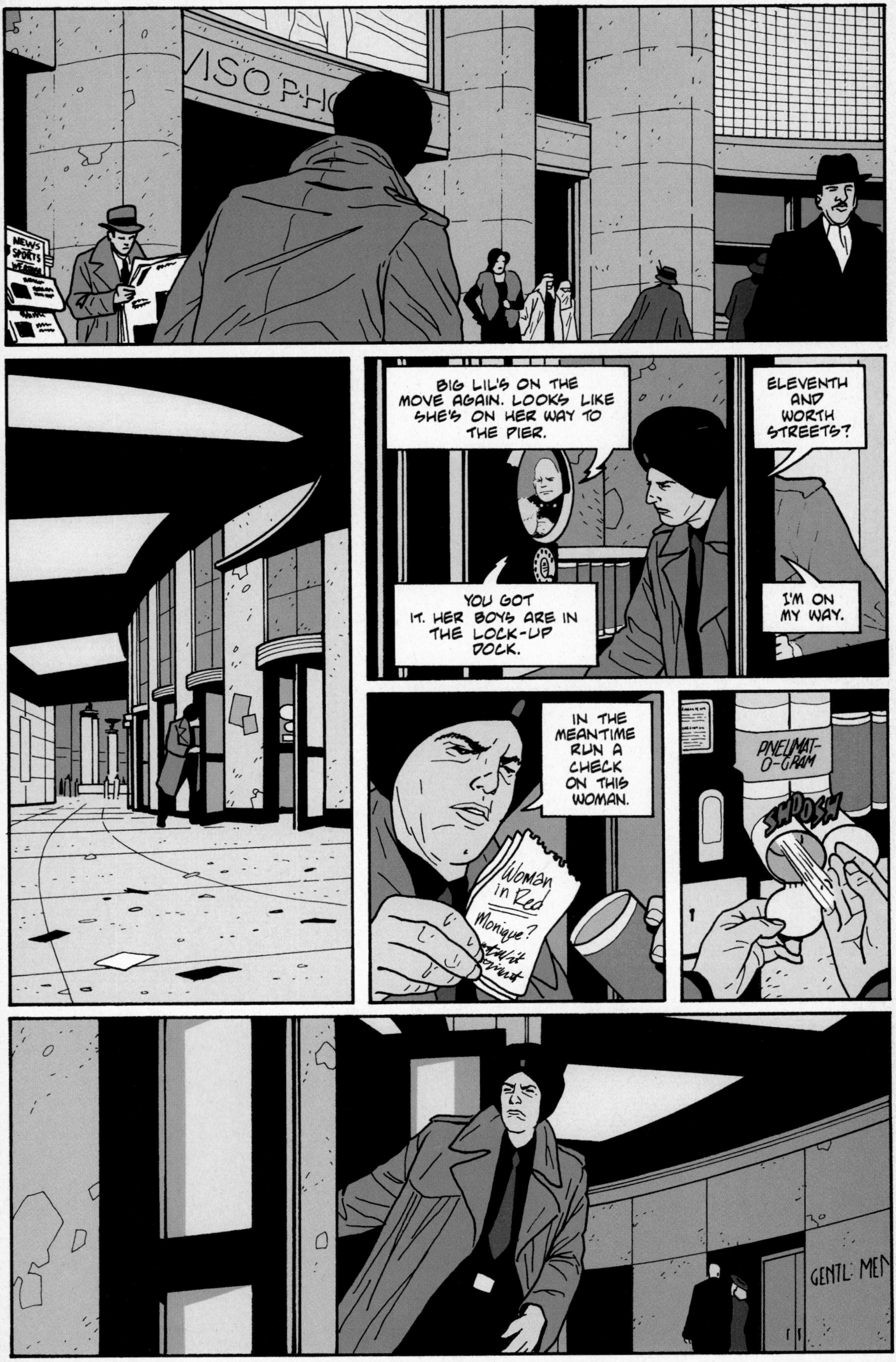
NEWS
SPORTS
BIG LIL'S ON THE MOVE AGAIN. LOOKS LIKE SHE'S ON HER WAY TO THE PIER.
ELEVENTH AND WORTH STREETS?
YOU GOT IT. HER BOYS ARE IN THE LOCK-UP DOCK.
I'M ON MY WAY.
IN THE MEANTIME RUN A CHECK ON THIS WOMAN.
Woman in Red
Monique?
PNEUMAT-O-GRAM
SHPOSH
GENTL·MEN

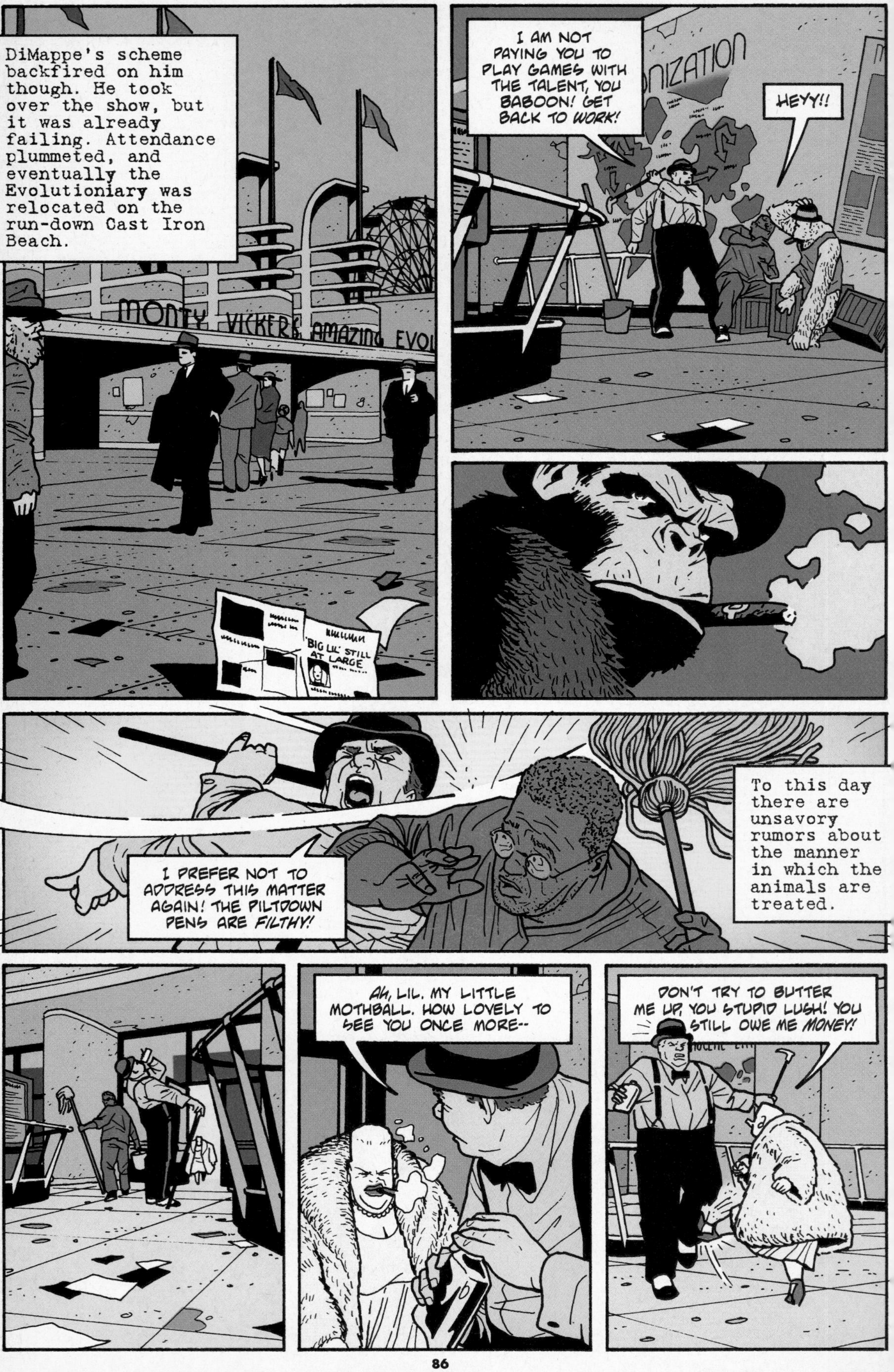
DiMappe's scheme backfired on him though. He took over the show, but it was already failing. Attendance plummeted, and eventually the Evolutioniary was relocated on the run-down Cast Iron Beach.
MONTY VICKERS AMAZING EVOL
BIG LIL' STILL AT LARGE
I AM NOT PAYING YOU TO PLAY GAMES WITH THE TALENT, YOU BABOON! GET BACK TO WORK!
NIZATION
HEYY!!
I PREFER NOT TO ADDRESS THIS MATTER AGAIN! THE PILTDOWN PENS ARE FILTHY!
To this day there are unsavory rumors about the manner in which the animals are treated.
AH, LIL. MY LITTLE MOTHBALL. HOW LOVELY TO SEE YOU ONCE MORE--
DON'T TRY TO BUTTER ME UP, YOU STUPID LUSH! YOU STILL OWE ME MONEY!

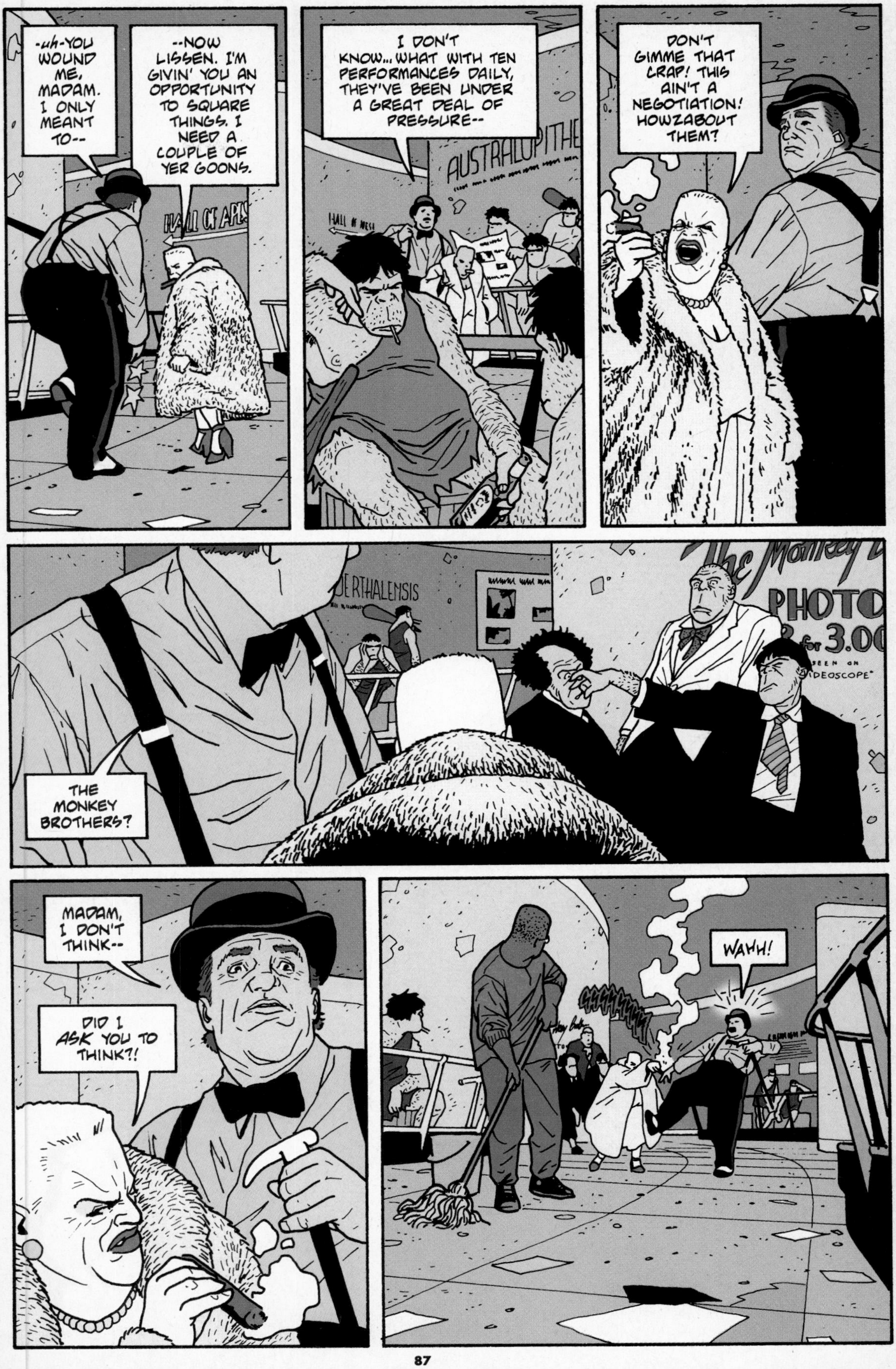
-uh-YOU WOUND ME, MADAM. I ONLY MEANT TO--
--NOW LISSEN. I'M GIVIN' YOU AN OPPORTUNITY TO SQUARE THINGS. I NEED A COUPLE OF YER GOONS.
I DON'T KNOW... WHAT WITH TEN PERFORMANCES DAILY, THEY'VE BEEN UNDER A GREAT DEAL OF PRESSURE--
AUSTRALOPITHE
DON'T GIMME THAT CRAP! THIS AIN'T A NEGOTIATION! HOWZABOUT THEM?
THE MONKEY BROTHERS?
DERTHALENSIS
PHOTO
3.00
MADAM, I DON'T THINK--
DID I ASK YOU TO THINK?!
WAHH!

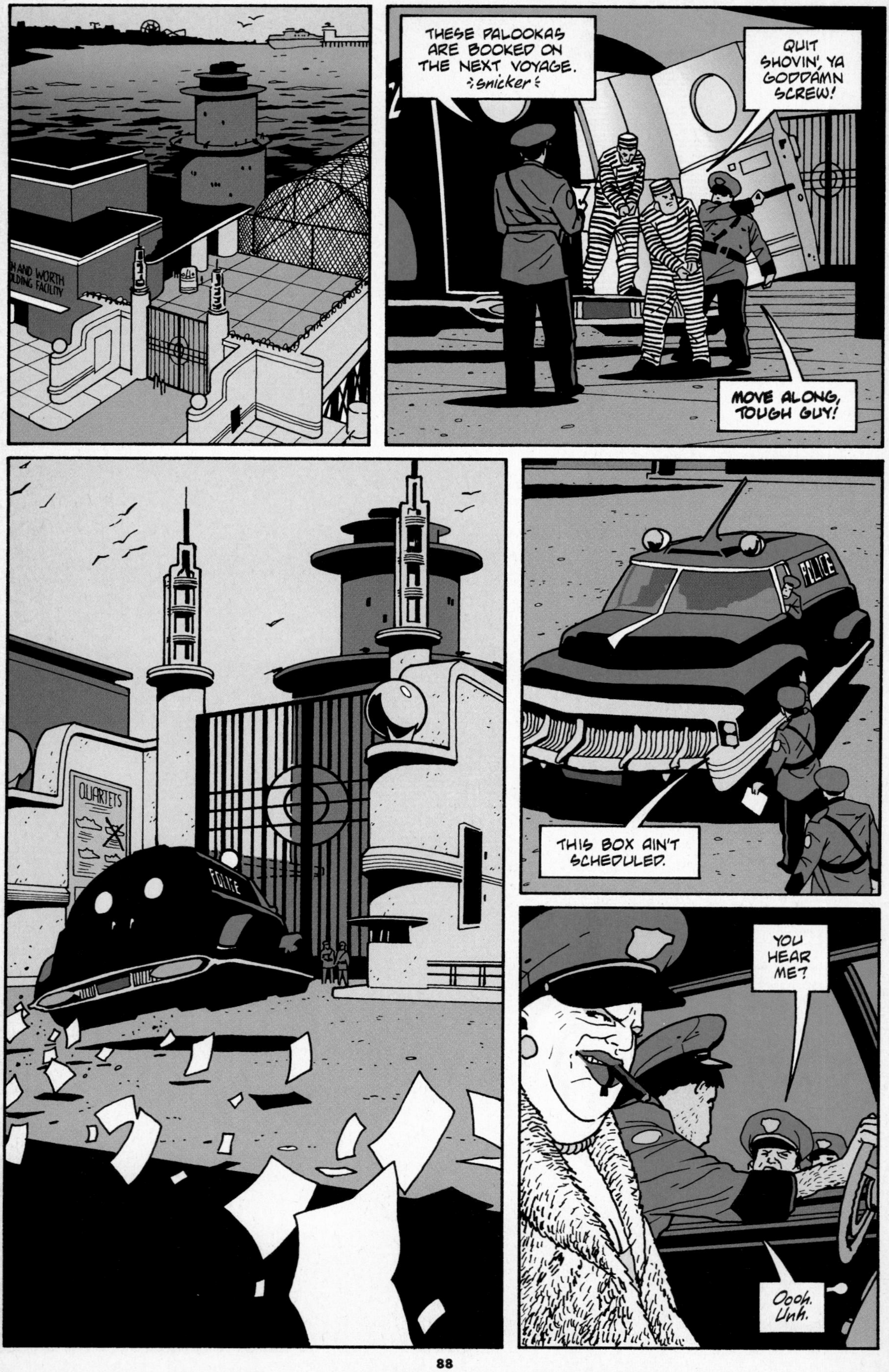
AND WORTH
THESE PALOOKAS ARE BOOKED ON THE NEXT VOYAGE.
snicker
QUIT SHOVIN', YA GODDAMN SCREW!
MOVE ALONG, TOUGH GUY!
QUARTETS
POLICE
POLICE
THIS BOX AIN'T SCHEDULED.
YOU HEAR ME?
Oooh. Unh.

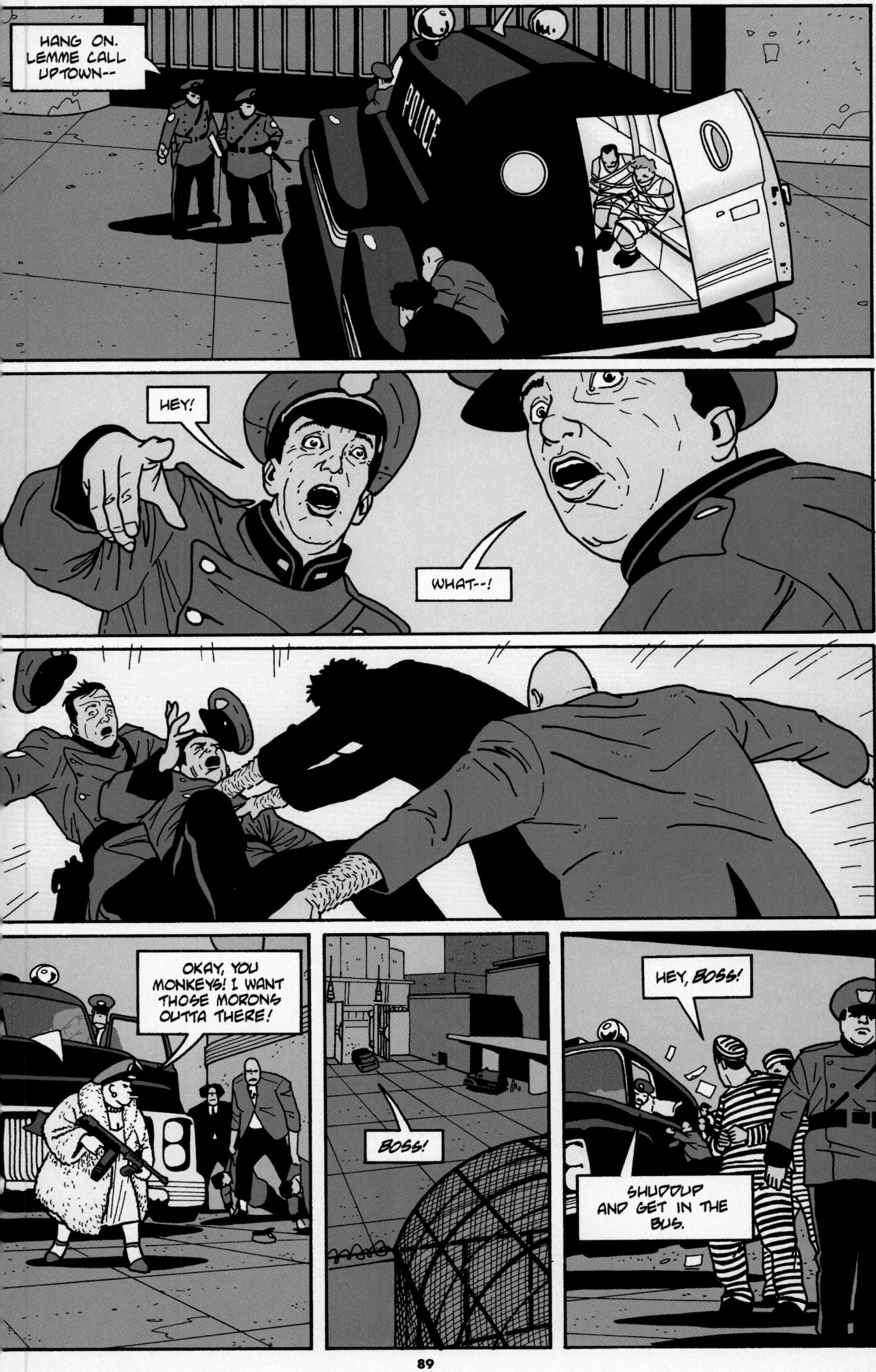
HANG ON. LEMME CALL UPTOWN--
HEY!
WHAT--!
OKAY, YOU MONKEYS! I WANT THOSE MORONS OUTTA THERE!
BOSS!
HEY, BOSS!
SHUDDUP AND GET IN THE BUS.

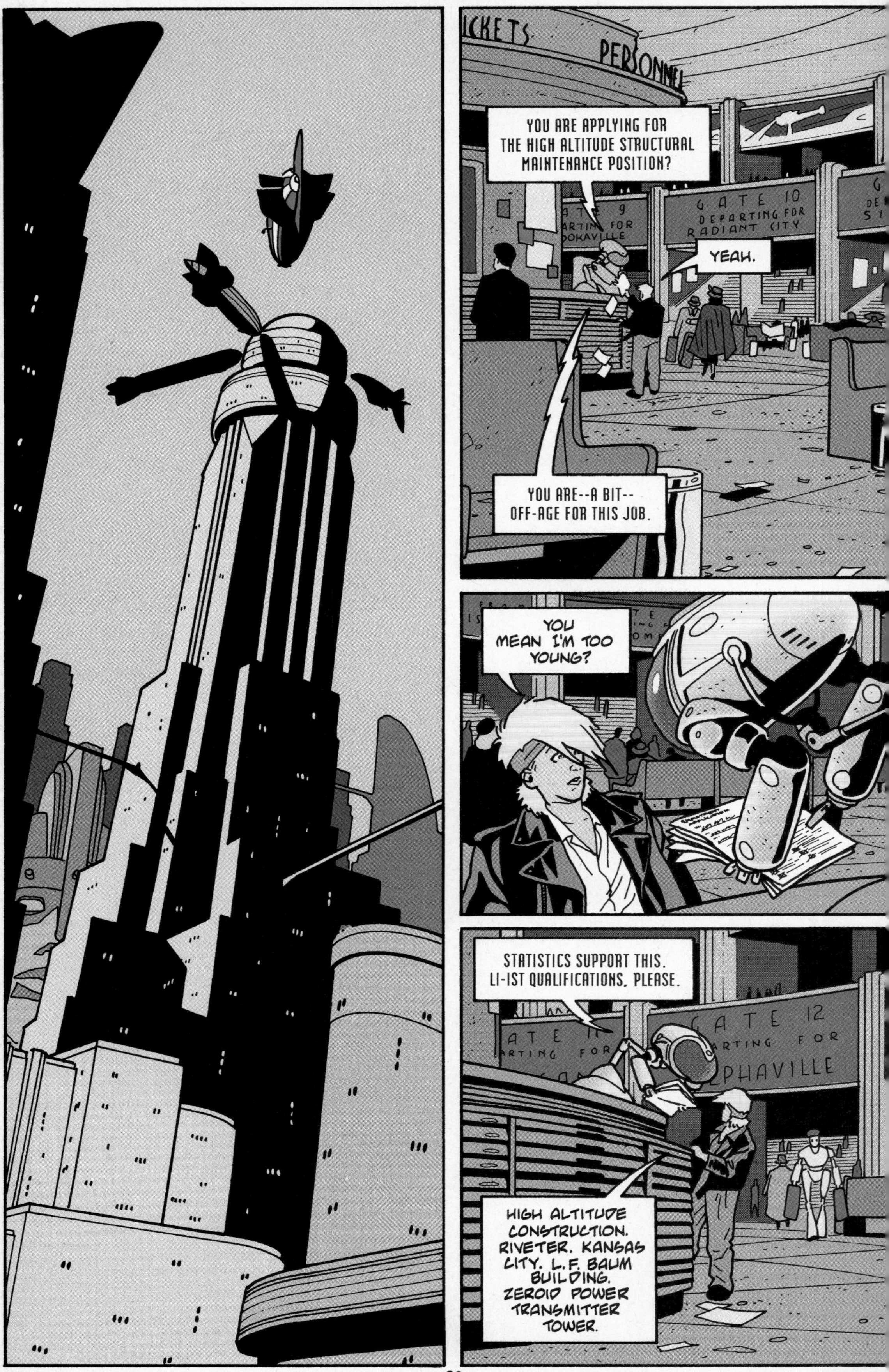
TICKETS
PERSONNEL
YOU ARE APPLYING FOR THE HIGH ALTITUDE STRUCTURAL MAINTENANCE POSITION?
GATE 10 DEPARTING FOR RADIANT CITY
YEAH.
YOU ARE--A BIT--OFF-AGE FOR THIS JOB.
YOU MEAN I'M TOO YOUNG?
STATISTICS SUPPORT THIS. LI-IST QUALIFICATIONS, PLEASE.
GATE 12
HIGH ALTITUDE CONSTRUCTION. RIVETER. KANSAS CITY. L.F. BAUM BUILDING. ZEROID POWER TRANSMITTER TOWER.

Occasionally an inhabitant will become disoriented. This may be due to catastrophic weather, changing migration patterns of their prey, even lengthy pursuit by other predators.

They often lose their way for extended periods of time, but their instincts almost always brings them back to the veldt.

ANY ZEPPELIN-RELATED EXPERIENCE?

NO.

AEROSHIP-RELATED EXPERIENCE?

NO.

FORM ONE LINE HERE

MON-NO-NO-RAIL?

NO...

ANY TRANSPORTATION EXPERIENCE AT ALL?

WELL, NO...

VERY WELL, CITIZEN. YOUR PROFILE WILL BE PROGRAMMED INTO CENTRAL MEMORY. RECOMMENDED YOU APPLY PROMETHEAN CONSTRUCTION. -zip-THA--NK YOU.

HAVE THESE SENT TO THE ARMS.

BUT, WAIT. WILL SOME-ONE?

GATE 35 ARRIVING FROM GOTHAM CITY

GATE 36 ARRIVING FROM METROPOLIS

GATE DEPARTING OPAL CITY

PLEASE STEP AWAY FROM THE YELLOW RUBBER LINE. THA-NK YOU.

SHIT. NOW WHAT AM I GOING TO DO?

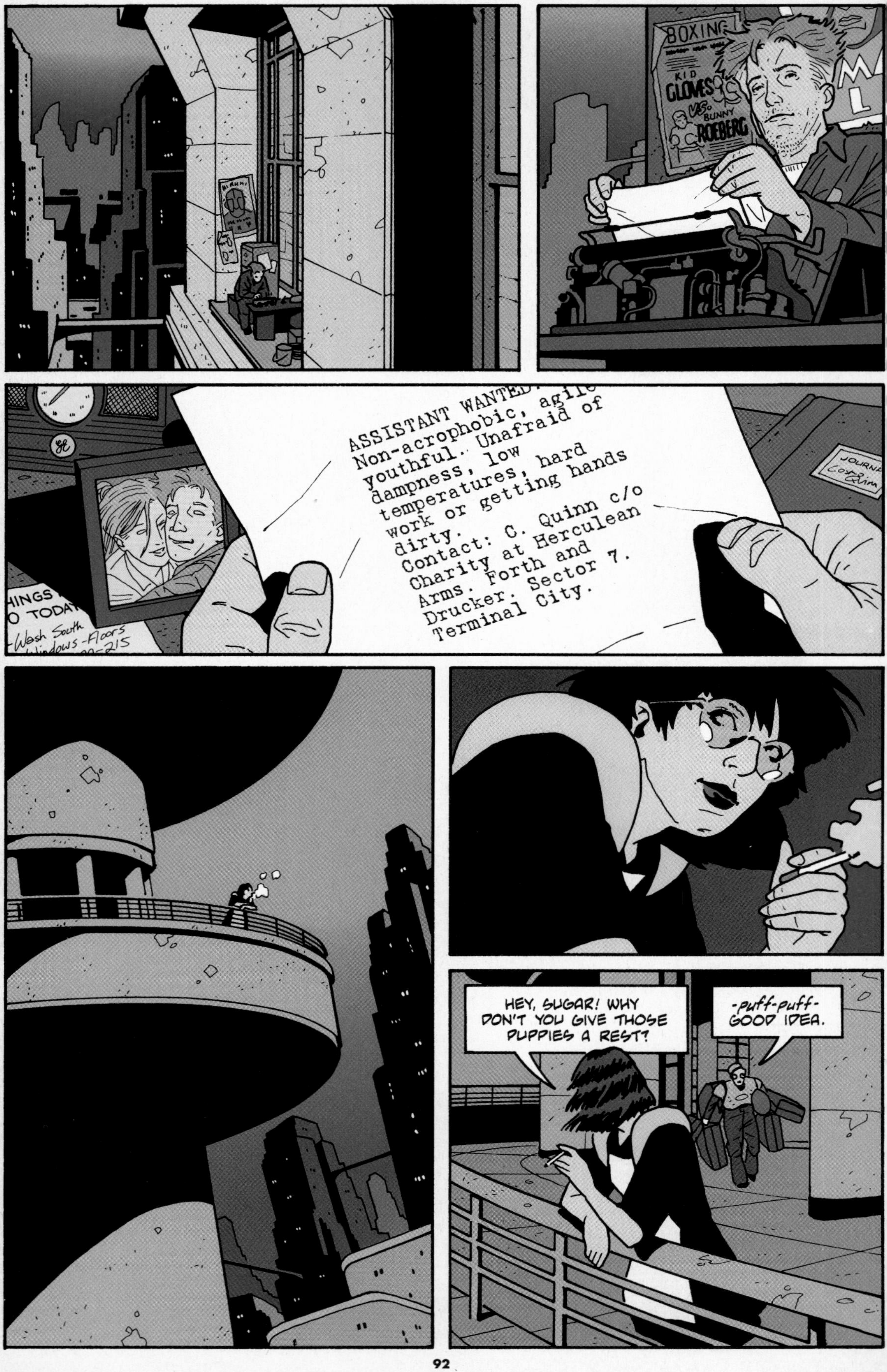
BOXING
KID GLOVES VS. BUNNY ROEBERG
ASSISTANT WANTED: Non-acrophobic, agile youthful. Unafraid of dampness, low temperatures, hard work or getting hands dirty.
Contact: C. Quinn c/o Charity at Herculean Arms. Forth and Drucker. Sector 7. Terminal City.
-Wash South
HEY, SUGAR! WHY DON'T YOU GIVE THOSE PUPPIES A REST?
-puff-puff- GOOD IDEA.

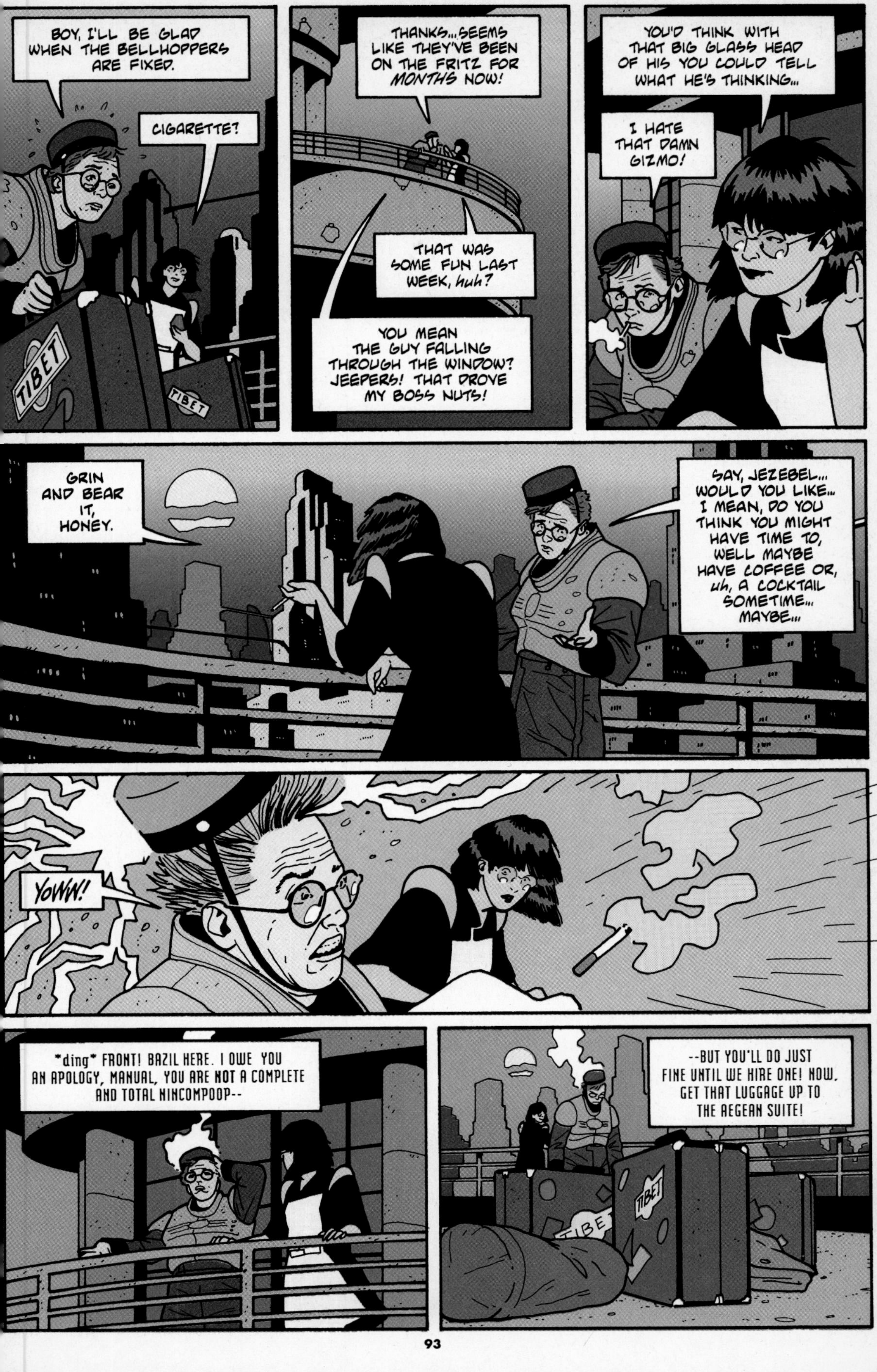
BOY, I'LL BE GLAD WHEN THE BELLHOPPERS ARE FIXED.
CIGARETTE?
TIBET
TIBET
THANKS... SEEMS LIKE THEY'VE BEEN ON THE FRITZ FOR *MONTHS* NOW!
THAT WAS SOME FUN LAST WEEK, *huh*?
YOU MEAN THE GUY FALLING THROUGH THE WINDOW? JEEPERS! THAT DROVE MY BOSS NUTS!
YOU'D THINK WITH THAT BIG GLASS HEAD OF HIS YOU COULD TELL WHAT HE'S THINKING...
I HATE THAT DAMN GIZMO!
GRIN AND BEAR IT, HONEY.
SAY, JEZEBEL... WOULD YOU LIKE... I MEAN, DO YOU THINK YOU MIGHT HAVE TIME TO, WELL MAYBE HAVE COFFEE OR, *uh*, A COCKTAIL SOMETIME... MAYBE...
YOWW!
ding FRONT! BAZIL HERE. I OWE YOU AN APOLOGY, MANUAL, YOU ARE NOT A COMPLETE AND TOTAL NINCOMPOOP--
--BUT YOU'LL DO JUST FINE UNTIL WE HIRE ONE! NOW, GET THAT LUGGAGE UP TO THE AEGEAN SUITE!
TIBET
TIBET

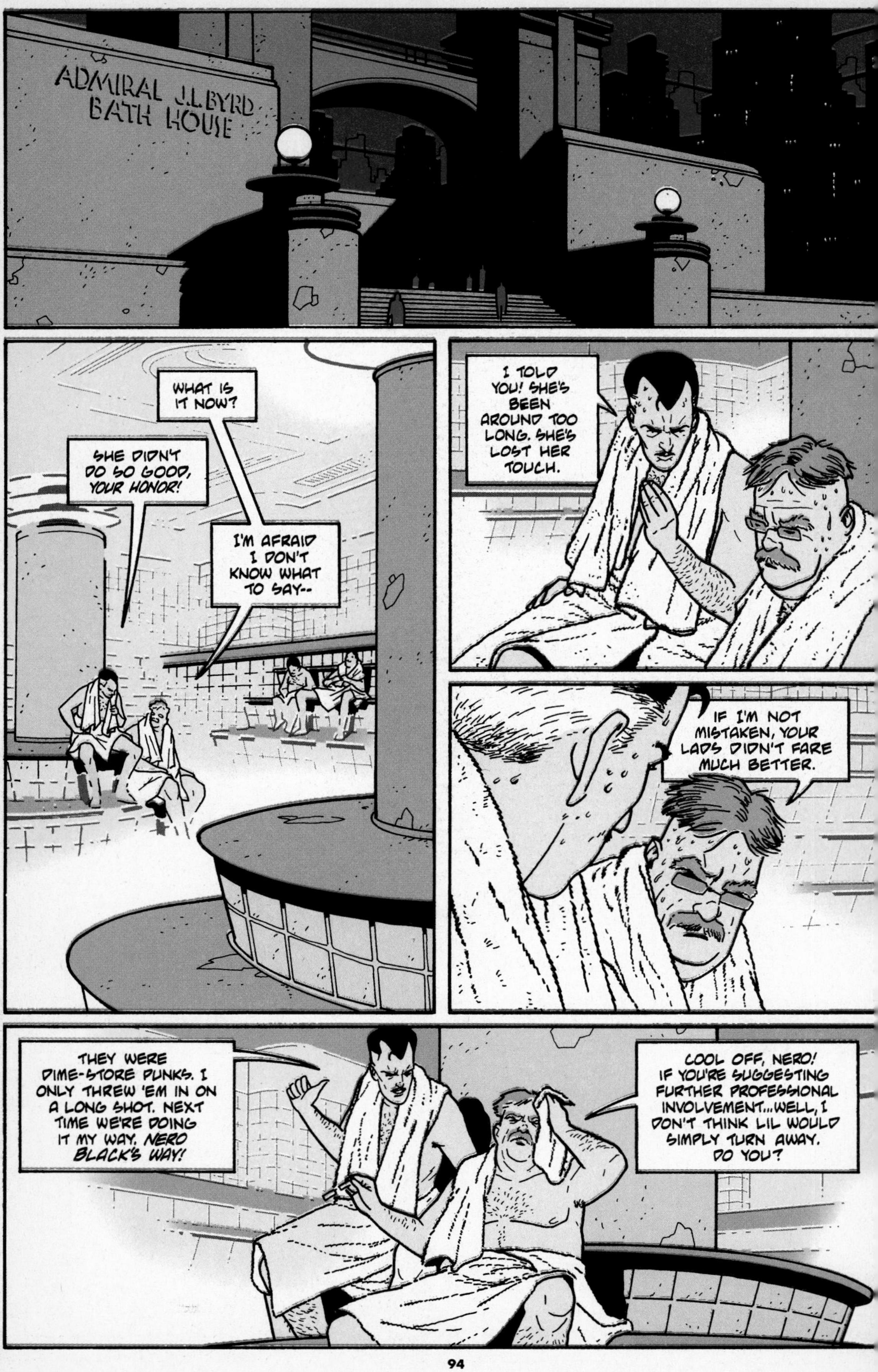
ADMIRAL J.L. BYRD BATH HOUSE
SHE DIDN'T DO SO GOOD, YOUR HONOR!
WHAT IS IT NOW?
I'M AFRAID I DON'T KNOW WHAT TO SAY--
I TOLD YOU! SHE'S BEEN AROUND TOO LONG. SHE'S LOST HER TOUCH.
IF I'M NOT MISTAKEN, YOUR LADS DIDN'T FARE MUCH BETTER.
THEY WERE DIME-STORE PUNKS. I ONLY THREW 'EM IN ON A LONG SHOT. NEXT TIME WE'RE DOING IT MY WAY. NERO BLACK'S WAY!
COOL OFF, NERO! IF YOU'RE SUGGESTING FURTHER PROFESSIONAL INVOLVEMENT...WELL, I DON'T THINK LIL WOULD SIMPLY TURN AWAY. DO YOU?

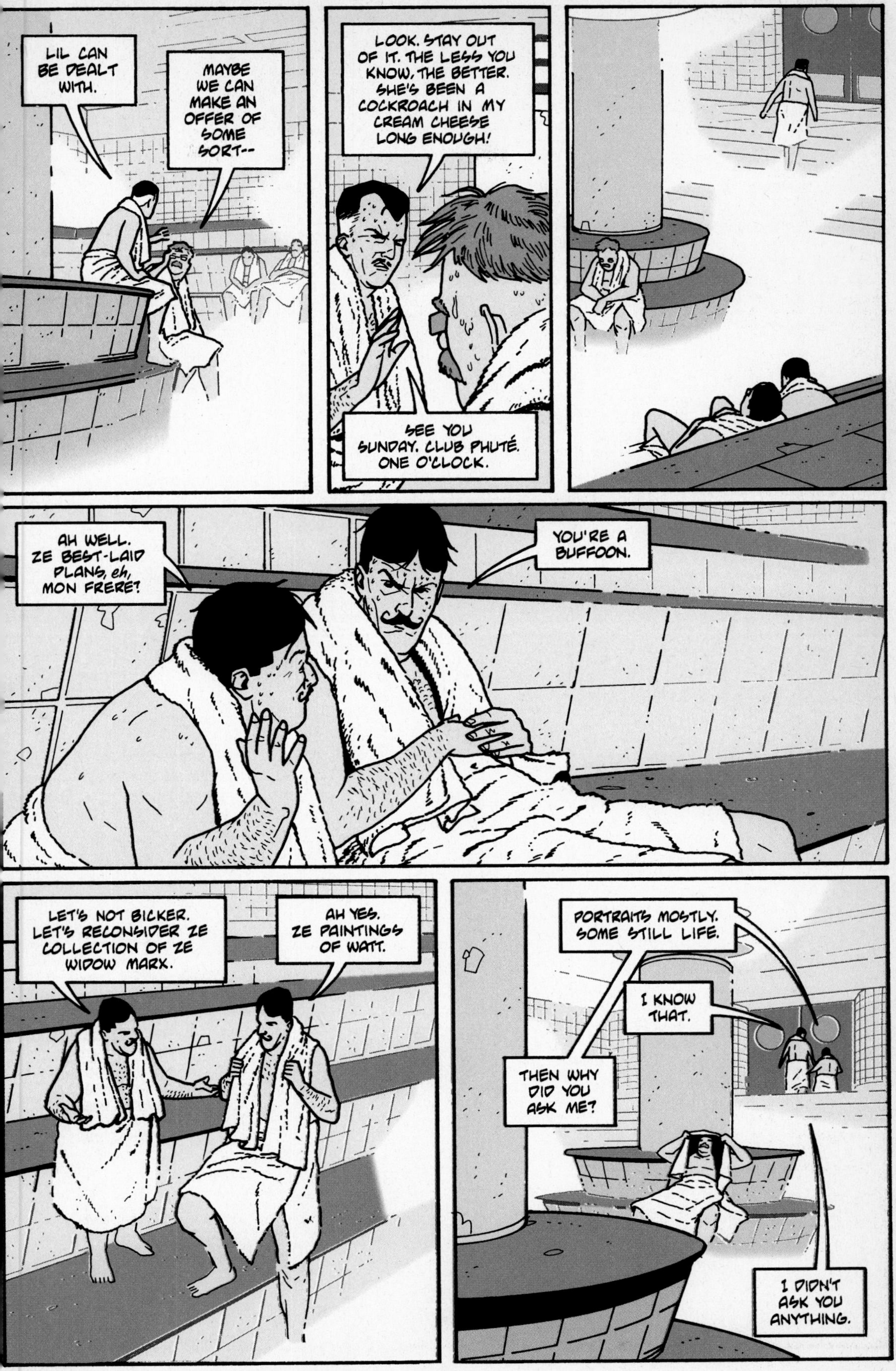
LIL CAN BE DEALT WITH.
MAYBE WE CAN MAKE AN OFFER OF SOME SORT--
LOOK. STAY OUT OF IT. THE LESS YOU KNOW, THE BETTER. SHE'S BEEN A COCKROACH IN MY CREAM CHEESE LONG ENOUGH!
SEE YOU SUNDAY. CLUB PHUTÉ. ONE O'CLOCK.
AH WELL. ZE BEST-LAID PLANS, eh, MON FRERE?
YOU'RE A BUFFOON.
LET'S NOT BICKER. LET'S RECONSIDER ZE COLLECTION OF ZE WIDOW MARX.
AH YES. ZE PAINTINGS OF WATT.
PORTRAITS MOSTLY. SOME STILL LIFE.
I KNOW THAT.
THEN WHY DID YOU ASK ME?
I DIDN'T ASK YOU ANYTHING.

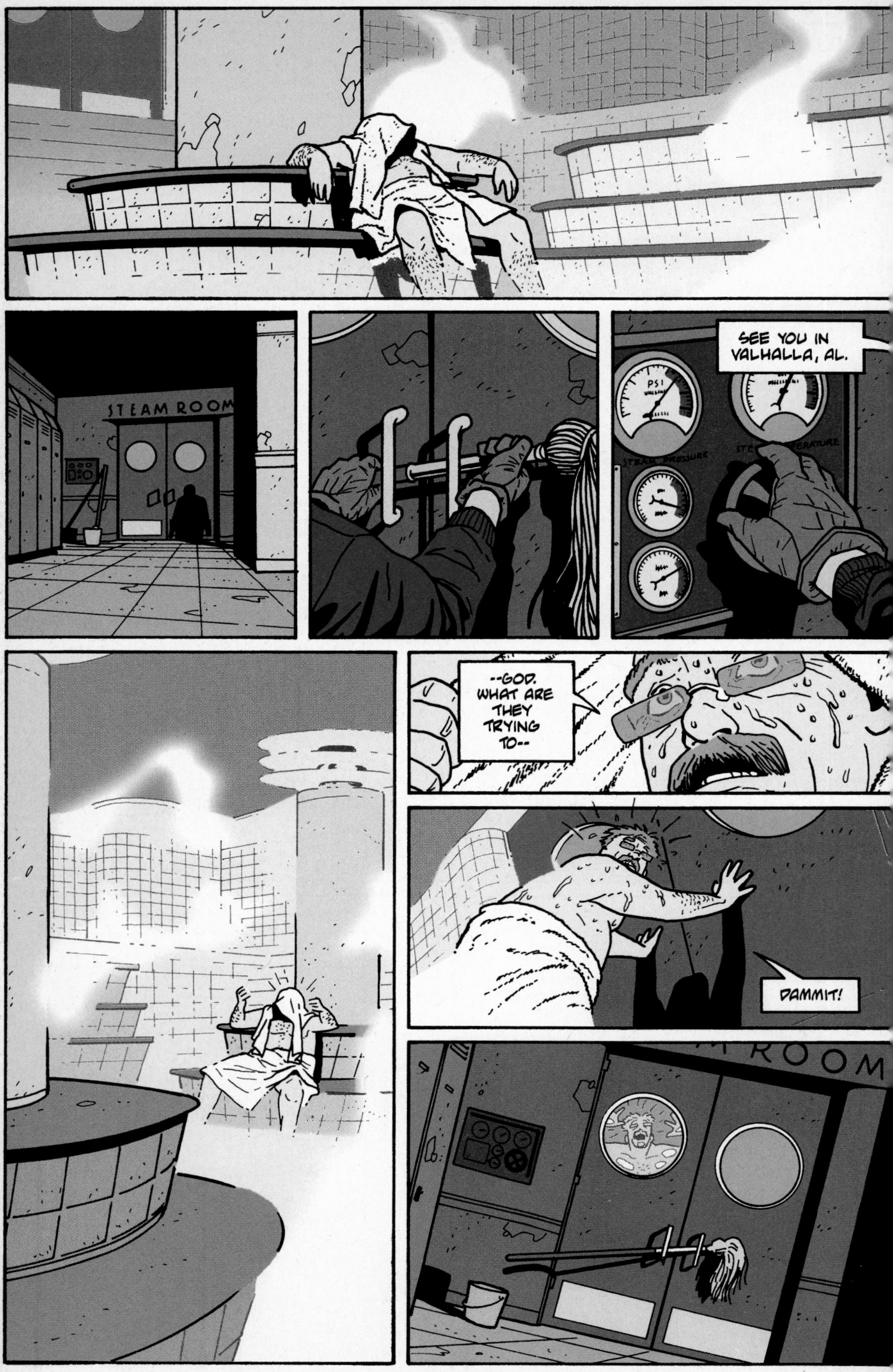
STEAM ROOM
SEE YOU IN VALHALLA, AL.
PSI
STEAM PRESSURE
STEAM TEMPERATURE
--GOD. WHAT ARE THEY TRYING TO--
DAMMIT!
M ROOM

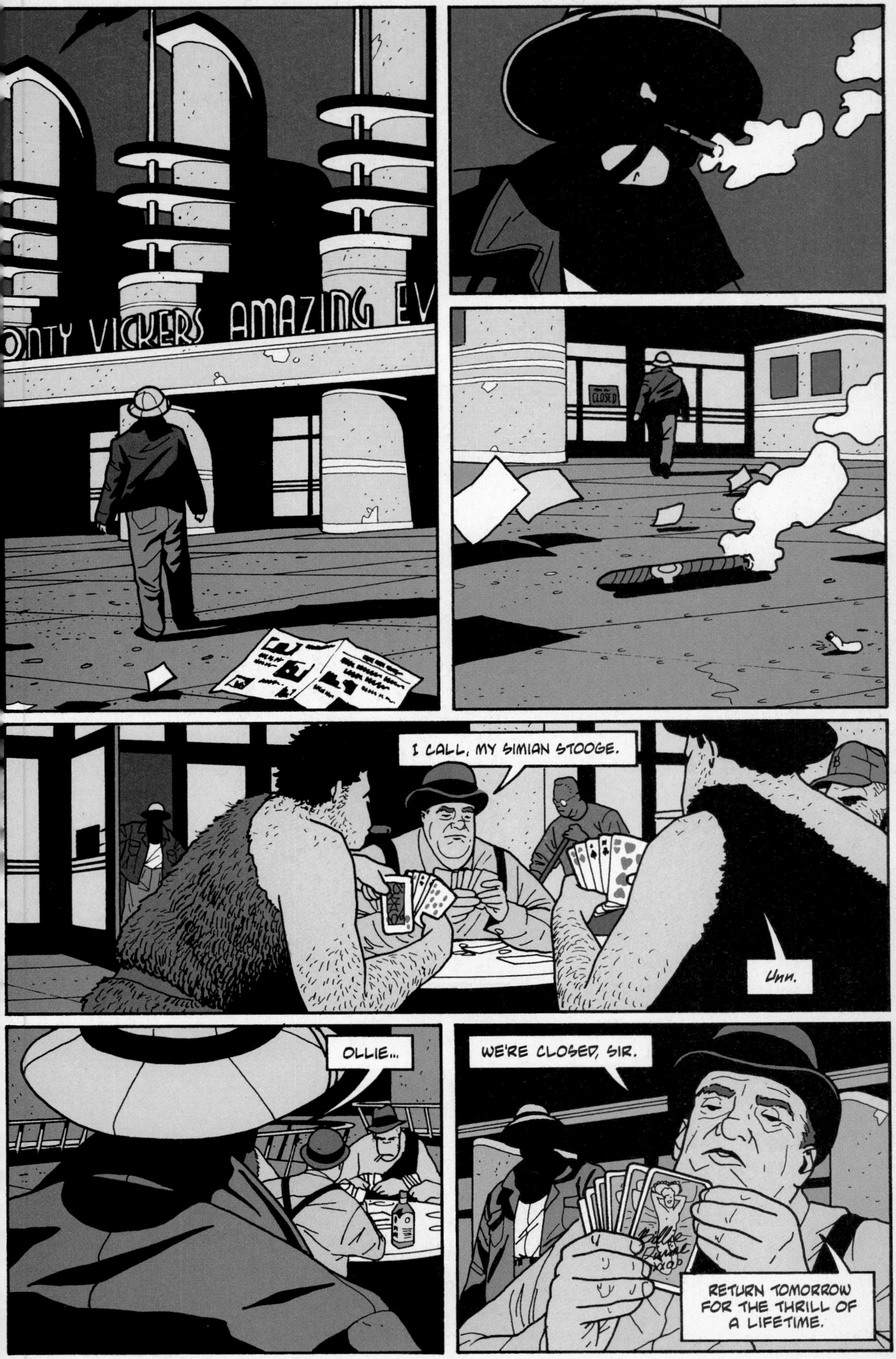
ONTY VICKERS AMAZING EV
CLOSED
I CALL, MY SIMIAN STOOGE.
Unn.
OLLIE...
WE'RE CLOSED, SIR.
RETURN TOMORROW FOR THE THRILL OF A LIFETIME.

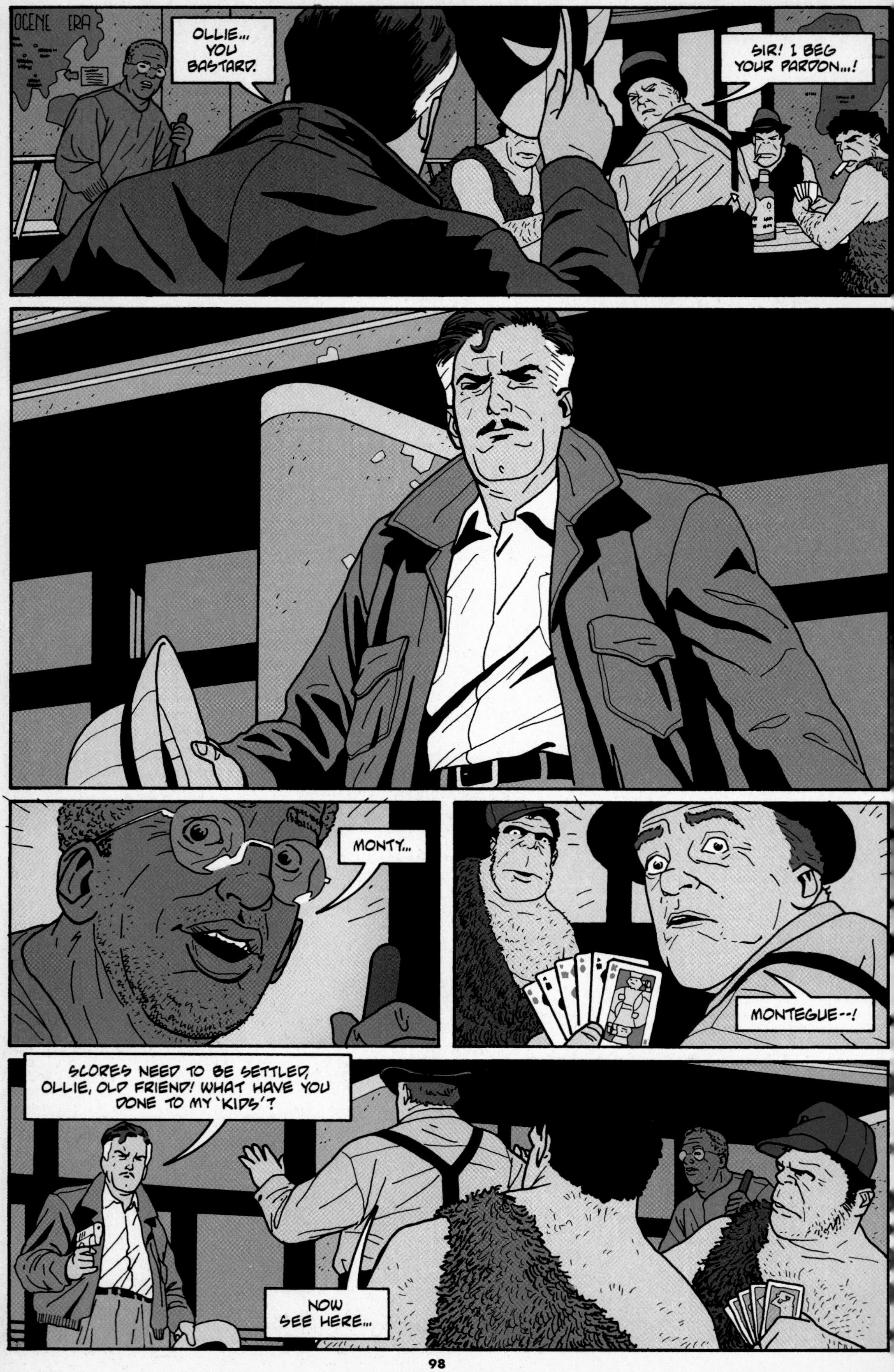
OLLIE... YOU BASTARD.
SIR! I BEG YOUR PARDON...!
MONTY...
MONTEGUE--!
SCORES NEED TO BE SETTLED, OLLIE, OLD FRIEND! WHAT HAVE YOU DONE TO MY 'KIDS'?
NOW SEE HERE...

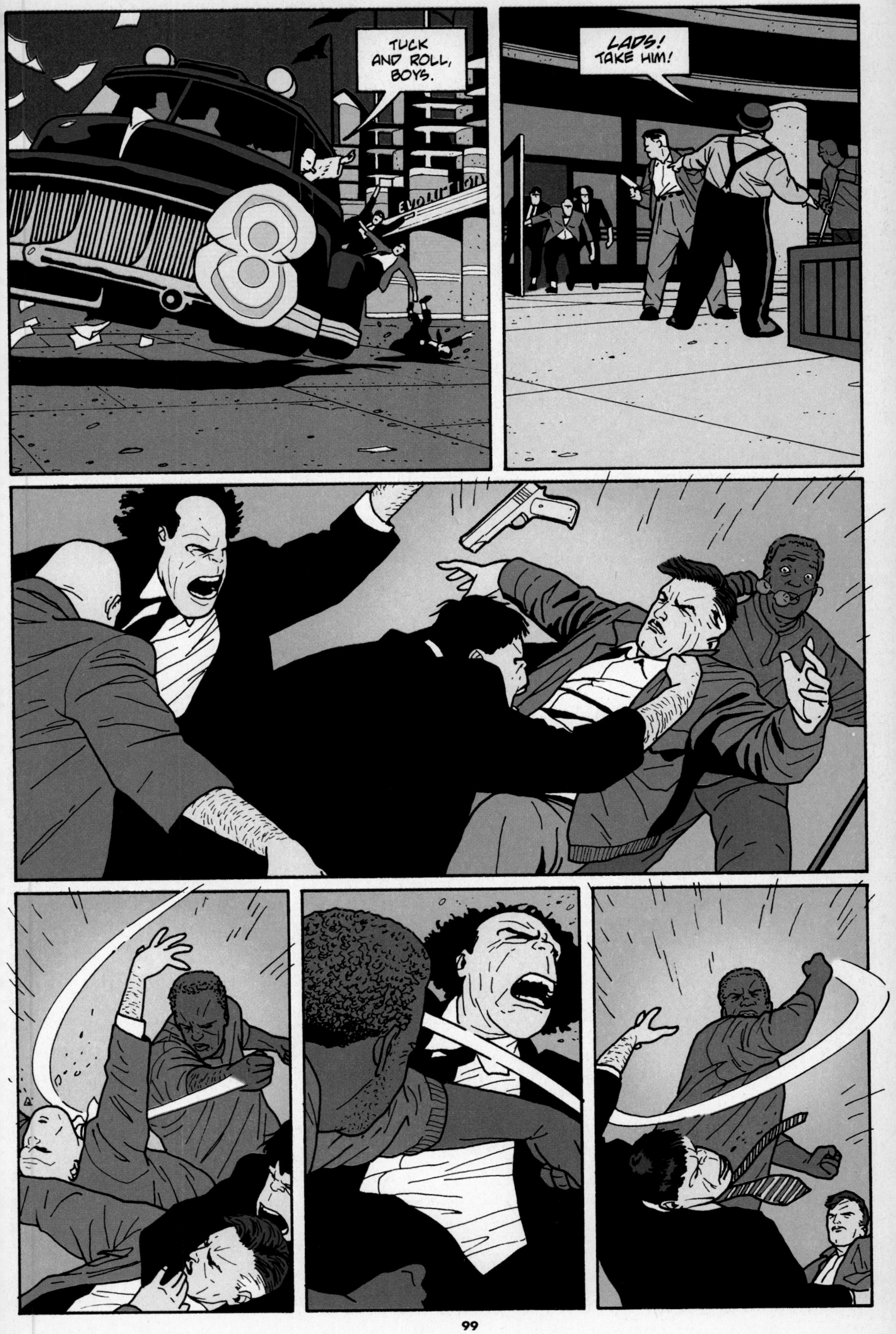
TUCK AND ROLL, BOYS.
EVOLUTION
LADS! TAKE HIM!

THANK YOU, MY OLD FRIEND. THANK YOU.

S'OKAY, BOSS.

Hmm...

Sorry... We're CLOSED

NEANDERTHAL

Episode Five

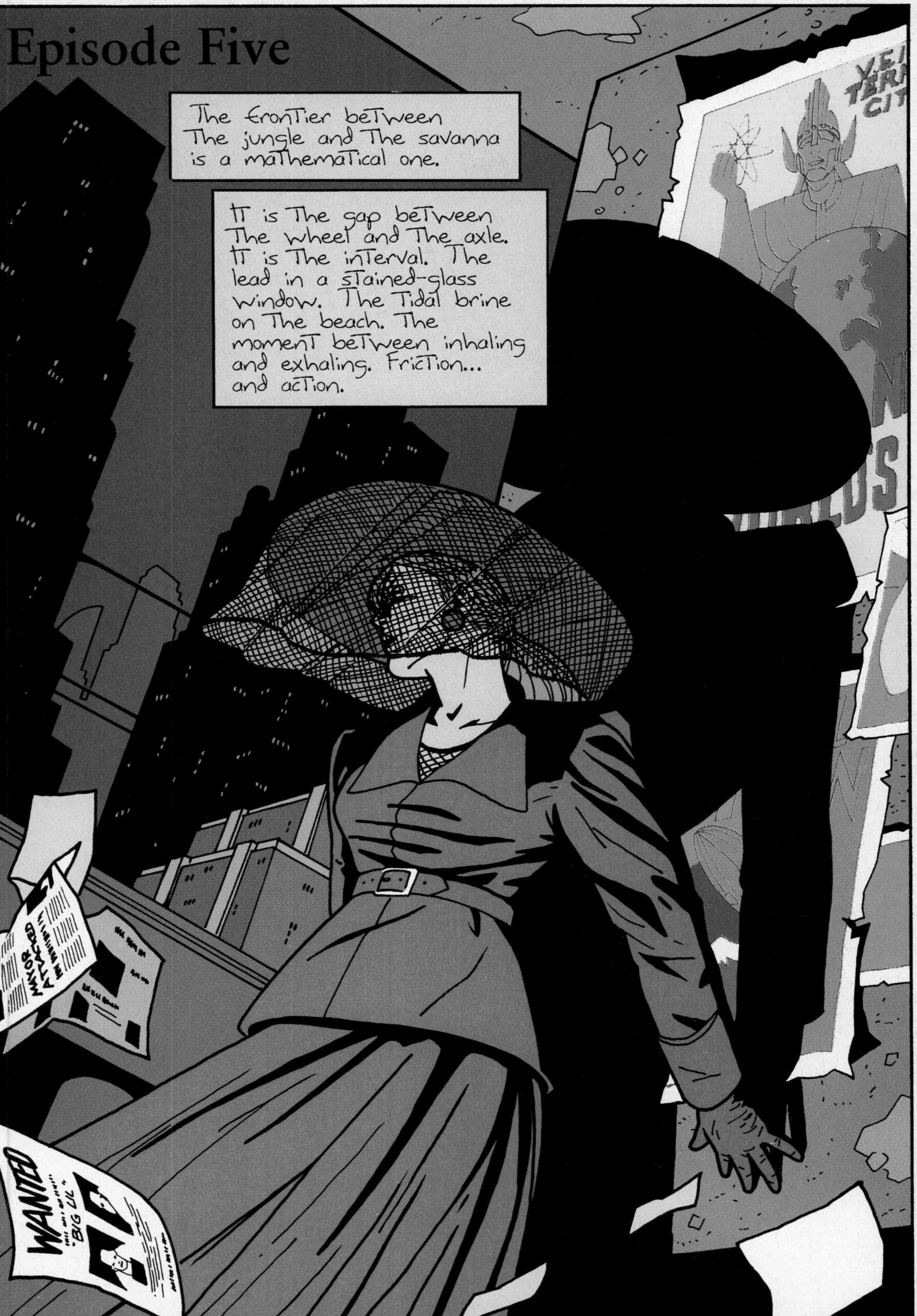

The frontier between the jungle and the savanna is a mathematical one.
It is the gap between the wheel and the axle. It is the interval. The lead in a stained-glass window. The tidal brine on the beach. The moment between inhaling and exhaling. Friction... and action.
MAYOR ATTACKED
WANTED
"BIG LIL"

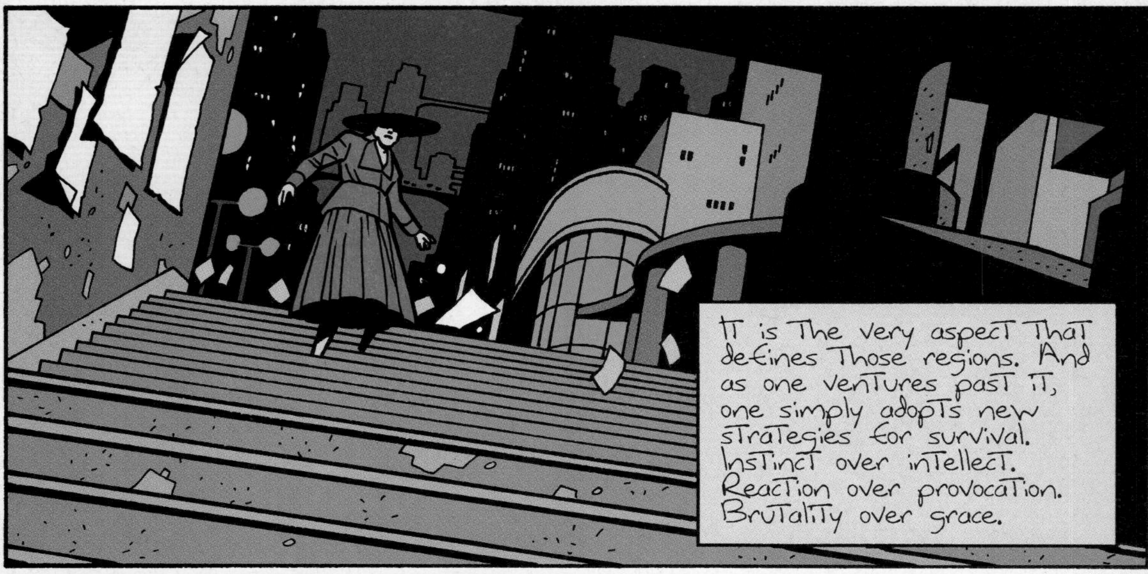
It is the very aspect that defines those regions. And as one ventures past it, one simply adopts new strategies for survival. Instinct over intellect. Reaction over provocation. Brutality over grace.

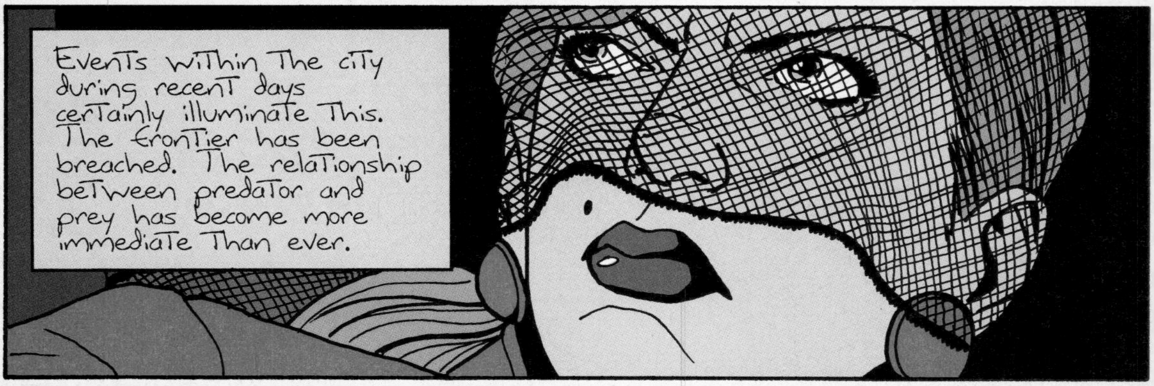
Events within the city during recent days certainly illuminate this. The frontier has been breached. The relationship between predator and prey has become more immediate than ever.

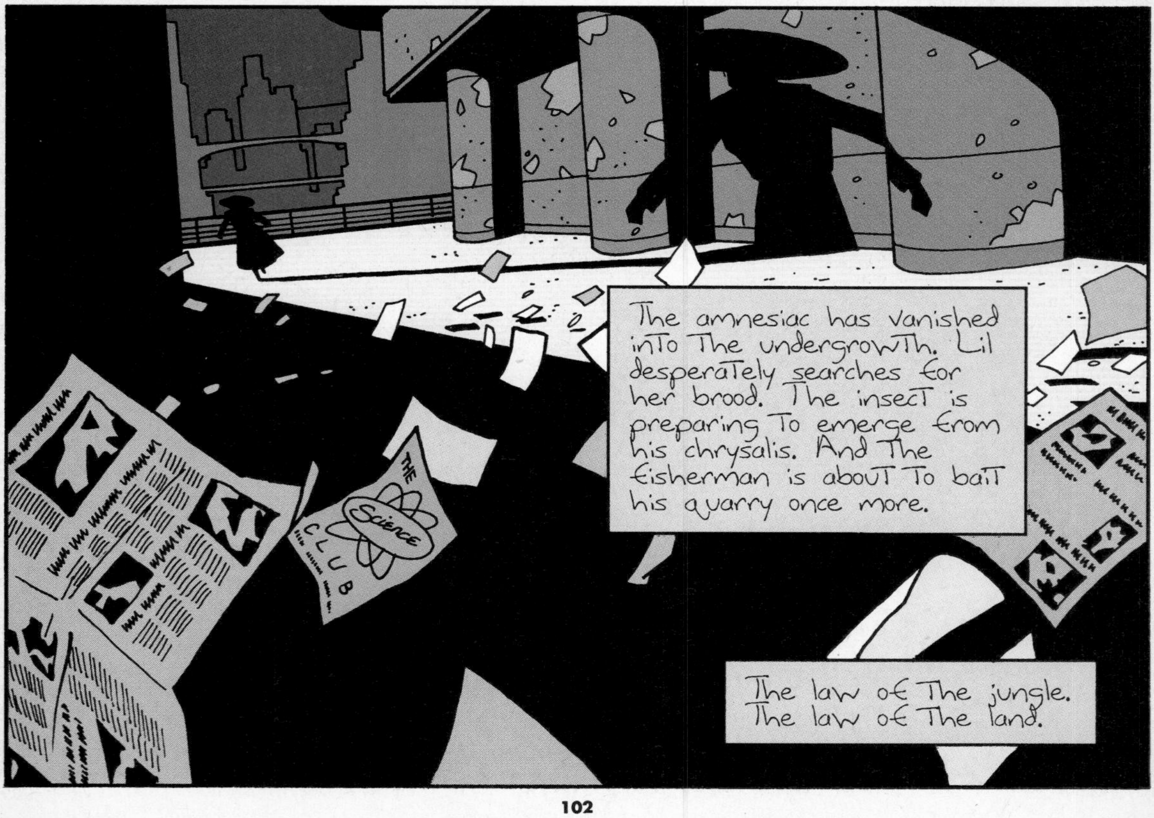
The amnesiac has vanished into the undergrowth. Lil desperately searches for her brood. The insect is preparing to emerge from his chrysalis. And the fisherman is about to bait his quarry once more.
The law of the jungle. The law of the land.
The Science Club

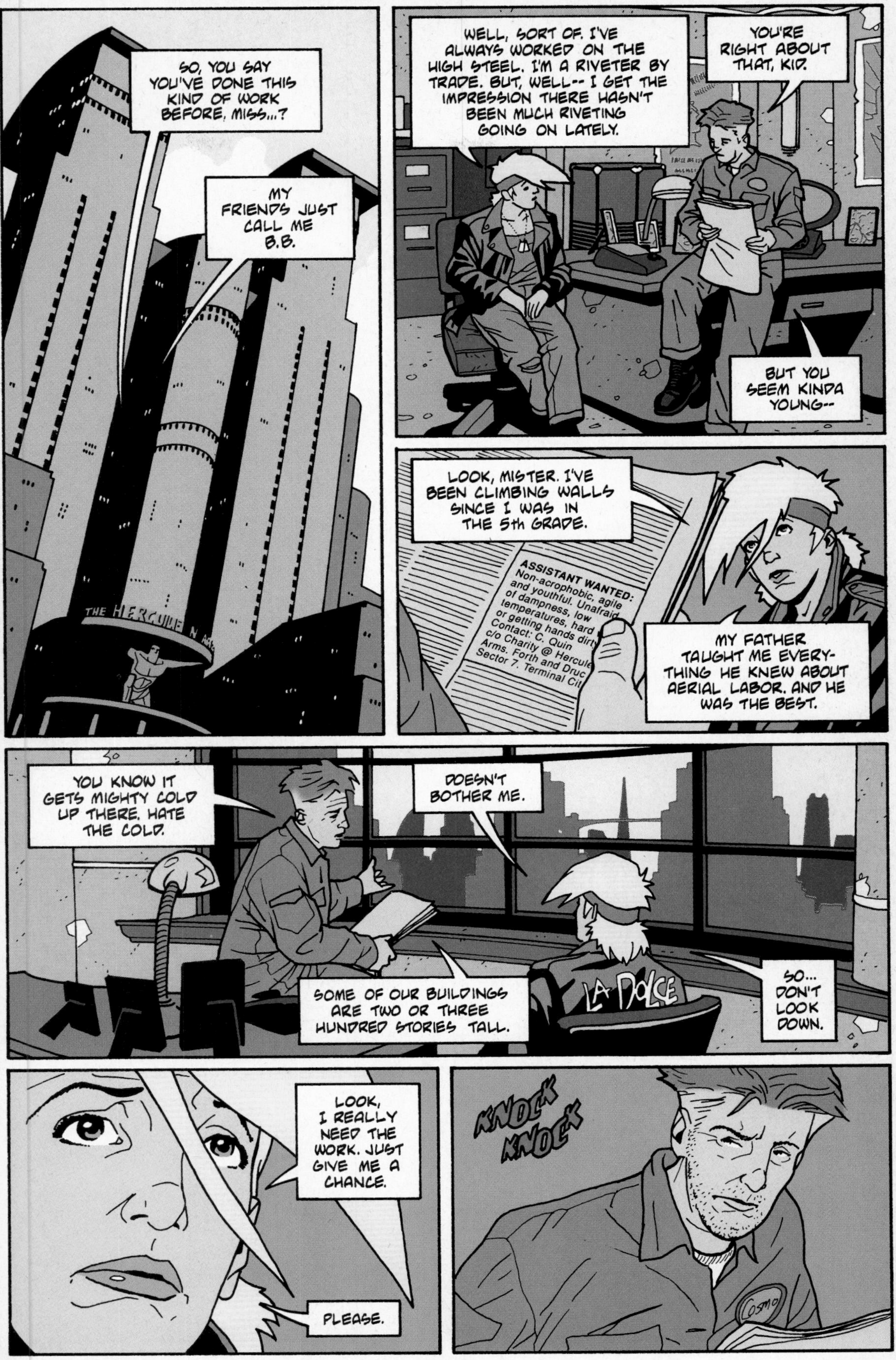

SO, YOU SAY YOU'VE DONE THIS KIND OF WORK BEFORE, MISS...?
MY FRIENDS JUST CALL ME B.B.
WELL, SORT OF. I'VE ALWAYS WORKED ON THE HIGH STEEL. I'M A RIVETER BY TRADE. BUT, WELL-- I GET THE IMPRESSION THERE HASN'T BEEN MUCH RIVETING GOING ON LATELY.
YOU'RE RIGHT ABOUT THAT, KID.
BUT YOU SEEM KINDA YOUNG--
LOOK, MISTER. I'VE BEEN CLIMBING WALLS SINCE I WAS IN THE 5th GRADE.
ASSISTANT WANTED:
Non-acrophobic, agile
and youthful. Unafraid
of dampness, low
temperatures, hard
or getting hands dirt
Contact: C. Quin
c/o Charity @ Hercule
Arms. Forth and Druc
Sector 7. Terminal Cit
MY FATHER TAUGHT ME EVERYTHING HE KNEW ABOUT AERIAL LABOR. AND HE WAS THE BEST.
YOU KNOW IT GETS MIGHTY COLD UP THERE. HATE THE COLD.
DOESN'T BOTHER ME.
SOME OF OUR BUILDINGS ARE TWO OR THREE HUNDRED STORIES TALL.
LA DOLCE
SO... DON'T LOOK DOWN.
LOOK, I REALLY NEED THE WORK. JUST GIVE ME A CHANCE.
PLEASE.
KNOCK KNOCK
COSMO

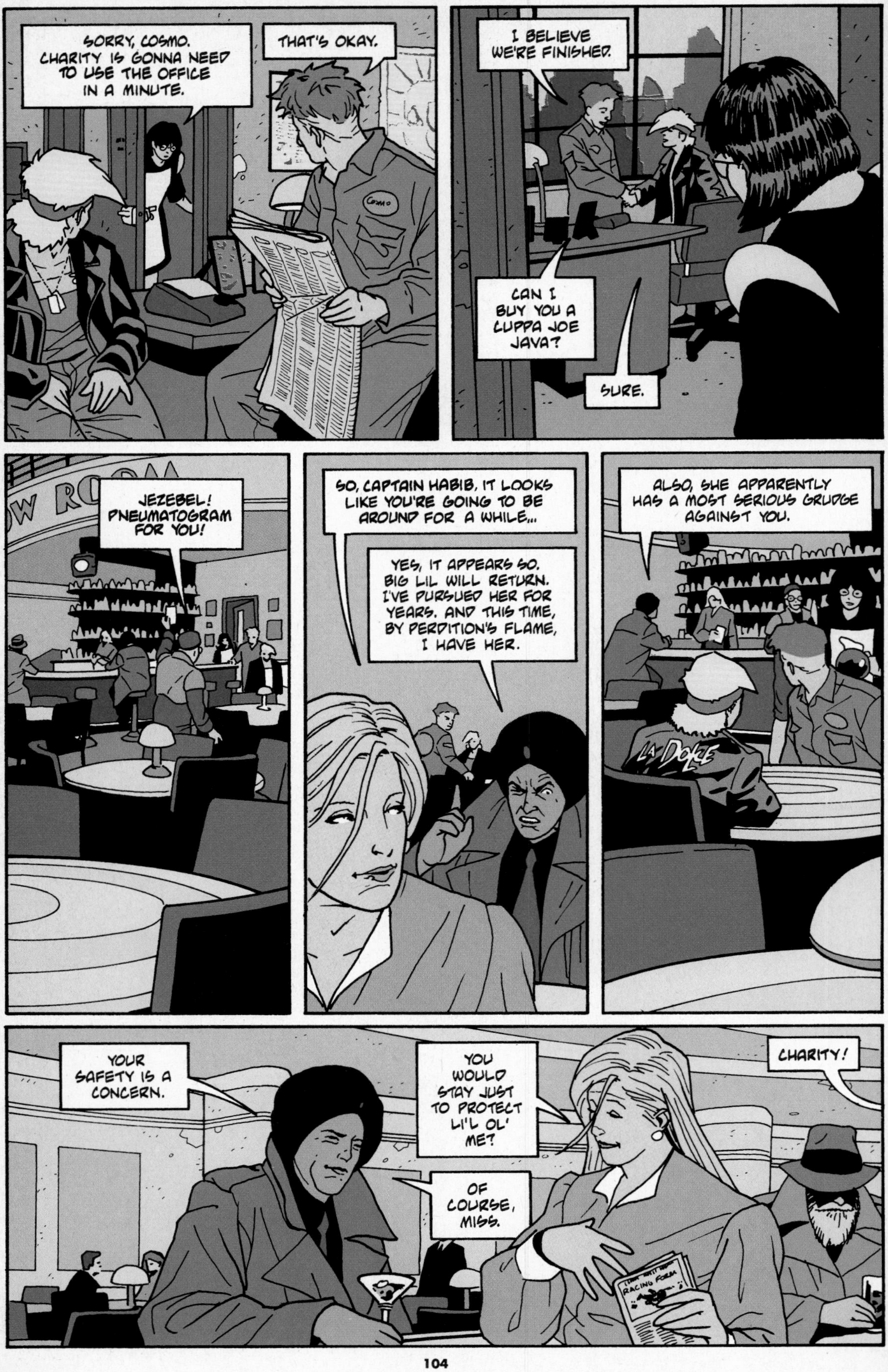
SORRY, COSMO. CHARITY IS GONNA NEED TO USE THE OFFICE IN A MINUTE.
THAT'S OKAY.
COSMO
I BELIEVE WE'RE FINISHED.
CAN I BUY YOU A CUPPA JOE JAVA?
SURE.
JEZEBEL! PNEUMATOGRAM FOR YOU!
SO, CAPTAIN HABIB, IT LOOKS LIKE YOU'RE GOING TO BE AROUND FOR A WHILE...
YES, IT APPEARS SO. BIG LIL WILL RETURN. I'VE PURSUED HER FOR YEARS. AND THIS TIME, BY PERDITION'S FLAME, I HAVE HER.
ALSO, SHE APPARENTLY HAS A MOST SERIOUS GRUDGE AGAINST YOU.
LA DOLCE
YOUR SAFETY IS A CONCERN.
YOU WOULD STAY JUST TO PROTECT LI'L OL' ME?
OF COURSE, MISS.
CHARITY!
RACING FORM

OFFICE IS FREE, BOSS.

EXCUSE ME. I HAVE TO CALL MY BOOKIE.

A DOLCE

--AUTHORITIES CONTINUE THEIR INVESTIGATION INTO THE ATTEMPTED STEAMBATH MURDER OF MAYOR HUXLEY. A HALLOWEEN MASK FOUND AT THE SCENE HAS SPARKED SPECULATION ON THE RETURN OF--

WOULD YOU PLEASE CHANGE THE CHANNEL, MISS?

GOOD MORNING TERMINAL CITY

--DOCTOR STUART PITT, HERE TO DISCUSS WHAT HAS BECOME KNOWN AS THE ESCHER SYNDROME.

TELL US, DOCTOR PITT, WHAT EXACTLY CHARACTERIZES THIS SYNDROME?

WELL, TRUDY, THIS CONDITION REALLY DEFIES ANY SATISFACTORY EXPLANATION. THERE HAVE BEEN A GROWING NUMBER OF CASES OF SOMNAMBULISM WHEREIN THE SUBJECTS ARE FOUND IN STRANGE AND PRECARIOUS SITUATIONS.

THEY AWAKEN ON LEDGES OR ROOFTOPS, OFTEN HUNDREDS OF STORIES ABOVE THE STREET. IN MANY CASES THERE IS NO PHYSICAL ACCESS TO THOSE PLACES. THEIR MEANS OF GETTING THERE ARE COMPLETELY WITHOUT EXPLANATION. AND THEY SEEM TO HAVE NO MEMORY OF--

I DON'T BELIEVE THIS!

JEZ--!

E V I C T I O N

To Miss J. Chaney

Due to immediate demolition, the owners of Futura Estates have elected not to renew your lease. Please vacate the premises on or before July 15. Thank you for your co-operation in this matter.

Yours Truly,
The Management

PROMETHEAN REAL ESTATE

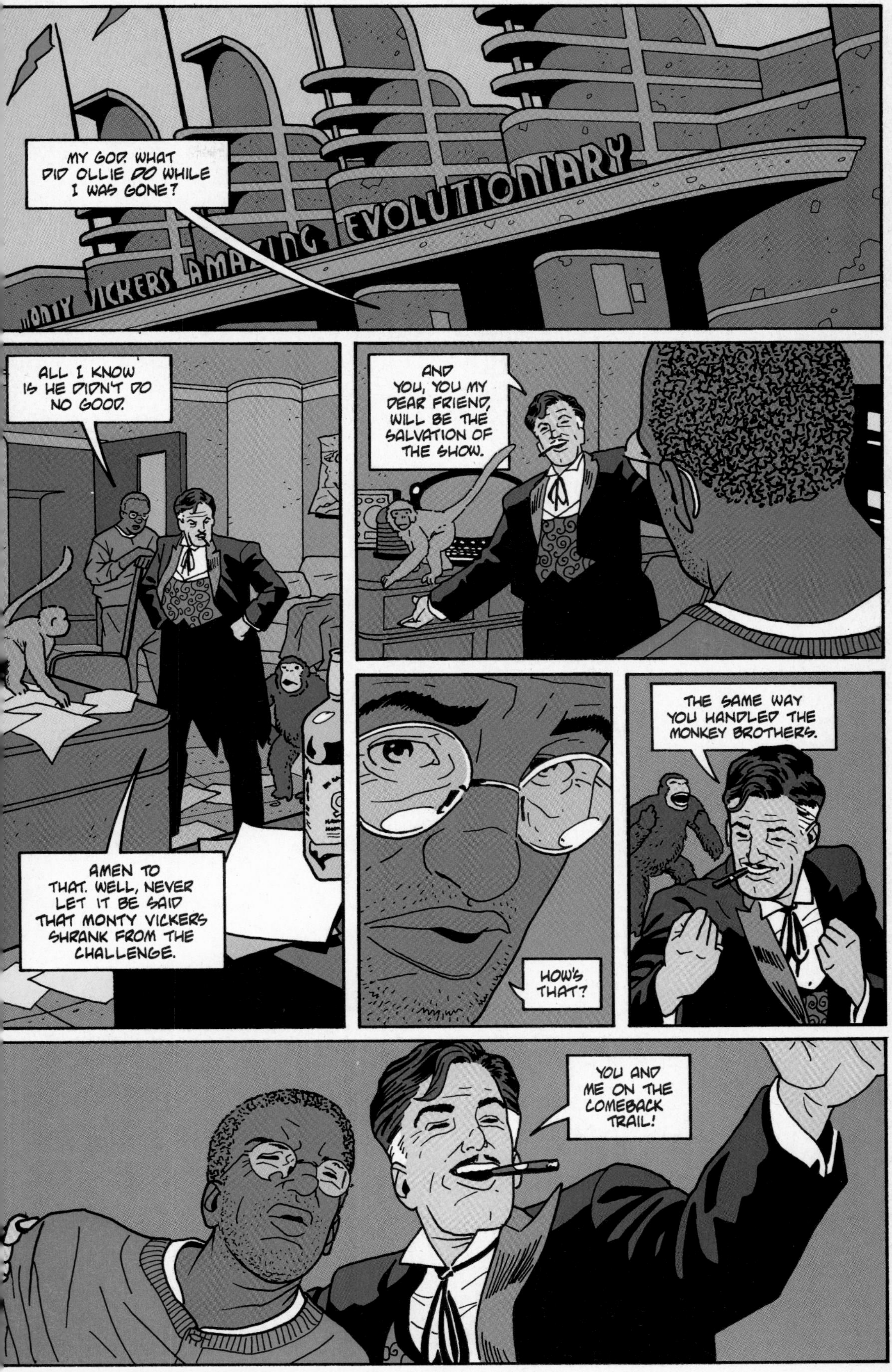
MY GOD. WHAT DID OLLIE DO WHILE I WAS GONE?
MONTY VICKERS AMAZING EVOLUTIONIARY
ALL I KNOW IS HE DIDN'T DO NO GOOD.
AMEN TO THAT. WELL, NEVER LET IT BE SAID THAT MONTY VICKERS SHRANK FROM THE CHALLENGE.
AND YOU, YOU MY DEAR FRIEND, WILL BE THE SALVATION OF THE SHOW.
HOW'S THAT?
THE SAME WAY YOU HANDLED THE MONKEY BROTHERS.
YOU AND ME ON THE COMEBACK TRAIL!

TERMINAL CITY. CROSSROADS OF THE NATION. SITE OF THE BRAVE NEW WORLD'S FAIR. AND HOME TO YET ANOTHER SCANDAL IN THE BUSINESS OF PUBLIC SPECTACLE. KID GLOVES. THE REMARKABLE CONTENDER FOR THE NATIONAL HEAVYWEIGHT CHAMPIONSHIP.

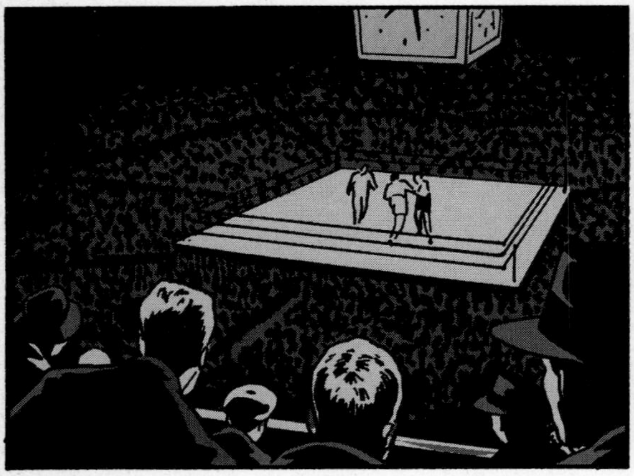

BORN IN THE STARKNESS OF SLANT-TOWN, THIS IRON-WILLED YOUNGSTER'S DETERMINATION SERVED HIM WELL. HIS METEORIC RIS TO BECOME THE EINSTEIN OF THE SWEET SCIENCE WAS A CINDERELLA STORY UNLIKE ANY OTHER.

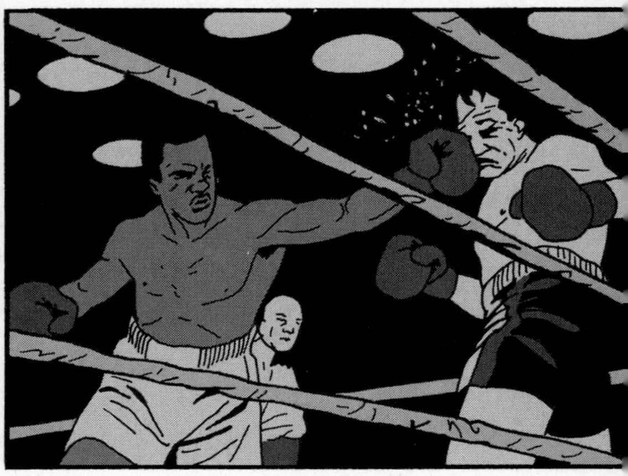

THEN, DISGRACE. ON THE EVE OF HIS FATEFUL BOUT TO USURP THE TITLE FROM TUGBOAT ANDY HE IS PHOTOGRAPHED TAKING A BRIBE FROM THIS MAN: HASBRAU MARX, THE LATE RACKETEER.

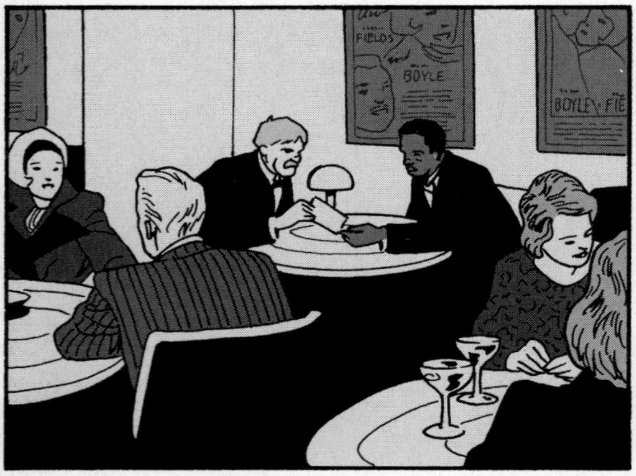
FIELDS
BOYLE

AN INVESTIGATION BY DETECTIVE OTTO REX REVEALS THAT MANY OF HIS MOST DRAMATIC VICTORIES WERE RIGGED BY MARX. MANY OF HIS KNOCKOUTS— NOTHING BUT DIVES.

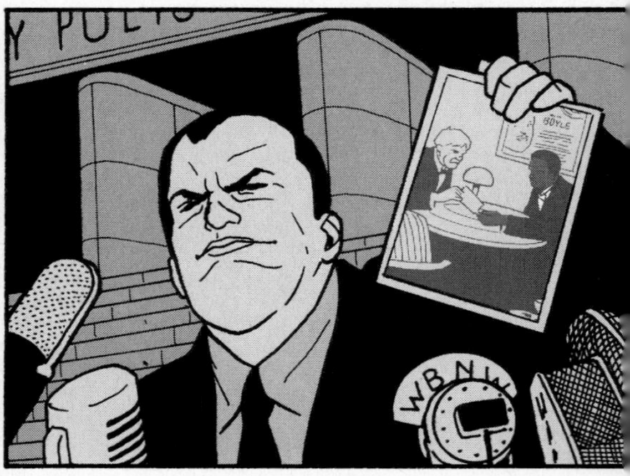
BOYLE

KID GLOVES RETIRES IN DISGRACE, STEADFASTLY INSISTING THAT HE WAS IGNORANT OF ANY RIGGED FIGHTS. INDEED, THAT THEY HAD BEEN MADE TO APPEAR RIGGED LONG AFTER HE LEGITIMATELY WON THE BOUTS.

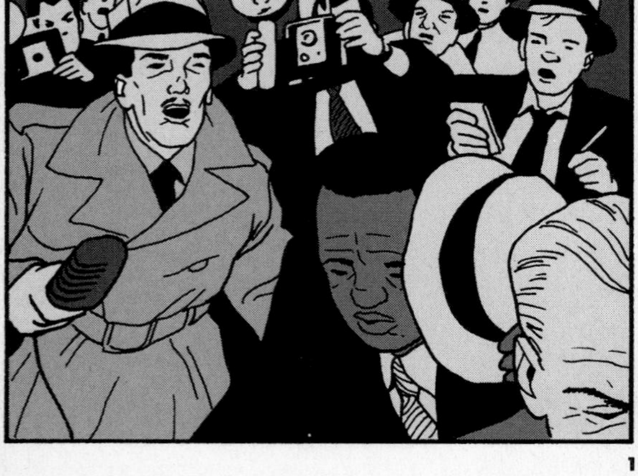

THE FORMER HEAVYWEIGHT CHAMPION MAINTAINS HIS INNOCENCE TO THIS VERY DAY.

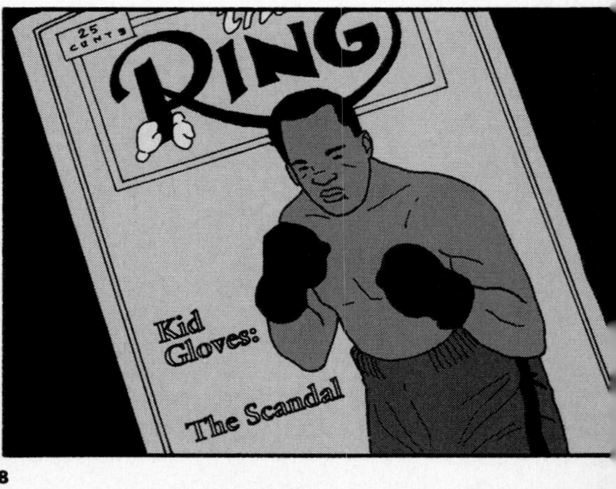
25 CENTS
RING
Kid Gloves:
The Scandal

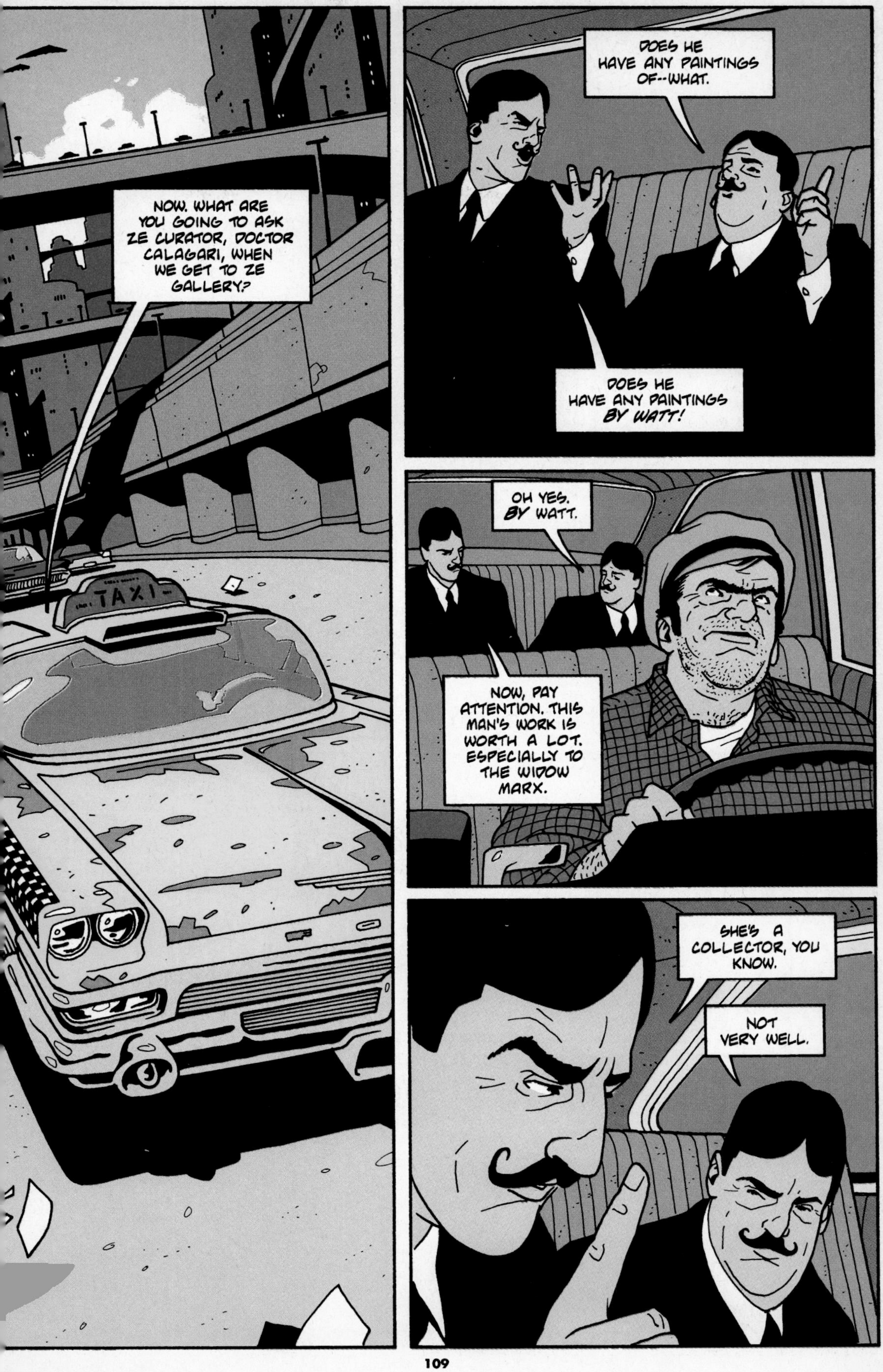
NOW. WHAT ARE YOU GOING TO ASK ZE CURATOR, DOCTOR CALAGARI, WHEN WE GET TO ZE GALLERY?
TAXI
DOES HE HAVE ANY PAINTINGS OF--WHAT.
DOES HE HAVE ANY PAINTINGS *BY WATT!*
OH YES. *BY* WATT.
NOW, PAY ATTENTION. THIS MAN'S WORK IS WORTH A LOT. ESPECIALLY TO THE WIDOW MARX.
SHE'S A COLLECTOR, YOU KNOW.
NOT VERY WELL.

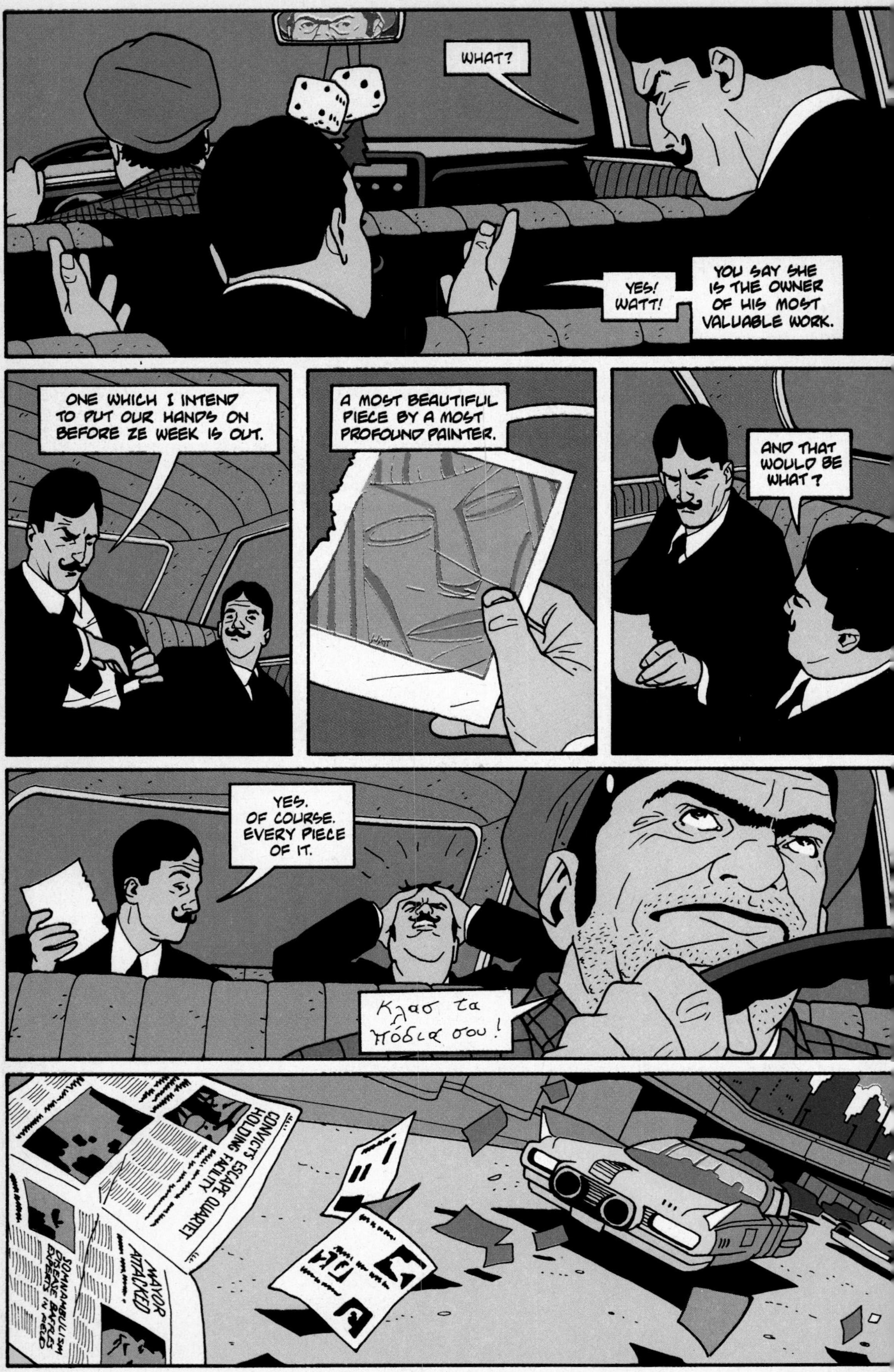
WHAT?
YES! WATT!
YOU SAY SHE IS THE OWNER OF HIS MOST VALUABLE WORK.
ONE WHICH I INTEND TO PUT OUR HANDS ON BEFORE ZE WEEK IS OUT.
A MOST BEAUTIFUL PIECE BY A MOST PROFOUND PAINTER.
WATT
AND THAT WOULD BE WHAT ?
YES. OF COURSE. EVERY PIECE OF IT.
Κλασ τα πόδια σου!
CONVICTS ESCAPE HOLDING FACILITY QUARTET
MAYOR ATTACKED
SOMNAMBULISM DISEASE BAFFLES EXPERTS IN FIELD

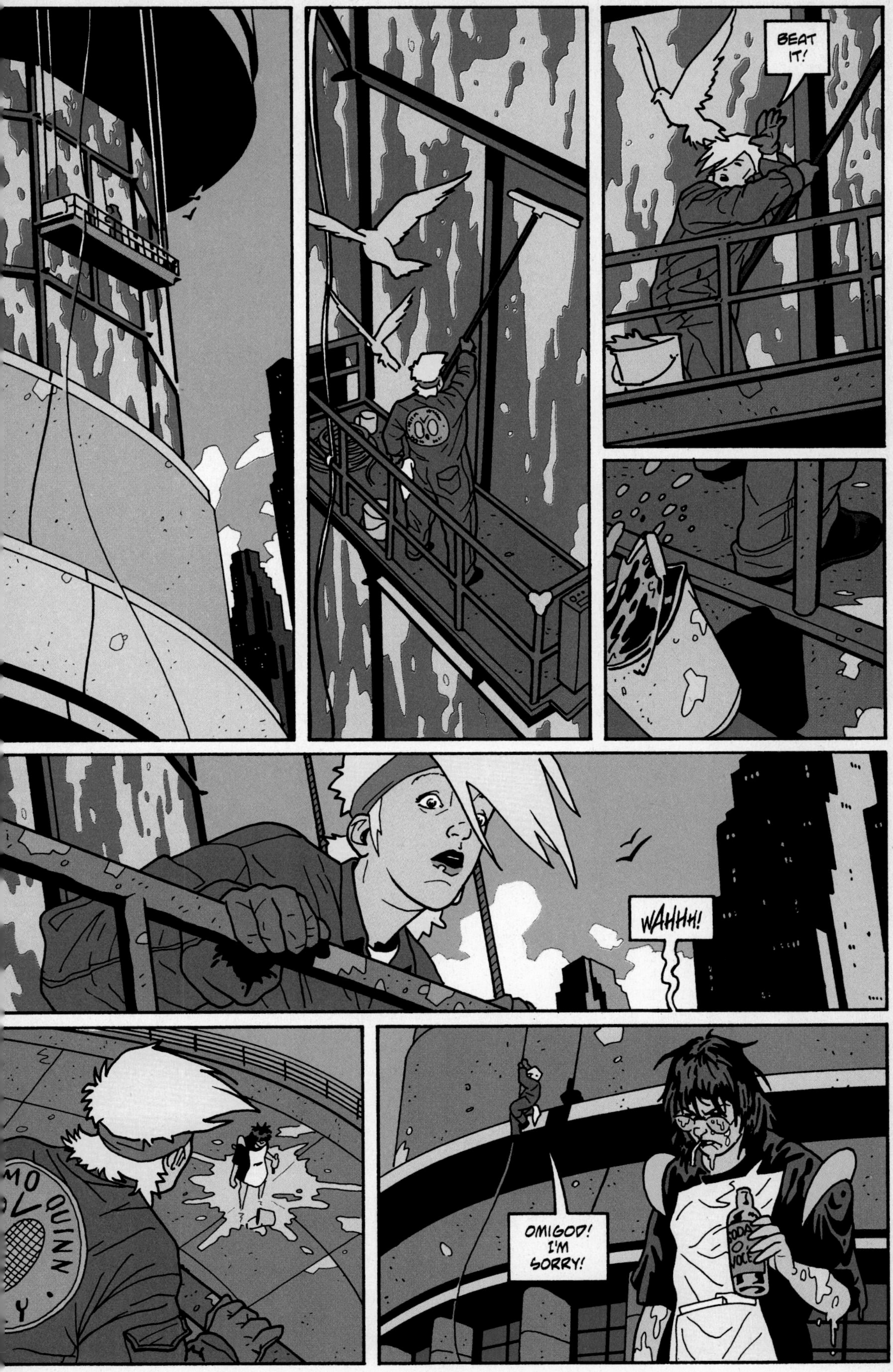
BEAT IT!
WAHHH!
OMIGOD! I'M SORRY!

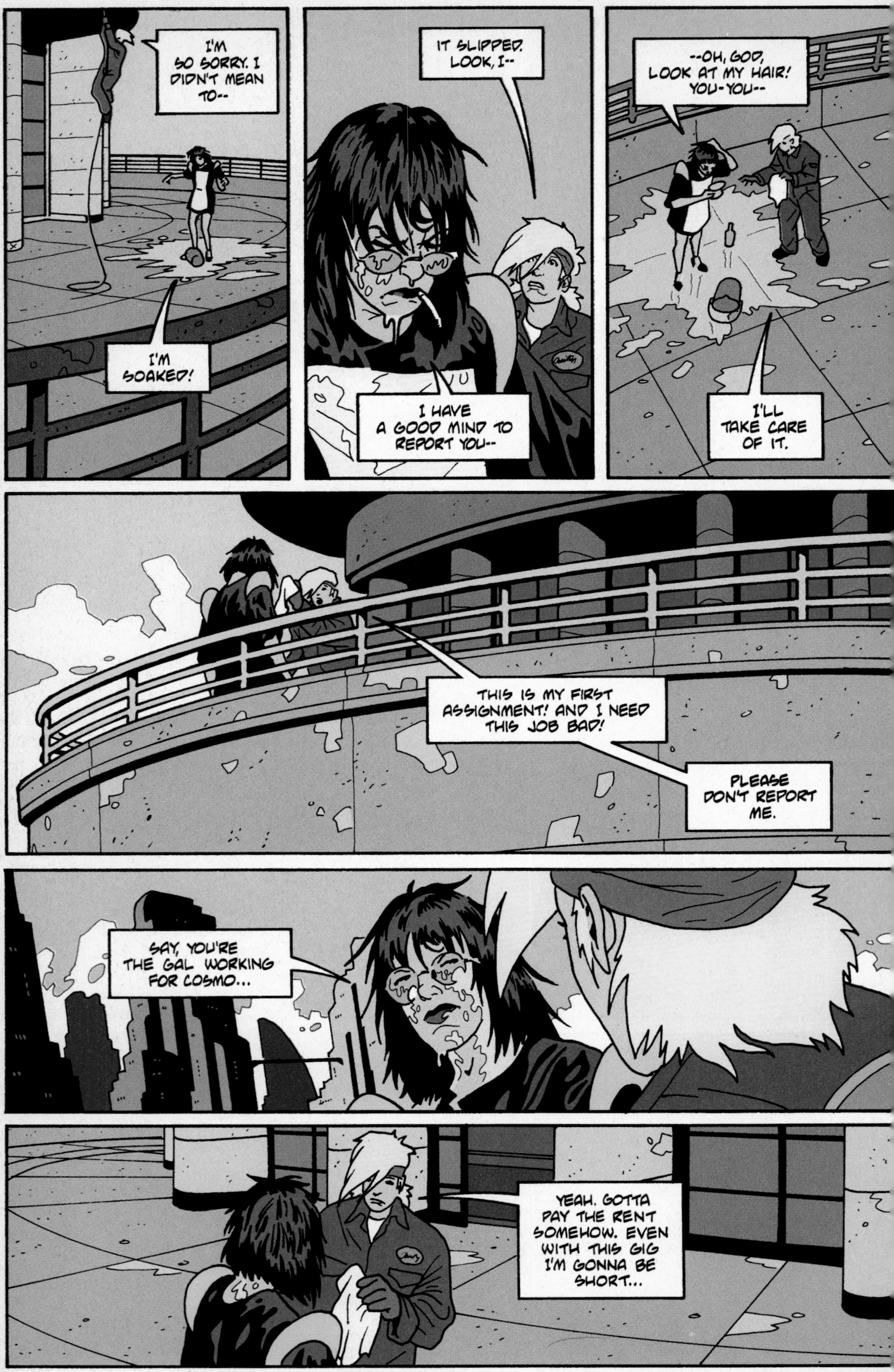
I'M SO SORRY. I DIDN'T MEAN TO--
I'M SOAKED!
IT SLIPPED. LOOK, I--
I HAVE A GOOD MIND TO REPORT YOU--
--OH, GOD, LOOK AT MY HAIR! YOU-YOU--
I'LL TAKE CARE OF IT.
THIS IS MY FIRST ASSIGNMENT! AND I NEED THIS JOB BAD!
PLEASE DON'T REPORT ME.
SAY, YOU'RE THE GAL WORKING FOR COSMO...
YEAH. GOTTA PAY THE RENT SOMEHOW. EVEN WITH THIS GIG I'M GONNA BE SHORT...

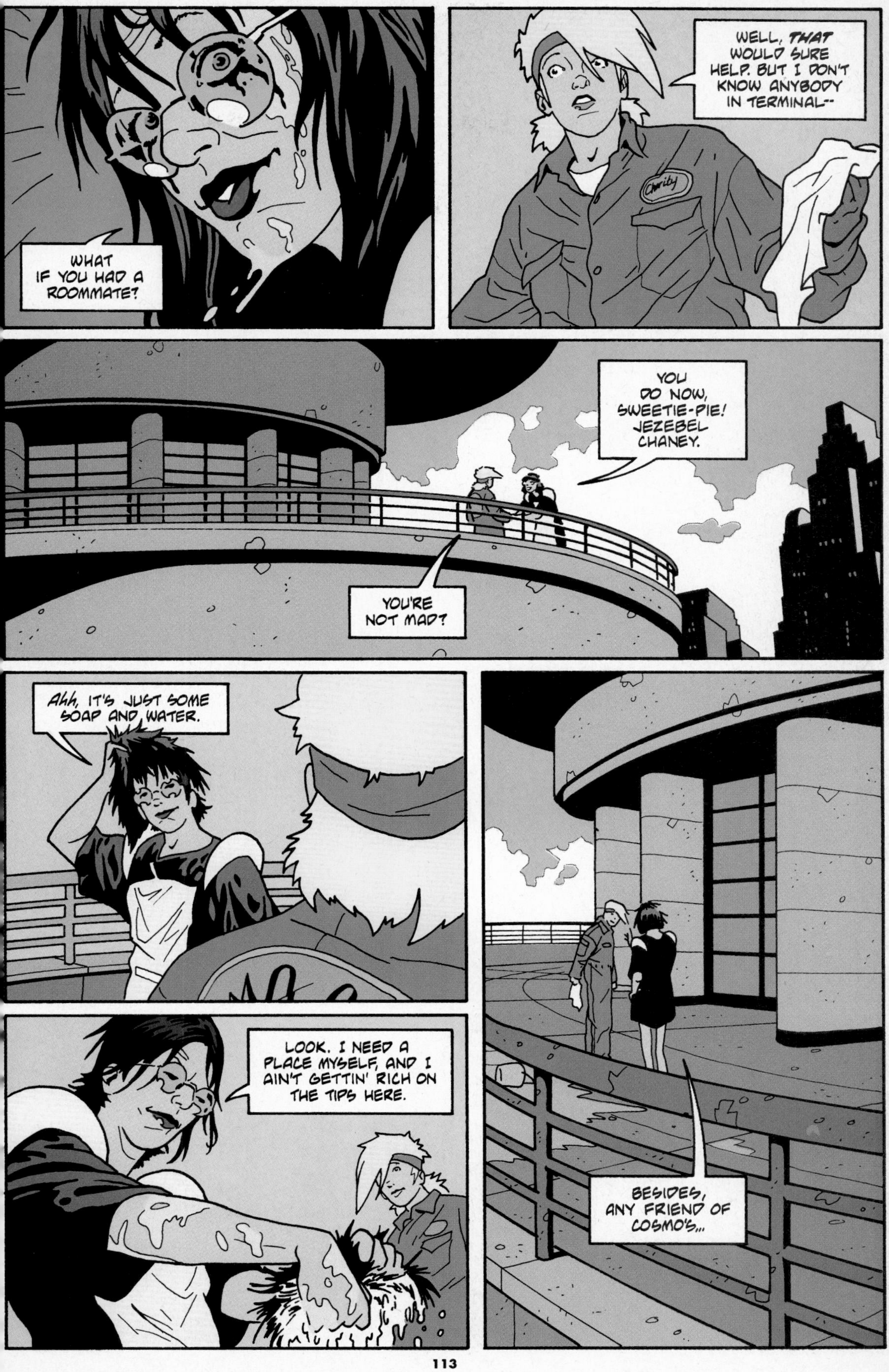
WHAT IF YOU HAD A ROOMMATE?
WELL, THAT WOULD SURE HELP. BUT I DON'T KNOW ANYBODY IN TERMINAL--
Charity
YOU DO NOW, SWEETIE-PIE! JEZEBEL CHANEY.
YOU'RE NOT MAD?
Ahh, IT'S JUST SOME SOAP AND WATER.
LOOK. I NEED A PLACE MYSELF, AND I AIN'T GETTIN' RICH ON THE TIPS HERE.
BESIDES, ANY FRIEND OF COSMO'S...

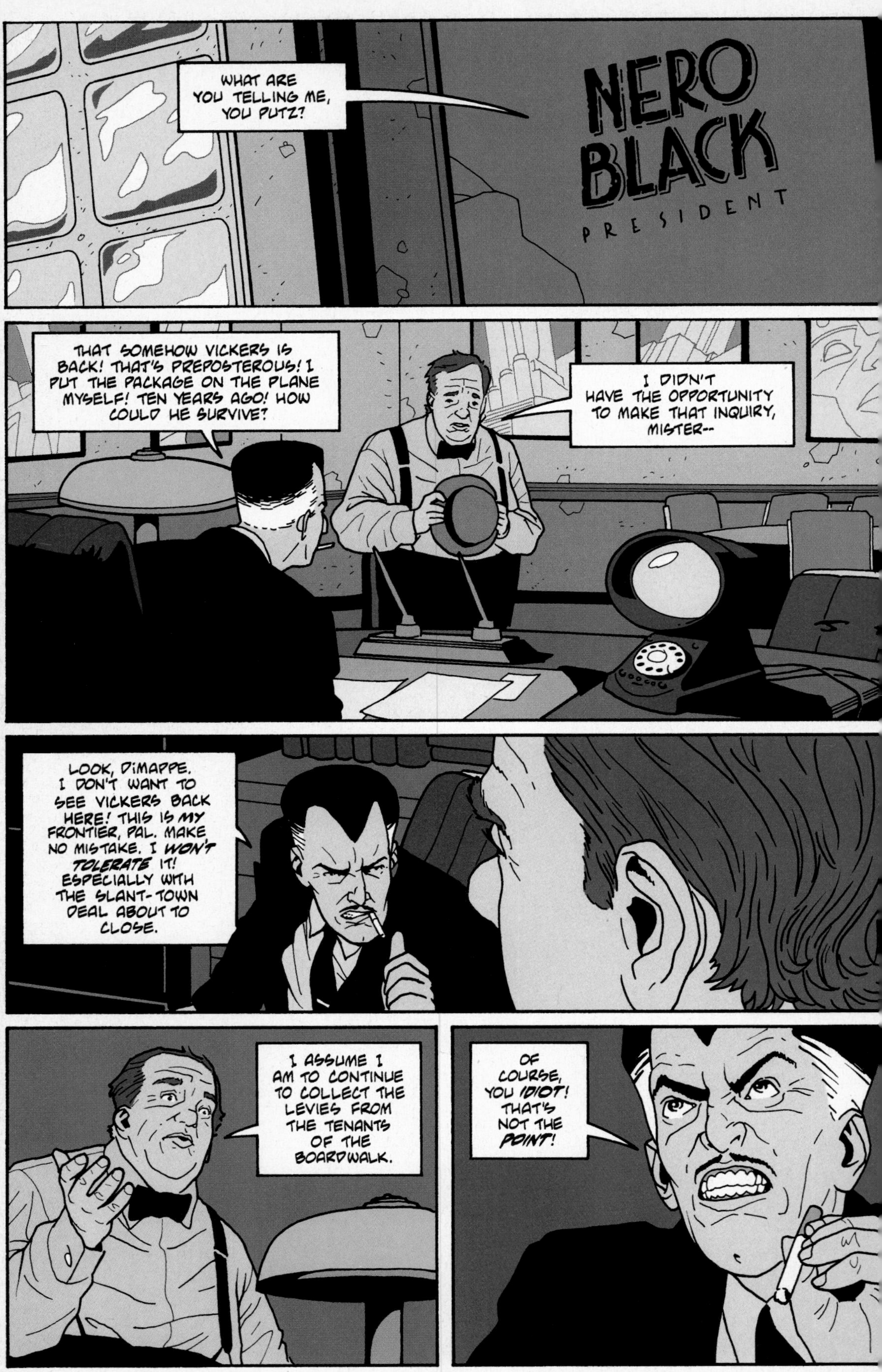
WHAT ARE YOU TELLING ME, YOU PUTZ?
NERO BLACK
PRESIDENT
THAT SOMEHOW VICKERS IS BACK! THAT'S PREPOSTEROUS! I PUT THE PACKAGE ON THE PLANE MYSELF! TEN YEARS AGO! HOW COULD HE SURVIVE?
I DIDN'T HAVE THE OPPORTUNITY TO MAKE THAT INQUIRY, MISTER--
LOOK, DIMAPPE. I DON'T WANT TO SEE VICKERS BACK HERE! THIS IS MY FRONTIER, PAL. MAKE NO MISTAKE. I WON'T TOLERATE IT! ESPECIALLY WITH THE SLANT-TOWN DEAL ABOUT TO CLOSE.
I ASSUME I AM TO CONTINUE TO COLLECT THE LEVIES FROM THE TENANTS OF THE BOARDWALK.
OF COURSE, YOU IDIOT! THAT'S NOT THE POINT!

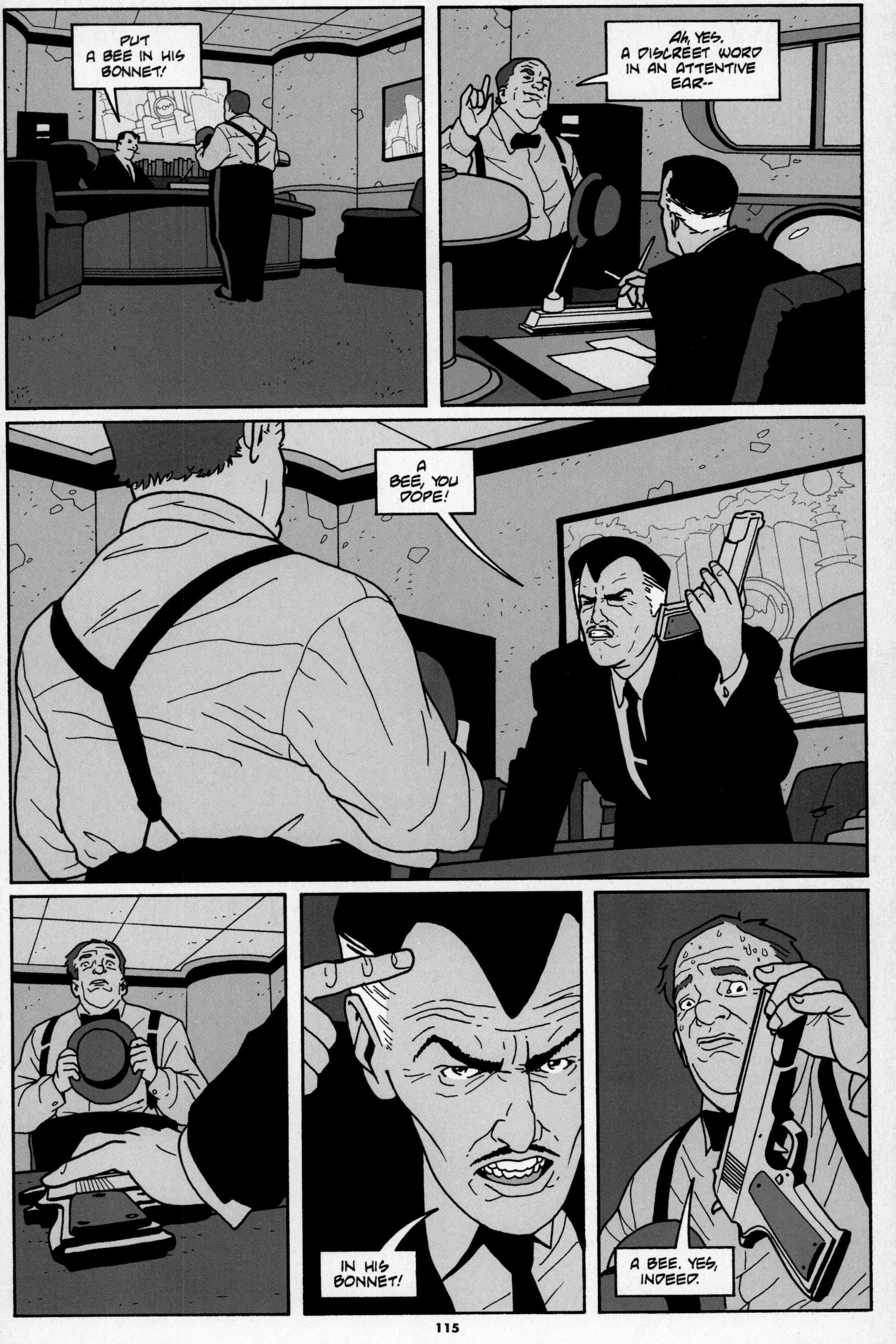
PUT A BEE IN HIS BONNET!
Ah, YES. A DISCREET WORD IN AN ATTENTIVE EAR--
A BEE, YOU DOPE!
IN HIS BONNET!
A BEE. YES, INDEED.

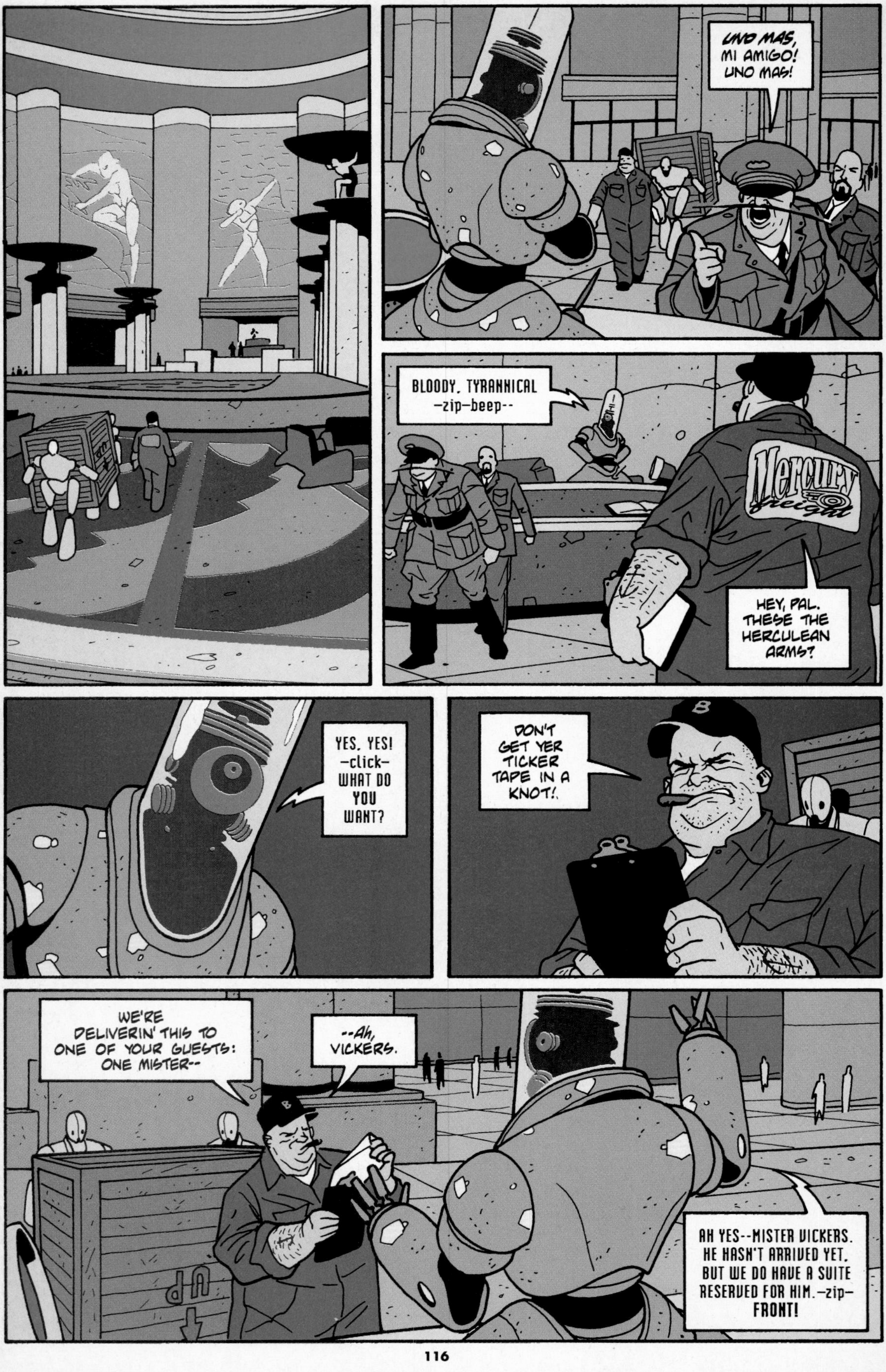
UNO MAS, MI AMIGO! UNO MAS!
BLOODY, TYRANNICAL -zip-beep--
HEY, PAL. THESE THE HERCULEAN ARMS?
Mercury freight
YES, YES! -click- WHAT DO YOU WANT?
DON'T GET YER TICKER TAPE IN A KNOT!.
WE'RE DELIVERIN' THIS TO ONE OF YOUR GUESTS: ONE MISTER--
--AH, VICKERS.
AH YES--MISTER VICKERS. HE HASN'T ARRIVED YET, BUT WE DO HAVE A SUITE RESERVED FOR HIM. -zip- FRONT!
UP

MANUAL, SHOW THESE-uh-GENTLEMEN TO THE—beep— AEGEAN SUITE.

WAITAMINNIT! THIS IS A DOOR-TO-DOOR DELIVERY!

YOU TAKE IT UPSTAIRS.

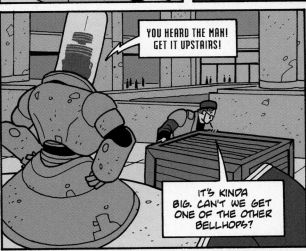

YOU HEARD THE MAN! GET IT UPSTAIRS!

IT'S KINDA BIG. CAN'T WE GET ONE OF THE OTHER BELLHOPS?

THEY'VE BEEN TAKEN BACK TO THE SHOP.

I DON'T EXPECT —beep-snik— THEM BACK BEFORE SATURDAY.

I HAVE TO MAKE DO WITH YOU!

MIND YOU, A TRAINED APE WOULD—pop—DO AS WELL...

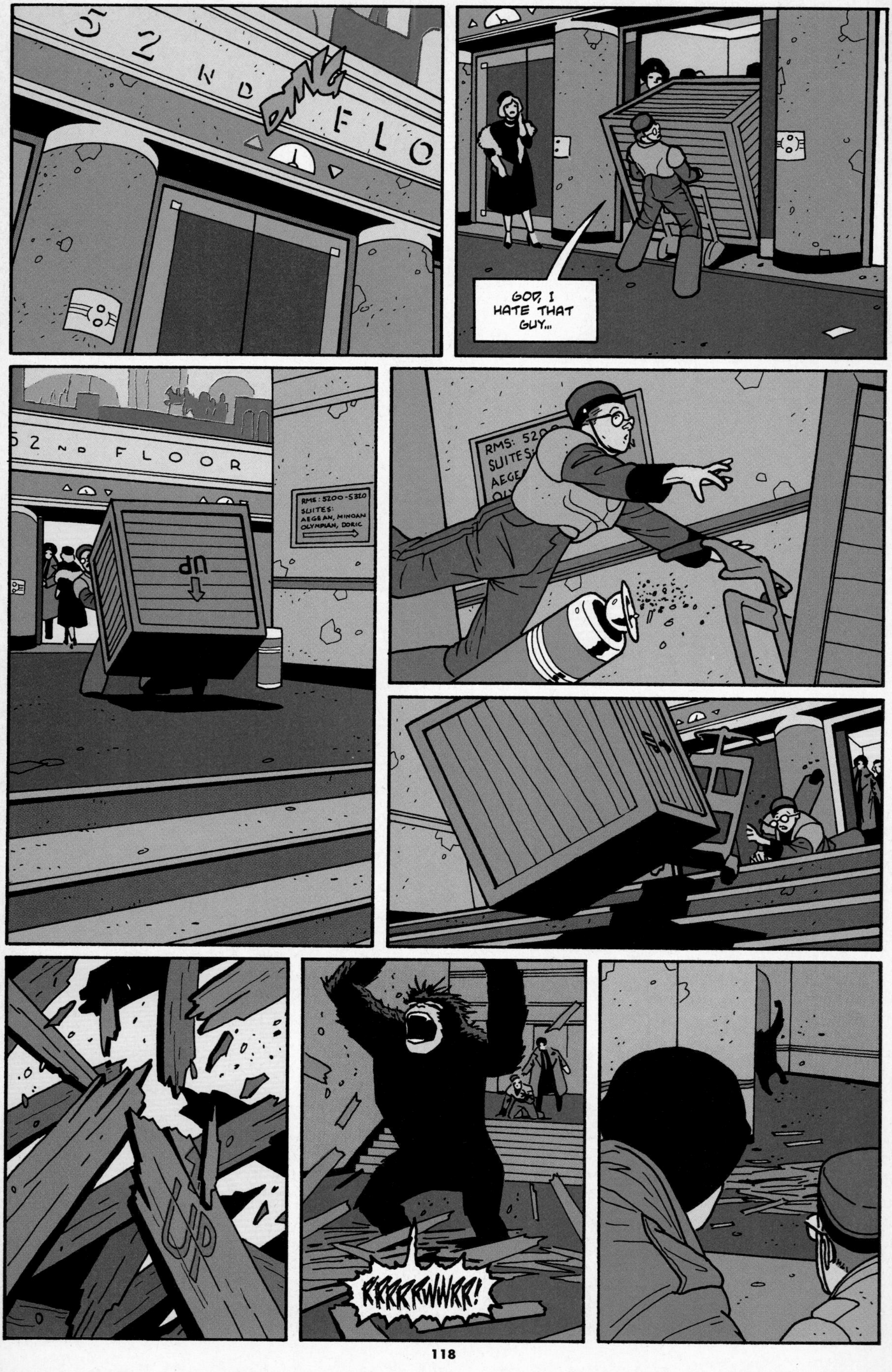
52ND FLO
DING
GOD, I HATE THAT GUY...
52ND FLOOR
RMS: 5200-5310
SUITES:
AEGEAN, MINOAN
OLYMPIAN, DORIC
UP
RRRRRWWRR!

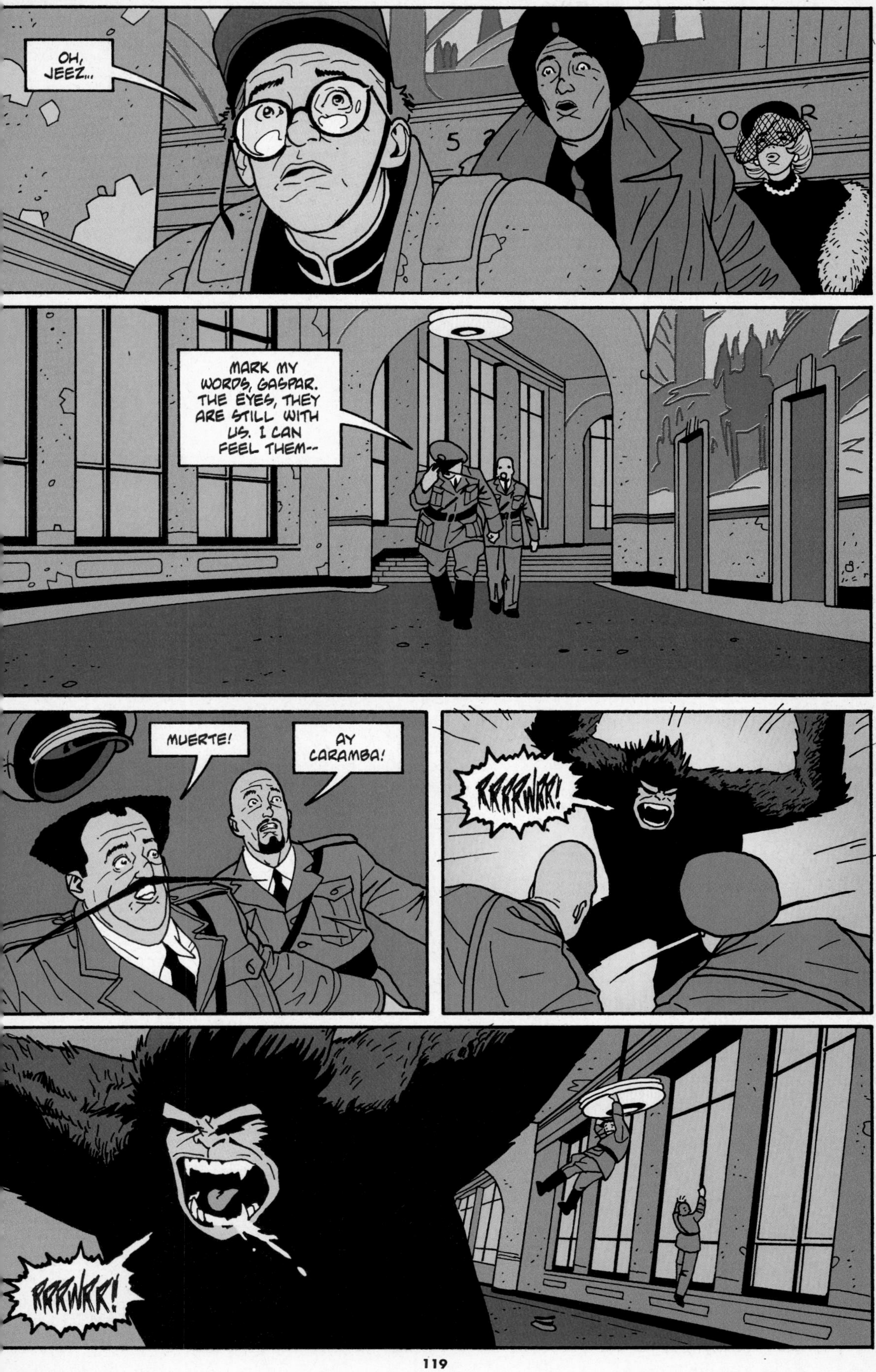
OH, JEEZ...
MARK MY WORDS, GASPAR. THE EYES, THEY ARE STILL WITH US. I CAN FEEL THEM--
MUERTE!
AY CARAMBA!
RRRRWRR!
RRRWRR!

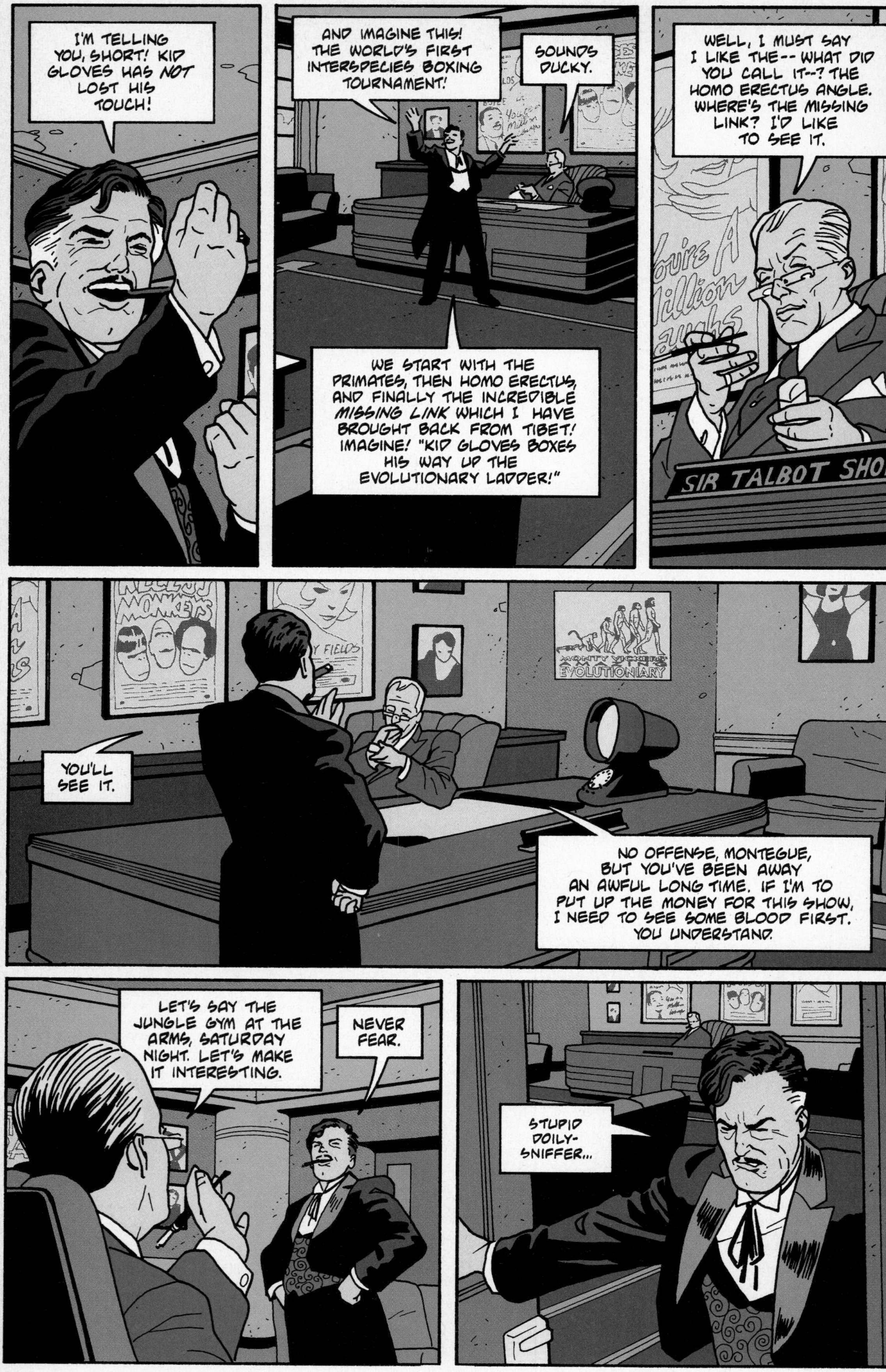
I'M TELLING YOU, SHORT! KID GLOVES HAS NOT LOST HIS TOUCH!
AND IMAGINE THIS! THE WORLD'S FIRST INTERSPECIES BOXING TOURNAMENT!
SOUNDS DUCKY.
WE START WITH THE PRIMATES, THEN HOMO ERECTUS, AND FINALLY THE INCREDIBLE MISSING LINK WHICH I HAVE BROUGHT BACK FROM TIBET! IMAGINE! "KID GLOVES BOXES HIS WAY UP THE EVOLUTIONARY LADDER!"
WELL, I MUST SAY I LIKE THE-- WHAT DID YOU CALL IT--? THE HOMO ERECTUS ANGLE. WHERE'S THE MISSING LINK? I'D LIKE TO SEE IT.
SIR TALBOT SHOR
MONTY VICKERS' AMAZING EVOLUTIONARY
YOU'LL SEE IT.
NO OFFENSE, MONTEGUE, BUT YOU'VE BEEN AWAY AN AWFUL LONG TIME. IF I'M TO PUT UP THE MONEY FOR THIS SHOW, I NEED TO SEE SOME BLOOD FIRST. YOU UNDERSTAND.
LET'S SAY THE JUNGLE GYM AT THE ARMS, SATURDAY NIGHT. LET'S MAKE IT INTERESTING.
NEVER FEAR.
STUPID DOILY-SNIFFER...

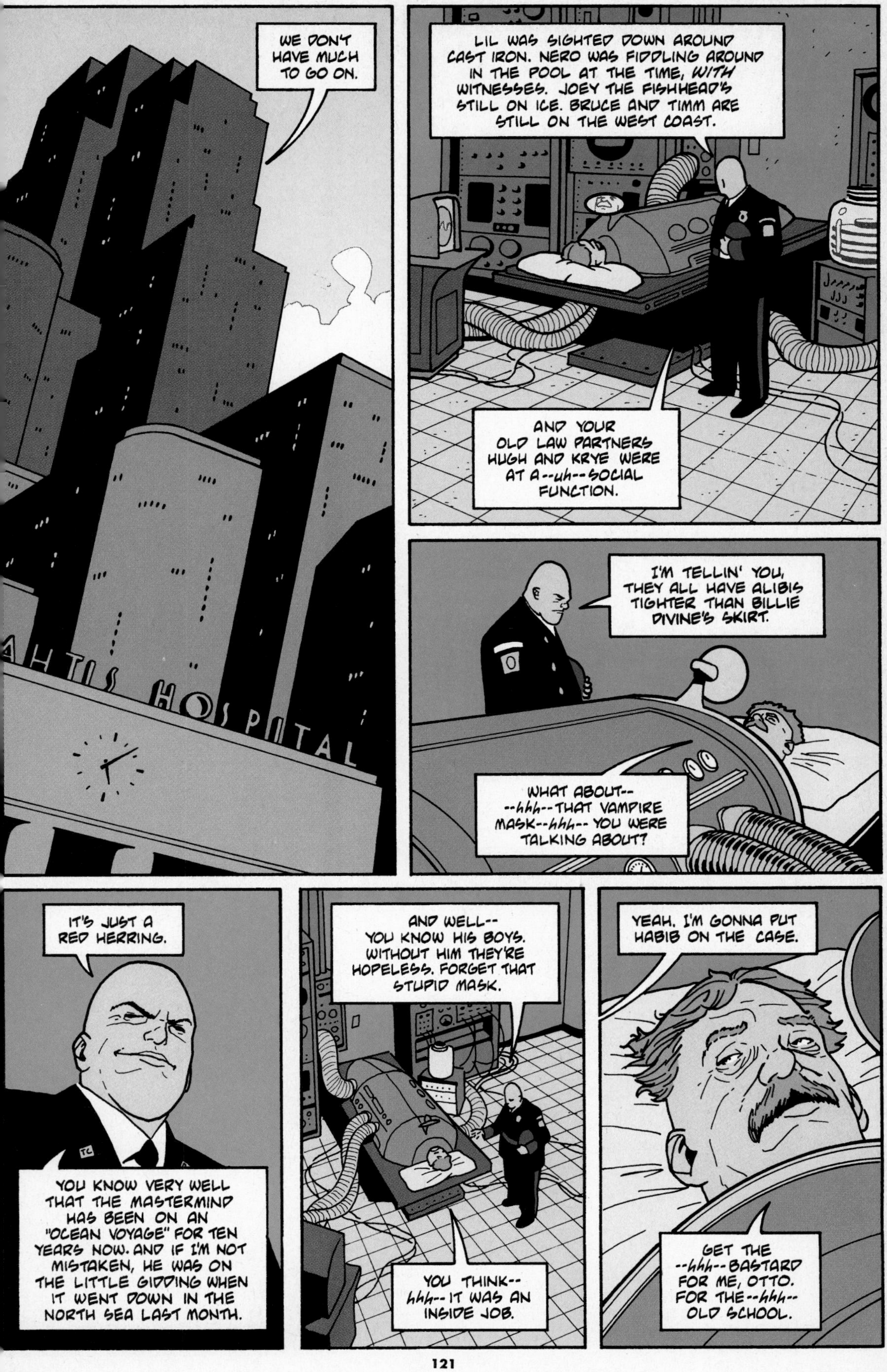
WE DON'T HAVE MUCH TO GO ON.
HOSPITAL
LIL WAS SIGHTED DOWN AROUND CAST IRON. NERO WAS FIDDLING AROUND IN THE POOL AT THE TIME, WITH WITNESSES. JOEY THE FISHHEAD'S STILL ON ICE. BRUCE AND TIMM ARE STILL ON THE WEST COAST.
AND YOUR OLD LAW PARTNERS HUGH AND KRYE WERE AT A--uh--SOCIAL FUNCTION.
I'M TELLIN' YOU, THEY ALL HAVE ALIBIS TIGHTER THAN BILLIE DIVINE'S SKIRT.
WHAT ABOUT-- --hhh--THAT VAMPIRE MASK--hhh-- YOU WERE TALKING ABOUT?
IT'S JUST A RED HERRING.
YOU KNOW VERY WELL THAT THE MASTERMIND HAS BEEN ON AN "OCEAN VOYAGE" FOR TEN YEARS NOW. AND IF I'M NOT MISTAKEN, HE WAS ON THE LITTLE GIDDING WHEN IT WENT DOWN IN THE NORTH SEA LAST MONTH.
AND WELL-- YOU KNOW HIS BOYS. WITHOUT HIM THEY'RE HOPELESS. FORGET THAT STUPID MASK.
YOU THINK-- hhh-- IT WAS AN INSIDE JOB.
YEAH. I'M GONNA PUT HABIB ON THE CASE.
GET THE --hhh--BASTARD FOR ME, OTTO. FOR THE--hhh-- OLD SCHOOL.

31 G

HUXLEY, A—

I WILL, AL. I WILL.

ATION

EL

CAUTION

IRON LUNG
IN USE

ELEVATORS →

31 G

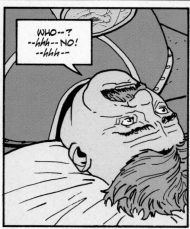

WHO--?
--hhh--NO!
--hhh--

LUNG PRESSURE

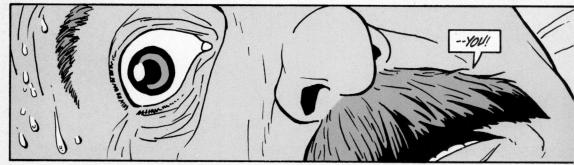

--YOU!

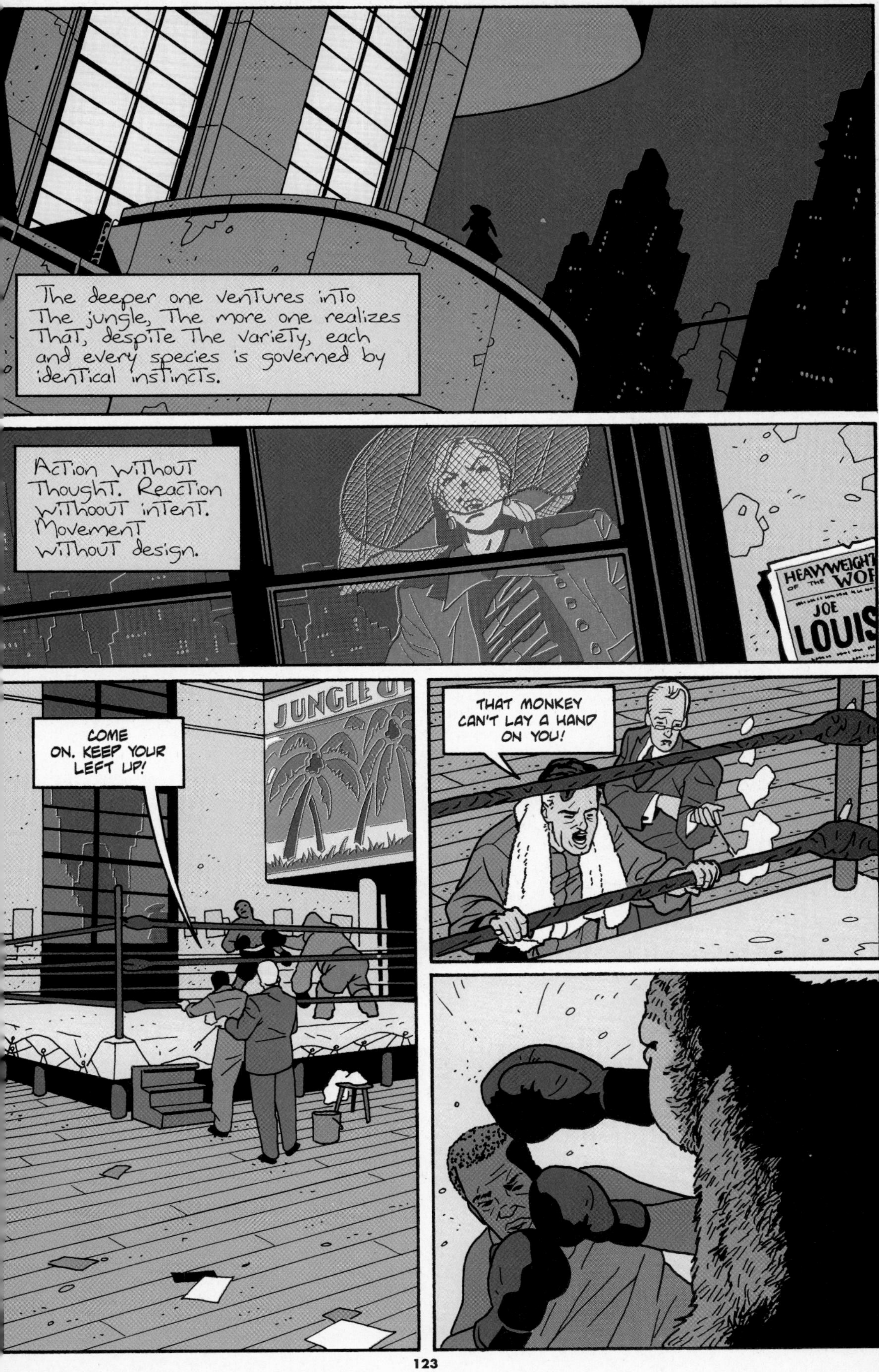

The deeper one ventures into the jungle, the more one realizes that, despite the variety, each and every species is governed by identical instincts.
Action without thought. Reaction without intent. Movement without design.
HEAVYWEIGHT OF THE WOR
JOE LOUIS
JUNGLE
COME ON. KEEP YOUR LEFT UP!
THAT MONKEY CAN'T LAY A HAND ON YOU!

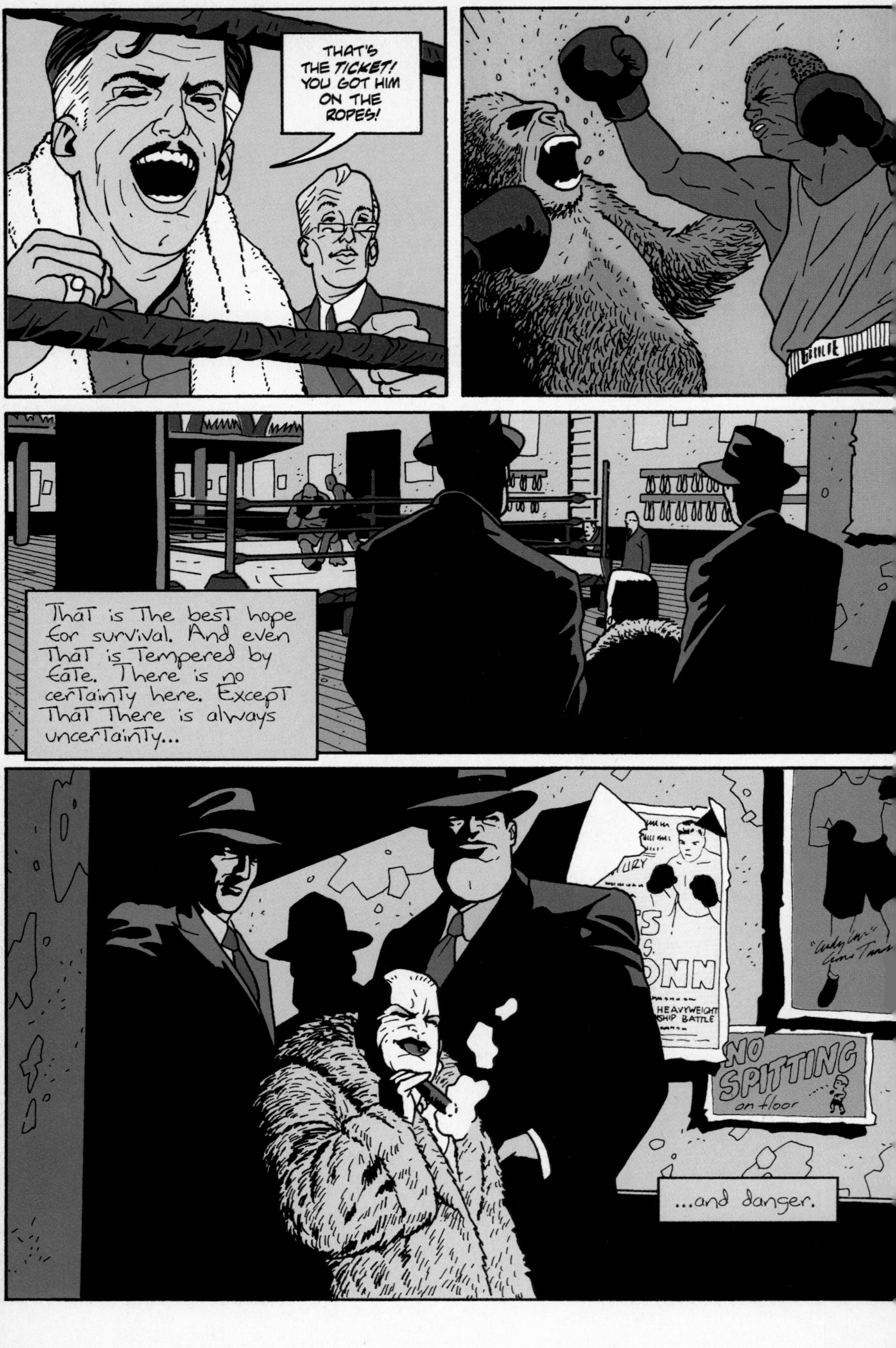
THAT'S THE TICKET! YOU GOT HIM ON THE ROPES!
That is the best hope for survival. And even that is tempered by fate. There is no certainty here. Except that there is always uncertainty...
NO SPITTING on floor
...and danger.

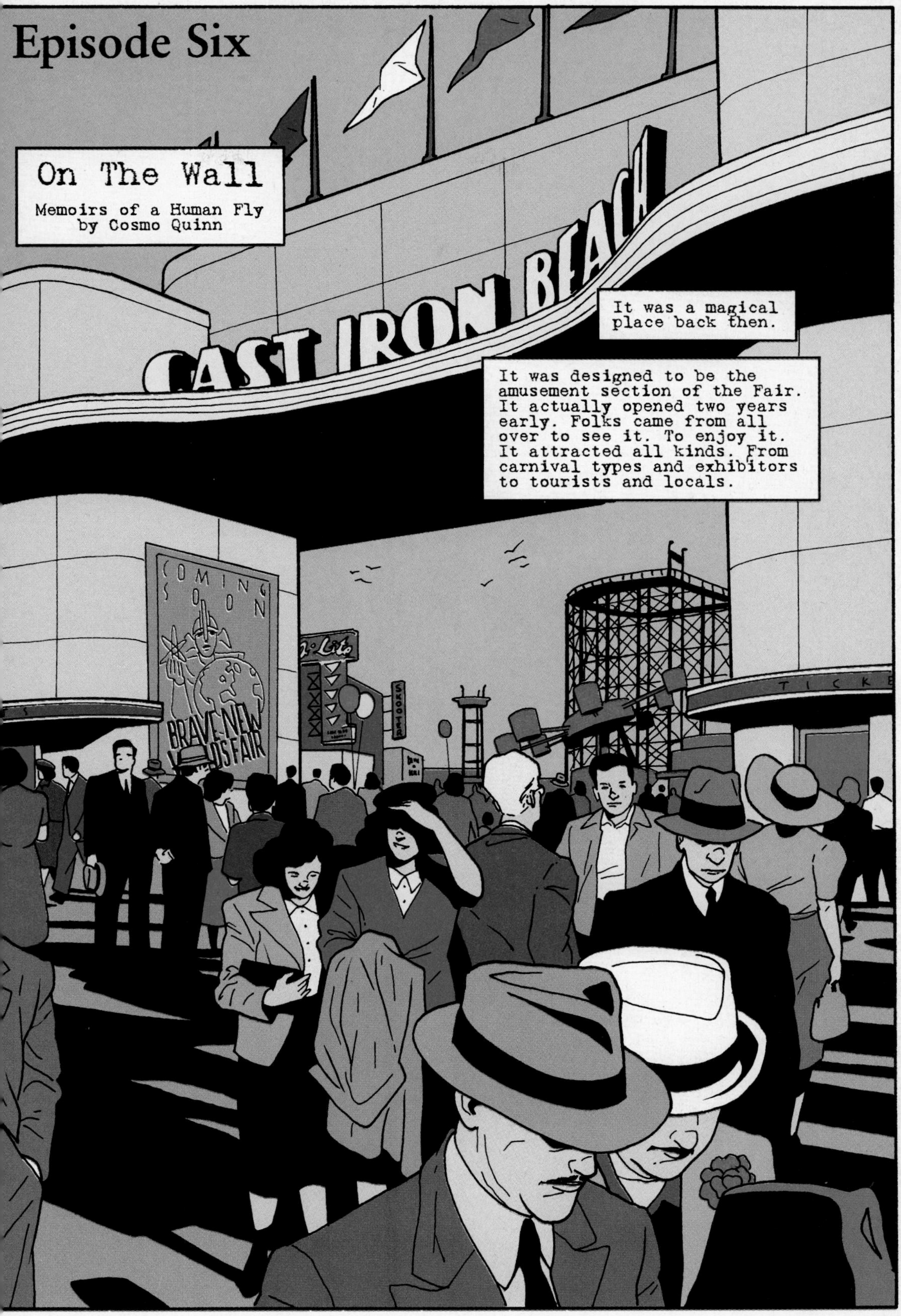
Episode Six
On The Wall
Memoirs of a Human Fly
by Cosmo Quinn
CAST IRON BEACH
It was a magical place back then.
It was designed to be the amusement section of the Fair. It actually opened two years early. Folks came from all over to see it. To enjoy it. It attracted all kinds. From carnival types and exhibitors to tourists and locals.
COMING SOON
SKOOTER

Promethean had artificially extended the beach out into the ocean. Back then the metal substructure was covered with sand.

It wasn't unusual for there to be half a million people at Cast Iron Beach on a Sunday.

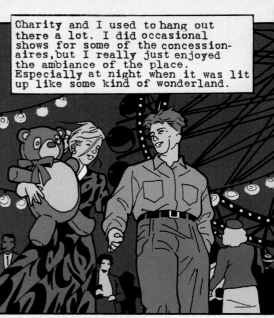

Charity and I used to hang out there a lot. I did occasional shows for some of the concession-aires, but I really just enjoyed the ambiance of the place. Especially at night when it was lit up like some kind of wonderland.

Charity posi-tively thrived there. Besides the miniature horse races there were the exhibition matches.

And she was a sucker for both. If Charity had a vice, it was gambling on the ponies and the palookas.

Me, I was spending my money in other ways.

Too bad about the way that place ended up. It's almost a ghost town these days. The sand is gone. A FEW of the rides are still running. And there is still a hint of its history in the air-- but it is a quiet and forlorn one.

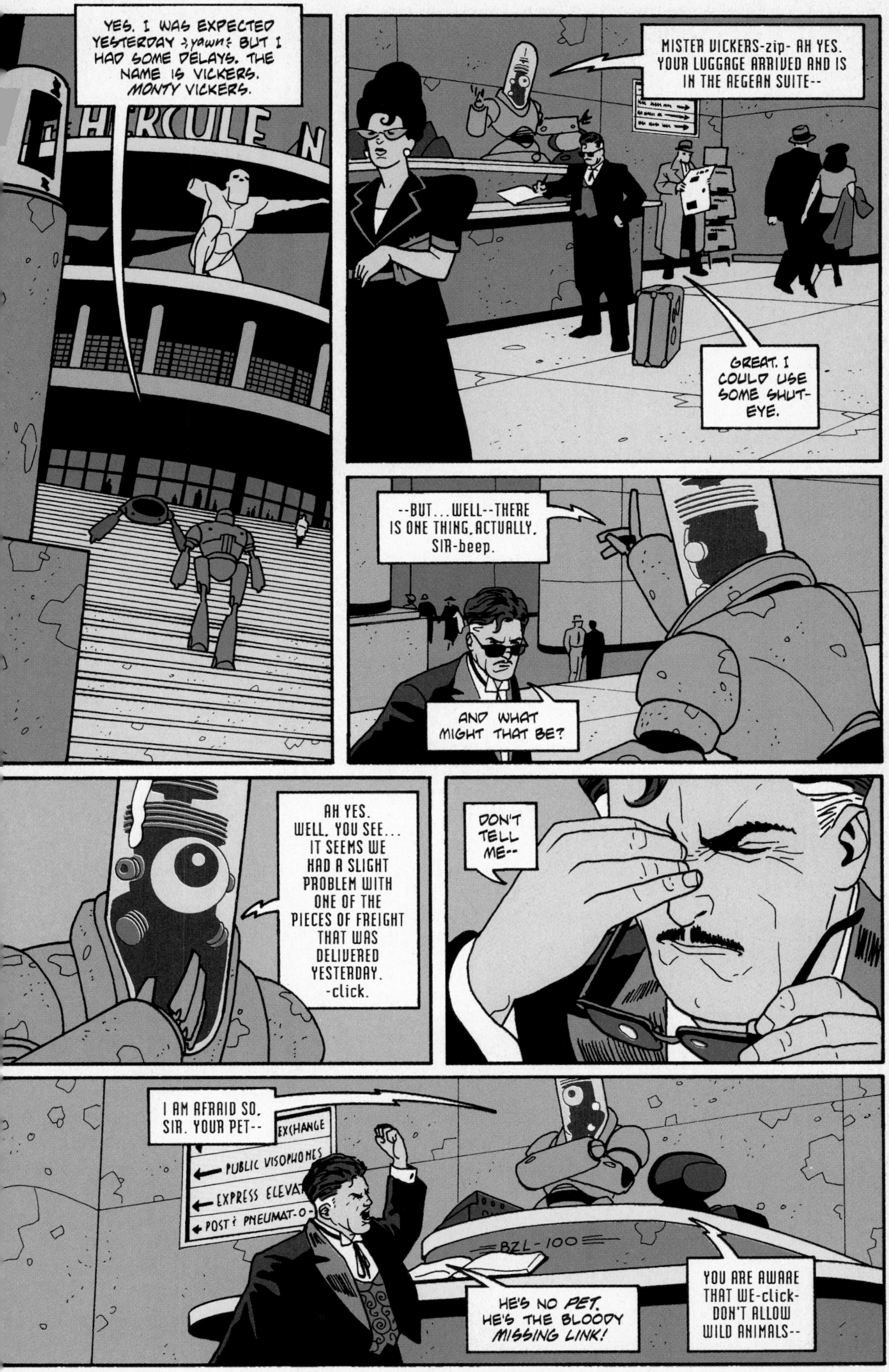

YES. I WAS EXPECTED YESTERDAY -yawn- BUT I HAD SOME DELAYS. THE NAME IS VICKERS. MONTY VICKERS.
HERCULE N
MISTER VICKERS-zip- AH YES. YOUR LUGGAGE ARRIVED AND IS IN THE AEGEAN SUITE--
GREAT. I COULD USE SOME SHUT-EYE.
--BUT...WELL--THERE IS ONE THING, ACTUALLY, SIR-beep.
AND WHAT MIGHT THAT BE?
AH YES. WELL, YOU SEE... IT SEEMS WE HAD A SLIGHT PROBLEM WITH ONE OF THE PIECES OF FREIGHT THAT WAS DELIVERED YESTERDAY. -click.
DON'T TELL ME--
I AM AFRAID SO, SIR. YOUR PET--
EXCHANGE
PUBLIC VISOPHONES
EXPRESS ELEVAT
POST & PNEUMAT-O
BZL-100
HE'S NO PET. HE'S THE BLOODY MISSING LINK!
YOU ARE AWARE THAT WE-click- DON'T ALLOW WILD ANIMALS--

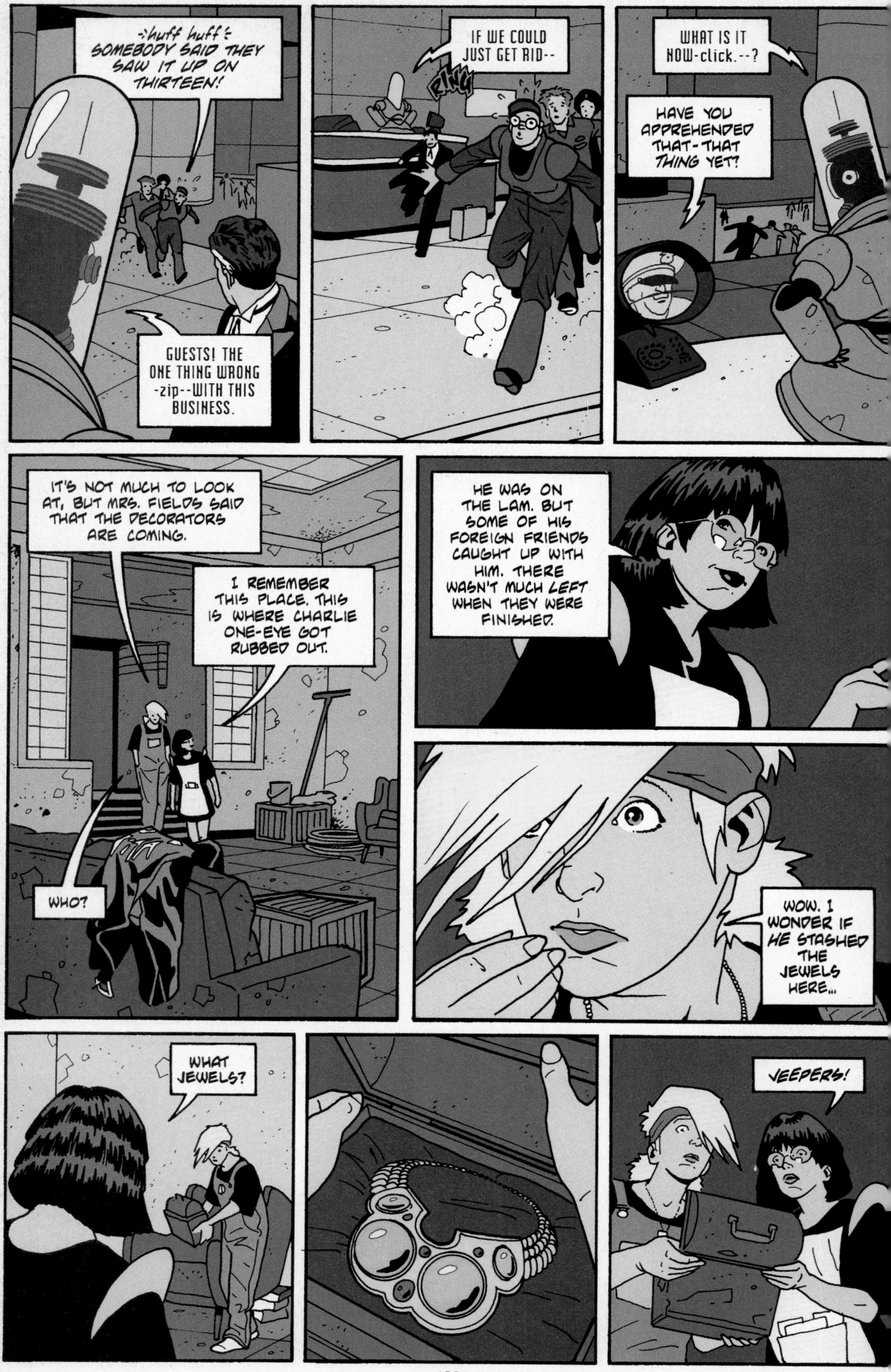
-huff huff- SOMEBODY SAID THEY SAW IT UP ON THIRTEEN!
GUESTS! THE ONE THING WRONG -zip--WITH THIS BUSINESS.
IF WE COULD JUST GET RID--
RING
WHAT IS IT NOW-click.--?
HAVE YOU APPREHENDED THAT-THAT THING YET?
IT'S NOT MUCH TO LOOK AT, BUT MRS. FIELDS SAID THAT THE DECORATORS ARE COMING.
I REMEMBER THIS PLACE. THIS IS WHERE CHARLIE ONE-EYE GOT RUBBED OUT.
WHO?
HE WAS ON THE LAM. BUT SOME OF HIS FOREIGN FRIENDS CAUGHT UP WITH HIM. THERE WASN'T MUCH LEFT WHEN THEY WERE FINISHED.
WOW. I WONDER IF HE STASHED THE JEWELS HERE...
WHAT JEWELS?
JEEPERS!

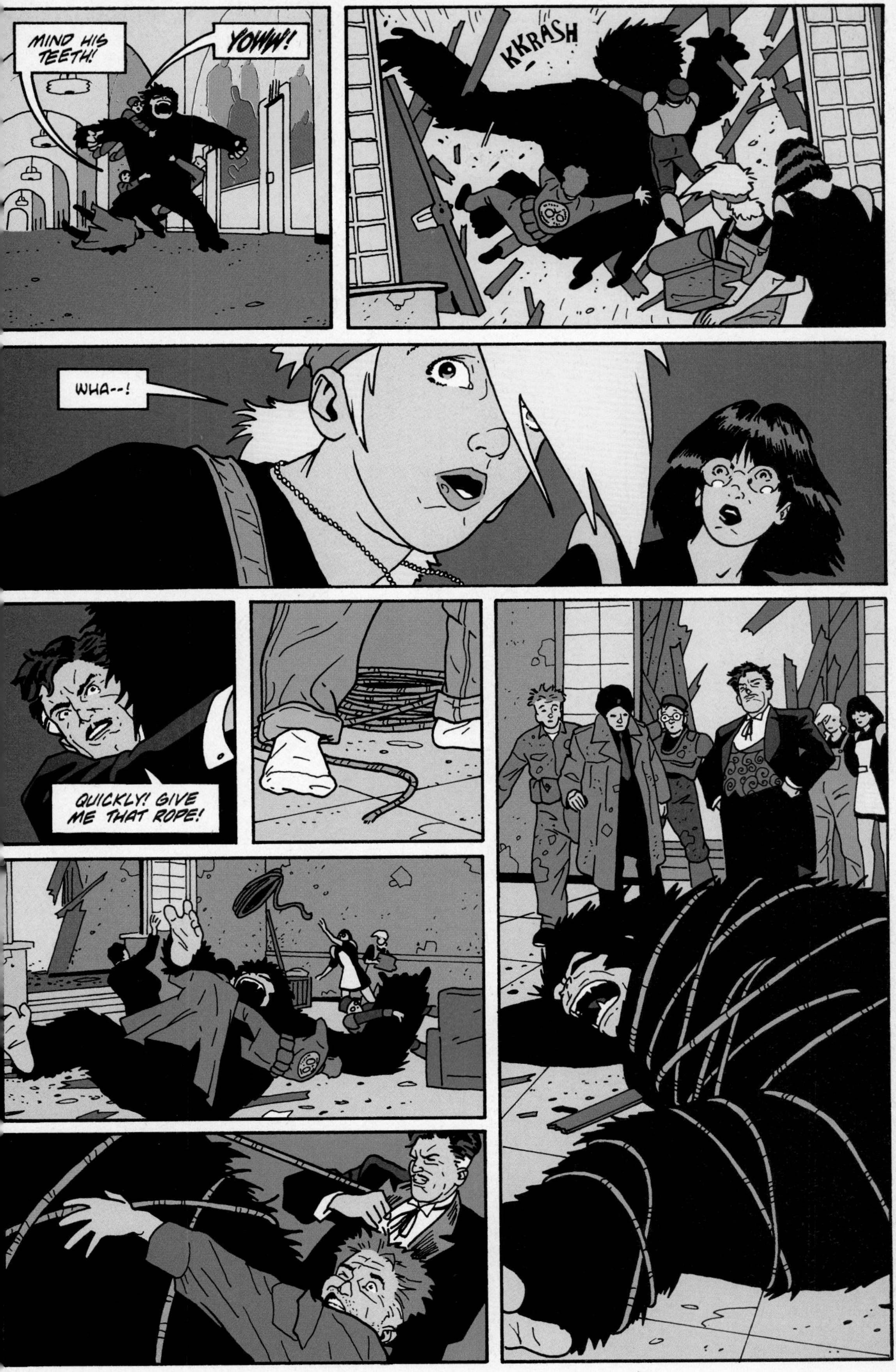
MIND HIS TEETH!
YOWW!
KKRASH
WHA--!
QUICKLY! GIVE ME THAT ROPE!

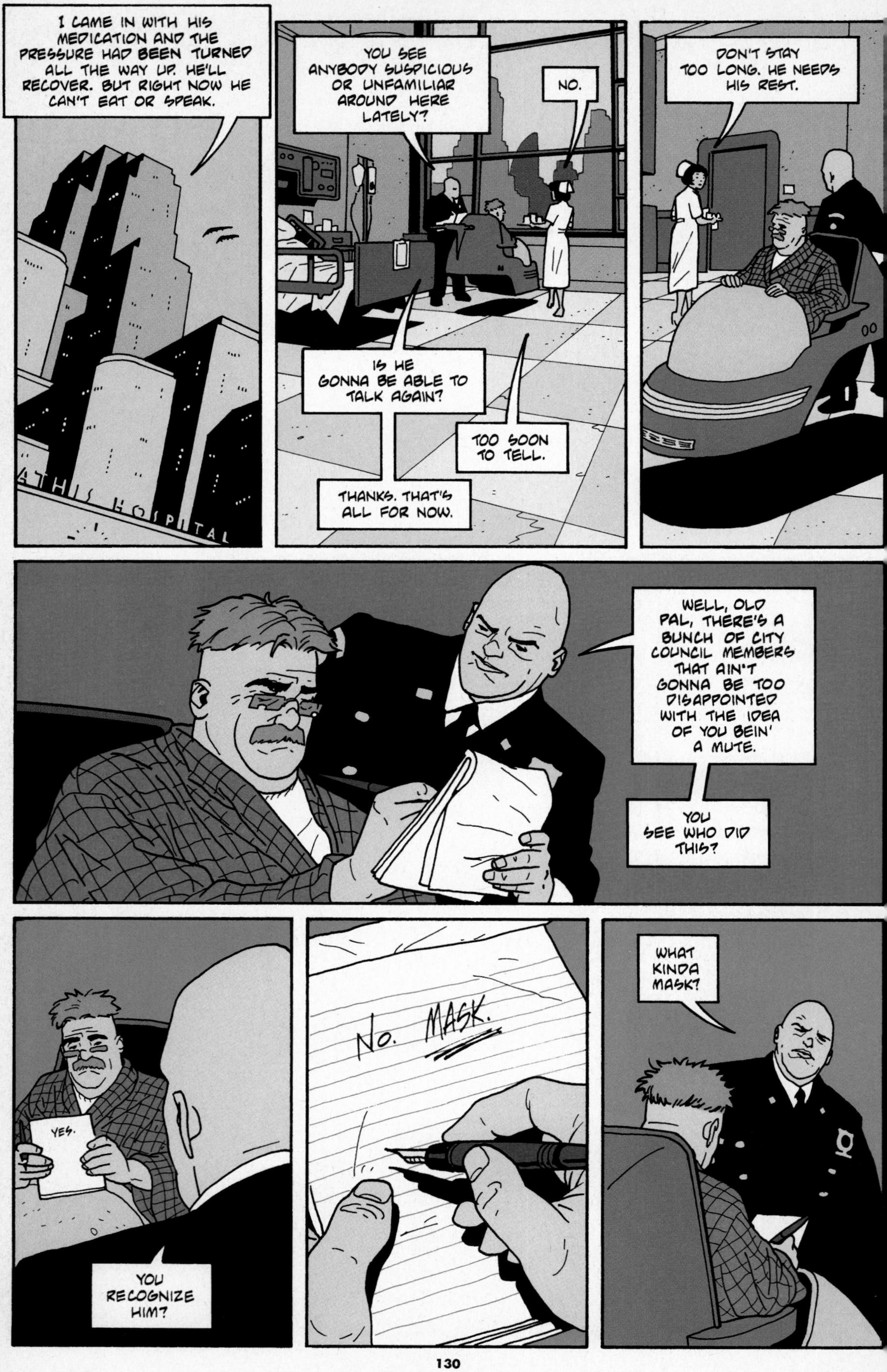
I CAME IN WITH HIS MEDICATION AND THE PRESSURE HAD BEEN TURNED ALL THE WAY UP. HE'LL RECOVER. BUT RIGHT NOW HE CAN'T EAT OR SPEAK.
ATHIS HOSPITAL
YOU SEE ANYBODY SUSPICIOUS OR UNFAMILIAR AROUND HERE LATELY?
NO.
IS HE GONNA BE ABLE TO TALK AGAIN?
TOO SOON TO TELL.
THANKS. THAT'S ALL FOR NOW.
DON'T STAY TOO LONG. HE NEEDS HIS REST.
WELL, OLD PAL, THERE'S A BUNCH OF CITY COUNCIL MEMBERS THAT AIN'T GONNA BE TOO DISAPPOINTED WITH THE IDEA OF YOU BEIN' A MUTE.
YOU SEE WHO DID THIS?
YES.
YOU RECOGNIZE HIM?
No. MASK.
WHAT KINDA MASK?

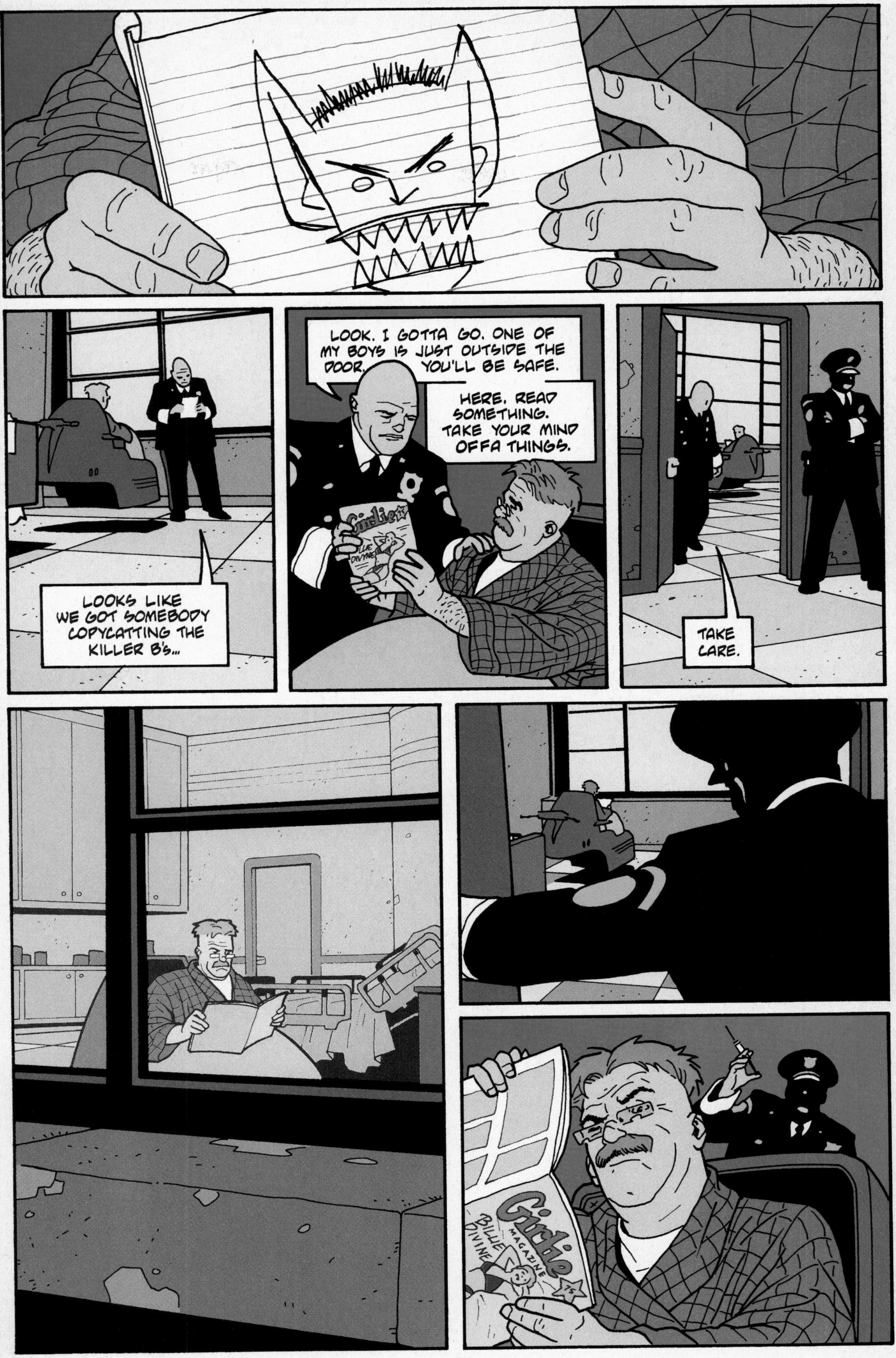
LOOKS LIKE WE GOT SOMEBODY COPYCATTING THE KILLER B's...
LOOK. I GOTTA GO. ONE OF MY BOYS IS JUST OUTSIDE THE DOOR... YOU'LL BE SAFE.
HERE. READ SOMETHING. TAKE YOUR MIND OFFA THINGS.
TAKE CARE.
Girlie
MAGAZINE
BILLIE DIVINE

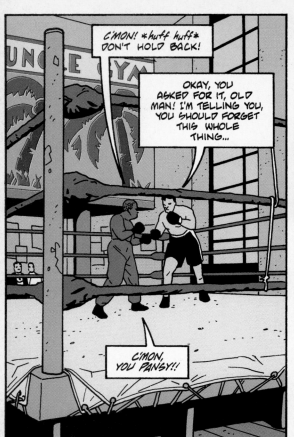

C'MON! *huff huff* DON'T HOLD BACK!

OKAY, YOU ASKED FOR IT, OLD MAN! I'M TELLING YOU, YOU SHOULD FORGET THIS WHOLE THING...

C'MON, YOU PANSY!!

BRAVO! WELL DONE!

WHAT DID I TELL YOU?

YOU'RE A MAN OF YOUR WORD, VICKERS. AS ALWAYS. LET'S GO PUT SOME INK ON PAPER.

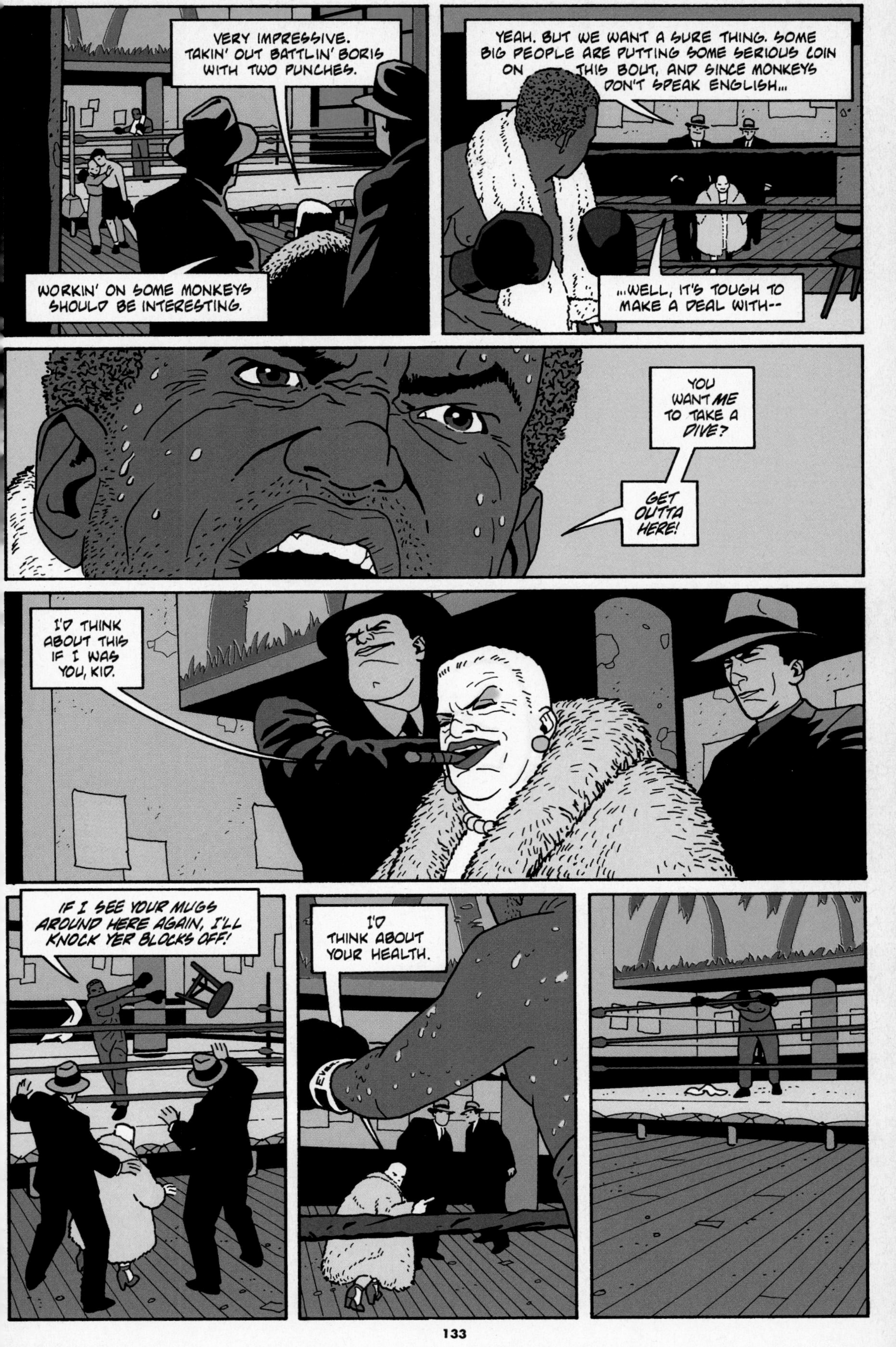

VERY IMPRESSIVE. TAKIN' OUT BATTLIN' BORIS WITH TWO PUNCHES.
WORKIN' ON SOME MONKEYS SHOULD BE INTERESTING.
YEAH. BUT WE WANT A SURE THING. SOME BIG PEOPLE ARE PUTTING SOME SERIOUS COIN ON THIS BOUT, AND SINCE MONKEYS DON'T SPEAK ENGLISH...
...WELL, IT'S TOUGH TO MAKE A DEAL WITH--
YOU WANT *ME* TO TAKE A *DIVE?*
GET OUTTA HERE!
I'D THINK ABOUT THIS IF I WAS YOU, KID.
IF I SEE YOUR MUGS AROUND HERE AGAIN, I'LL KNOCK YER BLOCKS OFF!
I'D THINK ABOUT YOUR HEALTH.

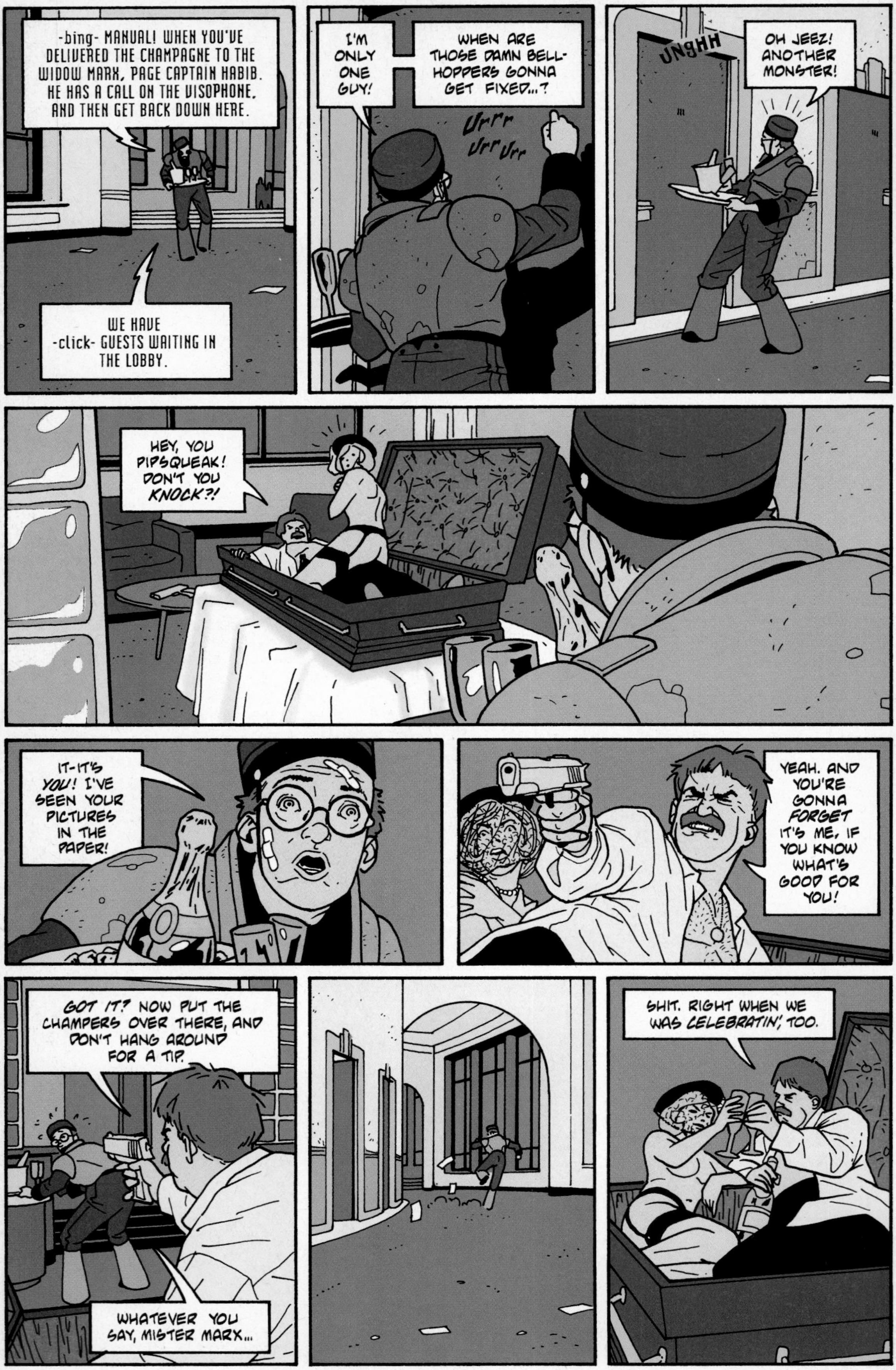
-bing- MANUAL! WHEN YOU'VE DELIVERED THE CHAMPAGNE TO THE WIDOW MARX, PAGE CAPTAIN HABIB. HE HAS A CALL ON THE VISOPHONE, AND THEN GET BACK DOWN HERE.
WE HAVE -click- GUESTS WAITING IN THE LOBBY.
I'M ONLY ONE GUY!
WHEN ARE THOSE DAMN BELL-HOPPERS GONNA GET FIXED...?
Urr'r Urr Urr
UNGHH
OH JEEZ! ANOTHER MONSTER!
HEY, YOU PIPSQUEAK! DON'T YOU KNOCK?!
IT-IT'S YOU! I'VE SEEN YOUR PICTURES IN THE PAPER!
YEAH. AND YOU'RE GONNA FORGET IT'S ME, IF YOU KNOW WHAT'S GOOD FOR YOU!
GOT IT? NOW PUT THE CHAMPERS OVER THERE, AND DON'T HANG AROUND FOR A TIP.
WHATEVER YOU SAY, MISTER MARX...
SHIT. RIGHT WHEN WE WAS CELEBRATIN', TOO.

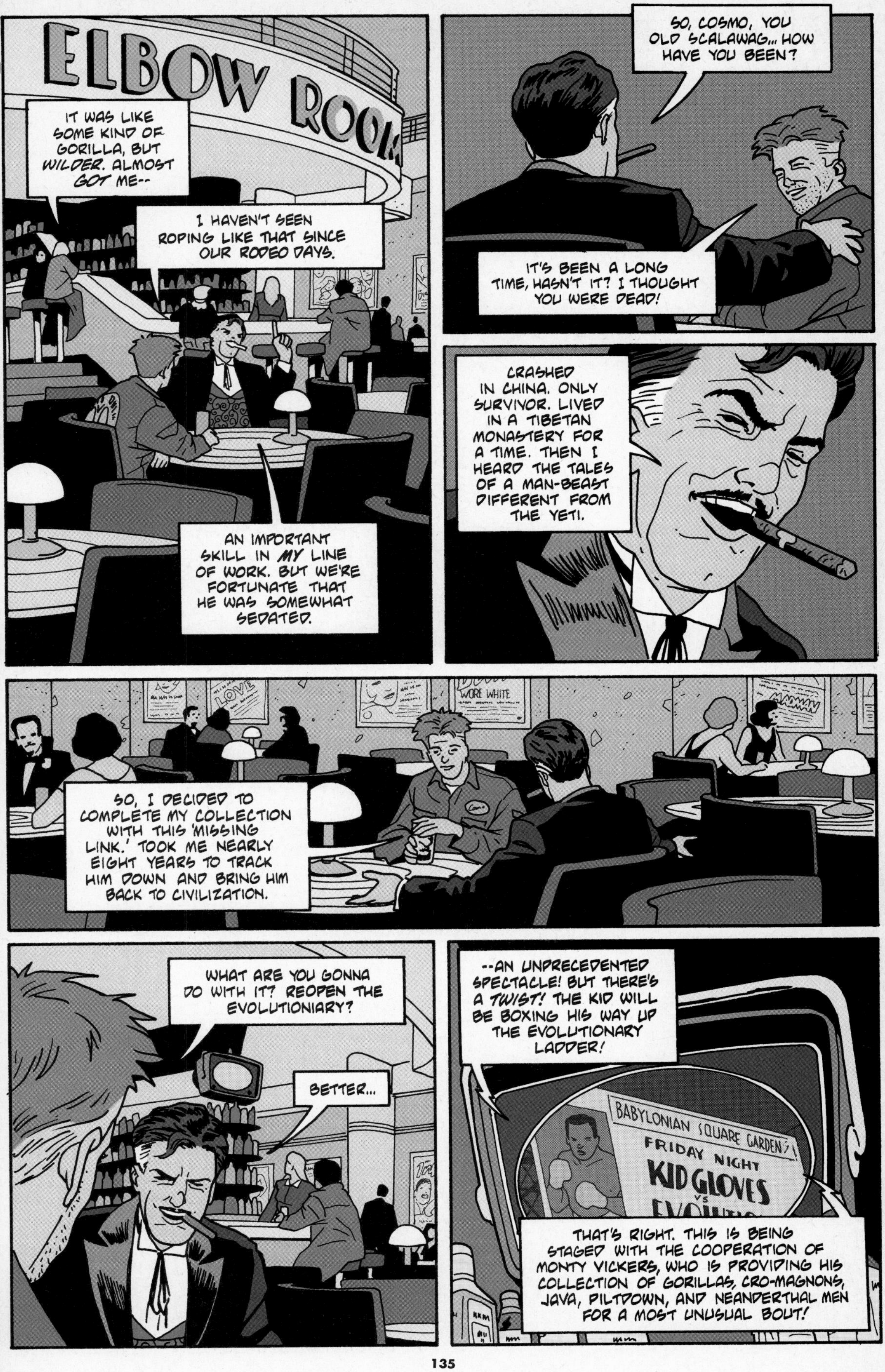
ELBOW ROOM
IT WAS LIKE SOME KIND OF GORILLA, BUT WILDER. ALMOST GOT ME--
I HAVEN'T SEEN ROPING LIKE THAT SINCE OUR RODEO DAYS.
AN IMPORTANT SKILL IN MY LINE OF WORK. BUT WE'RE FORTUNATE THAT HE WAS SOMEWHAT SEDATED.
SO, COSMO, YOU OLD SCALAWAG... HOW HAVE YOU BEEN?
IT'S BEEN A LONG TIME, HASN'T IT? I THOUGHT YOU WERE DEAD!
CRASHED IN CHINA. ONLY SURVIVOR. LIVED IN A TIBETAN MONASTERY FOR A TIME. THEN I HEARD THE TALES OF A MAN-BEAST DIFFERENT FROM THE YETI.
SO, I DECIDED TO COMPLETE MY COLLECTION WITH THIS 'MISSING LINK.' TOOK ME NEARLY EIGHT YEARS TO TRACK HIM DOWN AND BRING HIM BACK TO CIVILIZATION.
WHAT ARE YOU GONNA DO WITH IT? REOPEN THE EVOLUTIONIARY?
BETTER...
--AN UNPRECEDENTED SPECTACLE! BUT THERE'S A TWIST! THE KID WILL BE BOXING HIS WAY UP THE EVOLUTIONARY LADDER!
BABYLONIAN SQUARE GARDEN
FRIDAY NIGHT
KID GLOVES
VS
THAT'S RIGHT. THIS IS BEING STAGED WITH THE COOPERATION OF MONTY VICKERS, WHO IS PROVIDING HIS COLLECTION OF GORILLAS, CRO-MAGNONS, JAVA, PILTDOWN, AND NEANDERTHAL MEN FOR A MOST UNUSUAL BOUT!

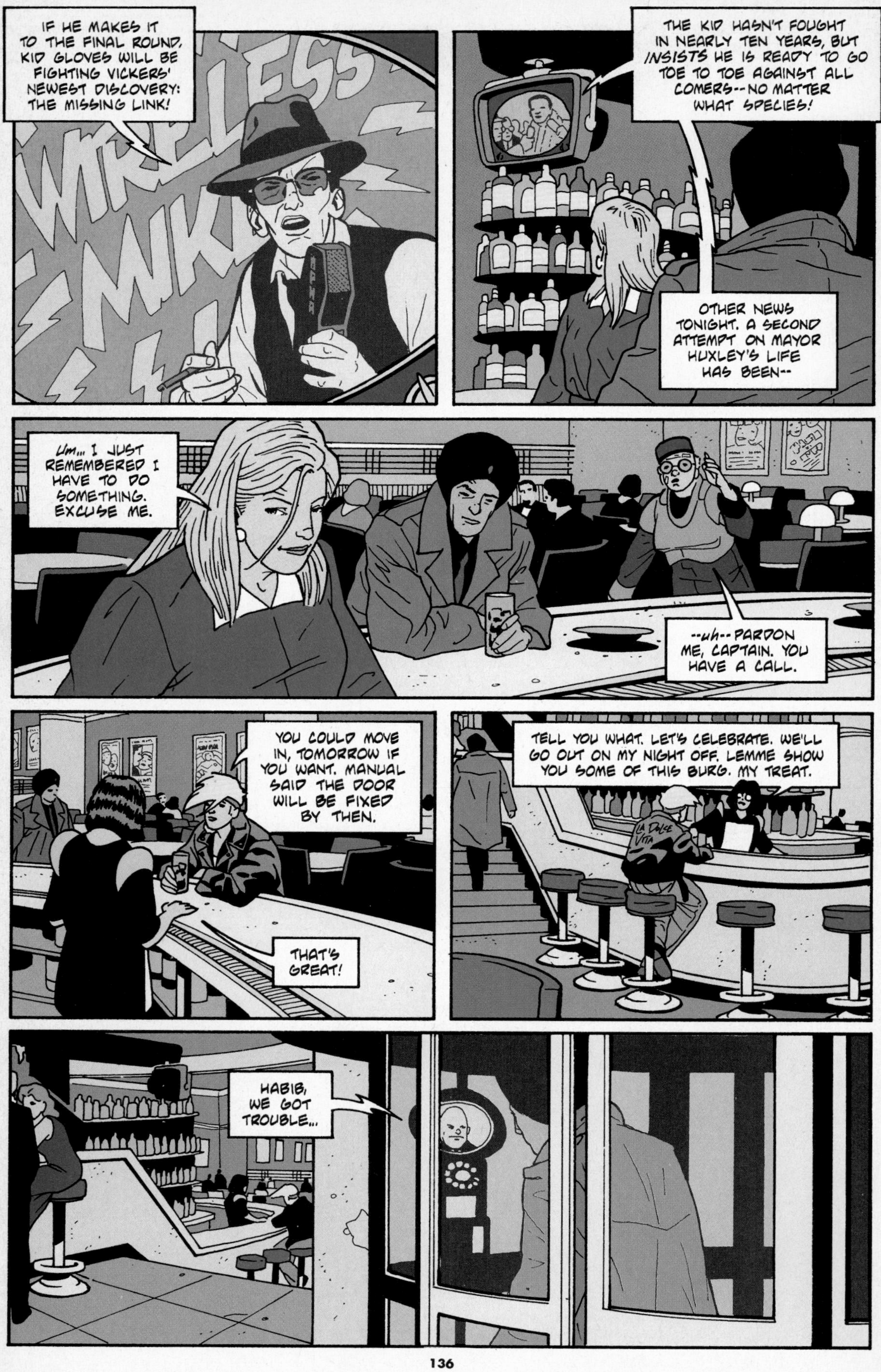
IF HE MAKES IT TO THE FINAL ROUND, KID GLOVES WILL BE FIGHTING VICKERS' NEWEST DISCOVERY: THE MISSING LINK!
THE KID HASN'T FOUGHT IN NEARLY TEN YEARS, BUT INSISTS HE IS READY TO GO TOE TO TOE AGAINST ALL COMERS--NO MATTER WHAT SPECIES!
OTHER NEWS TONIGHT. A SECOND ATTEMPT ON MAYOR HUXLEY'S LIFE HAS BEEN--
UM... I JUST REMEMBERED I HAVE TO DO SOMETHING. EXCUSE ME.
--UH--PARDON ME, CAPTAIN. YOU HAVE A CALL.
YOU COULD MOVE IN, TOMORROW IF YOU WANT. MANUAL SAID THE DOOR WILL BE FIXED BY THEN.
THAT'S GREAT!
TELL YOU WHAT. LET'S CELEBRATE. WE'LL GO OUT ON MY NIGHT OFF. LEMME SHOW YOU SOME OF THIS BURG. MY TREAT.
LA DOLCE VITA
HABIB, WE GOT TROUBLE...

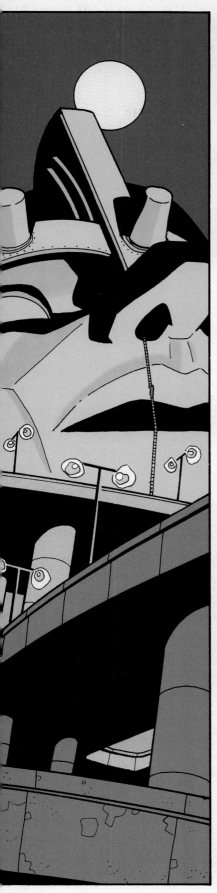

WELL, WHAT IS IT NOW, BLACK? IT'S RISKY SHOWIN' UP HERE.

IT'S VICKERS. HE'S BACK. HE'S GONNA BE TROUBLE. AFTER THIS PUBLICITY STUNT, I THINK HE'S GONNA EXPOSE THE SLANT-TOWN DEAL.

I THOUGHT HE WAS DEAD.

SO? THEY THINK YOU'RE DEAD TOO.

YOU WANT ME TO DEAL WITH HIM?

OF COURSE.

I'VE TOLD DIMAPPE TO DO IT, BUT HE'S A PUTZ. HE'LL BLOW IT.

IT'S GONNA TAKE SOME SOMOLIANS. AND IT'S GONNA HAVE TO WAIT TILL I'VE FINISHED ANOTHER "PROJECT" I'M WORK- ING ON.

THE DOUGH IS NO PROBLEM. BUT I NEED IT DONE BY NEXT WEEK.

FINE.

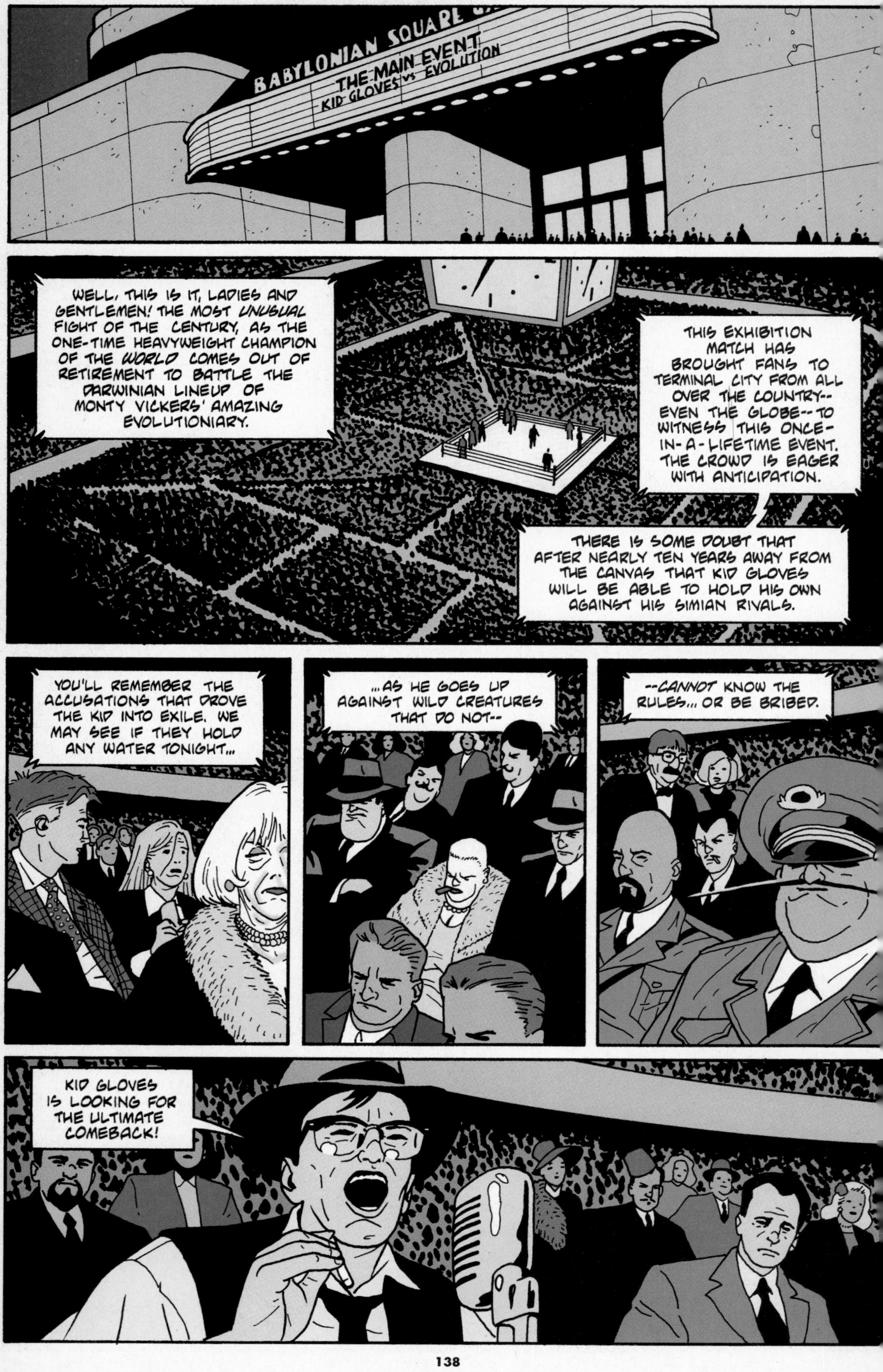
BABYLONIAN SQUARE
THE MAIN EVENT
KID GLOVES VS EVOLUTION
WELL, THIS IS IT, LADIES AND GENTLEMEN! THE MOST UNUSUAL FIGHT OF THE CENTURY, AS THE ONE-TIME HEAVYWEIGHT CHAMPION OF THE WORLD COMES OUT OF RETIREMENT TO BATTLE THE DARWINIAN LINEUP OF MONTY VICKERS' AMAZING EVOLUTIONIARY.
THIS EXHIBITION MATCH HAS BROUGHT FANS TO TERMINAL CITY FROM ALL OVER THE COUNTRY-- EVEN THE GLOBE-- TO WITNESS THIS ONCE-IN-A-LIFETIME EVENT. THE CROWD IS EAGER WITH ANTICIPATION.
THERE IS SOME DOUBT THAT AFTER NEARLY TEN YEARS AWAY FROM THE CANVAS THAT KID GLOVES WILL BE ABLE TO HOLD HIS OWN AGAINST HIS SIMIAN RIVALS.
YOU'LL REMEMBER THE ACCUSATIONS THAT DROVE THE KID INTO EXILE. WE MAY SEE IF THEY HOLD ANY WATER TONIGHT...
...AS HE GOES UP AGAINST WILD CREATURES THAT DO NOT--
--CANNOT KNOW THE RULES... OR BE BRIBED.
KID GLOVES IS LOOKING FOR THE ULTIMATE COMEBACK!

A HUSH GOES OVER THE CROWD AS THE M.C., MISTER PHILLIP McCANN, ENTERS THE RING!

LADIES AND GENTLEMEN! IN THIS CORNER, WEIGHING 256 POUNDS, FORMER HEAVYWEIGHT CHAMPION OF THE WORLD! *KID GLOVES!*

AND IN THIS CORNER! WEIGHING APPROXIMATELY 600 POUNDS--

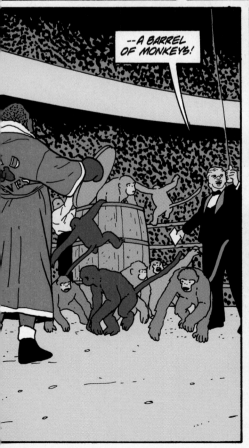

--A BARREL OF MONKEYS!

BUT SERIOUSLY, LADIES AND GENTLEMEN...

...IN THIS CORNER, WEIGHING 1500 POUNDS: A MOUNTAIN GORILLA FROM DEEPEST DARKEST AFRICA!

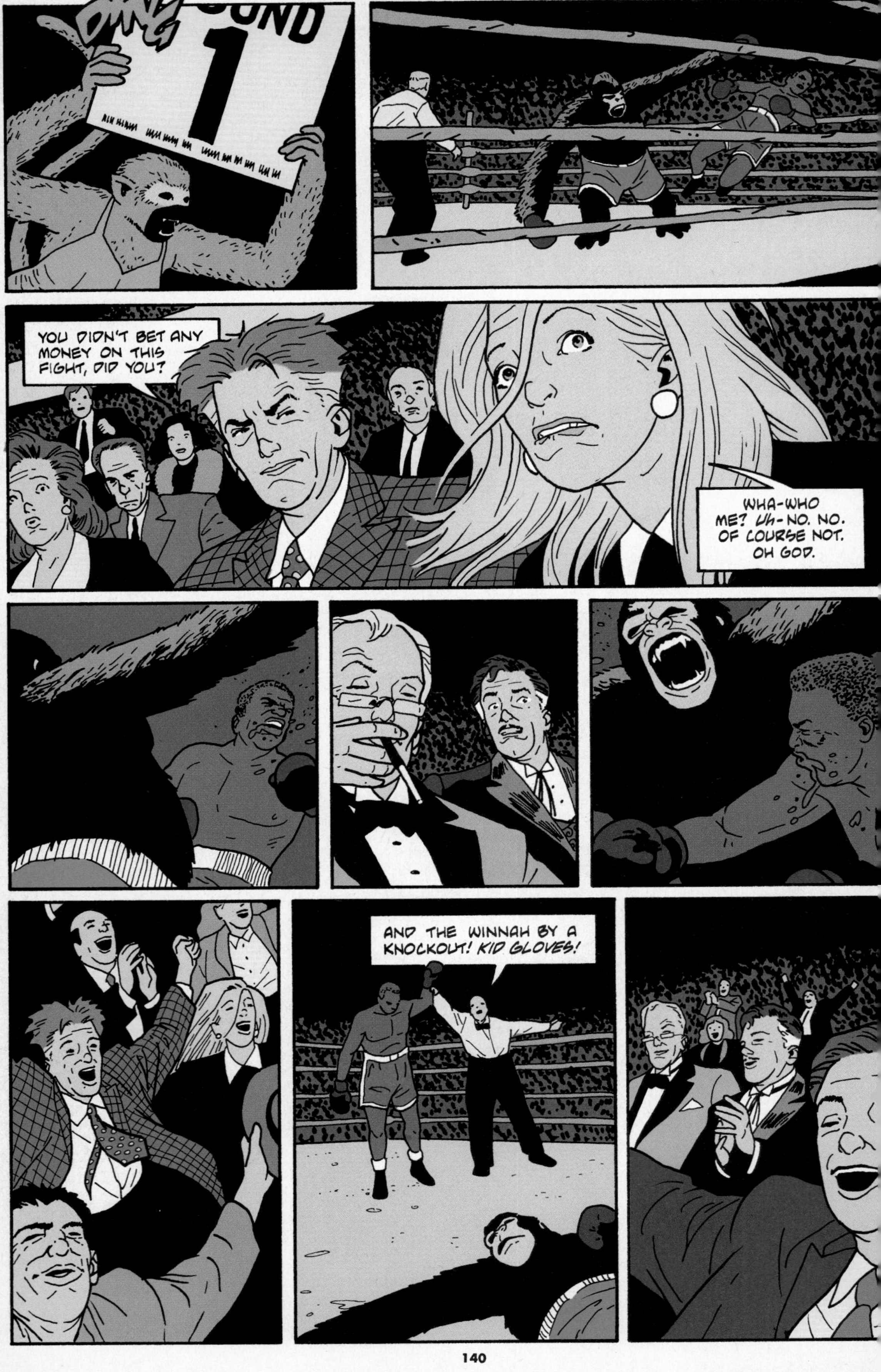

DING
1
YOU DIDN'T BET ANY MONEY ON THIS FIGHT, DID YOU?
WHA-WHO ME? UH- NO. NO. OF COURSE NOT. OH GOD.
AND THE WINNAH BY A KNOCKOUT! KID GLOVES!

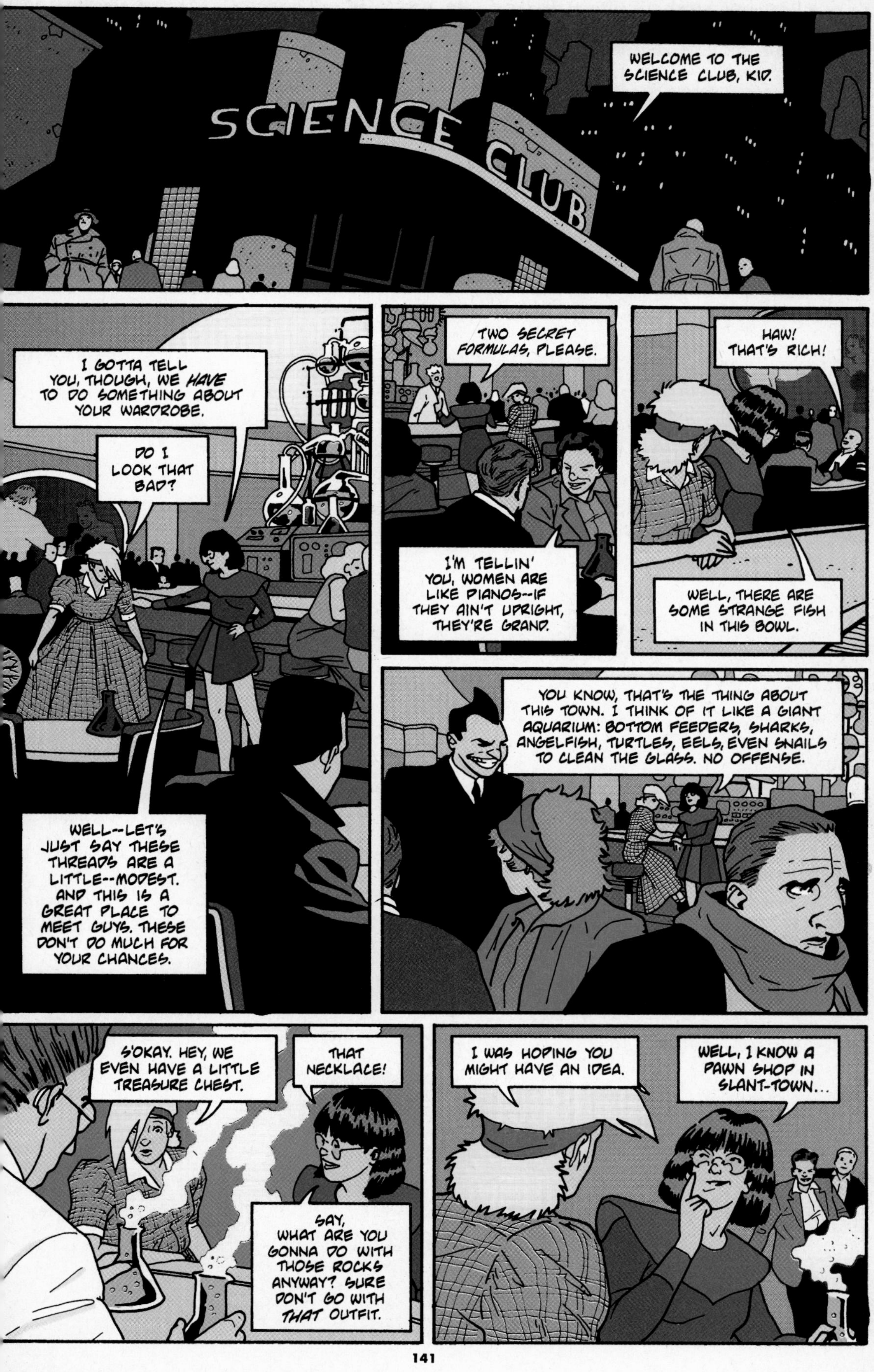
SCIENCE CLUB
WELCOME TO THE SCIENCE CLUB, KID.
I GOTTA TELL YOU, THOUGH, WE HAVE TO DO SOMETHING ABOUT YOUR WARDROBE.
DO I LOOK THAT BAD?
WELL--LET'S JUST SAY THESE THREADS ARE A LITTLE--MODEST. AND THIS IS A GREAT PLACE TO MEET GUYS. THESE DON'T DO MUCH FOR YOUR CHANCES.
TWO SECRET FORMULAS, PLEASE.
I'M TELLIN' YOU, WOMEN ARE LIKE PIANOS--IF THEY AIN'T UPRIGHT, THEY'RE GRAND.
HAW! THAT'S RICH!
WELL, THERE ARE SOME STRANGE FISH IN THIS BOWL.
YOU KNOW, THAT'S THE THING ABOUT THIS TOWN. I THINK OF IT LIKE A GIANT AQUARIUM: BOTTOM FEEDERS, SHARKS, ANGELFISH, TURTLES, EELS, EVEN SNAILS TO CLEAN THE GLASS. NO OFFENSE.
S'OKAY. HEY, WE EVEN HAVE A LITTLE TREASURE CHEST.
THAT NECKLACE!
SAY, WHAT ARE YOU GONNA DO WITH THOSE ROCKS ANYWAY? SURE DON'T GO WITH THAT OUTFIT.
I WAS HOPING YOU MIGHT HAVE AN IDEA.
WELL, I KNOW A PAWN SHOP IN SLANT-TOWN...

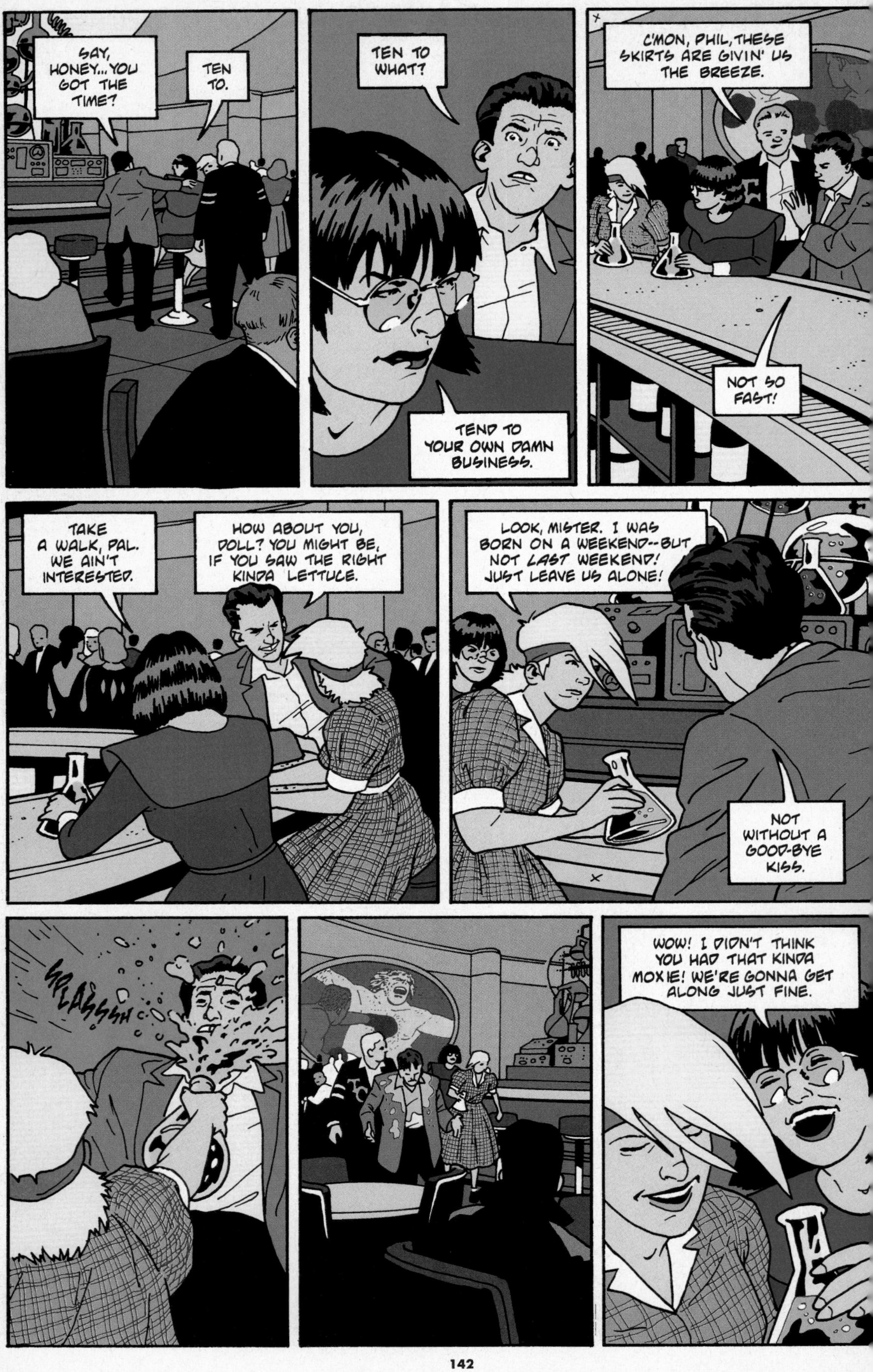
SAY, HONEY... YOU GOT THE TIME?
TEN TO.
TEN TO WHAT?
TEND TO YOUR OWN DAMN BUSINESS.
C'MON, PHIL, THESE SKIRTS ARE GIVIN' US THE BREEZE.
NOT SO FAST!
TAKE A WALK, PAL. WE AIN'T INTERESTED.
HOW ABOUT YOU, DOLL? YOU MIGHT BE, IF YOU SAW THE RIGHT KINDA LETTUCE.
LOOK, MISTER. I WAS BORN ON A WEEKEND--BUT NOT *LAST* WEEKEND! JUST LEAVE US ALONE!
NOT WITHOUT A GOOD-BYE KISS.
SPLASSSH
WOW! I DIDN'T THINK YOU HAD THAT KINDA MOXIE! WE'RE GONNA GET ALONG JUST FINE.

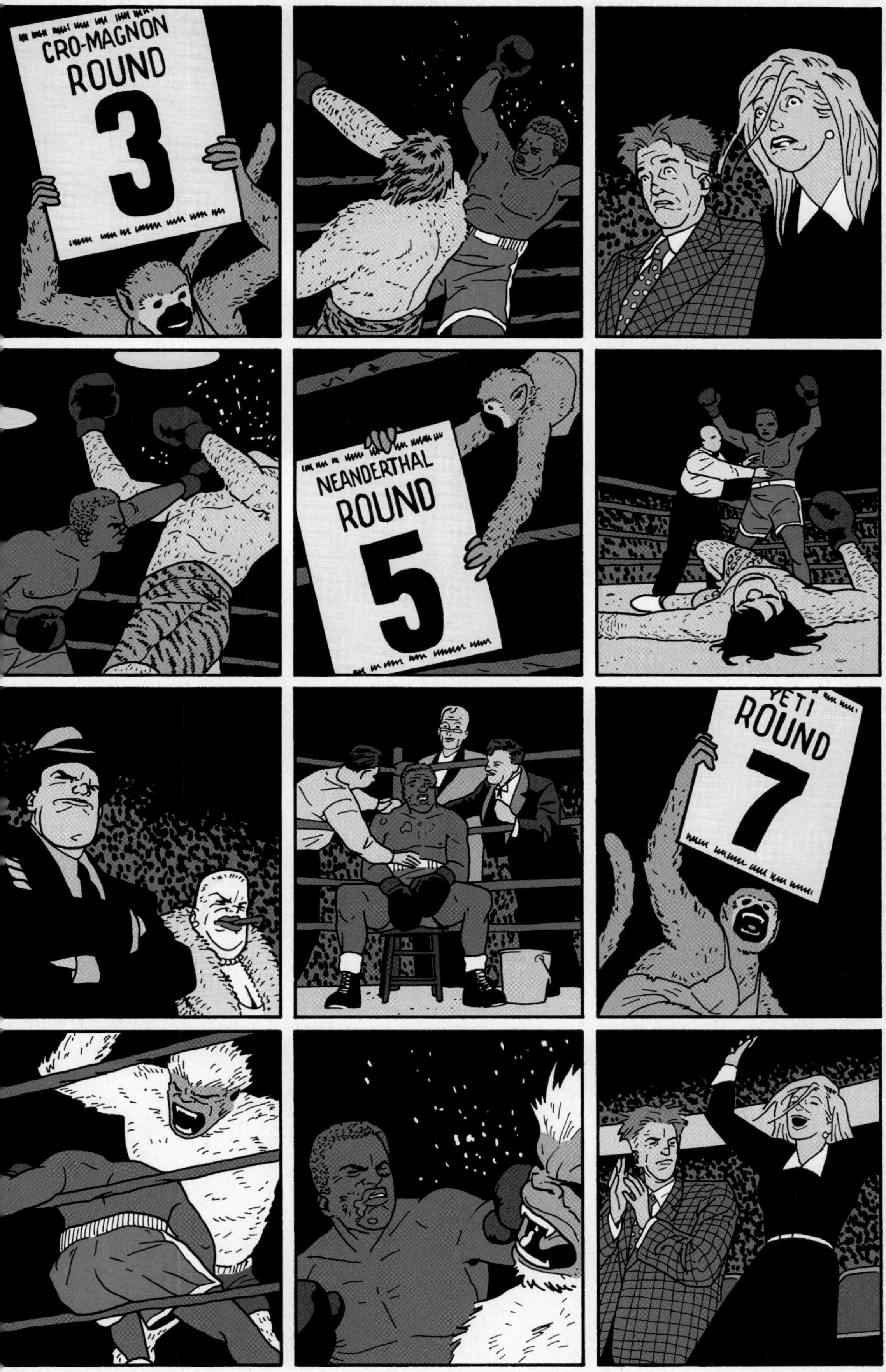
CRO-MAGNON
ROUND
3
NEANDERTHAL
ROUND
5
YETI
ROUND
7

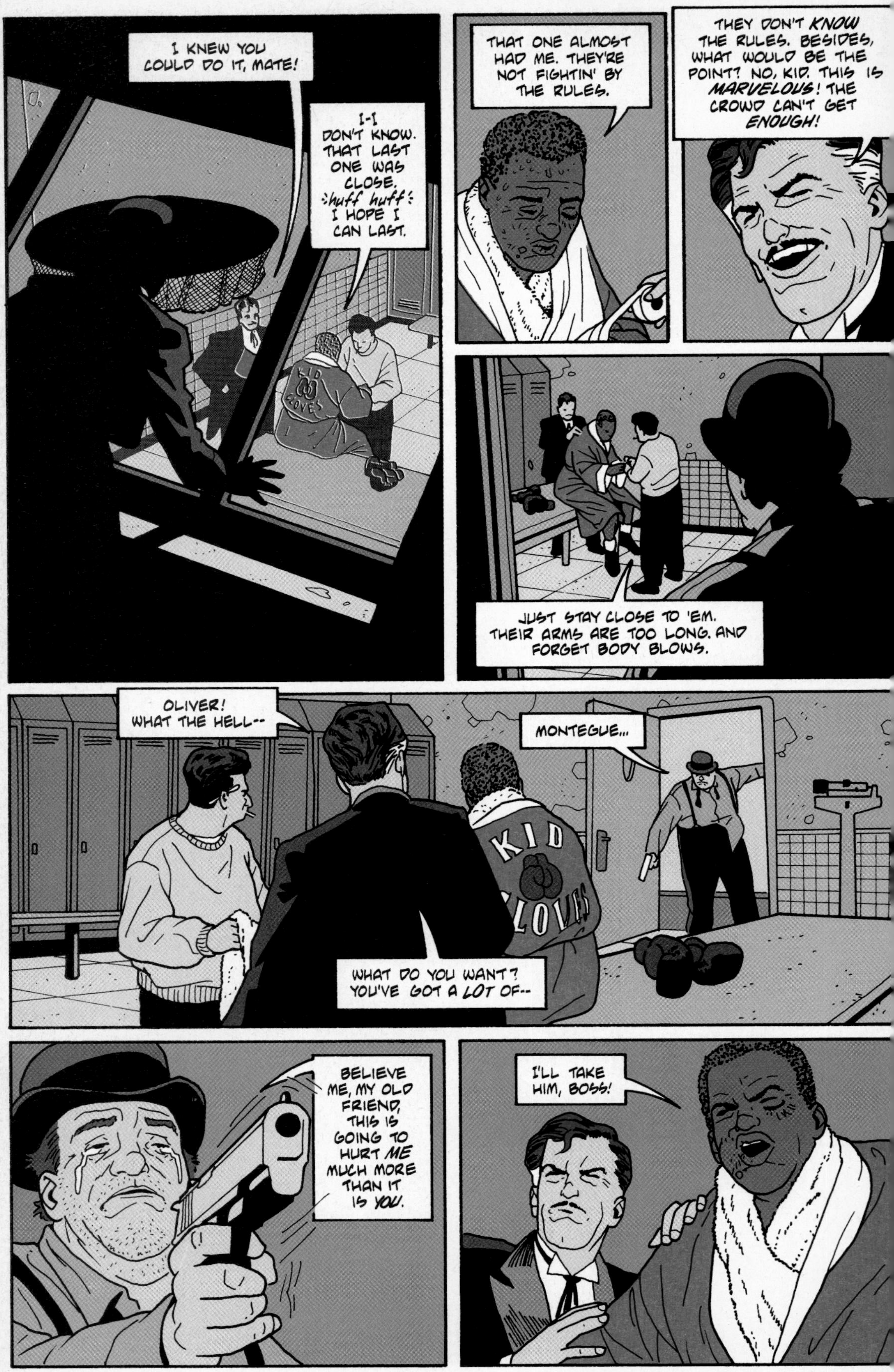

I KNEW YOU COULD DO IT, MATE!
I-I DON'T KNOW. THAT LAST ONE WAS CLOSE. *huff huff* I HOPE I CAN LAST.
THAT ONE ALMOST HAD ME. THEY'RE NOT FIGHTIN' BY THE RULES.
THEY DON'T KNOW THE RULES. BESIDES, WHAT WOULD BE THE POINT? NO, KID. THIS IS MARVELOUS! THE CROWD CAN'T GET ENOUGH!
JUST STAY CLOSE TO 'EM. THEIR ARMS ARE TOO LONG. AND FORGET BODY BLOWS.
OLIVER! WHAT THE HELL--
MONTEGUE...
WHAT DO YOU WANT? YOU'VE GOT A LOT OF--
BELIEVE ME, MY OLD FRIEND, THIS IS GOING TO HURT ME MUCH MORE THAN IT IS YOU.
I'LL TAKE HIM, BOSS!

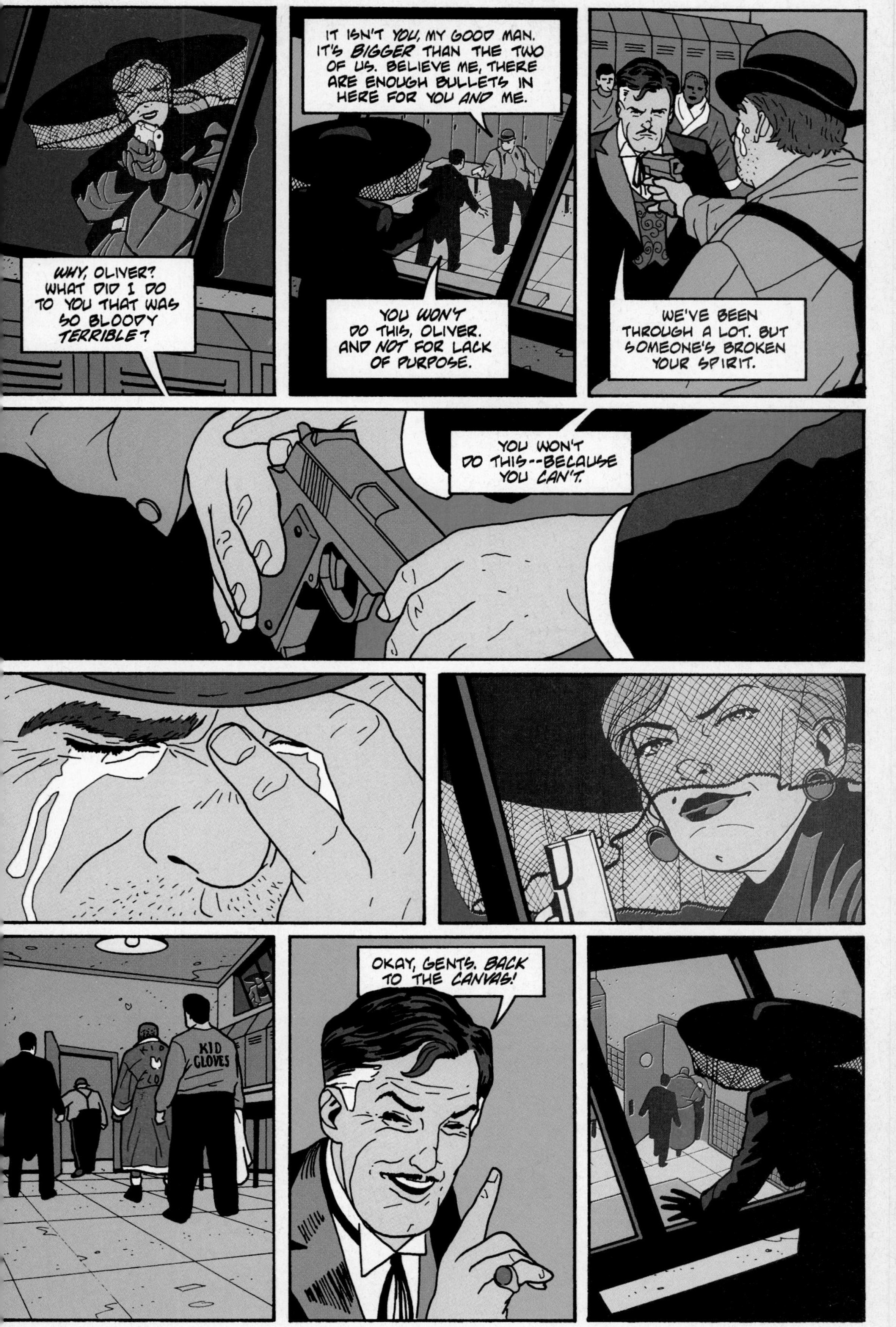
WHY, OLIVER? WHAT DID I DO TO YOU THAT WAS SO BLOODY TERRIBLE?
IT ISN'T YOU, MY GOOD MAN. IT'S BIGGER THAN THE TWO OF US. BELIEVE ME, THERE ARE ENOUGH BULLETS IN HERE FOR YOU AND ME.
YOU WON'T DO THIS, OLIVER. AND NOT FOR LACK OF PURPOSE.
WE'VE BEEN THROUGH A LOT. BUT SOMEONE'S BROKEN YOUR SPIRIT.
YOU WON'T DO THIS--BECAUSE YOU CAN'T.
KID GLOVES
OKAY, GENTS. BACK TO THE CANVAS!

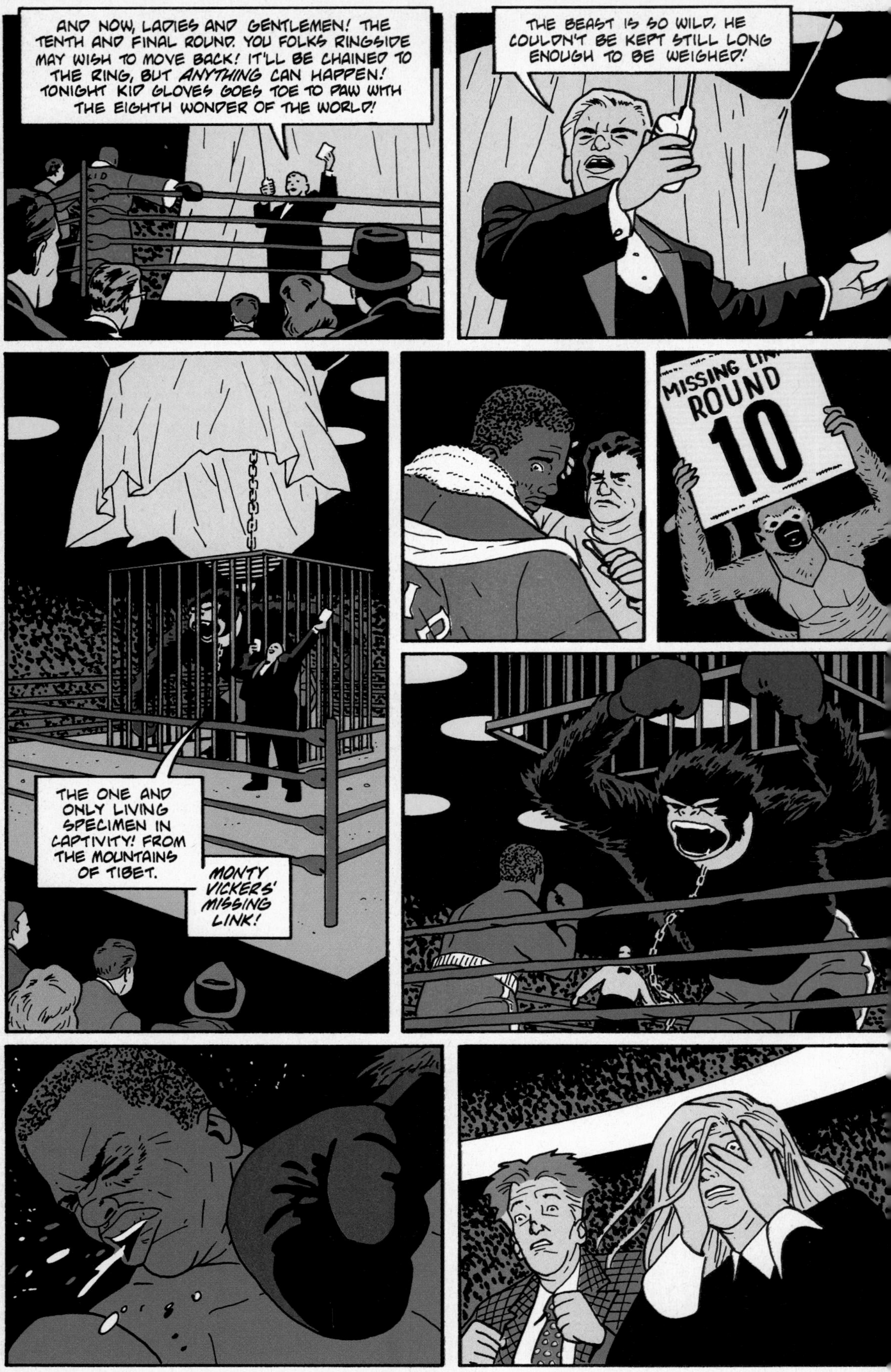
AND NOW, LADIES AND GENTLEMEN! THE TENTH AND FINAL ROUND. YOU FOLKS RINGSIDE MAY WISH TO MOVE BACK! IT'LL BE CHAINED TO THE RING, BUT ANYTHING CAN HAPPEN! TONIGHT KID GLOVES GOES TOE TO PAW WITH THE EIGHTH WONDER OF THE WORLD!
THE BEAST IS SO WILD, HE COULDN'T BE KEPT STILL LONG ENOUGH TO BE WEIGHED!
THE ONE AND ONLY LIVING SPECIMEN IN CAPTIVITY! FROM THE MOUNTAINS OF TIBET.
MONTY VICKERS' MISSING LINK!
MISSING LI
ROUND
10

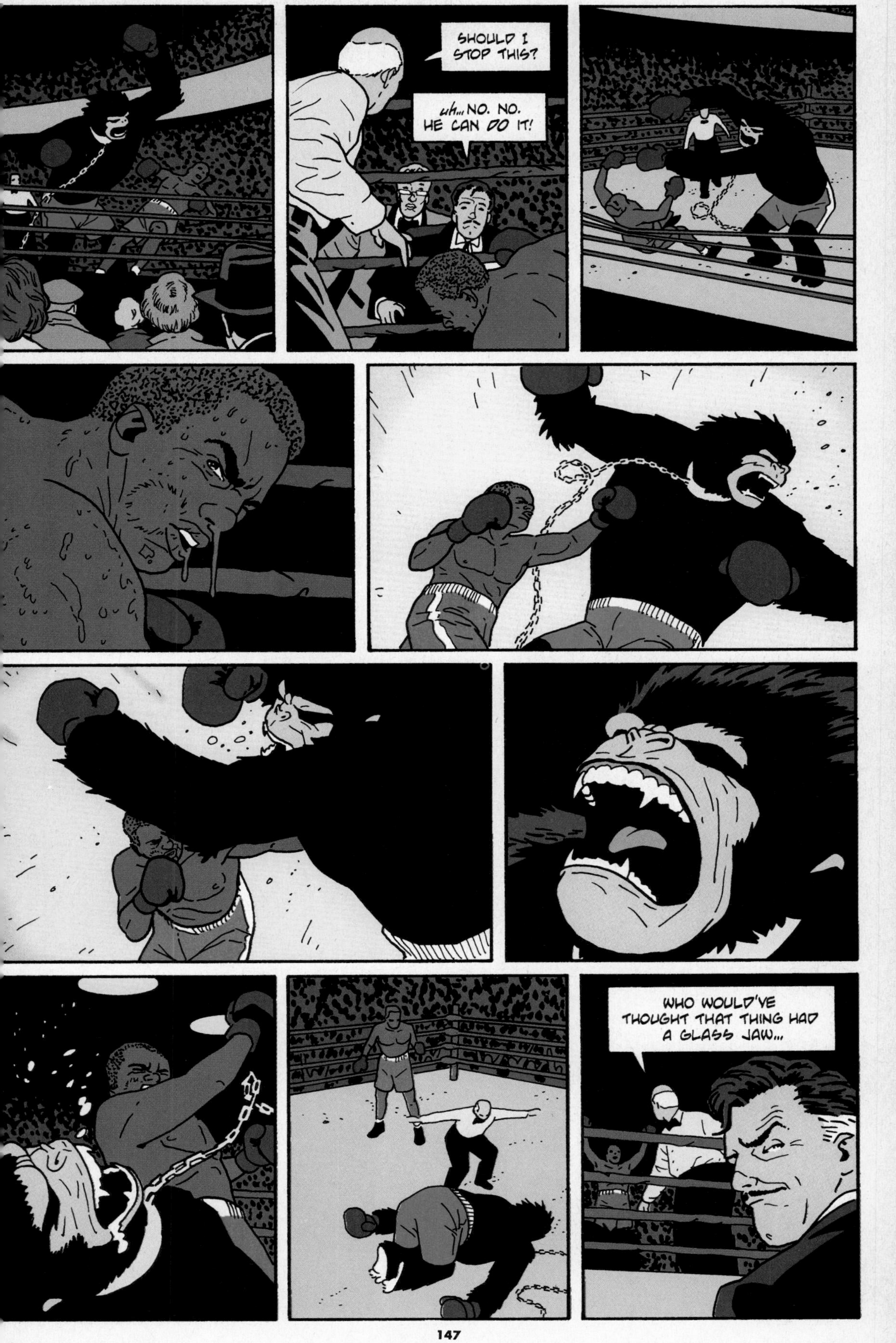
SHOULD I STOP THIS?
uh... NO. NO. HE CAN DO IT!
WHO WOULD'VE THOUGHT THAT THING HAD A GLASS JAW...

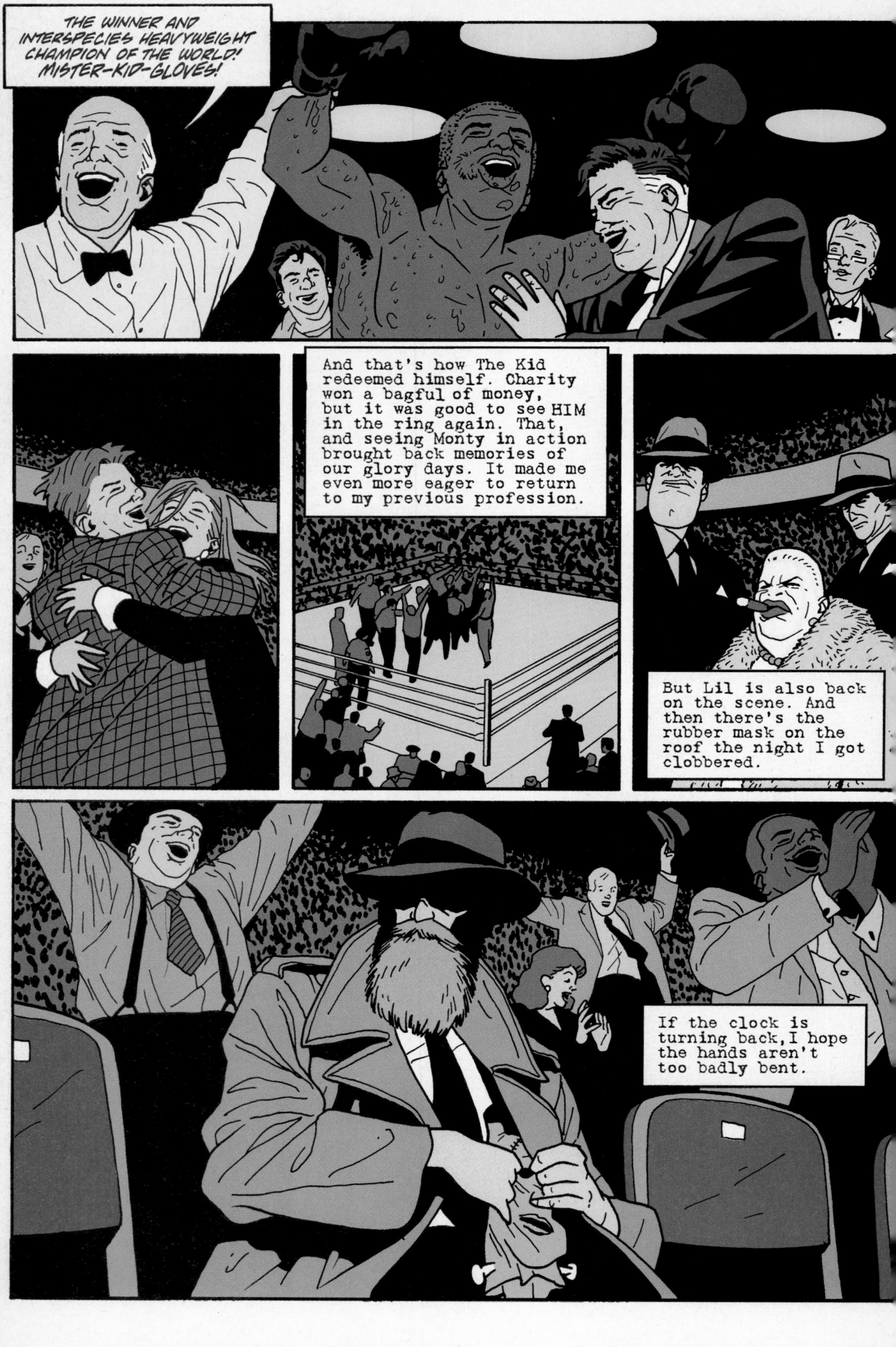
THE WINNER AND INTERSPECIES HEAVYWEIGHT CHAMPION OF THE WORLD! MISTER-KID-GLOVES!
And that's how The Kid redeemed himself. Charity won a bagful of money, but it was good to see HIM in the ring again. That, and seeing Monty in action brought back memories of our glory days. It made me even more eager to return to my previous profession.
But Lil is also back on the scene. And then there's the rubber mask on the roof the night I got clobbered.
If the clock is turning back, I hope the hands aren't too badly bent.

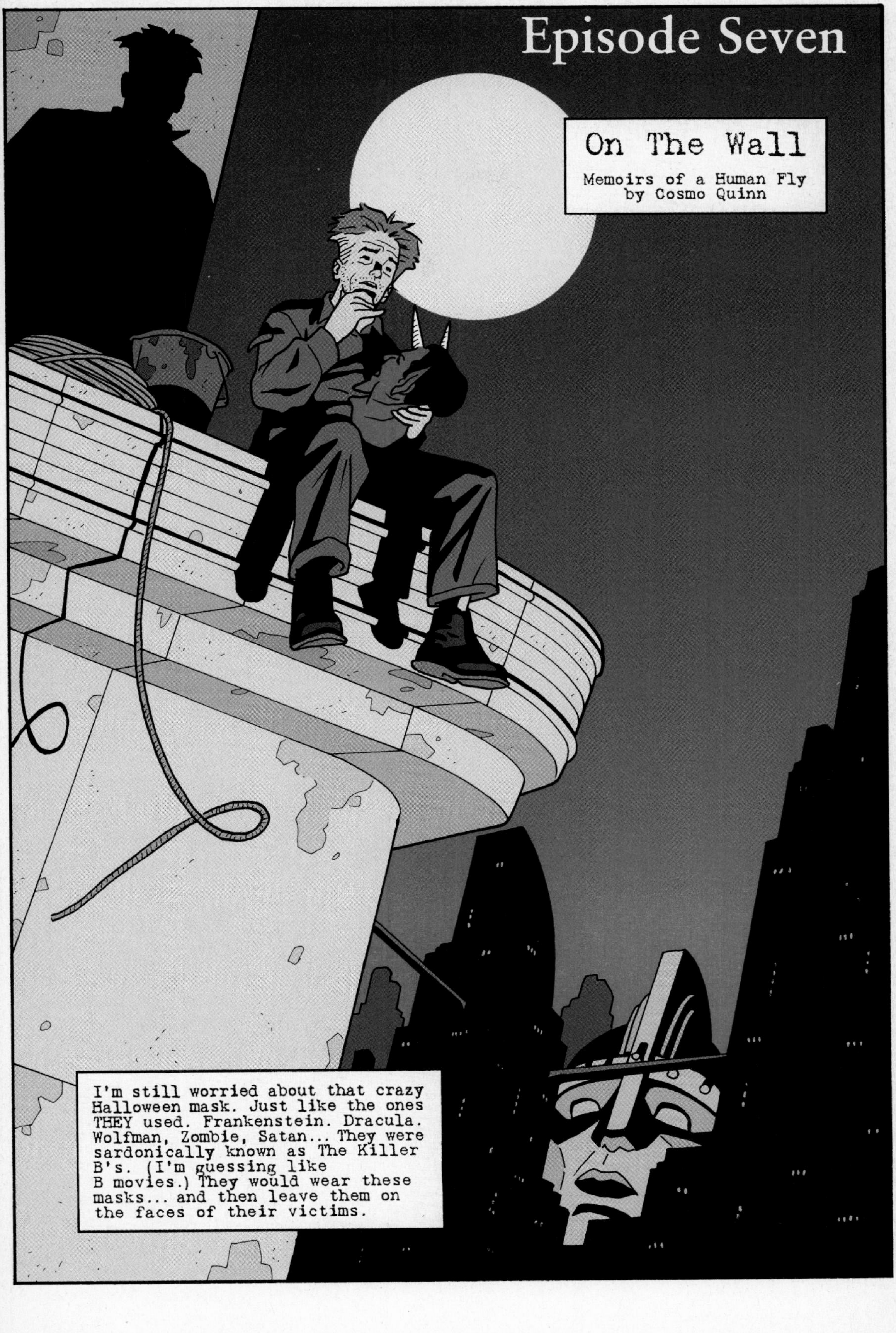

Episode Seven
On The Wall
Memoirs of a Human Fly
by Cosmo Quinn
I'm still worried about that crazy Halloween mask. Just like the ones THEY used. Frankenstein. Dracula. Wolfman, Zombie, Satan... They were sardonically known as The Killer B's. (I'm guessing like B movies.) They would wear these masks... and then leave them on the faces of their victims.

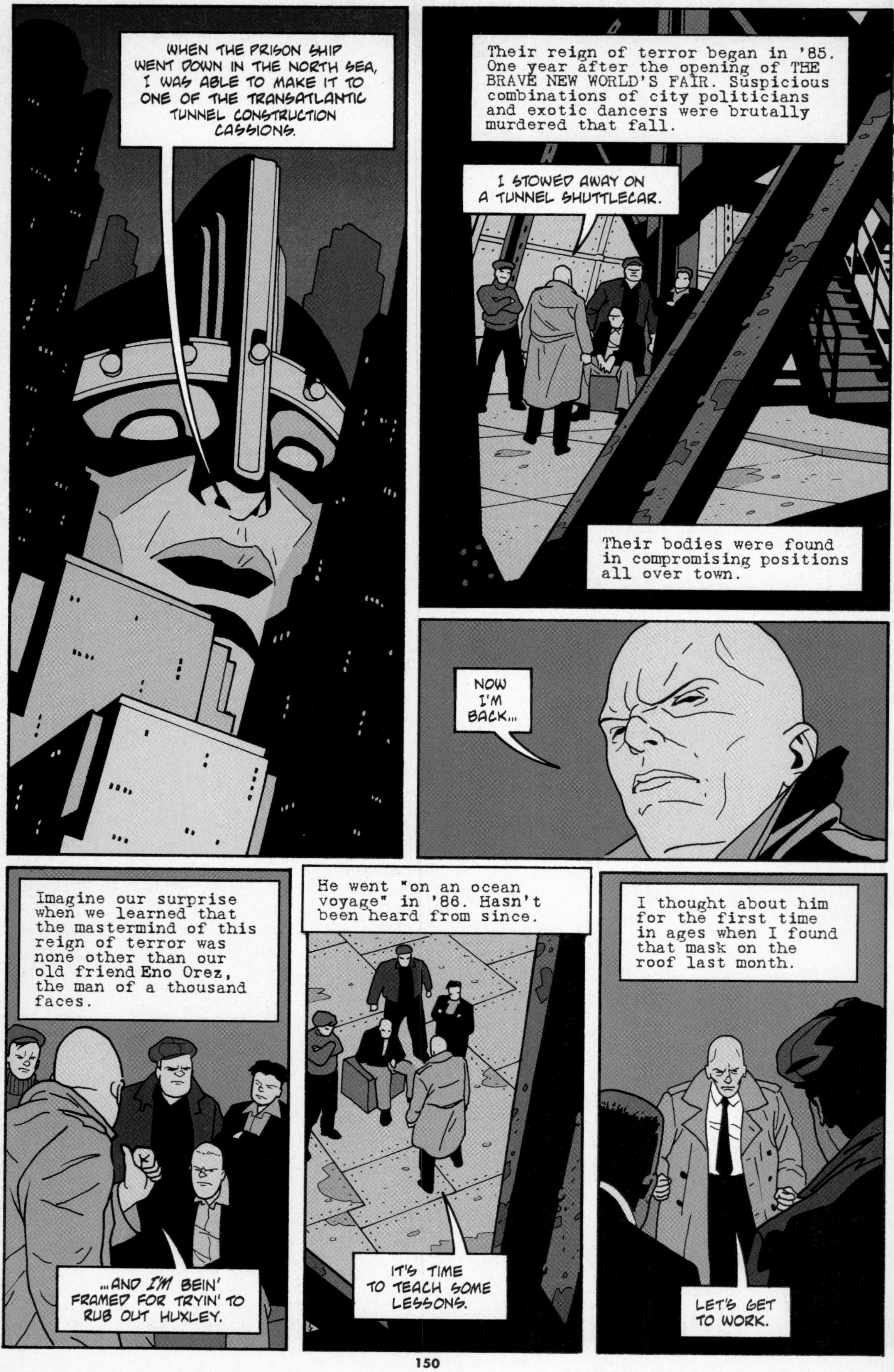
WHEN THE PRISON SHIP WENT DOWN IN THE NORTH SEA, I WAS ABLE TO MAKE IT TO ONE OF THE TRANSATLANTIC TUNNEL CONSTRUCTION CASSIONS.
Their reign of terror began in '85. One year after the opening of THE BRAVE NEW WORLD'S FAIR. Suspicious combinations of city politicians and exotic dancers were brutally murdered that fall.
I STOWED AWAY ON A TUNNEL SHUTTLECAR.
Their bodies were found in compromising positions all over town.
NOW I'M BACK...
Imagine our surprise when we learned that the mastermind of this reign of terror was none other than our old friend Eno Orez, the man of a thousand faces.
...AND I'M BEIN' FRAMED FOR TRYIN' TO RUB OUT HUXLEY.
He went "on an ocean voyage" in '86. Hasn't been heard from since.
IT'S TIME TO TEACH SOME LESSONS.
I thought about him for the first time in ages when I found that mask on the roof last month.
LET'S GET TO WORK.

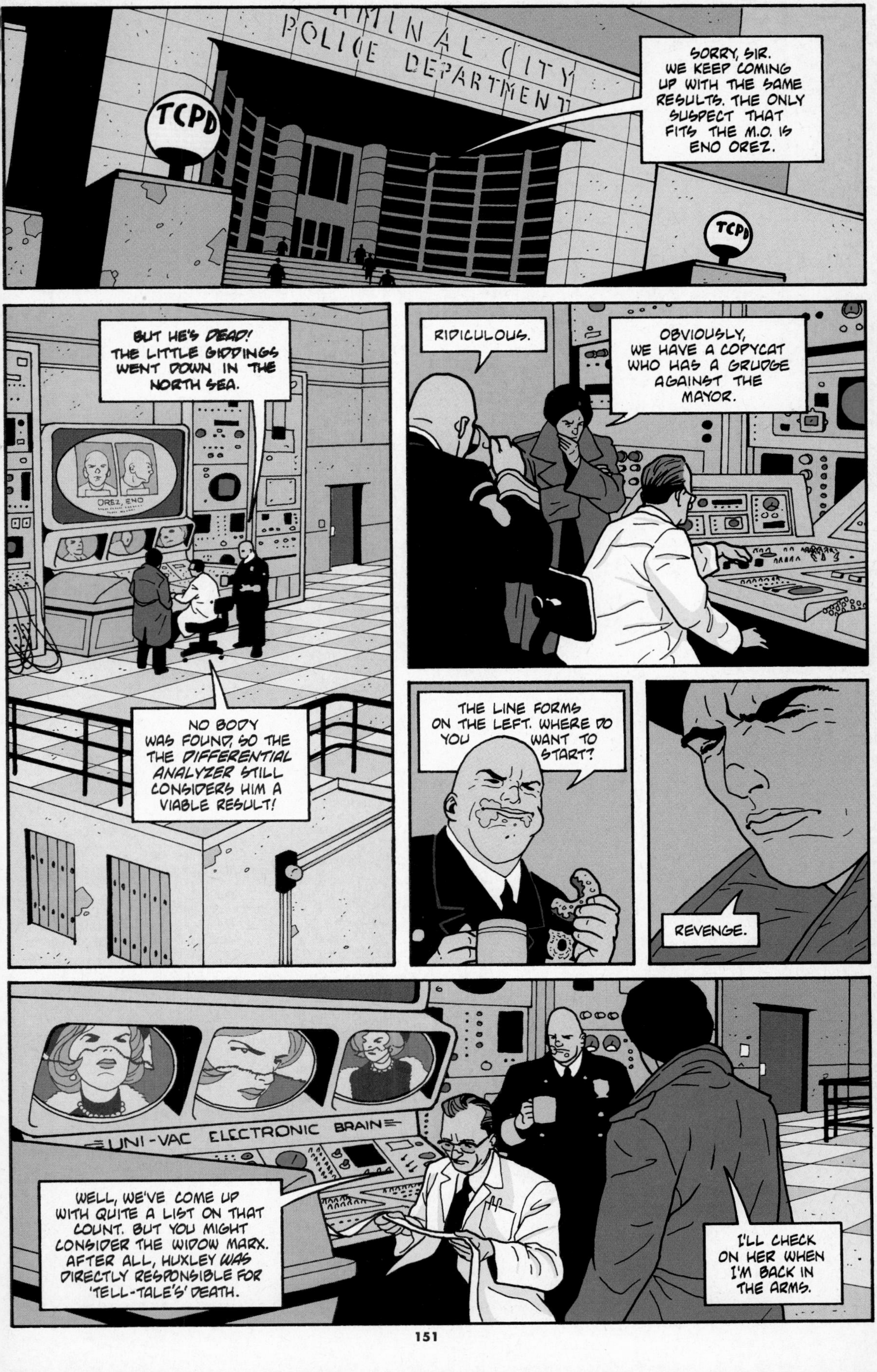

POLICE DEPARTMENT
TCPD
SORRY, SIR. WE KEEP COMING UP WITH THE SAME RESULTS. THE ONLY SUSPECT THAT FITS THE M.O. IS ENO OREZ.
TCPD
BUT HE'S DEAD! THE LITTLE GIDDINGS WENT DOWN IN THE NORTH SEA.
OREZ, ENO
NO BODY WAS FOUND, SO THE THE DIFFERENTIAL ANALYZER STILL CONSIDERS HIM A VIABLE RESULT!
RIDICULOUS.
OBVIOUSLY, WE HAVE A COPYCAT WHO HAS A GRUDGE AGAINST THE MAYOR.
THE LINE FORMS ON THE LEFT. WHERE DO YOU WANT TO START?
REVENGE.
UNI-VAC ELECTRONIC BRAIN
WELL, WE'VE COME UP WITH QUITE A LIST ON THAT COUNT. BUT YOU MIGHT CONSIDER THE WIDOW MARX. AFTER ALL, HUXLEY WAS DIRECTLY RESPONSIBLE FOR 'TELL-TALE'S' DEATH.
I'LL CHECK ON HER WHEN I'M BACK IN THE ARMS.

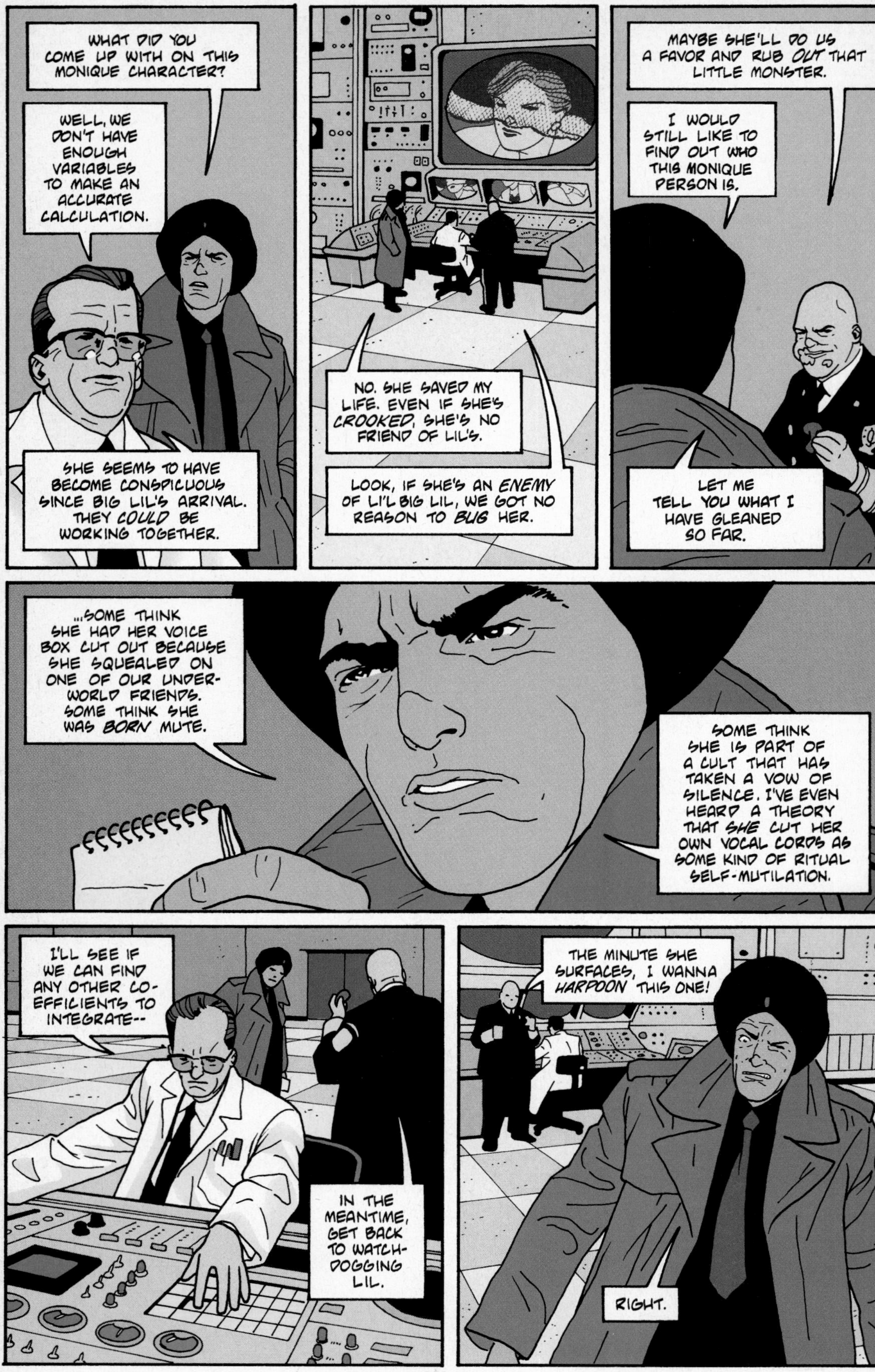
WHAT DID YOU COME UP WITH ON THIS MONIQUE CHARACTER?
WELL, WE DON'T HAVE ENOUGH VARIABLES TO MAKE AN ACCURATE CALCULATION.
SHE SEEMS TO HAVE BECOME CONSPICUOUS SINCE BIG LIL'S ARRIVAL. THEY COULD BE WORKING TOGETHER.
NO. SHE SAVED MY LIFE. EVEN IF SHE'S CROOKED, SHE'S NO FRIEND OF LIL'S.
LOOK, IF SHE'S AN ENEMY OF LI'L BIG LIL, WE GOT NO REASON TO BUG HER.
MAYBE SHE'LL DO US A FAVOR AND RUB OUT THAT LITTLE MONSTER.
I WOULD STILL LIKE TO FIND OUT WHO THIS MONIQUE PERSON IS.
LET ME TELL YOU WHAT I HAVE GLEANED SO FAR.
...SOME THINK SHE HAD HER VOICE BOX CUT OUT BECAUSE SHE SQUEALED ON ONE OF OUR UNDER-WORLD FRIENDS. SOME THINK SHE WAS BORN MUTE.
SOME THINK SHE IS PART OF A CULT THAT HAS TAKEN A VOW OF SILENCE. I'VE EVEN HEARD A THEORY THAT SHE CUT HER OWN VOCAL CORDS AS SOME KIND OF RITUAL SELF-MUTILATION.
I'LL SEE IF WE CAN FIND ANY OTHER CO-EFFICIENTS TO INTEGRATE--
IN THE MEANTIME, GET BACK TO WATCH-DOGGING LIL.
THE MINUTE SHE SURFACES, I WANNA HARPOON THIS ONE!
RIGHT.

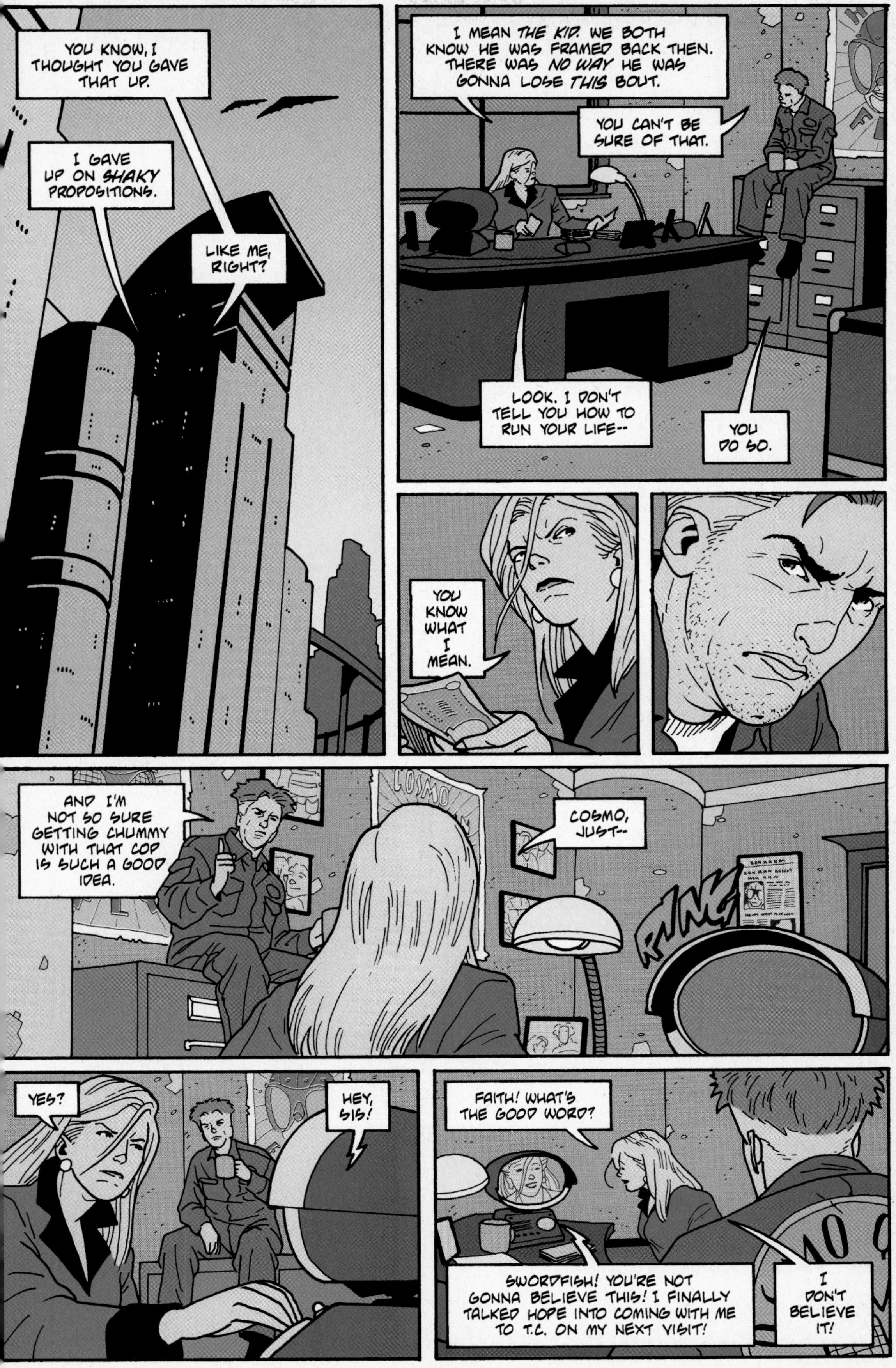
YOU KNOW, I THOUGHT YOU GAVE THAT UP.
I GAVE UP ON SHAKY PROPOSITIONS.
LIKE ME, RIGHT?
I MEAN THE KID. WE BOTH KNOW HE WAS FRAMED BACK THEN. THERE WAS NO WAY HE WAS GONNA LOSE THIS BOUT.
YOU CAN'T BE SURE OF THAT.
LOOK. I DON'T TELL YOU HOW TO RUN YOUR LIFE--
YOU DO SO.
YOU KNOW WHAT I MEAN.
AND I'M NOT SO SURE GETTING CHUMMY WITH THAT COP IS SUCH A GOOD IDEA.
COSMO, JUST--
RING
YES?
HEY, SIS!
FAITH! WHAT'S THE GOOD WORD?
SWORDFISH! YOU'RE NOT GONNA BELIEVE THIS! I FINALLY TALKED HOPE INTO COMING WITH ME TO T.C. ON MY NEXT VISIT!
I DON'T BELIEVE IT!

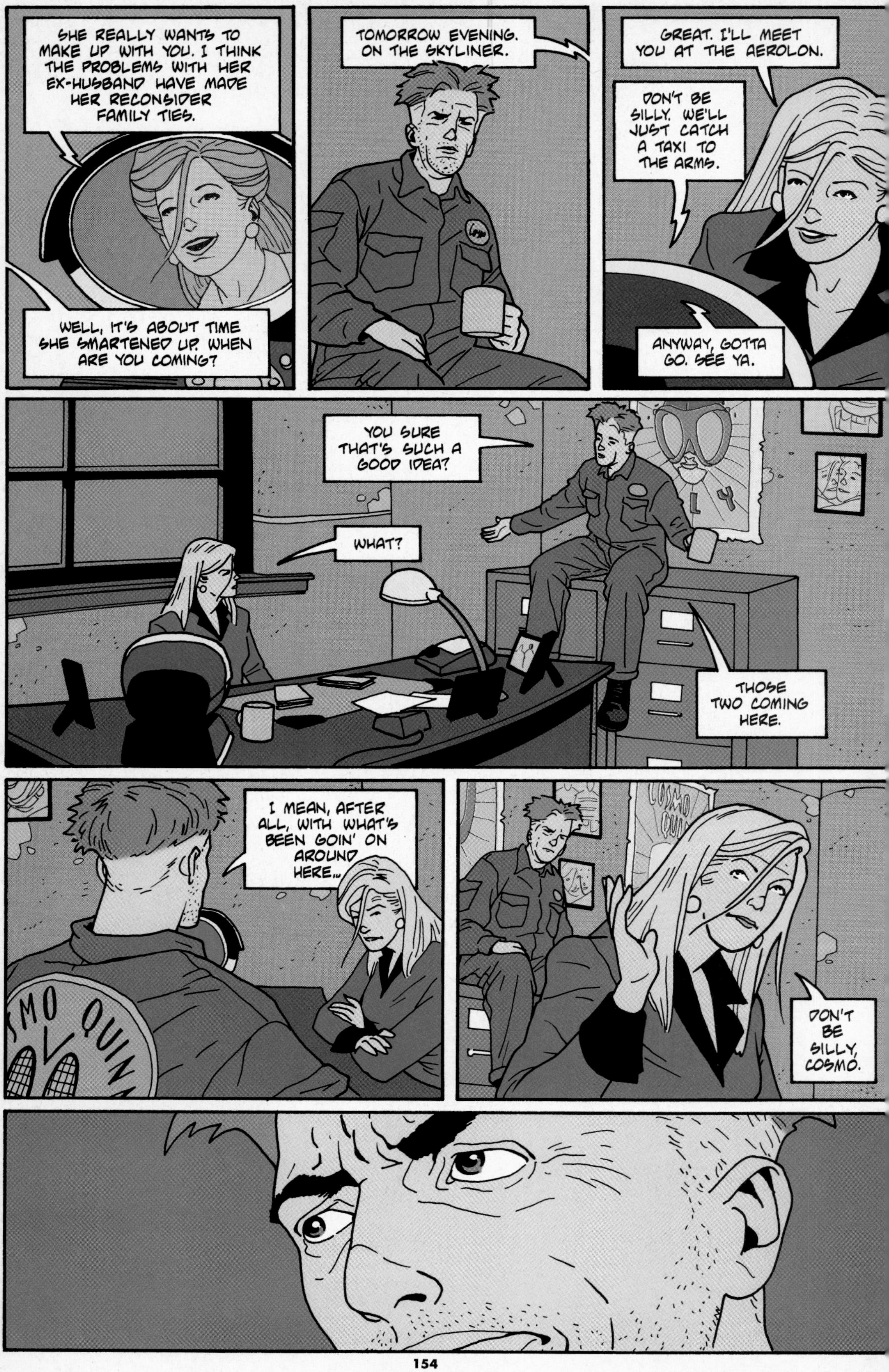
SHE REALLY WANTS TO MAKE UP WITH YOU. I THINK THE PROBLEMS WITH HER EX-HUSBAND HAVE MADE HER RECONSIDER FAMILY TIES.
WELL, IT'S ABOUT TIME SHE SMARTENED UP. WHEN ARE YOU COMING?
TOMORROW EVENING. ON THE SKYLINER.
GREAT. I'LL MEET YOU AT THE AEROLON.
DON'T BE SILLY. WE'LL JUST CATCH A TAXI TO THE ARMS.
ANYWAY, GOTTA GO. SEE YA.
YOU SURE THAT'S SUCH A GOOD IDEA?
WHAT?
THOSE TWO COMING HERE.
I MEAN, AFTER ALL, WITH WHAT'S BEEN GOIN' ON AROUND HERE...
DON'T BE SILLY, COSMO.

WHAT DO YOU HAVE *IN* HERE?

JUST SOME ODDS AND ENDS. GIRLIE STUFF.

CAREFUL WITH THAT THING!

Shoes

Records

WOOWH!

SKRASH

...SORRY. I'LL GET YOU ANOTHER ONE...

POOR GUY. HE TRIES SO HARD.

MAYBE WE CAN PICK UP ANOTHER AT THE PAWN SHOP.

WE GOT A TRUCKLOAD OF BELLHOPS OUT HERE. WHERE D'YA WANT'EM?

ACME ROBOT REPAIR

WELL, IT'S ABOUT BLOODY TIME, ISN'T IT?!

HEY! I'M JUST THE WHEELS, OKAY?

-tick-VERY WELL. PUT THEM IN THE FOYER.

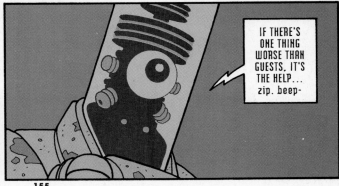
IF THERE'S ONE THING WORSE THAN GUESTS, IT'S THE HELP... zip. beep-

IT'S LUCKY YOU WERE HERE WHEN HE WENT INTO THAT SEIZURE.
HOSPITAL
YEAH...
I CAME AS SOON AS I HEARD. IS HE OKAY?
LUCKILY. SOMEONE INJECTED HIM WITH 100 CC'S OF ZERIUM. WE HAVE A SERIOUS SECURITY PROBLEM.
Girlie MAGAZINE
YEAH...
HIS HONOR WILL BE FINE.
WE WERE ABLE TO TREAT WHAT COULD'VE BEEN A FATAL ATTEMPT ON HIS LIFE.
DID ANYBODY SEE ANYTHING SUSPICIOUS?
AFRAID NOT.
MURDERERS... LIVING... IN... HEAD...
HE'S DELUSIONAL...
HE'S CUCKOO!

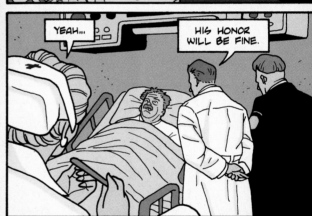

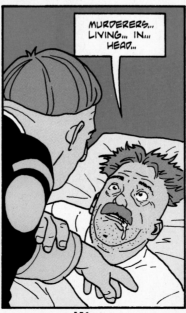

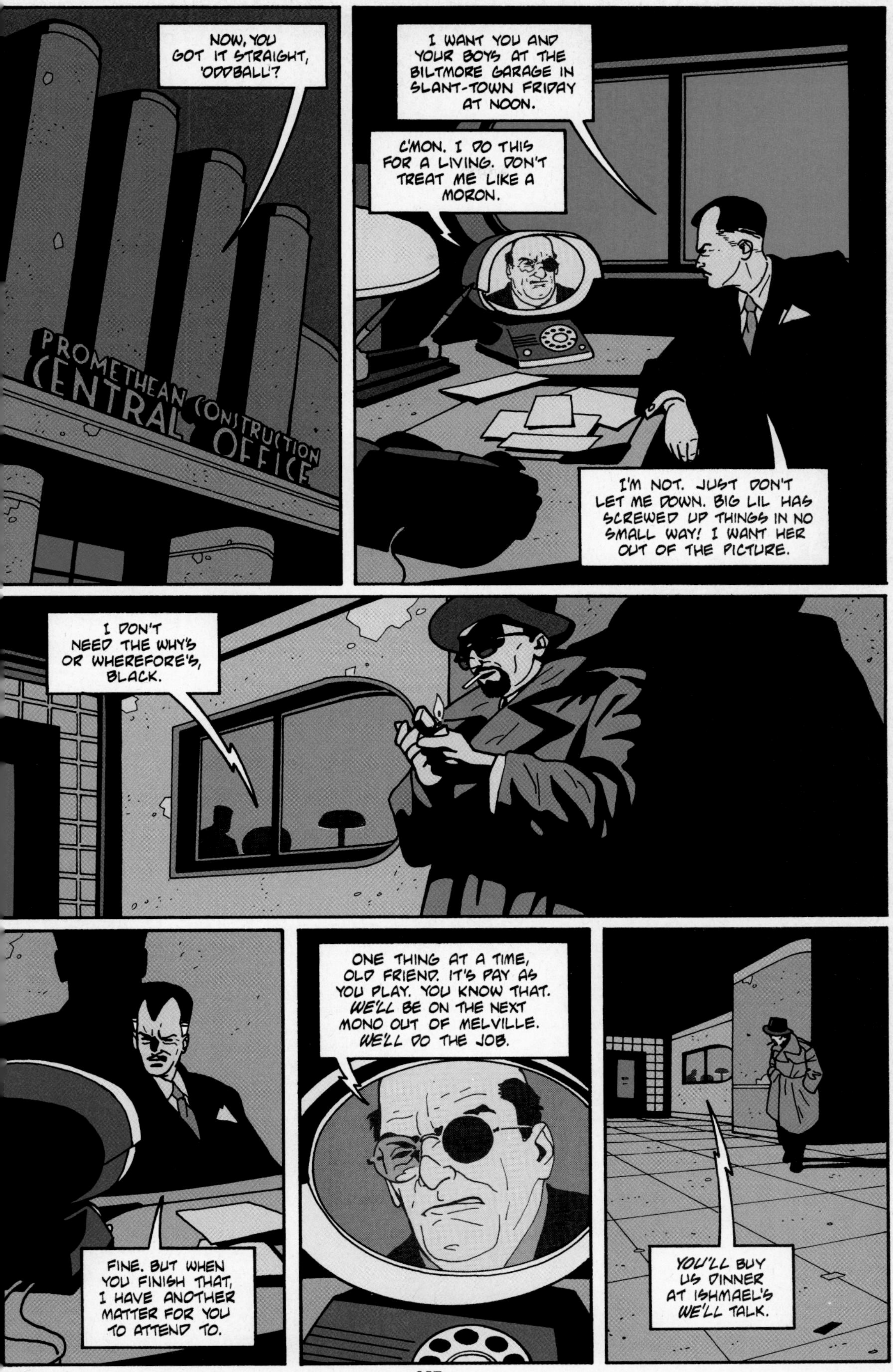
NOW, YOU GOT IT STRAIGHT, 'ODDBALL'?
PROMETHEAN CONSTRUCTION CENTRAL OFFICE
I WANT YOU AND YOUR BOYS AT THE BILTMORE GARAGE IN SLANT-TOWN FRIDAY AT NOON.
C'MON. I DO THIS FOR A LIVING. DON'T TREAT ME LIKE A MORON.
I'M NOT. JUST DON'T LET ME DOWN. BIG LIL HAS SCREWED UP THINGS IN NO SMALL WAY! I WANT HER OUT OF THE PICTURE.
I DON'T NEED THE WHY'S OR WHEREFORE'S, BLACK.
FINE. BUT WHEN YOU FINISH THAT, I HAVE ANOTHER MATTER FOR YOU TO ATTEND TO.
ONE THING AT A TIME, OLD FRIEND. IT'S PAY AS YOU PLAY. YOU KNOW THAT. *WE'LL* BE ON THE NEXT MONO OUT OF MELVILLE. *WE'LL* DO THE JOB.
YOU'LL BUY US DINNER AT ISHMAEL'S *WE'LL* TALK.

Huff. Huff.

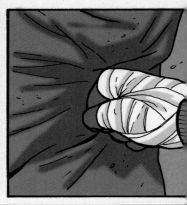

--WE CAN GET INTO THE UNIDROME ON THE FOURTH. HE'LL BE GOING UP AGAINST KIMINSKI.

TWO MORE BOUTS AND WE MAKE THE CHAMPION-SHIP AGAIN!

WITH THE KID BOXING HUMAN BEINGS ONCE MORE, WE'LL CLEAN UP!

FORGET THE HUMANS FOR A MINUTE, OLD CHAP. I'VE AN EVEN MORE INTERESTING PROPOSITION.

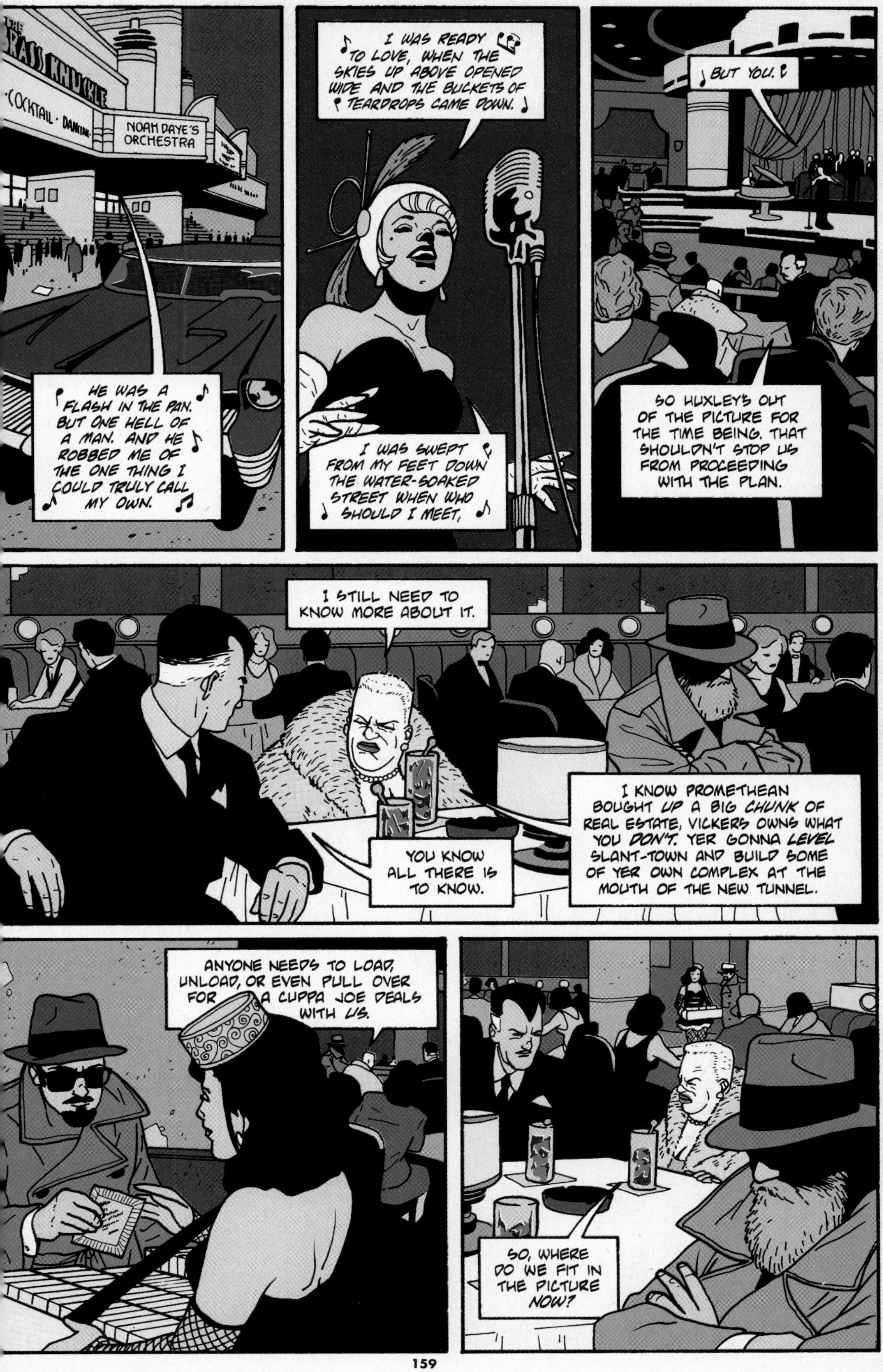
THE BRASS KNUCKLE
COCKTAIL · DANCING ·
NOAH DAYE'S ORCHESTRA
HE WAS A FLASH IN THE PAN. BUT ONE HELL OF A MAN. AND HE ROBBED ME OF THE ONE THING I COULD TRULY CALL MY OWN.
I WAS READY TO LOVE, WHEN THE SKIES UP ABOVE OPENED WIDE AND THE BUCKETS OF TEARDROPS CAME DOWN.
I WAS SWEPT FROM MY FEET DOWN THE WATER-SOAKED STREET WHEN WHO SHOULD I MEET,
BUT YOU.
SO HUXLEY'S OUT OF THE PICTURE FOR THE TIME BEING. THAT SHOULDN'T STOP US FROM PROCEEDING WITH THE PLAN.
I STILL NEED TO KNOW MORE ABOUT IT.
YOU KNOW ALL THERE IS TO KNOW.
I KNOW PROMETHEAN BOUGHT UP A BIG CHUNK OF REAL ESTATE, VICKERS OWNS WHAT YOU DON'T. YER GONNA LEVEL SLANT-TOWN AND BUILD SOME OF YER OWN COMPLEX AT THE MOUTH OF THE NEW TUNNEL.
ANYONE NEEDS TO LOAD, UNLOAD, OR EVEN PULL OVER FOR A CUPPA JOE DEALS WITH US.
SO, WHERE DO WE FIT IN THE PICTURE NOW?

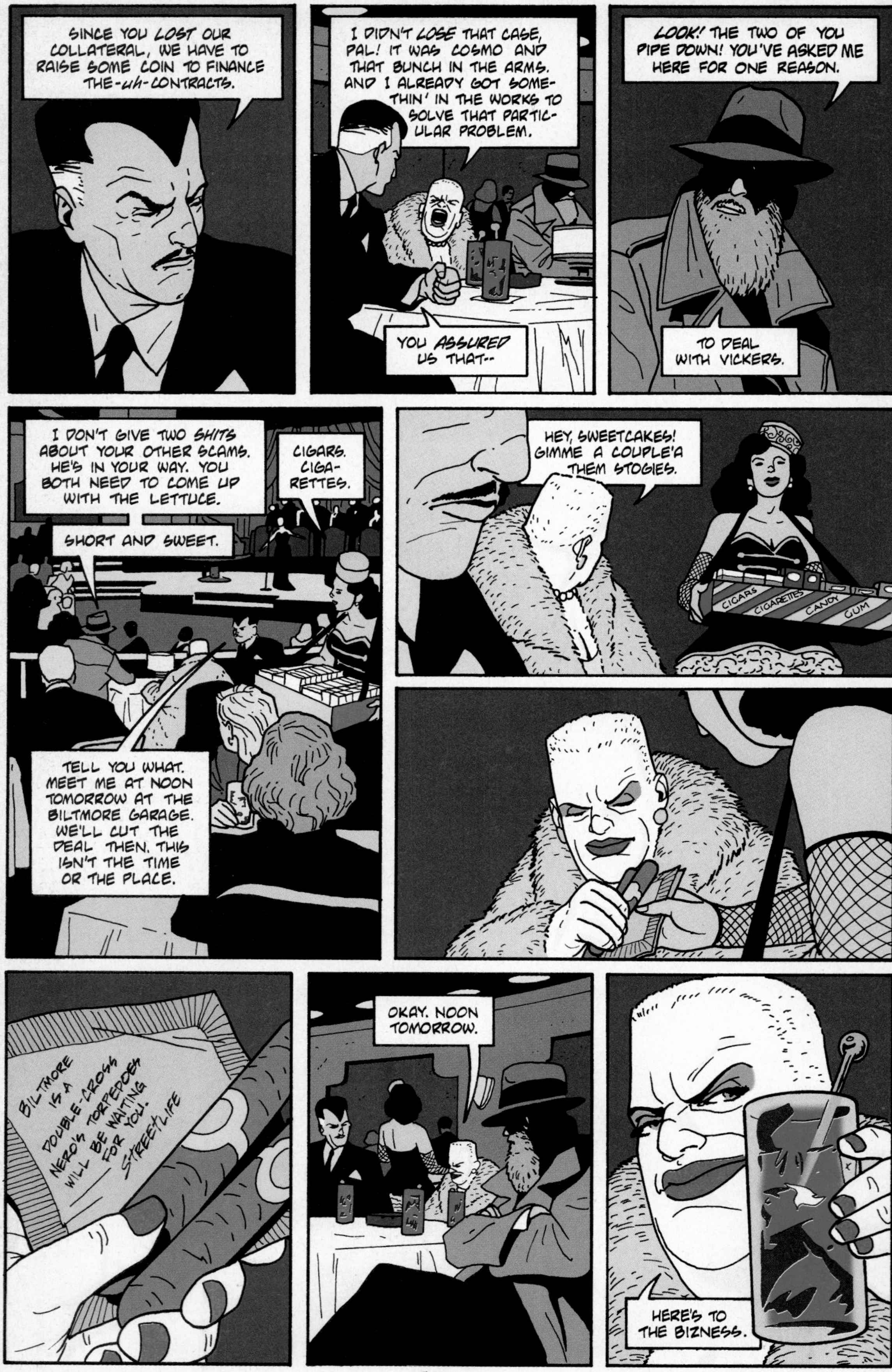

SINCE YOU LOST OUR COLLATERAL, WE HAVE TO RAISE SOME COIN TO FINANCE THE--uh--CONTRACTS.
I DIDN'T LOSE THAT CASE, PAL! IT WAS COSMO AND THAT BUNCH IN THE ARMS. AND I ALREADY GOT SOME-THIN' IN THE WORKS TO SOLVE THAT PARTIC-ULAR PROBLEM.
YOU ASSURED US THAT--
LOOK! THE TWO OF YOU PIPE DOWN! YOU'VE ASKED ME HERE FOR ONE REASON.
TO DEAL WITH VICKERS.
I DON'T GIVE TWO SHITS ABOUT YOUR OTHER SCAMS. HE'S IN YOUR WAY. YOU BOTH NEED TO COME UP WITH THE LETTUCE.
CIGARS. CIGA-RETTES.
SHORT AND SWEET.
TELL YOU WHAT. MEET ME AT NOON TOMORROW AT THE BILTMORE GARAGE. WE'LL CUT THE DEAL THEN. THIS ISN'T THE TIME OR THE PLACE.
HEY, SWEETCAKES! GIMME A COUPLE'A THEM STOGIES.
CIGARS
CIGARETTES
CANDY
GUM
BILTMORE IS A DOUBLE-CROSS NERO'S TORPEDOES WILL BE WAITING FOR YOU. STREETLIFE
OKAY. NOON TOMORROW.
HERE'S TO THE BIZNESS.

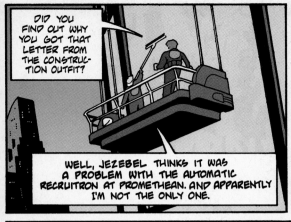

DID YOU FIND OUT WHY YOU GOT THAT LETTER FROM THE CONSTRUCTION OUTFIT?

WELL, JEZEBEL THINKS IT WAS A PROBLEM WITH THE AUTOMATIC RECRUITRON AT PROMETHEAN. AND APPARENTLY I'M NOT THE ONLY ONE.

THERE'S A GOOD DOZEN OR SO IN THE SAME BOAT.

SO, IS IT BACK TO KANSAS?

SHOULD I? AREN'T YOU HAPPY WITH MY WORK?

SURE. BUT THIS JOB DOESN'T EXACTLY HAVE A LOTTA ROOM FOR MOVIN' UP.

I MEAN, MY BEST DAYS ARE BEHIND ME, BUT YOU--YOU'RE ONLY TWENTY-TWO!

THERE'S NOTHING FOR ME BACK HOME. MY FOLKS ARE GONE. MY BROTHER LIVES IN EUROPE.

NO ONE SPECIAL?

I'VE ALWAYS BEEN A LONER.

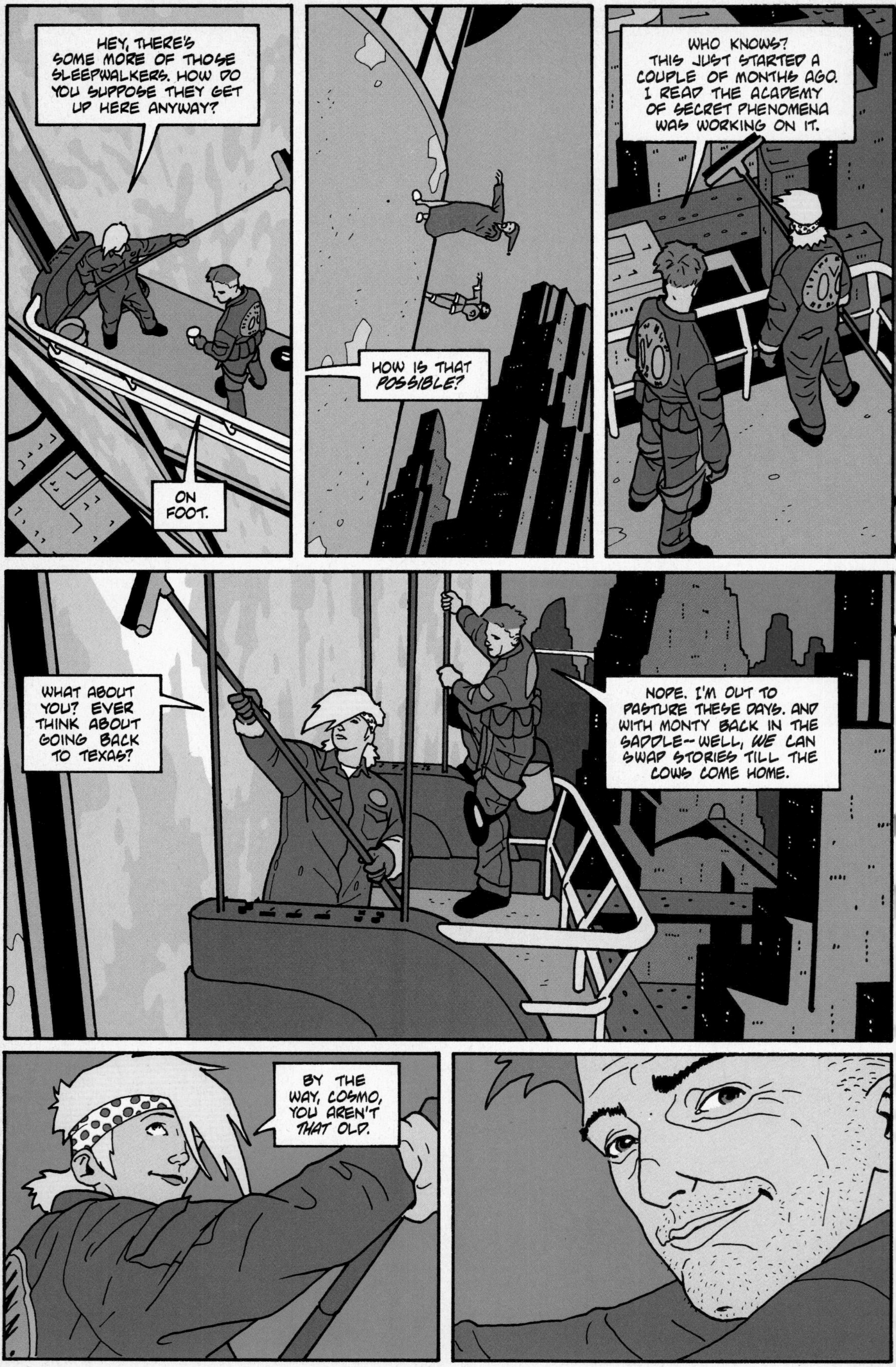
HEY, THERE'S SOME MORE OF THOSE SLEEPWALKERS. HOW DO YOU SUPPOSE THEY GET UP HERE ANYWAY?
ON FOOT.
HOW IS THAT POSSIBLE?
WHO KNOWS? THIS JUST STARTED A COUPLE OF MONTHS AGO. I READ THE ACADEMY OF SECRET PHENOMENA WAS WORKING ON IT.
WHAT ABOUT YOU? EVER THINK ABOUT GOING BACK TO TEXAS?
NOPE. I'M OUT TO PASTURE THESE DAYS. AND WITH MONTY BACK IN THE SADDLE--WELL, WE CAN SWAP STORIES TILL THE COWS COME HOME.
BY THE WAY, COSMO, YOU AREN'T THAT OLD.

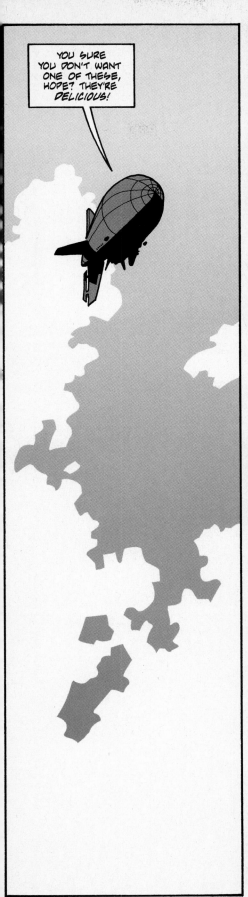

YOU SURE YOU DON'T WANT ONE OF THESE, HOPE? THEY'RE *DELICIOUS!*

I DON'T KNOW HOW YOU CAN *STAND* TO *EAT* THOSE THINGS!

YOU SHOULD TRY ONE. YOU'RE SO REPRESSED.

I'M NOT *REPRESSED!* I'M *CAUTIOUS.* THOSE THINGS ARE SCAVENGERS. THEY JUST LIE IN THE MUCK AND MIRE. GOOD LORD. THEY'RE NOT EVEN *COOKED!* YOU'RE EATING SEWAGE.

YOU'RE JUST BEING STUBBORN. LIKE SIS.

IF ANYONE IS LIKE CHARITY, IT'S *YOU.* CARELESS. TAKING *UNNECESSARY* CHANCES.

I'LL REMIND YOU THAT I'M NOT THE ONE WHO HAD THE FALLING OUT WITH HER--

IS THE ESCARGOT TARTÂR SATISFACTORY, LADIES?

JUST FINE, THANK YOU.

I'D LIKE SOME MORE SPRING-WATER, PLEASE. AND A SMALL PLATE OF CRUDITÉS.

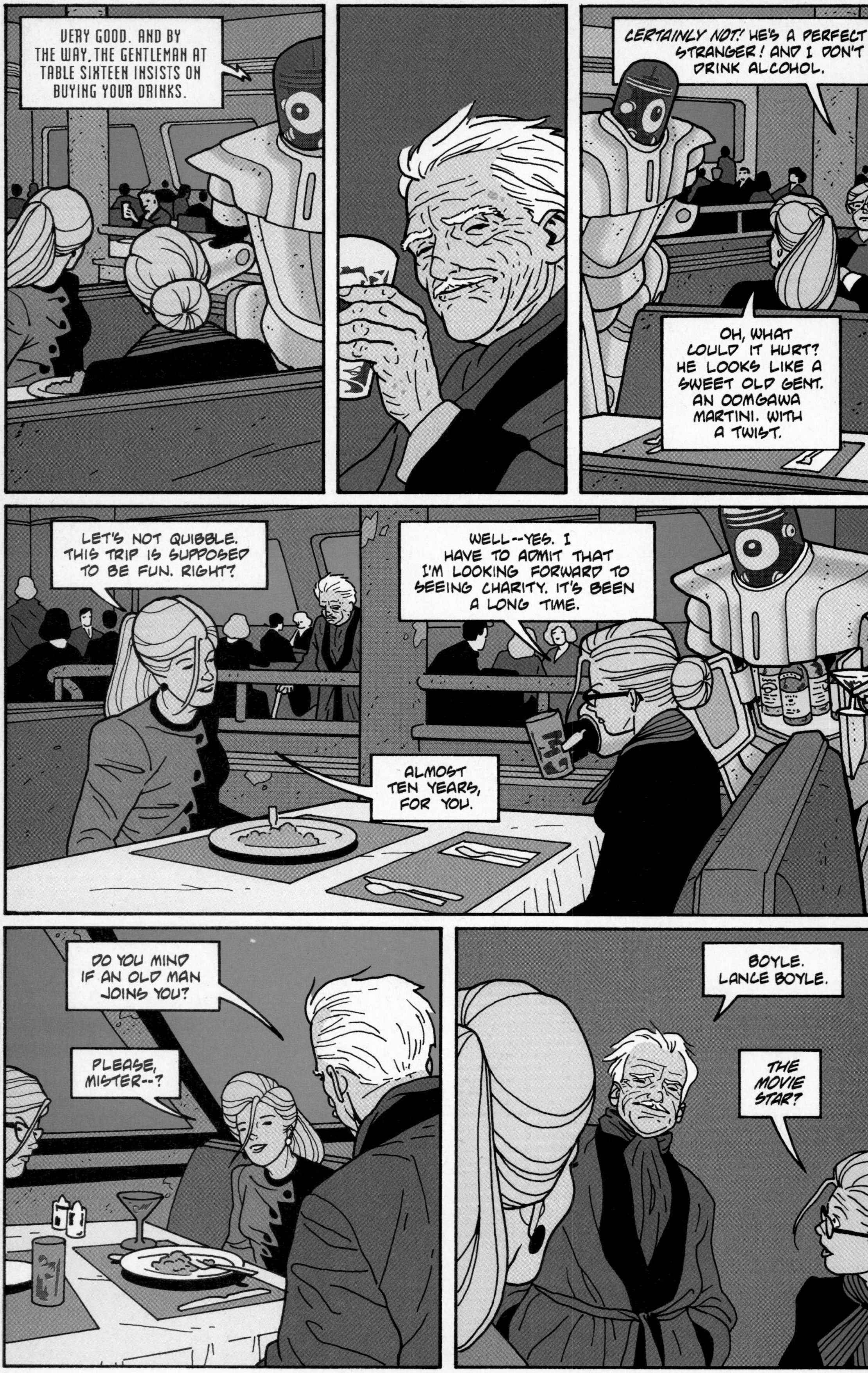
VERY GOOD. AND BY THE WAY, THE GENTLEMAN AT TABLE SIXTEEN INSISTS ON BUYING YOUR DRINKS.
CERTAINLY NOT! HE'S A PERFECT STRANGER! AND I DON'T DRINK ALCOHOL.
OH, WHAT COULD IT HURT? HE LOOKS LIKE A SWEET OLD GENT. AN OOMGAWA MARTINI. WITH A TWIST.
LET'S NOT QUIBBLE. THIS TRIP IS SUPPOSED TO BE FUN. RIGHT?
WELL--YES. I HAVE TO ADMIT THAT I'M LOOKING FORWARD TO SEEING CHARITY. IT'S BEEN A LONG TIME.
ALMOST TEN YEARS, FOR YOU.
DO YOU MIND IF AN OLD MAN JOINS YOU?
PLEASE, MISTER--?
BOYLE. LANCE BOYLE.
THE MOVIE STAR?

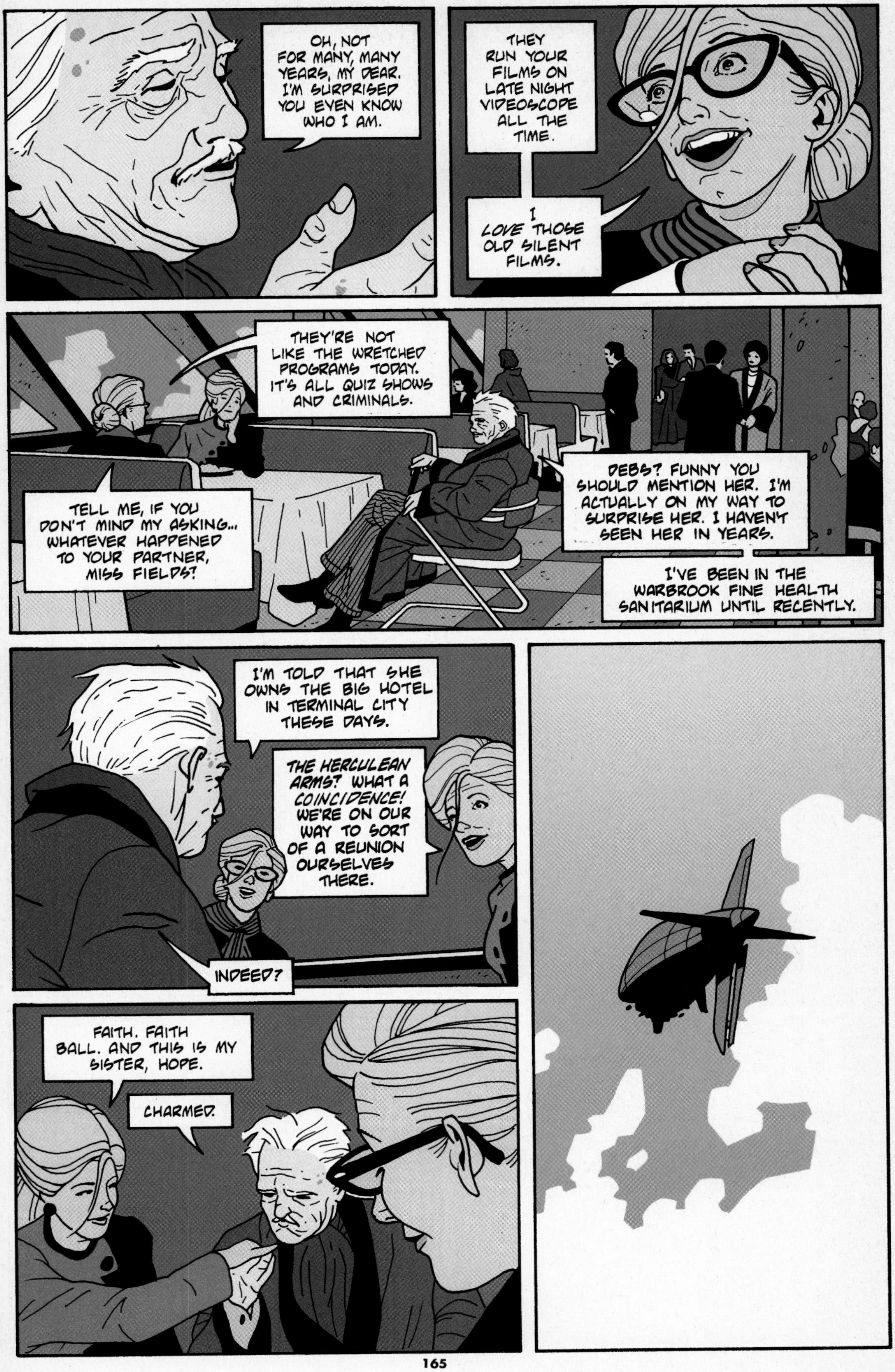
OH, NOT FOR MANY, MANY YEARS, MY DEAR. I'M SURPRISED YOU EVEN KNOW WHO I AM.
THEY RUN YOUR FILMS ON LATE NIGHT VIDEOSCOPE ALL THE TIME.
I LOVE THOSE OLD SILENT FILMS.
THEY'RE NOT LIKE THE WRETCHED PROGRAMS TODAY. IT'S ALL QUIZ SHOWS AND CRIMINALS.
TELL ME, IF YOU DON'T MIND MY ASKING... WHATEVER HAPPENED TO YOUR PARTNER, MISS FIELDS?
DEBS? FUNNY YOU SHOULD MENTION HER. I'M ACTUALLY ON MY WAY TO SURPRISE HER. I HAVEN'T SEEN HER IN YEARS.
I'VE BEEN IN THE WARBROOK FINE HEALTH SANITARIUM UNTIL RECENTLY.
I'M TOLD THAT SHE OWNS THE BIG HOTEL IN TERMINAL CITY THESE DAYS.
THE HERCULEAN ARMS? WHAT A COINCIDENCE! WE'RE ON OUR WAY TO SORT OF A REUNION OURSELVES THERE.
INDEED?
FAITH. FAITH BALL. AND THIS IS MY SISTER, HOPE.
CHARMED.

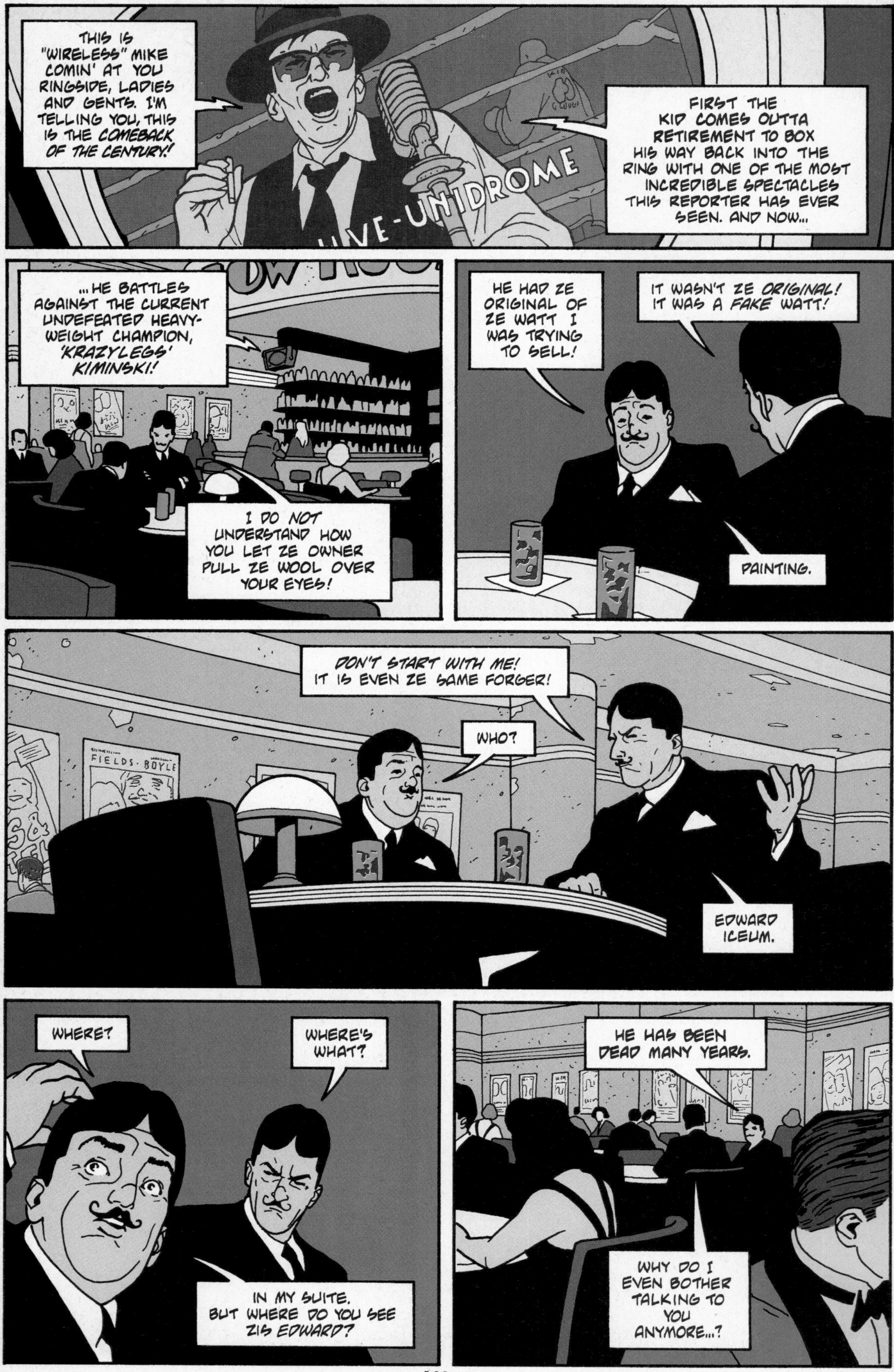
THIS IS "WIRELESS" MIKE COMIN' AT YOU RINGSIDE, LADIES AND GENTS. I'M TELLING YOU, THIS IS THE COMEBACK OF THE CENTURY!
FIRST THE KID COMES OUTTA RETIREMENT TO BOX HIS WAY BACK INTO THE RING WITH ONE OF THE MOST INCREDIBLE SPECTACLES THIS REPORTER HAS EVER SEEN. AND NOW...
...HE BATTLES AGAINST THE CURRENT UNDEFEATED HEAVY-WEIGHT CHAMPION, 'KRAZYLEGS' KIMINSKI!
I DO NOT UNDERSTAND HOW YOU LET ZE OWNER PULL ZE WOOL OVER YOUR EYES!
HE HAD ZE ORIGINAL OF ZE WATT I WAS TRYING TO SELL!
IT WASN'T ZE ORIGINAL! IT WAS A FAKE WATT!
PAINTING.
DON'T START WITH ME! IT IS EVEN ZE SAME FORGER!
WHO?
EDWARD ICEUM.
WHERE?
WHERE'S WHAT?
IN MY SUITE. BUT WHERE DO YOU SEE ZIS EDWARD?
HE HAS BEEN DEAD MANY YEARS.
WHY DO I EVEN BOTHER TALKING TO YOU ANYMORE...?

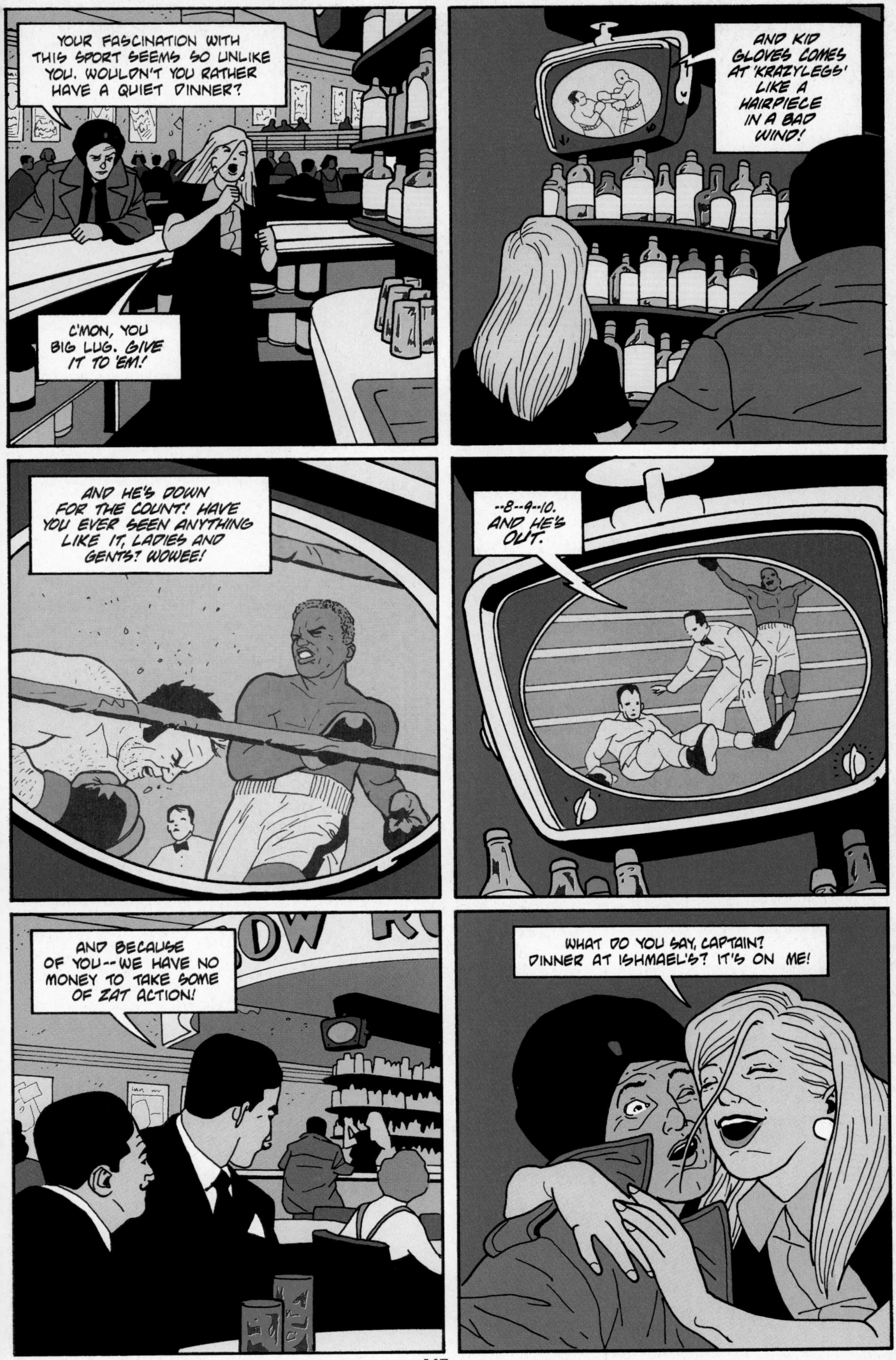
YOUR FASCINATION WITH THIS SPORT SEEMS SO UNLIKE YOU. WOULDN'T YOU RATHER HAVE A QUIET DINNER?
C'MON, YOU BIG LUG. GIVE IT TO 'EM!
AND KID GLOVES COMES AT 'KRAZYLEGS' LIKE A HAIRPIECE IN A BAD WIND!
AND HE'S DOWN FOR THE COUNT! HAVE YOU EVER SEEN ANYTHING LIKE IT, LADIES AND GENTS? WOWEE!
--8--9--10. AND HE'S OUT.
AND BECAUSE OF YOU--WE HAVE NO MONEY TO TAKE SOME OF ZAT ACTION!
WHAT DO YOU SAY, CAPTAIN? DINNER AT ISHMAEL'S? IT'S ON ME!

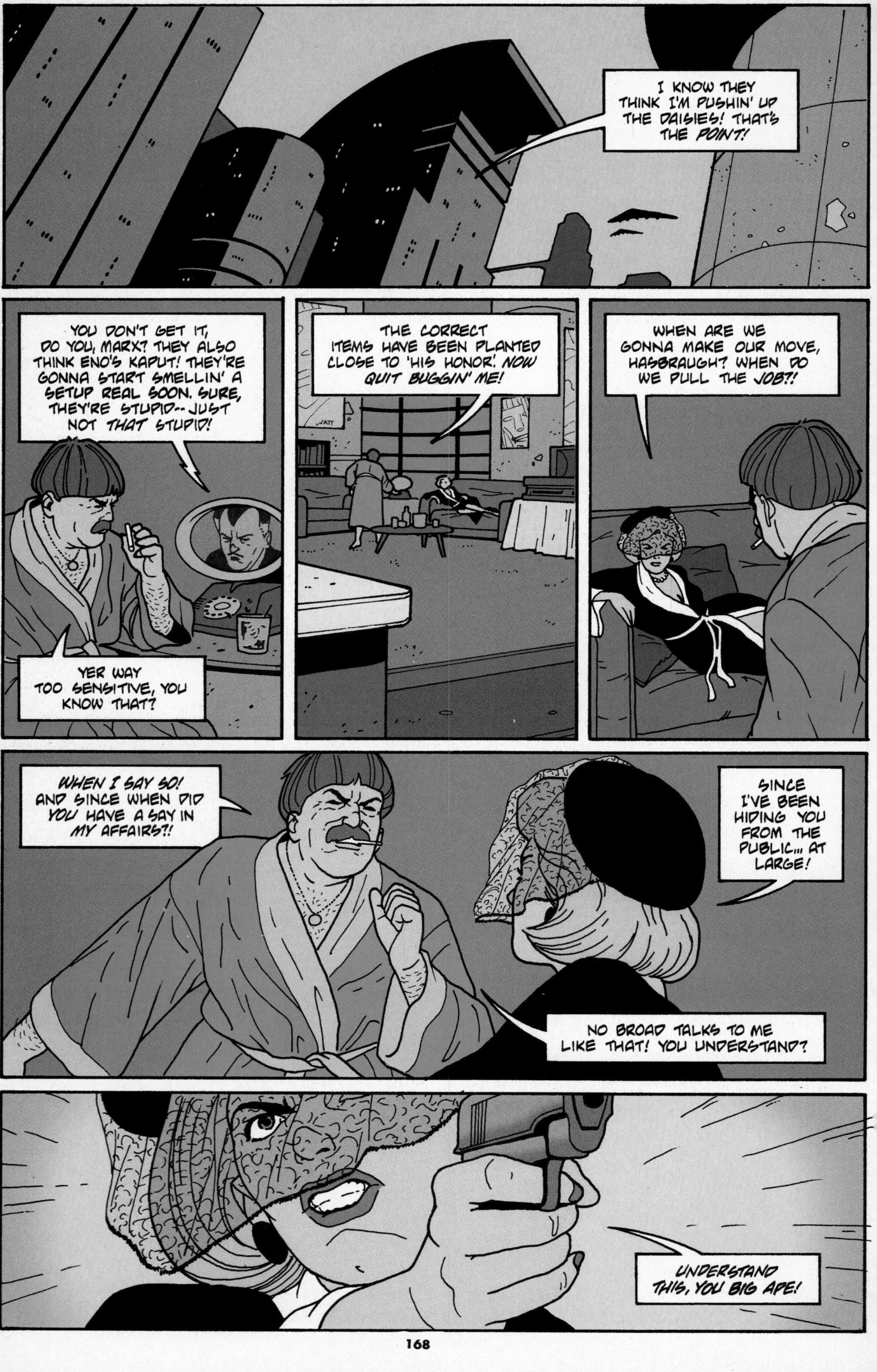
I KNOW THEY THINK I'M PUSHIN' UP THE DAISIES! THAT'S THE POINT!
YOU DON'T GET IT, DO YOU, MARX? THEY ALSO THINK ENO'S KAPUT! THEY'RE GONNA START SMELLIN' A SETUP REAL SOON. SURE, THEY'RE STUPID-- JUST NOT THAT STUPID!
YER WAY TOO SENSITIVE, YOU KNOW THAT?
THE CORRECT ITEMS HAVE BEEN PLANTED CLOSE TO 'HIS HONOR'. NOW QUIT BUGGIN' ME!
WHEN ARE WE GONNA MAKE OUR MOVE, HASBRAUGH? WHEN DO WE PULL THE JOB?!
WHEN I SAY SO! AND SINCE WHEN DID YOU HAVE A SAY IN MY AFFAIRS?!
SINCE I'VE BEEN HIDING YOU FROM THE PUBLIC... AT LARGE!
NO BROAD TALKS TO ME LIKE THAT! YOU UNDERSTAND?
UNDERSTAND THIS, YOU BIG APE!

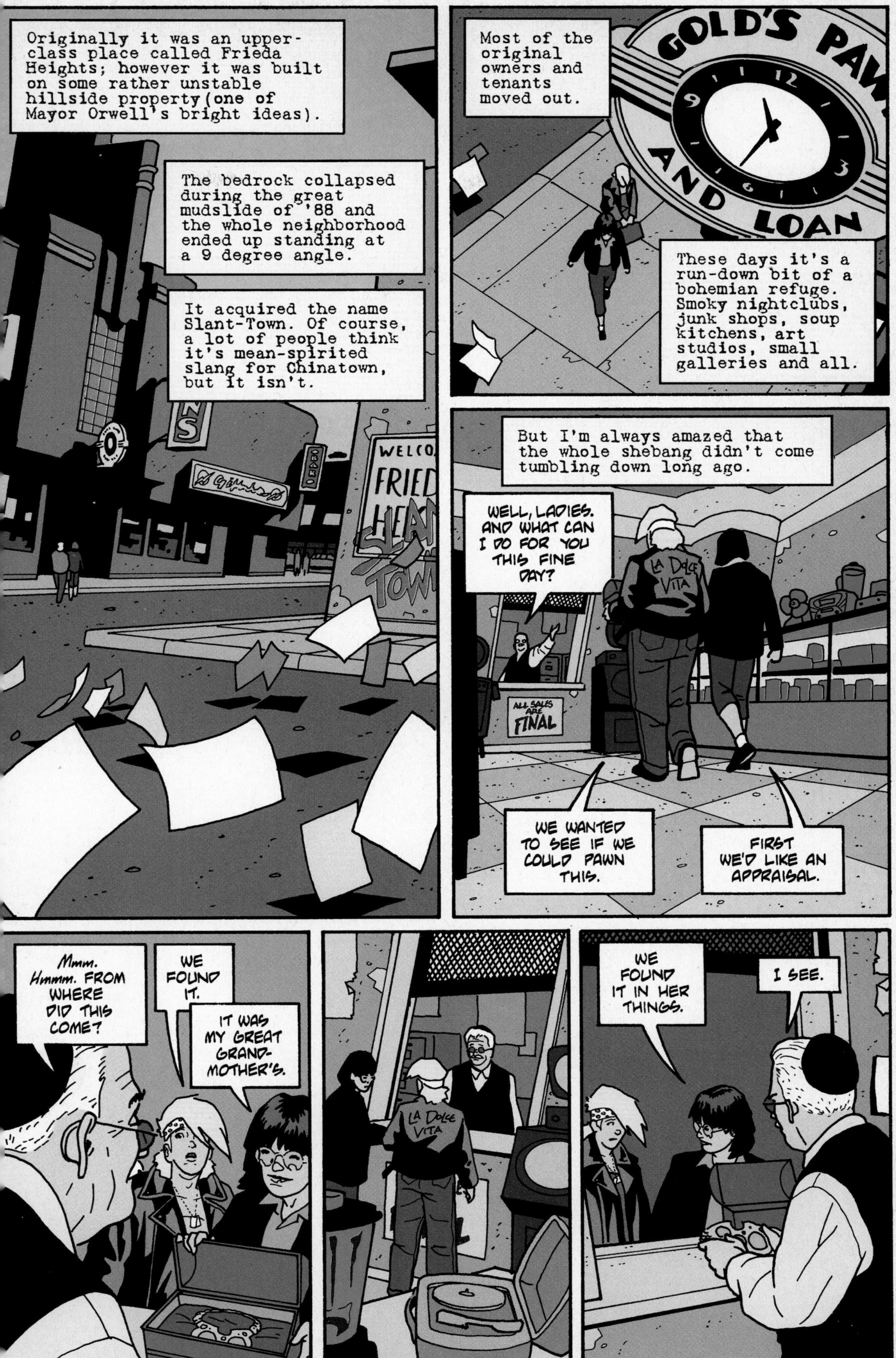
Originally it was an upper-class place called Frieda Heights; however it was built on some rather unstable hillside property(one of Mayor Orwell's bright ideas).
The bedrock collapsed during the great mudslide of '88 and the whole neighborhood ended up standing at a 9 degree angle.
It acquired the name Slant-Town. Of course, a lot of people think it's mean-spirited slang for Chinatown, but it isn't.
Most of the original owners and tenants moved out.
GOLD'S PAW
AND LOAN
These days it's a run-down bit of a bohemian refuge. Smoky nightclubs, junk shops, soup kitchens, art studios, small galleries and all.
But I'm always amazed that the whole shebang didn't come tumbling down long ago.
WELL, LADIES. AND WHAT CAN I DO FOR YOU THIS FINE DAY?
LA DOLCE VITA
ALL SALES ARE FINAL
WE WANTED TO SEE IF WE COULD PAWN THIS.
FIRST WE'D LIKE AN APPRAISAL.
Mmm. Hmmm. FROM WHERE DID THIS COME?
WE FOUND IT.
IT WAS MY GREAT GRAND-MOTHER'S.
LA DOLCE VITA
WE FOUND IT IN HER THINGS.
I SEE.

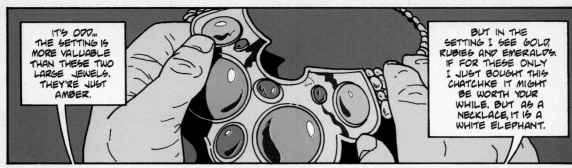

IT'S ODD... THE SETTING IS MORE VALUABLE THAN THESE TWO LARGE JEWELS. THEY'RE JUST AMBER.

BUT IN THE SETTING I SEE GOLD, RUBIES AND EMERALDS. IF FOR THESE ONLY I JUST BOUGHT THIS CHATCHKE IT MIGHT BE WORTH YOUR WHILE. BUT AS A NECKLACE, IT IS A WHITE ELEPHANT.

PERHAPS IF YOU KNEW SOMETHING ABOUT ITS BACKGROUND.

HOW MUCH?

WHERE IT CAME FROM. WHY IT WAS--

NO. HOW MUCH CAN WE GET?

THIS YOU WANT TAKEN APART? IT IS PROBABLY AN HEIRLOOM OF SOME KIND. I SUGGEST YOU HANG ONTO IT. SEE IF YOUR BUBBEH MENTIONED IT IN HER WILL.

YOU'LL THANK ME.

FOR NOTHIN.

BILTMORE GARAGE

PARKING

STOP - PLEASE OBTAIN TICKET

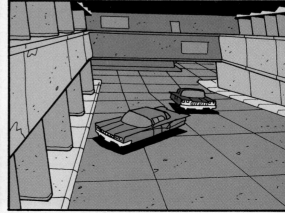

170

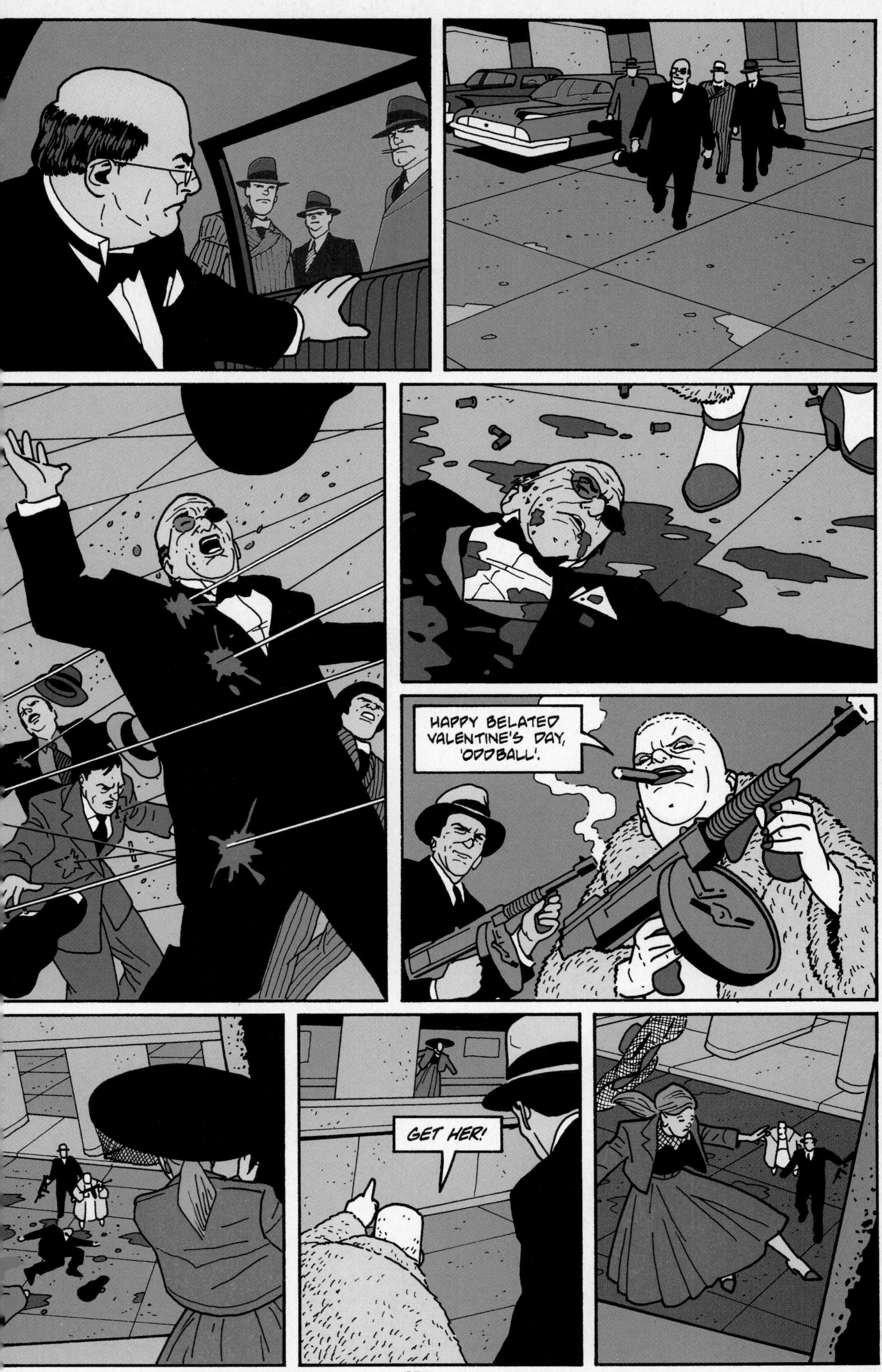
HAPPY BELATED VALENTINE'S DAY, 'ODDBALL'.
GET HER!

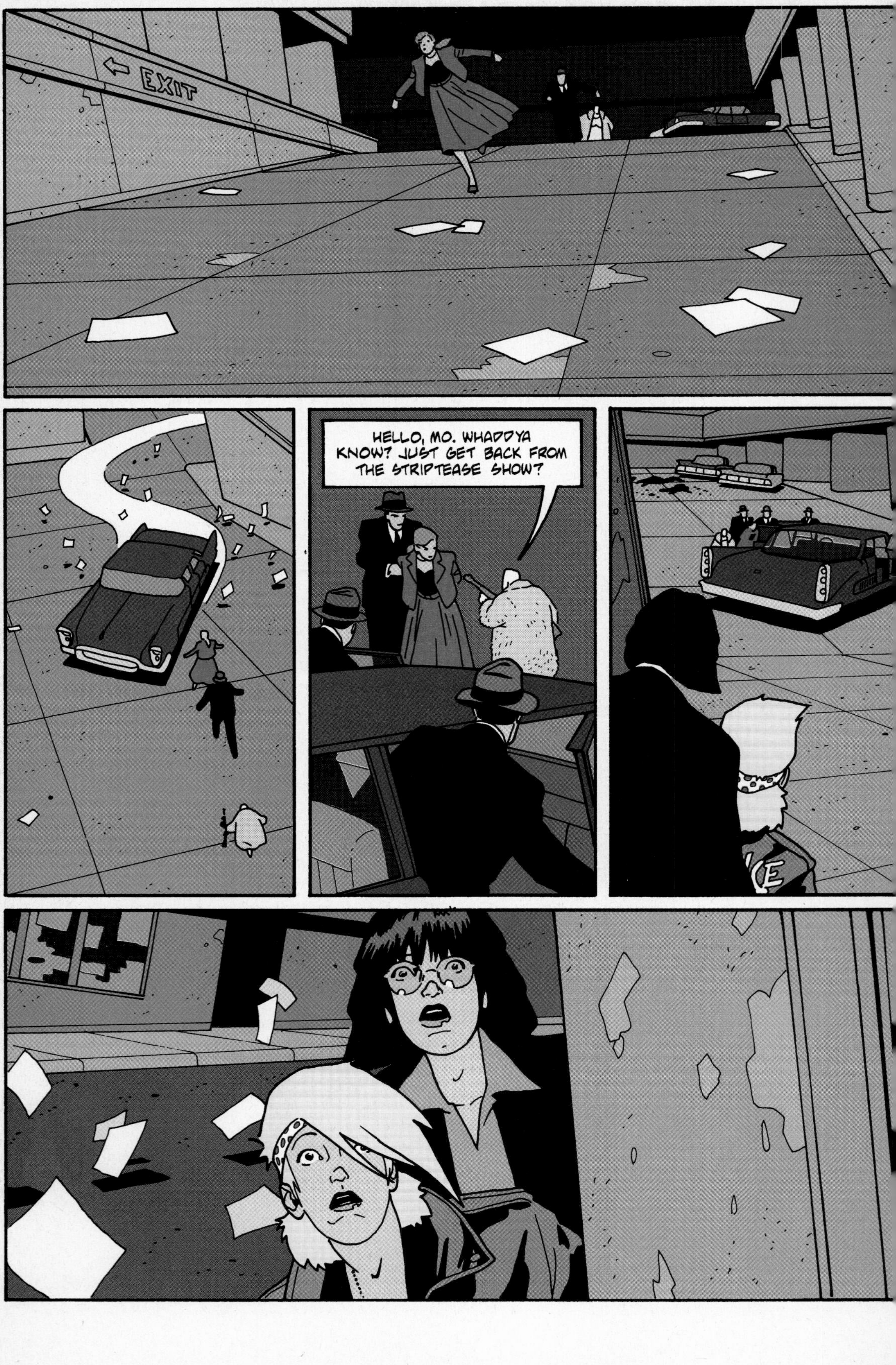
EXIT
HELLO, MO. WHADDYA KNOW? JUST GET BACK FROM THE STRIPTEASE SHOW?

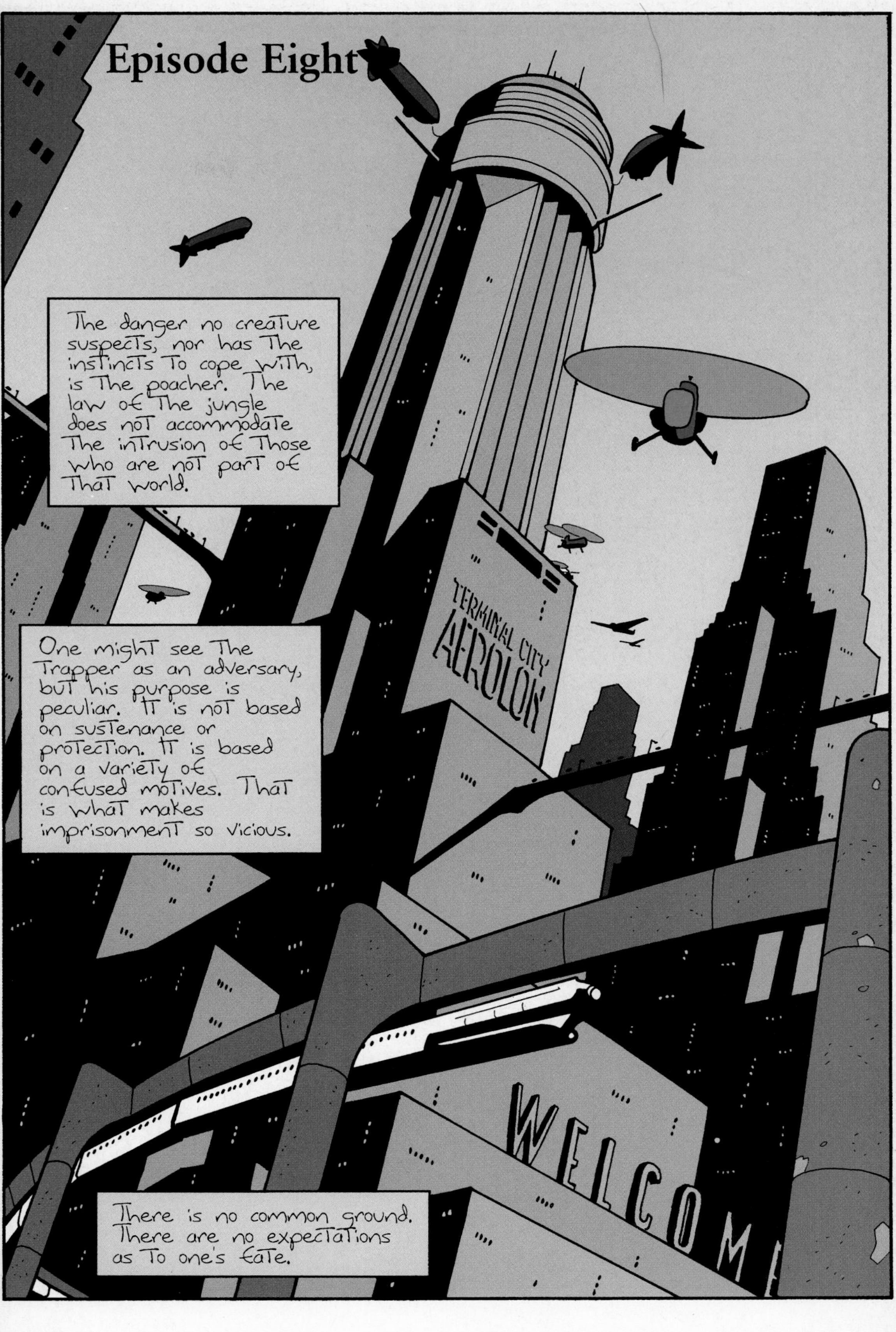
Episode Eight
The danger no creature suspects, nor has the instincts to cope with, is the poacher. The law of the jungle does not accommodate the intrusion of those who are not part of that world.
TERMINAL CITY AEROLON
One might see the Trapper as an adversary, but his purpose is peculiar. It is not based on sustenance or protection. It is based on a variety of confused motives. That is what makes imprisonment so vicious.
WELCOM
There is no common ground. There are no expectations as to one's fate.

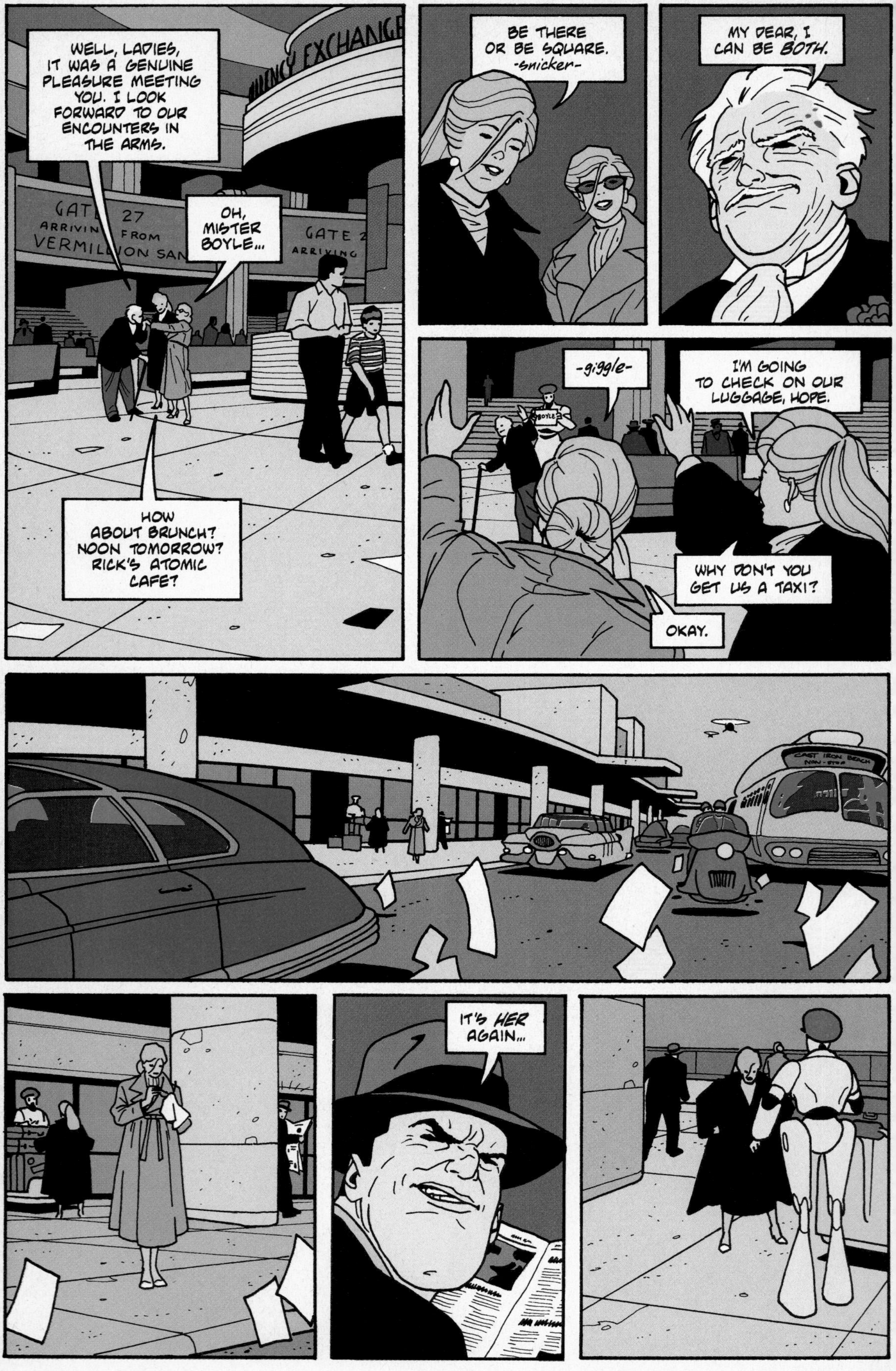
CURRENCY EXCHANGE
GATE 27 ARRIVING FROM VERMILION SANDS
GATE 2 ARRIVING
WELL, LADIES, IT WAS A GENUINE PLEASURE MEETING YOU. I LOOK FORWARD TO OUR ENCOUNTERS IN THE ARMS.
OH, MISTER BOYLE...
HOW ABOUT BRUNCH? NOON TOMORROW? RICK'S ATOMIC CAFE?
BE THERE OR BE SQUARE. -snicker-
MY DEAR, I CAN BE BOTH.
-giggle-
BOYLE
I'M GOING TO CHECK ON OUR LUGGAGE, HOPE.
WHY DON'T YOU GET US A TAXI?
OKAY.
CAST IRON BEACH NON-STOP
IT'S HER AGAIN...

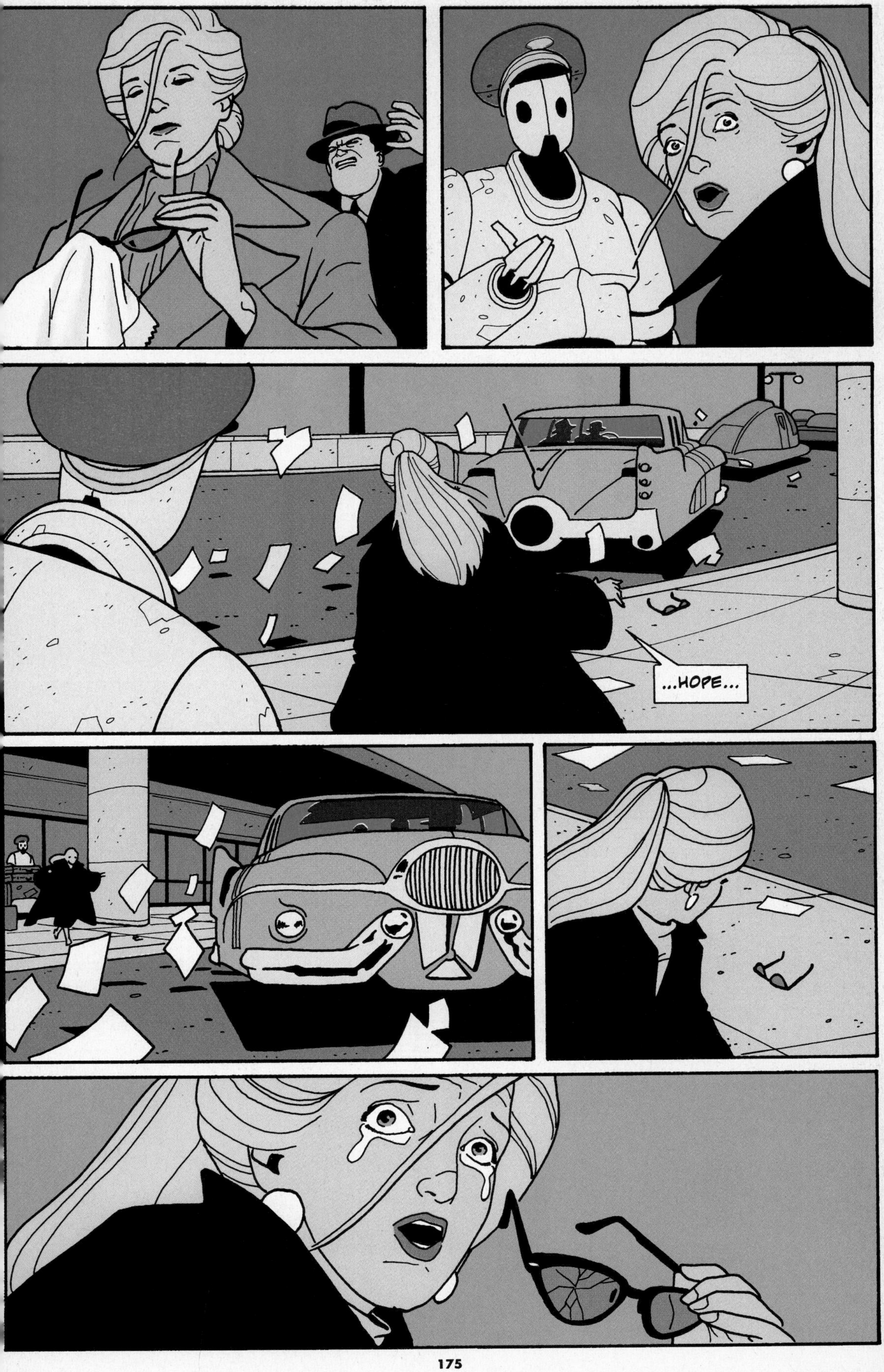
...HOPE...

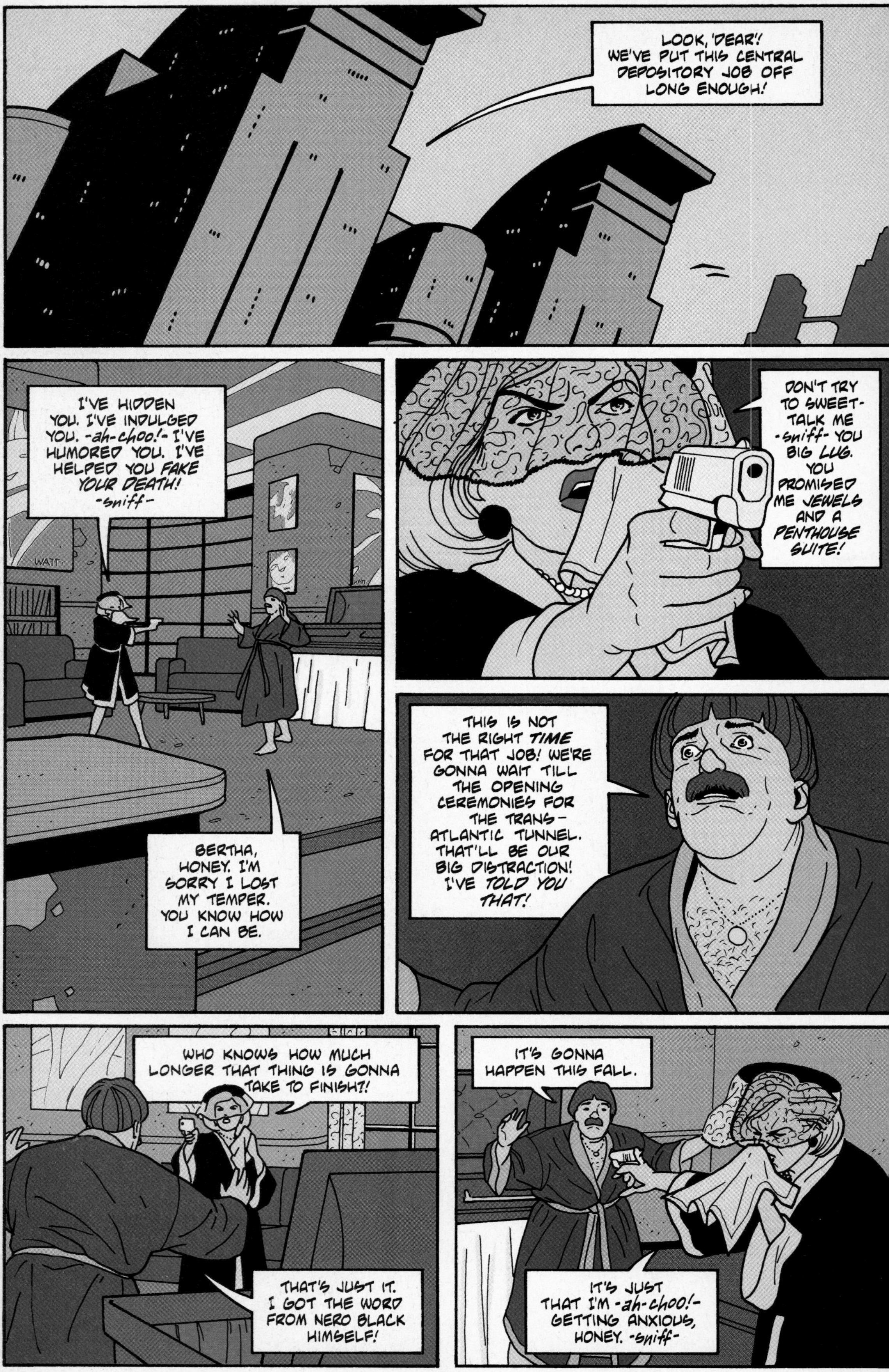

LOOK, 'DEAR'! WE'VE PUT THIS CENTRAL DEPOSITORY JOB OFF LONG ENOUGH!
I'VE HIDDEN YOU. I'VE INDULGED YOU. -ah-choo!- I'VE HUMORED YOU. I'VE HELPED YOU FAKE YOUR DEATH! -sniff-
DON'T TRY TO SWEET-TALK ME -sniff- YOU BIG LUG. YOU PROMISED ME JEWELS AND A PENTHOUSE SUITE!
BERTHA, HONEY. I'M SORRY I LOST MY TEMPER. YOU KNOW HOW I CAN BE.
THIS IS NOT THE RIGHT TIME FOR THAT JOB! WE'RE GONNA WAIT TILL THE OPENING CEREMONIES FOR THE TRANS-ATLANTIC TUNNEL. THAT'LL BE OUR BIG DISTRACTION! I'VE TOLD YOU THAT!
WHO KNOWS HOW MUCH LONGER THAT THING IS GONNA TAKE TO FINISH?!
THAT'S JUST IT. I GOT THE WORD FROM NERO BLACK HIMSELF!
IT'S GONNA HAPPEN THIS FALL.
IT'S JUST THAT I'M -ah-choo!- GETTING ANXIOUS, HONEY. -sniff-

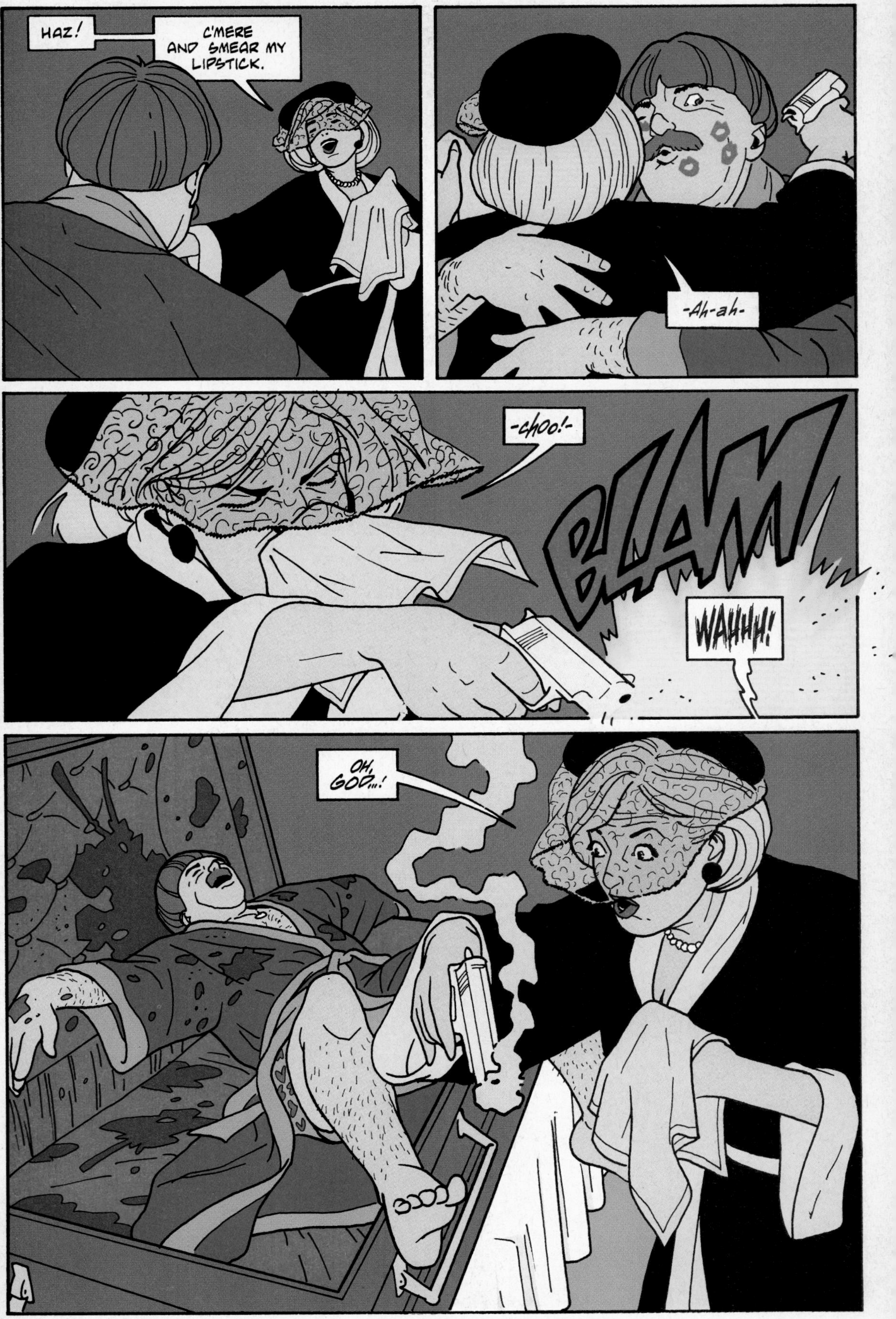
HAZ!
C'MERE AND SMEAR MY LIPSTICK.
-Ah-ah-
-CHOO!-
BLAM
WAHHH!
OH, GOD...!

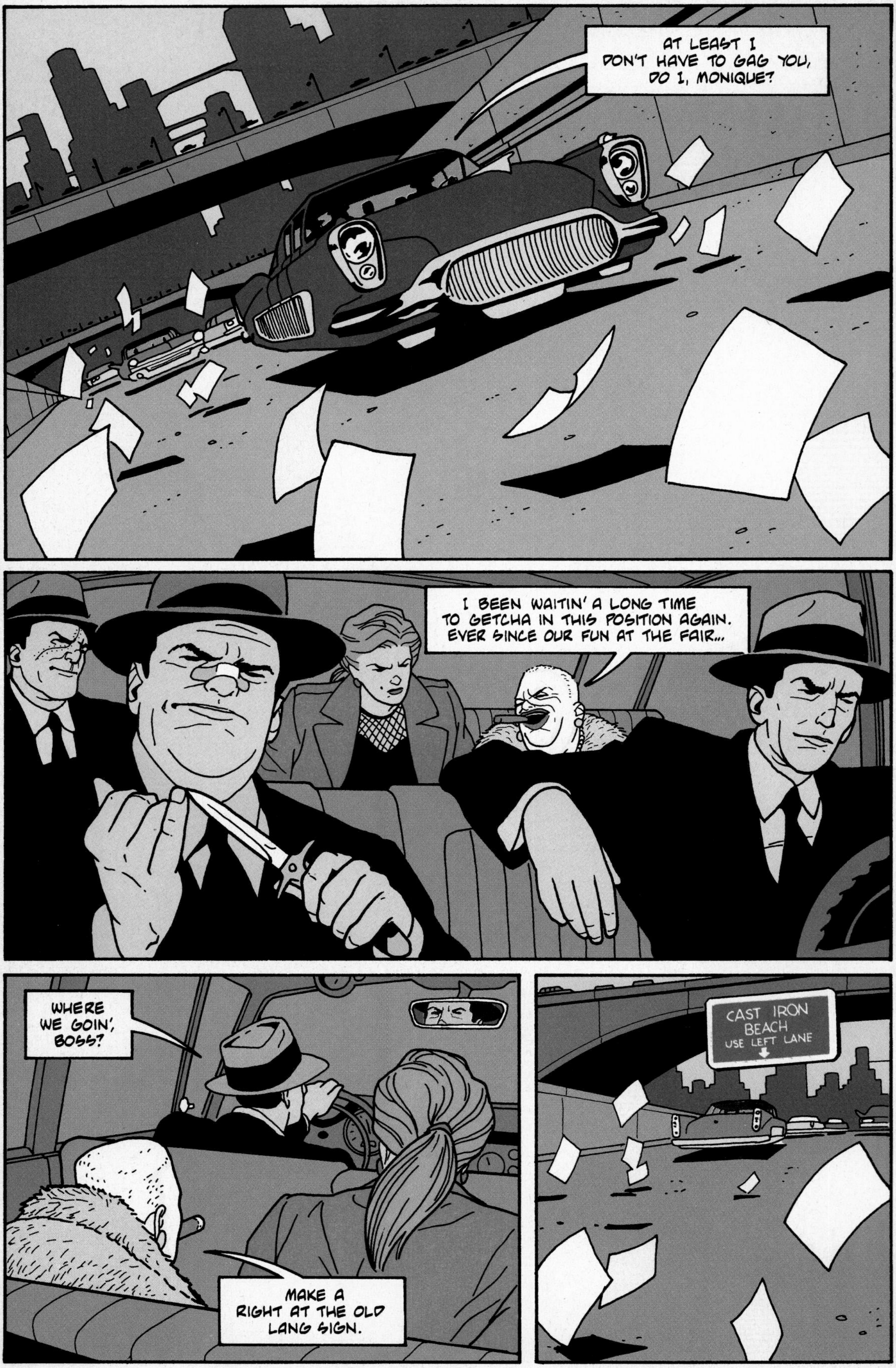
AT LEAST I DON'T HAVE TO GAG YOU, DO I, MONIQUE?
I BEEN WAITIN' A LONG TIME TO GETCHA IN THIS POSITION AGAIN. EVER SINCE OUR FUN AT THE FAIR...
WHERE WE GOIN', BOSS?
MAKE A RIGHT AT THE OLD LANG SIGN.
CAST IRON BEACH USE LEFT LANE

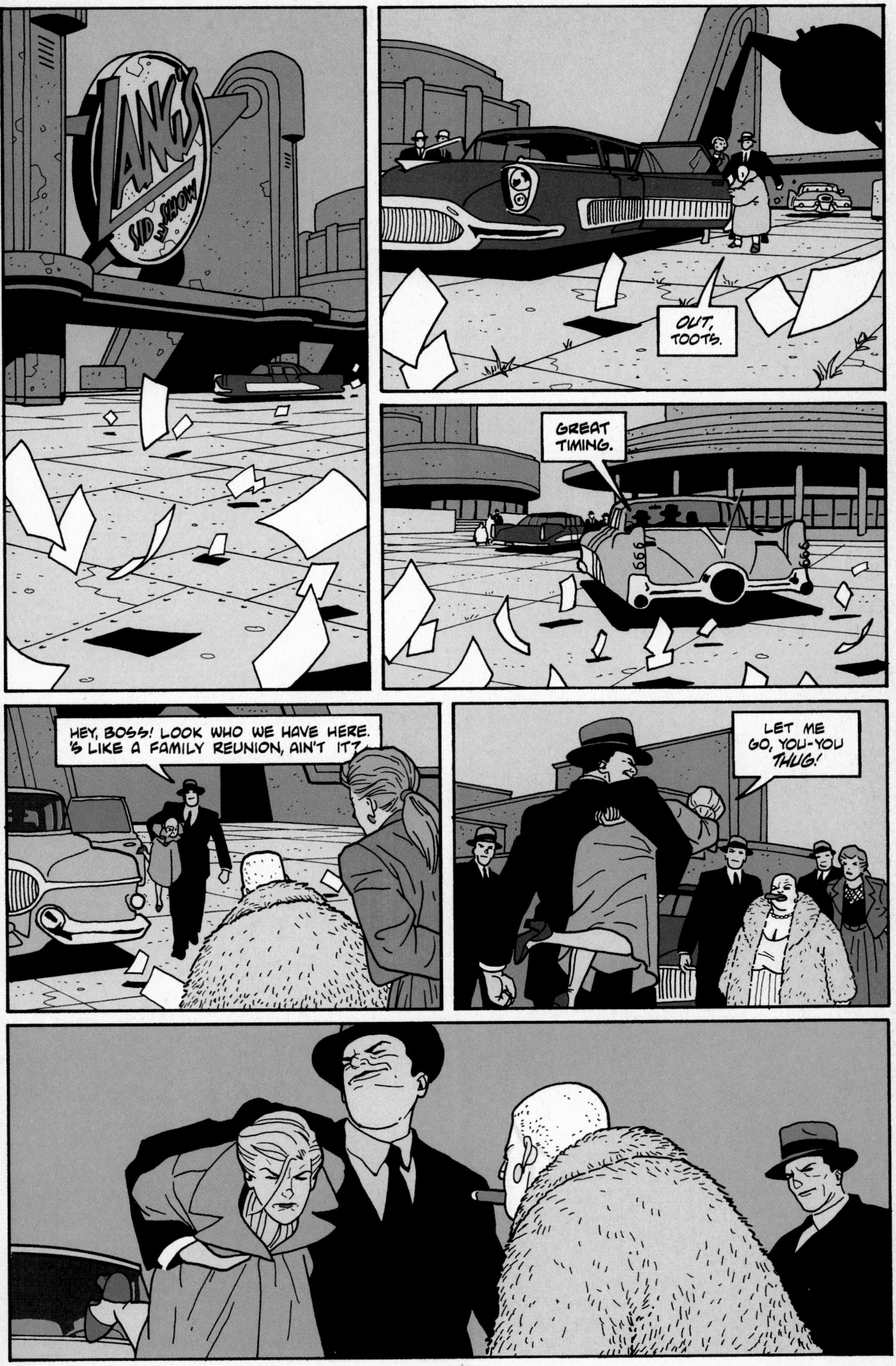
LANG'S
SIDE SHOW
OUT, TOOTS.
GREAT TIMING.
HEY, BOSS! LOOK WHO WE HAVE HERE. 'S LIKE A FAMILY REUNION, AIN'T IT?
LET ME GO, YOU-YOU THUG!

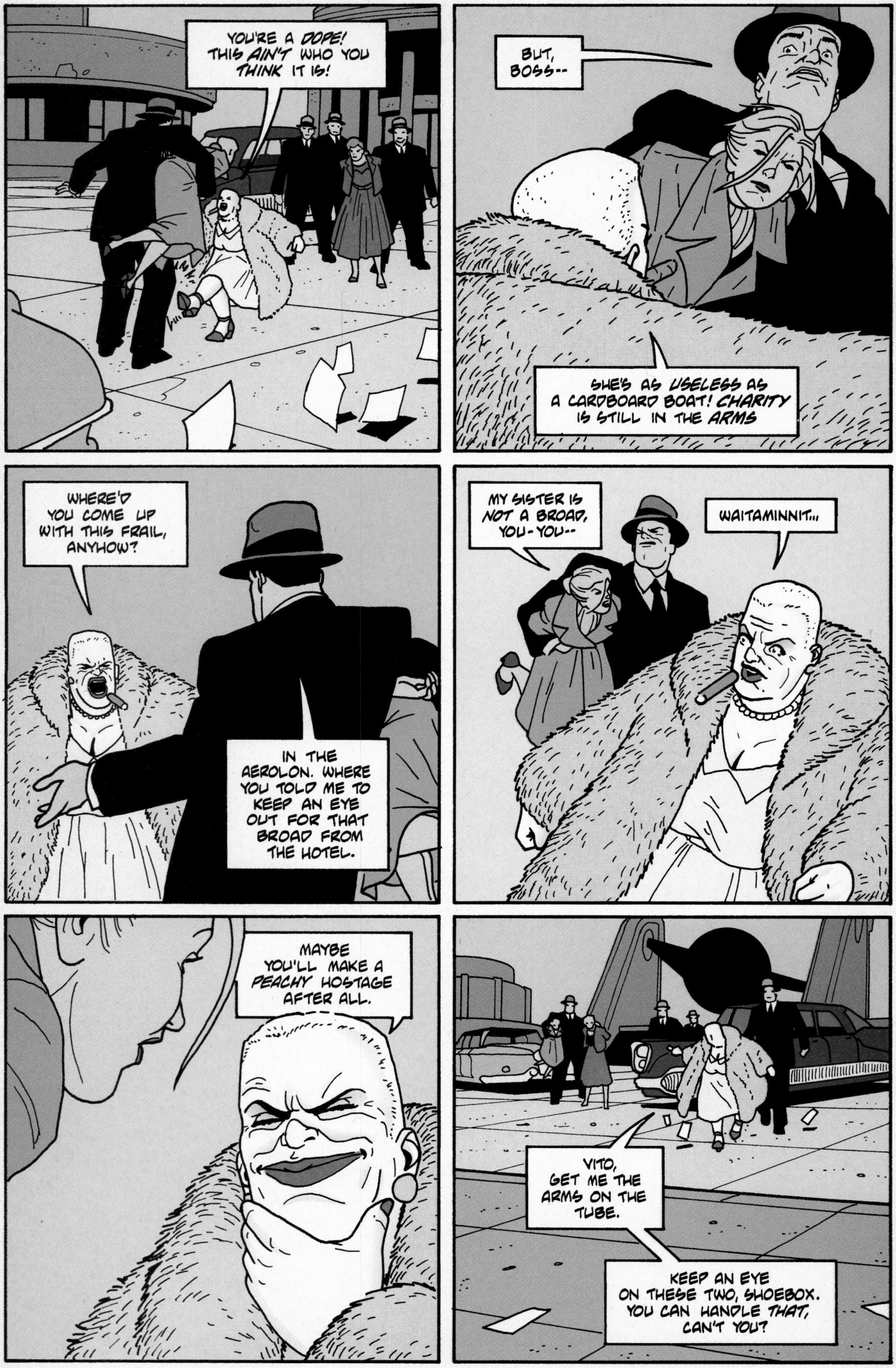
YOU'RE A DOPE! THIS AIN'T WHO YOU THINK IT IS!
BUT, BOSS--
SHE'S AS USELESS AS A CARDBOARD BOAT! CHARITY IS STILL IN THE ARMS
WHERE'D YOU COME UP WITH THIS FRAIL, ANYHOW?
IN THE AEROLON. WHERE YOU TOLD ME TO KEEP AN EYE OUT FOR THAT BROAD FROM THE HOTEL.
MY SISTER IS NOT A BROAD, YOU-YOU--
WAITAMINNIT...
MAYBE YOU'LL MAKE A PEACHY HOSTAGE AFTER ALL.
VITO, GET ME THE ARMS ON THE TUBE.
KEEP AN EYE ON THESE TWO, SHOEBOX. YOU CAN HANDLE THAT, CAN'T YOU?

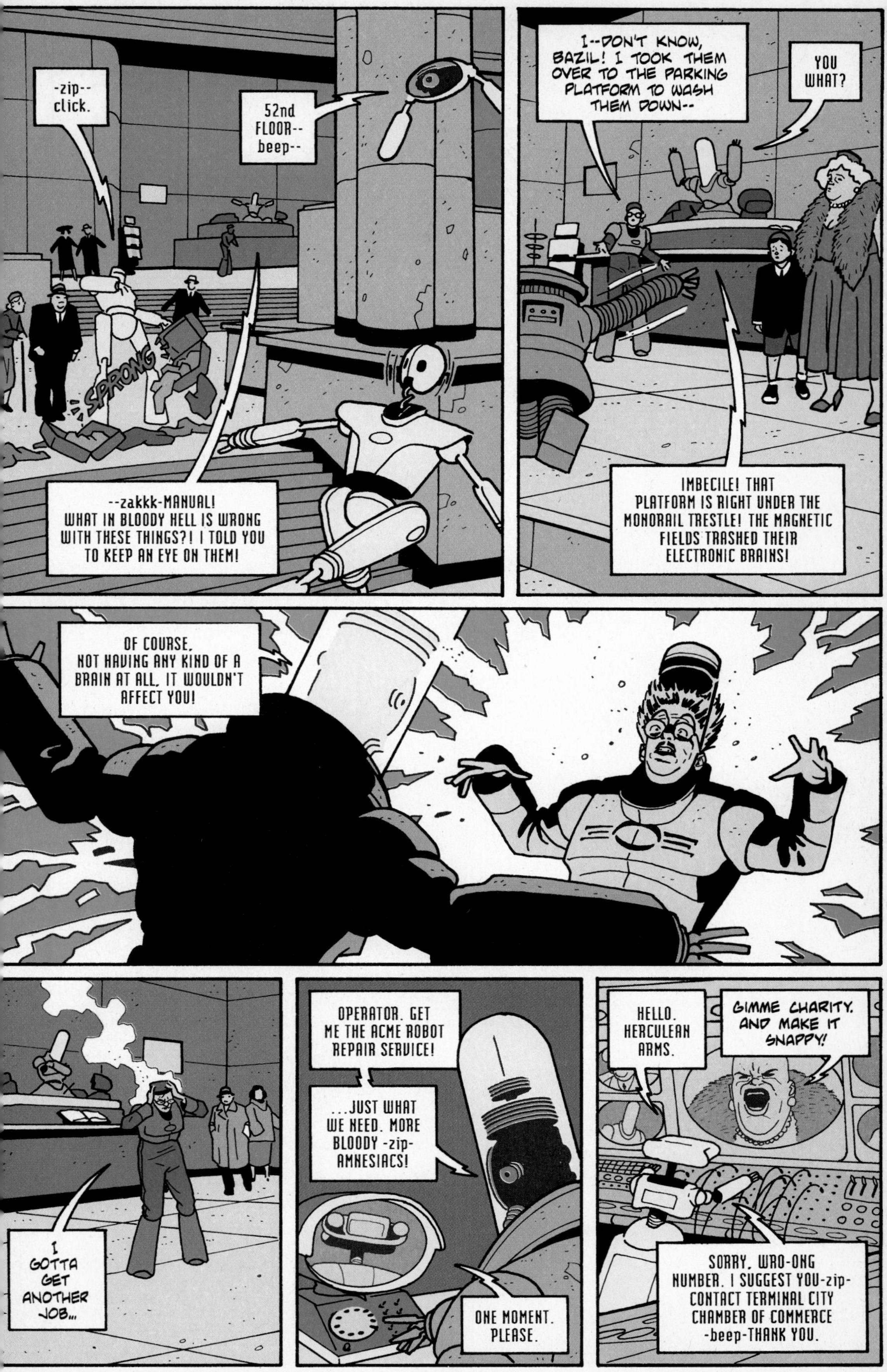
-zip--
click.
52nd
FLOOR--
beep--
SPRONG
--zakkk-MANUAL!
WHAT IN BLOODY HELL IS WRONG WITH THESE THINGS?! I TOLD YOU TO KEEP AN EYE ON THEM!
I--DON'T KNOW, BAZIL! I TOOK THEM OVER TO THE PARKING PLATFORM TO WASH THEM DOWN--
YOU WHAT?
IMBECILE! THAT PLATFORM IS RIGHT UNDER THE MONORAIL TRESTLE! THE MAGNETIC FIELDS TRASHED THEIR ELECTRONIC BRAINS!
OF COURSE, NOT HAVING ANY KIND OF A BRAIN AT ALL, IT WOULDN'T AFFECT YOU!
I GOTTA GET ANOTHER JOB...
OPERATOR. GET ME THE ACME ROBOT REPAIR SERVICE!
...JUST WHAT WE NEED. MORE BLOODY -zip- AMNESIACS!
ONE MOMENT. PLEASE.
HELLO. HERCULEAN ARMS.
GIMME CHARITY. AND MAKE IT SNAPPY!
SORRY. WRO-ONG NUMBER. I SUGGEST YOU-zip-CONTACT TERMINAL CITY CHAMBER OF COMMERCE -beep-THANK YOU.

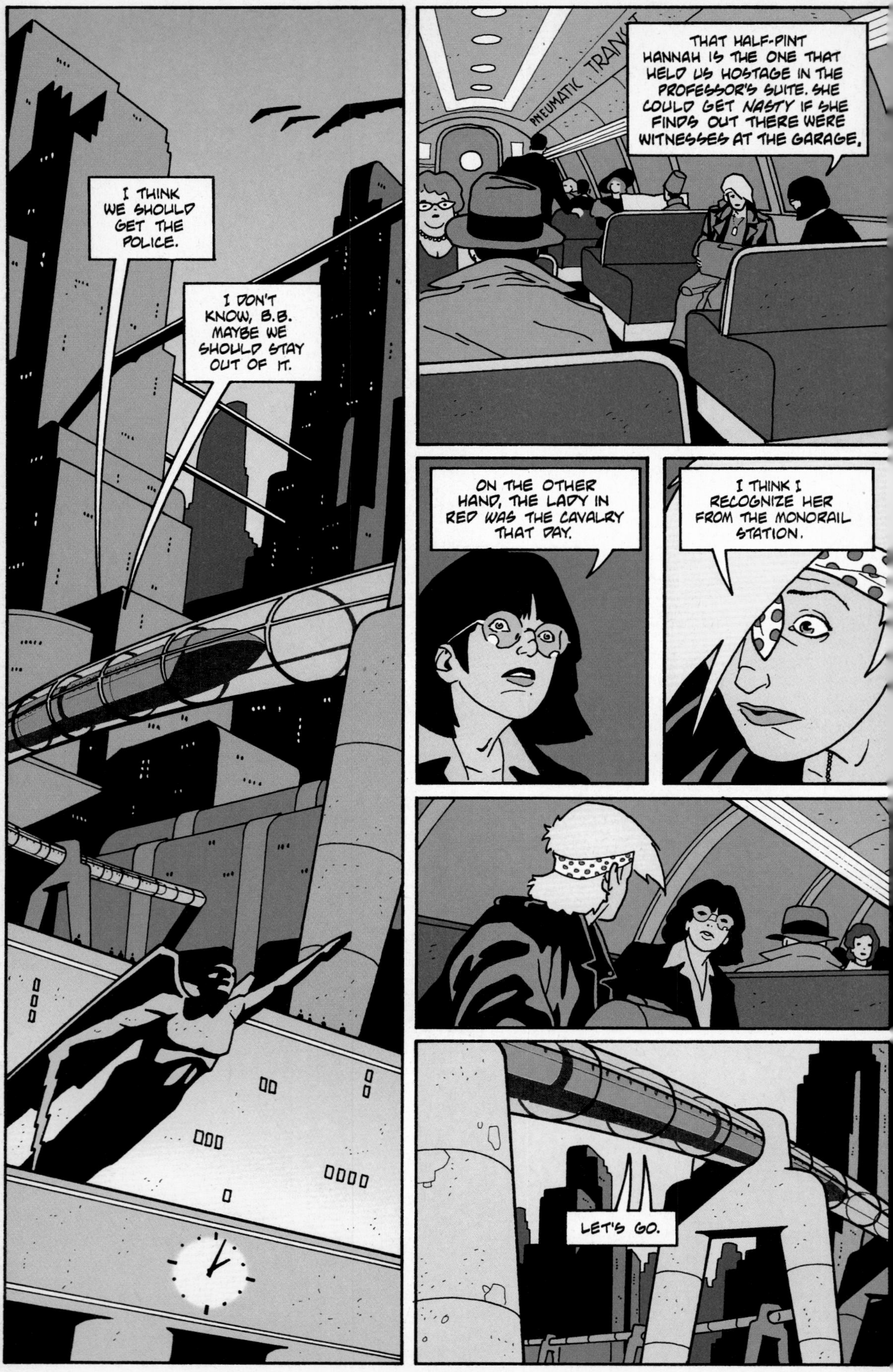
I THINK WE SHOULD GET THE POLICE.
I DON'T KNOW, B.B. MAYBE WE SHOULD STAY OUT OF IT.
PNEUMATIC TRANSIT
THAT HALF-PINT HANNAH IS THE ONE THAT HELD US HOSTAGE IN THE PROFESSOR'S SUITE. SHE COULD GET NASTY IF SHE FINDS OUT THERE WERE WITNESSES AT THE GARAGE.
ON THE OTHER HAND, THE LADY IN RED WAS THE CAVALRY THAT DAY.
I THINK I RECOGNIZE HER FROM THE MONORAIL STATION.
LET'S GO.

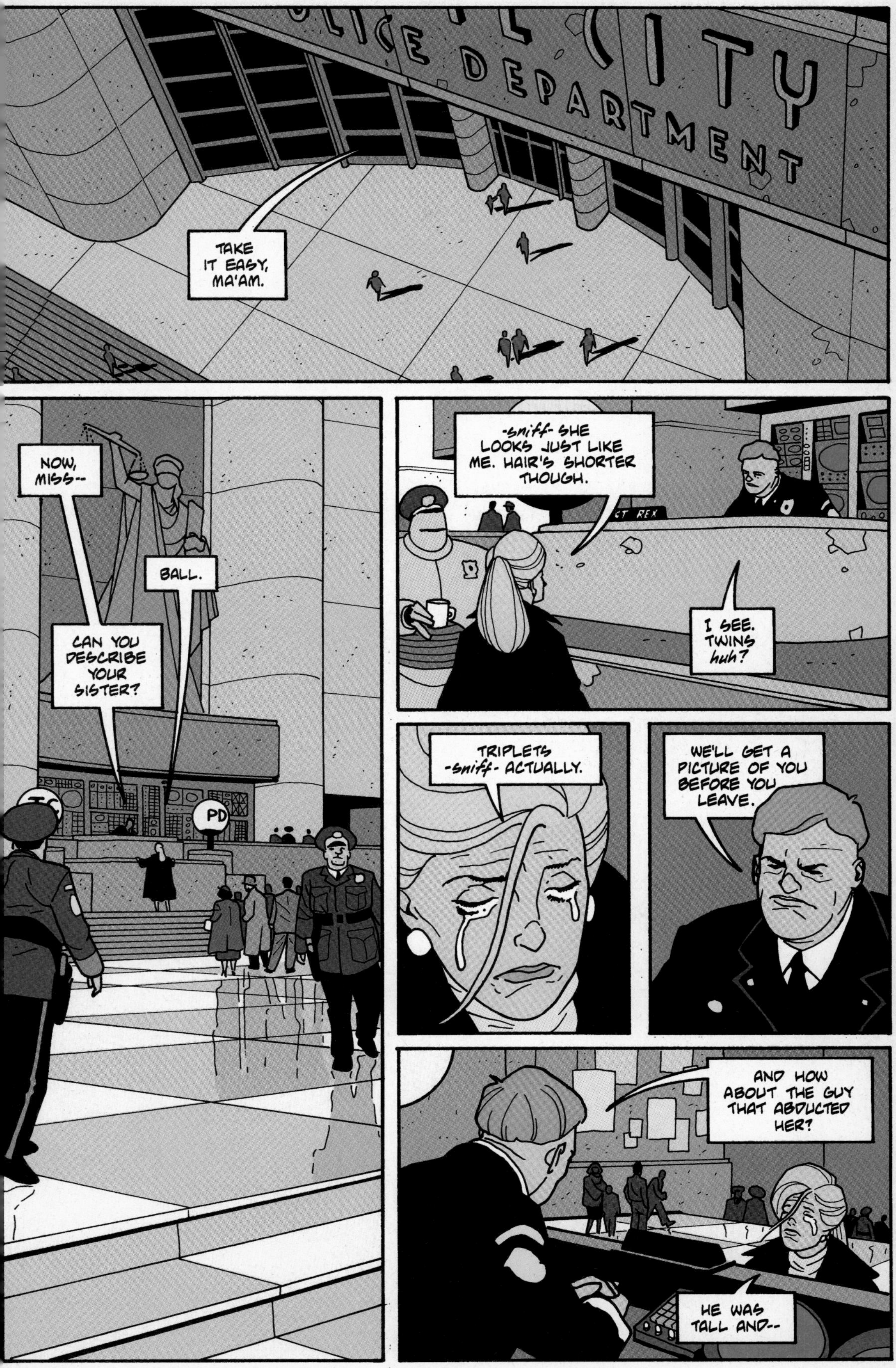

OLICE CITY
DEPARTMENT
TAKE IT EASY, MA'AM.
NOW, MISS--
BALL.
CAN YOU DESCRIBE YOUR SISTER?
PD
-sniff- SHE LOOKS JUST LIKE ME. HAIR'S SHORTER THOUGH.
I SEE. TWINS huh?
TRIPLETS -sniff- ACTUALLY.
WE'LL GET A PICTURE OF YOU BEFORE YOU LEAVE.
AND HOW ABOUT THE GUY THAT ABDUCTED HER?
HE WAS TALL AND--

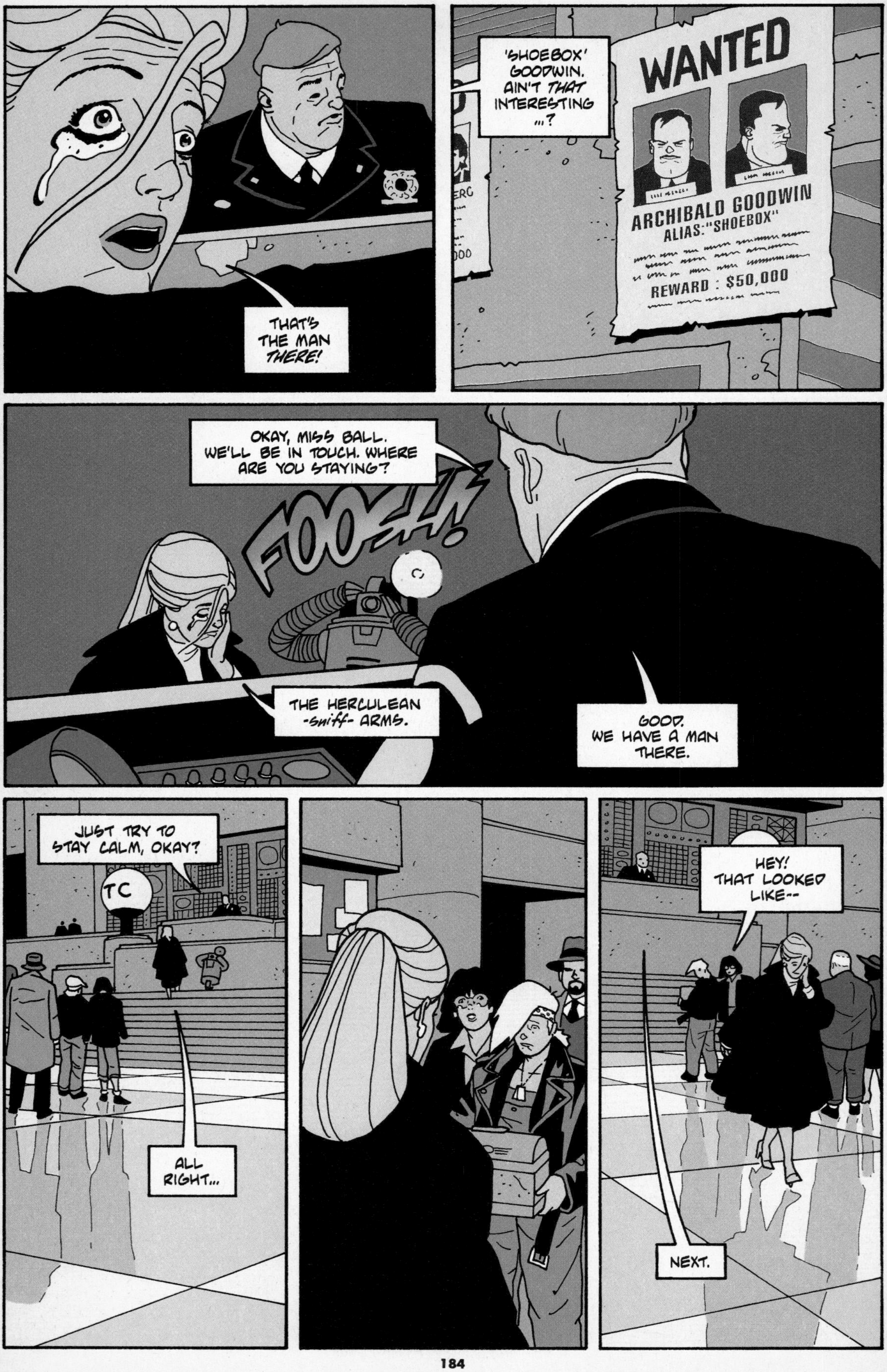
THAT'S THE MAN THERE!
'SHOEBOX' GOODWIN. AIN'T THAT INTERESTING ...?
WANTED
ARCHIBALD GOODWIN
ALIAS:"SHOEBOX"
REWARD : $50,000
OKAY, MISS BALL. WE'LL BE IN TOUCH. WHERE ARE YOU STAYING?
FOOSH!
THE HERCULEAN -sniff- ARMS.
GOOD. WE HAVE A MAN THERE.
JUST TRY TO STAY CALM, OKAY?
TC
ALL RIGHT...
HEY! THAT LOOKED LIKE--
NEXT.

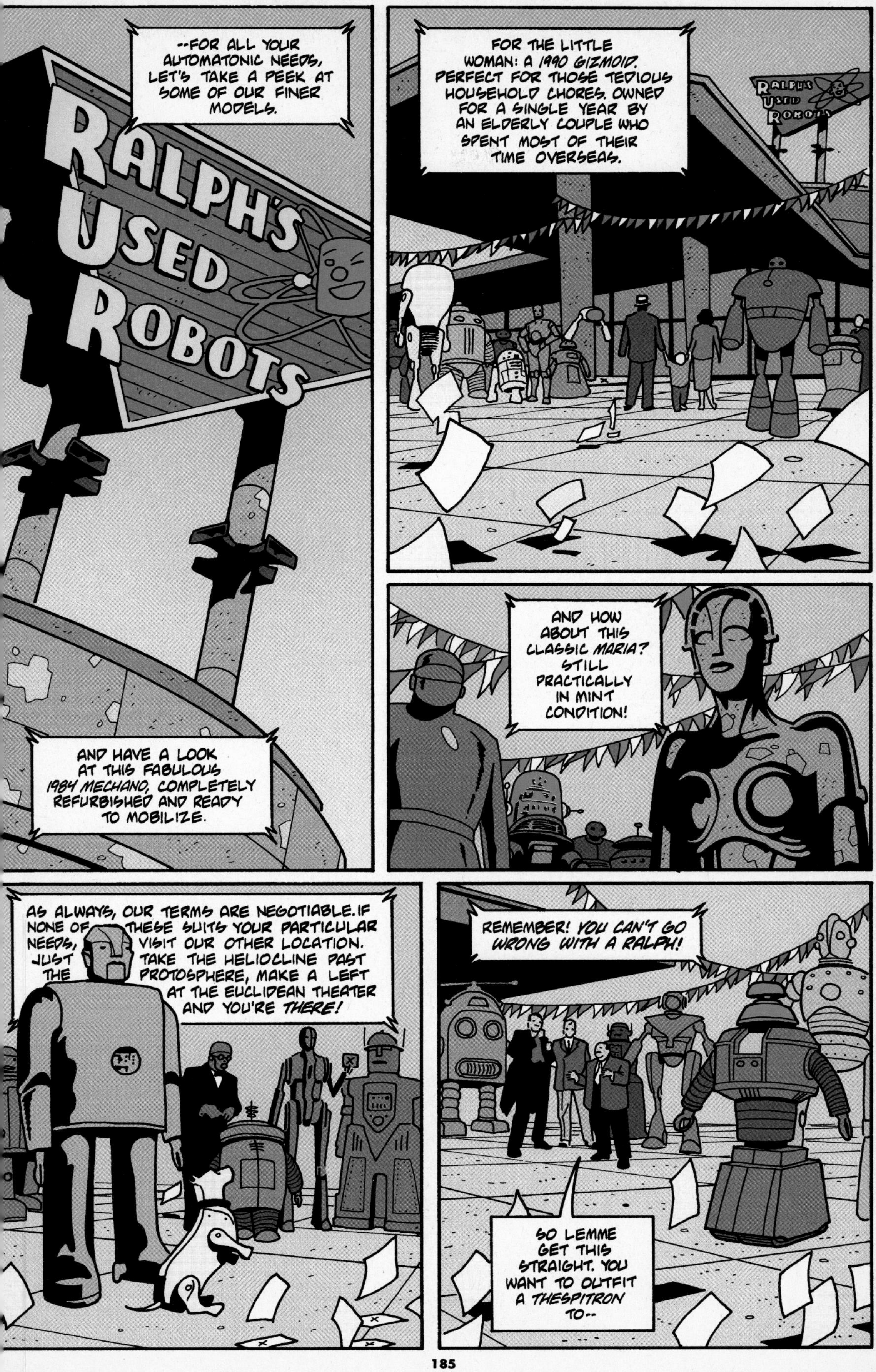

--FOR ALL YOUR AUTOMATONIC NEEDS, LET'S TAKE A PEEK AT SOME OF OUR FINER MODELS.
RALPH'S USED ROBOTS
AND HAVE A LOOK AT THIS FABULOUS *1984 MECHANO*, COMPLETELY REFURBISHED AND READY TO MOBILIZE.
FOR THE LITTLE WOMAN: A *1990 GIZMOID*. PERFECT FOR THOSE TEDIOUS HOUSEHOLD CHORES. OWNED FOR A SINGLE YEAR BY AN ELDERLY COUPLE WHO SPENT MOST OF THEIR TIME OVERSEAS.
RALPH'S USED ROBOTS
AND HOW ABOUT THIS CLASSIC *MARIA*? STILL PRACTICALLY IN MINT CONDITION!
AS ALWAYS, OUR TERMS ARE NEGOTIABLE. IF NONE OF THESE SUITS YOUR PARTICULAR NEEDS, VISIT OUR OTHER LOCATION. JUST TAKE THE HELIOCLINE PAST THE PROTOSPHERE, MAKE A LEFT AT THE EUCLIDEAN THEATER AND YOU'RE *THERE!*
REMEMBER! *YOU CAN'T GO WRONG WITH A RALPH!*
SO LEMME GET THIS STRAIGHT. YOU WANT TO OUTFIT A *THESPITRON* TO--

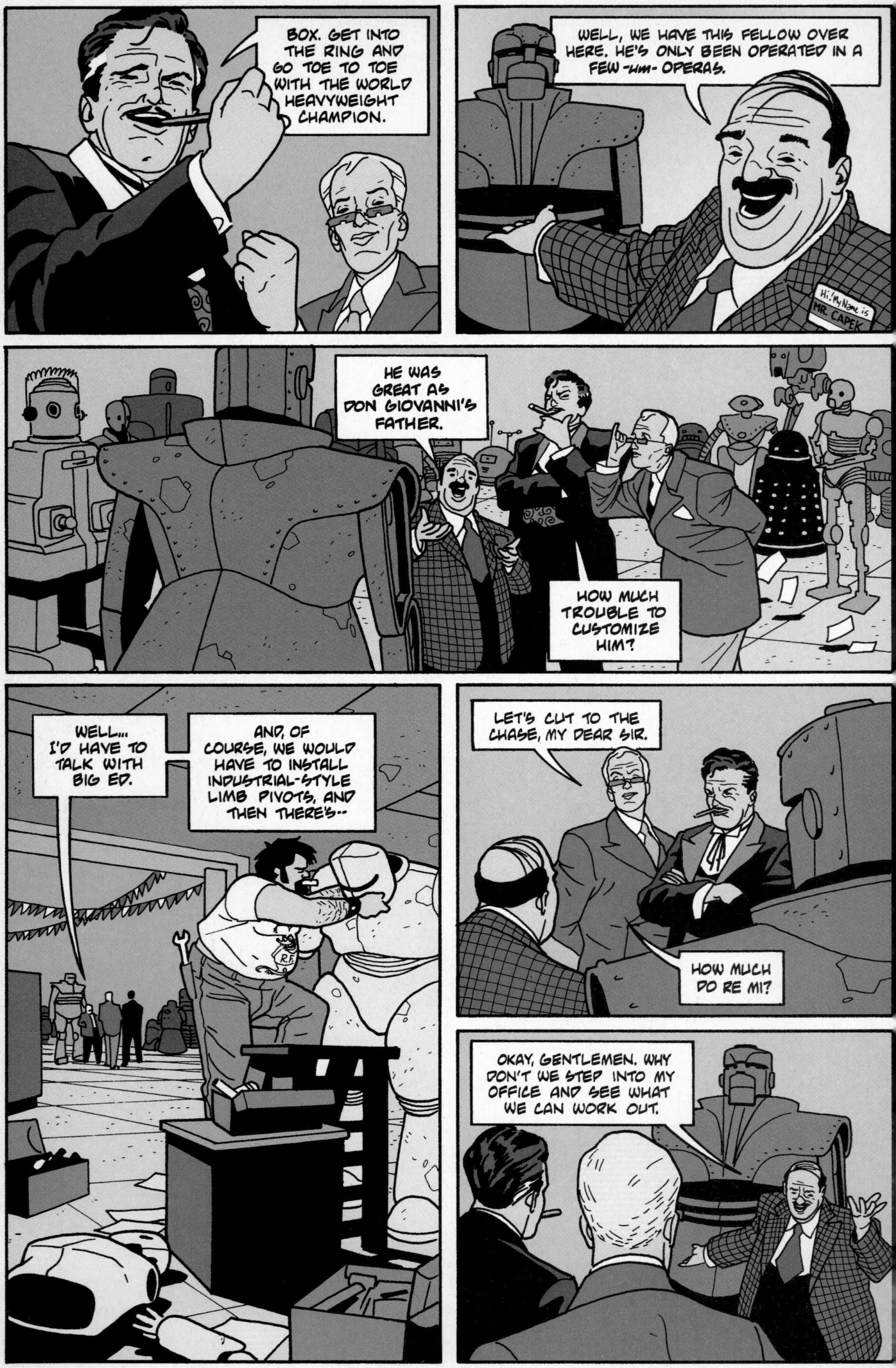
BOX. GET INTO THE RING AND GO TOE TO TOE WITH THE WORLD HEAVYWEIGHT CHAMPION.
WELL, WE HAVE THIS FELLOW OVER HERE. HE'S ONLY BEEN OPERATED IN A FEW -*HM*- OPERAS.
Hi! My Name is MR. CAPEK
HE WAS GREAT AS DON GIOVANNI'S FATHER.
HOW MUCH TROUBLE TO CUSTOMIZE HIM?
WELL... I'D HAVE TO TALK WITH BIG ED.
AND, OF COURSE, WE WOULD HAVE TO INSTALL INDUSTRIAL-STYLE LIMB PIVOTS, AND THEN THERE'S--
R.F.
LET'S CUT TO THE CHASE, MY DEAR SIR.
HOW MUCH DO RE MI?
OKAY, GENTLEMEN. WHY DON'T WE STEP INTO MY OFFICE AND SEE WHAT WE CAN WORK OUT.

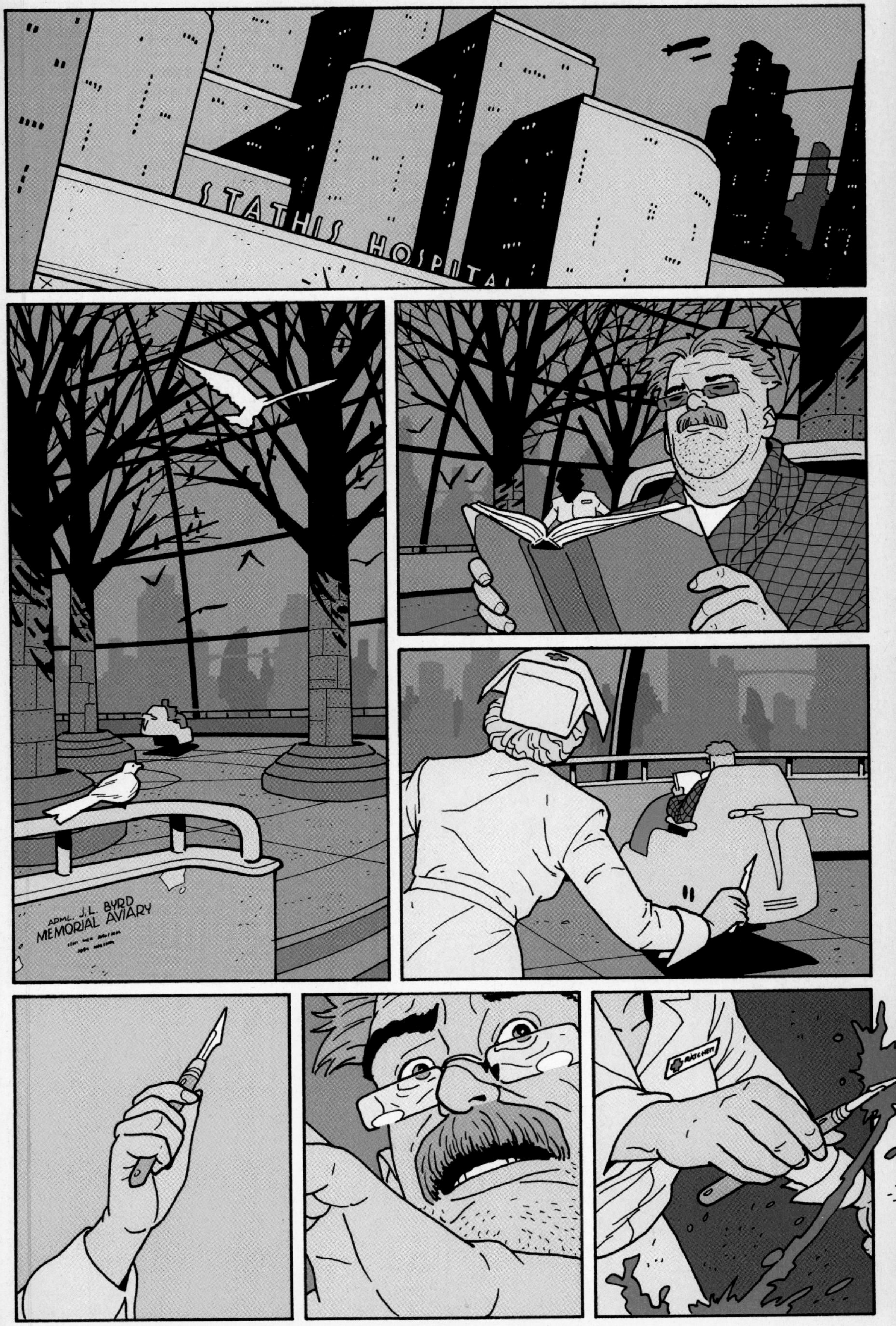
STATHIS HOSPITAL
ADML. J.L. BYRD MEMORIAL AVIARY
RATCHETT

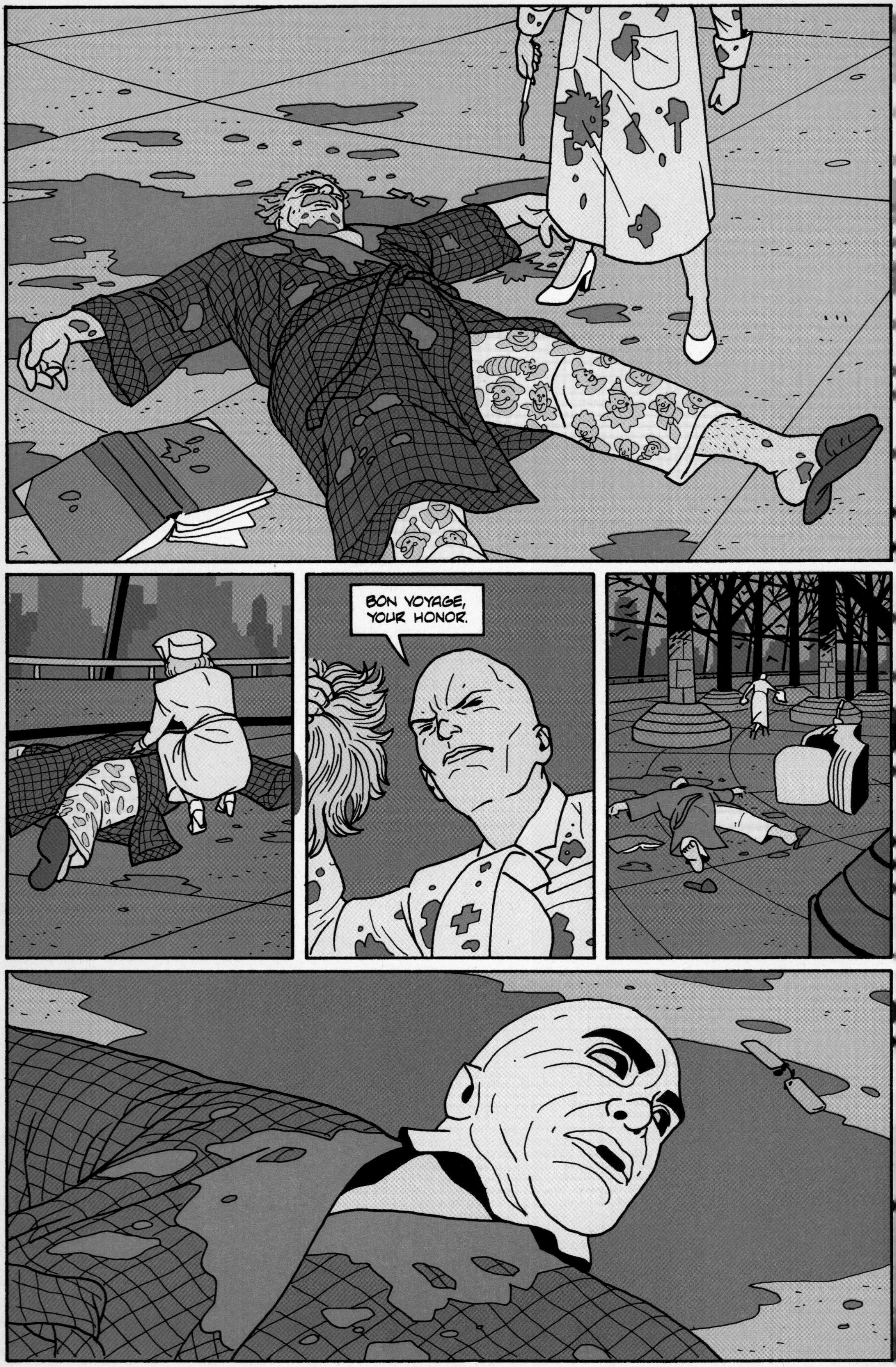
BON VOYAGE, YOUR HONOR.

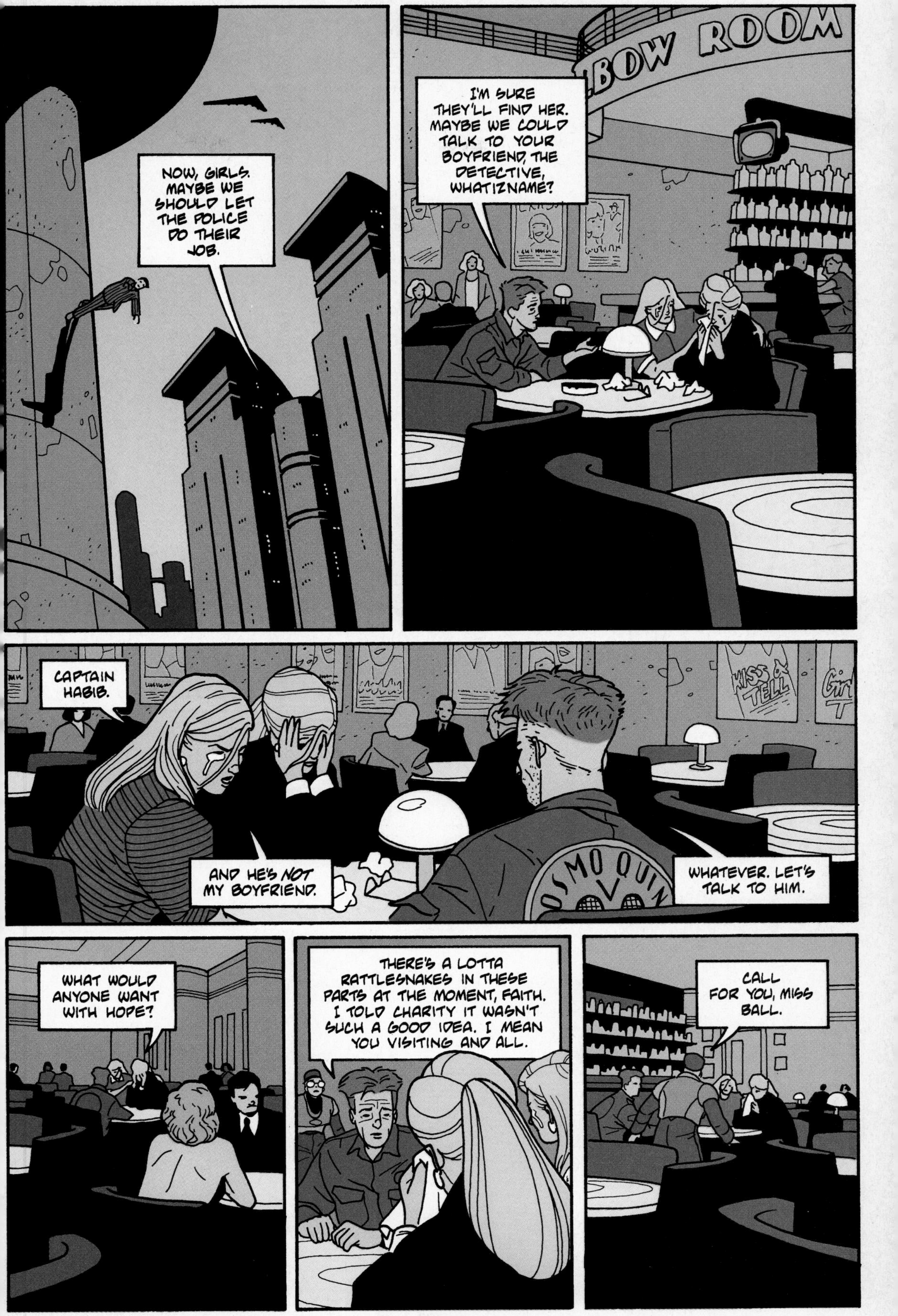
NOW, GIRLS. MAYBE WE SHOULD LET THE POLICE DO THEIR JOB.
BOW ROOM
I'M SURE THEY'LL FIND HER. MAYBE WE COULD TALK TO YOUR BOYFRIEND, THE DETECTIVE, WHATIZNAME?
CAPTAIN HABIB.
AND HE'S NOT MY BOYFRIEND.
KISS & TELL
WHATEVER. LET'S TALK TO HIM.
WHAT WOULD ANYONE WANT WITH HOPE?
THERE'S A LOTTA RATTLESNAKES IN THESE PARTS AT THE MOMENT, FAITH. I TOLD CHARITY IT WASN'T SUCH A GOOD IDEA. I MEAN YOU VISITING AND ALL.
CALL FOR YOU, MISS BALL.

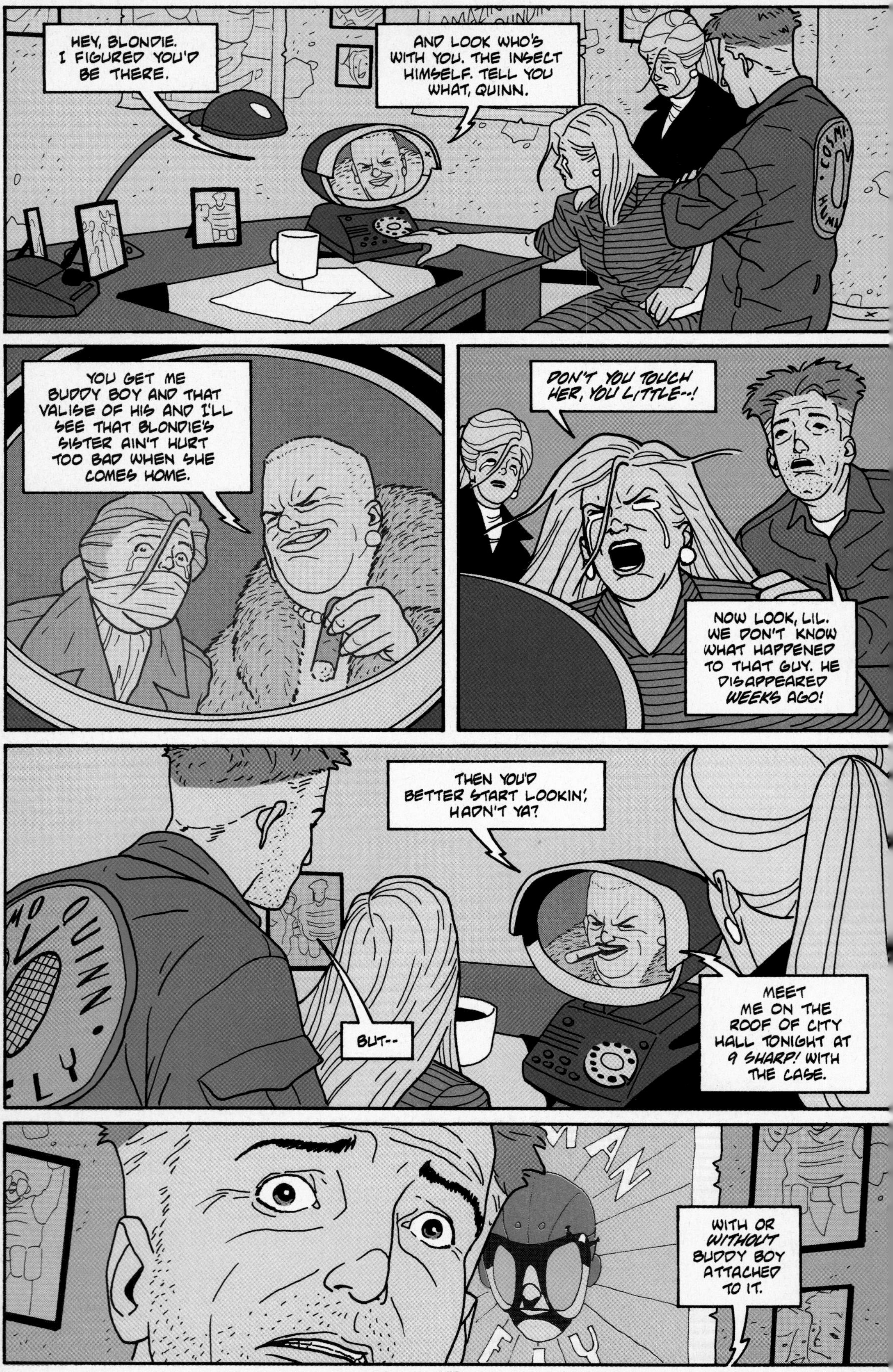

HEY, BLONDIE. I FIGURED YOU'D BE THERE.
AND LOOK WHO'S WITH YOU. THE INSECT HIMSELF. TELL YOU WHAT, QUINN.
YOU GET ME BUDDY BOY AND THAT VALISE OF HIS AND I'LL SEE THAT BLONDIE'S SISTER AIN'T HURT TOO BAD WHEN SHE COMES HOME.
DON'T YOU TOUCH HER, YOU LITTLE--!
NOW LOOK, LIL. WE DON'T KNOW WHAT HAPPENED TO THAT GUY. HE DISAPPEARED WEEKS AGO!
THEN YOU'D BETTER START LOOKIN', HADN'T YA?
BUT--
MEET ME ON THE ROOF OF CITY HALL TONIGHT AT 9 SHARP! WITH THE CASE.
WITH OR WITHOUT BUDDY BOY ATTACHED TO IT.

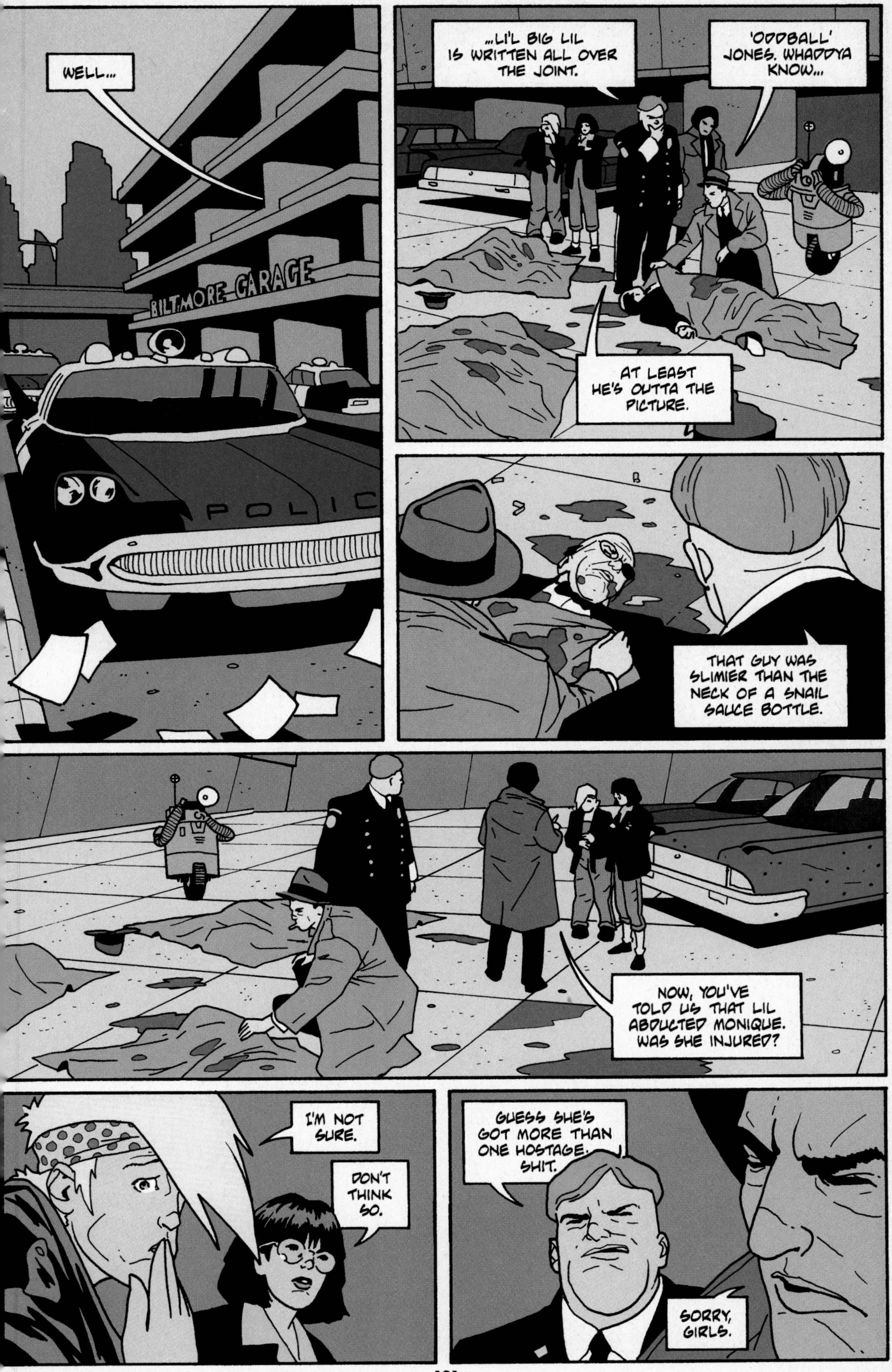
WELL...
BILTMORE GARAGE
POLIC
...LI'L BIG LIL IS WRITTEN ALL OVER THE JOINT.
'ODDBALL' JONES. WHADDYA KNOW...
AT LEAST HE'S OUTTA THE PICTURE.
THAT GUY WAS SLIMIER THAN THE NECK OF A SNAIL SAUCE BOTTLE.
NOW, YOU'VE TOLD US THAT LIL ABDUCTED MONIQUE. WAS SHE INJURED?
I'M NOT SURE.
DON'T THINK SO.
GUESS SHE'S GOT MORE THAN ONE HOSTAGE. SHIT.
SORRY, GIRLS.

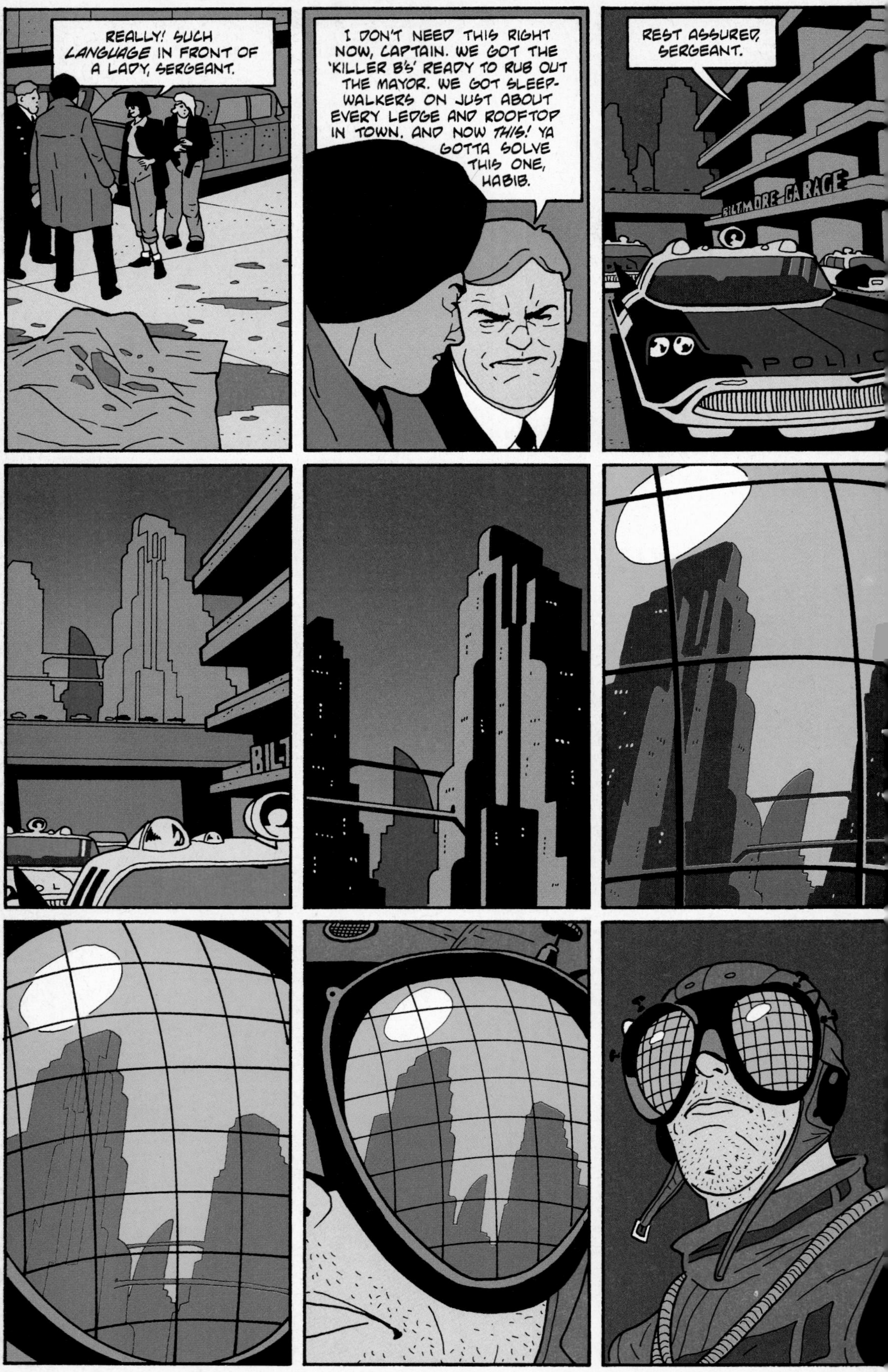
REALLY! SUCH LANGUAGE IN FRONT OF A LADY, SERGEANT.
I DON'T NEED THIS RIGHT NOW, CAPTAIN. WE GOT THE 'KILLER B'S' READY TO RUB OUT THE MAYOR. WE GOT SLEEP-WALKERS ON JUST ABOUT EVERY LEDGE AND ROOFTOP IN TOWN. AND NOW THIS! YA GOTTA SOLVE THIS ONE, HABIB.
REST ASSURED, SERGEANT.
BILTMORE GARAGE
POLIC
BILT

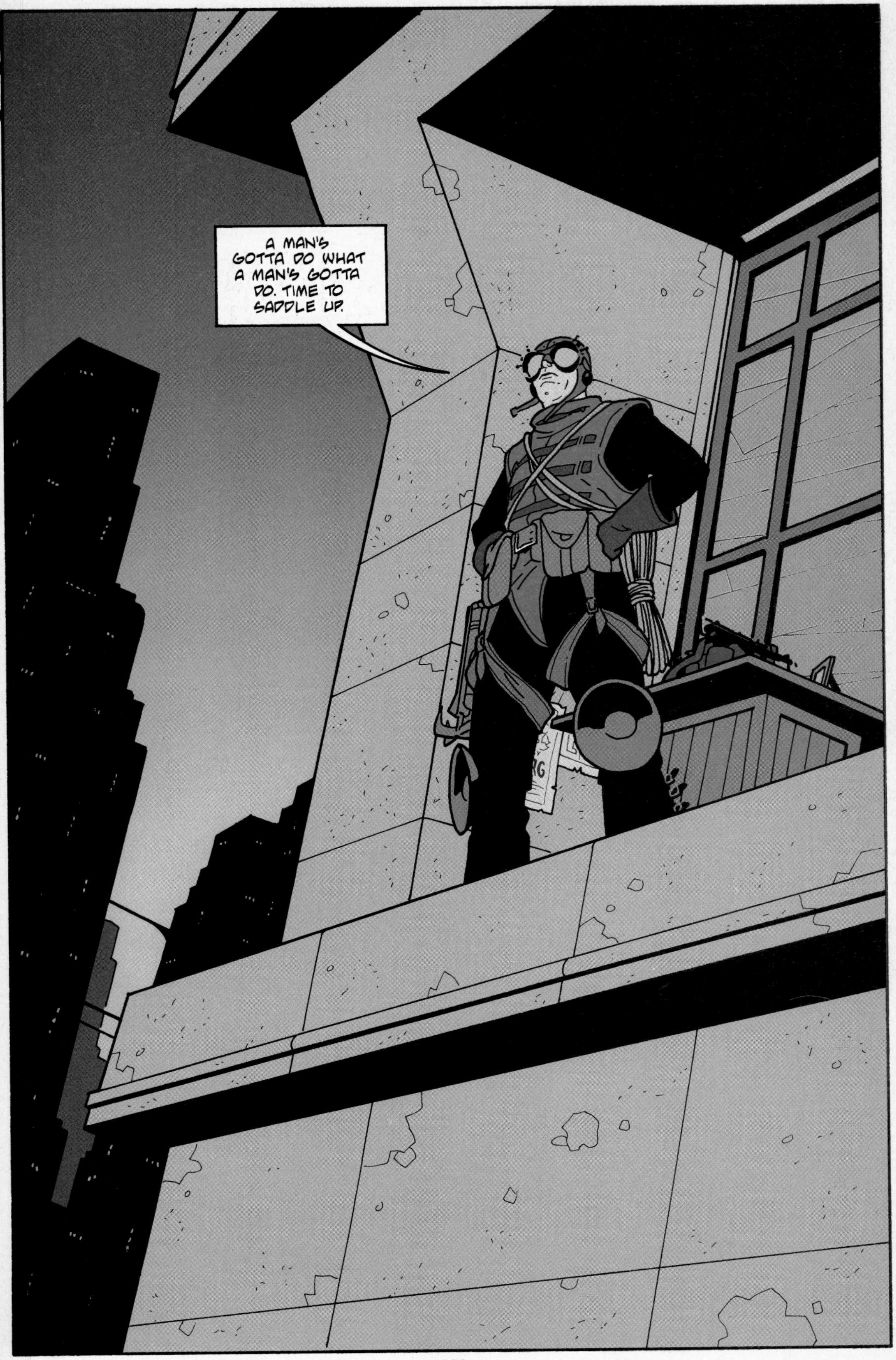
A MAN'S GOTTA DO WHAT A MAN'S GOTTA DO. TIME TO SADDLE UP.

I DUNNO, MONTY.

HOW CAN I GO UP AGAINST A *MACHINE?*

THAT'S JUST THE *POINT,* MY FRIEND! WE'RE ALL MACHINES, IN A WAY, AREN'T WE?

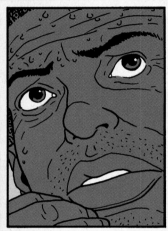

WHAT'S IT GONNA BE CALLED AGAIN?

BOLT. BOLT UPRIGHT.

LOOK, MY OLD FRIEND. HE'LL BE PROGRAMMED WITH THE SAME SKILL AND INJURY RATIOS AS ANY PROFESSIONAL BOXER. NOT *ONE BIT MORE.* IT'LL BE AN EVEN MATCH.

AND *WE* KNOW WHO WINS THOSE.

IT'LL BE GREAT! FIRST IT WAS KID GLOVES VS. EVOLUTION. NOW, KID GLOVES VS. SCIENCE. WE'LL *CLEAN UP!*

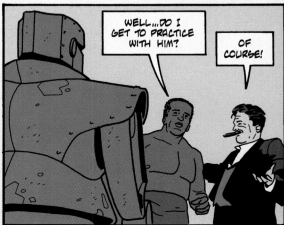

WELL...DO I GET TO PRACTICE WITH HIM?

OF COURSE!

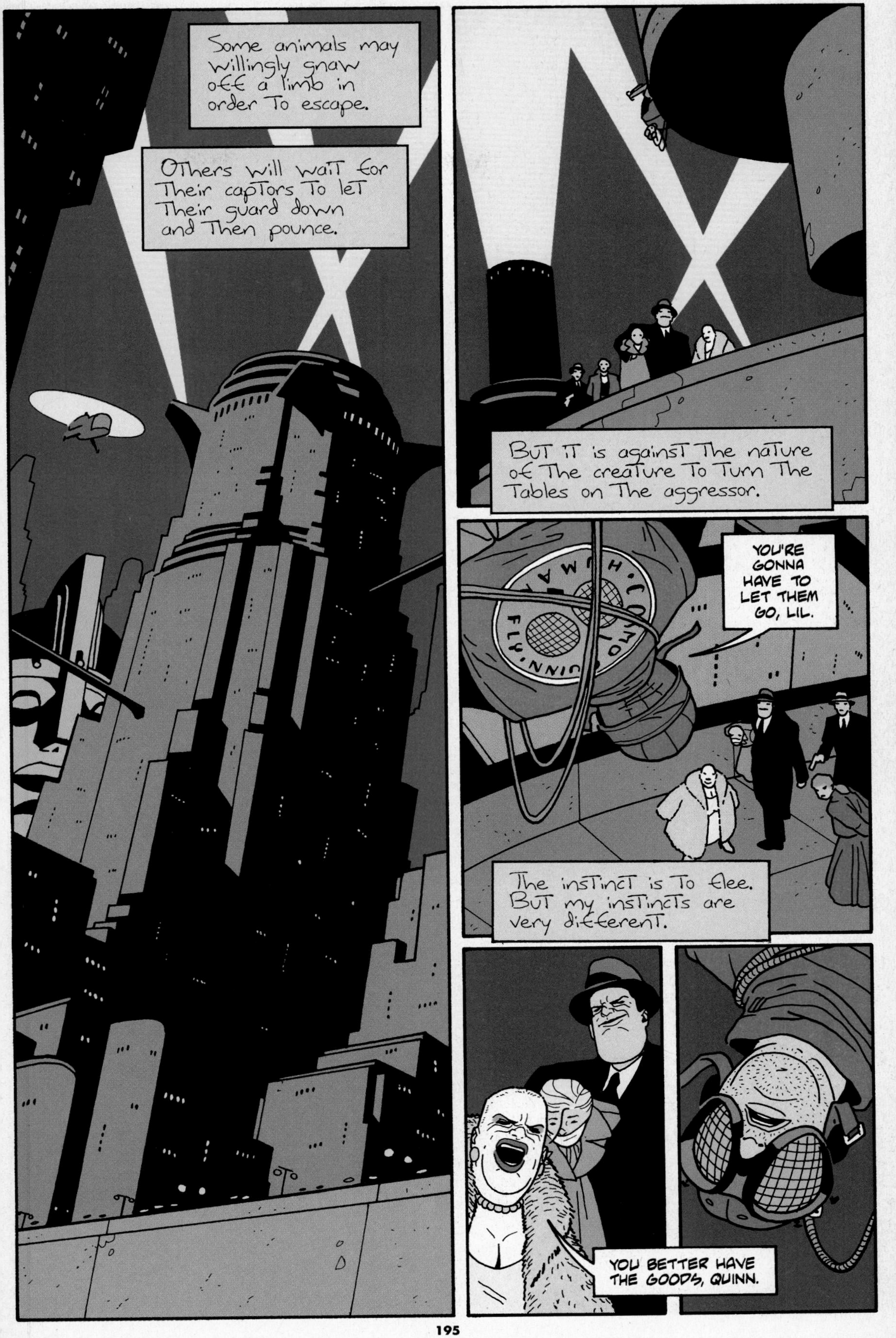
Some animals may willingly gnaw off a limb in order to escape.
Others will wait for their captors to let their guard down and then pounce.
But it is against the nature of the creature to turn the tables on the aggressor.
YOU'RE GONNA HAVE TO LET THEM GO, LIL.
The instinct is to flee. But my instincts are very different.
YOU BETTER HAVE THE GOODS, QUINN.

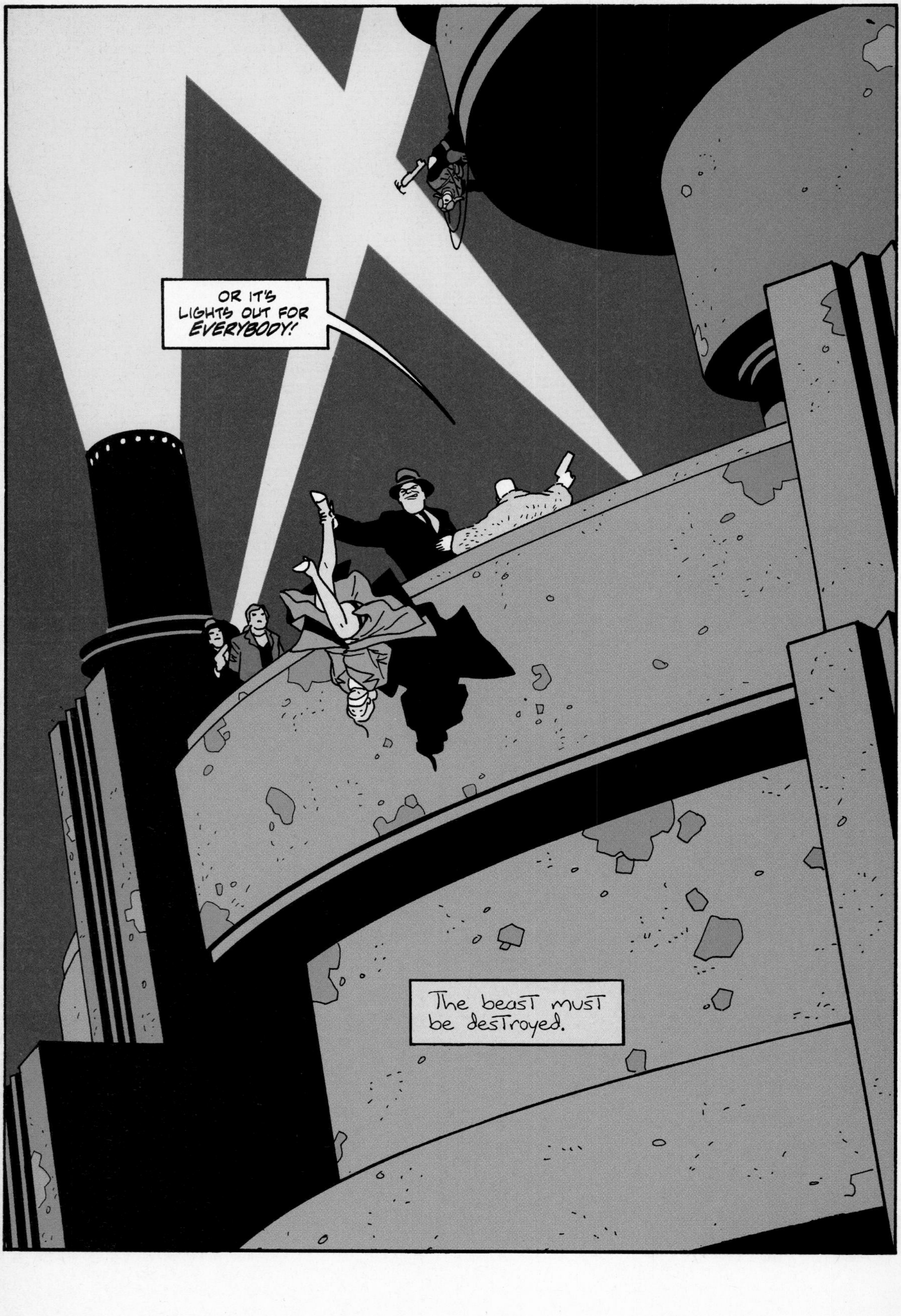
OR IT'S LIGHTS OUT FOR EVERYBODY!
The beast must be destroyed.

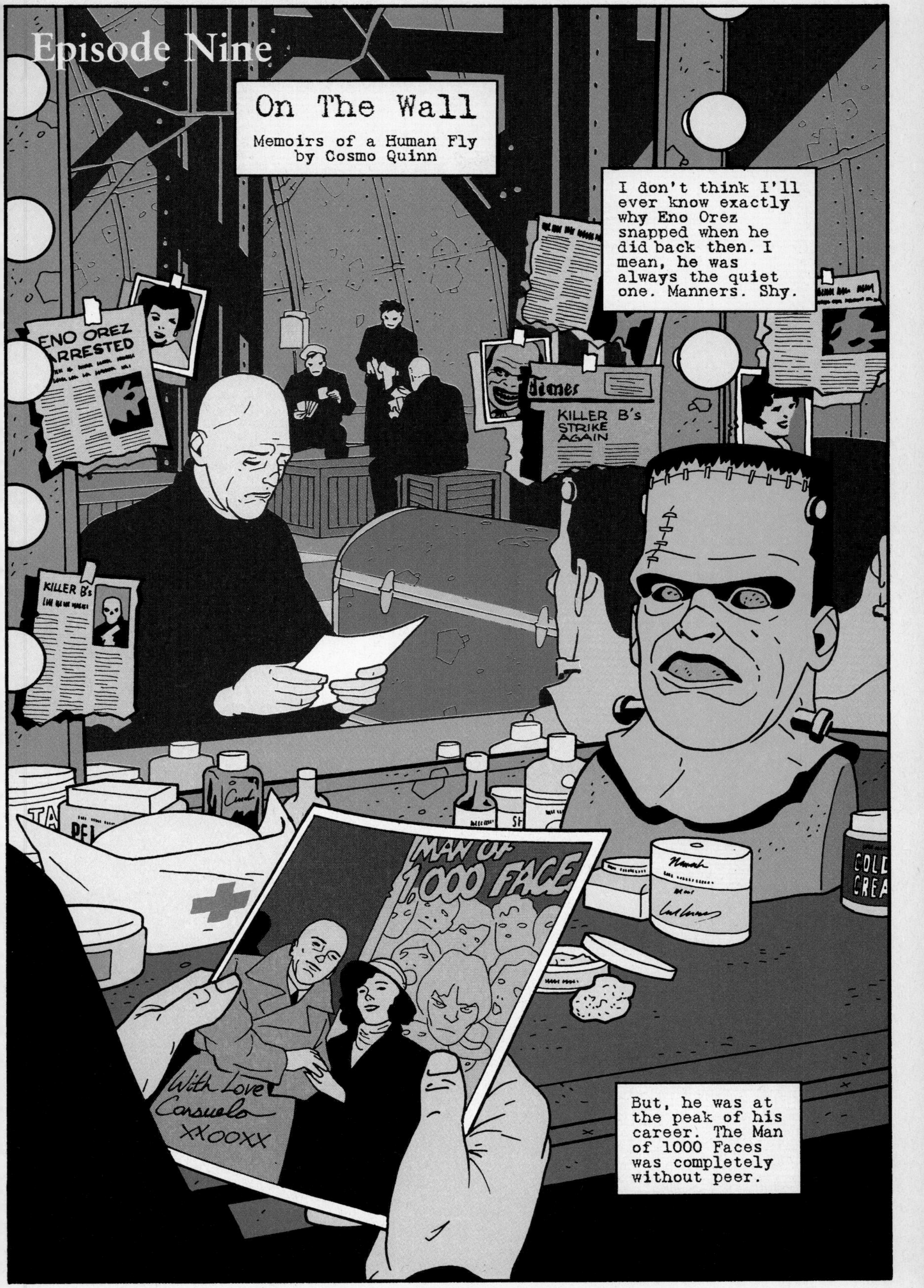
Episode Nine
On The Wall
Memoirs of a Human Fly
by Cosmo Quinn
I don't think I'll ever know exactly why Eno Orez snapped when he did back then. I mean, he was always the quiet one. Manners. Shy.
ENO OREZ ARRESTED
Times
KILLER B's STRIKE AGAIN
KILLER B's
MAN OF 1,000 FACE
With Love Consuelo XXOOXX
COLD CREA
But, he was at the peak of his career. The Man of 1000 Faces was completely without peer.

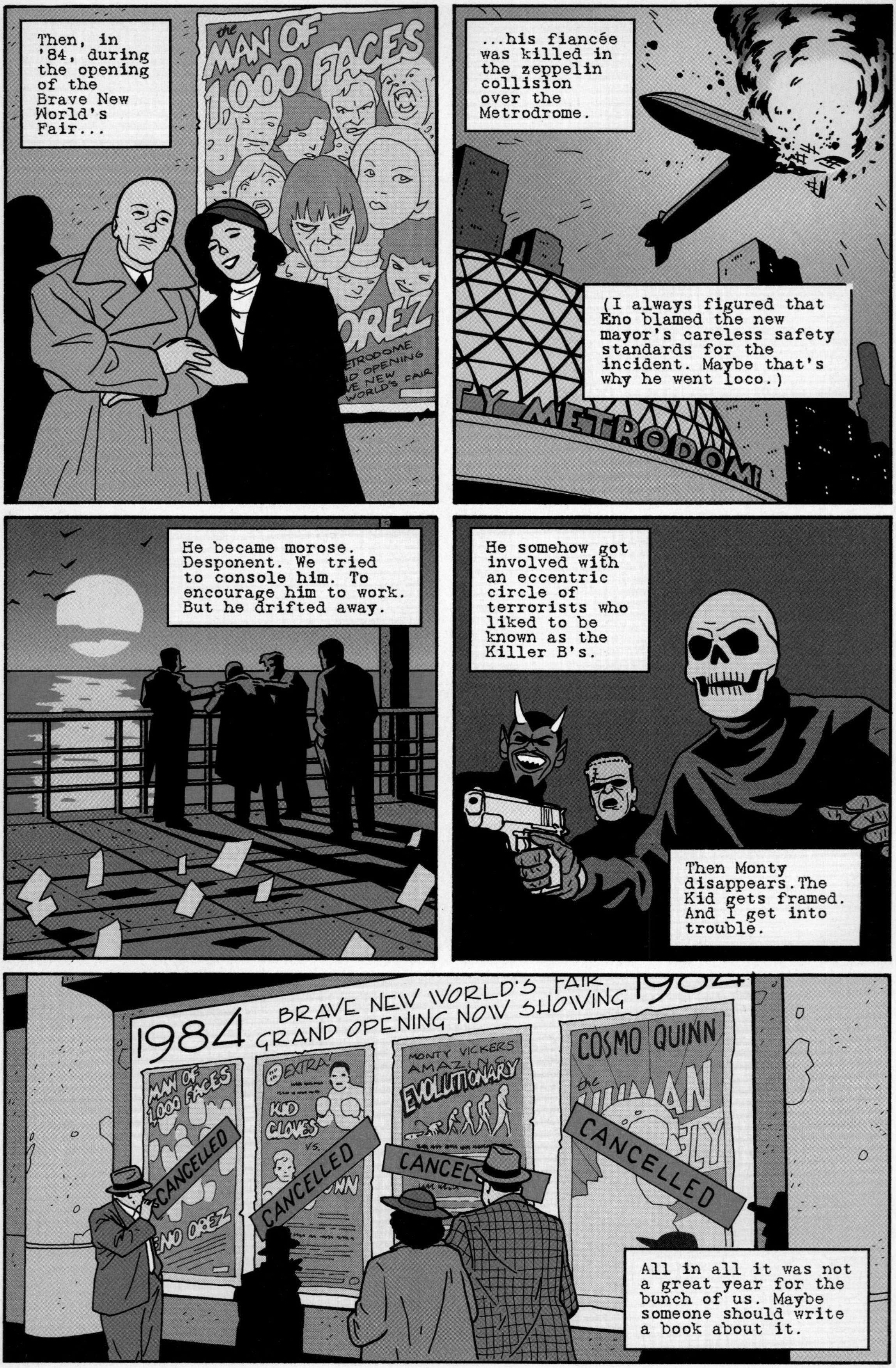
Then, in '84, during the opening of the Brave New World's Fair...
the MAN OF 1,000 FACES
...his fiancée was killed in the zeppelin collision over the Metrodrome.
(I always figured that Eno blamed the new mayor's careless safety standards for the incident. Maybe that's why he went loco.)
He became morose. Desponent. We tried to console him. To encourage him to work. But he drifted away.
He somehow got involved with an eccentric circle of terrorists who liked to be known as the Killer B's.
Then Monty disappears. The Kid gets framed. And I get into trouble.
1984 BRAVE NEW WORLD'S FAIR GRAND OPENING NOW SHOWING
MAN OF 1,000 FACES
ENO OREZ
EXTRA!
KID GLOVES VS.
MONTY VICKERS AMAZING EVOLUTIONARY
COSMO QUINN
CANCELLED
CANCELLED
CANCELLED
All in all it was not a great year for the bunch of us. Maybe someone should write a book about it.

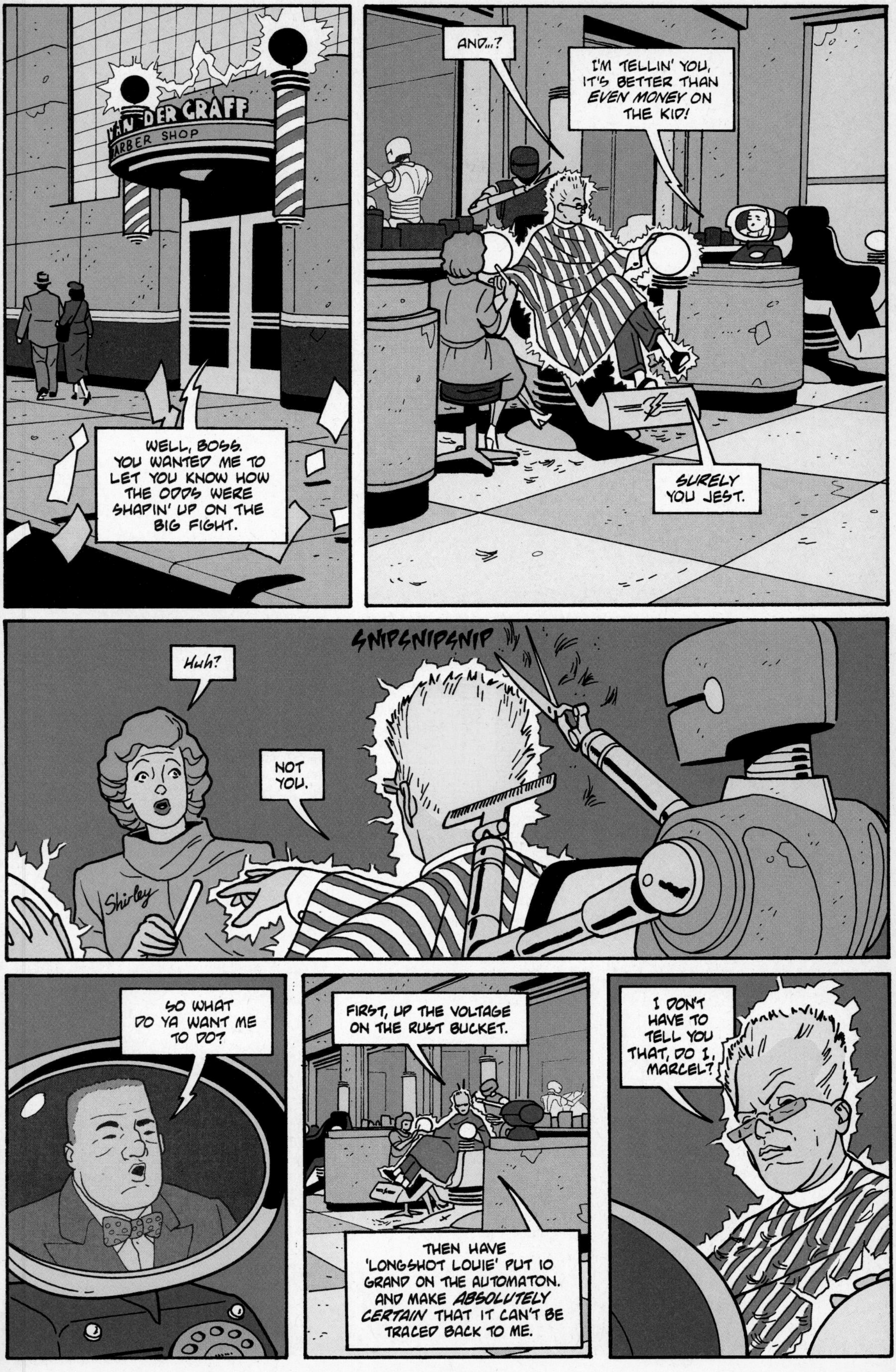
VAN DER GRAFF
BARBER SHOP
WELL, BOSS. YOU WANTED ME TO LET YOU KNOW HOW THE ODDS WERE SHAPIN' UP ON THE BIG FIGHT.
AND...?
I'M TELLIN' YOU, IT'S BETTER THAN EVEN MONEY ON THE KID!
SURELY YOU JEST.
SNIPSNIPSNIP
Huh?
NOT YOU.
Shirley
SO WHAT DO YA WANT ME TO DO?
FIRST, UP THE VOLTAGE ON THE RUST BUCKET.
THEN HAVE 'LONGSHOT LOUIE' PUT 10 GRAND ON THE AUTOMATON. AND MAKE ABSOLUTELY CERTAIN THAT IT CAN'T BE TRACED BACK TO ME.
I DON'T HAVE TO TELL YOU THAT, DO I, MARCEL?

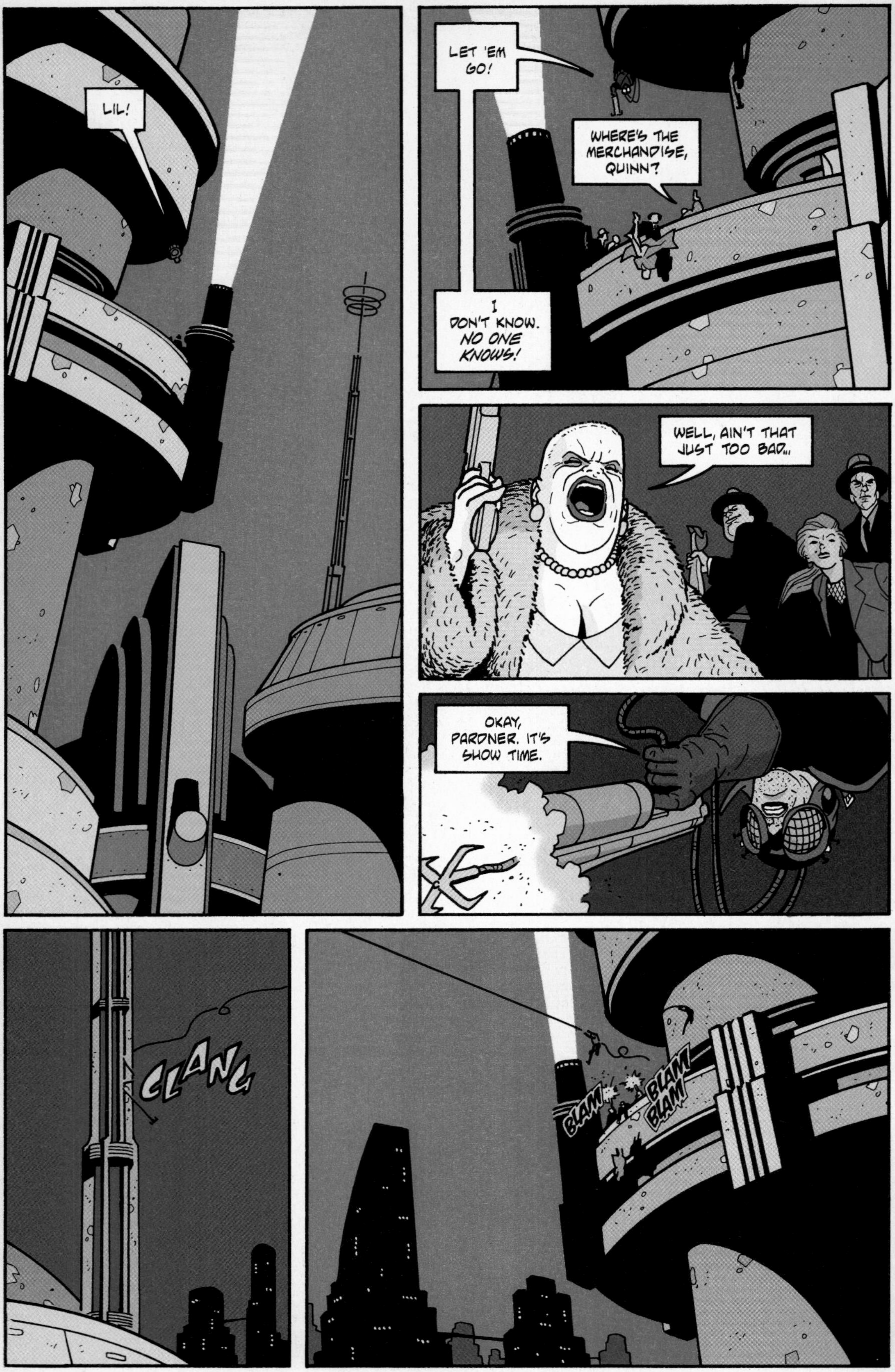
LIL!
LET 'EM GO!
WHERE'S THE MERCHANDISE, QUINN?
I DON'T KNOW. NO ONE KNOWS!
WELL, AIN'T THAT JUST TOO BAD...
OKAY, PARDNER. IT'S SHOW TIME.
CLANG
BLAM
BLAM
BLAM

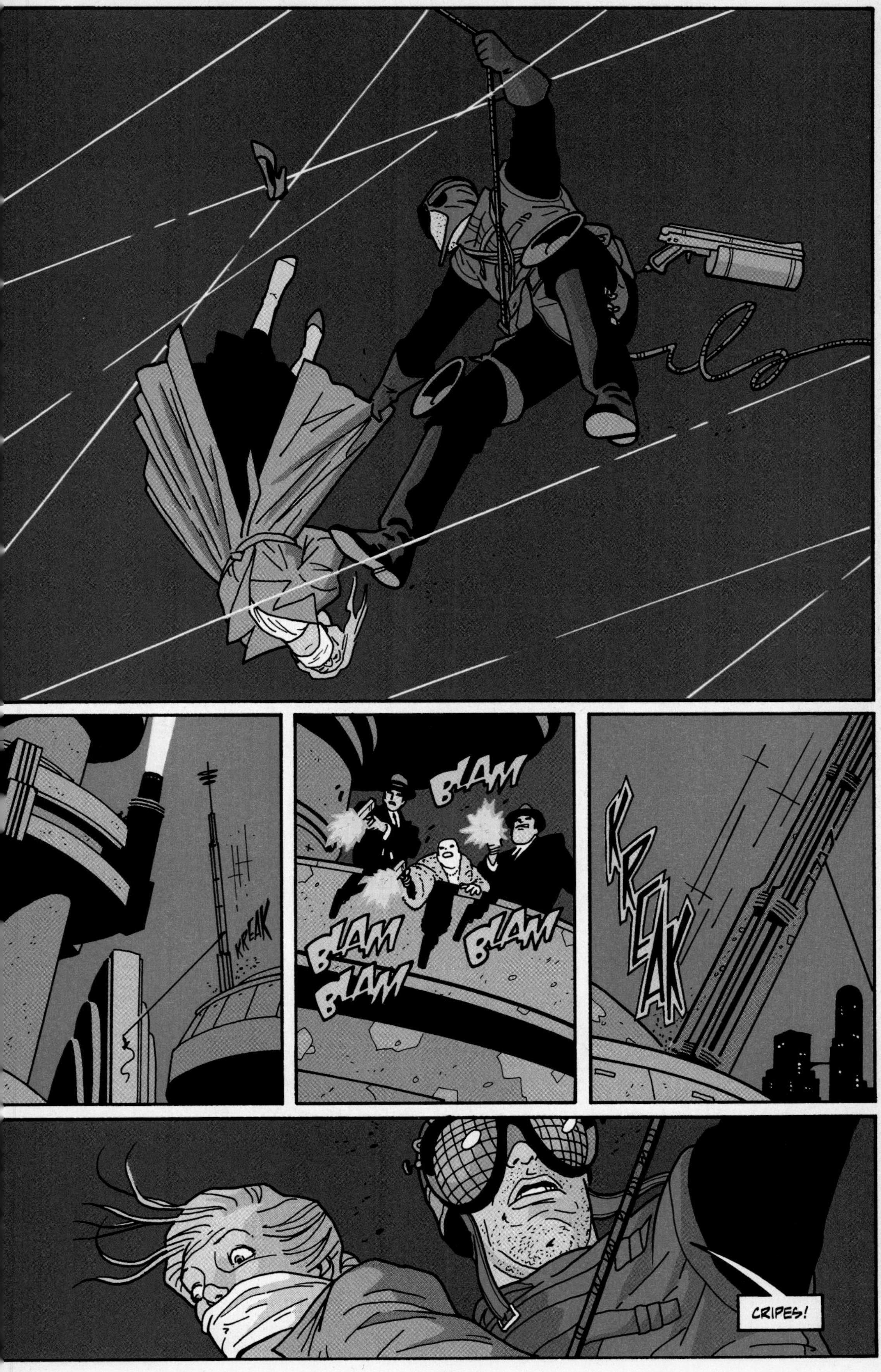
KREAK
BLAM
BLAM
BLAM
BLAM
KREAK
CRIPES!

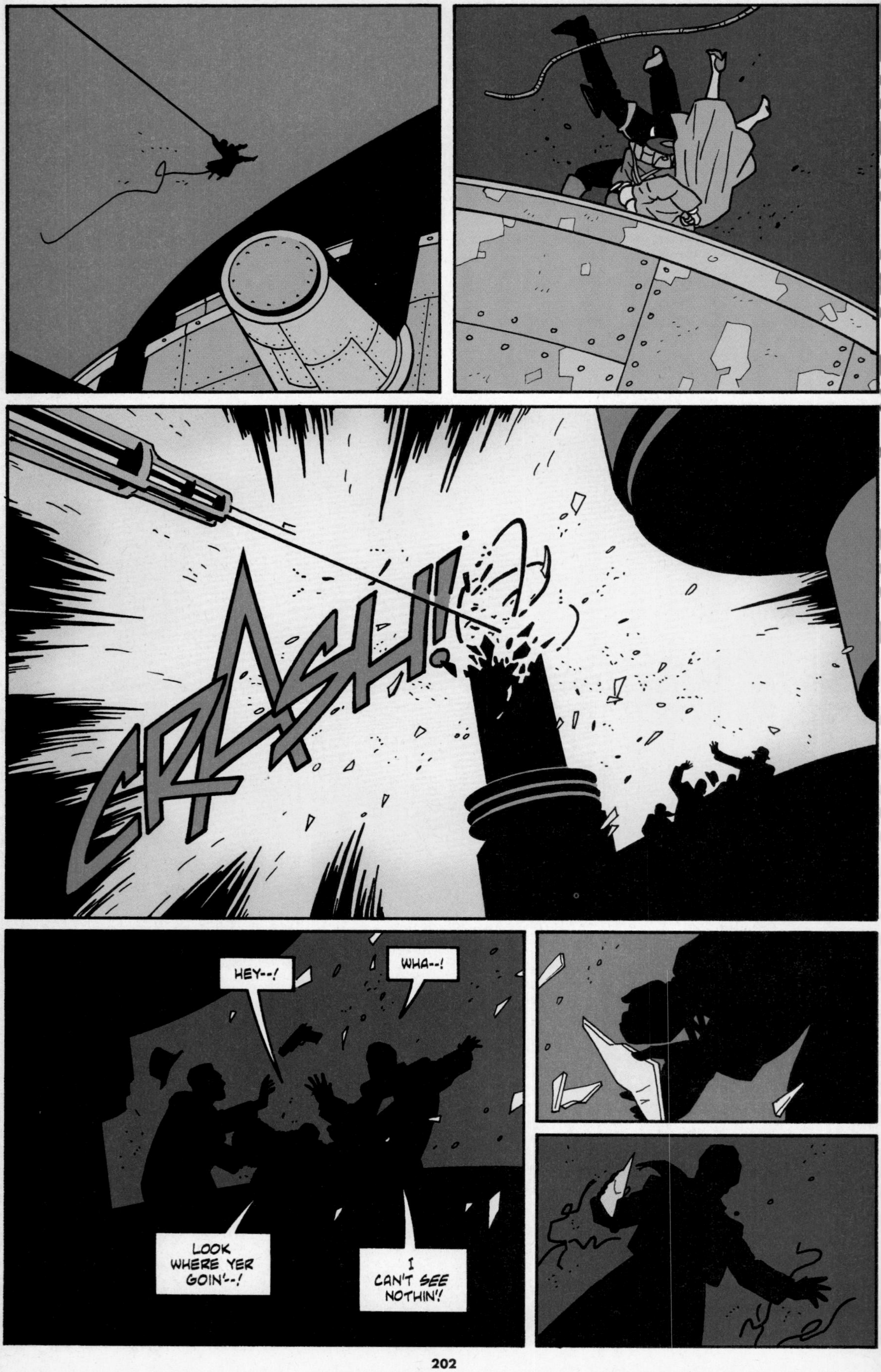
CRASH!
HEY--!
WHA--!
LOOK WHERE YER GOIN'--!
I CAN'T SEE NOTHIN'!

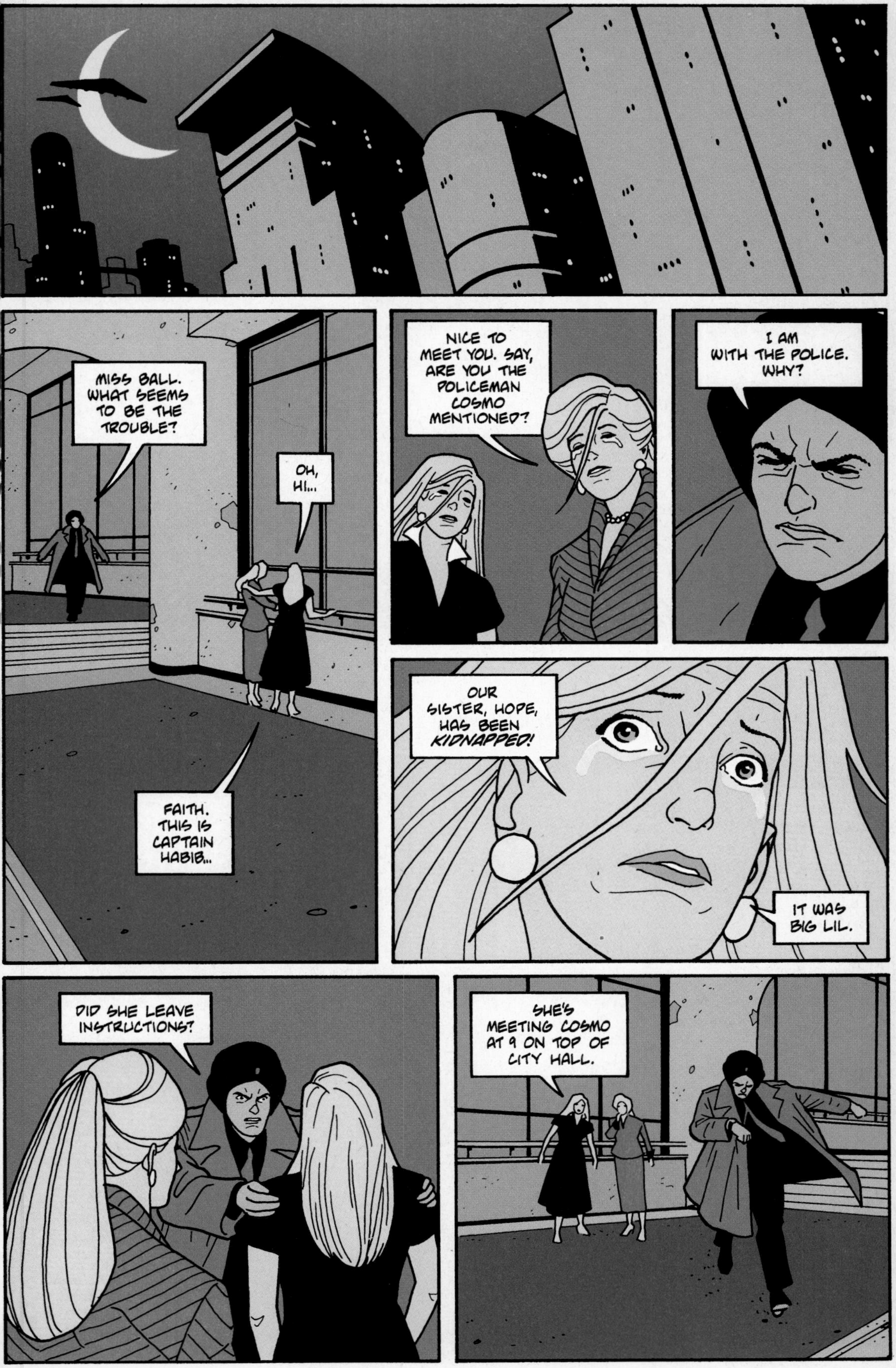

MISS BALL. WHAT SEEMS TO BE THE TROUBLE?
OH, HI...
FAITH. THIS IS CAPTAIN HABIB...
NICE TO MEET YOU. SAY, ARE YOU THE POLICEMAN COSMO MENTIONED?
I AM WITH THE POLICE. WHY?
OUR SISTER, HOPE, HAS BEEN *KIDNAPPED!*
IT WAS BIG LIL.
DID SHE LEAVE INSTRUCTIONS?
SHE'S MEETING COSMO AT 9 ON TOP OF CITY HALL.

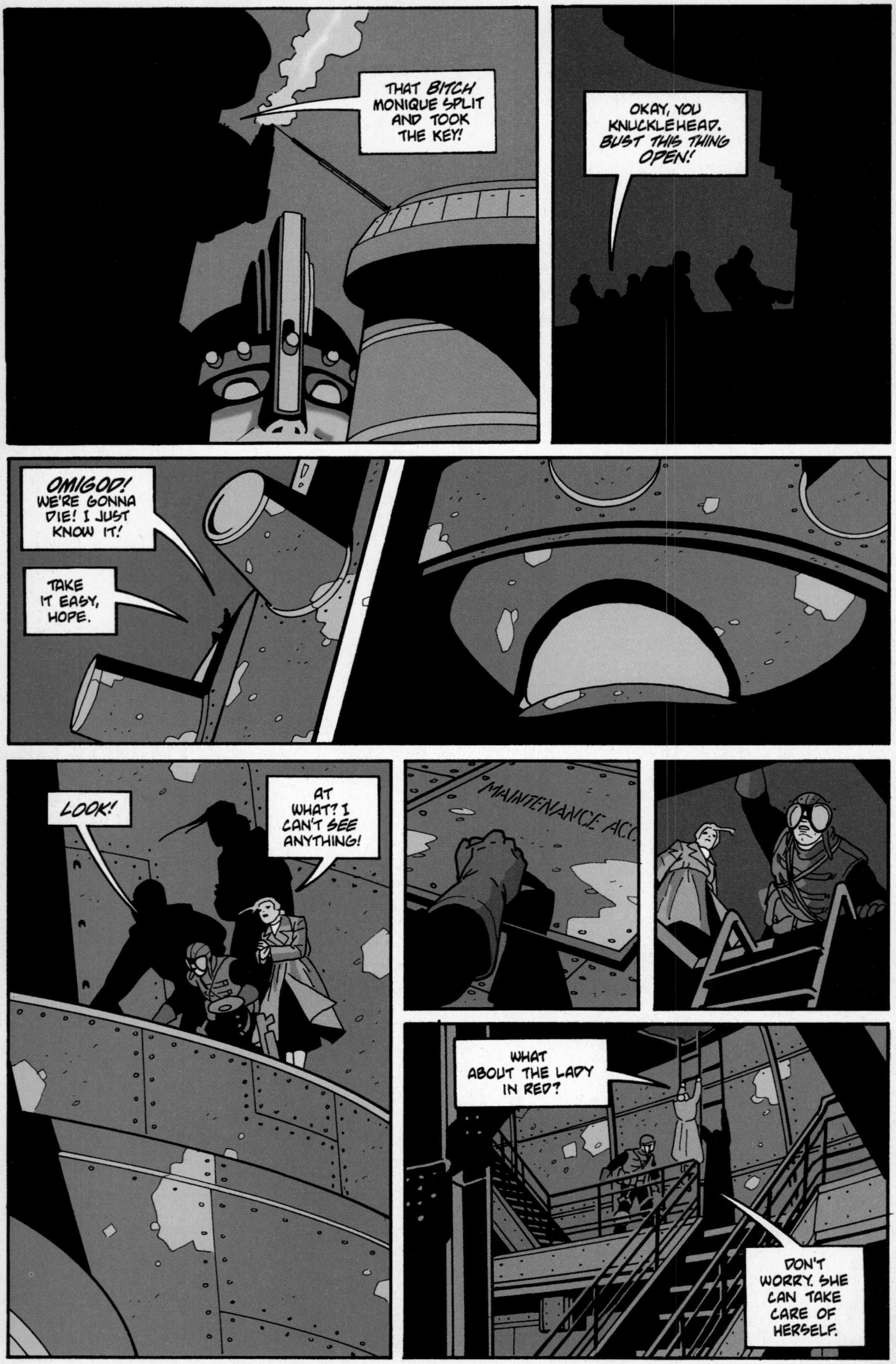
THAT BITCH MONIQUE SPLIT AND TOOK THE KEY!
OKAY, YOU KNUCKLEHEAD. BUST THIS THING OPEN!
OMIGOD! WE'RE GONNA DIE! I JUST KNOW IT!
TAKE IT EASY, HOPE.
LOOK!
AT WHAT? I CAN'T SEE ANYTHING!
MAINTENANCE ACC
WHAT ABOUT THE LADY IN RED?
DON'T WORRY. SHE CAN TAKE CARE OF HERSELF.

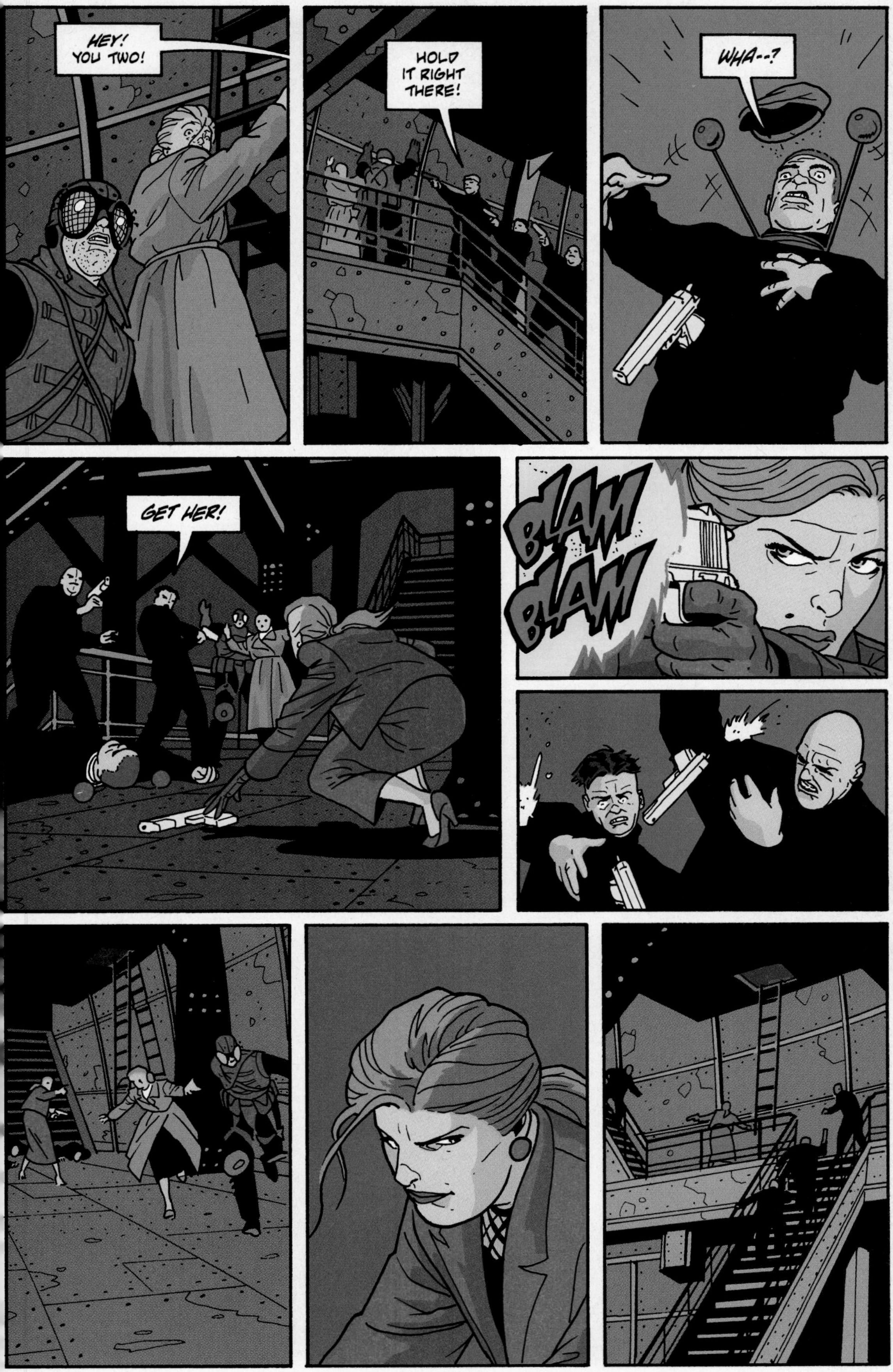

HEY! YOU TWO!
HOLD IT RIGHT THERE!
WHA--?
GET HER!
BLAM BLAM

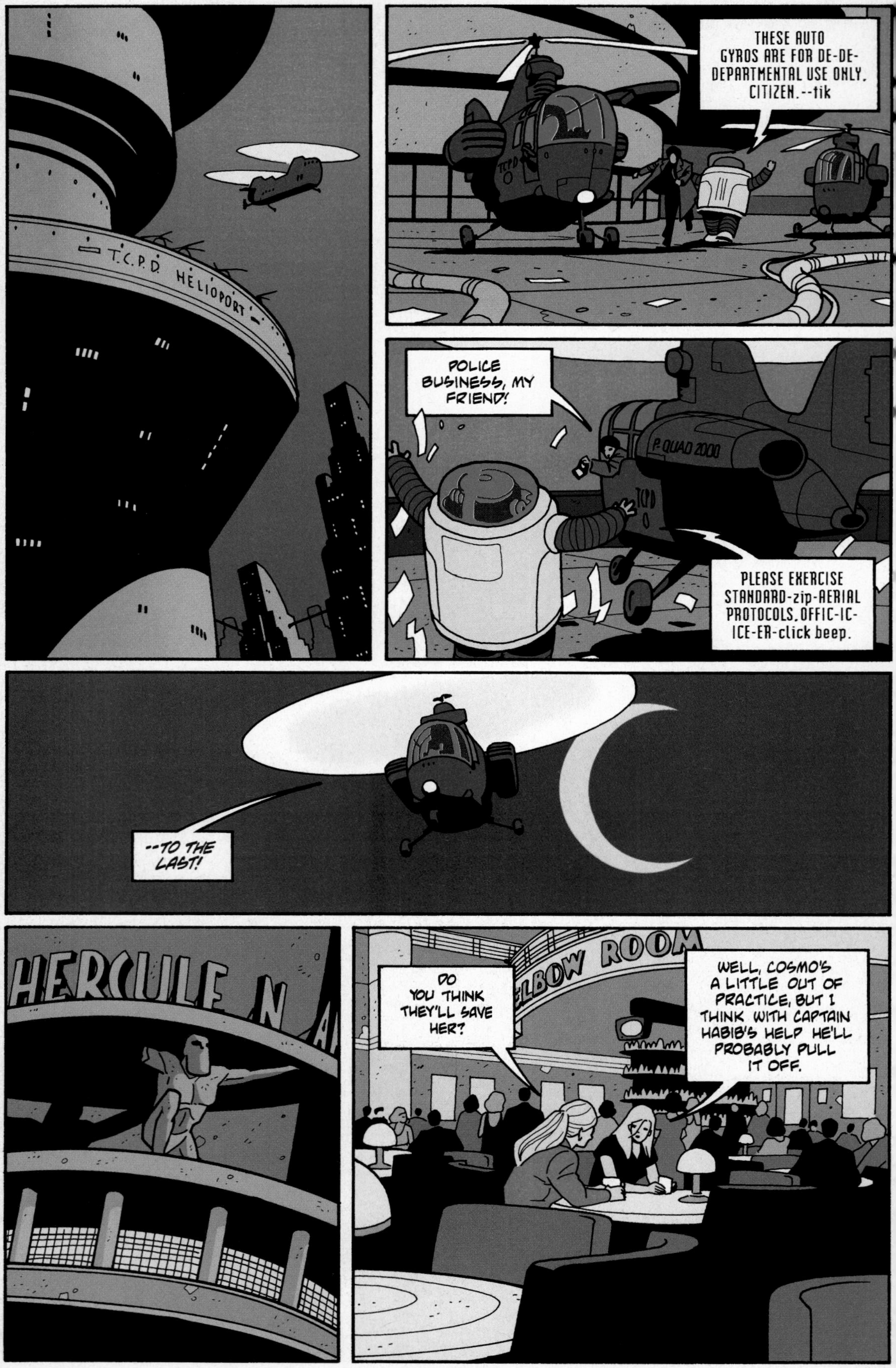
T.C.P.D. HELIOPORT
THESE AUTO GYROS ARE FOR DE-DE-DEPARTMENTAL USE ONLY, CITIZEN.--tik
POLICE BUSINESS, MY FRIEND!
P. QUAD 2000
PLEASE EXERCISE STANDARD-zip-AERIAL PROTOCOLS. OFFIC-IC-ICE-ER-click beep.
--TO THE LAST!
HERCULE N
ELBOW ROOM
DO YOU THINK THEY'LL SAVE HER?
WELL, COSMO'S A LITTLE OUT OF PRACTICE, BUT I THINK WITH CAPTAIN HABIB'S HELP HE'LL PROBABLY PULL IT OFF.

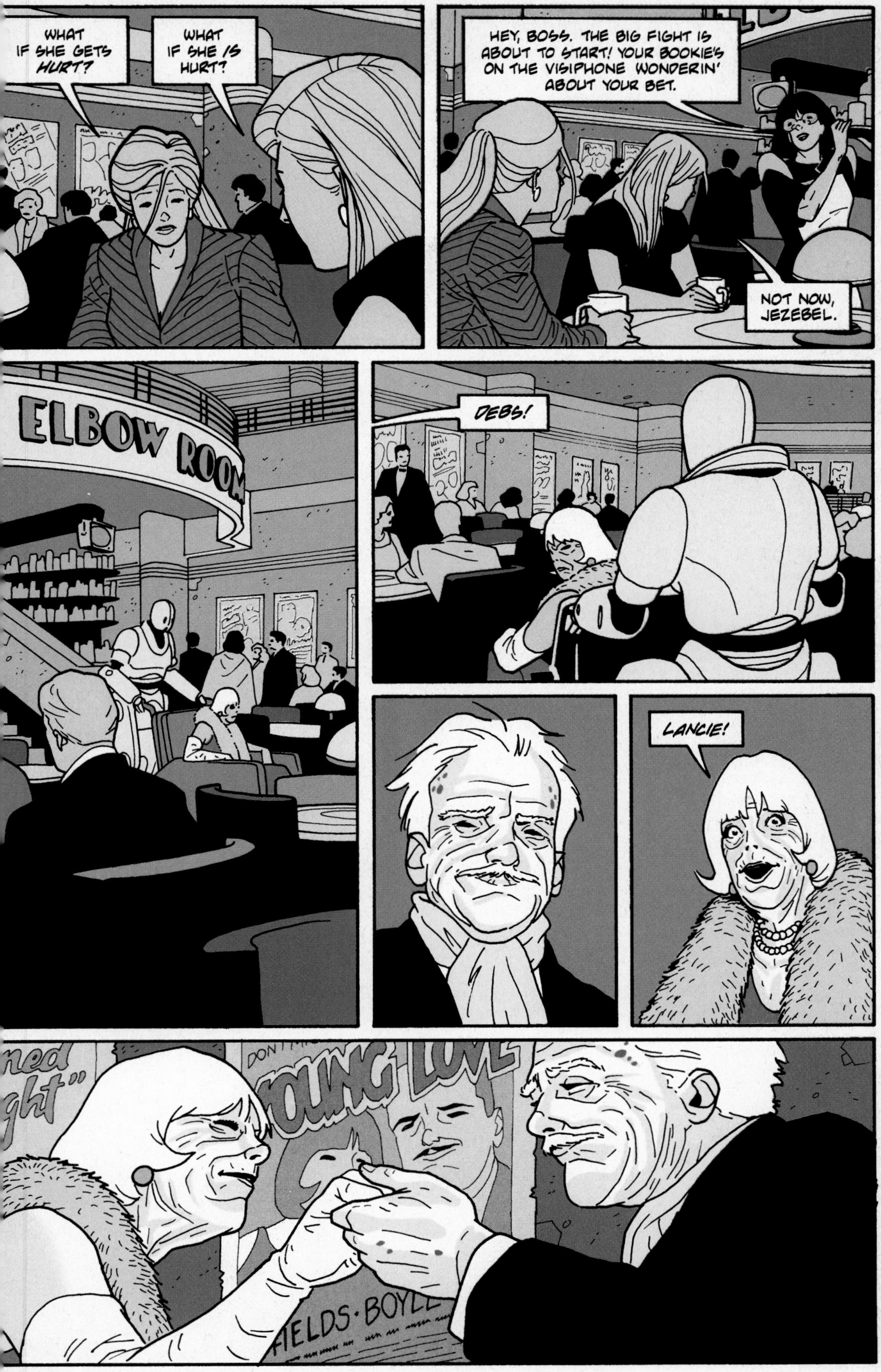
WHAT IF SHE GETS HURT?
WHAT IF SHE IS HURT?
HEY, BOSS. THE BIG FIGHT IS ABOUT TO START! YOUR BOOKIE'S ON THE VISIPHONE WONDERIN' ABOUT YOUR BET.
NOT NOW, JEZEBEL.
ELBOW ROOM
DEBS!
LANCIE!
YOUNG LOVE
FIELDS · BOYLE

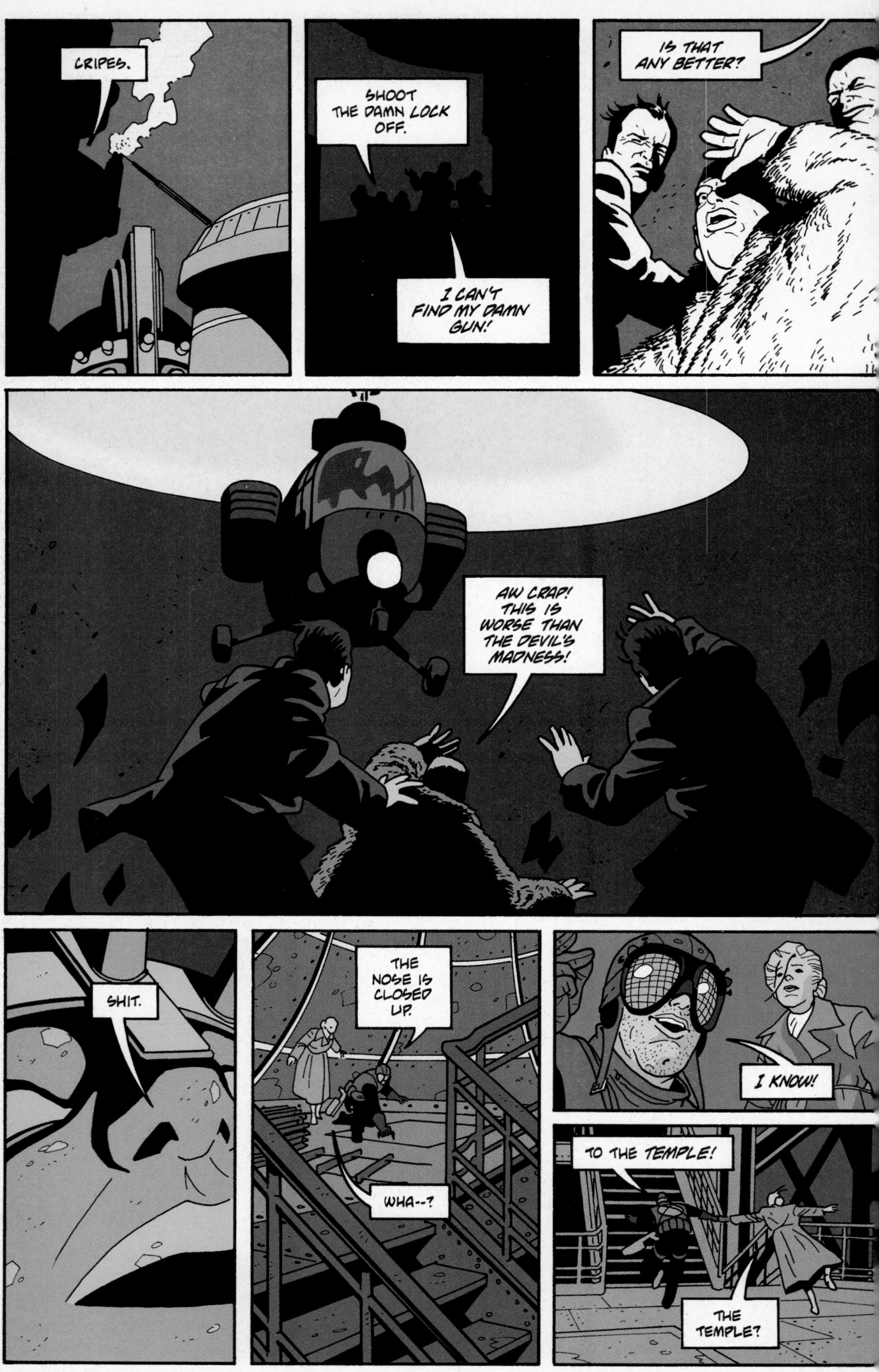
CRIPES.
SHOOT THE DAMN LOCK OFF.
I CAN'T FIND MY DAMN GUN!
IS THAT ANY BETTER?
AW CRAP! THIS IS WORSE THAN THE DEVIL'S MADNESS!
SHIT.
THE NOSE IS CLOSED UP.
WHA--?
I KNOW!
TO THE TEMPLE!
THE TEMPLE?

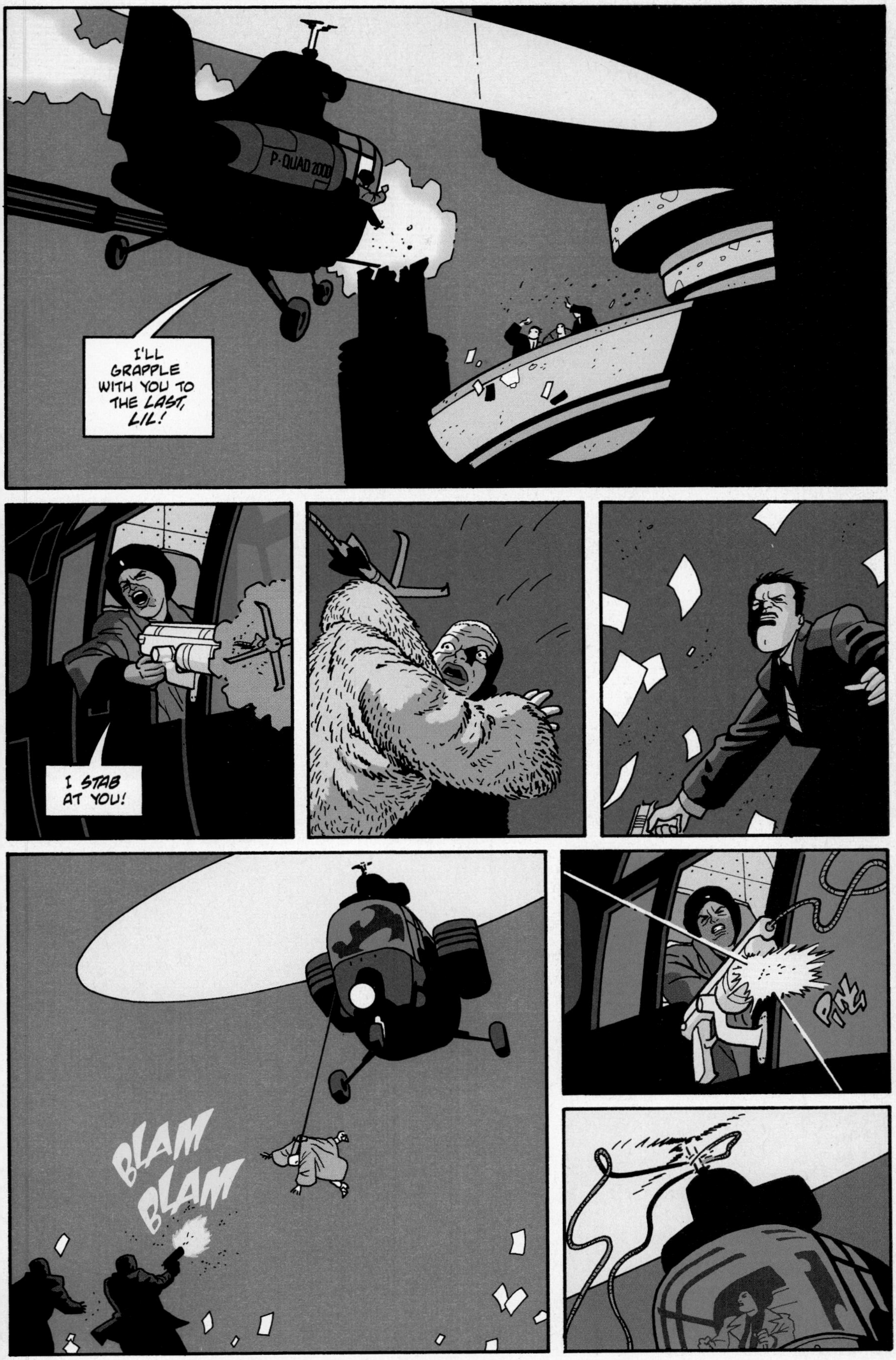
P-QUAD 2000
I'LL GRAPPLE WITH YOU TO THE LAST, LIL!
I STAB AT YOU!
BLAM BLAM
PING

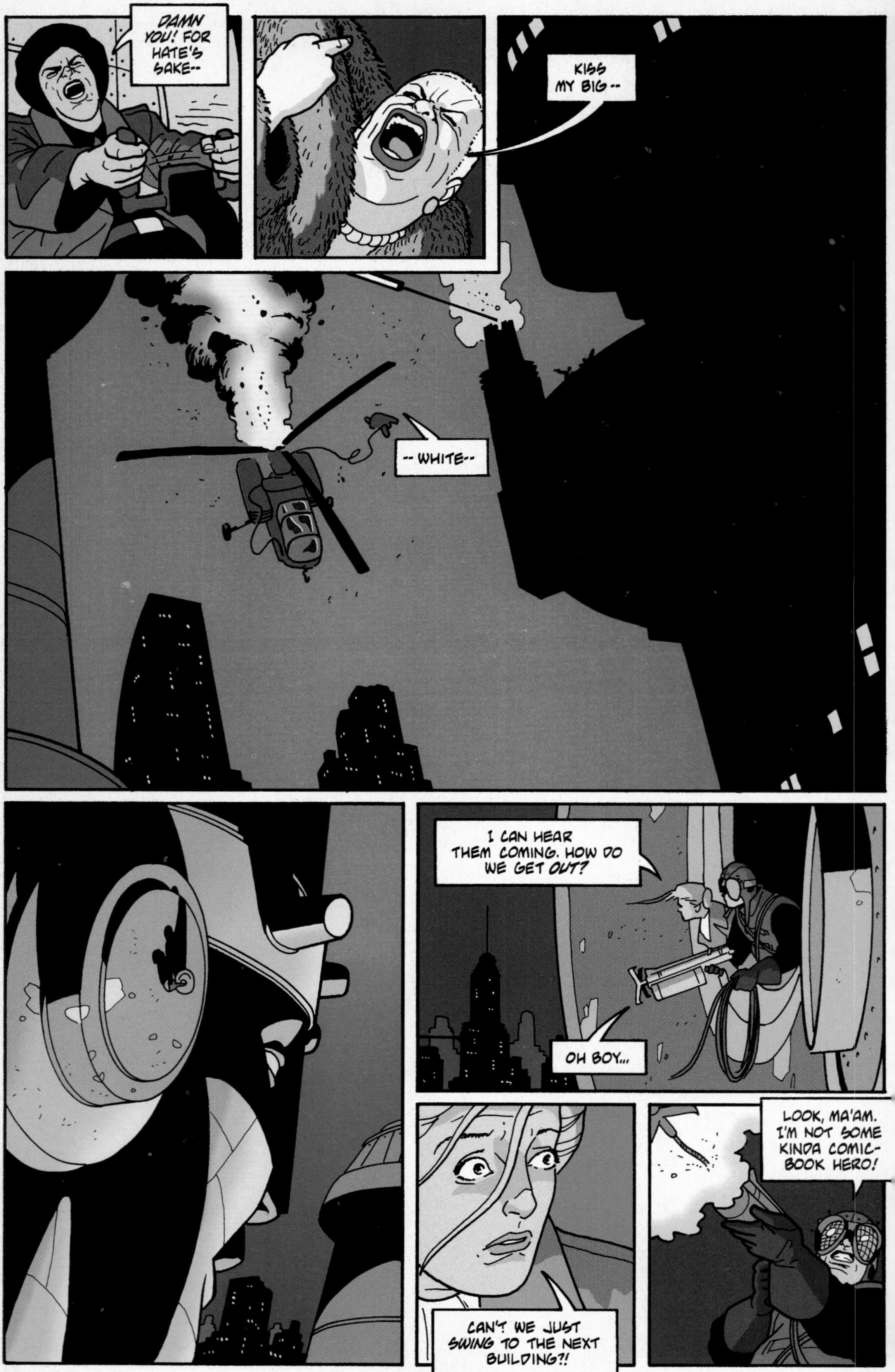
DAMN YOU! FOR HATE'S SAKE--
KISS MY BIG--
--WHITE--
I CAN HEAR THEM COMING. HOW DO WE GET OUT?
OH BOY...
CAN'T WE JUST SWING TO THE NEXT BUILDING?!
LOOK, MA'AM. I'M NOT SOME KINDA COMIC-BOOK HERO!

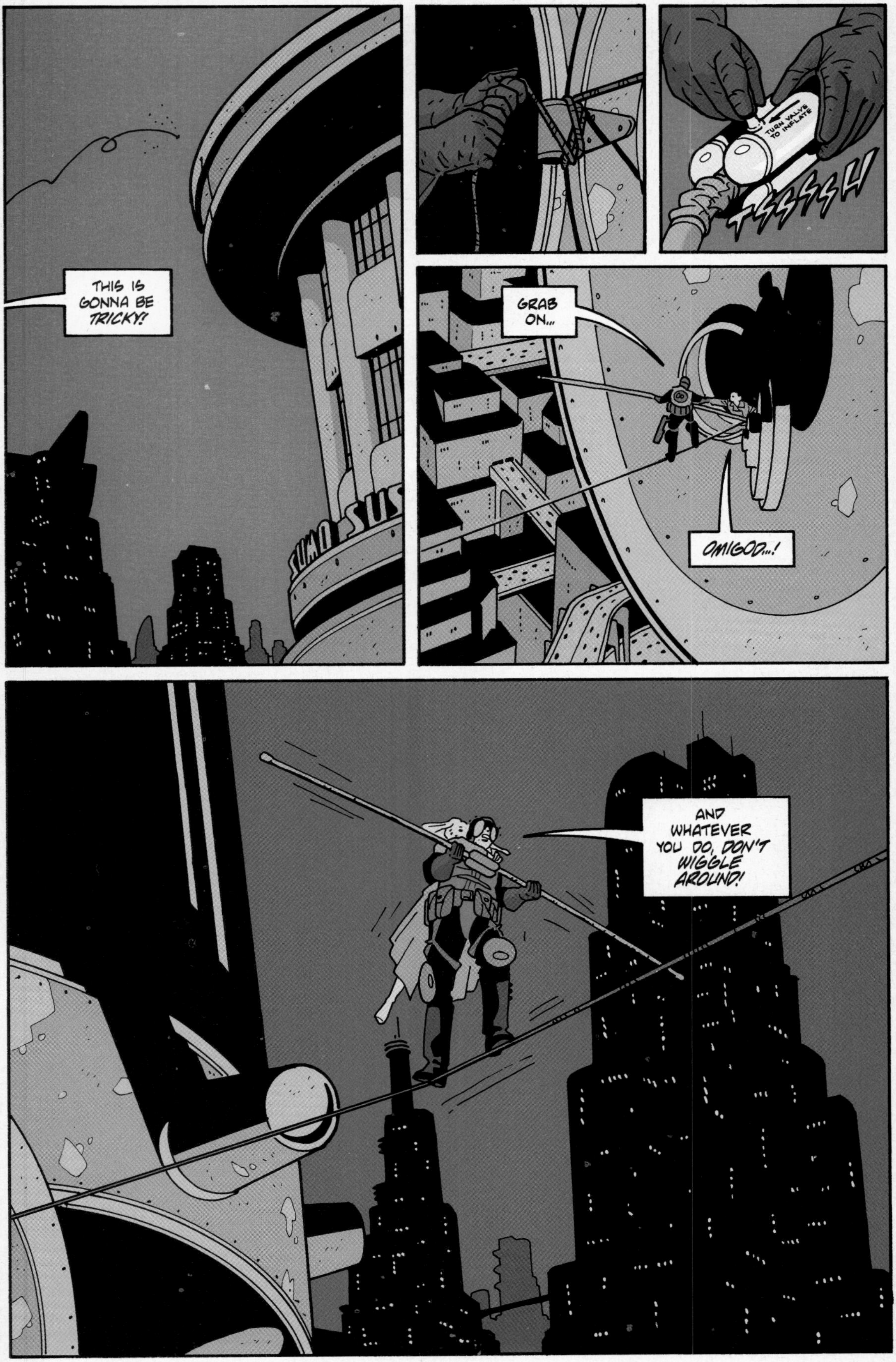
THIS IS GONNA BE TRICKY!
TURN VALVE TO INFLATE
TSSSSH
GRAB ON...
OMIGOD...!
AND WHATEVER YOU DO, DON'T WIGGLE AROUND!

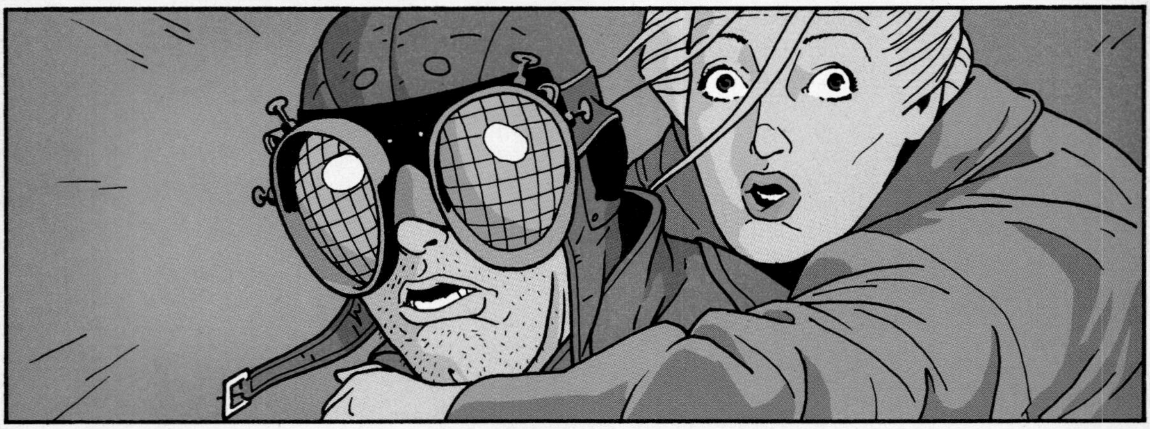

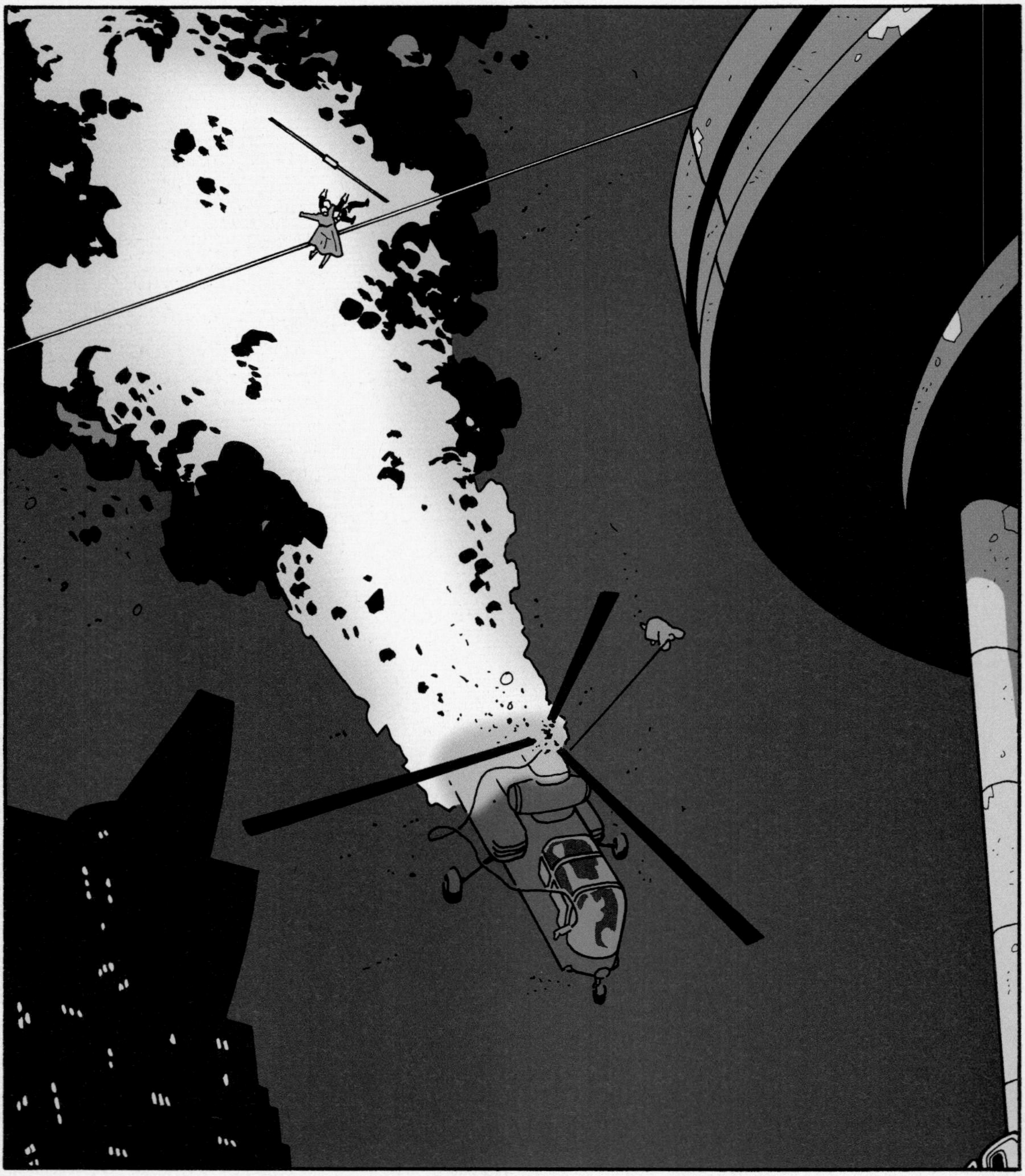

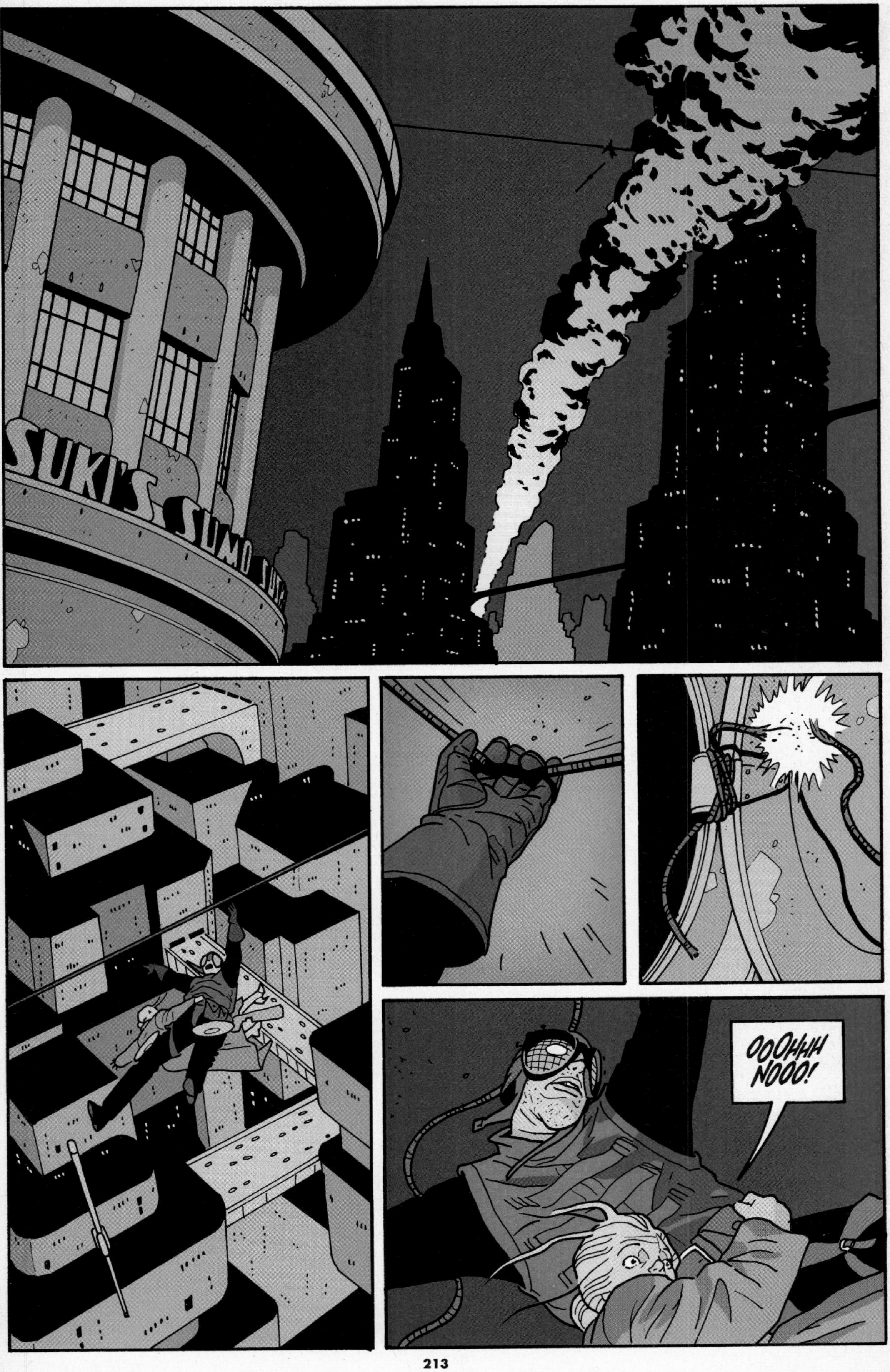
SUKI'S SUMO
OOOHHH NOOO!

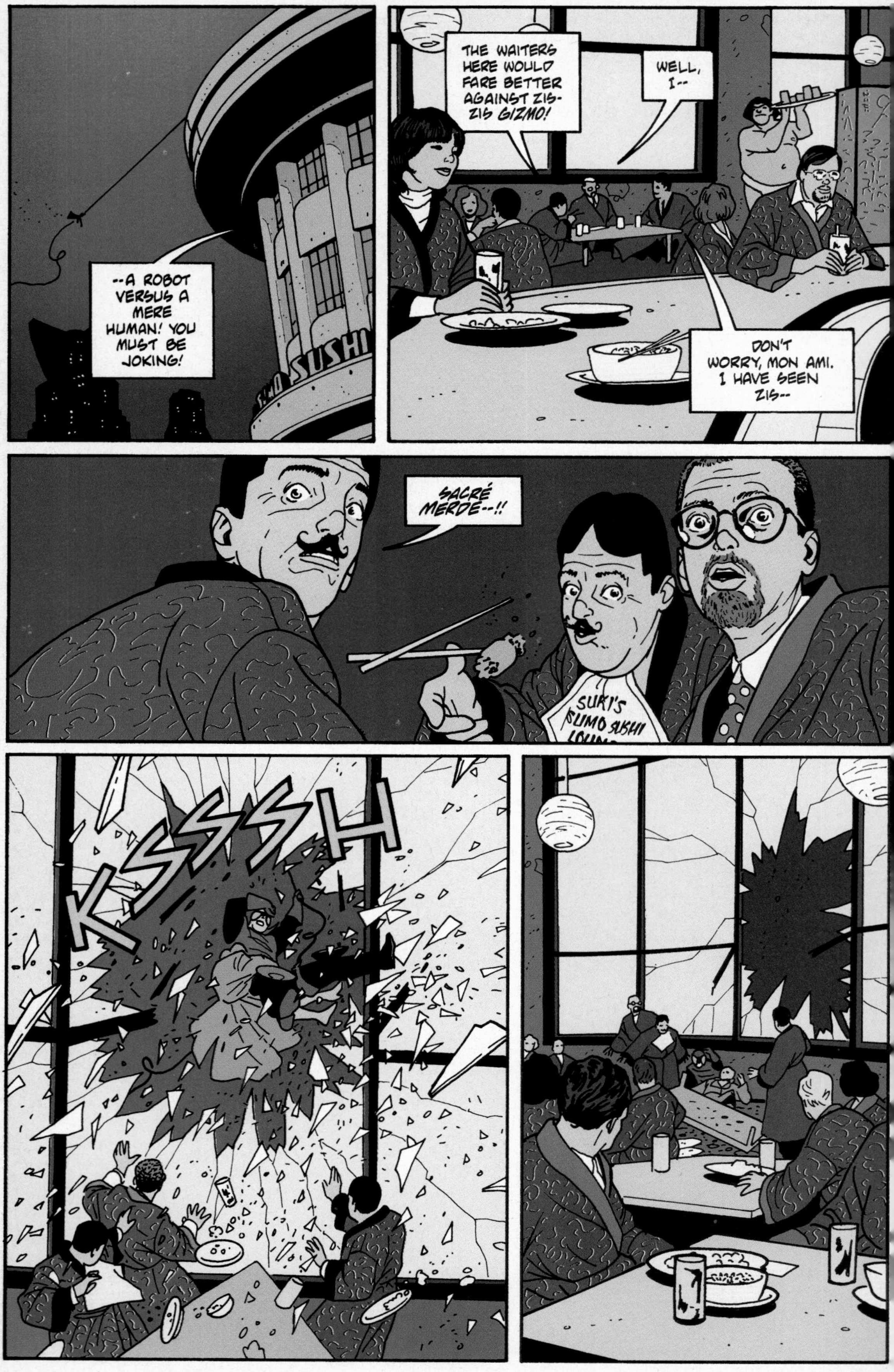
--A ROBOT VERSUS A MERE HUMAN! YOU MUST BE JOKING!
SUSHI
THE WAITERS HERE WOULD FARE BETTER AGAINST ZIS-ZIS GIZMO!
WELL, I--
DON'T WORRY, MON AMI. I HAVE SEEN ZIS--
SACRÉ MERDE--!!
KSSSH

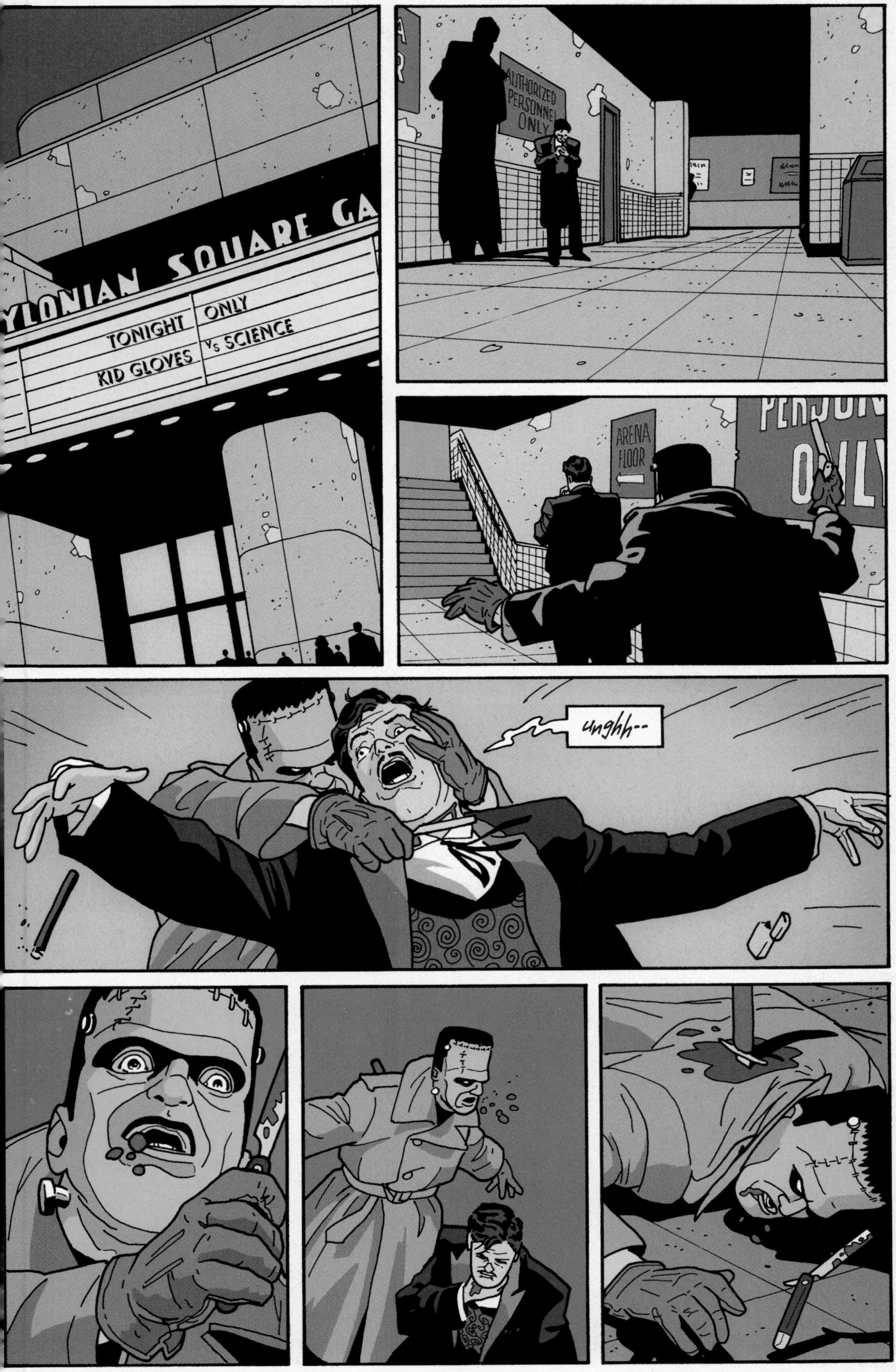
YLONIAN SQUARE GA
TONIGHT ONLY
KID GLOVES Vs SCIENCE
AUTHORIZED PERSONNEL ONLY
ARENA FLOOR
unghh--

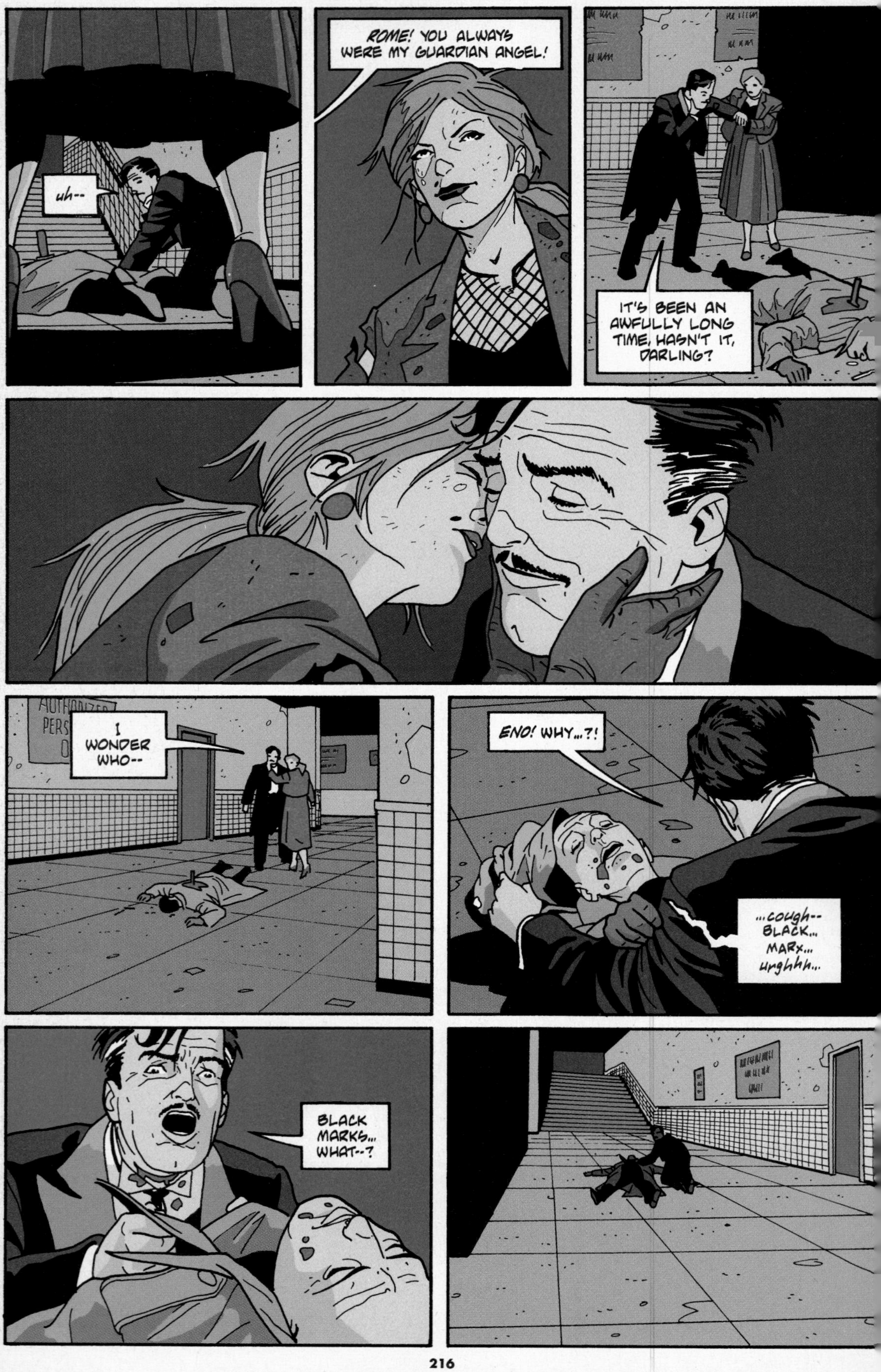
uh--
ROME! YOU ALWAYS WERE MY GUARDIAN ANGEL!
IT'S BEEN AN AWFULLY LONG TIME, HASN'T IT, DARLING?
I WONDER WHO--
ENO! WHY...?!
...cough-- BLACK... MARX... urghhh...
BLACK MARKS... WHAT--?

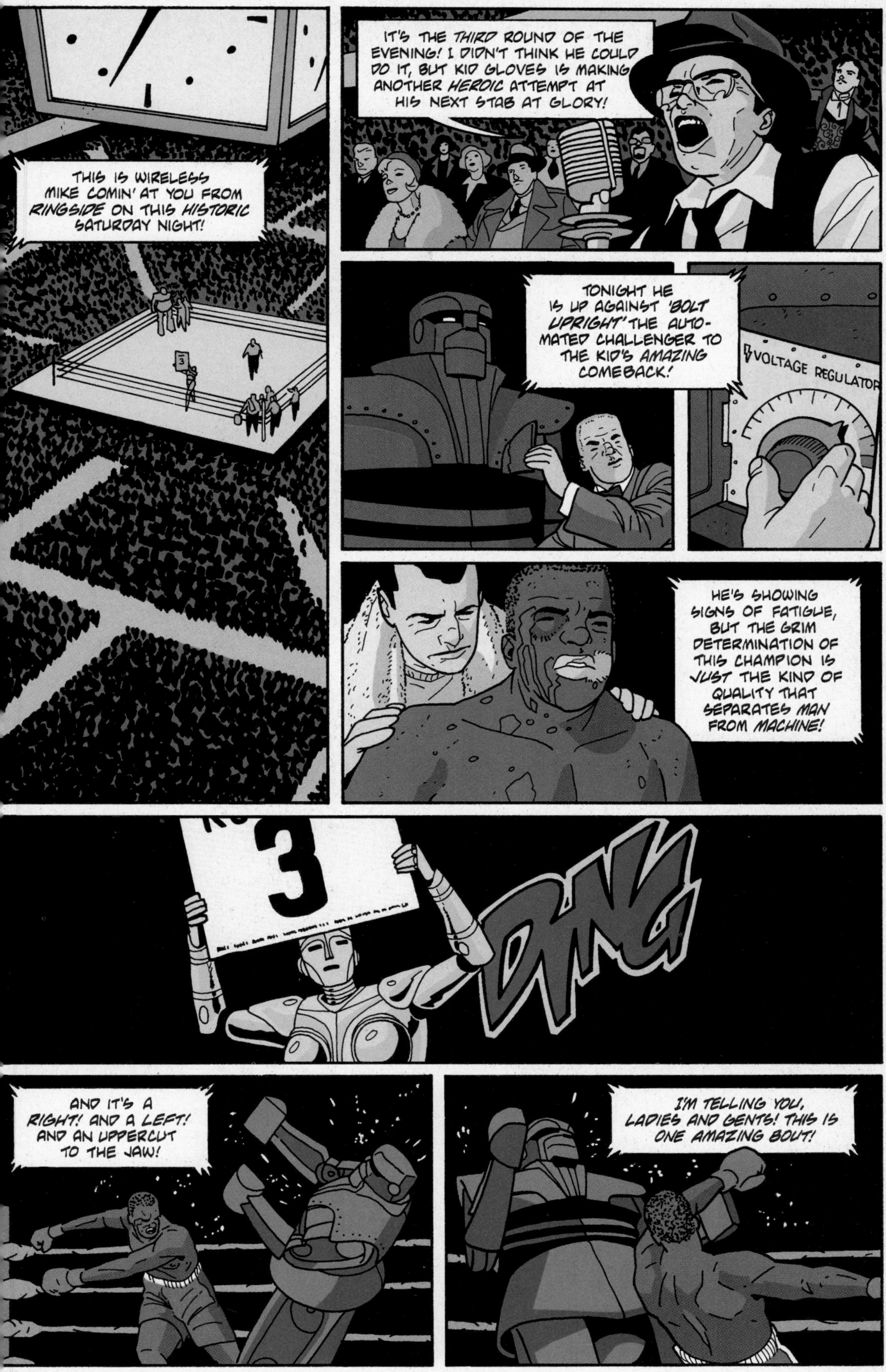
THIS IS WIRELESS MIKE COMIN' AT YOU FROM RINGSIDE ON THIS HISTORIC SATURDAY NIGHT!
IT'S THE THIRD ROUND OF THE EVENING! I DIDN'T THINK HE COULD DO IT, BUT KID GLOVES IS MAKING ANOTHER HEROIC ATTEMPT AT HIS NEXT STAB AT GLORY!
TONIGHT HE IS UP AGAINST 'BOLT UPRIGHT' THE AUTO-MATED CHALLENGER TO THE KID'S AMAZING COMEBACK!
VOLTAGE REGULATOR
HE'S SHOWING SIGNS OF FATIGUE, BUT THE GRIM DETERMINATION OF THIS CHAMPION IS JUST THE KIND OF QUALITY THAT SEPARATES MAN FROM MACHINE!
3
DING
AND IT'S A RIGHT! AND A LEFT! AND AN UPPERCUT TO THE JAW!
I'M TELLING YOU, LADIES AND GENTS! THIS IS ONE AMAZING BOUT!

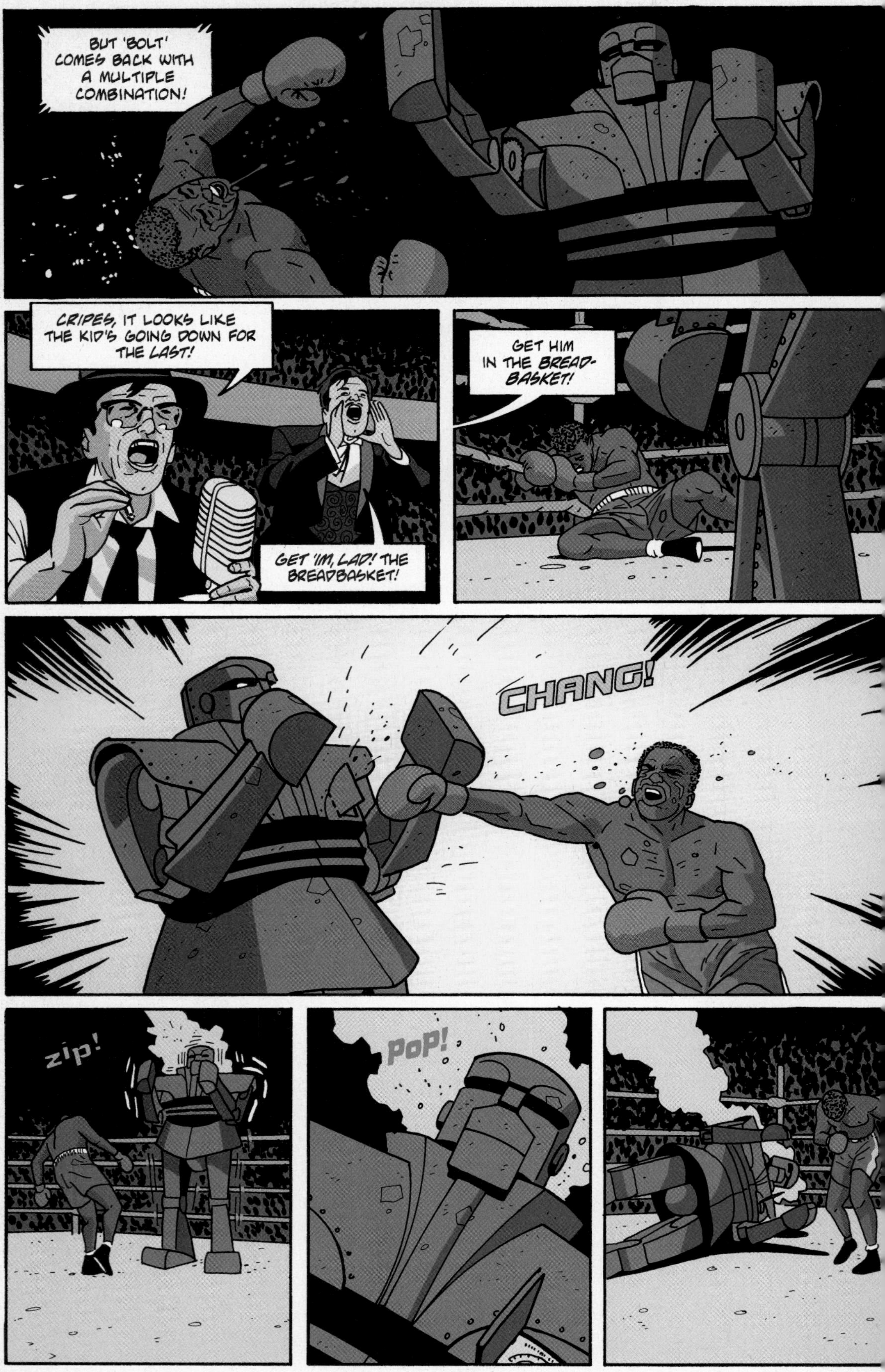
BUT 'BOLT' COMES BACK WITH A MULTIPLE COMBINATION!
CRIPES, IT LOOKS LIKE THE KID'S GOING DOWN FOR THE LAST!
GET 'IM, LAD! THE BREADBASKET!
GET HIM IN THE BREAD-BASKET!
CHANG!
zip!
PoP!

THE WINNAH AND STILL CHAMPEEN! KID GLOVES!

COME ON, OLD FRIEND!

...OLD FRIEND...

S'OKAY, BOSS...

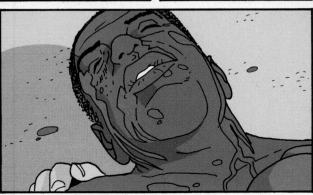

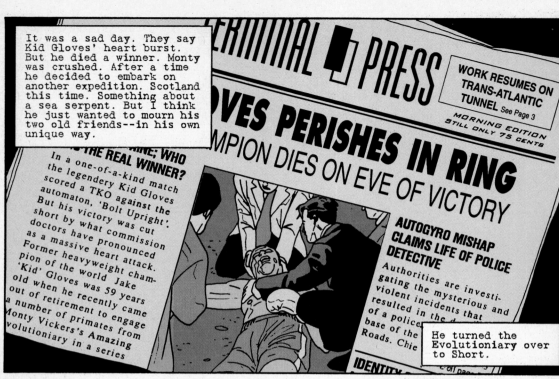

It was a sad day. They say Kid Gloves' heart burst. But he died a winner. Monty was crushed. After a time he decided to embark on another expedition. Scotland this time. Something about a sea serpent. But I think he just wanted to mourn his two old friends--in his own unique way.

KID GLOVES PERISHES IN RING
CHAMPION DIES ON EVE OF VICTORY

TERMINAL PRESS

WORK RESUMES ON TRANS-ATLANTIC TUNNEL See Page 3

MORNING EDITION STILL ONLY 75 CENTS

...THE REAL WINNER?

In a one-of-a-kind match the legendary Kid Gloves scored a TKO against the automaton, 'Bolt Upright'. But his victory was cut short by what commission doctors have pronounced as a massive heart attack. Former heavyweight champion of the world Jake 'Kid' Gloves was 59 years old when he recently came out of retirement to engage a number of primates from Monty Vickers's Amazing Evolutioniary in a series

AUTOGYRO MISHAP CLAIMS LIFE OF POLICE DETECTIVE

Authorities are investigating the mysterious and violent incidents that resulted in the d... of a police... base of the... Roads. Chie...

IDENTITY...

He turned the Evolutioniary over to Short.

With the demise of Big Lil, things quieted down a bit. I held off telling Charity of Habib's fate, though. After all, he was the first man who had shown interest in her in years.

But life in the Arms goes on.

I've said it before, Terminal City is a strange and extraordinary place.

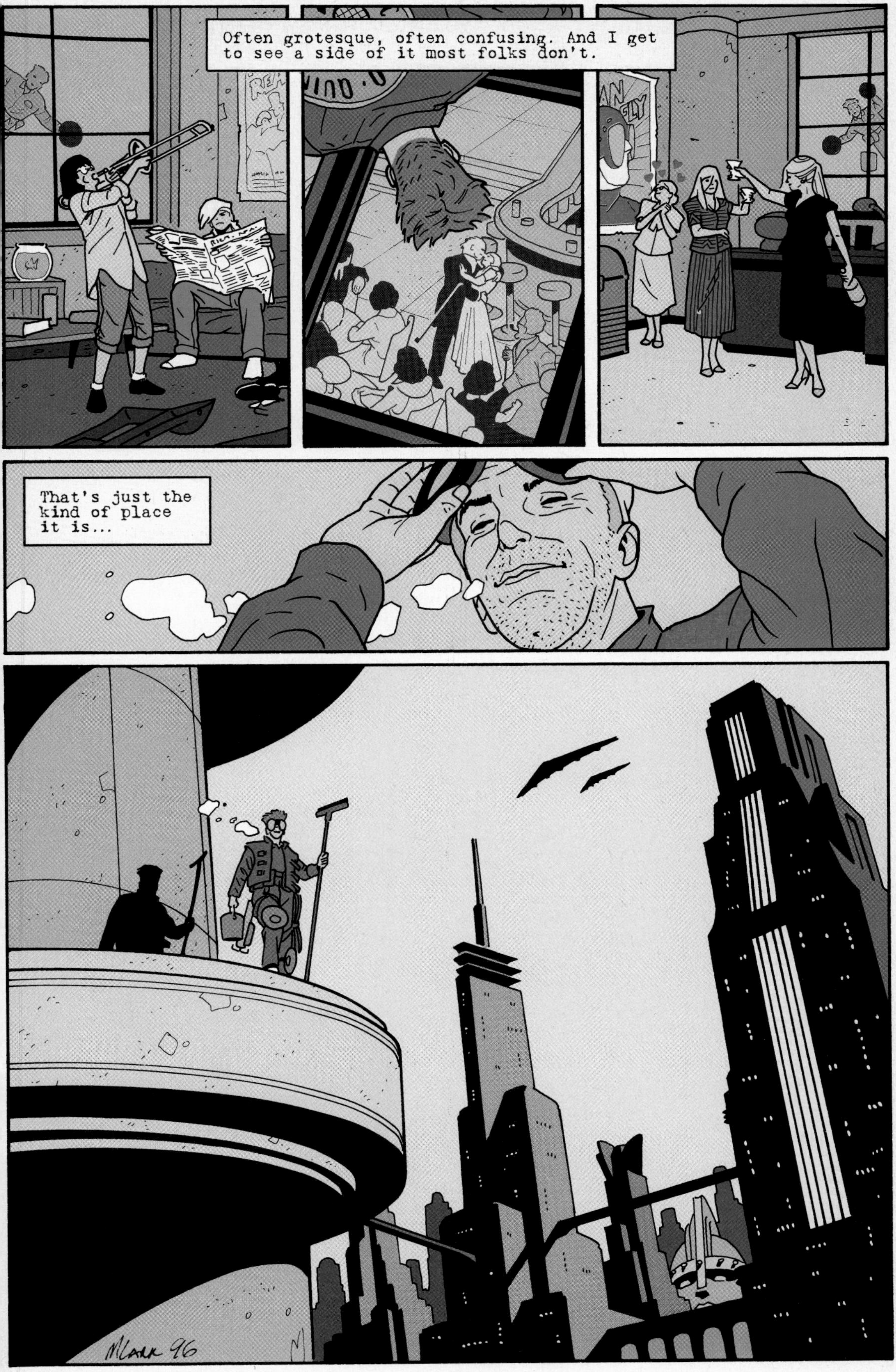
Often grotesque, often confusing. And I get to see a side of it most folks don't.
That's just the kind of place it is...
Mlark 96

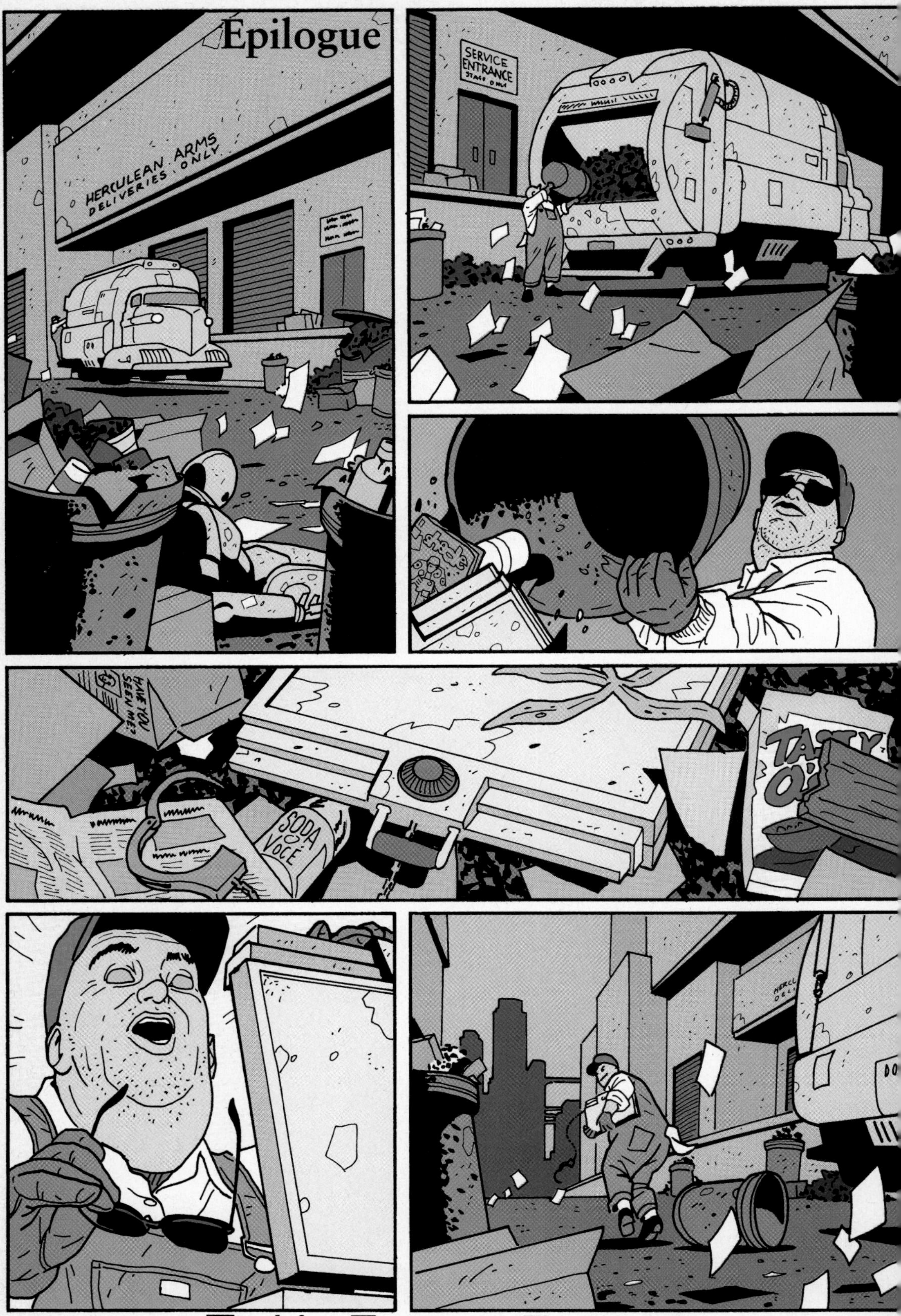
Epilogue
HERCULEAN ARMS
DELIVERIES ONLY
SERVICE
ENTRANCE
HAVE YOU SEEN ME?
SODA
VOCÊ

THE END

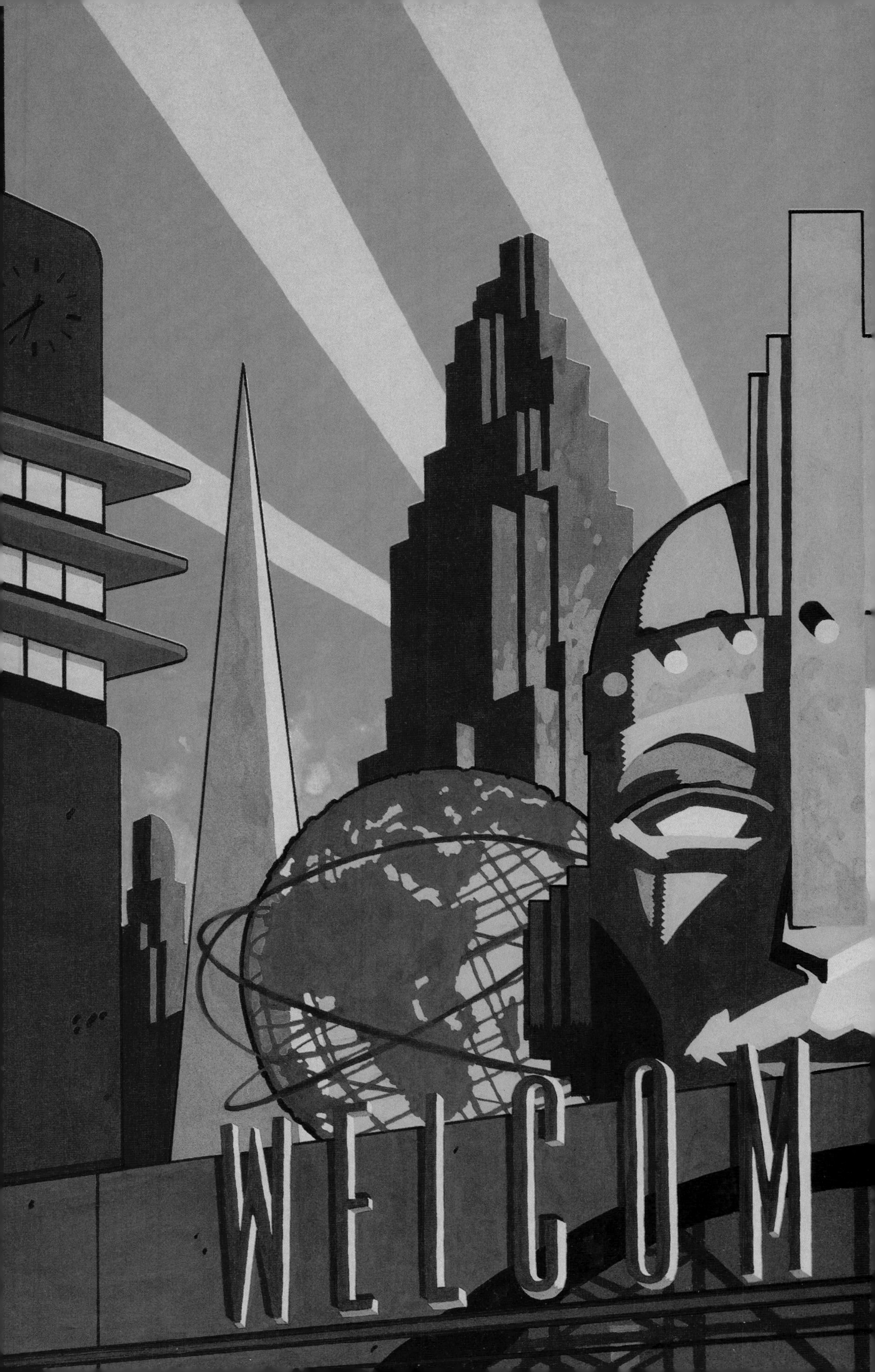
WELCOM

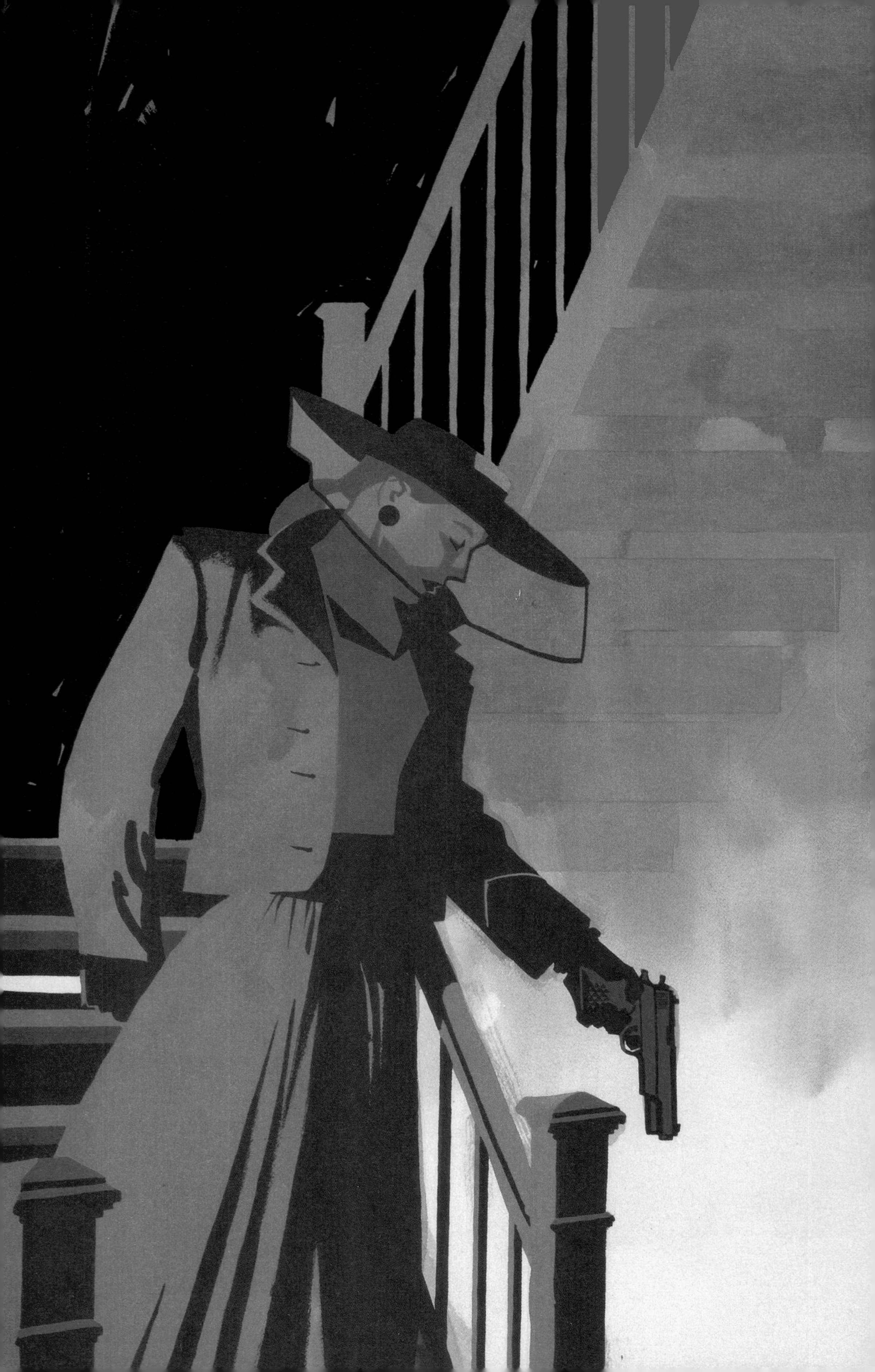

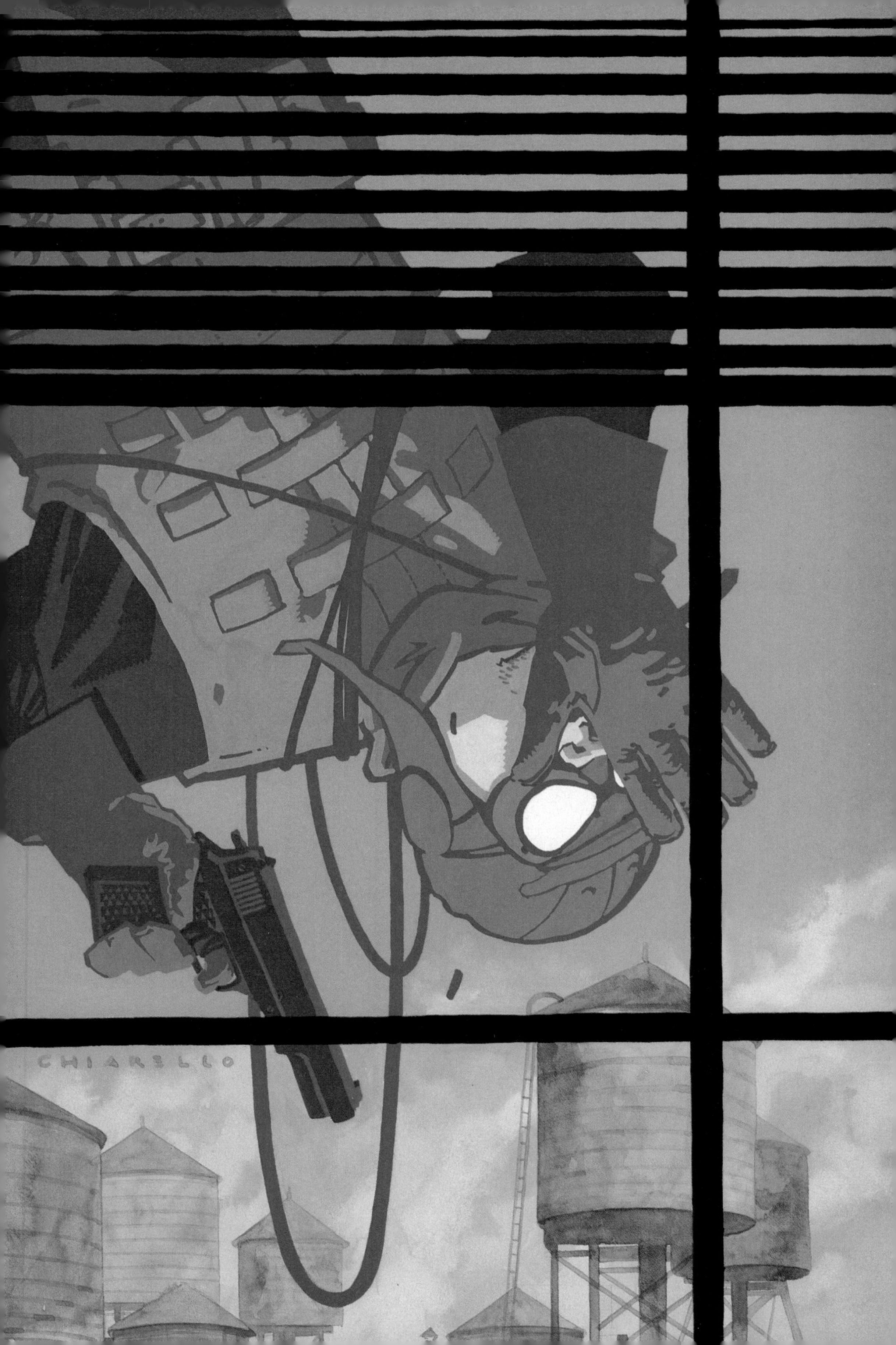
CHIARELLO

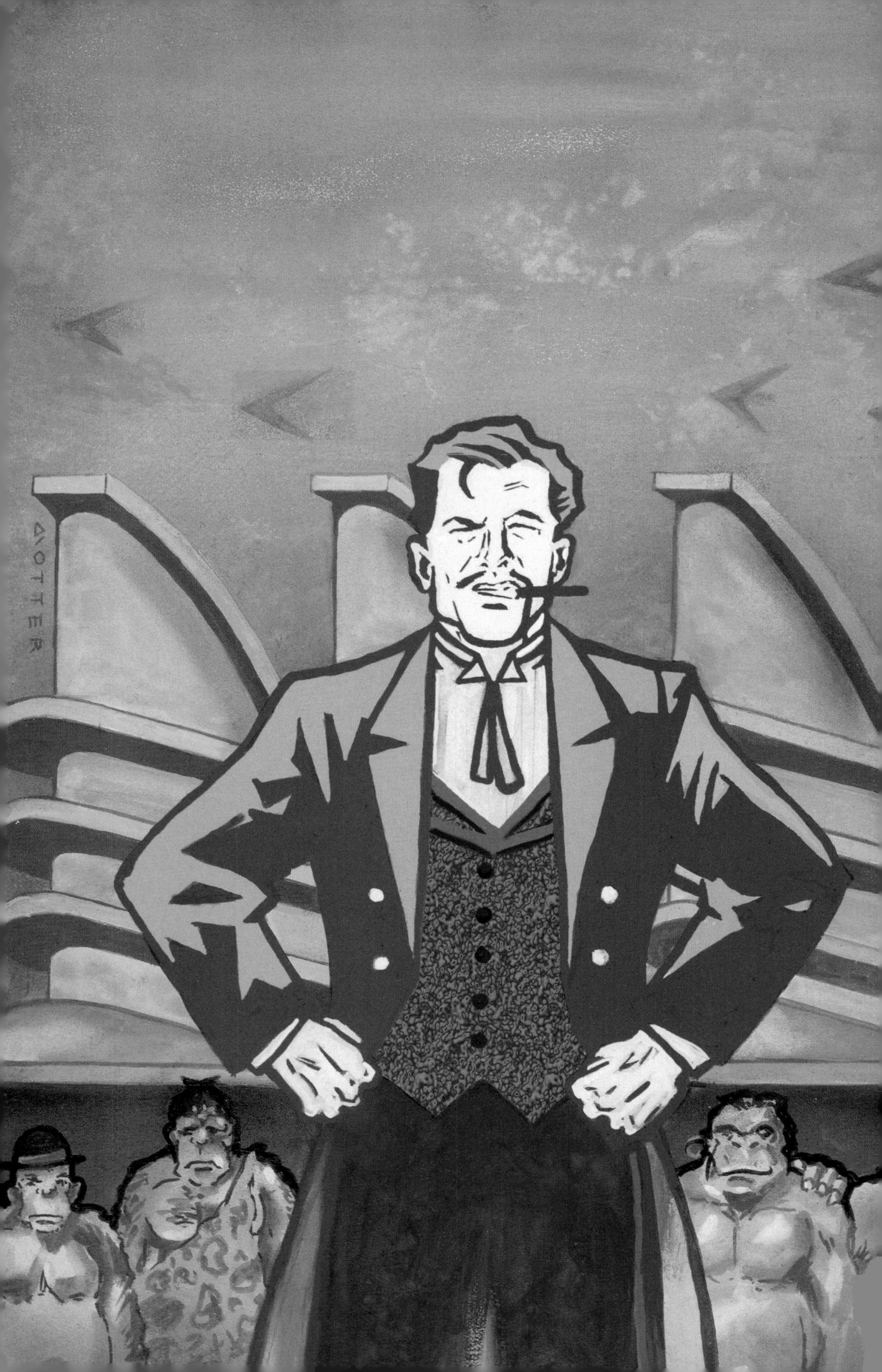

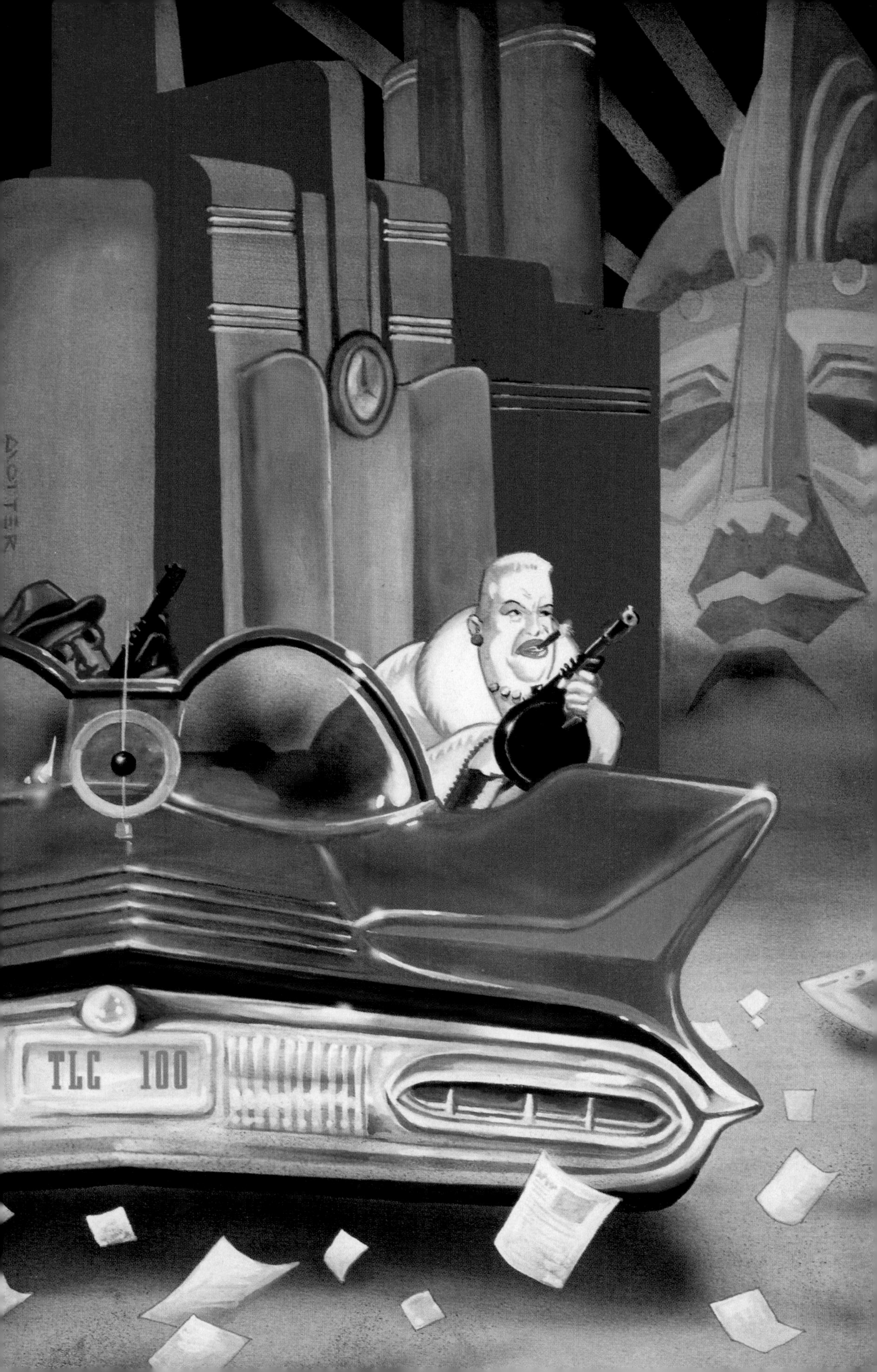
TLC 100

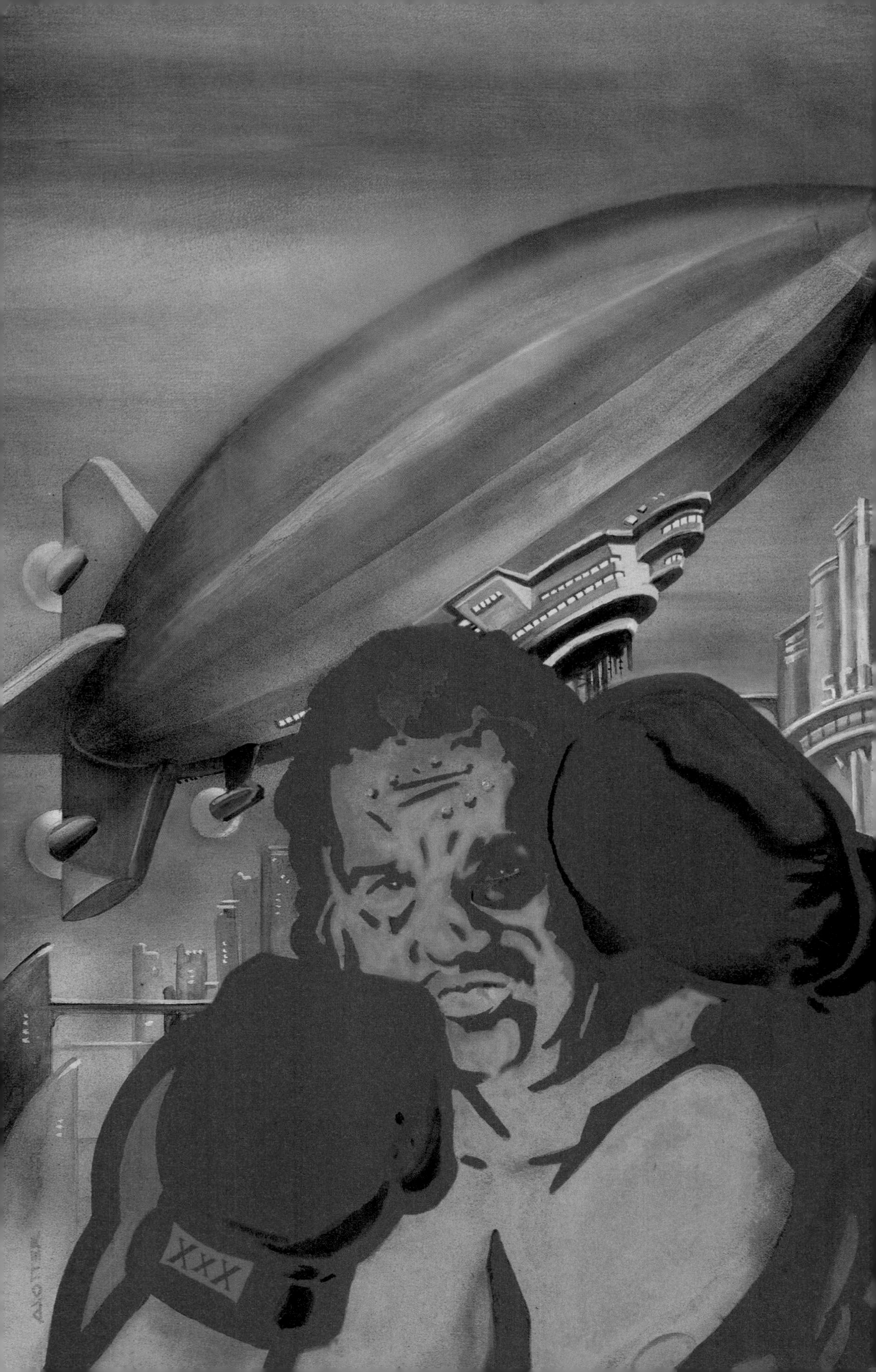
XXX

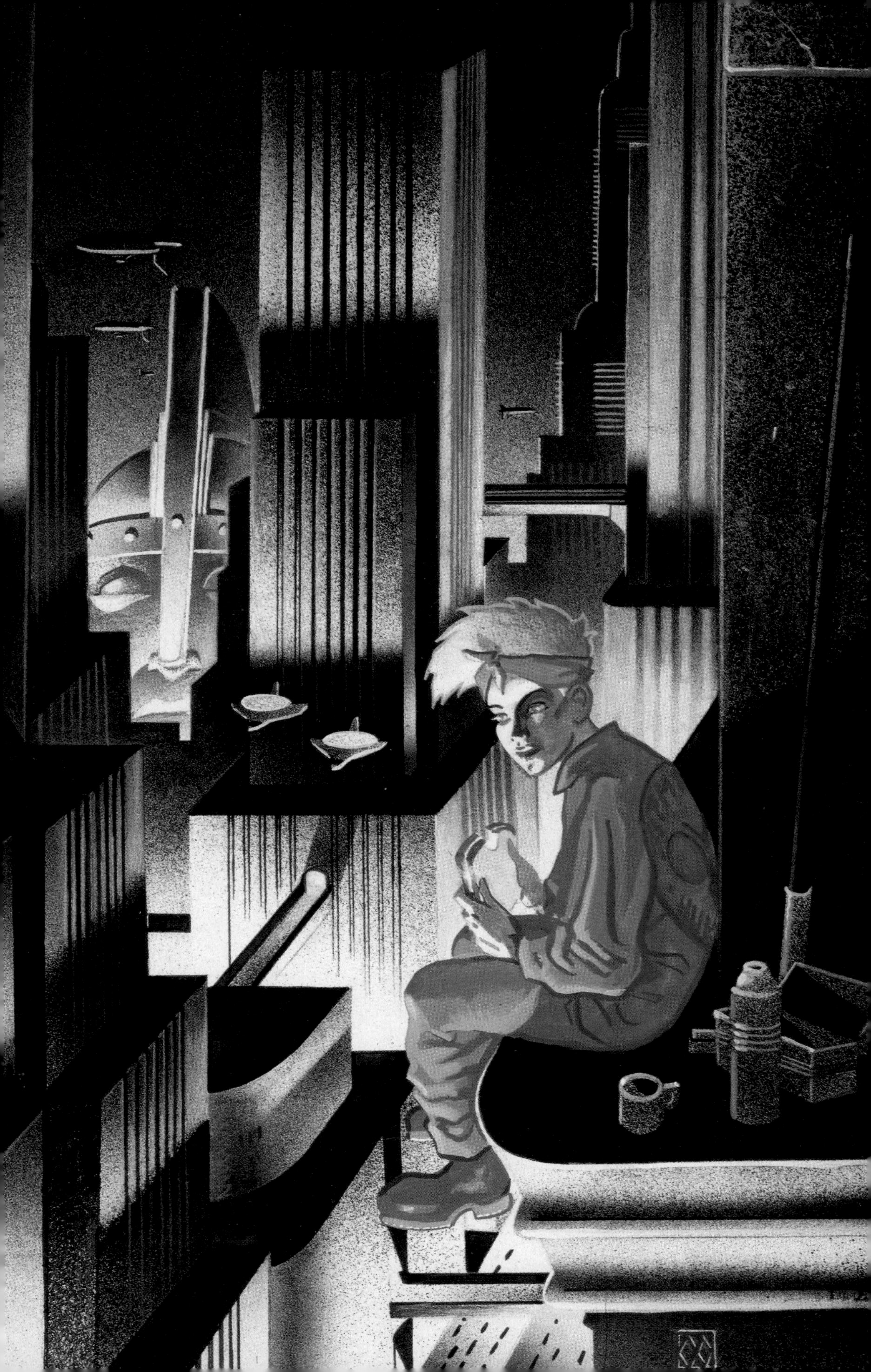

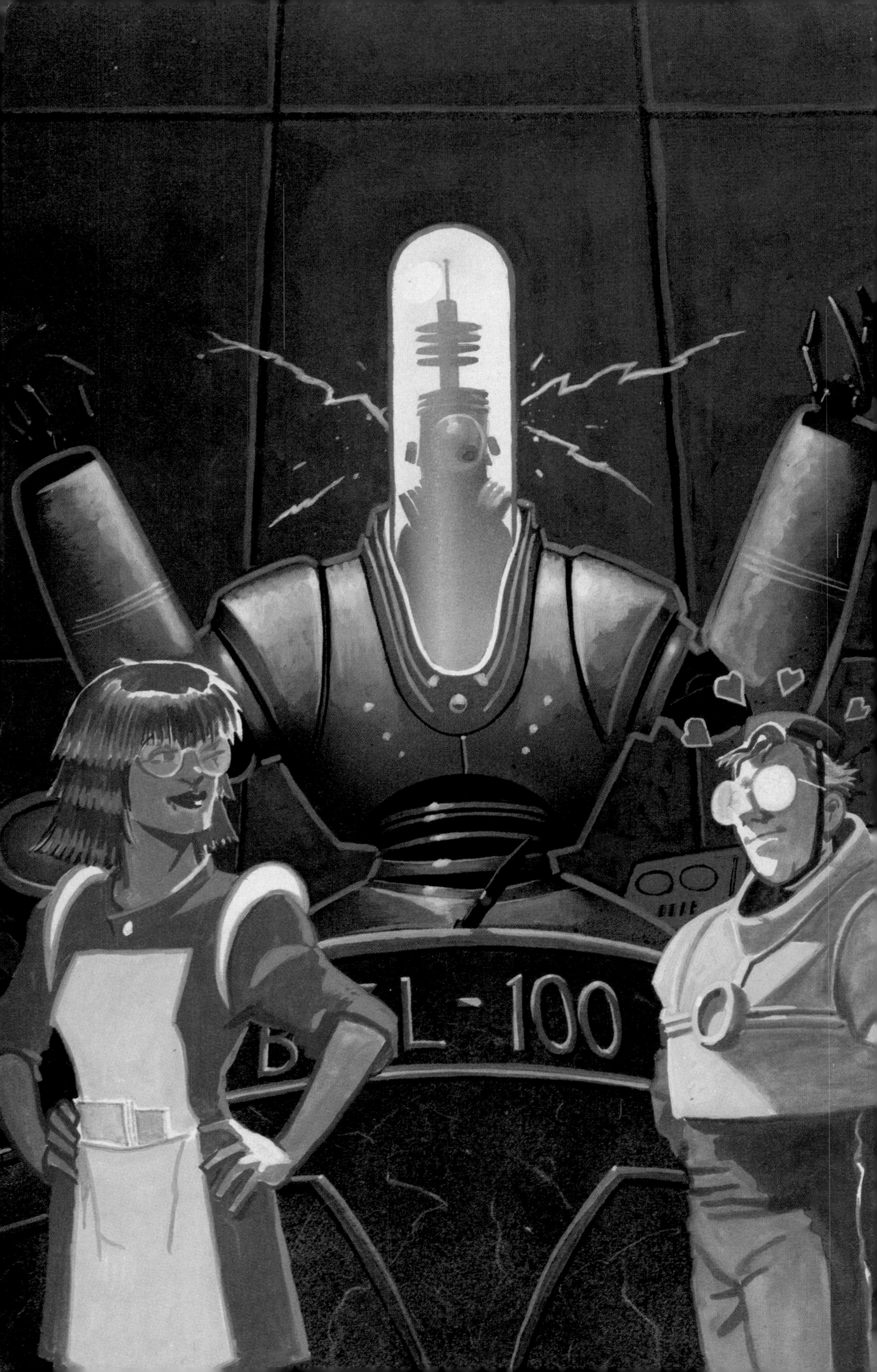
B L-100